It was time to make a name for our-selves.

"We're finally sixth graders, Gretch! Top of the heap!" I said.

"But next year, we'll be back down at the bottom again, Kobie. When we go to junior high."

"Don't think about that. Concentrate on making this our most memorable year at Centreville."

"How are we going to make this year memorable?" Gretchen wanted to know.

"We need a new project," I declared. "Something that will make us famous."

Now that we were both almost twelve, it was time to make a name for ourselves.

**Other Apple Paperbacks
you will enjoy:**

GOING ON TWELVE

Candice F. Ransom

AN
APPLE
PAPERBACK

SCHOLASTIC INC.
New York Toronto London Auckland Sydney

ISBN 0-590-40848-8

12 11 10 9 8 7 6 5 4 3 2   8 9/8 0 1 2 3/9

Printed in the U.S.A.   01

First Scholastic printing, August 1988

For Howard,
who has crossed the equator
for the last time

Chapter 1

"I'll bet anything he's the Hammer Man," I said. Actually, the legend of the Hammer Man had just popped into my mind. But the thought lodged there and grew fizzy, like an m&m dropped in a Coke bottle. Suddenly it seemed more than possible — no, absolutely *right* — that the old man on the hill was really the Hammer Man.

Gretchen took the digging spoon from its place in the dogwood tree. "The Hammer Man? Who's that?"

I parted the heavy veil of honeysuckle to spy on the gray house on the hill above our school. In a mysterious voice, I told Gretchen the story, making up only a little. "Years and years ago, before we were born, the Hammer Man used to sneak around Manassas after dark and hit people over the head with this big hammer he carried hooked in his belt."

"Did he kill them?" Gretchen looked up from digging in the floor of our hideout, her blue eyes wide. Usually she didn't mind scary stories, as long as it was broad daylight.

"Well, he didn't do them any good," I replied, quoting my father. Sometimes my parents talked about stuff in the newspaper at supper, forgetting I was there, taking it all in. My father would mention somebody got hit by a car or something and my mother would say, "Isn't it a shame a person couldn't walk down the street?" and then I'd ask if the guy died and my father would answer, "Well, it didn't do him any good."

Gretchen shivered in the dappled light of our Honeysuckle Hideout, even though it was September and still warm. "Kobie, if he's the Hammer Man, how come he's here in Centreville? Manassas is only six miles from here. Why haven't the police caught him yet?"

"Because" — I paused dramatically — "he's very clever. Sure, you'd think a murderer would run as far away as he could. Alaska or someplace. But the Hammer Man was smart. He decided to go where people would least expect to find him. Centreville was perfect. People are so out of it here, even if he went screaming down Braddock Road with his hammer, nobody'd notice."

Gretchen sat back on her heels, the digging spoon loose in her fingers, and stared at the house looming above our hideout. "A real-live murderer right next to our school," she murmured. "Do you think we should report him to the principal?"

I could see us storming into Mr. Magyn's office with the shocking news. Mr. Magyn would react the way he always did, whether a kid came in with a hurt knee or somebody whacked a baseball through the window. Before he'd move from behind his desk, he'd ask Miss Warren, the school secretary, for the proper form. Miss Warren would paw through the filing cabinet, looking under "H" for "Hammer," and then "M" for "Murderer."

I shook my head. "We need evidence first."

"What kind of evidence?"

I let the curtain of honeysuckle fall back. "Hammers," I said. "He probably has a whole rack of them in his basement, maybe with little tags on them so he could remember who — "

The bell rang. Recess was over. It was time to line up on the blacktop.

"Darn. We haven't put our dues in yet.

Gretch, hurry up." Today was Dues Day. We couldn't leave without putting our dues in the tin box.

She scraped dirt off the lid of our buried box with her bare hands and pried it open. I threw in the nickel I had been saving. Gretchen tossed in a quarter. She always had more money than I did. Then we piled the dirt back in the hole and stamped on the earth so no one would realize anything had been buried there. Not that anybody had discovered our secret hideout yet.

Because Gretchen was the tallest, she wedged the digging spoon in a V-shaped branch of the dogwood tree. Then we scrambled out of the tunnel, yanked the honeysuckle vines over the secret entrance, and scurried up the hill to join the rest of our class.

We got in line behind Vincent Wheatly, the meanest boy in the whole school, let alone the sixth grade, and giggled. We had done it again! Mrs. Harmon never missed us — we had spent the entire recess period in our hideout instead of playing dumb old four-square.

"Class!" Mrs. Harmon blew her whistle so hard I expected to see smoke fly out of her ears. "Next week we begin physical fitness training. Boys and girls are to bring shorts and T-shirts for that week. I'll pass out the permission slips at the end of the day."

I groaned. The President's program for fitness was the pits. Last year, in fifth grade, our teacher forced us to jump and throw and catch like trained seals. We performed dashes and sit-ups and the most loathsome event of all, the six hundred. Now, I don't mind running ten or even fifty yards, but eight times around the blacktop is ridiculous. I walked the course, pulling the worst time in the history of Centreville Elementary, thirteen minutes and twenty-three seconds. And I didn't even get out of breath.

"It's not so bad." Gretchen tugged her strawberry-blond ponytail over one shoulder. "We'll probably be partners again like we were last year."

"I'm going to get a doctor's note," I said, knowing full well my mother would eagerly sign the permission slip. She was forever driving me out of the shade where I liked to sit and read, into the hot, broiling sun and urging me to play like a normal kid. "Maybe I'll break my leg before next week," I said hopefully.

Mrs. Harmon herded us back inside. In room 10, I sat down and scratched "Kobie Roberts" in the soft wood of my desktop with the end of my pen. I'd been working on my name-carving since the first day of school. Mrs. Harmon caught me in the act the second day and gave me a lecture about defacing school property and how I'd have to pay for my desk. But then I showed her the fifteen other signatures carved on the seat and the back of the desk and she clammed up.

In the desk beside me, Gretchen took out her history book. She was always ready to start the lesson, even before the teacher told us to take out our books. She looked over and saw me inking the "K" in my carving.

"Kobie, you shouldn't write on your desk."

"Why not? Everybody else does." I indicated the signatures I wasn't sitting on. "I want all those nerdy little kids coming after us to know I was here. We're finally sixth graders, Gretch! Top of the heap!"

She thoughtfully chewed the end of her pencil. "That's true. After five years, we're number one. But next year, we'll be back down at the bottom again, Kobie. When we go to junior high."

"Don't think about that. Concentrate on making this our most memorable year at Centreville. When we leave, I want people to say, 'The old place will never be the same without Kobie Roberts and Gretchen Farris.' "

"Well, they'll have the 'old' part right, anyway," Gretchen laughed.

That was another reason I didn't sweat over carving my name in my desk. All the furniture and equipment were practically falling apart. Centreville Elementary was one of the oldest schools in Fairfax County, Virginia. My father went here when he was a little boy, so our school was either forty or a hundred and eight years old, I forget which. My father worked for the grounds department of Fairfax County schools and he was always telling me about the nice new schools the kids in Annandale and Burke went to. Next year Gretchen and I might go to one of those new schools.

"How are we going to make this year memorable?" Gretchen wanted to know. Mrs. Harmon was late getting the history lesson started. She was busy yelling at Vincent Wheatly for cutting a chunk out of Marcia Dittier's hair. With Marcia's looks, one hank of hair wasn't any great loss.

Instead of answering Gretchen, I stared out the window to the playground below. Just beyond the edge of the blacktop, I could see our hideout, last year's secret project. One day at recess, we discovered that the honeysuckle-tangled dogwoods bordering the school property would make a terrific hiding place. We sneaked away from the rest of the class every day during recess to tunnel out weeds and vines. We also got terrible poison ivy but it was worth it. When we were finished, our hideout had a packed-earth floor and a thick canopy of vines that let us see out but kept outsiders from looking in.

I brought an old spoon from home and Gretchen found an old tin box which we buried in the dirt floor. Every other Thursday was Dues Day. We added to the treasury whatever we could afford. At the end of the year, we planned to buy the Nancy Drew books we didn't have.

If I craned my neck a little, I could spot the old man's house on the hill above the Honeysuckle Hideout. At least, an old man was *supposed* to live there, but no one ever saw him. I didn't even know his name.

The biggest problem with dinky places like Centreville and Willow Springs, where I lived, was that nothing ever happened. *Nothing*. In the mystery books Gretchen and I checked out of the library, kids were always having adventures, tracking down jewel thieves or finding long-lost treasures. All we ever did was get up, go to school, do homework, and go to bed. In between, our parents made us clean our rooms and sometimes we visited relatives in Mannassas, the next town over. That was it.

"We need a new project," I declared. "Something that will make us famous."

"Like what?" Gretchen asked.

"Like — " My eyes went to the gray house on the hill again. "Like finding out the truth about that old hermit next door. That he really was — is — the Hammer Man."

"Gosh, Kobie, I don't know. . . ." Gretchen's voice trailed off. She turned to the end-of-the-chapter questions in her history book, already leery of my project. Okay, so one or two of my schemes hadn't worked out. That was no reason to reject the best idea ever.

I wasn't too worried about Gretchen. We'd been best friends since second grade. No matter what I wanted to do, she'd go along. Now that we were both almost twelve, it was time for us to make a name for ourselves. And revealing the true identity of the Hammer Man would do it.

I jumped off the bus, feeling weightless and free the way I always did at the end of the school day. Setting my books on a flat rock, I opened the mailbox and pulled out two bills and an ad. I noticed my father's hand-painted "Roberts" was coming off again. He'd painted our name on the mailbox so many times I could see faint outlines of the old letters peering around the new ones like jiggly ghosts.

Gretchen and I both lived in Willow Springs, a place so dinky it didn't qualify as a town. Gretchen lived a few miles down Lee Highway. We rode the same bus, but I got off first. After supper, she'd call me and we'd do our homework together over the phone.

I headed up our long, steep driveway. In the summer, briar roses and morning glories spilled down the bank next to the garden. Now the garden was weedy, September-neglected. A few dead-ripe tomatoes, hidden among the weeds, the skins wrinkled and split, reminded me of forgotten Easter eggs. Summer was definitely over.

At the crest of our driveway, I planted one foot firmly on a fist-sized white rock I called the Moonstone. It was embedded in the gravel and polished smooth by the tires of our car. Every single day, whether I was going up the driveway or down, I stepped on the rock because I believed it brought me luck. Today I skipped back to tromp on the Moonstone a second time, for good measure. If Gretchen and I were going to expose a desperate criminal like the Hammer Man, we needed all the luck we could get.

In the kitchen, I found my mother ironing a plain white dress. Another white cotton dress, freshly-pressed, hung from the doorway. On the windowsill, a cooling apple pie scented the air with cinnamon. It was nice to be home.

"Did you make me those little pie dough things?" I asked, heaving my books onto a chair.

"Don't I always?" my mother replied. "Over there on the stove."

I poured myself a glass of cherry Kool-Aid, totally unsweetened the way I like it, and took the pie plate and my glass over to the table. Whenever my mother made a pie, she rolled the dough scraps in cinnamon and sugar and baked them for me. To me, the scraps tasted better than the pie.

"How was school?" My mother adjusted a sleeve before pressing it.

"Boring, as usual." Of course, I couldn't tell her about the Honeysuckle Hideout or the new project Gretchen and I had dreamed up just today. My mother believed kids should be thrilled to go to school and learn long division. If I told her I had fun, she'd automatically assume I was carrying on and not listening to the teacher.

I ate the last pie dough roll-up and stared at the white dress as she slipped it on a hanger. "That looks like a uniform."

"It is. I've got a job."

"A job! Where? You can't even drive!"

She unfolded a stack of aprons and began pressing them. "I don't need to drive to this job. I can take the bus."

"When did you get a job?" I couldn't believe it. My mother was always home, like the shabby old sofa in the living room. It would be funny not to see her when I came home from school.

"Today." She bent over the ironing board, concentrating on a wrinkle. "I was up at your school and you didn't even know it."

"You were at my school? Why?"

"To get a *job*, silly. I work in the cafeteria now — well, starting Monday."

I nearly splashed the apron with cherry Kool-Aid. "You're going to be a cafeteria lady? In *my* school?" My voice shrilled like Mrs. Harmon's when she was trying to get Vincent Wheatly to behave. "How could you *do* this to me?"

She stopped ironing. "Do what? Kobie, we need the money. Taxes this year are sky-high . . . and I'd like to buy new living room furniture. So I decided to get a job. I wish you wouldn't stare at me like that. It's not the end of the world."

"Yes it is!" I shrieked. "Mom, you *can't* work in my school! It's — against the law! There's some law that says a parent can't go to the same school as her kid!"

"There is not. Mrs. Wright teaches sixth grade and her two girls go to Centreville. Maryruth is in your class instead of her mother's and it's no problem."

Not unless you considered the fact that Maryruth Wright was a 'fraidy-cat wimp scared of her own shadow. And who wouldn't be? Maryruth could hardly misbehave or talk back to the teacher, not with her own mother in the very next classroom. Now *my* mother was going to be downstairs in the cafeteria. This was worse than the time in fourth grade when she volunteered to be room mother. Whenever we had a party, my mother would sail in with her box of cookies and party hats and stay until it was time to go home. Needless to say, I never had much fun.

Instead of bringing cookies to my class four or five times a year — a punishment I'd gladly endure — now my mother would hand me my plate in the lunch line *every single day*. She'd watch me eating and giggling with Gretchen. She'd see me blowing straw wrappers. She'd know when I traded my entire lunch for somebody's dessert. I'd never be out of her sight. The image was too horrible to bear.

"Why did you get a job as a cafeteria lady?" I wailed. "Why didn't you try the fountain at Centreville Pharmacy if you wanted to cook so bad?"

"Kobie, I wasn't really looking for a cooking job," she explained. "I wanted a job that would let me be here when you got home from school. Working in your school seemed the best solution. And of course, there's the bus."

A nasty feeling squirmed in the pit of my stomach. "What bus?" I asked warily.

"Your bus. I can take the school bus to and from work every day. I won't have to beg rides. It works out perfectly."

"You mean, you're going to ride my *bus*, too? Stand out at *my* bus stop and wait for the bus with *me*?" This was getting worse by the minute. "Mom, you can't do that! The school bus is just for kids. The only grown-up allowed is Mr. Bass, the bus driver."

"I don't know where you get these strange ideas. I've already talked to Mr. Bass and he said he'd be delighted to have me ride his bus." She frowned. "But you aren't. What's bothering you?"

I was too overwhelmed by her news to reply. My mother working in the cafeteria, riding my bus . . . I wouldn't have one speck of privacy, anywhere!

"Kobie, this job is a good thing. We'll have more money — your father won't have to work so much overtime. He'll be able to build you that tree house you've been wanting."

I perked up a little at that. Ever since my father saw me attempting to build a tree house with one board and four nails, he promised to build me a real tree house, with walls and a roof and everything. But summer had come and gone and still no tree house. My father had worked every Saturday and spent the evenings in the garden.

"Do you think Dad will start my tree house this weekend?" I asked, tears springing to my eyes. Even if my father built me a tree house city, it wouldn't help the fact that my wonderful sixth grade year was over before it began. Gretchen and I might as well kiss our secret project good-bye. No way could we trap the Hammer Man with my mother hovering around.

She came over and gave me a squeeze.

"It's tough being an only child, isn't it? We try to make time for you, Kobie, but it isn't always possible, with all the bills we have."

If she hadn't acted nice, I would have been okay. If we had gone on arguing about her stupid job at my school, I wouldn't have started crying like a baby. I hated to cry — I was going on *twelve*, for Pete's sake.

I broke away from her, blubbering like a first grader. "I don't care what you do!" I yelled. "But don't expect me to sit by you on the bus! And I'm fixing my own lunch from now on — I'd rather die than eat your dumb old food!"

Chapter 2

When I called Gretchen and told her about my mother's new job, she didn't seem to think it was the end of the world, either.

"Your mother can give you double helpings of French fries," she said. "And sneak you extra butter cookies." The great big round butter cookies the cafeteria served, usually on Flying Saucer Sandwich days, were worth buying lunch for.

"I'll get double helpings, all right," I said bitterly. "A double dose of problems. Gretch, can you just *imagine* having your mother work in the cafeteria of your school? Can't you just hear my mother nagging me to eat all my lima beans in front of everybody?"

"Kobie, it probably won't be so bad. Don't worry yourself sick over it." Papers rustled on her end of the line. "I hate to change the subject, but have you done your arithmetic?"

"I looked at it. You know I can't do long division. Will you give me your answers?" I wheedled.

"Yeah, but Mrs. Harmon wants to see how you got them."

"I know." In the drawer of the phone stand, I scrounged up a pencil stub and an old envelope. "Maybe I can figure it out backward once I have the answers."

"Kobie, long division is easy. Wait till we get to fractions and decimals." Gretchen always peeked ahead in her textbooks to see what was coming up next. As for me, I always hoped that after the chapter we were working on, my book would be filled with blank pages.

"Why did you have to bring that up? I'll never be able to do fractions or decimals or long division. I can't even do short division."

She sighed. "Kobie, short division is like multiplication, only in reverse, kind of."

I didn't want to talk about arithmetic. Gretchen could explain it to me until she was blue in the face, but I only knew my times tables up to five and that was why I couldn't divide. The rest of the times tables — six, seven, eight and especially nine — were too slippery to stay in my brain.

"This was supposed to be such a great school year," I grumbled. "First we have that awful physical fitness training. Then we have long division. Now my mother will be spying on me in the cafeteria and riding my bus! What else will go wrong?"

"Nothing," Gretchen replied confidently. "Bad things come in threes. Only good things can happen from now on."

After we hung up, I went down to the basement. Usually I watched TV or talked to my mother while she cooked supper, but today I wanted to be by myself.

I sat on the steps, breathing in the cool, musty air. The basement was one of my favorite places. Both sides of the white plaster stairwell were covered with my drawings. Once a long time ago when I was bored and didn't have any paper, I started drawing in the stairwell. Naturally my mother complained, but my father told her my drawings were cheaper than wallpaper.

I didn't feel very creative, so I went over to my swing. When my old, rusty swing set had to be hauled to the dump, my father salvaged one of the swings, looping the chains over a big, square metal beam in the basement. I rocked back and forth, glad nobody from school could see me. The chains grated overhead, *skreek! skreek!*

Next to the swing was a mildewed carton

of ancient encyclopedias. The encyclopedia we used at school was divided alphabetically — "Timbuktu to Wombat," for example. But each volume of my old encyclopedia was a separate subject, like *Science, Peoples of the World*, etc. The books had rich-looking dark blue bindings, and were filled with old-fashioned pictures. The information in them was mostly out of date. Once my teacher asked me how many planets were in the solar system and I told her seven. "My encyclopedia says so," I argued when she informed me I was wrong.

I loved to idle in my swing and leaf through those books. It made me feel content. I picked up the Children's volume, which had the neatest pictures, and opened it on my lap.

But all I could think about was my mother in her white uniform standing at the bus stop with me Monday morning. The bus would come and we'd get on together. She'd make me sit with her, in the seat right behind the driver where the goody-goodies sat.

The encyclopedia grew heavy in my lap. The cellar seemed gloomy and damp, no longer pleasantly cool. Suddenly I knew what my name would be this year, the name everyone would remember me by: Mama's Baby.

On Monday morning, I stood as far away from my mother as I possibly could and still legally be in our driveway. We waited for the bus without speaking to each other. She was mad at me for acting so childish over a little thing like her riding my bus. Little thing!

When the bus came, I charged on first, butting in front of my mother to save a seat for Gretchen. My mother took forever getting up the steps and then she had to stop and talk to Mr. Bass, the bus driver. It was so embarrassing. Mr. Bass wasn't allowed to start the bus again until everybody was sitting down. Traffic backed up behind us something terrible.

My mother looked around uncertainly. She glanced over where I was stubbornly claiming the middle of an empty seat, then glanced away. A little red-haired girl piped up, "You can sit with me!" My mother slid next to the little girl, smoothing her uniform over her knees. We did not look at each other.

When Gretchen got on, she said hi to my mother and would have said more but I pulled her away.

"Don't encourage her. Maybe she'll leave us alone."

"But she's not bothering us," Gretchen pointed out.

"She will."

At the unloading zone at school, my mother poked down the steps in her thick-soled white shoes.

"Your mother is very nice," Mr. Bass said as I stomped off the bus. "I'm glad she'll be riding with us."

"Well, *I'm* not." It was beginning already. Pretty soon everybody would be associating me with my mother. I was doomed.

The little kid my mother had sat with on the bus was having trouble with the front door. She smiled at me as I opened it for her. "Is that lady your mother?" she asked.

"What's it to you?" I asked sourly.

In room 10, I threw the paper sack containing the shorts and T-shirt I had to wear during recess in the cloakroom, stuffed my lunch bag under my desk, and flopped in my seat. I was too depressed to work on my name-carving.

It was an awful day, just as I expected. First, we had to switch arithmetic homework to mark in class. When I handed mine to Gretchen, Mrs. Harmon plucked it out of her fingers and gave it to Kathy Stall on the other side of the aisle.

"You girls are too chummy," Mrs. Harmon declared. "I want you to start mixing with your classmates more, Kobie."

As the teacher called out the answers to the arithmetic questions, I saw Kathy cheerfully checking every one of mine wrong, because I hadn't written out the whole problem. Kathy, of course, got them all correct. I wrote a very small, very faint "A" in the corner under Kathy's name.

"You failed," Kathy said loudly as we switched papers back. "You missed them all," she added unnecessarily. The "F" she had scrawled at the top of my paper was as big as the Empire State Building.

And Mrs. Harmon wanted me to "mix" with the other kids. Everybody in my class, in the whole school even, except Gretchen, was a total nerd. I mean, with friends like Kathy Stall, who needed enemies? Mrs. Harmon didn't understand that Gretchen and I were more than friends — we were practically sisters. We liked exactly the same things, mystery stories and butter cookies and talking about how we were going to be famous when we grew up. The other girls were dull as sticks — all they ever wanted to do was play jumprope. The reason Gretchen and I made the Honeysuckle Hideout was to get away from them.

Recess made the morning seem like a picnic. We changed into shorts and T-shirts in the girls' room and met the boys on the blacktop. Vincent Wheatly whistled at Kathy Stall, who looked nice in shorts. In fact, all the girls but me looked good in shorts. I had the skinniest legs in both sixth grade classes. Nobody whistled at me.

The first event was the broad jump. We were supposed to jump across this sawdust-filled pit as far as we could. Mrs. Harmon marked everyone's jump with a yardstick. She didn't need a yardstick to measure mine — a six-inch ruler was more than adequate. When I lumbered to my feet, brushing sawdust off my shorts, I was mortified to see my footprints were barely over the starting line. My broad jump was more like a bunny hop.

"Let's hear it for Bony Maroni! Hey, Skinny Minnie!" Richard Supinger yelled. He was Vincent Wheatly's sidekick.

I wanted to run down the hill to the Honeysuckle Hideout, but Mrs. Harmon's whistle urged us on to the next event.

"Don't pay any attention to them," Gretchen said. "They're just stupid boys."

"Gretchen, I can't broad jump and I

can't do long division. I'm a sixth grade failure. Washed up at eleven!"

After we had sprinted and hopped and choked ourselves at the chin-up bars, Mrs. Harmon decided we had been tortured enough for one day and let us go early. As I changed into my dress, I realized I still had lunch, with my mother as a cafeteria lady, to look forward to.

But when we got back to class, two things happened to make me forget about my mother, for a little while, at least.

We had a new kid. He shuffled shyly beside Mrs. Harmon's desk, staring at the floor while she introduced him.

"Class, I want you to welcome John Orrin to room 10," she said. "His family moved to Centreville last week. Let's show John how glad we are to have him join us."

I applauded with two fingers, smirking at Gretchen.

John Orrin was a shrimp, even smaller than me. He had hay-colored hair and watery gray eyes. When he walked back to the desk Mrs. Harmon assigned him, two seats over from me, he ducked his head and loped like a camel.

Gretchen and I cracked up behind our geography books. He was so funny-looking! He reminded me of a scarecrow, with that straw hair and those too-short pants. On the back of my "F" arithmetic paper I sketched a scarecrow. Scribbling the caption "John Oreo" at the bottom, I passed the drawing to Gretchen. She spluttered with laughter.

Mrs. Harmon was down the aisle like a shot. "What's going on here?"

"N-nothing," Gretchen stammered. She tried to slide my sketch under her geography book, but the teacher snatched it from her.

Mrs. Harmon stuffed the drawing in her pocket, flashing her glasses in my direction. "Kobie, see me before lunch."

The whole class was staring at me, including the new boy. My face burning, I pretended to read a terribly interesting paragraph in my geography book. When I looked up again, only the new boy was still watching me. He was actually smiling, as if he thought it was hilarious that I was in trouble with the teacher. I stuck my tongue out at him and he turned away.

Then Mrs. Harmon made her second announcement.

"Settle down, people. As you know, our annual Back-to-School Night is October 15. Every year, all the classes do special projects for the parents to see. This year, the two sixth grade rooms will compete to display their project on the bulletin board by the office." Immediately a buzz of excitement swelled and Mrs. Harmon had to flick the lights on and off to get everybody quiet again. "Mrs. Wright and I have already selected the subject and type of project. We are going to do a mural sewn on burlap. A medieval tapestry showing a scene from the Middle Ages we're learning about in history."

Right away there were a million comments, mostly from the boys, who didn't like the idea of sewing. I wasn't crazy about the sewing part myself, but I knew somebody had to draw the picture on the burlap and I wanted to be that person.

"Everyone will participate in the project," Mrs. Harmon said, bringing a chorus of groans from the boys. "We will all help design the mural and each of you will take a turn stitching the design — "

I couldn't stand it any longer. "Who's going to draw the picture?" I blurted out.

"Did I see your hand raised, Kobie?"

I waggled my fingers and waited for her to call on me. "Who's going to be the one who draws the picture?"

"Why, everyone," Mrs. Harmon replied.

"Won't the design look better if *one* person draws it?" I said. "If a whole bunch of people work on it, it'll look like something from Miss Dede's room." Miss Dede taught first grade. A few kids snickered.

Gretchen held up her hand. "Mrs. Harmon, I think the best artist in the class should draw the design." Surprisingly, Kathy Stall and Marcia Dittier and a couple others agreed with her.

"I don't know," Mrs. Harmon hesitated. "It hardly seems fair to let one person do the entire drawing. . . ."

"But we want to win!" Vincent Wheatly bellowed. "We want to beat Mrs. Wright's class!"

"Yeah!"

Mrs. Harmon relented. "We'll take a vote. All those in favor of one person drawing the mural, raise your hand."

I raised both of mine. The majority ruled; it was decided that one person would draw the tapestry.

"How are we going to determine who the artist should be? Suggestions?" Mrs. Harmon perched on top of her desk.

That was easy. The best artist was seven seats away from her. But I couldn't nominate myself. I elbowed Gretchen.

"Mrs. Harmon," Gretchen spoke up. "Kobie Roberts is the best artist in our class. Last year, Kobie and Lynette

O'Bannon were picked to do the theater show."

The fifth grade in room 8 did a theater show every year. Two artists illustrated a fairy tale on a long paper scroll. Then the scroll was stretched on dowels in a fancy little wooden theater and rolled like a filmstrip. Last year, Lynette and I drew "Cinderella." We copied the pictures from a Golden Book, working during free periods. Then we wheeled the portable theater around to all the lower grades. Lynette turned the scroll while I read the story to the little kids.

"Lynette will probably draw the mural for Mrs. Wright's class," Kathy Stall said. Lynette O'Bannon was in room 11, the other sixth grade class.

"If we want to win, we ought to let Skinnie Minnie — I mean, Kobie draw ours," Richard Supinger said, grinning at me.

"Richard, do you want to spend lunch in Mr. Magyn's office?" Mrs. Harmon said sternly. "All right, let's take another vote. Those who want Kobie Roberts to draw the design for our mural, raise your hands."

It was unanimous! I was elected to draw the tapestry. But, then, I *was* the best artist in the class.

On my way to lunch, Mrs. Harmon snared me. Gretchen waited at the door, but the teacher motioned her on. When everyone had left, Mrs. Harmon took the scarecrow drawing of John Orrin from her pocket. She laid it on her desk between us.

"One thing I won't tolerate in my class is cruel humor," she began. "You didn't have to write John's name below your drawing — you *are* a good artist. Your caricature is quite accurate."

"What's a cari — what you just said?" I asked.

"A picture of a person with their features exaggerated and distorted. I suppose you think this is very funny."

"Well, yes. Don't you? You said yourself it looks just like him — "

"Kobie, don't get smart with me. You are deliberately misreading my point. What if John Orrin had seen this picture? How do you think he would have felt?"

But he *hadn't* seen the drawing, I almost protested. Why worry over something that hadn't even happened? However, I suspected my best-artist title was at stake. "It probably would've hurt his feelings," I said humbly.

"Exactly. Now would you have wanted to

hurt his feelings? A brand-new student, his first day here?"

I shook my head. Mrs. Harmon tore the drawing to shreds and dropped the pieces in her trash can.

"Can I go to lunch now?"

"You may. But remember, Kobie — the other students voted you best artist in the class, a great honor, but I will take that privilege away from you any time I see you abusing it. Do you understand?"

I nodded that I did. Then I grabbed my lunch bag and skipped down the stairs to the lunchroom. Maybe I couldn't do long division or broad jumps, but I was the best artist in my class. Soon I'd be Best Artist in Centreville Elementary, when our mural won the contest. Now *that* was a name people would remember.

Chapter 3

The rackety engine of my father's old Ford tractor coughed twice, then died. My father clambered down from the seat and came over to sit by me on the big flat rock at the edge of the garden.

"Just look at that sky," he said, tipping his cap back. "Not a cloud in it. October is my favorite month."

"Mine, too." I hugged my notebook to my chest. Every year when October rolled around, cool and serene after a muggy September, we made the same statement.

"Great month to work outdoors," my father went on. "Not too hot. No birds twittering."

We both listened. Though woods surrounded our property, we didn't hear a single bird.

I liked having the same favorite month

as my father. "I wish my birthday was in October. On Halloween. That'd be neat."

"I wish my birthday was in October, too." He stretched out his legs. The cuffs of his dark green pants were caked with red clay. "But we had to be born in July, didn't we? I guess that makes us appreciate October even more."

In the fall my father plowed the garden one last time before winter, turning over the tasseled weeds and dried-up cornstalks until the earth was red and clean again. Usually I rode on the tractor with him, snugly wedged between his shoulder and the chipped fender. I'd watch the action behind us, hoping the plow blades would bring a white quartz arrowhead or a battered Confederate bullet to the surface.

But today I was too busy to help plow. Since I was going on twelve, I figured riding the tractor was for kids, and anyway, I hardly ever found an arrowhead or a musket ball.

I sat on the flat rock at the edge of the garden and worked on the mural sketches. Our class had finally decided on a scene for our medieval tapestry — a medieval castle, a dragon running from some knights on horseback, and a unicorn grazing in a flowery meadow. Yesterday Mrs. Harmon excused me from social studies so I could go to the library and check out books on the Middle Ages.

"What are you doing?" my father asked. "Every time I look, you've got a pencil in your hand."

I showed him my picture of the castle. "It's for our Back-to-School Night project."

He held the tablet out at arm's length, studying my drawing. "That's really something, Kobie, the way you can draw. I couldn't draw a straight line with a ruler. I can't even draw flies."

I giggled because he always said that. "I'm having trouble with these horses." On the next page were sketches of stump-legged horses. "I can't get their legs right."

"They look fine to me." He tilted his head. "Did you hear that one snort?"

"Oh, Dad." I swatted him with my drawing tablet.

"Well, with the garden all plowed, I've got a little free time next weekend," he said. "Have you thought about where you want your tree house?"

My heart leaped. He was actually going to build my tree house! I pointed to an oak on the other side of the driveway. "Over there."

"Kobie, that tree doesn't have any low branches to hold a tree house. The trunk goes straight up for twenty feet. It won't work."

I flipped to the last page in my drawing tablet. "It'll work if you make it like this." In science class last year, I had designed a tree house that didn't need to be built around large, sturdy branches. Instead, the structure was fastened to the *side* of the tree, with braces underneath.

"Yes, that'll work," he acknowledged. "I would never have thought of building it tacked to the tree like that."

"I got the idea from a book about these kids trying to build a clubhouse, only they don't have a tree big enough so they just build a house on stilts." Now for the sticky part. "Can you make me stairs like this, Dad, with rails on both sides?"

"You don't want a ladder? Most tree houses have rungs nailed to the trunk of the tree."

I shook my head. As desperately as I wanted a tree house — a secret place all my own, away from my mother — I was afraid of heights. Once I got *up* there, I knew I'd be okay, but I couldn't stand to climb ladders. I hardly ever went into our attic because the pull-down stairs were so narrow they scared me.

"I can build a staircase, if that's what you want."

"And don't make it very high," I said. Then I added hastily, afraid he'd change his mind if I made too many demands, "I mean, you won't have to build such a *long* staircase if the tree house is kind of close to the ground."

"A close-to-the-ground tree house. Sounds more like a bush house to me." He chuckled. "Tell you the truth, I don't like high places, either. When I was in the Navy, they put me in the crow's nest once for a four-hour watch. The crow's nest was way above the deck and every time the ocean pitched, that pole dipped so low I thought I'd have to bail water."

"How did you get down?" For me, getting down from a high place was almost as bad as climbing up.

"I skinned over the fella coming up to relieve my watch. Practically ripped his shirt off him."

I loved to hear my father talk about his Navy days in the Pacific. He had been to Australia and a lot of islands with magical-sounding names like Guam, Borneo, and New Guinea. One island had nothing on it but pure white sand like sugar and big dumb birds that couldn't fly. No people, no animals, not even any trees. It sounded so different from dreary Willow Springs.

"Tell me about the time you crossed the equator," I asked.

"Oh, you've heard that old one a hundred times. You don't want to hear it again."

"Yes, I do! Please, Dad!"

When he laughed, I knew he intended to tell me all along. He was always teasing me. "When I was in basic training up in Great Lakes, Illinois, some of the guys told awful tales about crossing the equator. Seamen who'd never been that far south before had to pass an initiation ceremony."

"Like eating cold spaghetti blindfolded and they tell you it's worms?" One year at the school Halloween party, the older kids did that to the younger kids.

"I wish it had been cold spaghetti. Well, the day arrived. Our ship was about to cross the equator. All of us who were going to be initiated were blindfolded and lined up on deck. Some guy slammed me in a barber chair and the ship's barber shaved me bald. Then he flicked a lever under the chair and threw me backward over the railing. The whole way down I thought I'd been thrown overboard! I landed in a big tub of seawater on the lower deck, only I didn't know it. I thrashed around like a whale, trying to get that blindfold off and get to the top! When I climbed out, everybody was laughing. But I was one of them — I had crossed."

With my pen I aided a sluggish ladybug on her descent from the rock to the grass. "Did you feel any different?"

"I was wet — and plenty mad."

"No, I mean, when your ship was right at the equator. Did you feel funny being on the line?"

"Kobie, the equator isn't actually a line, like you draw on paper. It's an imaginary circle around the earth that divides the Northern Hemisphere from the Southern Hemisphere. You can't really see it."

"But you must have seen *something*," I insisted.

"No, I didn't. Those are just numbers, Kobie, coordinates the captain uses to guide the ship. The equator marks the base line for latitude. Have you learned about latitude and longitude in geography yet?"

I shook my head, more interested in what it felt like to be right on the equator, not really in the Northern Hemisphere and not really in the Southern Hemisphere. Now that I was going on twelve, I seemed to be drifting toward some kind of equator myself. I wouldn't be a real teenager until I was thirteen, my mother had told me, and I was phasing out being a kid. In July, I'd turn twelve . . . and be right on the line. I wanted to know what I was in for.

My father thought I was still stuck on latitude and longitude. "I've got a paper somewhere," he said. "When I passed the initiation."

"What kind of paper?" I'd never heard this part of the story before.

"A certificate signed by King Neptune. Everybody got one when we crossed. It had the latitude and longitude and some other stuff about the mysteries of the deep, or some such craziness."

A paper signed by King Neptune, about crossing a mysterious line! If I had that paper, I'd really *know*. "Where is it, Dad? Do you still have it?"

He shrugged. "Your mother has all my military papers. She'll get it for you."

My heart sank. Ever since my mother had begun working at my school, she had less time for me than she usually did. On weekends, she was busy cleaning the house and doing laundry.

"No, she won't," I said.

"All you have to do is ask her."

I could ask *him* to do things for me, like build my tree house and tell me stories, but my mother wasn't at all like my father.

* * *

Our special table in the lunchroom was conveniently located near the garbage cans and away from the monitors. To discourage anyone else from sitting with us, I propped the extra chairs against the edge of the table, like the janitor did when he mopped the floor. It was the only way Gretchen and I could have complete privacy.

While Gretchen was inching through the lunch line, I dumped out the contents of my lunch bag. A few minutes later, she sat down with her tray.

"Here's your milk," she said, handing me the extra carton off her tray. "Your mother wants to know when you're going to stop acting silly and come through the line to buy your own milk."

I unwrapped the sandwich I had slapped together that morning — Vienna sausage, sliced lengthwise and lined up on the bread. "Fingers again."

Gretchen stopped buttering her roll to give me a dark look. "Kobie, why do you always have to be gross at lunch?"

"That's the only time it counts." I laughed, but I was really angry with my mother, passing that message to Gretchen. The serving line was so noisy, I knew my mother had to yell it out. Probably every kid in school heard her tell Gretchen how silly I was behaving.

"Your mom also said to eat all of your lunch," Gretchen reported. "She knows you threw your banana away yesterday."

"That banana was rotten," I said. "She made me take it, even after I told her I didn't want it. You see how she is? My mother has spies everywhere in here but under the table — I have to bring my lunch to save my reputation."

I finished half my sandwich, but put the other half on Gretchen's tray to throw away without my mother noticing. Today I had slathered too much mayonnaise on my sandwich. I was tired of Vienna sausage anyway, and that made me even madder because normally I loved it. Another favorite thing down the tubes since my mother started working at my school.

"Look who's coming," Gretchen whispered suddenly.

John Orrin was ambling in our direction, clutching his tray and scanning the room for an empty seat. His head swiveled like a lighthouse beam. John was last in the lunch line every single day, not just because he hadn't made any friends who would let him cut in front, but because he was so slow. A snail crawling over molasses moved faster than he did.

"He's on free lunch," I said. Actually it

was no big secret. Everybody knew he was on free lunch because Mrs. Settinger, the cafeteria lady who collected the lunch money, screamed, "Go on through!" to the kids who didn't have to pay.

"So what?" Gretchen said. "Lots of kids can't afford to buy lunch."

"I know," I replied quickly. My mother was forever reminding me how poor *we* were, yet we always had enough to eat. Whenever I went through the serving line behind a kid on the free lunch program, I always felt a little peculiar. Lunch was just lunch to me, but according to my mother, lunch to those kids was often the only meal they got all day.

Today I didn't care whether John was a welfare case or not; I didn't want our meeting interrupted. "He can't sit here." I jerked the extra chairs around us, barricading our table from the intruder.

"I think he's going to. The monitor probably sent him over here."

"Rats. I wanted to talk about the old man next door."

"We'll talk about it some other time," Gretchen said, as John approached.

I didn't want to be put off. Too many portions of my life were out of my control now. "Go away," I told John as he gingerly set his tray down.

"Kobie!" Gretchen looked shocked.

"The lady told me to sit here," John drawled. He had a weird accent, real hicky.

"She didn't ask *us* if you could sit here." I glared at him. "This is a private table. Members only."

Gretchen shoved one of the extra chairs toward John. "Kobie was just fooling. Sit down. Your food will get cold."

"Who cares?" I muttered, but John sat down anyway, undaunted by my glare.

Gretchen kicked me under the table. "Kobie, what's the matter with you?" she hissed.

I kicked her back, hard. "What's the matter with *you*? Why don't you roll out the red carpet for him? Buy him a box of Oreos? You got a crush on him or what?"

She bit her bottom lip. Her shin must have hurt from my kick, but she didn't cry.

"I don't think I want to be friends with you anymore," she said softly.

I flung my trash in the garbage can. "Fine! I don't want to be friends with you, either."

Down the table, John Orrin dug into his lunch. Apparently terminal slowness did not affect his appetite. He smiled at us placidly around a mouthful of mexi-corn, either secretly glad or completely unaware of the tension he'd caused between me and Gretchen.

For the rest of the day, Gretchen and I avoided each other, which wasn't easy considering our desks were side by side. We didn't play hangman or giggle like we usually did. It was a long afternoon and I was glad when the last bell rang.

I followed Gretchen on the bus. She paused before our special seat, third from the front on the left. Then she saw me and stepped back to let me pass.

"Go ahead," I told her.

"No, you go in."

"You were here first."

Gretchen took the seat, sliding over close to the window. "Aren't you going to sit here?"

"Are you sure you want me to?" I was blocking the aisle but dynamite couldn't have moved me. Gretchen and I hardly ever fought. I was desperate to make up with her.

"Are you sure *you* want to?" she countered.

I sat down beside her. "I'm sorry — "

"I'm sorry — " she began at the same instant.

Automatically we chorused "Thumbs up" and held up our right thumbs in the required signal. We kept on chanting

"Thumbs up! Thumbs up!" at the same time, until Gretchen collapsed with laughter.

"We have to link pinkies," I instructed. We crooked our pinky fingers together to end the jinx of talking at the same time. "I hate it when we fight."

"Me, too. I didn't mean it when I said I didn't want to be friends with you anymore."

"Neither did I. I've been miserable all day," I confessed. Never again, I vowed, would I fight with Gretchen over something as stupid as John Orrin sitting at our lunch table. It wasn't worth it.

"There's your mother," Gretchen said. "She looks tired."

My mother *did* look tired as she plodded down the aisle, but it was her own fault. Nobody forced her to get a job at my school.

"Who's that girl who saves your mother a seat every day?"

"I don't know." I pretended not to notice my mother and the first grader, one seat ahead of us. "Some dumb kid. Her name's Beverly."

"She really seems to like your mother."

Beverly and my mother were going to town up there, chattering like they hadn't seen each other in years.

"My mother loves little kids who don't

have any front teeth," I remarked sarcastically.

Now Beverly pulled a wad of paper from her Barbie lunch box. The paper was a big, oatmeal-colored sheet of construction paper, the cheap kind issued to the lower grades. On it Beverly had crayoned a lopsided house and a messy-looking thing that could have been either a person or an elephant with measles — it was impossible to tell.

"Isn't that cute?" Gretchen cooed.

"What a crummy picture! I could draw better with my feet!" An unfamiliar emotion churned in my stomach, like the time I had too much grape soda at the fireman's carnival and then got on the Round-Up ride.

My mother exclaimed over Beverly's picture, praising it enthusiastically.

"Your mother thinks it's cute," Gretchen observed.

"She doesn't know *anything* about art," I said. "She doesn't know anything about anything. I wish she'd never got that dumb job. All she does is bug me."

"How can you say that? She's not bothering us one bit. You don't want your mother sitting with us and she isn't. What's eating you?"

What was eating me was the sight of

Beverly's gap-toothed grin as she hugged my mother's arm. Gretchen was half right — I didn't want my mother sitting with us. But I didn't want anybody *else* sitting with her, either.

Chapter 4

"One of us could go up and knock on his front door and ask him directions or something. You know, distract him, while the other peeps in his windows." I kept my voice low since we were in the library at school. "Then, when we find which room has the evidence we need, we go back and try to get it."

Gretchen frowned. "And just how do we get in his house? Walk up and say, 'Pardon me, but my friend wants to borrow one of your hammers. We're going to take it to the police and have you arrested.' Kobie, if the Hammer Man's been hiding out here all these years, he's not about to let two kids go off with one of his hammers."

"Of course we're not going to *ask* him for a hammer," I said, forgetting to keep my voice down. "What kind of a jerk do you think I am?"

"Just an ordinary, everyday one." Gretchen grinned, unable to resist making the crack.

"Very funny." I surveyed the library over the book I was holding in front of us to help muffle our conversation. Another class was filing in to join ours. "We have to come up with a foolproof plan. This is a desperate criminal we're dealing with, Gretchen."

"How do you know that? I mean, why does the old man on the hill have to be the Hammer Man? Suppose he's just some old man who doesn't like to leave his house?"

"Honestly, Gretch, you're getting as fussy as Harmon. Why *can't* he be the Hammer Man?" Mrs. Sharp, the librarian, warned me with a nod. I lowered my voice again. "The Hammer Man disappeared without a trace years ago, right after his last murder. The police never found a single clue and you know why? Because he's right here, that's why."

Gretchen turned the pages of a horse book until she found a picture I could copy. "Here's a good one. He's running like the horse in your mural. I still don't see what makes you think he's the Hammer Man."

I began sketching the running horse in my notebook. I had finished the castle and the meadow parts of the mural. The horses, and the unicorn, which was basically a white horse with a horn, were driving me nuts. I couldn't get their legs right to save me.

"That's just it," I said briskly. "I *think* he's the Hammer Man. You have to think of something first, before you find it out. That's how electricity got invented. Benjamin Franklin thought it up first — he probably got tired of drippy candles — and then he went out with his kite and got struck by lightning."

Since she needed further convincing, I elaborated on my theory. "Take Nancy Drew. She doesn't sit around waiting for criminals to fall in her lap. She *deduces* who they are, by using her mind. I've already deduced he's the Hammer Man — all we have to do is think of a plan to catch him."

Capturing a murderer would make me instantly famous. I'd be the Centreville Heroine. Of course, having the name Best Artist in Centreville Elementary wouldn't be so bad, either. I could handle both.

"One more thing, Sherlock," Gretchen said.

I concentrated on the horse's legs, trying to get the proportions accurate. "What's that?"

"How are we going to catch the Hammer

Man when we're not allowed off school property?"

I looked up from my sketch to stare at her. Sometimes Gretchen was so sensible, it was annoying. "We sneak off school property, that's how."

"But, Kobie, it's against the rules. Mr. Magyn could suspend us. My mother would kill me if I got suspended."

I wasn't surprised Gretchen was worried about a minor detail like leaving school property. She never turned in homework papers full of eraser holes. And she never yelled in class or threw spitballs. At the beginning of the year when Mrs. Harmon told us to put covers on our schoolbooks to keep them nice, Gretchen spent one entire evening converting grocery bags into book covers. She wasn't exactly a teacher's pet or anything like that, but she never caused any trouble, either. The most daring thing Gretchen did was skip recess with me to meet in the Honeysuckle Hideout.

"Gretchen, if we get caught, it'll be for a good reason. It won't be like we're running off to the Dairy Queen."

The ice-cream stand, Centreville's no-man's-land, was located at the bottom of the hill opposite the old man's front yard, like an oasis in a desert. Occasionally a kid would get a craving for frozen custard and slip away during lunch. The principal forbade the students on pain of death to walk over to the Dairy Queen during school hours. We even thought twice about going to the Dairy Queen *after* school.

I could see this was a big thing with Gretchen. Our project was in danger of disintegrating before it ever got off the ground unless I did something.

The other class, Mr. Breg's fifth grade, swarmed over the bookshelves. Two classes at once packed the tiny library. Mrs. Sharp came over to our table.

"I haven't had a chance to speak to you girls this morning," she said. "Kobie, I see you're still drawing."

"She's working on the mural for our room." Gretchen told her about the sixth grade competition.

"Is there anything I can do for you? Any books you need?" Mrs. Sharp was the neatest person in the whole school. She had long dark hair she wore pulled back and sparkling black eyes. She was never too busy and always had interesting articles and books in her office she saved just for Gretchen and me. Library period was very special because of her.

"Do you have anything about wringing a confession from a criminal?" I asked seriously.

Mrs. Sharp laughed. "Oh, dear, I'm afraid we're fresh out of books on that subject. What are you two up to now? Last year you kept hounding me for books on buried treasure."

"Oh, we're still interested in treasure books," I put in quickly, with a sidelong glance at Gretchen. You couldn't always trust grown-ups, even the nicest ones. If Mrs. Sharp knew what we were really up to, she'd probably feel obligated to go to Mr. Magyn and blab. "Do you have any new ones?"

"Not at the moment, Kobie, but I did come across an article in *Life* about a lost mine somewhere out west. It's just the kind of thing you'd like. I don't have the magazine with me, but I'll bring it in next week." The other class was getting rowdy. Before she went over to calm them down, she wished me good luck on the mural.

"She's really nice," Gretchen said. "I like her a lot."

"Me, too," I replied absently. I was staring at a straw-haired girl in Mr. Breg's class. "Is that John Orrin's sister? Another one? Boy, those Orrin kids are everywhere."

Orrins overran Centreville Elementary like field mice in a granary. They were easy to spot since they all had the same haystack hair and pale gray eyes. There was an Orrin boy or girl in every grade and two Orrins in the sixth grade, one in each class. John's older sister Brenda, who was at least fourteen and had obviously flunked out, was in Mrs. Wright's class.

"Maryruth told me they ride her bus," Gretchen said. "She said when the Orrins get on, there's no room for anybody else."

"They ought to have a bus of their own," I commented. "Where do they live?"

"On that dirt road off Union Mill. Maryruth says it's sort of a shack. It must be awful to be that poor."

I didn't want to think about how poor John Orrin's family was. It wasn't my fault his family didn't have enough money. Library period was almost over. We still had to figure out a way to trap the Hammer Man. But first, I had to get Gretchen over her silly fear of leaving school property.

When Mrs. Harmon announced it was time to begin social studies, I stood up, stretched importantly, then strolled over to the long row of cabinets where the art supplies were stored.

I was excused from social studies every day until I finished drawing the mural. Yesterday Mrs. Harmon asked how much longer I would be and I told her artists shouldn't be rushed. After all, Michelangelo had lain on his back for years painting the ceiling of the Sistine Chapel and nobody bugged him to hurry up, it was almost Back-to-School Night.

While the others labored over boring old social studies, I took out my box of colored chalk and prepared to hoist myself up on the cabinet. Mrs. Harmon had tacked the length of burlap that was going to be our tapestry mural over the supply cabinets, the only available wall space. In order to transfer my drawings in chalk onto the burlap, I had to climb up on the cabinet and sit cross-legged on the countertop. After a while in this position, my legs cramped and I realized how much in common I had with Michelangelo.

The cabinet was too high for a short person like me — not so high I was scared to climb up, but high enough to make me look ridiculous getting up there. Today I was chalking in the outlines of the knights and horses, which meant I would be working practically in the sink.

I put my hands on the edge of the cupboard, hoping to spring up in one smooth, coordinated move. But the toe of my shoe bumped the stupid cabinet knob and threw me off balance. Scrambling to gain a foothold on the slick wood, I dove headfirst into the sink. Fortunately it was not filled with water, but my cool move was certainly demolished.

With my tennis shoes braced against the faucet, I began sketching with a piece of dark blue chalk. The rest of the class had their heads bent over their textbooks, reading. Everybody except John Orrin. He was staring at me, with a sliver of a smile. I knew he had seen my giraffe-leap up on the cupboard and thought it was funny. For some reason, his little smile irked me so bad I smudged the horse I was outlining.

Recess followed social studies. Physical fitness training was over. I had scored the lowest in both sixth grades in every event, but I didn't care. Sports were dumb.

For the first time in over two weeks, I led the way into the Honeysuckle Hideout.

"Boy, I thought we'd never get back here," I said to Gretchen, closing the screen of vines that concealed the secret entrance.

"It has been a while," Gretchen agreed as she checked to make sure the digging spoon was still in the dogwood tree. "Everything's just like we left it."

I parted the vines so I could see the games in progress on the blacktop. "I wonder why nobody has discovered this place yet. We've been coming here almost two years."

"Maybe it's because only the swings and merry-go-round are down here. The boys usually play in the softball field and the girls are always up on the blacktop. Only little kids come down here to play."

"I guess that's it." The dodgeball game certainly didn't fascinate me. I moved to the other side of the hideout so I could spy on the Hammer Man's house. "I bet he's up in that house, probably going through his scrapbook of all his favorite unsolved murder cases. Murders that he committed — "

"Kobie, don't start that," Gretchen said, nervously finger-combing her ponytail.

"Okay." I could tell she wasn't in the mood for spooky stories. Maybe because it was October and there was a strangeness in the air, a deadly quiet. The house on the hill was creepy, occupied, yet you never saw a living soul around the place. Still, I had to get her over being scared to leave school property. And then I spotted the perfect excuse.

"What's that?" I said suddenly.

Gretchen looked in the direction I was pointing. "What's what?"

"That. Over there in the vines. Looks like an old fence." The area beyond the hideout, on the old man's property, was carpeted with brambles and more honeysuckle. A rusty-black bar arrowed up through the weeds. "Let's go see."

"I don't know. . . ." Gretchen glanced back over her shoulder to see if Mrs. Harmon was watching us.

"Gretch, don't worry about Harmon," I told her. "We're only going two steps from the hideout. The bushes will be in the way. She'll never see us."

Actually it was more like ten yards from our hideout to the fence section. The weeds were so thick it took us ages to get there. Beggar's-lice clung to our socks.

"Here's your old fence," Gretchen said. "That's all it is. Now let's go back."

I tried to lift the fence, but it was too heavy. "People don't put up fences just for the fun of it. This was here for a reason, either to keep people out of something . . . or to keep something in."

"It's just a fence, Kobie. Come on." From here we were in plain view of the old man's house. Gretchen kept flinging uneasy glances up the hill.

I felt a little funny myself. The old man could be watching us from his window. It was time to go back anyhow. I was about to tell Gretchen that she had left school property and nothing drastic had happened to her when I tripped over a rock and went sprawling. The rock, half-buried under a snarl of vines, was square and solid.

"Now I know why this fence is here," I cried. "This is a cemetery! I've found a gravestone!"

Gretchen blanched. The idea of a cemetery on the property of a possible murderer obviously gave her the willies. "Kobie, let's get out of here. Right now!"

I was tearing honeysuckle away from the tombstone. "Darn. It's just a rock, after all. It's only shaped like a gravestone."

"Good. Now we can leave." She yanked impatiently at my jacket.

"No, wait. Gretch, here's another rock. And another one. I wonder why somebody put these rocks here. They go in a circle, see? Help me." I uncovered five square stones from a jungle of honeysuckle. The rocks had been set in a circular pattern, and were webbed with vines. Nobody had been down here in years.

Reluctantly she helped me clear the weeds from the last rock. The last weeds came away in one big bunch, revealing a deep hole beneath the vines. My arms plunged into nothingness. I skittered away from the rock-rimmed edge, my heart pounding. To me, a deep hole in the ground was just as frightening as climbing a ladder.

"It's a well," Gretchen noted. "An old dried-up well. I guess somebody had it fenced off at one time. Do you think we should tell Mrs. Harmon about it?"

Recovered from my fright, I headed toward the Honeysuckle Hideout again. When we were inside I answered her. "She won't care. It's not on school property."

Gretchen flared with anger. "Kobie Roberts, you did this on purpose! You couldn't rest until you got me to leave school property, could you? Suppose Mrs. Harmon saw us?"

"But she *didn't*. Gretch, you've got to stop being so afraid of teachers. Mrs. Harmon doesn't run the world."

"Neither do you, Kobie!" She was madder that I had ever seen her, even madder than the day I wouldn't let John Orrin sit at our table.

"Gretch, I did it for your own good."

She never lost her temper with me, not even the time I pleaded with her to give me all her book-fair money to buy an Advent calendar simply because I liked the sparkly village scene and the little doors to open each day before Christmas. But now she was furious. "You didn't do it for my own good. You did it to see if your plan would work. Just because you come up with the best ideas doesn't mean I'm going to follow you and get in all kinds of trouble. Ever since we've been friends, you've always told me what to do and I'm tired of — "

"Shhhhhh!" I clamped my hand over Gretchen's mouth. "Somebody's out there. They probably heard you yelling."

We stood stock-still in the center of our hideout. As long as no one discovered the secret entrance, we were safe.

"Who is it?" Gretchen whispered.

I twitched aside a blackberry vine to see better. The person lurking outside our hideout stooped as he peered into the bushes. I drew back, more shocked than upset.

"It's John Orrin," I breathed. "What's *he* doing here?"

Chapter 5

I had forgotten about my father's King Neptune paper until I was cleaning some old drawings out from under my bed one Saturday and suddenly remembered it. My mother would know where it was. The sooner I found that paper, the sooner I'd know what I'd be in for after I turned twelve.

My mother was baking cupcakes to put in the freezer. She was also making a big pan of lasagna to freeze for supper one night when she didn't feel like cooking.

"Cook, cook, cook," she said as I walked in the kitchen. "That's all I ever do. Some days I get so sick of it, I wish I could — "

"Could what? Quit your job?" I supplied for her, hoping she'd take me up on the offer.

"I can't do that," she said, vigorously stirring the frosting. "We need the money."

I gazed longingly at the frosting bowl. As usual, my mother had made only enough icing to barely cover the cupcakes, so I had no chance of licking the bowl. "I hope that's not your usual flour-and-water icing. That stuff hardens like plaster of paris."

"I do *not* make frosting out of flour and water," she retorted. "I'll have you know I use powdered sugar and milk and real butter."

"Then how come it gets so hard? I almost broke my teeth last week." Now that I took my lunch instead of buying, I begged her to buy lots of goodies like Twinkies and those little bags of Fritos. But my mother claimed that five packs of Twinkies every week was too expensive so she baked cupcakes and put them in the freezer for my lunches. "Gretchen's mother makes the fluffiest frosting. Her cakes are yummy."

My mother paused to give me her you're-skating-on-thin-ice look. I got that look from her a lot lately. I decided to drop the cupcake issue while I was still ahead.

"Dad said you had his Neptune paper. Would you get it for me?"

"What? A Neptune paper? What on earth are you talking about?"

I hooked my finger in the frosting bowl while she was busy knocking cupcakes out of the muffin tins. "It's this paper he got in the Navy when he crossed the equator, signed by King Neptune. He says it's with his military papers and that you know where they are. He told me I could have his Neptune paper."

"I don't know anything about any Neptune paper." She put a teaspoon of icing on a cupcake. "I have his discharge paper from the Navy and that's it."

"But you have to have the Neptune paper," I cried. "He said you do. Look for it, please!"

"Kobie, I've got a hundred things to do this morning without stopping to dig through a bunch of papers. I have to finish these cupcakes and that lasagna . . . iron my uniform and polish my white shoes. I don't have time for your foolishness."

"You never have time for anything I want to do," I accused, swiping a big hunk of frosting. She caught me this time and cracked my knuckles with the frosting spoon. "All you ever do is work."

"Do you think I love serving all those ungrateful kids who come through my line and gripe?" she said. "When you get older, you'll have to work, too. Either at home or at a job or both."

Being a grown-up sounded like a real drag to me, endless worrying about taxes and fuel oil and new tires for the car. In a way, I felt sorry for my mother. But in a way I didn't. After all, she had gone to my school and got that job in the cafeteria on her own — nobody made her do it. Then it occurred to me that she really hated her job and didn't know how to get out of it.

"Listen," I told her conspiratorially. "All you have to do is not wash your uniform or polish your shoes. Mrs. Settinger will see you're messy and she'll fire you. That's what I did when I wanted to get out of bus patrols."

Last year in fifth grade, the captain of the patrols selected me to replace a patrol who couldn't keep up his "B" average. At first I was thrilled to be a patrol. I got to wear a white canvas belt with a silver badge. Every Monday morning, I was excused from the pledge of allegiance to go to a patrols' meeting and I was allowed to leave class early at the end of the day. I felt really cool when I marched out on the highway with my red flag to halt the cars.

But after a while, I hated going to those meetings and I never had any fun on the bus because I had to sit up front with Mr. Bass and hold the flag. It was like being in the Army. I decided to get myself kicked out by not washing my patrol belt. We were supposed to wash our belts over the weekend so the patrol captain could inspect

them on Monday. My patrol belt got grubbier and grubbier and when the captain
asked me if I had washed my belt I kept
telling him I forgot. The kid I was replac-
ing raised his grade average and the captain kicked me off patrols. I gladly turned
in my badge and belt.

My mother smiled at my suggestion. "I'm
afraid that won't work in my case, Kobie.
Anyway, I don't want to get fired. Some
days aren't so bad." She finished icing the
cupcakes and began wrapping them in
waxed paper, leaving two on the plate.

"Can I have those?" I asked, caving in
with hunger. It had been a whole hour since
breakfast and then all I'd had was four
measly slices of French toast and some
sausage.

"You may have one cupcake. I'm saving
the other."

"For me to have later?"

She ran water in the pan and bowl. "No.
It's for somebody else."

"Who? Dad?"

"If you must know, I'm going to give it
to Beverly, the little girl I sit with on the
bus."

Cupcake crumbs flew out of my mouth
as I sputtered indignantly. "*Bev*-erly!
You're giving *my* cupcake to that little
twerp?"

"It's not *your* cupcake. And she's not a little twerp."

"She is a little twerp. I've seen the way she acts when you get on the bus."

"What's wrong with the way she acts? She's a sweet child."

"She's dumb."

"She is not dumb. You're talking like a child, Kobie. Beverly's six years younger than you are. How do you think you acted when you were her age?"

"I didn't act like that. And I could draw better."

"Yes," my mother agreed. "You're a real artist. But your disposition leaves a great deal to be desired."

"There's nothing wrong with my disposition!" I argued. "It's that little kid, hanging all over you all the time, showing you her pictures and now you're bringing her cupcakes. Next thing, you'll adopt her!"

She laughed at that. "Why, Kobie Roberts, I believe you're jealous!"

"I am not!" I denied hotly. "Why should I be jealous of some little twerp who can't draw and hasn't got any front teeth?"

"Stop calling her that name, Kobie, I'm warning you." Then she put her hand on my forehead, brushing my bangs aside. "What's the matter with my little girl today? Have you got growing pains?"

"My legs don't hurt." Whenever I used to run a lot, my legs would sometimes ache and she'd tell me I had growing pains. I'd measure myself against the sewing room door to see if I had grown any, but I'd always be the same height.

"Your legs don't have to hurt to have growing pains," my mother explained. "You seem out of sorts lately."

I *was* out of sorts and with good reason. Gretchen and I still hadn't come up with a plan to approach the Hammer Man. Report cards would be out in a few weeks and I knew I was flunking arithmetic. And I was really bothered by that new kid, John Orrin. After two years of keeping the Honeysuckle Hideout a secret, some stupid new kid finds it right away. Gretchen and I stayed quiet until he left, but I think he knew we were in there.

My mother slid the lasagna dish in the oven. "Okay," she said, wiping her hands on a tea towel. "I'll go look for that Neptune paper you're pitching a fit over."

In her room, she lifted the green strongbox down from the closet shelf and set it on the bed to unlock it. I hung eagerly over her shoulder. There were loads of documents in the box, insurance policies and birth certificates and contracts. At the very bottom was my father's Navy discharge paper, with a photograph of his ship, the U.S.S. *Griffin*, in the center. But no King Neptune paper.

"It's not in here." My mother began cramming the insurance folders back in the box. "I told you I've never seen such a paper."

"But Dad says he has it." I *had* to have that paper.

"If he does, I don't know where it is. You'll have to ask him again."

"It could be in his drawer," I said, hopping off the bed. My father stored personal belongings in the top drawer of his bureau.

In a flash, my mother collared me. "You know better than to go nosing in your father's things without his permission. You're getting a little too big for your britches these days, young lady."

I jerked away from her. "Well, you were the one who said I was growing up! What do you expect?" I ran before she could scold me for talking back.

But as I dashed out the back door, I heard her call after me, "My mother always told me girls started carrying on when they hit twelve. She didn't miss it by much!"

It felt good to be outside in the fresh autumn air. I barely remembered my grandmother, my mother's mother, because she died years ago. Evidently all she did was run around spouting mottoes for my mother to pass on to me. Stuff like, "Were you brought up in a barn?" when I forgot to shut the door and the one I detested the most, "Life is what you make of it." How could I possibly make anything of my life with my mother breathing down my neck?

Yet her parting remark shook me. According to my grandmother's dire predictions, I was supposed to start carrying on when I hit twelve! I probably wouldn't be able to help it, either. The second I turned twelve, I'd lose control. This was the important stuff I wanted to know. My mother wasn't a very reliable source. I still needed the Neptune paper.

I went out to the shed to ask my father if he knew where the paper was. I found him piling lumber on the wheelbarrow.

"What's that for?"

"Your tree house. Grab my carpenter's apron, will you?" He rolled the wheelbarrow out of the shed.

"You're going to start my tree house right now?" I snatched up his carpenter's apron and hurried after him.

"You bet."

The ladder and the rest of the lumber were already heaped around the base of the tree I had chosen. I watched my father saw the braces that would hold up the tree house and then build the platform. It was tough, slow work, but we talked and that made the time pass faster.

"What's your mother doing?" he asked once.

I looked up from the design I was making with his nails, lining them up by size. "Nothing much. She's so grouchy, I can't stand to be in the same room with her."

"Grouchy, huh?" He planed a board, then said, "Are you sure it's not the other way around?"

"I'm not grouchy! I don't know what her problem is these days, but she just won't get off my case. I can't ever seem to do anything right anymore." I rearranged the nails into a sunburst pattern.

"I know why you can't get along with your mother," he said. "It's because the two of you are exactly alike."

"Mom and me alike? You've got to be kidding. She's *years* older than I am. And we don't look at all alike . . . she's bigger than I am and her eyes are dark brown and her hair's getting gray — "

"I don't mean those things," he interrupted. "I'm talking about the way you both act in general."

I still couldn't see his point. "I don't act like my mother. She's *boring*."

"I guess the things she does seem boring

to you, but believe me, it's easy to tell you're her daughter."

"If we're so much alike, then how come we fight so much? Gretchen and I like the same things, and we hardly ever fight."

"Taking after somebody isn't necessarily the same as liking the same things," he said. "When you get older, you'll understand what I mean."

I hated it when my parents wormed out of telling me the truth by saying I'd understand when I got older. By the time I was old enough to understand all the stuff I'd been trying to figure out since the day I was born, I'd be too old to do anything about it. But never in a million years could my mother be the slightest bit like me. We had absolutely nothing in common.

We stopped for lunch, then went back to work. By three o'clock the platform was fastened to the side of the tree. My father climbed up on the platform to construct the walls, while I stayed on the ground.

"Kobie, don't you want to come up here? You can help me with the roof after I get these walls done."

I shook my head, squinting up at him. "I'll just stay down here."

There was only one way up to the platform, up that skinny, wobbly ladder. Until he built my staircase, I had no hope of getting up to my tree house.

My father leaned out the doorway and looked down at me. "How about if I come down and help you up the ladder? I'll be right behind you every step of the way. I won't let you fall."

I would have given anything to be up where he was, but my feet seemed rooted, earthbound. "I can't," I said, ready to cry. "I just can't."

"Okay. Nobody's going to force you to do anything you don't want to." He ducked back inside and reappeared at one of the long windows, resting his level on the ledge. "Kobie, are you sure you're going to be able to get up the staircase when I build it? This tree house is pretty high. I'd hate to see you too scared to come up here."

That horrible thought had entered my mind, too. What if I couldn't use the staircase, either? What if my father built me this fabulous tree house and it just sat there vacant because I was such a sissy? If the kids at school found out I was too cowardly to climb up to my own tree house, I'd have another name besides Mama's Baby: Kobie the Chicken.

Chapter 6

It sounds pretty dumb to throw away the Best-Artist-in-the-Whole-School title over a cloud, but that's exactly what I did.

On Monday, Mrs. Harmon questioned my progress on the mural. "You're taking too long, Kobie," she said. "Why don't I let some of the others start stitching the castle? We need to get moving on this. Back-to-School Night is a week from today."

Mrs. Harmon might have known about fractions and decimals, but she didn't know beans about art — or the way true artists work.

"I can't finish the background with a bunch of people in the way," I told her. "Just give me one more good day. I could probably finish if I missed arithmetic," I added coyly.

"No, you couldn't, either. You can stay in library period and use that time."

So I remained behind in room 10 while the rest of the class trooped off to the library. The background part of the mural, which I had saved to outline last, was taking forever. Every tree, each flower and blade of grass had to be drawn just so, or the whole effect of the tapestry would be destroyed.

I was working on the sky when the class came back, carrying library books.

Mrs. Harmon came over to check on me. "Kobie, we're going to start stitching after lunch, whether you're done or not."

I resisted the temptation to stick my tongue out at her tweed-covered back. Sometimes Mrs. Harmon was just too pushy, even on projects that were supposed to be fun. She ordered Kathy Stall and Marcia Dittier to untangle and sort the big bag of colored yarns she had brought in. The girls dumped the yarns on the floor right below where I was drawing. I tried to ignore them.

"What is *that*?" Kathy Stall asked suddenly.

I turned around slowly. "What's what?"

"That! That thing you're drawing. What is it?" Kathy pointed to the cloud I had just finished outlining in purple chalk.

Some people are so stupid it's unbelievable. "It's a cloud, dummy. What do you think it is?"

"Looks more like a turtle to me."

"A turtle that was run over by a car!" Marcia commented and they fell over giggling.

Immediately Mrs. Harmon was on the scene. "What's the trouble over here? Marcia? I gave you girls something to do and I expect you to do it *quietly*." Her voice boomed across the room. The entire class was staring at us.

"It's Kobie's cloud," Kathy giggled. "It looks so funny."

Mrs. Harmon stared at my purple cloud. "That's a cloud?"

"Of course!" What was the matter with her? How did she get to be a teacher if she didn't know a cloud when she saw one?

"It looks rather — well...." She pressed her lips together, at a loss to describe my cloud.

"Like a turtle that was run over by a car!" Marcia Dittier repeated, still trying for a cheap laugh.

Mrs. Harmon silenced Marcia with a scowl. "Kobie, that cloud doesn't go with the rest of the mural."

"But, Mrs. Harmon, this is the way you

draw clouds! I learned how from Frank Forrester."

"Who?"

"The weatherman on channel four."

Marcia and Kathy went off into peals of giggles again. "Kobie learned to draw from the weatherman!" Kathy shrieked.

I glared down at them. There was no point explaining to those turkeys — or to my teacher, for that matter — how I spent years lying on my stomach in front of the television while my father watched the news, waiting for Frank Forrester to come on. The weatherman could draw so cool, he just grabbed a Magic Marker and made fast, practiced motions and there was a sun hidden by a fog or big splashy raindrops. His clouds were the best — flat on the bottom, swoopy-scalloped on the top, the way clouds really *are*, most of the time. My version of Frank Forrester's cloud was particularly good.

But you couldn't expect peasants to understand anything about art. "Mrs. Harmon," I said tightly. "This is the right way to draw a cloud."

"But it doesn't *look* like a cloud," she maintained. "It spoils the rest of the mural."

"It does!" Kathy said, sticking her two

cents' worth in. "I think we ought to let somebody else draw the clouds."

I nudged her head with my foot. "Who asked you?"

"Kobie, stop it," Mrs. Harmon commanded. "You shouldn't be so sensitive. After all, other people are entitled to have opinions."

"Not if they're stupid!"

"That's enough, Kobie." Then she said, "It's really too much work for one person, this whole mural. You're probably tired. We'll see what the others think. All those in favor of keeping Kobie's cloud, raise your hands."

Two hands waved in the air, mine and Gretchen's. John Orrin had his arm half lifted, as if he couldn't make up his mind whether he liked my cloud or not. But he didn't count. Why weren't Vincent Wheatly and Richard Supinger supporting me? They were the most influential boys in room 10 — if they voted yes, everyone else would, too. But their hands stayed stubbornly down.

I wanted to punch out Kathy Stall and Marcia Dittier. It was all *their* fault this whole mess got started. They had been so eager to have me draw the mural in the first place and now they were criticizing my cloud. That was another reason I never mingled with those girls: they were two-faced.

"We'll get someone to help Kobie with the background," Mrs. Harmon declared. "It's better this way, Kobie." She smiled to cushion the blow. "With two of you working, we'll be able to begin stitching this afternoon. You've worked very hard on the mural and you've done a wonderful job. Won't it be nice to have someone help you finish?"

"No, it won't!" But I didn't say it very loud.

Mrs. Harmon scouted the class for a suitable helper. Kids whose arms were apparently made of lead a few minutes before now waved wildly, dying to be picked. My only hope was that she would choose Gretchen. A hope that was quickly dashed.

"How about . . . John! John Orrin. You've been very quiet." Sure he was quiet — nobody ever talked to him. "Come up here, John. Kobie will show you what to do."

I would? Of all the people she had to pick! The *one* kid who got under my skin, and now he was going to work on my mural.

"Mrs. Harmon," I said brusquely. "I've changed my mind about putting clouds in the mural. We really don't need them. A bunch of clouds only makes the picture too fussy — "

"Don't be silly, Kobie. Of course we're going to have clouds." She handed John another piece of purple chalk. "Start by redrawing Kobie's cloud."

He had even more trouble than I did climbing up on the cabinet. With a sheepish glance at me, he rubbed out my beautiful Frank Forrester cloud with the heel of his hand and awkwardly drew a plump, marshmallowy cloud, like a woolly sheep without legs.

"That's perfect!" Mrs. Harmon beamed at John. "Exactly right for our tapestry. Kobie, your co-artist is very talented, don't you think?"

If she knew what I truly thought, she'd send me to the office so fast my tennis shoes would leave skid marks down the hall.

John grinned at me, obviously thinking I liked his cloud, too. His crooked teeth reminded me of a jack-o'-lantern. I'd hated his smile since the first day he joined our class, the way he looked at me when Mrs. Harmon caught me with the "John Oreo" cartoon. How could the teacher actually prefer John's stupid powderpuff cloud to my artistic Frank Forrester cloud? And to call him my co-artist, as if he had worked on the tapestry all along! It was too much.

I plunked my chalk on the countertop, breaking it in half with the force of my decision. "Mrs. Harmon," I announced. "I quit."

"What are you talking about?" she demanded. "You can't quit. You have to finish that mural."

"John can finish the mural," I said, scooting off the supply cupboard. "I quit. Q-U-I-T, quit!"

"I know how to spell it." Mrs. Harmon's tone bordered on the dangerous. "I don't like your attitude, Kobie Roberts. Your problem is, if you can't be the center of attention, you don't want to be involved at all."

"And your problem is you wouldn't know a decent cloud if you tripped over it!" As soon as the words left my mouth, I knew I had gone too far. Even John Orrin was gaping at me, still clenching the purple chalk.

Mrs. Harmon's face flushed a dull red. "Do you want me to call your mother, Kobie? She's right downstairs. I'm sure she'd want to hear how her daughter is misbehaving and acting like a poor sport."

I wasn't acting at all — I really *was* a poor sport, but who wouldn't be? I had slaved for days on that mural and she ruined the whole thing by picking a country bumpkin to be my co-artist. If she had any sense, she'd realize artists worked *alone*, not in pairs.

But she had me and she knew it. Mrs. Harmon wouldn't have to bother writing a note home — a note that just might get lost on the bus. Or phone my mother to come in for a conference. Not with my mother merely a hop, skip, and a tattle away.

"Well?" She tapped a pencil on the black-board, waiting for my response.

"I'm sorry," I mumbled, hating the way I had to grovel in front of her when *I* had been wronged.

"Now apologize for disrupting the class."

Actually, the others were delighted by the interruption. Nobody in their right mind was anxious to do social studies. I dutifully apologized to the class.

Mrs. Harmon seemed satisfied. "If you hurry, you and John could have the mural finished by lunch."

"No." I stood firmly by my desk. "I'm not working on the mural anymore."

"Kobie — " she cautioned.

"Mrs. Harmon, I apologized for the things I said, but I meant it about quitting. I'm not working on the project."

The tension between me and my teacher was like a cold steel wire. Nervous per-spiration trickled down my backbone. I was petrified. Talking back was bad enough, but I had never defied a teacher in my life. But then, my refusing to work on the mural was small potatoes compared to the stuff Mrs. Harmon had to put up with from Vincent Wheatly and Richard Supinger all the time. Maybe that was why she relented, without sending me to the office or downstairs to my mother.

"If you want to let your classmates down, then that's your business," she said coolly. "John will finish the tapestry. Open your social studies book to page 143."

I sat down, shaking. "I didn't have any choice," I whispered to Gretchen across the aisle. "Look how she messed up my mural by letting John draw my cloud over. You think I did the right thing, don't you?"

"Sure you did," Gretchen said loyally. "You stuck by your principles and that's what counts."

I wasn't sure what principles were involved and I certainly didn't feel as if I had scored any great victory. While I was catching up on all the social studies I had missed the last few weeks, John Orrin was adding the final touches to *my* mural.

My father came home early that evening to finish my tree house. "Might as well use what little daylight we have left before the time goes back," he said.

As he nailed the bannister rails to the staircase, I fooled around the edge of the woods, collecting huge poplar leaves. Except for the railing, the staircase to my tree house had been completed for a week. Every day after school, I'd stand at the bottom of the steps, longing to be hidden among the branches of my very own tree house, but too scared to climb up there.

Gretchen and the others on my bus could see my tree house from the road. "Boy, are you lucky," Gretchen said. "I can't wait to come over and see your tree house."

"It's not quite done yet." I put her off, not wanting her to find out her best friend was really a jellyfish.

So I gathered poplar leaves as big as fans and hoped that my fear of heights would be miraculously cured by the time my father hammered the last nail.

"Okay," he said after a while. "Want to try it out?"

"You're done?" I jumped, scattering the leaves. Zero hour had arrived. Do or die. Looking up the length of the long, long staircase, I decided dying was probably easier than doing.

My father tested the bannisters to demonstrate their sturdiness. "These won't come off in a hurricane. And I made the steps extra-shallow, so you shouldn't be afraid to climb up."

I shouldn't be afraid, but I was. Putting one faltering foot on the bottom step, I said, "Maybe if you weren't watching. . . ."

"I'll be in the shed," he said. "If you need me, just holler."

Gripping the side rails like a drowning man clinging to a life preserver, I slowly crawled up five steps. Then I stopped and looked back to see how high I was. About twelve inches, by my estimation. My father had made the steps shallow, as he said, but the tree house was at least fifteen feet off the ground. My heart thumped, a sure sign I was about to wimp out. Then I remembered what had happened in school earlier. If I could defy my teacher and quit a class project, I could get up those dumb stairs.

My feet carried me up a few more steps. The doorway to the tree house seemed miles away yet. *Don't look down,* I instructed myself, but of course I did. Way, way below me, the poplar leaves I had dropped lay in a yellow puddle. Surprisingly, I didn't feel dizzy.

Gretchen's voice echoed in my head: *You stuck to your principles and that's what counts.* That got me up a couple more steps.

And then I was at the top, swinging

through the doorway into my tree house. The man who scaled Mt. Everest the first time must have felt this great!

I went over to one of the long windows and bravely leaned out. My father was walking back to the shed with his tools. The sun was setting behind him, casting a giant shadow on the path. "I made it!" I yelled. "See? I'm here!"

He turned and touched his cap, saluting my accomplishment. "How do you like it?"

"I love it! Thanks, Dad!"

It was amazing. I didn't mind the height the least bit! Now I could probably do all sorts of high-up things like hang from the monkey bars at school and shinny up the persimmon tree next to my father's shed. A whole new world had opened up to me.

Things looked different from fifteen feet up in the air. Our house appeared to be mostly roof and my father, striding back from his shed, seemed smaller.

Through the red-gold leaves of the oak tree, I gazed at the horizon. The sun was sinking below the distant Blue Ridge mountains, tinting the clouds a hazy pink. I noticed the clouds were neither flat on the bottom with swoopy-scalloped tops nor plump like marshmallows. These clouds were something in between, a shape I couldn't describe.

Chapter 7

Three days later, Gretchen and I saw the old man on the hill for the first time.

We were skipping recess in the Honeysuckle Hideout. I was busy digging up the treasury box because it was Dues Day.

"I think the mural looks awful," I said, furiously shoveling dirt. "The trees and clouds and flowers that John drew are terrible. Mrs. Harmon doesn't have any taste. She thinks John's stuff looks great. I don't even want my name on it now."

"Don't worry about it," Gretchen reassured me. "We'll still win. The castle and the horses you did are so good we have to."

I couldn't let it go. "A medieval tapestry is supposed to have a certain style and that's the way I tried to make it. Those marshmallow clouds and broccoli-stalk trees John put in ruin the whole thing, but do you think Mrs. Harmon cares? No, she just — "

"Kobie!" Gretchen broke in excitedly. "That's him!"

"Who? If John Orrin is sneaking around our hideout again, I'm going to give him what for — " I brandished the digging spoon like a club.

"Not John! The old man on the hill! He just came out of his house!" She gestured for me to get up and look.

I scrambled to my feet. The vines of our hideout were starting to wither, so I only had to separate a few strands to view the house up on the hill. A shambling figure was making its way toward a gray weathered outbuilding. It was the old man, all right. No mistake.

His sparse white hair was fluffed by the breeze, like a dandelion gone to seed. He wore khaki "wash" pants and a plaid shirt. I strained my eyes looking for a telltale hammer or even a screwdriver. He appeared clean from this distance.

"The Hammer Man in the flesh!" I said, awestruck. The legend lived! "On the FBI's Ten-Most-Wanted list and there he is, just walking around his yard like he's perfectly innocent. Little does anyone know how dangerous he really is."

"He doesn't look very dangerous to me,"

Gretchen said. "He looks like an ordinary old man. In fact, I think he's kind of cute, in a grandfatherly sort of way."

I stared at her. "Cute! I suppose you think Frankenstein is cute! And the Werewolf reminds you of a cuddly little puppy! Honestly, Gretch, how dumb can you get?"

"Well, does he look like a murderer to you?"

"Dangerous criminals don't advertise with a big sign, you know. They look like regular people, most of the time." We watched as the Hammer Man reached the outbuilding and fumbled to unlatch the door. "That's actually a clever disguise, going around like somebody's grandfather. People would never suspect who he really is."

"He certainly is slow," Gretchen observed. "I bet he wouldn't hurt a flea."

"All part of his disguise. And it's working. He already has you fooled." I continued my observations, knowing Gretchen was fuming.

"I am not fooled!" she returned, stung by my remark. "You don't know everything, Kobie Roberts. You could be wrong!"

I gave her a smug look that said I was never wrong. And I wasn't — well, hardly ever. I felt it in my bones that the old man with the sweet, white hair and the shuffling gait was in reality the dangerous man who skulked out of Manassas one hot summer night years ago.

Gretchen was still huffy. "If he's so dangerous, then what is he doing in that shed?" The old man had finally disappeared inside and shut the door. "Probably potting geraniums."

"I doubt it." I deepened my voice for effect. "That's where he keeps them. The hammers. The evidence we need to prove who he really is."

"Ohhh, no!" She shook her head, her ponytail lashing back and forth. "I know what you're thinking. I'm not going anywhere near that man's shed. Not in a million years."

"How about for a million *dollars*?" Gretchen had an obstinate streak but, sooner or later, I knew she'd come around.

"What do you mean, a million dollars?"

"Reward money! Gretch, this guy's been at large for ages — I bet the reward money is worth a fortune by now!" I envisioned sacks of coins and mounds of cash piled up like the loot in Scrooge McDuck's money bin. But even more tantalizing, in my mind, was the star-spangled acclaim that came with turning in the Hammer Man. Fame was within our grasp. I had to make Gretchen see that.

She was weakening. "I don't know . . . he seems harmless enough. What if he gets violent?"

"He won't," I told her confidently. "We just have to be smarter than he is. I've got a plan."

"Your last plan almost got us arrested," she said, referring to the Great Indian Pottery Fraud of fifth grade.

Last year, while we were tunneling out the Honeysuckle Hideout, I found some broken crockery. When I suggested we sell the pieces as ancient Indian pottery, Gretchen had to be convinced over and over that we wouldn't get in trouble. Then we went behind the baseball diamond and sold five pieces for a nickel each, before our teacher heard about it. She made us give the kids back their money and told us if we ever tried a hoax like that again, we'd go to jail. Personally, I felt if some kids were gullible enough to believe a piece of a stone crock was really a fragment of Indian pottery, they deserved to lose five cents.

"We didn't almost get arrested," I said, setting the record straight. "Miss Price screamed a lot, but she hardly did anything. It was still a good idea — I almost earned twenty-five cents for the treasury."

Gretchen sighed. "All right. What's your plan?"

"It's really very simple. We wait till he's in the shed — not today, because recess is nearly over. You go up to the door and knock — "

"Me? Why me?"

"Listen to the whole thing before you squawk." I went on, "When he answers, you fall down like you're sick or something. He'll run over to help you and while he's doing that, I'll creep in the shed and grab one of his hammers. When you see me coming out, you get well fast. After I've gone down the hill, you jump up and — "

"How come *I'm* the one who has to pretend to be sick?"

"Because," I said smoothly, "you're a better actress than me. If I pretended to be sick, he'd see right through me in a flash."

"I don't know. . . ." She wasn't quite hooked yet.

Now it was my turn to sigh. These days it was harder and harder to get people to do things. What was the world coming to, when a person could dangle the possibility of a million dollars plus overnight glory, and yet her best friend still wouldn't leap at the chance? Gretchen's assignment was kid's stuff compared to mine. All she had to do was roll around on the ground and gag. *I* had to sneak into the shed, right under the Hammer Man's nose, take one of the murder weapons and any other evidence I could lay my fingers on, then sneak back out before he saw me. Talk about dangerous!

We put our dues in the treasury box and buried it again before the bell rang. I had plenty of time to persuade Gretchen the plan would work. One thing was for sure, the Hammer Man wasn't going anywhere.

Room 11's mural was displayed prominently in the place of honor by the main office when I walked into the school Monday morning. I recognized Lynette O'Bannon's sharp line in the jousting tournament the tapestry illustrated. Room 11's tapestry was very, very good.

Our tapestry was hanging on the wall outside the door to room 10. Whoever had stitched John Orrin's lamb's-wool cloud had made the stitches too loopy. The cloud drooped over the flag-topped tower of my beautiful castle like an old rag. That stupid cloud spoiled the entire mural. No wonder we didn't win.

When the parents came on Back-to-School Night, they'd spot room 11's tapestry first thing because everyone had to go by the office and they'd know that the best artist in the school drew the scene. Only the parents of sixth graders would trudge all the way up the hall to see the mural of the losing class. After taking one look at John Orrin's cloud, they probably wouldn't even want to see the rest of the mural, the parts *I* drew.

Next to the mural, Mrs. Harmon had posted the names of all the students in room 10. Uncapping my pen, I scratched my name off the list. I didn't want the parents to think I had anything to do with that awful tapestry.

As I took my seat, I heard rumbles of discontent over the contest decision from the other kids. Some of them seemed to be aimed in my direction.

"Mr. Magyn said the contest was close," Mrs. Harmon claimed. "He said he wished he had room by the office to hang both tapestries." I didn't believe a word of it. She was only trying to make us feel better.

Kathy Stall prodded me with her pencil. "It's your fault we lost," she hissed. "You quit and made us lose."

"My fault!" I couldn't believe the nerve of that girl. "You were the one who griped about my cloud. If you hadn't opened your mouth, I would have finished the mural."

Marcia Dittier twisted around. "Your cloud was dumb. I'm glad Mrs. Harmon got somebody else to do it over. But you shouldn't have quit."

"I had to quit," I said, thinking that Vincent Wheatly should have chopped off the rest of Marcia's ugly hair. "The idea was, *one* person would draw the mural. And that person was me. You voted for me, so you ought to know."

"That was before we found out you took art lessons from the weatherman." Kathy cackled at her own stupid joke.

I thought how wonderful Kathy Stall would look staked to an anthill.

"Quitter, quitter, quit-ter," Kathy chanted. "Kobie Robert's a quitter!" To my delight Mrs. Harmon wryly asked her which she'd rather do, pay attention to fractions or take a little walk to the office? Kathy shushed, but from time to time she and Marcia would sing in voices no one but me could hear, "Quitter, quitter, quit-ter!"

I sensed a chilliness in the room. The whole class was blaming me for losing the competition. I could feel it.

It was worse at recess. Vincent Wheatly and Richard Supinger cornered Gretchen and me on the playground before we could escape to the Honeysuckle Hideout. Kathy and Marcia and some other kids joined them.

Richard grabbed my arm. "You blew it, Roberts."

I rubbed my arm, scanning the blacktop

for Mrs. Harmon. She was busy setting up a four-square game. "I didn't blow anything. It wasn't my fault Mr. Magyn liked room 11's mural better. You can't blame me."

"You dropped out," Vincent jeered. "If you'd finished it instead of running off like a baby, we would've won."

Gretchen sprang to my defense. "Kobie did more work than anybody on that project. Don't you dare say it's her fault."

"It *is* her fault," Richard stated flatly. Vincent agreed. You couldn't argue with those two. They ran room 10 with their big mouths and their big muscles and nothing Gretchen could say would make any difference.

"Come on," I told her, hoping the boys would let us go if we just walked past them.

Vincent shoved me into Richard. "Where's the quitter going?"

"Probably down to those bushes she likes so much," Kathy taunted.

Vincent stood on the toes of my tennis shoes so I couldn't budge. Richard Supinger pinned Gretchen's arms behind her back.

"Leave us alone," I yelled. "Or I'll tell the teacher!"

"Tattletale, tattletale, hang your pants

on a rusty nail!" Vincent sang, wiggling his eyebrows. He had funny little peaked eyebrows and eyelashes so blond they were almost white. When I doodled cartoons of Vincent Wheatly, I made his eyes oblong and blank like Little Orphan Annie's.

"Shut up, Whitey," I said, daringly calling him a name I knew he despised. One way to get them off the subject of the mural was to make them mad about something else.

Vincent reacted instantly, twisting the material of my jacket around his fist. "What did you call me?"

Gretchen pulled away from Richard and ran over to Mrs. Harmon. As soon as the boys saw where she was heading, they let me go, pushing me so hard I fell on the blacktop and scraped my knee. I just lay there, holding my knee and blinking back tears. I could see Gretchen telling Mrs. Harmon what had happened, pointing at Vincent and Richard, who were down on the softball field acting as if they'd been there for hours.

Mrs. Harmon ordered me to the nurse's office to get patched up. She let Gretchen go with me. I hobbled back into the building, blood dribbling down my leg and into my sock.

"Vincent and Richard are in for it now," Gretchen consoled me. "They'll be sorry they knocked you down."

"No, they won't. They'll probably do it again." At the water fountain I wet a tissue and wiped most of the blood off my leg.

"They're bullies," she said. "You can't expect them to behave like normal human beings."

"It's not just them. It's everybody in the whole class. They hate me, Gretchen, I know they do. They hate me because I quit the project and our mural lost."

For once, she didn't say anything and I knew she thought I was right about the class hating me. Maybe she hated me, too.

"You don't blame me, do you?" I said, almost crying. If my best friend turned against me, I couldn't stand it. "You don't think it's my fault?"

She found a used tissue in her pocket and handed it to me. "Of course I don't blame you, Kobie. You did the best you could. Mrs. Harmon should have let you finish the project the way you wanted."

There wasn't anybody else around. I let the tears flow, not caring that Gretchen was watching, not caring that I was going on twelve, too old to cry. I should have been the Best Artist in Centreville Elementary.

Instead, the others thought I was the Benedict Arnold of room 10. There was only one way I could redeem myself — I absolutely *had* to discover the true identity of the Hammer Man. If I helped the police capture a dangerous criminal, everybody would forget about the stupid mural contest.

"Somebody's coming," Gretchen murmured.

I stopped sniveling. It sounded like only a kid coming down the hall, but I didn't want anybody to see me bawling. My reputation was already a disaster.

Gretchen peeked around the corner. "Don't worry. It's just John Orrin."

He clumped down the hall, evidently on an errand for Mrs. Harmon. He smiled as he went by, then said, idiotically, "Your leg's bleeding, Kobie."

"No kidding," I said stonily.

My heart hardened like a lump of coal. It wasn't my fault at all that our class lost the contest. It was *John's*. His dumb puffy cloud ruined our mural. *He* should have been the one Vincent pushed on the blacktop, not me.

John always managed to get off scot-free, while I always got dumped on. Thanks to John, Mrs. Harmon chewed me out over the "John Oreo" cartoon. Thanks to John,

I was forced to quit the project. Thanks to John, our class lost the contest. Everything was John Orrin's fault, yet I was the one taking the blame.

Well, that was about to change, I decided, anticipating the sting of iodine the nurse would swab on my knee. Starting tomorrow, John Orrin was going to pay me back.

Chapter 8

I licked the tip of my pencil and scribbled faster, trying to finish my one-page science report before the bus came. Mrs. Harmon was making us give our reports orally, so my writing didn't have to be that great. This report was super-important. Not for my grade, but for the beginning of the downfall of John Orrin.

From the doorway of my tree house, I could see at least a quarter of a mile down Lee Highway. I'd be able to spot the blunt yellow snout of the bus as it cruised over the hill and still have plenty of time to gather my books and run down to the stop, where my mother was standing alone.

I had fixed my tree house up really cool. A sign on one of the braces warned away trespassers: *Abandon Hope All Ye Who Enter*. My mother had donated a plastic shower curtain set and her old tin kitchen cannisters. With my father's help, I covered the roof with the shower curtain. On rainy days, I could let down the sides of the curtain over the windows. I put little things in the cannisters — small notebooks, pencils, even candy. The cannisters had tight lids that kept squirrels out.

My father gave me a three-legged wooden footstool and an old bunch of keys on a ring. The keys didn't go to anything, but I liked the solid "house" look of keys hanging on a peg. My father said those great big keys gave my place more of a jailhouse look.

Because I didn't like it down in the basement anymore, I moved my ancient encyclopedias to my tree house, covering the heavy books with the plastic window curtain that came with the shower curtain set. The books came in handy when I had to whip up a quick report, like today.

For science, though, the old encyclopedias were kind of a hindrance. Gretchen was doing her report on dinosaurs. I couldn't even find dinosaurs in my encyclopedia, which made me wonder how old the books really *were*. Having learned my lesson not to trust the astronomy section in the Science volume, I stuck to the safer subject of Animals, deciding to do my report on a toad with scaly trapdoors in its skin, where it carries its babies. No one else in room 10 would write about trap-door toads, I was sure.

Trying to describe the toad in my own words was hard. You had to *see* this toad to understand how the trapdoors worked, how the tiny baby toads hold up their own little doors like sewer workers lifting up manhole covers. I filled half of my one page report with an illustration. But Mrs. Harmon didn't like reports with drawings anymore than she liked long division problems answered but not worked out, so I had to write a few paragraphs. Somebody ought to tell that woman that a picture is worth a thousand words.

Already I'd run into a problem. According to my encyclopedia, trap-door toads lived in Italian West Africa. Even I was aware no such country existed anymore, but since I didn't know what the new name was, I had to leave it.

"Bus!" somebody shouted.

Forgetting where I was for an instant, I looked up in surprise to see my mother waving at me to hurry up, the bus was coming. The way she yelled "Bus!" startled me. She could have been a kid. There's always someone who dawdles and someone who tells other kids to get moving.

I stuffed my report in my notebook and

trotted down the steps. I made it just as the bus was pulling up.

"Your hair is a mess," my mother commented, swiping at my bangs with one hand. The illusion that she might be a regular kid waiting for the bus burst like a soap bubble. She was only my mother, a horrible embarrassment I had to endure, like a bad case of hives.

Gretchen didn't know I was out to get John Orrin. When she sat next to me on the bus, I resisted telling her about my plan and instead showed her my illustrated report.

"Look at those tiny frogs coming out of the warts!" she squealed. "Kobie, what a gruesome picture!"

"They aren't frogs," I explained patiently. "They're toads. And those bumps aren't warts, but little trapdoors the babies live in to stay safe. Isn't it neat?"

Gretchen let me read her copied-over-three-times report on the brontosaurus. I stared at her neat, round handwriting, in reality thinking about the little trap I was going to set for a certain warty toad named John Orrin.

At school while the others were milling around and talking before the late bell, I dropped my notebook right in front of John's desk. Papers fluttered all over the place. I got down on my hands and knees to pick them up. When nobody was paying attention, I crammed my science report in the cubbyhole under John's desk.

As usual, slowpoke John was the last kid to take his seat. He stowed his books under his desk without ever noticing the piece of paper that didn't belong there. I stifled a snicker. In an hour or so, John would probably be expelled. Or at the very least ordered to the principal for a good bawling out.

Mrs. Harmon preferred to start oral reports right away, so the students wouldn't have to agonize all day about getting up in front of the class, a policy she instituted after Danny Blevins threw up on the world globe. Danny said he felt sick waiting to give his report.

Our one-page science reports were supposed to last three minutes. Mine wouldn't take that long, since it was mostly picture, but it didn't matter. After the ruckus was over, Mrs. Harmon would probably forget all about making me give my report.

For obvious reasons, Danny Blevins was called on first. Then Marcia Dittier, who giggled through her presentation, and then Vincent Wheatly, who told Mrs. Harmon his cat had her kittens on his report and he couldn't move her. The whole class cracked up at this original excuse. Mrs. Harmon pursed her lips and marked a zero in the grade book.

"Kobie Roberts," she called.

I clasped my hands on my desk and tried to make my face blank.

"Come up here, Kobie," Mrs. Harmon said, still irritated over Vincent Wheatly's excuse. "We haven't got all day."

"I can't," I told her solemnly.

"Why can't you?" she demanded. "Didn't you do your report, either?"

"Yes, ma'am." I hadn't said "ma'am" in so long, the word tasted funny in my mouth, like water sitting overnight in the bottom of a glass.

Mrs. Harmon ruffled her curly hair, exasperated. "Then get up here, Kobie! We're waiting."

"I can't."

She sighed. "I thought you said you did your report."

"I did."

Mrs. Harmon enunciated every word carefully, as if I had suddenly grown stupid. "Do you or do you not have your science report?"

"She probably quit in the middle like she did with the mural," Richard Supinger said.

Everybody in the class still blamed me for losing the mural contest. Only Gretchen treated me like a normal person. The others either snubbed me or else picked on me constantly.

"Be quiet, Richard," Mrs. Harmon barked, her patience just about gone, "unless you want a zero alongside your name, too. Kobie, if you're not up here in two seconds with your report — "

"I wrote my report, Mrs. Harmon," I said, "but I don't have it."

"If you left it at home, that's the same as not doing it and you get a zero."

I spoke up before she marked a goose egg beside my name in the grade book. "I didn't leave it at home. *He's* got it and he won't give it back." Standing up dramatically like a witness in a courtroom drama, I pointed at John Orrin.

John's face crumpled in shock, too stunned to deny my accusation.

"Kobie, I would like to get through science before midnight," Mrs. Harmon said wearily. "Why does John have your report?"

"He took it," I lied. "He took it away from me so I'd get a bad grade."

"John, is this true?"

John worked his mouth like a gasping

fish. At last he managed to say, "Mrs. Harmon, I don't know nothing about Kobie's report."

"She says you took it." Mrs. Harmon whirled on me again. "Kobie, when did John take your report?"

I hadn't thought that far ahead. "This morning. Before the late bell." I remembered that Mrs. Harmon had been out of the room then, talking to Mrs. Wright across the hall.

She looked at me dubiously, reluctant to believe her pet was capable of such a spiteful deed, then said, "John, give Kobie her report."

"I don't have it!" he cried. "I never saw no report! She's — " He stopped and stared at me. I knew what he'd been about to say, that I was lying.

I glared back at him, determined not to buckle under even though I was lying through my teeth. My entire future in room 10 depended on pulling this off. "If you don't believe *me*, Mrs. Harmon," I said with an injured sniff, "go through his desk. That's where he put it. Under his books."

Mrs. Harmon made John take his books out one by one. When he pulled out my trapdoor toad report, he gaped as if he'd been caught with the floor plan to the National Bank of Virginia.

"I don't know how this got in my desk," he stuttered.

Mrs. Harmon delivered the wadded-up report to me, her eyes flashing. I couldn't tell if she was annoyed by the delay or if she suspected I had set the whole thing up. As it turned out, John wasn't expelled or even sent to the office and I got a "C—" on my presentation because I had drawn a picture instead of writing a full page.

Gretchen gawked at me when I sat down again. I knew she had figured out the truth. She passed a scrap of paper torn from her notebook with a single question mark on it. I didn't answer her note, too busy plotting my next move.

At recess, Gretchen headed for the Honeysuckle Hideout, but I pulled her into a dodgeball game instead.

"Kobie, what — ?" she asked as I found two spaces in the circle.

"I want to play this for a change."

It wasn't easy getting into the game. On my other side, Kathy and Marcia jostled me, but I held firm. John Orrin was the last one on the blacktop. He stood timidly at the edge of the circle, waiting for Rack Carter to chuck the ball to him. The object of the game was to strike a person in the center of the ring. Then you got to trade places with them, and dodge other people's throws. John didn't even try to hit anyone, but one of the kids in the middle got in the way of the ball, so John got to take his place.

When the ball bounced over to me, I hefted its weight. John watched me steadily, but didn't flinch when I pretended to throw the ball. I threw again, this time with all my might, hoping to wallop him a good one. I was a rotten thrower, unable to hit the side of a parked tractor-trailer, much less a moving target, but I struck John's arm with a glancing blow. John was a rotten player. He stayed outside the circle, feebly tossing the ball and missing everyone, until Gretchen stepped in the way of his throw.

With a defiant glance at me, she exchanged places with John. Because I didn't want to hit my best friend when the ball came into my hands again, I deliberately missed her. Then I caught Danny Blevins on the elbow with the ball and took his place in the circle.

But when I saw the looks on the other kids' faces, I realized it wasn't the safest place to be. They creamed me, pelting me with fast, hard throws that didn't let up until Mrs. Harmon blew her whistle.

Gretchen avoided speaking to me until

we were sitting at our table in the lunch-room.

"What's with you, Kobie?" she asked. "John never took your science report."

I bit happily into my Vienna sausage sandwich, mayonnaise spurting up between the neatly sliced meat. "I know. I made it up."

She was aghast. "But why? You almost got him in trouble with the teacher. What's he ever done to you?"

"What's he done to me? Plenty, that's what! He got Mrs. Harmon mad at me the first day he came. And then he had to horn in on the mural project and cause us to lose the contest. It's all John's fault nobody in our class likes me. I'm just paying him back."

Gretchen twirled her fork in her mashed potatoes, breaking the dam so gravy leaked into the Swiss steak. "I don't see how being mean to John will make the kids like you again."

It was difficult to explain. For one reason, everybody liked Gretchen. She'd never experienced the humiliation of having kids squirt her at the water fountain, knock her over on the playground, or make snide remarks in the halls. The other reason was that I wasn't too sure it would work. Picking on John Orrin might make the other kids hate me even worse. But that was a risk I'd have to take. Maybe, just maybe, they'd think I was a big shot and I'd *be* somebody again in room 10.

"It's the only thing left for me to do," I said. "Gretchen, there's something about that kid that drives me crazy. He's always so . . . calm. Even when he was getting clobbered in recess today, he just stood there like a ninny. He brought all this on himself."

"Your favorite person is heading this way. The other tables must be full again."

John Orrin! Coming to sit at our table after all that had happened this morning! The kid was either calmer than I imagined or unbelievably stupid.

"Howdy," he drawled. "Okay if I sit here?"

I shrugged, knowing I had no choice, not with the lunchroom warden monitoring us. Still, I could tell John was uneasy sitting next to me.

"Good lunch today," he said, tucking his napkin in his belt. "What's this?" He dunked his spoon into the little dish of fruit.

"Mandarin oranges," Gretchen said. "You've never had mandarin oranges before?"

"Actually," I spoke up, "they're dead goldfish."

John goggled at me. "Goldfish?"

I was on a roll. "Yes, the cafeteria ladies pull off the little fins so you can't tell. You eat them whole — they slide right down. If you chew them, you'll crunch up — "

"Kobie, will you stop?!" Gretchen admonished. To John she said, "Kobie always does this during lunch."

"Not just lunch," I said to no one in particular. I wanted John to realize that I was after him, if he didn't already know it.

"About this morning," Gretchen said suddenly. "That mix-up over Kobie's report? It was just a joke, John. Kobie's a terrible kidder."

"Oh, it was a *joke!*" John's face split into a smile, as if we had given him an unexpected present. "Like the goldfish. Boy, you really had me going for a while," he admitted to me.

I wanted to throttle Gretchen. How could I ever get even with John Orrin when she had him thinking I was the class clown?

"You took it pretty good," Gretchen said, still on the subject of my "joke." "Most kids would tell the teacher."

"I couldn't do that," John said. "If it

was only a joke, why get Kobie in trouble? Right, Kobie?"

He regarded me with his watery gray eyes, calm as a pond on a summer's day, and smiled. He had me and he knew it.

I hastily revised my opinion of John Orrin. He wasn't stupid at all. He was actually quite smart, knowing all along the mandarin oranges weren't goldfish and managing to reduce my clever trap to a crude sixth-grade prank. If I was going to regain my self-esteem in room 10 by waging war on John Orrin, I had my work cut out for me.

Chapter 9

My life suddenly became very busy.

Every morning, I had to check the seat of my desk for bubble gum. Whenever I went up to the front of the class to sharpen my pencil, I had to pry a chipped piece of lead out of the sharpener that always seemed to be there. Broken lead would only gnaw my pencil to a nubbin instead of sharpening it. The back of my jacket often had a "Kick Me" sign taped to it and once I came in from recess to find one of my best drawings, a Halloween cat, tampered with. Someone, probably Kathy Stall, had scrawled a stuck-out tongue and a cartoon balloon over my cat's head with the caption, "Kobie Roberts is a stinker."

The kids — at least four of them — were still blaming me for losing that stupid mural contest.

When I wasn't heading off possible sabotage, I watched out the window to catch the Hammer Man going out to his shed. Gretchen and I planned to put our fake-sickness scheme into action the next recess period we knew the Hammer Man was out of the house.

In between, I did a little schoolwork. My first-six-weeks report card was dismal, "D"s in arithmetic, science, and social studies. Under "Growth and Participation," the section where teachers loved to snitch on kids, Mrs. Harmon gave me the lowest mark for "Uses Time Wisely" and "Gets Along Well With Others." My folder of "A" papers my parents had to ooh and aah over on Back-to-School Night was pitifully scanty.

But mostly I was busy trying to get even with John Orrin.

He was driving me crazy! *Nothing* I did to him seemed to faze his maddening calmness. If I accidentally-on-purpose tripped him as he was coming down the aisle, *he'd* apologize to *me* for stepping on *my* foot! When I told him I'd never seen hair the color of his before, he took it as a compliment. Another time I commented on his too-short pants, asking him if he was expecting a flood and he laughed as if this was the funniest thing he'd ever heard. He never whined the day I threw spitballs at him, even when one landed in his ear, and he didn't tattle when I tore his history essay almost in half and he had to copy it over.

"I can't shake that kid no matter what I do," I said to Gretchen as we did our homework over the phone one evening.

"Kobie, why don't you leave him alone?" she said. "He's not hurting you."

"He is, too! He's the cause of my troubles at school. Nobody would be picking on me if John had stayed wherever he came from. It's all his fault."

"I still don't see how picking on John will make the other kids stop picking on *you*." Sometimes I hated the way Gretchen was always so logical, but that was probably why she understood fractions and long division and I didn't.

"If I could beat John *just once*, the others will know I'm a — a force to be reckoned with." I borrowed that phrase from an old movie I had seen the other night.

"I don't like it," Gretchen said. "I don't like it when somebody picks on another kid."

"What do you think Richard and Kathy and Vincent and the others are doing to *me*?" I flung back.

"It's different because you aren't by yourself. John doesn't have any friends."

True, but it didn't change the way I felt

about him one bit. Then I began to wonder if Gretchen was trying to tell me something without coming right out and saying it.

"Will you still be my friend?" I asked. "Even if I keep after John?"

Her sigh hummed through the phone wires. "I'll always be your friend, Kobie, even when you do things I don't like."

That was a relief. Without Gretchen, I wouldn't have the strength to face those hostile kids in room 10 day after day. Of course John didn't have any friends, but that was his own tough luck, barging into class so late in the year after everybody had already paired off.

"You know," Gretchen mused. "John isn't so bad, if you'd just talk to him. Why don't you bury the hatchet and try to be friends?"

"Friends with *John*? Gretchen, are you delirious?"

"Well, maybe not be a friend-friend," she backed down. "But would it be so terrible if he ate lunch with us?"

"That's the only time we have to ourselves except recess." Next, she'd want to invite him into our hideout.

"It's just a suggestion, Kobie. Sometimes it gets a little lonesome at lunch, just you and me."

"How can it be lonesome? I'm there. Who else do you need?" Years ago, we decided not to include anyone else in our group. I liked being exclusive. "We have a lot more fun than those other girls," I said. "Don't we?"

"I guess so." Gretchen's voice seemed thin.

The next morning, I jumped into my clothes and ran out to the kitchen. Dressed in her cafeteria uniform, my mother was jotting down a list and enjoying a last cup of coffee.

Before I put a fingernail on the cabinet handle, she said, "You have to buy lunch today, Kobie. There's nothing here to make your lunch out of until I get to the store."

"Buy my lunch!" I shrieked, as if she just said she'd enrolled me in sword-swallowing lessons. "I can't do that! I never buy my lunch." At least, not since she started working at my school.

She finished the list and put it in her purse. "Well, you'll have to suffer today and buy. I told you we don't have anything in the house."

"Why don't we? What kind of a mother are you, not buying groceries when you're supposed to?" She didn't realize what she was making me do, go through *her* serving line, when my reputation in sixth grade was already floundering.

"This is a house, not a restaurant," she said tersely. "And it's not run to suit you, missy. I don't want to hear anymore back talk, do you hear?"

I changed my tune in a hurry. Feverishly rummaging through the cupboards, I found the end of a loaf of bread, a jar of mustard, and a few stale Fritos.

"Look! There's plenty of stuff here," I sang out. "I can make — a mustard-and-Fritos sandwich! I love Fritos and mustard!"

"I'm sure you do, but that's hardly a nutritious combination." Working in a cafeteria had given my mother all sorts of notions about what a person should eat.

"Okay, you want vitamins . . . how's this?" I flourished a shriveled apple from the crisper in the refrigerator. The apple was so old my fingers sunk into the mealy flesh. Ordinarily I wouldn't even touch a piece of fruit that gross, much less consider eating it, but I was desperate.

"Throw that nasty thing in the garbage," my mother said. "And take your lunch money. You're buying and that's final."

"I'll starve first! I don't want to go through your old line!" I was on the verge of crying again. My father wouldn't have been so mean to me. He would have driven me to George's Store to buy a pre-made sandwich or let me fix whatever I wanted. But he wasn't here and my mother was.

She got up and came over to me, ominous in her spanking-white uniform and rubber-soled shoes. Anger sparked her dark brown eyes. "I've had enough out of you for one morning, Kobie Roberts. You don't think I can't make you eat your lunch? What if I jerked you up and dragged you through the lunch line, right in front of everybody? What if I stood over you and made you eat? What if I *fed* you, like a little baby?"

She'd do it, too. I had pushed her as far as she was going to be pushed. Snatching up my lunch money, I ran out the door without another word.

When lunchtime arrived, I walked very slowly down to the cafeteria.

"How come you're so poky today?" Gretchen asked. "I'm starving."

"Go on," I urged. "I have to buy and I want to make sure I'm last in line."

"Are you still down on your mother because she works here? Honestly, Kobie, nobody really cares whether your mother hands you your lunch or not."

"You don't know my mother, Gretch. She'll make a scene today, I just know it.

We had a big hairy fight this morning and she's going to get even with me." I loitered down the stairs, placing both feet on each step to take longer to reach the bottom.

"Kobie, mothers don't get even with their kids. You've got revenge on the brain lately. I don't know what's the matter with you." Disgusted, she went ahead without me.

I managed to be the very last one in line, right behind — who else? — John Orrin.

John selected his flatware with exaggerated care, as if he were having lunch at a fancy restaurant instead of our dumpy old cafeteria, placing his knife and fork and spoon squarely on his napkin. Behind him, I impatiently snatched a handful from the bins, winding up with four knives and one spoon, slinging the cutlery on my tray with a noisy clatter.

At the milk cooler, John took two milks, then offered one to me. I was so outraged at his nerve — handing me a milk as if we were buddies — that I leaned in and got a *chocolate* milk, knowing perfectly well kids on free lunch weren't permitted to have chocolate milk.

Actually, I wasn't permitted to have chocolate milk, either. As soon as my mother saw the brown carton on my tray, she flew up like a skyrocket. Pushing back a tendril of hair that had escaped her hair net, her cheeks flushed from working over the steam tables, she said, "Put that back right this instant and get regular milk! What have I told you about eating too much junk?"

I could have died of shame. I slunk back to the cooler and swapped the chocolate milk for regular.

John crowed, "Oh, we're having turkey today! Can I have a little extra dressing, Mrs. Roberts?"

My mother smiled at him. "You certainly may, John. I'm giving you extra turkey, too. Eat it all, now."

"Yes, ma'am!" He accepted his plate so eagerly you would have thought it was Baked Alaska rather than the tired old turkey and dressing the school always dished up when they were getting ready to clean out the freezer. "You're the best cook."

I was thoroughly nauseated. John's Oliver Twist act had my mother fawning all over him, but it didn't fool me a bit. How dare he con my mother into giving him extras? Yet if she took requests from him, I might as well put in mine.

"No peas for me today," I said airily to my mother.

"You're getting peas and you're going to eat them." She thrust a plate at me positively brimming with the hateful little green things.

I slammed the plate on my tray and shoved it up the line. John was waiting for me.

"You're mother's nice," he said. "Sometimes she lets me have two rolls."

"Bully for you." It was bad enough going through the serving line behind John — being in the same *country* was too much, really — but to have him smugly tell me the favors my mother granted him, *my mother*, was the absolute limit.

We had reached the cashier's desk by now. John was about to pick up his tray and leave the line when I suddenly yelled, "Where's your MONEY, John? You can't go through without PAYING."

Mrs. Settinger, the cafeteria manager and money-taker, glowered at me. "Go on through," she told John.

"He didn't PAY!" I bellowed. "How come HE doesn't have to pay and I have to? Here's MY dollar! John, where's YOUR DOLLAR?"

John looked as if he wanted to fall through the floor. "I — I — " he stammered painfully.

"It's all right," Mrs. Settinger reassured him. "Go sit down." John grabbed his tray and fled.

"But he didn't PAY!" My throat hurt from yelling so much.

"If you don't keep quiet, you're going to the principal," Mrs. Settinger said menacingly.

I fished four quarters from my pocket. "I didn't want him to get away without paying," I said with mock concern. "My mother says you have to watch some of these kids."

"Yes, you do." Mrs. Settinger dropped the coins into her cash box with a resounding clunk. "I know one kid I'd like to watch getting the tar whaled out of her."

Of course I knew who she meant. As I carried my tray back to our special table, I passed John Orrin sitting by himself, hunched miserably over his lunch. I felt guilt wash over me.

"What was *that* all about?" Gretchen asked.

"You'd have to be there to understand." I didn't feel good about what I had done, but it was over and there wasn't anything I could do about it.

However, someone else could. Mrs. Harmon stalked over to our table and said in a clipped voice, "Three minutes to eat, Kobie, then to the office."

I managed to choke down a few bites of

dry turkey before my time was up. "I wish you could come with me."

"I do, too." Gretchen stared at me with big scared eyes, probably wondering when she'd ever see me again.

The office was empty of other kids on Death Row when I slipped through the door. Behind the counter Miss Warren was pecking at her typewriter, undoubtedly typing a form of some kind. "Yes?" she inquired.

"I'm supposed to see Mr. Magyn."

"Have a seat." She went back to her typing.

This was only the second time I had actually been sent to the office, despite numerous threats from my teachers. Last year I popped a milk carton in the lunchroom and the monitor sent me upstairs. I waited an eternity, dying a thousand deaths, before Mr. Magyn summoned me to his inner office. He asked me my name and what awful thing I had done, then told me not to do it again and let me go back to class. I had a feeling I wouldn't get off so easy today.

I sat on the edge of the vinyl couch. My palms were sweaty. How long would he make me wait? Didn't he know that kids got awfully nervous when they had to wait for the principal? I might even throw up on his globe, the way Danny Blevins did.

At last Miss Warren told me Mr. Magyn would see me. I walked into the inner office with trembling knees. Mr. Magyn sat behind his form-littered desk.

"Sit down, Kobie," he said. A bad sign. He already knew my name, which meant he was probably going to expel me. Then the door opened and my mother came in! I wouldn't even get a chance to clear out my desk; my mother was going to take me straight home. Or to Juvenile Hall.

"Mrs. Roberts," Mr. Magyn greeted her as if we were at a tea party. "Please have a seat."

My mother took the chair next to me. "I'm sorry it took me so long," she apologized. "I had to finish on the line."

"That's quite all right. Kobie needed time to think about her behavior in the lunchroom."

"I'm so ashamed of you, Kobie," my mother said. "Humiliating that boy the way you did! What's gotten into you?"

Mr. Magyn interrupted. "Kobie, you know why you're here. Is there anything you'd like to say?"

"No, sir," I mumbled.

"Why did you do it?" my mother asked.

"Knowing that poor boy is on free lunch, why did you embarrass him that way? You *know* better!"

Yes, I knew John Orrin and all his brothers and sisters were on free lunch and I knew *better*, but I couldn't explain to her in a zillion years what happened on the serving line.

Mr. Magyn leaned forward. "How do you think John felt, Kobie, when you made such a fuss over his not paying?"

"Awful." But, then, so did *I*, yet nobody seemed to care about me.

"What do you think you should do?"

"Pay for his next lunch?" Maybe a little humor would lighten things up.

The principal frowned. Now he was really angry. "Do you think this is funny, Kobie?"

"No," I said lamely. "Sir."

"Usually I like to make the punishment fit the crime. You should be made to apologize to John Orrin at the top of your lungs, the way you humiliated him, in public. But that would only draw more attention to the boy's unfortunate situation." It wouldn't have done much for *my* unfortunate situation, either, but for once I kept quiet.

"I want to see you in my office tomorrow morning at eight-thirty," he continued.

"You will apologize to John Orrin and you will mean it." I nodded. "Also, I want you to write five hundred times in your best handwriting, 'I will not shout in the cafeteria.' Your sentences are due on my desk by noon tomorrow."

In the main office, my mother let me have it. "I was never so embarrassed in my whole life! Hearing that fracas on the line and then having to come up here! You think you got off the hook, apologizing to that boy and writing a few sentences, but just wait till I tell your father when he comes home tonight."

I could stand hearing my mother yell because I was used to it. If she got mad at me, it was no big deal. But I couldn't bear to have my father know what I did. He might tear down my tree house or prevent me from trick-or-treating with Gretchen next Sunday night. But mainly, I didn't want him to find out that going on twelve was making me into a terrible person.

Chapter 10

My mother didn't tell my father what I did, for some reason, but she wouldn't let me write my sentences in my tree house, either. She said it was too cold to sit up there half the evening.

So I stayed in my room with the door shut, writing "I will not shout in the cafeteria." When I finished, hours later, the sentences covered both sides of ten sheets of lined notebook paper.

The next day was more torturous than writing those stupid sentences. In the principal's office, I muttered an apology to John Orrin, who seemed as uncomfortable as I was.

"Kobie is genuinely sorry," Mr. Magyn emphasized. "I hope you two can be friends after this."

I really *was* sorry! But, still, it was all John's fault I said those things in the first place! If he hadn't gushed all over my mother, like she was *his* mother, I wouldn't have made such a scene. No way could I ever be friends with him. Never in a thousand million years.

We went back to class together, but I walked on the opposite side of the hall. He didn't speak. He didn't have to — he'd won and we both knew it.

At least it was library day. Gretchen and I secured a private table by the window, hidden by the nonfiction bookshelves. Gretchen didn't grill me about my ordeal in the principal's office — she was that kind of a friend. She read me silly riddles from this book, like What did the baby chick say when he found an orange in his mother's nest? Oh, look at the orange marmalade!

Soon we were giggling over jokes even dumber than that one.

"I need a drink of water," I gasped. "I'm getting a little hoarse."

"Hope you've got a little hay," Gretchen quipped. "Whinny-whinny, neigh-neigh, nicker-nicker." She was reciting an old gag we started years ago when Lori Bass, who was playing a horse in a puppet show, pronounced her lines phonetically, instead of making horse sounds.

It was really great having a friend like

Gretchen. She always cheered me up when I was down.

"If everything was just like now," I said after our laughter subsided, "we wouldn't need the Hammer Man. I mean, it wouldn't matter if we were famous or not. It would just be you and me having fun."

"I know." Then she said, "Kobie, why don't we forget about this Hammer Man business?"

For a second, I wished we could. I wasn't as brave as I let on — sneaking into a murderer's shed to steal evidence wasn't my idea of fun. But the other kids in room 10 were still on my case. They wouldn't quit until I either moved away or did something heroic.

"We can't forget him," I declared. "The very next time we see him go out to his shed, we'll nab him."

"He never leaves his house. We've only seen him go to his shed once when we were in the Honeysuckle Hideout."

"He'll go out there again." I glanced out the window at his shuttered house. The barren trees and dead grass made the place look even more forbidding.

"It's almost November," she pointed out. "If we didn't see him when the weather was nice, why should we see him when it's practically winter?"

"You have to think positively, Gretch. Let's send him a thought message: Hammer Man, go to your shed. Maybe if we both concentrate hard enough, he'll do it." I was starting to believe the power of my own imagination, visualizing the Hammer Man sleepwalking to his shed, arms outstretched as if he had no control over his body.

We closed our eyes so we could communicate better. But instead of willing the Hammer Man to leave his house, I thought about how my wonderful year was turning out so crummy. I lost the mural contest, forfeiting the title Best Artist in Centreville Elementary (yet I knew I really *was*). I hadn't found my father's King Neptune paper, the one he received when he crossed the equator. So far I hadn't done anything to make a name for myself. At the end of the year I'd be promoted to junior high (maybe) and no one would remember me, even though I had spent six whole years in this school. Kobie *who*?

Gretchen was right about one thing. Winter was coming, which meant indoor recess, stupid stuff like square dancing and sing-alongs. No more running down to the Honeysuckle Hideout to get away from the nerds in our class until spring. If everyone continued to berate me for losing the contest, I didn't know how I'd survive being cooped up with them day after day.

"I can't sit here with my eyes closed," Gretchen said, breaking the silence. She leafed through the mystery book she had picked to check out for the week. "I bet I've read this before."

"I bet you haven't read *this*." Mrs. Sharp glided over to our table and handed Gretchen a magazine article. "Remember that treasure story I promised you? Well, I finally remembered to bring it in."

We pounced on the article, spreading the pages so we both could read it at the same time. It was the greatest treasure story ever, about the Lost Dutchman Mine in the Superstition Mountains in Arizona. Apparently a Dutch prospector in the Wild West days found this gold mine hidden in the desert mountains. He etched coded directions to the mine on stone tablets. Then he died in his mine, too greedy to leave his gold.

Years later, the tablets were discovered and people were searching for the Dutchman's mine. The article told about one prospector whose campsite kept getting wrecked and who even claimed he'd been shot at. He believed it was the ghost of the old Dutchman, back from the dead to drive people away from his mine. Gretchen shivered as she read that paragraph.

"Look at those tablets," I said, referring to the photographs that accompanied the story. "It's like a treasure map."

The granite tablets were tombstone-shaped, with faint markings carved into the surface, arrows and double lines and strange symbols. But the prospector who owned the tablets didn't want people reading the magazine to decipher the code and go busting out to Arizona to find his mine, so he made the magazine photographer put pieces of black tape over the important clues on the tablets.

"I wish we could go out there and find that mine." I was already dreaming about how famous I'd be if I discovered a mine that had been lost for a hundred years and was cursed by a ghost besides.

"We'd never figure out where it was," Gretchen said. "Not without the clues under the tape. Anyway, I'm not too anxious to tangle with a ghost."

"Still, it'd be so neat. If we went out there, all we'd need is some camping equipment and this article."

We talked about the story, rereading parts of the article out loud to each other. My worries about my awful year suddenly evaporated. I'd never been any farther west than Front Royal, Virginia, but I could picture myself climbing rocks in the Superstition Mountains under the desert sun, stopping every now and then to consult the *Life* magazine article. When the blazing sun went down, Gretchen and I would roast hot dogs over a fire while the coyotes howled and the ghost of the old Dutchman roamed the hills, protecting his gold.

Mrs. Sharp came back to see how we liked the story. "I'm glad you enjoyed it," she said. "You know, John Orrin likes treasure stories, too. He asked me if I had any books about buried treasure and then I remembered the article. Why don't you share it with him?"

I stared at Gretchen in dismay. Share our wonderful *private* story with *him*! Why did John Orrin always have to meddle in everything we did?

Mrs. Sharp led John over to our table. "Kobie and Gretchen just finished reading this exciting story," she told him, practically pushing him in my lap in her enthusiasm to foist his company on us. "I'm sure they'll be happy to let you read it. Maybe the three of you can discuss it then. Isn't it nice to have a common interest?"

I spoke up before she left. "But, Mrs.

Sharp, it's *our* story. You saved it for us. You *gave* it to us."

A frown puckered her forehead. "Well, yes, I gave it to you girls first, but I brought it in for everyone to enjoy. You can take it home with you after the others have looked at it, if you like."

What good was an exclusive, saved-especially-for-us treasure story if she was going to let everybody read it? Of all people, Mrs. Sharp knew how much Gretchen and I liked our little secrets. Nobody else would appreciate the story of the Lost Dutchman Mine — the others would probably think it was dumb.

Then John had to open his mouth and make things worse, as usual. "I don't want to read it," he drawled. "I'll go over there and look at books instead."

"John, I thought you said you wanted to read about the lost mine. When I told you about it, you seemed excited."

"Well, obviously he's not," I said.

Mrs. Sharp's ever-present smile melted. "Kobie, I'm surprised at you! It's not like you to be stingy."

Yes, it was, she just didn't know it. This was the new going-on-twelve Kobie Roberts and she was a lot stingier, among other things, than the old Kobie Roberts.

"The library is for every student in Centreville Elementary," she went on crisply. "All the resources in this room are available to anyone who has a need or an interest. Do you understand?"

Gretchen and John nodded, but I tuned her out, thinking instead of the answer to that riddle: Oh, look at the orange marmalade!

"We're finished with the story," Gretchen told Mrs. Sharp, rescuing me. "John can have it."

The librarian left to stamp books, evidently satisfied we were going to behave ourselves.

"She probably hates me now," I said. "Here, take the stupid article." I shoved the papers across the table to John. "I hope you hate it."

"Kobie!" Gretchen cried. "She didn't mean it," she soothed John. "She never means half of what she says."

"Yes, I do. I meant every syllable. Since *you* came over here, you'll have to put up with me."

"I didn't ask to come over here," John corrected.

"Then why *are* you here?" I demanded. "How come every time I turn around, there *you* are, getting me in trouble? Why did you have to come to our school, anyway? Why didn't you just stay where you were?"

"Because my folks moved here," he answered, unruffled. "If you want to know the truth, when we first came, I sort of liked Centreville. But now I don't think I do."

"Then leave," I said, as if he could pack and go that very minute.

"I wish I could."

"That makes two of us."

John remained composed, calm as a boulder in a hurricane. "Where I came from, people are a lot friendlier."

"That's because they're all as dumb as you."

"Kobie — " Gretchen hated bickering. "If you can't say anything nice to John, don't say anything at all."

"She doesn't really rile me." John's lips curved in that tiny condescending smile that drove me insane.

He was like the ghost of the Lost Dutchman Mine; he would never stop haunting me, no matter where I went. I absolutely had to get in the last word or explode.

"I hate you," I said and turned my back to John.

Then I realized there was one other tactic I hadn't tried yet. Cold War. Instead of losing my temper at him, I'd snipe *indirectly* at him. That way I could still get my licks in and John wouldn't be able to complain.

"Do you smell something rotten?" I asked Gretchen, ignoring John as if he weren't sitting next to me.

She knew what I was up to. "No," she said, prickly with disapproval. "I don't smell anything except books and library paste."

"Well, I do. It smells like — like a dead rat. That's it. Mrs. Sharp probably trapped a rat behind the bookcase and it's rotting."

John was absorbed in the article. "Wow! Did you read the part about how much money they think the gold is worth?" he asked Gretchen, roundly ignoring *me*. "Millions and millions of dollars! I'd like to find that mine, wouldn't you?"

Before Gretchen could reply, I said, "Did you hear anything, Gretch? Must be the wind."

John said, "Those clues shouldn't be too hard to figure out. The patches only cover one or two spots, you can see the rest plain as day. I bet we could figure out where that mine is."

"Awfully loud wind," I remarked. "And hot, too." I fanned myself with the riddle book. "Just a lot of hot air."

When library period was finally over, I breezed past Mrs. Sharp's desk without saying good-bye to her the way I usually did.

"Kobie." Her voice reeled me back.

"Yes, Mrs. Sharp?"

"You didn't take the article." It was lying on the table where John had left it. "I thought you wanted to take it home."

"No, thanks." I wasn't about to touch it after John had his grubby paws all over it. "You can let other kids read it," I offered grandly, although my image was already tarnished.

Mrs. Sharp regarded me while my class streamed out behind us. When Gretchen paused at the desk, too, the librarian indicated she'd like to speak to me alone. When I was the last one in the library, she said, "Kobie, lately you seem a little unhappy. Is there anything you'd like to talk about?"

"No."

"I'd like to help, if I can."

"I don't need any help. I'm fine." But I did need help. I felt weird, as if I were plummeting down an endless mine shaft. Nothing was going right and it seemed as if nothing would, ever again.

"Well, if you feel like talking, my door is always open."

My gaze traveled past her ear, outside the window to the gray house on the hill. What would I talk to her about, even if I decided to trust her again? What the little chick said when he found an orange in his mother's nest? Mrs. Sharp would never understand that, besides the falling feeling, I also felt shuttered and closed-in, like the Hammer Man's house.

In fact, finding somebody who *would* understand was as remote as getting the Hammer Man to come out of his house.

Chapter 11

That night in bed I thought of a plan. The ultimate revenge. A plan that would fix John Orrin's wagon permanently and help me regain my position in room 10.

The weird feeling was still hanging over me as I brushed my teeth and changed into my pajamas. I felt sort of lonely, but it was too late to call Gretchen and I didn't want to talk to my parents. It wasn't that kind of loneliness.

Instead I piled my stuffed animals on my bed. All twenty-seven of them, ranging in size from my two-foot-tall panda bear to Ellsworth, a miniature elephant.

I had a system for arranging the stuffed animals and it took me about fifteen minutes to get them in the proper order. The big panda went against the wall, Dixie the mouse was next to him and below him the white rabbit with the music box in its tummy that didn't work anymore, and so on until there was just enough room left for me to crawl under the covers.

It was very cozy with all my old friends crowded around me. Of course I was much too old to sleep with stuffed animals, but I figured it wouldn't hurt to have them there a little while. When I was younger, I used to sleep with my stuffed animals because I was afraid of the dark. But then after I'd fallen asleep, I'd pitch them out one by one so I'd have room to turn over. One time I bonked my head on the white rabbit with the broken music box in its stomach, nearly giving myself a concussion. I transferred the rabbit down to the foot of the bed, where it wouldn't do any damage.

I lay back against my pillow with Ellsworth in the crook of my elbow, watching the headlights from the cars on Lee Highway graze my ceiling. The events of the day tumbled through my head like socks in an automatic dryer. So far John Orrin had evaded me at every junction. I just couldn't win, no matter what I did. It wasn't fair.

What could I do to get back at him?

I heard my mother in the hall, adjusting the thermostat on the wall outside my room. We had a constant battle over the furnace. My room was like a deep freeze all year long except in July and August, when it became a sauna. I tweaked the thermostat dial up to eighty degrees or so every night before I went to bed. Naturally my mother would hear the blower come on and come down the hall to turn it back down.

Sometimes my mother came in my room to kiss me good night again or just look in to see if I was still breathing. Once I was dozing off with my arm dangling over the side of the mattress. She tiptoed into my room and moved my arm, to keep the circulation from being cut off, I guess. It felt good when she did that, like hitting a warm spot while wading in a cold lake. Lately my mother hardly ever checked on me after I went to bed. Maybe she was too tired . . . or maybe she didn't care anymore.

Hearing her now, I flopped over in bed and dangled my arm over the edge of the mattress. When my mother switched the thermostat outside my door, I pretended to be asleep. Through my squinched eyelids, I sensed her inspecting me, but she didn't come in and move my arm. She eased the door shut, until the light from the hallway narrowed to a strip of yellow across my rug, then left.

Well! Obviously my mother didn't care whether her only daughter's arm turned black and dropped off before morning. I tried to convince myself I was too old anyway to be tucked into bed. After all, I was going on twelve. Only babies like Beverly, the twerp who sat with my mother on the bus, slept with stuffed animals and wanted to be kissed good night every two seconds. I flung my animals on the floor, then slumped back against my pillow, fighting tears of anger. Why was I crying? Not over my mother — *she* certainly didn't care. If I died from gangrene of the arm, my mother would probably give all my stuffed animals to Beverly. I think I despised Beverly almost as much as I despised John Orrin.

If only I could get rid of Beverly and John just by hating them to another place, another planet, even, the way I tried to will the Hammer Man to leave his house. I had as much chance of getting rid of John as I did of finding the Lost Dutchman Mine.

And then it hit me. The wonderful, brilliant plan.

Maybe I couldn't send John Orrin to another planet, but I *could* cause him to get suspended, maybe sent away from Centreville forever.

I couldn't wait until morning came so I could get started.

* * *

"A fake treasure map?" Gretchen echoed the next day in the Honeysuckle Hideout. "That's the joke you're going to play on John?"

"We already know he's nuts over buried treasure stories," I said, zipping my jacket up to my neck. It was pretty chilly in the hideout. Our days of outdoor recess were numbered, which meant I had to hurry and put my plan into motion. "I draw this fake treasure map and plant it in his desk. He finds it." I slackened my jaw, miming John discovering the map.

"Then what?" Gretchen prompted.

I resumed my normal expression. "He starts following the clues. First he has to go over to the baseball diamond, then he has to go over to the monkey bars, and then the swings — "

"Wait a minute," she interrupted. "You mean the map will be this playground? Kobie, why would anyone believe there's a treasure buried on the playground?"

"Let me finish. He goes back up to the blacktop, then around to the water fountain. He goes all over the place and gets confused. Then the map leads him back down the hill and over to the old fence we found, until he winds up — " I paused triumphantly, having reached the best part. "At the Dairy Queen!"

"The Dairy Queen?" Gretchen still didn't catch on. "The treasure's going to be buried at the Dairy Queen?"

"There is no treasure! The whole idea is to get him *over there* so we can tell Mrs. Harmon! That's the joke!" Of course my plan was more than a joke. The principal was sure to suspend John for sneaking over to the Dairy Queen, the one rule he couldn't stand to have disobeyed. "Won't it be a riot? And it's sure to work!"

"I hate to tell you this," Gretchen said, "but your idea is full of holes."

"What holes? I've thought of every angle. I can't lose on this one."

"Kobie, what makes you so sure that John will fall for a phony treasure map? He wasn't born yesterday, you know. He gets pretty good grades, better than mine. Better than *yours*." She *would* have to bring up my miserable report card.

"Have you forgotten who the best artist in the school is? I can draw a map that would fool anyone. My map will make him believe there's a buried treasure out here somewhere. It can't fail."

She jammed her hands into the pockets of her coat. "I don't like the idea of getting John in trouble."

"What trouble? It's a *joke*, Gretch. Jokes

are supposed to be funny. Why aren't you laughing?"

She looked at me, her blue eyes serious. "Because this one isn't funny. I know you, Kobie Roberts. I know how your devious pea brain works. Mr. Magyn suspends kids who are caught at the Dairy Queen. That's what you want, isn't it? To get him suspended."

"So what if I do? He's always getting me in trouble, why can't I try to get him back once? You won't say anything, will you? You're still my best friend," I added, as if that prevented her from telling on me.

Gretchen was quiet. I suddenly sensed our friendship straining at the seams. Would I lose her, my one and only friend, over my need for revenge?

"I won't tell," she promised, "but don't expect me to help, either."

She really believed in sticking to her principles. So did I, though I wasn't sure what they were. I only knew that I had to go through with this.

I started my map as soon as I got home from school. In order for the map to be credible, it had to look old-timey, kind of brown and ragged around the edges. A wrinkled grocery sack ripped into a rough rectangle looked fairly authentic by the time I was done "aging" it. Sepia crayon gave the map a faded, hundred-years-ago appearance, like the brown inks people used in the olden days.

"Kobie! What are you doing?" my mother shouted from the kitchen. "Have you swept the basement yet?"

"I'm busy," I called back.

"Doing what, your homework?"

"No," I answered truthfully. "I'm working on a project."

As if transported by magic, my mother materialized at my door, still wearing her cafeteria uniform. "I asked you an hour ago to sweep the basement. The man is coming tomorrow morning to fix the hot water tank and the basement is a hog pen."

"Basements are supposed to be dirty," I said, not looking up from my map. "He won't mind. In fact, he'd probably be more suspicious if it was clean. You know, wonder what we really do in our basement to keep it so clean. Instead of fixing the hot water heater, he'd spend all his time hunting for a printing press, thinking we're counterfeiters or something — "

"Stop changing the subject. Why haven't you done it?"

"I told you, I'm busy." Carefully I drew a north-west-south-east compass in one corner of my map. If I messed up, it would be her fault, yammering at me.

"If you're not doing your homework, then you're not too busy to do what I asked you," she said. "Every time I want you to do something, I have to whoop and holler to get you to do it. I'm tired of telling you things over and over, Kobie. In this house, we all have to do our share."

Her complaints were the same ones I've heard for years. I almost wished my mother would dredge up a new set of gripes. "I'll sweep the basement in a little while," I told her.

"No, you won't. You'll drag out whatever it is you're doing until tonight or the next day so you conveniently won't have to work. You won't turn your hand to do a thing around here anymore. My mother told me girls your age got lazy and she was right."

"If you knew I was going to get lazy, why do you try to make me work?" I was swimming in deep water, but it was too late to take the words back.

"If your father heard how you sass me . . . but no, you're nice when he's around."

"That's because he's nice to *me*. He tells me stories and makes me things. He doesn't scream at me night and day to clean the house."

Her eyes got moist as she chewed her bottom lip. I had hurt her feelings, but it was the truth. My father *was* nicer. "I hate this stage you're going through," she said. "I wish you were a cute little first grader again, like Beverly."

I had that coming but it still rankled, being compared to that little twit. "Then get Beverly to sweep your old basement," I snapped. "Since you're so crazy about her."

"Are you jealous of that little girl? Kobie, you should be ashamed."

"Well, you sit with her every single day on the bus."

"Where am I supposed to sit? On the hood?" she countered. "You don't want me sitting with you, you've made it quite clear."

I didn't know what I wanted anymore, except for this conversation to end. "All right! I'll sweep the basement, even though I think it's dumb to put on airs for the hot water tank man."

"We don't put on airs!" she retorted. "The place is filthy. When you used to swing down in the basement, you swept it every week. Now you don't go down there anymore, so you couldn't care less if the dirt piles up to the ceiling. You only do something when it suits your purpose."

"I *said* I'd do it, didn't I?"

"I'll do it myself," my mother said curtly. "Asking you to help a little around here is like asking a stick." She flounced into her room to change out of her uniform.

Through the heat register in my room, I could hear my mother down in the basement, sweeping the floor with resentful strokes of the push broom. I felt a twinge of guilt. If only she hadn't asked me to do a chore when I was working on my fake treasure map. But the map was more important to me than impressing some guy coming to fix our hot water tank.

I had to put the map aside to eat supper. As we ate beans and franks, I expected my mother, who came to the table with dust in her hair, to blab to my father. She never said a word about our argument.

After supper, my father went into the living room to watch the news. I lay on the rug beside him with my arithmetic book (merely a front) and my map. Usually my mother watched television with us, but tonight she attacked the dishes immediately after supper.

I decorated the margins of my map with dragons and sea monsters, like the old maps back when people thought there were only boundless oceans and strange creatures beyond their land.

"That looks like something I've seen before," my father said, glancing over my shoulder.

"What?"

"Those monsters you're drawing. Remind me of . . . I don't know." He scratched his head. "Oh, yeah, that paper I got when I crossed the equator."

I held my breath. Did he also remember where it was? "Dad, you told me I could have that paper but we can't find it. Do you remember where you put it?"

"Oh, it's around here someplace." He clicked off the TV and went back out to the kitchen.

I stared at the picture tube as the square of light diminished until it vanished altogether. If only I had the King Neptune paper, my troubles would be over. I would have a map of my own to guide me. Then going on twelve wouldn't be so murky and mysterious.

Planting the fake treasure map in John Orrin's desk turned out to be the simplest part of the entire scheme. John took a pirate book out of the library and brought it to school every day to read during free period. The library book was left conspicuously on top of his textbooks stacked in the compartment under his desk. I could see it from where I sat, two seats back.

Because it rained the whole week, Mrs. Harmon kept us indoors during recess. On the second day of indoor recess, we played a boisterous game of musical desks to this hilarious record. I positioned myself so that when Mrs. Harmon lifted the needle of the record player, I was sitting in John's desk. When the song started again, I slipped the folded treasure map in the back of his library book. Easy as pie.

Now all I had to do was wait. Wait for John to discover the map in his book. Wait for the rain to stop so we could have recess outside. Wait for the stupid country fly to blunder into the crafty spider's web.

Chapter 12

Alert as a bird dog, I watched John Orrin every day during free period. He would open his pirate book and read, slowly and methodically, following along with his finger. John made good grades, as Gretchen said, but he wasn't what you'd call a genius. He studied fiercely, memorizing lists of history dates and spelling words. He read the same way, so it took him forever to get through that stupid library book.

And then he found it. One morning he turned the page and my map drifted out. I held my breath as he unfolded it. Did it *really* look like a map or just a grocery bag with brown crayoned marks on it? If John immersed himself in stories the way I did, he'd be *ready* to believe it was a treasure map. After he'd been reading about pirates and buried treasure for a week, his head should have been brimming with visions of gold dubloons and Jolly Roger flags.

I couldn't see his face as he examined my map, but he stuck it in his shirt pocket and patted the flimsy material, as if guarding a secret.

"He fell for it," I whispered to Gretchen.

We had outdoor recess that day for the first time since the rain let up. It was sunny, but a stiff breeze chased leaves ahead of us as Gretchen and I loped down the mud-slicked hill to the Honeysuckle Hideout. Inside the tunnel, I crouched on the sodden floor so I could spy on John.

"He's by the basketball net, right on schedule," I reported gleefully. "He's checking the map. Now he's counting off the paces. In thirty-three steps he should be behind the baseball diamond. Take bigger steps, dummy! He won't reach the baseball diamond in a hundred steps, the dumb way he walks."

Gretchen refused to watch John bumble around the playground with my phony treasure map. "I still think it's mean," she commented in a low voice.

"What's mean?" I said. "He's having a great time out there, Gretch. Nobody ever invites him to play. For the first time since he came here, he's actually got something to do during recess."

"You know what I'm talking about. When he winds up at the Dairy Queen."

I clucked my tongue. "Into each life a little rain must fall," I said, quoting my father again.

She stared at the old man's house on the hill, defiantly ignoring my running commentary of John's progress.

Her objection didn't bother me much. As long as she was with me in the hideout, I knew she was still my friend. I resumed spying. John was spinning like a windmill on the blacktop, evidently trying to determine which way was north-by-northeast. I had deliberately made the directions tricky — if the map was too easy, he'd never buy it.

"Not that way," I coaxed. "Over *there*. At the rate he's going, he won't get to the Dairy Queen before next year. He can't even find the next clue, which is the water fountain. It's as plain as the nose on your face but he's too dumb — "

"Kobie, it's him! He's coming out! The Hammer Man!" Gretchen yanked me around.

The gray house above our hideout was blank-shuttered and unearthly silent, as usual. But the old man was indeed sauntering down the hill toward his shed. He wore a leather jacket and no hat — the wind tousled his long white hair. He didn't seem to be armed with a hammer or any other lethal weapon, but looks could be deceiving.

At last, the chance we'd been waiting for! With Gretchen distracting the Hammer Man, I could sneak in his shed and collect the necessary evidence. Then we'd go to the police and nail the Hammer Man. I grinned at my own pun. In one wonderful dazzling day, I would get rid of John Orrin and expose the Hammer Man! People would call me Famous Girl Sleuth like Nancy Drew, or maybe simply the Heroine of Centreville.

"We have to hurry," I said, pushing Gretchen toward the entrance. "He might not stay in his shed very long."

Gretchen balked halfway through the tunnel. "We're not going up there?"

"Yes! What do you think? We've talked about our plan a hundred times."

"Kobie, I don't want to do this."

"We *have* to," I screeched. "It's our last chance to be famous! We probably won't see the old man again till next spring."

Still she wouldn't budge. "If Mrs. Harmon sees us off school property, we'll be suspended just like John."

"Honestly, Gretch, do you want to be a nobody the rest of your life? Do you think a real hero like Admiral Byrd worried about leaving school property when he flew over the South Pole?" Then I remembered the reward money. "This time tomorrow," I said enticingly, "you could be in Woolworth's on the biggest shopping spree in the world. Don't forget the reward money."

"I don't want the money," she said and I realized she was nearly in tears. "I'm scared. I'm afraid to go up there."

In my exuberance to make a name for myself, I had overlooked the danger of our mission. "I'm scared, too," I admitted. "But we'll be together and it'll be over before you know it. Think of Admiral Byrd."

"He was in an airplane," she said, wiping her eyes and smiling. "We'll be on the ground."

"Then you'll do it?" Without Gretchen, I couldn't catch a gnat, much less a criminal.

She released a shuddering breath. "I'll do it. Let's go before I chicken out again." She parted the curtain of honeysuckle that concealed the entrance to our hideout.

Outside, I saw Mrs. Harmon gabbing with Mrs. Wright up on the blacktop. A few kids swung from the monkey bars, but they didn't notice us as we scuttled to the boundary of dense undergrowth that divided school property from the old man's property.

Heads down, we ran through rain-soaked weeds, wet horsetail, and snarly goose grass that tripped us about every other step. Briars snagged our socks and soon our legs were crisscrossed with whip-thin scratches.

Up on the hill, I glanced behind us again. The teachers were still talking. Bright figures of our classmates skipped around the blacktop, like scraps of colored construction paper. For an instant I longed to be with them, joining in their silly, ordinary games.

Then it dawned on me that what Gretchen and I were doing was *real*. Away from the safety of the hideout, we weren't idly speculating whether the man who lived in the gray house was a murderer, but were actually carrying out one of my schemes.

Thousands of acorns from the ancient oak trees, like marbles spilled from a giant bucket, made sneaking up on the Hammer Man even more treacherous. We slipped and slid, clutching each other to keep from falling, until we got the giggles.

"Shhh!" I cautioned as we approached the shed. The building was bigger than it appeared from the hideout. The warped boards hadn't seen a coat of paint this century.

Gretchen hung back, her eyes round and frightened.

"It'll be okay. Come on." I sounded braver than I felt. What if the Hammer Man had seen us? He might be sitting behind that door with his trusty hammer lying across his knees, just waiting. . . .

Gretchen nudged me, pointing to a knot-hole in the side of the shed.

"Good idea," I whispered. "Let's see if he's in there."

Before I could peek through the hole, Gretchen drew me back again. Her hand was over her mouth, muffling a laugh. Was she hysterical with fear?

"Kobie, suppose this isn't a shed at all, but an *outhouse* and he's in there — " Her pent-up laughter escaped in a spluttery outburst.

Laugh attacks were nothing new to us. They struck any time, any place, like a tornado. Last week in assembly when the second graders were doing the Hokey-Pokey, Gretchen and I had a giggle-fit. Mrs. Harmon separated us, but even then we couldn't quit. After Gretchen was moved four rows away from me in the auditorium, all I had to do was stick my left leg out in the aisle and shake it like the little kids were doing on stage, and Gretchen doubled up.

It was the same thing now. We collapsed in a heap in the acorn-studded grass, rolling on the acorns and laughing so hard a whole herd of criminals could have stampeded us.

The door to the outbuilding squeaked inward. The old man sat just inside the door, not on a toilet seat as we had pictured, but on a tool bench, surrounded by tools hanging from nails: saws and pliers and *hammers*. My plan suddenly winged out the window. The Hammer Man had caught us instead.

He wasn't at all the hardened criminal I expected to see. White feathery hair fringed a high forehead. His skin was the texture of leather, like his jacket. Behind rimless glasses, clear blue eyes appraised us.

He spoke first. "Well, hello there." His voice was creaky, like the chains of my basement swing, but friendly. "I know you two. You're the girls always hidin' in the brambles."

"You've seen us?" I asked, incredulous. After months of spying on his house, I was shocked to learn he'd been spying on *us* at the same time!

"Sure, I've seen you. I'm not blind." He

cocked his head at me. "You're the big-mouthed one, always yellin' at that little blond-haired fella."

My face reddened. The Hammer Man had heard me teasing John Orrin!

Gretchen grinned. "That's Kobie, all right. My name is Gretchen Farris. The big mouth is Kobie Roberts."

"I'm Thomas Robey. Pleased to meet you." He extended his hand. Gretchen shook it politely. "What're you girls doing up here? Payin' a social visit?" he asked.

"We were just —" Gretchen looked at me.

"Well, we were —" My voice died away. I couldn't very well tell him what we were *really* doing. "We were — hunting for buried treasure!"

Mr. Robey chuckled. "Buried treasure, huh? You won't find none on this place. I've been here eighty-four years and I ain't seen no treasure yet!"

"You've been here that long?" I marvelled.

"All my life. I was born here. 'Spect I'll die here."

It was obvious Mr. Robey wasn't the Hammer Man. Up close, he resembled somebody's nice old grandfather more than a murderer. Deep in my heart, I knew I had used the legend of the Hammer Man to create a new secret project. In order to convince Gretchen, I began believing my own story. Even deeper down inside, I think Gretchen knew I was making it up but went along with me because we were friends.

"What d'you girls do down in the bushes?" Mr. Robey demanded. "I see you down there pert' near every day."

Gretchen replied, "Oh, we read, mostly Nancy Drew mysteries, and sometimes Kobie draws pictures. She tells really neat stories, too."

"Is that so?" Mr. Robey focused his attention on me. "How come you don't play with the other children yonder? I never see you jumpin' rope or playin' ball. Why is that?"

"Those kids are morons," I said scornfully. "Gretchen and I have more fun by ourselves."

"It's nice you've got a good friend." Mr. Robey gazed at the activity on the blacktop. "My son and daughter-in-law live with me," he rambled. "The woman means well, but she's always fussin' over me." His voice cracked as he mimicked his daughter-in-law. " 'Don't sit in a draft, Dad. Put this rug over your legs.' Like I said, she means well. Ever' chance I get, I run out here and hide, like you all do in your bushes, just to have a minute's peace. But when she's babysittin' me, I park myself in a big easy chair by the parlor window and watch the children on the playground."

I couldn't imagine a more boring way to kill time. And I thought I had it bad, stuck in dull old Willow Springs.

"That little fella out there reminds me of when I was his age." A solitary figure stood by the empty monkey bars. John Orrin! "I was all by my lonesome, just like he is, day after day. Seems like nobody wants him around. Nobody liked me, neither, so I know just how he feels."

Mr. Robey's clear blue eyes were disarming, as if he could see right through me. I felt his remarks were mainly for my benefit. I didn't want to talk about John and how lonely he was.

I blurted out the first thing that flitted into my head. "You ought to come out west with us. Gretchen and I are going to Arizona someday." Her expression said this was news to her. "Out to the Superstition Mountains to find the Lost Dutchman Mine. It's loaded with gold. There'll be plenty for the three of us."

Mr. Robey chuckled again. "Go out west and find a gold mine! Glory be! My daughter-in-law won't let me out of her sight, much less let me go traipsin' off to Arizona."

"She would if you tell her about all the gold you'll bring back. It's hidden in the mountains, but we've got a map — " I broke off, suddenly remembering the trap I had set for John. He was still following the phony treasure map and only had one more clue to unravel before he'd be off school property.

Mr. Robey nodded, as if he were actually considering our expedition. "The riches of the world are often buried," he allowed. "Gold, diamonds. Gold is usually covered by ugly rock and you don't even know it's there. Diamonds don't show their fire till they're cut. Kind of like people."

"Like people?" Gretchen asked. "How?"

"Well sir, you have to take the time to dig beneath the surface on some people. Outside, they might look like a humble rock. But way down deep, they could be bright and shiny like a diamond, or gold. You have to look mighty hard." His sharp scrutiny was making me uncomfortable, as if he were judging me.

Down the hill, John measured off paces, skirting our hideout.

"We should go," Gretchen said to me. "Mrs. Harmon will probably blow her whistle any minute for us to line up on the blacktop." I suspected she planned to detour John away from the Dairy Queen so he wouldn't get in trouble. I didn't really care — the joke had gone far enough.

"You'd better skedaddle then," Mr. Robey agreed. "I like your company, but maybe you ought to come back another time, when you're not supposed to be in school. When I sold the land for your school, it was on the condition that no children would wander over the line on my property."

"Why?" I asked, sidetracked by curiosity. "What difference does it make if we play in the bushes at the bottom of the hill? We don't hurt anything."

"It's not my property I'm worried about. It's the children. There's an abandoned well somewhere in the brush down there. At one time I had it fenced off, but the fence keeled over. My son was going to locate the blamed thing and cover it proper, but the kids have been good at staying off my property." Until now, he implied.

"We know where it is! We could show your son so he could — " I stopped horrified.

John Orrin, intently following the final instruction on my map, was heading right for the well! Even if he stubbed his foot against one of the square rocks that bordered the rim of the well, he might not be able to catch himself in time.

"Kobie!" Gretchen cried. "The well — !"

I barreled down the hill, screaming at the top of my lungs. "John! Don't take another step! John — stop!"

He looked up from his counting, startled. Then his foot vaulted through the vines camouflaging the opening of the well and he crashed through the brambly net.

Chapter 13

I reached the well first, careful not to stumble over the slablike wall. My heart was thumping like crazy. If John was killed or hurt, it was all my fault! I never meant to hurt him, only have him suspended. And even that was terrible, now that I thought about it.

Slithering across the ledge on my stomach, I leaned over the yawning hole. My fear of heights came roaring back, forcing me to withdraw before I could look down. How deep was the well? And how could I help John get out? Even with a ladder, it was doubtful I'd have enough nerve to climb down there.

I cupped my hands in a megaphone. "John! Are you okay?"

"Kobie?" His voice didn't sound that far down. "Is that you? Yeah, I'm okay. Help me up, will you?"

He was asking me to help him! *Me!* After all I had done to him, humiliated him, called him names, plotted and planned and schemed to get rid of him. And still he wanted my help.

Gathering what little courage I could muster, I crawled out over the rock and looked down into the well. John Orrin's face tilted upward. To my everlasting relief, the well wasn't very deep at all! He teetered on a pile of debris, leaves and rocks and stuff that had either fallen or been dumped into the dried-up well, the top of his head only a few inches from the mossy rim. He really was okay!

I stretched my arm down into the pit, gripping the square stone with my other hand. He grabbed my arm with both hands, clinging tightly. When I pulled, he managed to gain a foothold on a rock protruding from the side of the well. By this time Gretchen had arrived. The two of us tugged on his belt and hauled him over the side.

Panting, he rested against the stone wall. "That was something! Like to scared me to death!"

"You aren't hurt, are you?" Gretchen asked anxiously.

"Naw. I bumped my knee going down but that's it."

"Let's see." He had no choice but to roll

up his pants leg. Above the frayed hem of his sock, a purplish knot was forming. "You'd better go to the nurse. It might be sprained. What do you think, Kobie?"

What did *I* think? That was like asking Dracula if he thought a mosquito bite should be treated. It was my fault John fell in the well in the first place. Me and my stupid treasure map.

Kathy Stall and Marcia Dittier tore through the brambles to drag us back on school property. From there, we went straight to the office.

Mr. Magyn was not nearly as lenient as he'd been the last time. He wrote notes for Gretchen and John to take to their parents before excusing John to the nurse's office and letting Gretchen return to class. But instead of writing a note for my parents, he had my mother paged over the PA system.

She must have raced upstairs because she got there in about four seconds flat. Her face was drained, as if she were afraid something awful had happened to me. When she saw me slouched in Mr. Magyn's office, obviously all right, she looked so relieved that I felt worse than ever.

"Kobie was caught off school property during recess," Mr. Magyn informed her. "Along with Gretchen Farris and John

Orrin. The Orrin boy fell into an unused well on Mr. Robey's property. Fortunately he was not hurt seriously, but he could have been. Because this is a first offense for these children, at least to my knowledge, I'm leaving disciplinary action up to their parents. But the next time — " He left his threat unfinished, letting my vivid imagination fill in a suitably horrid punishment.

I could tell my mother was infuriated by the incident. All she said after the principal dismissed us was a terse, "I'll deal with you later."

It was strange going back to class. Everybody in room 10 knew John and Gretchen and I were in trouble, but Mrs. Harmon continued the arithmetic lesson as if nothing had happened. Mrs. Harmon never made a big deal after a kid came back from the office, like some teachers did. I slipped into my seat and got out my arithmetic book. Kathy Stall tapped the corner of her own textbook, so I could find the right page. Usually she ignored me totally or made some remark to Marcia Dittier. I guess she felt sorry for me.

The door opened again and John Orrin limped to his seat.

"Are you all right, John?" Mrs. Harmon inquired.

"Yes, ma'am," he replied. He threw me

that funny little smile. Apparently his leg
wasn't sprained.

But my friendship with Gretchen was
definitely wounded. Because of my obses-
sion to get revenge, she was in as much
trouble as I was.

At lunchtime, Gretchen hurried ahead
of me to get into the serving line. I plopped
down at our table and emptied the contents
of my lunch bag. If Gretchen wanted to eat
with Kathy and Marcia from now on, I
could hardly blame her. When she marched
over to our table with John Orrin limping
behind her, I was so stunned I dropped my
finger sandwich on the floor.

"Kobie, you're such a slob," Gretchen
chided, breaking her butter cookie in two
and handing me half. "Here. So you won't
starve."

"Boy, I was scared. I thought Mr. Magyn
was going to suspend us," John said, pulling up a chair. "Didn't you?"

I stared at Gretchen, but she merely
shrugged. Why was John sitting at our
table? Didn't he realize my purpose all
along was to have him expelled? Surely he
must have known the map was a fake. He
probably even knew that I had drawn it
and stuck it in his library book. I still
couldn't understand why he wanted to eat
lunch with me.

Gretchen said, "Did you notice how sloppy Mr. Magyn's desk was? And he's always telling us in assembly how important it is to be neat and organized!"

"He couldn't even find his own telephone!" John laughed. You would never have thought that only an hour ago John was at the bottom of an abandoned well.

In a rare display of generosity, I gave my half of the butter cookie to him.

"That's your favorite," Gretchen said, surprised.

"I'm not hungry." I wasn't. Unrelated thoughts whirled around my brain. The Hammer Man, the fake map, the terror of watching John fall into the well. Events that I had caused. Recalling what Mr. Robey had said about looking beneath the surface for the true value in other people, I wondered what other people saw in me. Gold and diamonds . . . or brass and rhinestones.

My mother didn't speak as we walked up our steep driveway. I still felt terrible. The sky was November-gray, reflecting my mood. There was no point stepping on the Moonstone for luck. Wishing couldn't change what I had done. Much as I longed to retreat into my tree house, I had to face the music.

"Go to your room," my mother said, unlocking the door. "I'll be there in a minute."

I threw myself across my bed, clutched my stuffed panda to my chest, and began to sob. I *hated* to cry. Crying was for little kids, not somebody going on twelve. But it seemed like the closer I got to my twelfth birthday, the more I cried.

The mattress dented under my mother's weight as she sat next to me. "What's wrong, Kobie?"

"I'm miserable!" I was crying so hard, the word came out *mi-huh-is-huh-ra-huh-ble*. "Nobody knows!"

"I think I do," she said. "I was almost twelve myself, once."

"Are you going to tell Dad what I did today?"

"Shouldn't I? He has a right to know."

"Then he'll be mad at me, too!" I sobbed harder than ever.

"I expect so. Sit up, Kobie. I want to talk to you."

I obeyed, snuffling. She brushed my damp bangs out of my eyes. Her touch felt comforting, like the time she moved my arm when it was hanging over the side of the bed.

"You can't go on only showing your good side to your father," she said. "He knows you're not perfect, Kobie."

"But I don't want him mad at me."

"And I can be?"

I plucked at a tuft of chenille on my ratty old bedspread. "You know what I mean."

"You mean you like your father better than me." She stated this matter-of-factly, yet I knew her feelings were hurt. I didn't want to hurt anyone, but I seemed to be hurting people right and left lately.

"I don't like him *better*." I chose my words carefully. "It's just that he tells me stories and he makes me things. He doesn't yell at me all the time like you do."

"That's because he doesn't see your room like the wreck of the Hesperus, the way I do. And he doesn't know you'd only wash your hair once a year unless I got on you about it. Your father leaves for work early and he doesn't get home until suppertime. It's my job to see to it you get to school looking halfway decent and you do your homework. It's tough being a mother."

"It's no picnic being a kid, either."

"I know. Remember all those things my mother told me about girls growing up? How they get lazy and how they sass their mothers?"

I nodded. She could publish a book of my grandmother's corny sayings.

"Who do you think told my mother about raising girls? *Her* mother — your great-grandmother. And what my grandmother said still holds true. Because even though times change, people don't. Girls — and boys, too — go through the same stages. Growing up is no picnic, as you put it."

A pattern was beginning to emerge in my mind. "You were just like me when you were twelve, weren't you?"

"Exactly. That's why I can't come down on you too hard." My father had mentioned that my mother and I were alike in ways I wouldn't understand until I was older. Well, I was older now. And I was starting to understand.

"Remind me to tell you about the time I chopped the fur collar off Nancy Marsteller's coat because I was jealous." She laughed at the recollection.

I hadn't heard that story but I knew Nancy Marsteller was the doctor's daughter, the rich girl in town, and that my mother once snipped off Nancy's eyelashes with manicure scissors. Evidently my mother couldn't be trusted with sharp objects. But she had *picked on* Nancy Marsteller — did even worse things than I did to John. At least his clothes and eyelashes were intact. I wasn't proud of what I had done to him. Part of the reason I was feeling so guilty was that John never tried to fight back. Nancy Marsteller probably got her revenge when my mother had to go to Dr. Marsteller's for a shot, by making her father bring out his blunt needle. But John always took whatever I dished out. Maybe Gretchen was right again — maybe we *could* have a third person in our group at lunchtime.

"Were you and Nancy ever friends?" I asked.

"Yes. I thought she was stuck-up because she was rich, but when I got to know her, Nancy became one of my closest friends."

My mother had loads of friends back in the old days. Not one exclusive friend, but all kinds, both girls and boys. That was probably the key to being popular.

Then I remembered other stories my mother had told me, about her and her sister Lil when they were growing up in Manassas. I remembered all the things my mother had made me, too, like the pie-dough roll-ups she always fixed whenever she baked a pie and the skirts and blouses she sewed for me. My father wasn't any nicer than my mother, I realized — they were simply different people.

It was her turn to ask a question. "Think you can stand having me work in your school the rest of the year?"

So that had been a sore spot with her, too. I had to be honest. "Well . . . it sort of cramps my style."

"It cramps my style to have a daughter who won't sit with me on the bus or go through my serving line. Actually, it hurts," she said, equally sincere.

Tears welled up in my eyes again. "Mom — "

"It's okay," she said. "I didn't want to be seen with my mother either when I was your age. You could buy lunch once in a while, though, for old time's sake."

"I'm sorry I'm such a brat," I said, hoping she got my real message.

"So am I." She hugged me. "I'm afraid it's too late to send you back."

I snuggled in her arms for a moment.

"Sit still," she ordered. "I've got a couple of things for you." She came back a few moments later, with a yellowed paper and what looked like a packet of seeds. She gave me the paper first. "I found this the other day when I was rooting through the cedar chest."

The paper was fragile and worn along the creases, a certificate with some Latin jibberish lettered across the top. An anchor was stenciled over the words in the center and linked chains formed a nautical border.

" 'Domain of Neptunus Rex,' " I read

haltingly. "What's that mean?" My parents were forever bragging about taking Latin in school.

"The domain of King Neptune," she translated.

"The Neptune paper!" I yelled. "You found it!" The paper was strange, declaring to all "Mermaids, Whales, Sea Serpents, Porpoises, Sharks, Dolphins, Eels, Skates, Crabs, Lobsters and other Living Things of the Sea that on this day in Latitude 0000 and Longitude 175 degrees West there appeared within Our Royal Domain the U.S.S. *Griffin* bound South for the Equator."

I read the rest of the paper out loud. " 'That the said Vessel and Officers and Crew thereof have been inspected and passed by Us and Our Royal Staff and that Samuel Howard Roberts' — that's Dad! — 'having been found worthy to be numbered as one of Us has been initiated into the Solemn Mysteries of the Ancient Order of the Deep.' " Two signatures were scrawled in the lower left corner, Neptunus Rex, Ruler of the Raging Main, and Davy Jones, His Majesty's Scribe.

My father's Neptune paper. I gulped down a big lump of disappointment. It didn't explain anything about what it was *like* to cross the equator. None of the

"Solemn Mysteries of the Deep" were spelled out. I placed the paper on my bedside table. It was mine to keep, but I was still on my own, without any map or magic document to guide me.

"What's the other thing?" I asked my mother, feeling gloomy again.

She laid a packet of marigold seeds in my lap. The color photograph on the front was faded, the once-bright marigolds a pale, ghostly yellow. Tiny seeds rattled inside; the packet had never been unsealed.

"I'm going to tell you a story," she announced. "One you've never heard."

I settled back against my panda, holding the seed package loosely between two fingers.

"Not too long ago, or so it seems to me, somebody knocked on the door. It took me a while to answer it, because I was expecting you and I couldn't move too fast." So this happened before I was born. My mother went on, "A woman stood on the porch. She had blonde hair and spoke with an accent."

"Who was she?" I asked, mystified.

"A real estate agent, trying to drum up business, I guess. She handed me her business card and this packet of seeds and told me if we ever decided to sell our house, to call her. I was a little annoyed at having to get up for a salesperson, but then I looked at the card and a problem I'd been wrestling with was suddenly solved."

"What problem?"

"Your name." She laughed at the look on my face. "You see, I was positive the baby was going to be a girl so I was only considering girls' names. I had just about decided to call you Pamela before the real estate woman came to the door."

"Pamela! Ugh!" Pamela sounded like a snobby kid who wore lace dresses and ribbons in her hair. It wouldn't have suited me at all. I wasn't a bit like a Pamela.

"Well, it wasn't so bad then," my mother said. "And your father liked it. But when I saw the name on the card, I knew Pamela was all wrong. The woman's name was Kobie something. She was from Germany. I asked about her name and she said it wasn't a nickname. I liked the way the name looked on the card. So when you were born a month later, we named you Kobie. I knew that was a name people would remember."

"I'm glad she didn't hand you the seeds first or I would have been named Marigold," I said wryly. "What happened to the business card?"

"Oh, it got lost in the shuffle of having a baby. But I kept the seeds for you to have one day, a memento of how you got your name."

The story of how I got my name pleased me. I jiggled the seeds in the paper packet. Kobie Roberts. That was my name. A name people would remember. Not Best Artist or Girl Sleuth or Heroine of Centreville. Kobie Roberts was the name I carved in the soft wood of my desk in room 10. It was a name I would take with me as I charted my uncertain course through life. Going on twelve, going on thirteen, going on fourteen . . . no matter how old I was or who my friends were, I would always be Kobie Roberts.

And for now, that was enough.

About the Author

CANDICE F. RANSOM is the author of *Thirteen, Fourteen and Holding,* and *Fifteen at Last,* all involving the further adventures of Kobie Roberts and her best friend Gretchen. She has written thirteen books for Scholastic. Her fourteenth book, *My Sister, the Meanie,* will be published as a Scholastic Hardcover. Ms. Ransom lives in Centreville, Virginia, with her husband and her black cat.

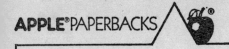

THE HISTORY
OF THE
HAYMARKET AFFAIR

THE HISTORY
OF THE
HAYMARKET
AFFAIR

A Study in the American Social-Revolutionary
and Labor Movements

By

HENRY DAVID Ph. D.

New York
RUSSELL & RUSSELL

TO
EVELYN

ACKNOWLEDGMENT

THIS study was begun at Columbia University in Professor Allan Nevins' seminar. To Professor Nevins, whose advice and keen critical sense were invaluable, I am profoundly indebted. Professors David S. Muzzey, John A. Krout, Evarts B. Greene, Samuel McCune Lindsay and Dr. Joseph Dorfman, all of Columbia University, read the galley proofs, and made suggestions for which I am grateful. Professors Nelson P. Mead and Holland Thompson of the Department of History of the College of the City of New York read a major portion of the volume in manuscript. Their kindly criticism was very helpful. I am indebted to my colleagues, Professors Oscar I. Janowsky, who read four chapters in manuscript, Michael Kraus, who read the galley proofs, and, especially, Joseph E. Wisan, who read the entire manuscript with painstaking care. Charles Hunt Page of the College of the City of New York and Dr. Harry Elmer Barnes likewise read the complete manuscript. Three former students, Daniel Thorner, Louis Eisenberg and Jesse Rubenstein have also aided me.

Donald L. Newborg and Morris A. Herson assisted extensively in the preparation of the legal sections. Agnes Inglis, in charge of the Labadie Collection of the University of Michigan Library, graciously supplied a wealth of material from the Collection. Lucy Parsons and George A. Schilling were kind enough to spend time with me discussing the Affair and to place much information at my disposal. Clarence Darrow was also good enough to grant me an interview.

I am grateful to my father for his continuous interest in this work, and I frequently called with profit upon his knowledge of the American and European revolutionary movements. At every stage in the preparation and writing of this study, the aid and critical judgment of my wife, Evelyn, were indispensable. My indebtedness to her is great indeed.

HENRY DAVID.

New York City
May, 1936.

From one point of view, the question of the identity of the person who threw the bomb on the night of May 4, 1886, may be said to have only trivial significance. No other aspect of the Haymarket Affair, however, has captured more interest or stimulated more strenuous exercise of the imagination. The identity of the bomb-thrower is still standard grist for the mills of newspaper feature story writers, and the seventy-first anniversary of the Haymarket bomb produced another alleged solution of the mystery. A story in the Chicago *Sun-Times* of May 5, 1957, reported an interview with Dr. Frank G. Heiner, a Chicago osteopath, shortly before his death in which he revealed that Emma Goldman had, in 1934, disabused him of the notion that the bombing was the act of an *agent provocateur*.

Dr. Heiner's recollection of his conversation with Emma Goldman was to the effect that she knew that the bomb-thrower was an anarchist; that he was not one of the defendants tried for the offense; that the defendants had not been parties to the deed; and that the defendants decided not to reveal the identity of the bomb-thrower because they were convinced that, if he was brought to trial, his conduct in court would be such as to injure irreparably the cause of anarchism. This kind of story "identifying" the bomb-thrower had long been current in social-revolutionary circles, and it would be fruitless to inquire whether Emma Goldman simply accepted it at face value or did in fact possess independent evidence which confirmed it.

Immediately after *The History of the Haymarket Affair* appeared in 1936, I received a number of letters from individuals claiming some firsthand knowledge of the episode. One or two communications pointed out minor errors. Thus, in a letter of February 23, 1937, Charles Edward Russell wrote that he had found "but one error and that slight enough though possibly you may wish to correct it in another edition. Engel it was that cried 'Hoch die Anarchie!' Not Fischer. I took down all their last words (during the execution) on the cover of a cigar box that I had smuggled in my overcoat pocket." Mr. Russell had also recorded a slightly different version of Albert Parsons' last words before the trap was sprung on November 11, 1887. According to Mr. Russell, Parsons said "in a tone of great surprise and disappointment, 'Are we not to be allowed to speak, Mr. Sheriff' and then in a loud, piercing tone 'LET THE VOICE OF THE PEOPLE BE HEARD!'" (Compare with the last words of the condemned quoted on p. 463.)

Other correspondents hopefully offered fresh evidence or leads to information which might enable one to name the bomb-thrower. Still others dug deeply into their memories to bring to the surface long-forgotten experiences linked directly or indirectly to the Haymarket Affair. One Chicagoan, John F. Kendrick, who was a boy of twelve in 1886, and who subsequently came to know George Schilling, Mrs. Albert Parsons, and others connected in some fashion with the Haymarket Affair, recalled, in a letter dated July 12, 1937, that he discovered in 1914 or 1915 that Oscar Neebe was a North Side neighbor. "I procured an introduction," he wrote, "and many evenings I sat and talked with Neebe, who was living with his second wife, was aged about 64 and going blind. I found it hard to believe that he was a native, he talked such broken Germanish English."

Mr. Kendrick did not keep a record of his conversations with Neebe, but he still remembered vividly—largely because he had had occasion to repeat them so frequently—many of Neebe's remarks. Neebe, he wrote, said:

"That Capt. Mike Schaack's book, after making allowance for the romantic bunk, came nearest of all to telling the truth; for Neebe was indignant at the 'defense' literature that made the victims bleating lambs. They were emphatically brave soldiers, and Engel was an out-and-out militarist. He firmly believed—

"That Schnaubelt threw the bomb as a police stool pigeon, and said the police believe that Schnaubelt threw it as an anarchist. He was firm in this belief....

"That while in the 'pen.' and later he found satisfactory evidence that the reason he, a ridiculously innocent business man, was railroaded, was because the Seipp Brewing Co. (well-known purveyor) was out to 'get' him for organizing its brewery wagon drivers, and that they spent judiciously $90,000 to do it. (Grinnell's ghost might testify at this point) He said—

"That one day he was in the office of the Arbeiter Zeitung and quite by accident learned that certain boxes, falsely marked, contained dynamite. Spies knew of it and was present. Parsons came in and Spies nudged Neebe to keep mum about the dynamite, later saying that Parsons would be very indignant and would have no hand in such doings. This I remember very distinctly; and when I asked Neebe as to what became of the explosive, he said it was for 'the southwest side Bohemians'. He said that when he was in jail the police knew all about the dynamite and grilled everybody repeatedly—that they were desperate to connect up Johan (sic) Most as the shipper. . . . When I asked Neebe if Most shipped it, I recall his headshake and slight smile—he would not tell me. I gathered that Most did. . . .

"That in the 'pen.' he learned that on the morning of Lingg's explosion (i.e., suicide) he was attended by a strange death-watch, and that this stranger had never been seen at the jail before or since. When Neebe was released (i.e., pardoned in 1893) he sought in vain for that man. Sheriff Matson and Jailer Folz (sic) were dead, but many of the old-timers were still at the jail and some of them (alas, for data on this point!), deeply sympathetic with Neebe, told him plenty and convinced him that Lingg was murdered to forestall gubernatorial action, since (Governor) Oglesby was (he said) weeping and protesting against 'one old man' having to make such decisions. . . . Neebe was very sure about all this, for the regular guards were as curious as he was to this man."

For the most interesting new documentary evidence to come to my attention subsequent to the publication of The History of the Haymarket Affair, I am indebted to Charlotte Teller, known also as Mrs. Charlotte Hirsch and John Brangwyn, her pseudonym. On the suggestion of Charles Edward Russell, as Miss Teller informed me in a letter dated December 14, 1936, she planned to use the Haymarket episode "as the background for a novel." It was probably in 1904 that she "went over the actual ground in Chicago" with Russell as her guide. According to Russell, he "took her over all the scenes in the drama from the Black Road to the County Jail" and told her what he knew about the affair. Shortly after Miss Teller's novel, The Cage, appeared in 1907, she received from John C. Richberg, the father of Donald R. Richberg, unpublished materials which, as she remarked, "would have been invaluable" to her earlier. Miss Teller, who made use of various facets of the Haymarket episode in the second half of her novel, strongly implied that the bombing was the act of a paid agent of business interests adamantly opposed to unionism.

The Richberg documents made available by Miss Teller consist of two memoranda and three affidavits. One memorandum was presumably prepared by Richberg at the very close of 1908 or early in 1909. It supports the judgment that the special bailiff, Henry L. Ryce, appointed by Judge Gary to facilitate the task of securing a jury, was strongly prejudiced against the eight defendants tried for murder. It also raises a question about the competence of the chief counsel for the defense, William Perkins Black. This memorandum reads as follows:

"On the 23rd day of December, 1908, I met Mr. Otis S. Favor, General Agent for more than thirty years of Enoch Morgan & Sons Sapolio. I have known Mr. Favor quite well for a quarter of a century and for a number of years he belonged to one of the clubs to which I belonged, during which time I knew him quite intimately. He is and has always been known in this community very favorably. In fact, one of the best known merchants. A man of his statements can be unquestionably relied upon.

"Knowing that after the trial and conviction of the 'anarchists' in 1886 Mr. Favor had made an affidavit which was used by the attorneys for the convicted in their efforts to obtain a new trial and that that affidavit cast a serious reflection upon the methods pursued by the then State's Attorney, I reffered (sic) to the same in my conversation at noon on this day and then Mr. Favor said to me, in substance:

"When the case was called for trial a special bailiff, by the name of Ryce, (whom Favor knew) was appointed to summons a jury, by agreement of the attorneys representing the defendant (sic) and the State's Attorney, to try the case. That he knew Harry (Henry) Ryce very well, having at various times befriended him, and, meeting him shortly after his appointment, told him that he could have the privilege of the use of a desk at his, Mr. Favor's, place of business, #6 Michigan Avenue, as he was summonsing men for jury service in that district (wholesale district).

"That he took advantage of this offer and took a desk there and made it his headquarters. It took some weeks before a jury was impanelled and Mr. Favor saw a great deal of this special bailiff and his methods. That while he, Favor, was not an anarchist or a socialist, yet he believed that the men should have a fair trial and, if they were not guilty of having thrown the bomb, they should be acquitted, although Mr. Favor had expressed no opinion to anyone in reference to his views. The general sentiment being that they ought to be convicted and, Favor says, that that was quite universal, especially among the people in that district. That one day this special bailiff said to him that he had gotten ten or twelve men that would be sure to hang those fellows. That he had in his employ a man by the name of Stevans, whom he afterwards learned was a socialist and who had been watching this special bailiff's actions and had been taking particular notice of the remarks he had made at various times, showing that he was only summonsing such men as would be sure to convict and that he made inquiries before he summoned a man for this jury as to what his general feelings and sentiments were, and if he found that he was in favor of conviction he would summons him. If he found the contrary to be the case, or that he was lukewarm, or was opposed to conviction, he would of course not summons him. Favor afterwards learned that during this time Mr. Stevans was in continuous communication with one of the attorneys for the defendants, reported to him and kept him posed as to the bailiff's actions and conduct. This attorney, William P. Black, never made this information public or brought it to the notice of the court until after the men had been tried and convicted. (This sort of conduct is inexcusable, but perhaps is in line with some of the ideosyncracies displayed by this attorney during the progress and trial of this case, of which the writer hereof has knowledge.) It was then, after the conviction and when the case was pending on a motion for a new trial, that Black came to Favor and asked him to make an affidavit in reference to the statement herein referred to, made by the special bailiff. Mr. Favor told Mr. Black that the statement was correct but he preferred to be placed on the witness stand instead of making a voluntary affidavit, and to make such a motion in court before Judge Gary, who tried the defendants, and he would come and submit to an examination and state the facts. That such a motion was made and denied by the Judge (Gary). (This was in line with his other infamous rulings in the case.) That, thereupon, Mr. Favor did make an affidavit of the facts as hereinbefore stated by him; that the same was read on a motion before Judge Gary for a new trial and that he overruled the motion and pronounced sentence. In overruling the motion he said that, assuming the affidavit to be true, it cut no figure in the case as the jurors who had tried the case had been subject to an examination by both sides, had been found qualified and accepted. (Of course a scoundrel who would tell a bailiff beforehand that he was in favor of hanging a man would lie in order to qualify to serve as a juror.)

"Mr. Favor told me that before the motion for a new trial came up that the State's Attorney, Julius S. Grinnell (*sic*) led him through a series of rooms and finally got him in a sort of dark chamber and as he got there turned the key in the lock and Favor found himself confronted with three policemen. That Grinell (*sic*), whom he had known for years and who knew him well in a neighborly way, then said to him: 'What's this about this affidavit?' Upon which Mr. Favor said: 'I will say nothing to you until you unlock that door and call in the special bailiff, to whom I referred in that affidavit. You can't bulldoze me, intimidate me nor scare me.' That Mr. Grennell (*sic*) hesitated; finally opened the door and sent for the special bailiff. That when the special bailiff arrived Favor said to him that he had made an affidavit stating those facts of what the special bailiff had said to him and asked him to verify it and if that was not true that he had so told him. The special bailiff admitted the truth of the affidavit and, thereupon, the conference ended and Mr. Favor departed. Mr. Favor expressed his utmost contempt of Judge Gary and the State's Attorney, Julius S. Grinell (*sic*). Neither of these worthies exist anymore."

The second memorandum prepared by John C. Richberg and given to Charlotte Teller details the manner in which the former stumbled upon evidence pointing to the innocence of those who stood trial for the Haymarket bombing. This evidence, moreover, indicated that the crime might have been perpetrated by one of two brothers known as Carl and Otto Blank. This memorandum, apparently written in 1893, when Governor Altgeld was considering the pardon of Fielden, Schwab and Neebe, also merits quotation in full.

"In the month of October 1886," wrote Mr. Richberg, "while I was professionally engaged in investigating a matter for a Client, incidentally facts were developed which to my mind threw considerable light upon the question of the bomb throwing at the Haymarket on the evening of May 4th 1886. I became deeply interested, and pursued my investigations in that regard until December 11th 1886, when I put the facts in writing as related to me by the parties who gave them to me; had them signed and sworn to. The testimony of these parties could not then be used, nor has there been an opportunity since, as that could only be done in the event of a new trial being granted to the seven (*sic*) condemned men as they had been sentenced, and the case was then taken to the Supreme Court of the State, where no new or extraneous evidence could be submitted.

"The United States Supreme Court having declined to allow a writ of error for the reason that no question involving a conflict with the U.S. Constitution was involved, of course could not pass upon the merits of the case. Hence this is the first time an opporunity has occurred to present the evidence before a power competent to receive and act upon it. Evidence discovered since the trial and sentence. If the same could have been presented at the trial, the verdict of the Jury might have been different, or the judgment either of the lower or Supreme Court would not have been as it now stands. The evidence hereto annexed (in the form of three affidavits), shows that the witness Thompson who gave testimony implicating Spies and Schwab; that they were together that night, plotting and conspiring, that he was mistaken; that the two persons he saw were Carl Blank and Otto Blank, both of whom bore a striking resemblance to Spies and Schwab respectively, and as Thompson had only seen them once, would readily mistake one for the other in the glimmer of a street lamp.

"My investigations were brought about mainly, by the fact that the Consul of the German Empire at Chicago, upon instructions from his Government, was investigating the career in America, of one Otto or Carl Blank who had been arrested at Dresden, Saxony, for an attack upon a police officer, and among whose effects were found Anarchistic Literature, Most's paper the "Freiheit" and papers showing he had been at Pullman, Illinois; that he had served five years in the Austrian Penitentiary for burglary under the name of Anderle. Blank's photograph was taken at Dresden, forwarded to the Consul here and identified by several residents of Pullman, as being the picture of a man known there as Carl Blank, who with his brother Otto, had lived there and left in June 1886. The evidence shows both these men were scoundrels of the worst type and professional thieves; they were in Chicago on May 4th 1886, and at the Haymarket meeting; that they returned to Pullman at 12 M. on the night of May 4th; that Carl between that hour and 9 A.M. of the 5th, shaved off his beard, the affidavits tend to show that either one or the other of them threw the bomb; that both had an ungovernable and violent personal hatred toward the police; that both fled about the time of the trial of the seven condemned men June 26th 1886; that one or the other threw the bomb of his own volition; that neither of them have ever in any way been connected with the seven (sic) condemned men."

Richberg's memorandum contains the gist of the information set forth in the three affidavits appended to it. These affidavits, signed by Emanuel E. Ertsman, Frank Smolar, and Oswald Carl, all residents of Pullman, Illinois, are not needed to impugn the testimony offered by M. M. Thompson, a "star" witness for the prosecution, which pointed to Schnaubelt as the bomb-thrower and implicated Spies and Schwab in the deed. While the affidavits encourage the belief that Carl and Otto Blank were thieves, that Otto resembled August Spies in appearance, and that Carl asserted that he stood close to the bomb-thrower on the night of May 4, they provide no basis for the conclusion that either one of the pair actually threw the bomb. They provide only hearsay evidence on this last point. The photographs of the Blank brother—now in my possession—which seemed to carry some weight with Richberg, add nothing to the credibility of the statements sworn to in the affidavits.

It would be gratifying to be able to solve the mystery of the bomb-thrower at this late date, but none of the evidence which I have encountered since 1936 has been compelling enough to warrant abandoning the judgments I reached in Chapter XXIII, "Who Threw the Bomb?" For me, at least, the precise identity of the bomb-thrower still remains unknown.

New York
November, 1957

HENRY DAVID

CONTENTS

CONTENTS

INTRODUCTION

O N the night of May 4, 1886, a dynamite bomb was thrown in the city of Chicago.

That bomb, designated as the "Haymarket Bomb"—though it was not hurled in Chicago's old Haymarket Square—and the events which followed have their place in American history as the "Haymarket Affair." The episode is of major significance in the annals of American labor and jurisprudence, while the background which made it possible and gives it meaning constitutes an important chapter of the social-revolutionary movement in the United States.

There has grown up about the Haymarket Affair a mass of judgments, half-truths and myths which have long passed as history. If the event has given rise to a strange medley of emotions, opinions, and ideas, it is because it was of such a character that it instantly aroused the sharpest individual and group prejudices, and lent itself with facility to the most varied interpretations.

For some rigid economic determinists it easily takes shape as a striking manifestation of the class-struggle between capitalists and proletariat. In this light the bomb becomes the instrument with which labor forcefully resisted the police who supported its oppressors. The machinery of law and government, coming to the assistance of capital interests, made the working-class pay dearly for its act by punishing its true leaders. To those whose approach is fixed by the belief in the sanctity of private property and existing authority and institutions, the Haymarket Affair stands as a conflict between the forces of "law and order" of a free republic and a handful of revolutionists. The latter suffered defeat, and a few of them met a well-merited end on the gallows after exploiting every legal means of escaping that fate.

Some take the Haymarket Affair as an instance of the use of provocative tactics by the police and employing classes to injure the cause of American labor and destroy a revolutionary movement. Others see in it the utilization of the law to "railroad" innocent men to their death for having spoken out boldly against the evils of capitalism. For still others it stands as an example of those historic episodes into which there enters the elusive factor of chance and which appear largely "accidental" in their nature.

It is the purpose of this study to present a full account of how the bomb came to be thrown in the city of Chicago on the night of May 4, 1886, and of its consequences; but that forms only the core of the present work. To this core are related those constituents of the American and European scenes which are directly and indirectly linked with it. This embraces an examination of certain phases of American industrial and labor history and a treatment of the origin, growth, form, and nature of the social-revolutionary movement in the country at large and especially in Chicago.

THE HISTORY
OF THE
HAYMARKET AFFAIR

I. THE LABOR SCENE

IN American labor history the tumultuous years of the middle 'eighties have long been marked as exceptional. The occurrences that packed the years 1884-1886 constitute what Selig Perlman calls the "great upheaval." [1] They are more deserving of this title than even the convulsive events of 1877 and the bitter struggles of 1893-1894. Norman J. Ware speaks of 1886 as a "revolutionary year," [2] and it is significant that in 1887 George E. McNeill [3] wrote with insight that the previous twelvemonth

"will be known as the year of the great uprising of labor. The future historian will say: Trades-unions increased their membership and their powers as never before. The Knights of Labor, who had for seventeen years struggled against all adverse influences, added to their membership by tens of thousands weekly. Trades and occupations that had never before been organized joined the . . . assemblies of the order. . . . Laboring men who had heretofore considered themselves as scarcely more than serfs, without rights or privileges, fearing to organize, or failing to do so because of the hopelessness of their condition, seemed imbued with a new spirit. . . . Strikes prevailed everywhere. Thousands of grievances were settled by peaceful arbitration. Every branch of labor was affected. . . . The skilled and the unskilled, the high-paid and the low-paid, all joined hands. . . . The press was filled with labor news." [4]

It is not strange that the decade of the 'eighties should have witnessed a pulsating labor movement accompanied by struggles of a vigor and scope which had hitherto been absent from nineteenth century America. They were the fruit of the sweeping industrialization of the country which characterized the Civil War years and the period following. Though the basis for the Industrial Revolution in America had been laid much earlier, it was not until after 1865 that the implications of the change in industrial technique became fully apparent. Concurrently, new areas in the trans-Mississippi West were being opened to agriculture, while the development of transcontinental railroads and the consolidation of trunk lines served to create a domestic market of national scope.

The half century following the Civil War witnessed the refashioning not only of American industry, but of the whole structure of American society. Manufacturing broke away from its dependence upon commerce. Changes in technology were paralleled by changes in the organization of industry and business enterprise in general. Through the corporate form huge "combinations" came to dominate industrial activity. Immense fortunes, far greater than those of earlier days, were founded. Urban centers were multiplying in number and mounting in population. In them a true industrial proletariat was growing rapidly. The stream of cheap European labor entering the country was becoming wider and creating new problems.

The 'eighties themselves were unmistakably marked by a definite quickening in the extension of the factory and machine technique. Not only was there an increase in the number of machines, but they also invaded fields in which they had been relatively absent. Factories and shops in general grew vastly in number, and the amount of capital invested in foundries and machine-shops alone increased two and one-half times in the decade. This, together with the notable increase in the number of patents issued during the 'eighties, offers further evidence of the tendency toward the completer mechanization of production.

This process characterized the whole field of American

industry. It was constantly asserted during this period that rapid mechanization was responsible for an over-production of goods which in turn caused industrial depressions. Carroll D. Wright, the first Commissioner of Labor, stated in his annual report of 1886, that manufacturers estimated that in the production of agricultural implements, machines had displaced fully one-half of the "muscular" labor necessary fifteen or twenty years earlier. In the shoe-making and textile industries, there was an equal reduction in the manual labor formerly employed. In the manufacture of small arms, one man with the use of power machinery and with a division of labor "turns out and fits the equivalent of 42 to 50 stocks in ten hours as against 1 stock in the same length of time by manual labor, a displacement of 44 to 49 men in this one operation."

By the 'eighties, striking evidence of the accelerated tempo of industrial life was available. Between 1874 and 1882, the production of Bessemer steel ingots jumped from 191,933 tons to 1,696,450. In Pennsylvania alone, in the ten-year period 1875-1885, it mounted from 148,374 to 1,109,034 tons. In 1884, there were 125,739 miles of railroad in operation, almost a four-fold increase since 1865. The total production of iron and steel rails in 1880, 1,461,847 tons, was more than double that of 1874. In 1860, 14,000,000 tons of coal were mined. In 1884 almost 100,000,000 tons of bituminous and anthracite coal were being extracted from the earth. Regardless of the field, evidences of the phenomenal growth of American industry abound. In Massachusetts, for example, 2,633,075 cases of boots and shoes were manufactured in 1885, compared with the 718,660 cases annually produced two decades earlier. The total value of manufactures estimated at $1,019,000,000 for 1849, came to $3,386,000,000 in 1869 and to $9,372,000,000 twenty years later.

The economic expansion of the two decades after the Civil War was reflected in the growth of international commerce. Exports and imports of the United States, totalling $687,-192,176 in 1860, rose to $828,730,176 in 1870, and to more than one and a half billion dollars in 1880. Between 1876 and 1885, the country enjoyed an unbroken annual excess of exports over imports. In the twenty year period 1860-1880, the total value of American imports and exports increased at a more rapid rate than that of the British Isles or France.[5]

In 1884, the *Commercial and Financial Chronicle* pointed out that "this country has already a commerce with the countries south of us on the American continent by no means inconsiderable, and not contemptible in comparison with that of England and France. It is quite equal to that of our rivals in point of variety, and, excepting a few great classes of articles like textiles, iron manufactures, boots, hats and clothing, it is also equal in amount." It urged that these markets be further developed for the consumption of American manufactures, and recommended that "Americans . . . establish foreign houses, and place them in charge of active, intelligent and pushing agents." American manufacturing had reached a point where it was imperative to seek foreign markets "not merely with the purpose of disposing of an occasional surplus of goods which temporary over-production or under-consumption leave undisposed of, but for the permanent supply of great populations which are to be clothed and fed and transported from place to place." [6] These observations clearly indicate that American industry had already outgrown its swaddling clothes.

The changes in industrial technique led to the increase of factory laborers, who in contrast to the handicraft worker, may be regarded as semi-skilled or unskilled. Differentiation between employer and employee became more striking, and the dominant conception of the worker as an impersonal commodity became more sharply confirmed. In M. A. Foran's *The Other Side, A Social Study Based on Fact,* published in 1886, a noteworthy though poorly conceived labor novel which is strongly pro-working class, but not opposed to capitalism as such, social cleavage between employers and employees is a constant theme. Antagonistic to radical doctrines, the novel nevertheless presents the average employer of the period just as unfavorably as did the revolutionary of the day, describing him as a domineering "master." [7]

The gulf which separated workingman and employer, either individual or corporate, was produced by the economic changes which the country had experienced. In some occupations it was a comparatively recent development. A brass-worker discussing this question in 1883, remarked: "Well, I remember that fourteen years ago the workmen and foremen and the boss were all as one happy family; it was just as easy and as free to speak to the boss as anyone else, but now the boss is superior, and the men all go to the foremen; but we would not think of looking the foreman in the face now any more than we would the boss. . . . The average hand growing up in the shop now would not think of speaking to the boss, would not presume to recognize him, nor the boss would not recognize him either." [8] Employers "adopt a superior standpoint," complained another workingman. "The employer has pretty much the same feeling towards the men that he had toward his machinery. He wants to get as much as he can out of his men at the cheapest rate. . . . That is all he cares for the man generally." [9]

One manufacturer bluntly declared, according to Samuel Gompers, "I regard my employés as I do a machine, to be used to my advantage, and when they are old and of no further use I cast them in the street." [10] The indifference to human values here displayed was neither an invention of Gompers nor wholly exceptional. A New England wool-manufacturer, complacently observed that when workers "get starved down to it, then they will go to work at just what you can afford to pay." [11] Such views accompanied the conviction that it is, as Jay Gould said, an "axiom . . . that labor is a commodity that will in the long run be governed absolutely by the law of supply and demand," [12]—an argument which justified adequately the manner in which workers were commonly treated. Labor was a commodity—though sometimes a peculiar and troublesome one —and there was no reason why it should be dealt with differently from other commodities. ". . . I never do my talking to the hands," said a New England mill owner, "I do all my talking with the overseers." [13]

As long as these attitudes were taken by a considerable body of employers, it is no wonder that the feeling between them and the workers was generally one of steadily increasing "distrust and dissatisfaction," as Joseph Medill, publisher of the Chicago *Tribune,* put it.[14] P. J. McGuire, a labor leader, was no less aware of the absence of amicable relations between workers and employers. Their respective activities and wealth— or lack of it—drove a powerful wedge between them. They had no social contacts. "They do not know each other on the street." [15] The more poorly paid workers, observed W. H. Foster, general secretary of the Federation of Organized Trades and Labor Unions, in 1883, exhibited an attitude of "sullen discontent" toward those who employed them. "They do not seem to have the courage to express openly what they think all the time, unless they are under the influence of liquor." [16]

In pre-Civil War days industry was smaller in scope; less of it was corporately organized; the independent artisan was still an important industrial factor; and escape from working-class ranks was less difficult. The relationship of employer and employee of that period had almost vanished by the 'eighties. As one writer sympathetic to labor observed of the 'eighties and 'nineties, "the old liberality of American employers is on the wane. Competition compels them to be close-fisted and to inaugurate a policy of aggressive resistance against the demands of organized labor." [17] As labor, becoming increasingly conscious of its condition, boldly voiced its complaints and demands, and resorted more widely to industrial action to gain its objectives, capital developed not only the normal defense mechanisms but a definite militancy. In an age dedicated to the business exploitation of the vast resources of America it would have been strange had there not been an aggressive capitalist class. The spirit of the Gilded Age can be understood when it is remembered that the business men of the period were pioneers—pioneers in industry, pioneers in the pursuit of wealth.[18]

The idealization of property so characteristic of the period was a natural result of the intensive pursuit of material possessions. Walt Whitman declared that "Democracy looks with suspicious, ill-satisfied eyes upon the very poor and on those out of business; she asks for men and women with occupations, well off, owners of houses and acres, and with cash in the bank."[19] John Hay's *The Bread-Winners,* with its hostile treatment of discontented labor, its "odor of property-morality," was a natural and early literary manifestation of this attitude.[20] Josiah Strong remarked that the "Christian man who is not willing to make the largest profits which an honest regard for the laws of trade permits is a rare man."[21] To the charge that the Vanderbilts' wealth was a monstrous injustice in a democratic republic, one writer replied that "Mr. Vanderbilt is receiving a proportionally small, and a well earned part of the profits of the greatest economical device of modern times." He was merely being rewarded for his father's great services to mankind and more particularly to American society.[22]

That tremendous appetite for wealth, which showed its worst side in the operations of Jay Gould, was amusingly satirized in the following bit of doggerel:

> "JAY GOULD'S MODEST WANTS
>
> My wants are few; I scorn to be
>   A querulous refiner;
> I only want America
>   And a mortgage deed of China;
> And if kind fate threw Europe in,
>   And Africa and Asia,
> And a few islands of the sea,
>   I'd ask no other treasure.
> Give me but these—they are enough
>   To suit my notion—
> And I'll give up to other men
>   All land beneath the ocean."[23]

The arrogance of wealth is illustrated by the words attributed to an American millionaire of the 'eighties who said of his class: "We are not politicians or public thinkers; we are the rich; we own America; we got it, God knows how, but we intend to keep it if we can. . . ." [24] The cry that American labor shared inadequately in the industrial wealth of the nation and that a large portion of the laboring class was impoverished was either never heard or flatly denied by capital. Andrew Carnegie, addressing the Nineteenth Century Club at the close of 1887, exclaimed, "I defy any man to show that there is pauperism" in the United States.[25] William Graham Sumner, closing his eyes to incontrovertible evidence, declared that pauperism did not characterize the American wage-earning class. "It is constantly alleged in vague and declamatory terms," he wrote, "that artisans and unskilled laborers are in distress and misery, or are under oppression. No facts to bear out these assertions are offered." [26]

If they admitted the existence of poverty among a considerable portion of the working-class, business men were ready to ascribe it to inadequate education,[27] drink, laziness, and improvidence. Occasionally, they placed part of the responsibility upon the activities of manipulators and gamblers who were not to be confused with sober, honest industrialists.[28] Joseph Medill declared that the primary "cause of the impecunious condition of millions of the wage classes of this country is due to their own improvidence and misdirected efforts. Too many are trying to live without labor . . . and too many squander their earnings on intoxicating drinks, cigars and amusements, who cannot afford it." [29] It was easy to place the responsibility for inadequate wages and penury upon unalterable economic laws which determined the share that labor received. Thus, the Commercial Club of Boston was informed that

"There is certainly a very general complaint just now that labor does not get its share, that capital gets more than its share, that things ought not to go on as they have gone. . . .

But complaints are not always well founded. Men as well as children often desire what they cannot and ought not to have. And complaining settles nothing. The existing mode of division is the work of certain natural laws. . . .

"It is perfectly right for the wage earner to get all he can. The employer will pay as little as he can. . . . It is the duty of the employer to sedulously regard the interests of those he employs, to deal fairly by them. Above all, every man imbued with the spirit of Christianity, the Christian in deed as well as in name, will strive to do as he would be done by.

"But after all, one inexorable law finally settles this as it does so many other economic questions, and that is the law of demand and supply." [30]

Not everyone, however, denied that the American worker had just ground for complaint, or ascribed such unfortunate conditions as existed to the operation of natural laws. In his first annual report in 1886, Commissioner Wright, discussing the effect of the industrial revolution upon the worker, declared that "if the question should be asked, has the wage-worker received his equitable share of the benefits derived from the introduction of machinery, the answer must be no. In the struggle for industrial supremacy in the great countries devoted to mechanical production, it probably has been impossible for him to share equitably in such benefits." [31] Some of the State bureaus of labor or labor statistics pointed to evidences of the maldistribution of wealth, and concluded that labor did not receive a fair share in the returns of industry. Such assertions were made by the bureau of New Jersey in 1881 and 1883, of Illinois in 1882, and of Michigan in 1884. [32] Some writers charged that State and Federal laws favored the few at the expense of the many. In an article in the *Contemporary Review*, Prof. Charles Kendall Adams reported that in 1886 a "very large proportion of our thoughtful writers were inclined to take it for granted that the wage-workers had a grievance that could, in some way, be corrected. The opinion was very general that . . . the masses of the people did not receive their fair share . . ." [33] When Francis A. Walker asserted that the "real labor problem of today" turned on the question of how the self-assertiveness of the working-class could be tempered, he made it clear that it was "rightful," and that it would make for an "equitable and beneficial distribution of wealth" which was then lacking.[34]

Labor's grievances sprang from the privileges and corruption of the American political system, the growth of a small, immensely wealthy class, the results of corporate industrial organization, and the economic and social condition of the wage-earners at large and certain groups of them in particular. Protests against monopolies and large corporations filled the air during the period. The latter were denounced as sources of "outrage" and "corruption" and destroyers of human rights. National and State governments, it was charged, had been captured by corporate interests, for whose benefit they legislated at the expense of the many. The courts were stigmatized as subservient tools of the vested interests. A contributor to the *Catholic Quarterly Review* summed up current attitudes in the assertion that "it is futile for the public press to be constantly preaching platitudes respecting patience and regard for the rights of the employers and respect for law, whilst evasions and defiant violations, constantly practised by mammoth capitalists and corporations, are ignored, condoned and tacitly approved." [35]

If one examines the economic and social condition of the American working-class during the 'eighties, one can understand why labor was restive and discontented.

Though statistical information on pauperism in the United States before 1890 is lacking, there is sufficient evidence to leave no doubt concerning its existence. It is safe to say that a considerable number of American wage-earners lived below the poverty level. Estimates for the early 'nineties indicate that ten per cent of the total population of urban districts was poverty-stricken.[36] This would probably be true, roughly speaking, for the preceding decade. Samuel Gompers offered, in

1883, some interesting conjectures on the extent of pauperism in the United States. Taking the census statistics of 1870 for the five greatest manufacturing States, New York, Massachusetts, Ohio, Pennsylvania and Illinois, he showed that the average annual wages for industrial workers came to about $405.64. With five individuals in the average family, the amount for the support of each one was $81.149. There were in those five States in 1870, Gompers pointed out, "62,494 paupers, maintained by the States at a cost of $6,161,354, or a fraction over $95 per individual. Thus it appears that the workingman was compelled to support himself above the degree of 'pauperism' on $14 less per annum than the State spent to support paupers as paupers. These figures are, of course, old, but they can be depended upon, except that the wage of the workingmen is less now than it was in 1870." [37] Gompers' argument is open to serious objections, but it is not incorrect in its insistence upon the existence of a pauper class. It was said more than once that "dire want" and "superfluity" [38] were characteristic of the American scene.

Implicit in the statistics of the distribution of national wealth and income is the fact that a considerable part of the American working-class lived neither far from nor securely above the poverty line. On the basis of the census of 1890, Charles B. Spahr concluded that 200,000 families had an annual income of $5,000 and over; 1,300,000 families an income of from $1,200 to $5,000; 11,000,000 families an income under $1,200. The average annual income from labor per family for the last group was $380. He computed that one per cent of the families received nearly a fourth of the national income, while fifty per cent of the families received barely a fifth. More than half of the aggregate income of the country was enjoyed by one-eighth of the families, and the richest one per cent received a larger total income than the poorest fifty per cent. The great majority of small property owners, both urban and rural, possessed barely one-eighth of the national wealth, and one per cent of the families had more wealth than the remaining ninety-nine per cent. Of the twelve million families in the country, about five and one-half million could be classed as propertyless.[39]

"I have a brother who has four children, besides his wife and himself," reported a workingman in 1883. "All he earns is $1.50 a day." This was the abbreviated life history of thousands. He continued: "He works in the ironworks at Fall River. He only works about nine months out of twelve. There is generally about three months of stoppage, taking the year right through, and his wife and his family all have to be supported for a year out of the wages of nine months—$1.50 a day for nine months out of the twelve, to support six of them. It does not stand to reason that those children and he himself can have natural food or be naturally dressed." [40] Speaking of the industrial population of Fall River, especially of the mill operatives, a physician of that city declared that as a class they were "dwarfed physically," and that their careworn attitude always impressed visitors. ". . . most of them," he asserted, "are obliged to live from hand to mouth, or, at least, they do not have sufficient food to nourish them as they need to be nourished." If they drank, it was to find escape from the realities of life and its oppressive ennui.[41] A Chicago printer, active in labor circles, made it clear in 1883 that the workingmen of his city bitterly resented their condition. "The very fact of their living in the squalor and wretchedness they do live in," he said, "has provoked discontent in their minds; and in all our labor agitations, wherever there is any particular excitement aroused, these men who feel that they are oppressed are ready for almost any remedy. Even if it reached a revolution, if you chose, they are ripe for it." The lower class workers found it impossible to save money. "They don't receive enough wages . . ." he explained. "Instead of laying up money or anything of that kind, they are not able to earn enough to support themselves and their families." [42]

This picture of the poorer working people of Chicago is perhaps overdrawn, but it is not entirely misleading. What was true of the pushing Lake City was roughly true of practically every urban center in the country. Careful investigation of the tenement areas of the city in 1883-1884, undertaken by the Citizens' Association of Chicago—interested not only in civic improvement,[43] but also in lower rents, which would mean reduced wages and a source of profitable real estate investment—disclosed the existence of frightful conditions. The report which followed the investigation speaks of "the wretched condition of the tenements into which thousands of workingmen are huddled, the wholesale violation of all rules for drainage, plumbing, light, ventilation and safety in case of fire or accident, the neglect of all laws of health, the horrible condition of sewers and outhouses, the filthy dingy rooms into which they are crowded, the unwholesome character of their food, and the equally filthy nature of the neighboring streets, alleys and back lots filled with decaying matter and stagnant pools." [44] For these "unwholesome dens" into which they were crowded, working-class families paid extravagant rents in proportion to the wages they received.[45] In many cases, they were "fleeced at a rate which returns 25 to 40 per cent per annum of the value of the property." [46] Those with small incomes had to live on the outskirts of the city—which was perhaps why Chicago spread like quicksilver—to secure decent housing, or else occupy "pigsties" in the city proper.[47] Chicago, it may be noted, with an average of over eight persons to a dwelling, and with about seventeen per cent of the dwellings containing three or more families, appears to have had housing facilities which were superior to other urban centers.[48]

There is little wonder that many of Chicago's inhabitants displayed "sullen discontent." Of a population of approximately 630,000 in 1884, a quarter of a million were classed as adult wage-earners, and the vast majority of these, caught between low wages and high rents for bad dwellings, had good ground for complaint. Dissatisfaction was keen among large groups of the foreign born. Slightly less than half of Chicago's inhabitants were of foreign origin, with the Germans far in the lead and

the Bohemians following with about 35,000 to 40,000. Many
of both nationalities had come to the United States hoping to
find both a haven and an earthly heaven. Among the Bohemians,
largely low-paid laborers who lived in a wretched quarter of
the city, dissatisfaction ran high.[49]

Jane Addams' *Twenty Years at Hull House*, though it
treats essentially of the years after 1889, is an indictment of
the social conditions under which tens of thousands of the
inhabitants of Chicago lived and labored during the entire
decade.[50] In it is the story of Chicago's squalid and crowded
tenements, of the lack of the necessary sanitation provisions,
adequate municipal legislation, charitable organizations, and
relief facilities, of the thousands sunk in dire poverty, of the
conditions that make for a diseased community, and of the
unawareness of all this. Nor was Chicago unique in this.
America of the 'eighties may not have been conscious of its
Chicagos—Jane Addams writes of the "unfounded optimism
that there was no real poverty among us" [51]—but they existed.

Standard of living and particular living conditions are,
of course, causally related to wages, both money and real.
Especially during the 'eighties, did the American worker insist
that he was being underpaid. He did not receive enough for
his labor as such, and he did not receive enough to lead a
decent existence. The industrial depression which was first felt
in 1882, made available a large labor surplus in certain occupations by 1883, led to keen competition for employment, and
tended to depress wages.[52] In the textile industry, for example,
this was the case. "I stand every morning in my factory," said
a New England manufacturer, "and am obliged to refuse the
applications of men who want to come to work for a dollar
a day . . . and women begging for the opportunity to work
for 50 cents a day. . . . It is evident . . . that there are a
large number of men who desire to be employed at the low
rates of wages now prevailing, and who cannot find employment." [53]

Despite the fact that the wage statistics gathered in the

period are not always reliable, it appears that hourly money wages, recovering in 1880 from the effects of the depression beginning in 1873, rose to 1883, dropped somewhat in the following year and, after slight upward and downward movements in 1886, started to climb again in 1887. A more optimistic, but probably less accurate version of wage movements for the years 1883-1886 gives the same index figure for hourly wages for four solid years. That is to say, money wages at best remained at a fixed point for 1883-1886.[54]

A glance at actual money wages has value. In a number of New England textile mills, the daily earnings for all types of employees, male and female, ranged from $.50 to $1.80. This was for a working day running somewhat above ten hours. Most of the skilled male hands earned slightly better than one dollar a day, while women, of course, received less. Average weekly wages of $7.50-8.00 were considered better than fair, and in general the average monthly income was not much above $20. Only in comparatively few cases did it reach twice that sum. The wages of carpenters in 1883 averaged $1.45 a day for the entire year, although their actual money wage for time worked came to about one dollar more than that. Compositors in Massachusetts in the same year earned, on the basis of piece-work, an average weekly wage of $7-9, which was probably what their income was elsewhere. The daily average wage of machine shop workers in 1883 was $2.00, although many earned as little as $1.25, and in some cases men were paid $4.00 a day. Certain classes of skilled shipyard mechanics received lower daily wages than the same class of labor in England. In Delaware they earned from $10-12 a week, while in New York their wages ran higher at $2.60-3.50 a day. P. J. McGuire, General Secretary of the Brotherhood of Carpenters and Joiners, claimed on the basis of government figures, that in 1883 the average earnings of workingmen throughout the United States came to slightly more than a dollar a day.[55]

Inadequate and incomplete statistical returns for the State

of Illinois in 1884, show that yearly earnings of heads of families ranged between $210 and $1,608. The average earnings were $525.27, and this sum was increased, on the average, by the income of other members of the family to $588. Yearly average living expenses were estimated at $507.56. Of the wage-earning heads of families investigated, twenty-four per cent failed to make a living, nine per cent barely made ends meet, and sixty-seven per cent enjoyed some surplus.[56] In Massachusetts, the average annual living costs of a workingman's family in 1883 were put at $754.42. The average income of wage-earning heads of families was $558.68. The difference between the two figures had to be supplied by the earnings of wives and children if the family was not to fall below the poverty line. This placed almost a third of the support of the average family upon others than its head.[57]

Broadly speaking, wages in Illinois were higher in 1882 than they were in 1886. Of 114 organized occupations for which there are adequate statistics, seventy-one show a decrease in average weekly wage between 1882 and 1886, twenty-three show an increase, and twenty remained the same. Excluding the occupations which experienced a drop in wages of five per cent or less, almost sixty per cent of the trades examined suffered wage decreases. The average weekly wages for all 114 occupations came to $15.34 in 1882 and to $14.51 in 1886. Since the workers were employed only seventy-five per cent of full time during the year, the average yearly wage came to $566.19. This was approximately $50 more than the annual average for the unorganized employees in the same occupations. The only trades which could boast of wage increases for the years 1882-1886 were those which were well organized; and trade unions reported greater success in maintaining or even increasing wages than assemblies of the Knights of Labor.[58]

Wage levels in these years in the State of Illinois appear representative of the country at large. An investigation of the earnings of almost 140,000 employees in 552 establishments scattered throughout twenty-eight States and covering some forty industries in 1886, shows that the average daily wage of male workers was almost two dollars. With an average of 282.6 working days a year, this gives an annual average income of $565.20. The income of women and children in industry was strikingly lower. The average daily wage of the first came to $1.11, and of the second to $.70. Though the figures cover a relatively small portion of the six million wage-earners in the country,[59] the industries and States considered are so representative that the conclusions may be safely accepted.[60]

For those employed with some regularity, the tendency of wages to remain fixed or move downward was more than equalized before 1886 by changes in commodity prices and the general cost of living. Commodity prices, recovering from the depression of 1873-78, had risen more rapidly than wages between 1879 and 1882. They began to fall precipitately after the last year, and did not move upward again until 1886. In purchasing power wages declined in 1880, only to be followed by a gradual upward movement in the next year which continued until 1885. The slight drop in real wages in 1886 became more pronounced in 1887, but in the following year there was again a recovery.[61]

Labor, however, did not gain as much as might be expected from the rise in real wages between 1881-1885, because of the irregularity of employment. While precise statistics for unemployment are lacking, there can be no doubt that a considerable portion of the wage-earning class were always unemployed for a part of the year, and that practically all workers experienced some irregularity of employment. These generalizations are supported by the findings in Massachusetts. In 1885, the industrial population of that State lost on the average 1.16 working months during the year. At the same time, almost thirty per cent of the industrial wage-earners were unemployed at their particular trades for 4.11 months during the year. The Massachusetts Commissioner of Labor concluded that about one-third of the persons engaged in remunerative labor were unemployed at their principal occupation for about one-third of the working time.[62] Statistics covering more than 85,000 industrial wage-earners in the State of Illinois for 1885-1886 show that they were employed, on the average, 37.1 weeks in the year. Three per cent received twenty or less weeks of work during the year; thirty-two per cent received between twenty and thirty weeks' work; thirty per cent received between thirty and forty weeks' work; and thirty-five per cent between forty and fifty-two weeks' work. These figures show that the average worker was normally idle about one-fourth of the possible working time during the year.[63]

If, in the best of times, there was a constant unemployed class of two and one-half per cent of the total wage-earners in the country, as was asserted at the time, Carroll D. Wright's estimate of almost one million unemployed persons in 1885 in agriculture, trade, transportation, mining, manufacturing, and mechanical occupations, may be regarded as conservative. Since the depression of 1882-1886 hit industry in particular, the vast majority of the unemployed were industrial wage-earners. This unemployment, it was computed, accounted for a daily loss of consumptive power of one million dollars. Other contemporary estimates of unemployment set much higher figures. Terence V. Powderly, General Master Workman of the Knights of Labor, spoke of the widespread unemployment that affected the country from 1883 on, and declared that from one and a half to two million men were out of work in 1885. It was shortly after asserted that the unemployed reached two million in 1886.[64] Inevitably the feeling became widespread among American workers that a decrease in hours would reduce unemployment, and that they were not adequately paid for the goods and values they produced during the normal working day.[65]

Most industrial problems and most labor discontent arose in connection with the primary questions of employment, wages and hours. There were, however, other sources of antagonism between employer and worker in the secondary conditions of labor and in a number of industrial practises to which employers resorted. The latter include the black-list, the iron-clad oath and the practise of assessing fines and charges. While these affected only some workers, they called forth protests from American labor at large.

Fining, most common in retail stores, hotels, and restaurants, was also found in factories, generally only in those employing large numbers of women and children. Workers were fined for coming late, for being absent without permission, for singing or talking with one another during working hours, for unusual noise, for imperfections in the work, and for a host of arbitrary reasons. Fines were sometimes assessed to the extent of two and three per cent of the weekly wages, without any statement of the reasons for their imposition. It is true, of course, that fining affected industry to a minor extent at this time, and there was almost none of it among male factory workers. It was most in evidence in the older manufacturing States, but was spreading to all. In severely condemning the system in 1886, the Bureau of Labor Statistics of Illinois pointed out that fining was a development of the past five years, and that while it had not yet made deep inroads, the practise was growing rapidly.[66]

A series of investigations by the Chicago *Times* of the factories of Chicago, especially those employing women and children, disclosed in 1888 that the fining practise had spread. Frequently employees lost a considerable portion of the $3-4 weekly they received for a ten hour day through fines.[67]

Other burdensome charges were levied upon employees. Female operatives, especially in the clothing industry, were sometimes forced to contribute a certain per cent of the weekly wage to pay for the machines upon which they worked. If the worker left her employ before the machine was paid for, she usually forfeited her "contributions." Payments for needles and thread were common, and frequently workers were required to cover the expense of repairing machines. In at least one instance, the employer levied a charge of twenty-five cents weekly upon each operative for the steam by which the factory was run. There were authenticated instances where female operatives lost one-half of their weekly wages—which generally came to about five dollars—because of such charges.[68] Another practise, also found widely among female workers, compelled new hands to turn over a portion of the first week's wages as surety against quitting the factory before the expiration of a six months' period or without giving two weeks' notice. If the proper notice were given or six months had elapsed, the money was returned. Where this rule was rigidly enforced, an employee would lose the sum deposited for failing to report to work on any one day before the half year was up.[69]

The iron-clad oath, comparable to the yellow-dog contract of the present day, was employed to prevent the unionization of factories and shops. The oath affirmed that the signer was not a member of a labor organization, did not contemplate joining and would never join one. In its broadest sense it prohibited the members of a shop from collective action or even consultation of any kind. It was usually accompanied by a pernicious system of spying by which employers were informed of infractions of the oath. Membership in a labor organization of any sort was, for one who had signed it, cause for instant dismissal. Where labor organizations were weak or were in process of formation, the iron-clad oath was a particularly potent weapon. Workers had no legal redress against it. It was successfully used on many occasions to drive workers out of their organizations, or at least make such membership secret.[70]

Against the black-list the worker was given statutory protection by some States and in practically all of them its use could be prosecuted as a conspiracy punishable at common law.[71] Few wage-earners were cognizant of this, however, and court action was rarely taken. In essence, the black-list was the employers' method of boycotting obnoxious workers. Names on the list were circularized among employers within the same trade, and workers thus distinguished found it impossible to secure employment within a given district or even in other regions. Commonly regarded by workers as the cause of the labor boycott, to which it was analogous, the black-list was employed almost solely against men engaged in union activities. It served, therefore, as a supplementary weapon to the iron-clad oath. In the 'eighties, and especially by 1886, it was increasingly popular among employers. It was most bitterly resented in organized labor circles, which regarded its employment as a blanket declaration of war against union labor by the employer.[72] Employers also often imported foreign and colored workers into a troublesome locality to prevent the formation of labor organizations or destroy those which already existed.[73]

A limited number of workers found a grievance in the fact that they received their wages partly in cash and partly in goods or orders for goods. This practise obtained largely in the coal industry, where the company store system was frequently found with it. In Illinois, about one-fifth of the wage-earners in the coal industry were subject to the burdens of the system. In most instances, these stores sold goods at prices above those prevailing in the locality, and frequently they profiteered to the extent of twenty per cent above normal prices.[74] In many regions, reported Carroll D. Wright in 1886, "employment depends partially upon taking goods out of the companies' stores." [75] Large numbers of workers likewise found the custom of paying wages at fortnightly or monthly intervals burdensome,[76] and some States passed laws to protect the worker from employers who withheld his earnings for too long a time.

Obviously, not all American workers were being subjected to the unjust conditions which produced the working-class discontent of the period. But the unpleasant elements in the industrial scene cannot be glossed over, and the latter cannot be presented in the roseate light in which many of its contemporaries saw it. The American worker, it is true, was less rigidly fixed in his economic class and function than the European; passage into another class was easier for him; he enjoyed a degree of social equality and freedom, as well as material advantages, which the European did not. All this was frequently pointed out at the time.[77] Yet it does not follow that the American workingman had no reason for complaint, or that he was not conscious of the inequalities in American society. In 1888, James Bryce observed that

"There are no struggles between privileged and unprivileged orders, not even that perpetual strife of rich and poor. . . . No one of the questions which now agitate the nation is a question between rich and poor. Instead of suspicion, jealousy, and arrogance embittering the relations of classes, good feeling and kindliness reign. Everything that government, as the Americans have . . . understood the term, can give them, the poorer class have already. . . . Hence the poorer have had little to fight for, no grounds for disliking the well-to-do, few complaints to make against them."

Bryce placed upon the shoulders of foreigners who brought "their Old World passions with them," responsibility for the cries of protest which were raised and the labor disturbances which occurred.[78]

His judgments, however, cannot be accepted as either adequate or accurate. The elements which disturbed the serenity of the industrial scene were not exceptional to it—they cannot be regarded as rare abnormalities—and it was not alone the "foreigner" who was cognizant of them. If the worker aired his grievances, it was because he had full reason. America had reached a stage in economic development where a tranquil industrial life and a contented working class were practical impossibilities.

NOTES CHAPTER I

1. John R. Commons and Associates, *History of Labour in the United States*, 2 vols., New York, 1926, vol. 2, title of Chap. IX.

2. Norman J. Ware, *The Labor Movement in the United States, 1860-1895. A Study in Democracy,* New York, 1929, p. 302.

3. George E. McNeill, 1836-1906, a respected labor leader of the 'seventies and 'eighties, was active in the eight-hour movement of the 'sixties and played a leading rôle in the establishment of the Massachusetts Bureau of Labor Statistics, of which he was deputy chief for several years.

4. George E. McNeill, editor, *The Labor Movement, The Problem of To-Day, Comprising a History of Capital and Labor, and Its Present Status,* New York, 1887, pp. 170-171.

5. For the statistical and quoted material in this section on economic development, see, *The First Annual Report of the Commissioner of Labor, March, 1886. Industrial Depressions,* Washington, 1886, pp. 67-71, 72-73, 80-87; Commons, *op. cit.,* vol. 2, pp. 358-359. Excellent textbook treatments of the period of industrialization are Fred Albert Shannon, *Economic History of the People of the United States,* New York, 1934, Chaps. XXII-XXIV; Louis M. Hacker and Benjamin B. Kendrick, *The United States since 1865,* Revised Edition, New York, 1934, Chap. X.

6. Vol. 39, no. 999, August 16, 1884, p. 171.

7. Published in Washington, D. C., and dedicated "To the Working Men and Women of America . . ." It has been overlooked by Parrington and Hicks in their studies of the literature of the period. See especially, pp. 75, 158-159.

8. *Report of the [Education and Labor] Committee of the Senate upon the Relations between Labor and Capital, and Testimony Taken by the Committee,* 4 vols., Washington, 1885, vol. 1, p. 473 (cited hereafter as *Rep. of the Sen. Com. on Lab.*). Senator Henry W. Blair of New Hampshire was chairman. The resolution as a result of which the Committee was appointed contemplated an inquiry concerning the relations between labor and capital, hours and wages of labor, the share of labor and capital in the national income, the causes of strikes, etc. The Report contains a mine of valuable information. A fifth volume containing the report of the Committee was probably suppressed. It never appeared.

9. *Ibid.,* vol. 1, pp. 681, 682.

10. *Ibid.,* vol. 1, p. 288.

11. *Ibid.,* vol. 3, p. 288.

12. New York *Times,* April 30, 1886.

13. *Rep. of the Sen. Com. on Lab.,* vol. 3, p. 38.

14. *Ibid.,* vol. 2, p. 990.

15. *Ibid.,* vol. 1, pp. 357-358.

16. *Ibid.,* vol. 1, p. 410.

17. Henry W. Cherouny, *The Burial of the Apprentice: A True Story from Life in a Union Workshop . . . and Other Essays on Present Political and Social Problems,* New York, 1900, p. 118.

18. Van Wyck Brooks, *The Ordeal of Mark Twain,* new and revised edition, New York, 1933, pp. 83 *ff.*

19. Quoted in *ibid.,* p. 82.
20. Vernon Louis Parrington, *The Beginnings of Critical Realism in America,* 1860-1920, New York, 1930, pp. 173 *et seq.;* Granville Hicks, *The Great Tradition, An Interpretation of American Literature since the Civil War,* New York, 1933, pp. 78-84; Tyler Dennett, *John Hay. From Poetry to Politics,* New York, 1933, Chap. X, *passim.*
21. Josiah Strong, *Our Country. Its Possible Future and Its Present Crisis,* revised edition, New York, 1891, p. 259; *cf.* p. 166.
22. M. L. Scudder, Jr., *The Labor-Value Fallacy,* third edition, Chicago, 1887, pp. 76-79.
23. S. W. Foss in *Tid-Bits,* undated clipping, New York Public Library Scrap-Books on Labor.
24. Quoted in Virginius Dabney, *Liberalism in the South,* Chapel Hill, 1932, p. 203.
25. Quoted in *Social Science Review,* vol. 1, no. 2, December 14, 1887, p. 9.
26. W. G. Sumner, "Industrial War," *Forum,* vol. 2, September, 1886, p. 3.
27. See, however, the statement of a New England mill owner who in 1883 declared: "There is such a thing as too much education for working people sometimes. I don't mean to say by that that I discourage education . . . or that I think that with good sense any amount of education can hurt anyone, but I have seen cases where young people were spoiled for labor by being educated to a little too much refinement." *Rep. of the Sen. Com. on Lab.,* vol. 3, p. 15.
28. R. Heber Newton, *The Present Aspect of the Labor Problem. Four Lectures Given in All Souls Church, New York, May, 1886,* New York, 1886, pp. 21-25. The Rev. Newton's second lecture gives capital's view of the labor problem and of the existing economic order, pp. 21-36.
29. *Rep. of the Sen. Com. on Lab.,* vol. 2, p. 959.
30. A. S. Wheeler, *The Labor Question. A Paper Read before the Commercial Club of Boston. October 16, 1886. Reprinted from the Andover Review for November, 1886,* Boston, 1886, pp. 3, 8.
31. *First Annual Report of the Commissioner of Labor,* pp. 88-89.
32. Cited in Richmond Mayo Smith, "American Labor Statistics," *Political Science Quarterly,* vol. 1, no. 1, March, 1886, p. 53.
33. "Contemporary Life and Thought in the United States," *Contemporary Review,* vol. 52, November, 1887, pp. 731-732.
34. Francis A. Walker, *The Labor Problem of Today. An Address Delivered before the Alumni Association of Lehigh University, June 22d, 1887,* New York, 1887, pp. 8, 14.
35. George D. Wolff, "The Wage Question," *The Catholic Quarterly Review,* vol. 11, no. 42, April, 1886, pp. 343-344. For characteristic and different types of protest in behalf of labor, see the *Rep. of the Sen. Com. on Lab.,* vol. 1-4, *passim; Newton, op. cit.,* pp. 3-20, *passim;* Richard T. Ely, *The Labor Movement in America,* new

and revised edition, New York, 1905, p. 61, Appendix I, No. VIII, pp. 371-373; The Hon. Stewart L. Woodford, *The Labor Problem. Annual Oration Before the New York Delta of Phi Beta Kappa* (New York, 1886), *passim;* McNeill, *op. cit.,* chap. XVII, *passim;* Walter B. Hill, *Anarchy, Socialism, and the Labor Movement. An Address Delivered Before the Literary Societies of the University of Georgia, July 19, 1886,* Columbus, Ga., 1886, pp. 23-25, 37 *et seq.*

36. Thomas Sewall Adams and Helen L. Sumner, *Labor Problems,* eighth edition, New York, 1911, p. 150.

37. *Rep. of the Sen. Com. on Lab.,* vol. I, pp. 291-292.

38. Strong, *op. cit.,* p. 174.

39. Charles B. Spahr, *An Essay on the Present Distribution of Wealth in the United States,* New York, 1896, pp. 128-129, 158-159, 68-69; *cf.* pp. 50-52; *Free Society,* May 6, 1900, p. 2; Strong, *op. cit.,* p. 174.

40. *Rep. of the Sen. Com. on Lab.,* vol. 3, p. 452.

41. *Ibid.,* vol. 3, pp. 408-415, *passim.*

42. *Ibid.,* vol. I, pp. 574-576, *passim.* The statements were made by P. H. Logan.

43. The Citizens' Association was a civic reform organization.

44. *Report of the Committee on Tenement Houses of the Citizens' Association of Chicago. September, 1884,* Chicago, 1884, p. 3.

45. *Ibid.,* p. 4.

46. *Ibid.,* p. 9.

47. *Ibid.,* p. 15.

48. Marcus T. Reynolds, *The Housing of the Poor in American Cities. The Prize Essay of the American Economic Association for 1892. (Publications of the American Economic Association,* vol. 8, nos. 2 and 3), London, March and May, 1893, pp. 19, 30; Strong, *op. cit.,* p. 184.

49. *Rep. of the Com. on Ten. Houses of the Cit. Assn. of Chicago,* p. 10; *The University,* Chicago, February 6, 1886, clipping, Labadie Scrap-Book; *Hull House Maps and Papers. A Presentation of Nationalities and Wages in a Congested District of Chicago, together with Comments and Essays on Problems Growing Out of the Social Conditions,* New York, 1895, Josepha Humpal Zeman, "The Bohemian People in Chicago," pp. 115-119 *passim;* Claudius O. Johnson, *Carter Henry Harrison I, Political Leader (Social Science Studies Directed by the Local Community Research Committee of the University of Chicago),* Chicago, 1928, p. 189.

50. New York, 1911, *passim* and especially pp. 99-100, 158, 194-195, 198-199, 201-202, 281; Strong, *op. cit.,* p. 186.

51. *Op. cit.,* p. 158.

52. For the causes of the depression, see, *First Annual Report of the Commissioner of Labor,* pp. 291-292. Wages in Massachusetts in 1885, were about five per cent lower than they were in 1880, Spahr, *op. cit.,* p. 98 note.

53. *Rep. of the Sen. Com. on Lab.,* vol. 2, p. 1117.

54. Willford Isbell King, *The Wealth and Income of the People of the United States*, New York, 1923, table XXXVII, p. 198; *Handbook of Labor Statistics, 1929 Edition. Bulletin of the United States Bureau of Labor Statistics, Miscellaneous Series, No. 491*, Washington, 1929, p. 760. For movements of mining wages bearing out these generalizations, see Spahr, *op. cit.*, p. 114.

55. These wage figures come from *Rep. of the Sen. Com. on Lab.*, vol. 3, pp. 4, 28, 74, 125; vol. 1, pp. 320, 552-553, 757, 838-839.

56. Smith, *loc. cit.*, p. 70; *cf.* Strong, *op. cit.*, pp. 147-148.

57. Strong, *op. cit.*, p. 147. Compare with the earnings in Massachusetts in 1890, Spahr, *op. cit.*, pp. 97-98.

58. *Fourth Biennial Report of the Bureau of Labor Statistics of Illinois, 1886*, Springfield, 1886, Tables XXXI-XXXV, pp. 335-361.

59. Paul H. Douglas, "An Analysis of Strike Statistics," 1881-1921, *Journal of American Statistical Association*, n. s. no. 143 (vol. 18), September, 1923, p. 869. Douglas gives 6,905,000 as the average number of industrial workers for 1886-1890.

60. *First Annual Report of the Commissioner of Labor*, p. 226.

61. King, *op. cit.*, table XXXVII, p. 198; *cf.* Adams and Sumner, *op. cit.*, p. 514.

62. Cited in Adams and Sumner, *op. cit.*, pp. 160-161; Spahr, *op. cit.*, pp. 100-102.

63. *Fourth Biennial Report of the Bureau of Labor Statistics of Illinois*, table XXVII, pp. 318-319.

64. *First Annual Report of the Commissioner of Labor*, pp. 65-66; Terence V. Powderly, "The Army of the Discontented," *North American Review*, vol. 140, April, 1885, p. 369; *Record of the Proceedings of the Ninth Regular Session of the General Assembly, Held at Hamilton, Ont., Oct. 5-13, 1885*, n. p., 1885, p. 11; *Labor: Its Rights and Wrongs. Statements and Comments by the Leading Men of Our Nation on the Labor Question of To-Day . . .*, Washington, 1886, pp. 305-306; McNeill, *op. cit.*, pp. 575-576. S. B. Elkins put the number of unemployed in 1885 at 350,000; Hon. S. B. Elkins, *The Industrial Question in the United States. Address Delivered before the Alumni Association of the University of the State of Missouri. June 3, 1885*, New York (1885), p. 7.

65. For hours, see below, pp. 34-35, 159-160.

66. *Fourth Biennial Report of the Bureau of Labor Statistics of Illinois*, pp. 501-506, 507-509, 510-526.

67. John P. Altgeld, *Live Questions: Including Our Penal Machinery and Its Victims*, Chicago, 1890, pp. 80-89 ("Slave Girls in Chicago").

68. *Proceedings of the General Assembly of the Knights of Labor of America. Eleventh Regular Session, Held at Minneapolis, Minnesota, October 4 to 19, 1887*, n. p., 1887 (cited hereafter as *Proceedings of G. A., K. of L., 1887*), pp. 1584-1588.

69. *Fourth Biennial Report of the Bureau of Labor Statistics of Illinois*, pp. 507-508.
70. *Proceedings of G. A., K. of L., 1887*, pp. 1715, 1737, 1776; *Alarm,* December 17, 1887 (contains reprint of typical iron-clad oath); *A Summary of the Third Annual Report of the Bureau of Labor Statistics of New York, January 21, 1886,* Albany, 1886, p. 25; Newton, *op. cit.,* pp. 39-40.
71. See below, pp. 42 *et seq.*
72. Newton, *op. cit.,* p. 17; Hill, *op. cit.,* p. 47; *Proceedings of G. A., K. of L., 1887,* pp. 1408, 1666, 1667.
73. *Proceedings of G. A., K. of L., 1887,* pp. 1669-1670.
74. *Fourth Biennial Report of the Bureau of Labor Statistics of Illinois,* pp. 321-327, 333-334.
75. *First Annual Report of the Commissioner of Labor,* p. 244.
76. *Fourth Biennial Report of the Bureau of Labor Statistics of Illinois,* p. 326.
77. James Bryce, *The American Commonwealth,* 2 vols., new edition, New York, 1927, vol. 2, pp. 300 *ff.,* 647-649, Chap. CXIX, *passim.*
78. *Ibid.,* vol. 2, pp. 647-648.

II. LABOR AND THE LAW

A N examination of certain aspects of the labor movement and a survey of the labor legislation of the period throws additional light on the condition of American workers. If all other evidence were lacking, the State laws relating to labor would sufficiently indicate the degree to which the interests of capital were guarded in the thirty-eight commonwealths which made up the United States in 1887. Tested by present-day standards, practically every State failed to establish the legal safeguards necessary to protect the workingman from all but the grossest injustices. Georgia cannot be regarded as typical, but it is significant that its protection for the worker was exhausted with the provisions "that hours of labor shall be from sunrise to sunset for persons under 21 in all manufacturing establishments and machine shops," and that employers who administered corporal punishment were "liable in an action." [1]

State legislatures were unwilling to concern themselves with the interests of the workers except when it was necessary to conciliate the labor vote. This is illustrated by the tardy establishment of bureaus of labor or labor statistics. Fifteen years after the creation of the first such agency by Massachusetts in 1869, there were only sixteen in existence including the national bureau at Washington. With one or two exceptions, none was equipped either in funds or personnel to function properly. Many served as sources for political jobs, and practically all were established merely to put an end to the demand for them. [2]

The States were even more backward in the passage of legislation relating to sanitary and safety provisions in factories, and in the establishment of adequate machinery for inspection and administration. Massachusetts, which so frequently showed the way in this field, was the first State to boast of broad legislative efforts along these lines. As early as 1877, it made provision for the inspection of factories. Most legislation of this type came after 1882, and by the close of 1886, Massachusetts, Maryland, New Jersey and Ohio had the beginnings of factory codes. The laws protected the worker, to some degree, from fire-hazards, from exposed belting, shafting, gearing and the like, from overcrowding and poor lighting, and from lack of cleanliness and proper ventilation. Where such legislation existed in other States, it generally stopped short with obvious precautions against fire-hazards and with extremely elementary safety measures. Frequently these laws only incidentally applied to factories. Eleven States in all, in addition to those listed, had passed laws of this nature by 1887. As late as 1900 only twenty-one of the forty-five States provided for the inspection of factories.[3]

Laws restricting the labor of women and minors constitute a primary step in the development of labor legislation. By the close of 1887, three States had made it illegal to compel a woman to work more than eight or ten hours a day, and four States prohibited the employment of females in coal mines.[4] The total number of statutes concerning child labor is much larger, and they fall roughly into four main categories: those setting an age limit below which minors could not labor; those restricting the occupations of children; those limiting their hours of labor; and those affecting the education of children employed in industry.

Only nine States established unqualified age limits below which child labor was prohibited, the highest being thirteen years and the lowest ten.[5] In these and in at least eleven other States, the age limits for child laborers were based upon school attendance or ability to read and write. This type of legislation is illustrated by the laws of Massachusetts, where the employment of a child under fourteen, except during vacation, was prohibited unless the child had attended public school or its equivalent for twenty weeks in the preceding year. Children under fourteen who could not read and write were not to be employed while the schools were in session.[6] It can safely be said that the age levels were so low, the means of escaping the restrictions so numerous, the penalties for violation so mild, and the machinery for administration so inadequate, that this legislation did not prevent the employment of young children in industry. In general the statutory provisions seem to have been far in advance of actual industrial conditions.

From only one industry, coal mining, were children excluded to any wide extent. Most coal-mining States prohibited children under a certain age, generally twelve, from working in the mines, and some measure of protection was offered to those who were older but had not yet reached their majority.[7] Indiana was unusual in that it excluded children under twelve from employment in the manufacture of iron, steel, nails, metals and tobacco,[8] and Maine made the employment of children under twelve and fifteen in cotton and woolen factories dependent upon school attendance during the previous year.[9]

The slight stimulus given to the education of the young by some of the legislation already considered was sometimes aided by laws which set aside for the local school fund all or a portion of the fines collected for violation of child labor laws. This was done in Maine and Massachusetts. New Jersey had a law designed to send children between the ages of twelve and sixteen to school when they were temporarily unemployed.[10]

A large number of States limited the hours minors could work, or be compelled to labor, in industrial or mercantile pursuits. Fourteen states and one territory had passed such laws. This type of legislation is difficult to summarize, but it may be said that the maximum number of hours which minors were permitted to work was generally ten a day or sixty a week.[11]

The passage of woman and child labor laws implied a recognition of the existence of social evils in the industrial life of the country. Occasionally the statutes reflected even more directly the injustices experienced by the working-class. The fact that laws were passed to mitigate them is, however, in no sense in conflict with the rule of capital interests in the State capitals. Perhaps the most pointless piece of legislation written in the United States to do away with industrial abuses was a Michigan law of 1885 which declared that "Employers taking advantage of the poverty or misfortune of any employé, or one seeking employment, are guilty of a misdemeanor and liable to a fine of from $5 to $50 for each offense." [12]

Three States, New Jersey, Ohio, and Pennsylvania, legislated against the company store system. There is, however, no contemporaneous evidence that the system was seriously affected.[13] Three States, likewise, Pennsylvania, Ohio, and Missouri, attacked the practise of paying wages in other than lawful money or orders redeemable in legal tender. Frequently, payment was made in tokens, checks, and the like, redeemable only at a discount. To aid the company store, wages were also paid in orders which would be discounted everywhere except at the store.[14] An effort was made in Pennsylvania, New Jersey and Indiana to prevent employers from withholding wages long after they were due, but such laws did not insure prompt payment when the employer was obdurate.[15]

Half-hearted protection was given to workers in the coal industry by most of the mining States. This legislation was generally designed to prevent the false weighing of coal brought to the surface, and commonly provided for the inspection of mines and machinery by workers' representatives in order to protect safety regulations.[16] There was as yet no thoroughgoing body of legislation safeguarding the worker from the individual hazards of his industrial occupation and from bad working conditions in general. The peculiar nature of the coal industry was, of course, responsible for its extensive set of safety and inspection provisions, but even there the idea of workmen's compensation resting on the responsibility of the employer was as yet unknown.[17] Only one other type of humane legislation was as wide-spread as the safety and inspection laws for coal mines. This was the body of laws that compelled the provision of seats for women in industrial and mercantile pursuits, to be used when they were not engaged in active duties.[18]

As a result of the shorter hour movements after the close of the Civil War,[19] a large number of States specified the number of hours that constituted a legal day's work. Superficially, these laws constituted a major gain by the working class in that they recognized eight or ten hours as a legal day's labor. Actually, they were little better than legislative sops to keep the worker quiet and happy. So limited were they by qualifications of one sort or another that they had no real effect in reducing the number of hours of toil.

The general nature of these laws is illustrated by that of Illinois. Section 1 of the Act of March 5, 1867 declared that, "On and after the first day of May, A. D. 1867, eight hours of labor, between the rising and the setting of the sun, in all mechanical trades, arts and employments, and other cases of labor and service by the day, except farm employments, shall constitute and be a legal day's work, where there is no special contract or agreement to the contrary." Section 2 exempted labor service by the year, month or week from the terms of the statute, and permitted any person to work as many hours over eight as he or she pleased.[20] The only real effect of such a law was to stimulate the workers to secure a shorter working day in fact.

By 1886, eleven other States had passed shorter-hour legislation. Four set the number of hours at eight, and the remaining seven established a ten hour legal standard. In New Hampshire the law also made it illegal to compel a person to work more than ten hours a day, but this was apparently meaningless since compulsion was taken to be physical coercion. Some States also established an eight-hour day for State or municipal work, and in two instances a limit was set for labor in certain occupations. Maryland forbade miners in two counties to work more than ten hours a day in the absence of a contract to the contrary, and Minnesota did not permit railroad locomotive engineers and firemen to be employed more than eighteen hours in one day except under urgent necessity. These laws, broadly speaking, established no rigid restrictions on the number of hours the American worker was free to toil.[21]

Two other types of labor legislation are found in more than one State during this period. One is represented by the Connecticut law which declared that persons or corporations employing laborers "and requiring from them, under penalty of a forfeiture of a part of the wages earned by them, a notice of intention to leave such employment," are liable to payment of a like forfeiture, if suit is brought, when they have failed to give notice of dismissal, except in case of incapacity or misconduct, or where there is a general suspension of labor by the employer. In providing that recovery was possible only through suit by the employee, however, much was done to nullify the intent of the measure. Similar laws had been passed by the legislatures of Massachusetts and New Jersey.[22] The second type of legislation involved the establishment of legal machinery to encourage the peaceful settlement of industrial disputes through arbitration. Pennsylvania, in 1883, made provision for voluntary trade tribunals to arbitrate in the iron, steel, glass, textile and coal industries. Maryland provided for voluntary arbitration boards as early as 1878, and New Jersey two years later.[23]

The legislation thus summarized covers, with several exceptions, the labor laws in existence in 1886 apart from those concerning labor combinations, conspiracies, strikes, boycotts and the like. The exceptions of note are: a New York law of 1884 prohibiting the home manufacture of cigars in cities of over 500,000 inhabitants; a Missouri law of 1885 providing that railroad, mining, express, telegraph, and manufacturing companies must give thirty days' notice of a reduction in wages; and an Indiana law which forbade railroads to exact from their employees, without written consent, any portion of their wages for company hospitals, reading rooms, gymnasiums, and libraries.[24]

It cannot be said that the legislation here briefly surveyed was adequate to the needs of industrial America of the 'eighties. Nor does it compare favorably with the factory and social legislation passed by 1886 in the leading industrial nations of Europe. The laws were seriously lacking in proper administrative provisions. There were many loopholes for escape, the inspectors were few and generally lax, and the penalties for violations were too mild. Thus, the law may give a more favorable picture of industrial conditions than was actually the case.

Of even greater importance to the working-class were the laws and judicial practises affecting its collective activities. In dealing with his employer, the individual worker was, as he is today, pathetically weak. The "freedom" of which he was constantly being reminded was at best an interesting subject for philosophic contemplation. If he examined his own experiences and those of his fellows in the light of his theoretical position as a free worker in a free society, enjoying freedom of contract, he might easily conclude that he was the butt of a sardonic jest.

The remedy for his individual helplessness lay in the collective strength which he derived from his union with others. Union in labor organizations, however, was meaningless unless the worker could effectively use the strike and boycott, and could bargain collectively. Fighting alone against the capitalist, he was doomed to defeat regardless of his objectives. The essential truth of this was recognized in the 'eighties even by those who had no labor affiliations. In the vast majority of cases, declared an acute observer in 1886, "It is sheer mockery to say that wage workers are free to accept or reject the terms and conditions proffered them." [25]

As a class, employers made no secret of their antipathy to the principle of labor organization and all that it implied. Whenever possible they refused to recognize the existence of organizations or to treat with committees representing them. Norvin Green, president of the Western Union Telegraph Company, declared in 1883 that his company "declined to treat with any committee assuming authority to speak for all our employés, and to direct what those employés should do if their demands were not complied with." Though he refused to admit that the Western Union had consistently attempted to break up such organizations, he did grant "that the company would certainly discourage them. . . . It certainly does not look favorably upon them." When an employee joined a labor organization, the company felt that his action had broken his contract, and that it was justified in dismissing him. [26] On another occasion Mr. Green asserted that labor

"organizations have produced a feeling of distrust between labor and capital. They have cultivated distrust on the part of the laborers, and a feeling that capital does not propose or intend to do them justice, while, on the other hand, they have produced a distrust on the part of capital of those laborers or employés that are at the head of the organizations. I think, on the whole, that such organizations have done more harm than good . . . I do not think they are calculated to promote the interests of the workingman. I think that organizations are right. I think that . . . nobody [has] any right to object to them, but I go farther and believe that for many purposes organizations of workingmen are good for their members; but whenever they assume the right to dictate the terms of their employment, just to the extent that they do that, they react upon their members, and do them harm, as a general thing, instead of good." [27]

Mr. Green was, of course, merely echoing his astute superior, Jay Gould, who was not opposed to labor organizations as long as they did not concern themselves with questions of working conditions, hours, or wages. These organizations would be of great benefit if their activities were restricted to the education of their members, to the weeding out of "black sheep," and to the development of life insurance.[28] Unfortunately, remarked Gould, the existing organizations had "ignoble purposes" and were led by "wicked" men. Even an employer who boasted of his liberality in his relations with labor, John Roach of the Morgan Iron Works of New York, was hostile to unions. Refusing to treat with his workers collectively, he insisted that all questions of hours, wages, and related matters had to be adjusted between himself and his workers as individuals.[29]

It cannot be too strongly emphasized that this attitude was dominant among members of the employing class in the period under consideration. Variation appeared only in the arguments advanced in support of it, and these naturally followed certain obvious patterns. Even Abram S. Hewitt, long a champion of labor and a man who vigorously defended the right of labor to organize, attacked the Knights of Labor when it grew in membership and resorted to the strike and boycott with frequency. He was convinced, he asserted, that intelligent workingmen would not long continue "to submit themselves to the intolerable oppression of strikes, boycotts and inability to earn their daily bread at the will of a secret body, whose mandates are given without explanations, and from whose orders there seems to be no appeal." Without the open shop and individual bargaining—that is, unless the workers are permitted "to exercise their undoubted right of individual choice"—labor is reduced to a condition of serfdom.[30] The New York *Times* opposed the activities of labor organizations in strikes and boycotts because of their "un-American" nature. The methods of the "strikers and boycotters . . . are entirely un-American," said the *Times*, "and show that those who employ them have no real conception of what American citizenship is or implies. They are all based upon some pretensions of exclusive privilege to persons of a particular class or members of a particular association. . . . It is of the utmost importance that this pretension should be once for all put down. . . ." [31]

Henry Clews, of Wall Street fame, set out to prove to the worker that if he organized and engaged in strikes he was changing the providential rôle of the United States in world history. With complete seriousness he declared that "Strikes may have been justifiable in other nations but they are not justifiable in our country. The Almighty has made this country for the oppressed of other nations, and therefore this is the land of refuge . . . , and the hand of the laboring man should not be raised against it." [32]

William Graham Sumner as a thoroughgoing economic liberal viewed the activities of organized labor with extreme distrust, and rationalized his position in an amazing fashion. "There are a great many cases in sociology," he wrote, "where the sum of the parts is not the whole, but is zero. The trades-union is one of them. A national trades-union . . . of all employés, instead of being invincible would be nil. If by all going out to-day could force an advance in wages, by all going back to-morrow all would restore the old rate. . . . If we want more wages," he concluded, "the only way to get them is by working, not by not working." [33] Comparable with this argument were the statements of a contributor to the *Journal of Social Science* who attempted to demonstrate that labor unions were not to be confused with labor. The formation of a union implies a "remove from the condition of the mere laborer." Unions possess capital, and, instead of representing the workers, "they occupy a position of necessary hostility to them." Great masses of workers, it appeared, cannot unite, for they have nothing in common but their poverty. [34]

The Knights of Labor, which had become the great bogey of the industrial scene by 1886, came in for repeated special attacks in the general assault upon organized labor. It was discovered that the K. of L. was antagonistic to the Constitution of the United States because it limited freedom of thought and action.[35] *The Independent,* a religious journal published in New York, bitterly denouncing the Knights, declared that "Society in this country does not propose to submit itself to their tyranny, in order that they may in their own way, and without restraint, redress what they claim to be the injustice done to labor." [36] A journal of liberal tendencies observed that a reading of the religious and conservative press would lead one to conclude "that the industries of the country are in the hands of a league of bandits known as the Knights of Labor." [37]

When the strike was condemned in the press it was generally not because it interfered with the profit-making of employers, but for other reasons. Thus, the strike was "wrong" because it meant the creation of a monopoly. It was cruel, said Edward Atkinson, because it brought great suffering to the workers, both to those who went on strike and those who did not. "A strike, in which the employés take possession of the plant (!) and hinder others from taking their places," wrote Sumner, "is inconsistent with the peace and order of a modern civilized state." [38] The boycott was attacked as an even more terrible invention than the strike.[39]

These attitudes toward organized labor were in existence long before 1886. The sharper industrial conflicts of that year, the eight-hour movement, and the Haymarket Affair, only served to strengthen and crystallize them. As labor organizations grew in number and membership, as their weapons were more widely employed, as the question of union recognition and union rules became more vital, and as friction over these problems became more frequent,—the law, the courts, and the police power were naturally called upon for greater aid to the employing-class.

Immediately before the inception of the eight-hour movement in May, 1886,[40] it was urged that the "best policy" to break it "would be to drive the workingman into open mutiny against the law." [41] It was proposed that a straightforward method of settling the strike question was "to indict for conspiracy every man who strikes and summarily lock him up. This method would strike wholesome terror into the hearts of the working classes. Another way suggested is to pick out the leaders and make such an example of them as to scare others into submission." [42] Boycotting, it was urged, could and should be promptly and effectively dealt with under the State conspiracy laws. [43] The *Independent* pointed out that a current boycott case offered a splendid opportunity "for teaching the Knights of Labor, and everybody else, that boycotting conspirators are criminals. The time has come for stamping out this system by the power of law." [44]

An editorial in the *Albany Law Journal,* inspired by widespread industrial disputes, expresses the views of the conservative propertied classes on the relationship of the strike to the law and the police authorities.

"Without discussing the right of the master to get service at the cheapest practicable rate, and without dwelling on the apparent hardships which moneyed power imposes on the needy laborer," said the *Law Journal,* "it is clear that the employed can have no just claim for sympathy so long as they resort to tyranny or violence to redress their grievances. If one man is not bound to work a certain number of hours for a certain compensation, surely another man is not bound to pay any more or consent to fewer hours, and the former has no right to stand in his way by intimidation, conspiracy or violence, to prevent his employing others . . . Still less right has the unwilling [the striker] to use violence to deter the willing [i.e., the man willing to go to work]. The worst tyranny of strikes is . . . in their control of the willing in their own ranks. In every strike there are many who join from fear or a sense of loyalty . . . and not from any conviction that the edict is right. Strikes as now managed are notoriously lawless, reckless and dangerous conspiracies against the public peace and safety. They mean terror, incendiarism, violence, and bloodshed, and with these characteristics the law should deal, if patiently, yet decisively. . . . A mob of strikers is entitled to no more leniency than a mob of lynchers or common ruffians." [45]

The general tenor of the court decisions previous to 1886 and the State laws existing in that year bearing upon labor combinations form a rather disheartening picture. Only three States, New York, New Jersey and Maryland, had passed legislation specifically encouraging combinations of workers to improve their material conditions and exempting strikes from being classed as criminal conspiracies punishable as such. The New York law of 1882 provided that "the orderly and peaceful assembling or co-operation of persons employed in any calling, trade, or handicraft, for the purpose of obtaining an advance in the rate of wages or compensation, or of maintaining such rate, is not a conspiracy." [46] This, taken with other provisions of the criminal code, meant that there was nothing in the Penal Code to prevent employees from demanding higher wages or from assembling and using all lawful means to induce employers to pay just wages. The words "lawful means," however, made it possible to punish labor activities, which were presumably legal, as criminal conspiracies. The New Jersey law of 1883 was more explicit in providing that "it shall not be unlawful for any two or more persons to unite, combine, or bind themselves by oath, covenant, agreement, alliance or otherwise, to persuade, advise or encourage by peaceful means, any person or persons to enter into any combination for or against leaving or entering into the employment of any person, persons or corporation." [47] Maryland's statute, passed in 1884, declared that combinations "to do, or procure to be done, any act in contemplation or furtherance of a trade dispute . . . , shall not be indictable as a conspiracy, if such act committed by one person would not be punishable as an offense," [48] and was in some respects more satisfactory than the others.

Only two states, Maryland and Michigan, had by 1886,

enacted laws expressly authorizing the formation of trade unions. The Maryland act (1884) provided

". . . That any five or more persons, citizens of the United States, a majority of whom are citizens of this state, who are engaged in the same occupation or employment, may organize and form as a corporation, to be known as a 'Trade Union,' with such additions to the said name as they may adopt and set forth in their certificate, to promote the well-being of their everyday life, and for mutual assistance in securing the most favorable conditions for the labor of its members, as a beneficial society. . . ." [49]

The Michigan law (1885) was much the same, but was more liberal in that there were no citizenship qualifications, and membership in an incorporated trade union was not restricted to persons in the same occupation. [50]

Thirty-six States, in 1886, failed to provide for the legal formation of labor organizations, and in thirty-five the activities of workers in combination were subject to limitations imposed by conspiracy statutes, or, where these were lacking, by judicial application of the English common law governing combinations. The nature of the existing conspiracy statutes of the period is well illustrated by the law of Illinois, where, after a series of strikes in the coal mines at La Salle, the General Assembly passed in 1863 what presently became known as the La Salle Black Law. Of the four sections of the law, two were general in nature and two referred only to the coal industry. The first section prohibited any person from trying to prevent any other person by threat, intimidation or "unlawful interference" [51] from working at a lawful business or occupation on any terms he saw fit. Violation was punishable by fine up to $100. The second section prohibited "any two or more persons" from combining "for the purpose of depriving the owner or possessor of property of its lawful use and management, or of preventing by threats, suggestions of danger, or any unlawful means, any person from being employed by or obtaining employment from such owner or possessor of property, on such terms as the parties concerned may agree upon. . . ." Violation was punishable by fine up to $500 or six months' imprisonment. The remaining sections punished entry into coal banks to commit injury, or to induce or threaten persons to leave employment, and entry without permission.[52]

The first two sections are representative of the general run of conspiracy statutes. In some States the laws were more rigid and harsher in the punishments prescribed, and in others they were more liberal.[53] Fortunately for the working-class, there was a general relaxation in the application of these statutes in many States during the 'eighties, and very frequently they were completely ignored. This occurred in Illinois, where the La Salle Black Law became a dead letter by 1880. Significantly enough, organized labor tried without success to have the law repealed, and in the twentieth century it was once more utilized to prosecute workers.[54]

In addition to these general conspiracy laws, no less than six States had statutes designed to prevent the obstruction of railway traffic. This was a product of the great railroad strikes of 1877, and the effect of these laws was practically to ban the strike as an industrial weapon. Abandonment of trains by railroad employees or failure to aid in moving them at the order of the company, for example, were widely punished by fine, imprisonment, or both.[55]

By the 'eighties the courts showed a willingness to abandon or at least liberalize the highly restrictive body of precedent which had developed in connection with labor combination cases during the century. The construction of the doctrine of conspiracy which obtained, with some exceptions, almost to 1880 was extremely narrow and destructive in its effect upon labor. A long line of notable court decisions condemned combinations to raise wages as unlawful. The dominant view, expressed by Judge Savage of the New York State Supreme Court in *The People* v. *Fisher and others* (1834), was that

"It is important to the best interests of society that the price of labor be left to regulate itself, or rather be limited by the demand for it. Combinations and confederacies to *enhance* or *reduce* the price of labor, or of any article of trade or commerce, are injurious." [56]

With the New York case of *Master Stevedores' Association* v. *Peter H. Walsh,* decided in 1867, there was a departure from the reasoning followed by Judge Savage. Judge Daly, who gave the decision in this case, after a careful review of the earlier cases, declared:

"That it is not unlawful for any number of journeymen or master workmen to agree, on the one part, that they will not work below certain rates, or on the other, that they will not pay above certain prices; but any association or combination for the purpose of compelling journeymen or employees to conform to any rule, regulation, or agreement fixing the rate of wages, to which they are not parties, by the imposition of penalties, by agreeing to quit the services of any employer who employs journeymen below certain rates, unless the journeymen pay the penalty imposed by the combination, or by menaces, threats, intimidations, violence, or other unlawful means, is a conspiracy for which the parties entering into it may be indicted."

He also pointed out that it never was "a rule of common law that any mutual agreement among journeymen for the purpose of raising their wages is an indictable offense, or that they are guilty of conspiracy if by preconcert and arrangement they refuse to work unless they receive an advance of wages." He drew a line between what is and is not lawful for employees to do, concluding that an unlawful combination is one where there is an attempt to control the rate of wages "by coercive measures." [57]

This did not involve a fundamental repudiation of the older construction of the doctrine of conspiracy as it applied to labor combinations, but it did furnish a much more liberal application of the doctrine. The courts of many States did not follow the ruling immediately, but the passage of the laws abrogating the common law doctrine of conspiracy in some States and the general tendency to liberalize the older conspiracy construction, brought by the early 'eighties a marked improvement in the legal standing of the worker in his collective activities.[58]

This was a major gain, but it was accompanied by developments in the 'eighties which were less happy in their effect upon labor. The courts by 1886 were beginning to punish the boycott, and even before that date were tentatively employing the injunction in labor disputes. The widespread labor troubles of 1886 and the Haymarket Affair caused, as will be seen,[59] a reaction against the liberal tendencies in the courts and State legislatures, with the result that in 1887 much that had been won was lost.[60]

In their careful study Frankfurter and Greene point out that "injunctions were issued in Baltimore in 1883, and at Kent, Ohio, to prevent inducing laborers under contract to quit. In 1884, an injunction was granted in Iowa. *Bradstreets'* for December 9, 1885, reports an injunction against a boycott and unfair list. In the great railroad strike of 1886, the injunction met repeated favor. During the remaining years of the century the cases grew in volume like a rolling snowball." [61] The record of the early use of the labor injunction is far from complete, but it is nevertheless certain that at least three injunctions were issued in Chicago alone in 1886.[62] Unfortunately for their own well-being, the workers of the period failed to grasp the significance of the injunction.

As the workers turned with increasing frequency to the boycott, students of law in 1886-87 began to consider its legality and the question of the liability of those who participated in it. Joel Prentice Bishop, a leading authority on criminal law, asserted that the boycott was illegal in nature and operation.[63] John H. Wigmore, another authority, argued "that the boycott in its legal significance falls within the general definition applicable to all cases of loss of service—*interference with a social relation, whereby there occurs a pecuniary loss capable of proof. . . ."* [64] A contributor to the *Chicago Law Times* declared that "all combinations and confederacies formed for the purpose of injuring third persons are highly criminal, and the boycott having for its object an unlawful coercion of third persons and directed to their injury and only practical by reason of vast combinations, the illegality and criminality of the boycott is beyond dispute." This writer found satisfaction in the fact that boycotting was being answered "with the punishments recently inflicted upon those participating in that criminal method of coercion for some time practised in our midst." [65]

The Theiss boycott case in New York City in 1886, offers an example of the "punishments" to which the author referred. In this case the defendants, who had been engaged in distributing circulars urging a boycott, were convicted and given prison sentences ranging from eighteen months to three years and eight months. The judge declared that the defendants had "violated public right and opinion. Your offense," he continued, "is not short of blackmail. The distribution of circulars by you in places of business is conspiracy and punishable as such. Your conduct if unpunished would lead to savagery." [66] It was not to be long before labor would be stripped of the boycott as a weapon.

Broadly speaking, it may be concluded that the law and the courts strongly favored the business interests of the employing class at the expense of the wage-earners. With exceptions, the law was so fashioned that it placed as little hindrance as possible in the way of money-making activities of the employer. Labor, on the other hand, was seriously hampered by the limitations upon its collective activities. Sometimes they were restrictive enough to outlaw completely all collective efforts to improve conditions. The employer was relatively free in his dealings with those who sold him their labor. Generally speaking, he could discharge them without cause; he could lock them out; he could force them to sign iron-clad oaths; he could black-list them without fear of suffering punishment. He could combine with other manufacturers to form associations injurious to a "third party," and remain untouched by the law. Labor knew all this. Nor was it passed over in silence. In 1887, the Committee on Conspiracy Laws of the Knights of Labor declared:

"The facts are, the great conservative masses, together with the wage-earners of the country, are not represented at court; their rights, in a majority of instances, owing to the persuasive blandishments of wealth, are compromised, and it seldom happens that they are fought and contended for to the bitter end, unless it should chance to be that the principles involved in the security and protection of these rights are immediately and intimately connected with the issues developed in some big legal fight between two huge corporations . . ." [67]

Furthermore, the employer could expect State and municipal authorities to place at his disposal the police, militia and other coercive instruments in times of serious industrial disputes. In Illinois, for example, the militia were a product of the labor disturbances of the 'seventies and of the resulting desire to create an instrument for the suppression of labor violence. During 1885-1886, many requests came to the governor for their use in connection with labor troubles. One of these disturbances also brought into sharp focus the whole question of the employment of private police with State sanction. In the course of a switchman's strike in East St. Louis, the railroad company imported men from Texas, Kentucky and Mississippi, and had them appointed as special deputies to guard its property. The deputies later fired upon a crowd and killed and wounded several people. When they were arrested the court and the grand jury failed to take action, and their employer promptly shipped them out of the State under guard. Labor protested, calling for a thorough investigation and legislative measures to correct abuses of this nature. The General Assembly of the State could not be induced to do more than

pass a law in 1887 which defined the powers of the governor
with reference to the use of the militia, limited the conditions
under which it might be employed, and attempted to prevent
the usurpation of the police power by private police agencies.
County sheriffs, however, were not checked from appointing
private detectives as deputies or employers from using them
as guards.

For years such agencies as the Pinkerton Detective
Agency and Pinkerton's Protective Patrol had flourished in
Illinois, their "detectives" being employed as guards, strike-
breakers, and labor spies. When they got into difficulties the
authorities were generally only too willing to deal leniently
with them. Many were the indictable offenses they committed
and for which they were not punished. It was charged early
in 1887 that the Pinkerton Detective Agency had a veritable
"army" of 1,600 men, many of whom were barracked in
Chicago, where a private Pinkerton jail was supposed to exist.
In Chicago the police could not have acted with more concern for the interests of the business men and manufacturers
if they were hired Pinkertons.[68] It is significant that riot and
bloodshed followed with disturbing frequency when the police
and Pinkertons were used to prevent disorder.

The intensity and rapidity of post-war industrialization,
the concentration of industrial workers in larger establishments, the development of greater industrial urban centers,
the flow of foreign labor into the country, and the economic
and social position of the American working-class provided the
causes for the labor unrest of the middle years of the 'eighties.
These factors give meaning to the avalanche of strikes in
1886, to the eight-hour movement and the Henry George campaign of the same year, to the extensive use of the boycott
between 1884-1886, to the incredible rise in the membership of
labor organizations, and to the relatively large number of
lock-outs in 1886-1887. They explain the "armed truce" which
appeared to exist between worker and employer.[69]

It is in this industrial setting that the Haymarket Affair

must be visualized. It explains, for example, why the affair was utilized to attack both the eight-hour and labor movements. But the industrial scene alone does not provide the complete setting for the affair. To comprehend it thoroughly, a group of influences which were largely European in origin must be examined in detail. These produced in the United States a body of confused revolutionary thought and an uncompromising revolutionary movement which are inextricably connected with the Haymarket Affair.

NOTES CHAPTER II

1. *First Annual Report of the Commissioner of Labor*, p. 461.
2. Smith, *loc. cit.*, pp. 48 *et seq.;* McNeil, *op. cit.*, p. 182.
3. William Franklin Willoughby, *Inspection of Factories and Workshops* (No. VII in *Monographs on American Social Economics* edited by Herbert B. Adams and Richard Waterman, Jr.), Boston, 1900, pp. 4, 5-23 *passim; First Annual Report of the Commissioner of Labor*, pp. 460, 461, 465-470 *passim*, 472-477 *passim*, 482, 485.
4. *First Annual Report of the Commissioner of Labor*, pp. 458, 462, 469, 470, 478, 480, 484-485. Women were not prohibited from working a greater number of hours if the element of compulsion was presumably absent.
5. *Ibid.*, pp. 465, 467, 469, 472, 473, 477, 481, 482, 483.
6. *Ibid.*, pp. 460, 465, 467-468, 468-469, 470, 471, 473, 475, 478, 481, 482, 483.
7. *Ibid.*, pp. 462, 463, 470, 477-478, 481, 483.
8. *Ibid.*, p. 464.
9. *Ibid.*, p. 465.
10. *Ibid.*, pp. 460, 465, 467, 474.
11. *Ibid.*, pp. 457, 460, 461, 462, 464, 465-466, 467, 469, 474, 477-478, 481-482, 483, 484-485.
12. *Ibid.*, p. 469.
13. *Ibid.*, pp. 472, 478-479.
14. *Ibid.*, pp. 470-471, 478-479.
15. *Ibid.*, pp. 463, 472, 478-479.
16. *Ibid.*, pp. 457, 458-459, 462, 463, 464-465, 471, 474, 476-477, 479-480, 483, 484.
17. *Ibid.*, pp. 457-459 *passim*, 462, 463, 465 *passim*, 469-470, 474, 476-477, 481, 483-484.
18. *Ibid.*, pp. 457, 465, 469, 471, 472, 474, 477. Nine states had such laws.
19. See below, pp. 157-159.

20. Earl H. Beckner, *A History of Labor Legislation in Illinois* (Social Science Studies directed by the Local Community research committee of the University of Chicago, no. 13), Chicago, 1929, p. 179; *First Annual Report of the Commissioner of Labor*, p. 462.
21. *First Annual Report of the Commissioner of Labor*, pp. 457, 460, 465, 466, 469, 471, 472, 475, 478, 482.
22. *Ibid.*, pp. 460, 468, 473.
23. *Ibid.*, pp. 466, 474, 478-479.
24. *Ibid.*, pp. 464, 470, 475.
25. Wolff, *loc. cit.*, p. 327.
26. *Rep. of the Sen. Com. on Lab.*, vol. 1, pp. 911-912.
27. *Ibid.*, vol. 1, p. 955.
28. *Ibid.*, vol. 1, pp. 1084-1090 *passim;* New York *Times*, April 30, 1886; *Bradstreets'*, May 1, 1886.
29. *Rep. of the Sen. Com. on Lab.*, vol. 1, pp. 1004, 1010, 1011.
30. Clipping, Labadie scrap-book.
31. April 25, 1886.
32. Henry Clews, "Shall Labor or Capital Rule?" Part I, "The Labor Crisis," *North American Review*, vol. 142, June, 1886, p. 601.
33. Sumner, *loc. cit.*, p. 8.
34. D. McGregor Means, "Labor Unions under Democratic Government," *Journal of Social Science* (containing the *Transactions of the American Association*), no. 21, September, 1886, pp. 73-75. Mr. Means urged that there was no need to fear the unions, p. 78.
35. Rufus Hatch, "Strikes, Boycotts, Knights of Labor," Part II, "The Labor Crisis," *North American Review*, vol. 142, June, 1886, p. 605.
36. Vol. 38, no. 1952, April 29, 1886, p. 536.
37. *The Truth Seeker*, vol. 13, no. 19, May 8, 1886, p. 296.
38. Sumner, *loc. cit.*, p. 6; Elliot F. Shepard, *Labor and Capital Are One*, New York, 1886, p. 46.
39. *Cf. Nation*, vol. 42, no. 1089, May 13, 1886, p. 392.
40. See below, pp. 175 *et seq.*
41. New York *Tribune*, cited in *Social Science*, vol. 1, no. 12, September 21, 1887, p. 8.
42. New York *Times*, April 25, 1886, quoted in *idem.*
43. Hatch, *loc. cit.*, p. 606; *The Truth Seeker*, vol. 13, no. 19, May 8, 1886, pp. 296-297; New York *Times, Tribune,* and *Post* for the close of April, 1886.
44. Vol. 38, no. 1951, April 22, 1886, p. 501.
45. May 1, 1886, pp. 341-342. This was *before* the eight-hour strikes were fully under way.
46. Quoted in *Third Annual Report of the Commissioner of Labor, Strikes and Lockouts, 1887*, Washington, 1888, p. 1158; *First Annual Report of the Commissioner of Labor*, p. 475.
47. Quoted in *Third Annual Report of the Commissioner of Labor*, p. 1158.

48. Quoted in *ibid.*, p. 1154.
49. *Idem.*
50. In contrast to the present-day position, labor organizations of the period desired incorporation because it was felt that they would thus gain some protection from common law rulings and conspiracy statutes. Today, employers are eager for incorporated trade-unions, which, having the fiction of personality, might be sued for damages resulting from strikes and the like.
51. These words were added by an act of 1873.
52. *Ibid.*, p. 1150; Beckner, *op. cit.*, pp. 9-10.
53. *Third Annual Report of the Commissioner of Labor,* pp. 1146-1164 *passim.*
54. Beckner, *op. cit.*, p. 10; *Proceedings of G. A., K. of L., 1887* (Introduction to the Report of the Committee on Conspiracy Laws), p. 1668.
55. *Third Annual Report of the Commissioner of Labor,* pp. 1147-1148, 1150, 1152, 1153, 1155, 1159. The States were Delaware, Illinois, Kansas, Maine, Michigan, Pennsylvania. Louisiana had a similar law with reference to steamboat shipping, p. 1152.
56. Quoted in *ibid.*, p. 1128; see pp. 1124-1129 for the whole case.
57. Quoted in *ibid.*, pp. 1141-1142.
58. This section is based upon *ibid.*, pp. 1111-1143; Clifford Brigham, "Strikes and Boycotts as Indictable Conspiracies at Common Law," *American Law Review,* vol. 21, January-February, 1887, pp. 63-67; *Proceedings of G. A., K. of L., 1887,* p. 1668; George Gorham Groat, *Attitude of American Courts in Labor Cases* (Columbia University *Studies in History, Economics and Public Law,* vol. 42, Whole no. 108), New York, 1911, chap. III-IV *passim;* Walter Nelles, "Commonwealth v. Hunt," *Columbia Law Review,* vol. 32, no. 7, November, 1932, pp. 1128-1169.
59. See below, pp. 537-538.
60. *Proceedings of G. A., K. of L., 1887,* p. 1668.
61. Felix Frankfurter and Nathan Greene, *The Labor Injunction,* New York, 1930, p. 21.
62. Beckner, *op. cit.*, pp. 12-13.
63. *Proceedings of G. A., K. of L., 1887,* p. 1666.
64. John H. Wigmore, "Interference with Social Relations," *American Law Review,* vol. 21, September-October, 1887, p. 764. This is the second half of a paper read before the Langdell Society of the Harvard Law School. The first half was printed as "The Boycott and Kindred Practises as Ground for Damages," *American Law Review,* vol. 21, July-August, 1887, pp. 509-532.
65. Lyn Helm, "Legal Aspects of the Boycott," *Chicago Law Times,* vol. 1, no. 1, November, 1886, pp. 38-39.
66. Quoted in *ibid.*, p. 42.
67. *Proceedings of G. A., K. of L., 1887,* p. 1665.
68. Beckner, *op. cit.*, pp. 61-66; *Life of Albert R. Parsons with Brief History of the Labor Movement in America. Also Sketches of the*

Lives of A. Spies, Geo. Engel, A. Fischer and Louis Lingg, second
edition, Chicago, 1903, pp. 148-149.

69. See the statement of James A. Waterworth in William E. Barnes,
editor, *The Labor Problem. Plain Questions and Practical Answers,*
New York, 1886, p. 17.

III. THE SOCIAL-REVOLUTIONARY MOVEMENT

THE first serious penetration of Marxian Socialism into the United States came at the close of the Civil War.[1] At the same time, as a product of the post-Civil War industrial scene, there occurred a diffusion of trade union ideas and a growth of labor organization on a hitherto unknown scale. The presence of modern Socialism in America, however, is to be traced to European influences. The United States, especially during the period of the 'eighties, did not offer an unfertile soil for the spread of European revolutionary theories. Economic discontent and obvious abuses in the American political system prepared the ground for the spread of revolutionary doctrines.[2] Some infusion of socialist ideology into the beliefs of the American working-class was to be expected. At least one notable labor leader, William H. Sylvis, had even earlier been affected by socialist thought.[3]

But the vast majority of native-born workers were largely untouched by the socialist stream which was making headway in Europe. As late as 1883, Samuel Gompers pointed out that the trade unions were generally opposed to "socialistic" ideas, and declared that "those who try to inject socialism into the labor movement are generally opposed by the trade unions at large." [4] Another labor leader believed that trade unions even retarded the growth of socialistic or communistic tendencies.[5] By far the most active socialist units were the German labor organizations, and these, of course, also provided a connection with the European socialist movement. Had it not been for the death of Sylvis in 1869, it is possible that the American

54

labor movement—and especially the National Labor Union —would have been colored by socialist principles to a greater degree than was actually the case.[6]

In that same year there was reason to expect that the National Labor Union would join hands with the slightly older Marxian International Workingmen's Association. While the former had rejected an offer of formal affiliation with the International in 1867, two years later it sent A. C. Cameron as a delegate to the Basle convention of the First International. Its convention the following year resolved that "The National Labor-Union declares its adherence to the principles of the International Workingmen's Association, and expects to join the said association in a short time." This expectation was never realized, but active contact with the International was initiated by socialist groups which became American sections of the International. These, largely German in membership, were found in New York, Chicago and San Francisco. Some French and Bohemian sections were also formed. By 1872, it is asserted, the total number of sections in the country came to thirty, but only twenty-two sections were represented at the first national convention of the International held at New York City in July of the same year. Although a small number of American intellectuals were drawn into the fold of the International, and two native American sections were founded in New York City, the vast majority of the 5,000 members credited to the International in the United States at this date, were recruited from among the foreign born.[7]

With the removal of the General Council of the International from London to New York City in 1872—a move designed to save the European movement from further Bakuninist [8] influence—the American movement gained temporarily in vitality. Then, under the triple impact of internal dissension and strife, the dissolution of the International abroad, and the effects of the panic of 1873, the life of the American branch was irreparably injured. By 1874 inner controversies, inspired by questions of principle and policy, had led to the formation of two rival socialistic organizations, the Social Democratic Working-Men's Party of America, established in New York, and the Labor Party of Illinois. Except for the formulation of a notable platform in relation to political action, the national convention of 1874 of the American sections which remained affiliated with the International gave little cause for joy to their members. Two years later the pathetic last convention of the International was held at Philadelphia, when no alternative remained but officially to declare the death of the organization.[9]

Despite the differences of opinion on platform and policy which had already disrupted the young American socialist movement, there were present sufficient common elements and a strong enough desire to consolidate the socialist forces to unite the various wings in 1876 into the single Working-Men's Party of the United States. A year later this new party changed its name to the Socialist Labor Party of North America.[10]

The unity thus achieved was in many respects more nominal than real. The S.L.P. had been welded out of many smaller organizations, and the process did not act as an immediate solvent for their differences. A basic cause of disagreement lay in the opposition of "trade-union" socialists to "political action" socialists, a reflection of the European division into the older Internationalists and Lassalleans. The political actionists succeeded in carrying the day, and by the close of 1877, the S.L.P. was officially in the political ring. At the same time, however, there was present within the party the source of a more serious schism. This was the question of whether force was to be employed as a measure of defense by socialists and workers and as an instrument of propaganda. To accept the use of force as an integral part of the revolutionary movement would inevitably react upon the favorable position already taken upon political action.

As early as the summer of 1875, a handful of German

socialists in Chicago formed an armed club to which the name *Lehr und Wehr Verein* was given. In part, this organization was designed to provide protection for socialists, and it was hoped that it and similar armed bodies would produce greater respect for the socialist groups. More significantly, however, the *Lehr und Wehr Verein* was presented as the workingman's answer to the "servile militia" which the "bourgeoisie" of Chicago was creating to be employed against labor. The *Vorbote,* a German socialist organ, urged all workers to join the *Lehr und Wehr Verein* and to "contribute freely the few dollars necessary to arm and uniform themselves." Had the workers been properly prepared, pointed out the *Vorbote,* they would not have been treated as they were by the police when they made demands which were no more than just. Union in such an organization showed the way to ultimate victory. Some time later, another armed group, a *Jägerverein,* was organized in Chicago in opposition to the *Lehr und Wehr Verein,* because its members wanted a German commander.

The labor disturbances in Chicago which grew out of the great strike of 1877 were marked by an extensive and unwarranted use of force by police and militia. In the notorious Turner Hall episode, for example, the police were guilty of an indefensible assault upon workers. An historian of the Chicago police department writes that "the policemen turned upon the mob with their clubs, striking right and left, and breaking a large number of heads and limbs within a few minutes." A pitched battle between militia and police and a "mob" at the Halsted Street viaduct, the climax of the labor troubles of that year, resulted in a heavy toll of dead and wounded. Such occurrences stimulated the formation of armed groups not only in Chicago but in other cities. Quasi-military societies were established in Cincinnati and San Francisco during the summer of 1878, where workers had suffered especially at the hands of armed special deputies. In Chicago, the disruption of labor gatherings by forcible means and the arrest of labor leaders convinced many workers that their rights were being invaded. The public press supported these police activities, and the courts offered no real protection against them. It was therefore quite understandable if many workingmen concluded that only by arming and protecting themselves could they secure justice.

The strength of the *Lehr und Wehr Verein* and other armed groups cannot now be determined. It is extremely unlikely that they possessed the thousand members claimed for them around 1879. Nor can it be said to what extent they were armed. In any case, the armed groups were numerous enough to produce a movement for repressive legislation. In 1879 a bill was introduced in the General Assembly of Illinois to prevent persons, exclusive of the members of the State militia and United States troops, from forming a military company and drilling. When several armed groups in Chicago held a demonstration to express their contempt for this measure, its proponents had little difficulty in mustering sufficient strength to pass it.

The first case tried under this law involved Frank Bielfeld, who was arrested early in July, 1879, for drilling publicly; but it failed to go to the State Supreme Court because of a legal technicality. In a later case, however, the higher court upheld the constitutionality of the statute, declaring "that the parading with arms in populous communities is within the regulation and subject to the police power of the state." The law did not cause the disruption of *Lehr und Wehr Vereine,* the *Jägerverein,* Bohemian Guards, and Labor Guards, all armed societies in Chicago, though it did create much resentment among socialists and workers.

Most of the members of the armed groups were drawn from the ranks of the S.L.P. The national executive committee of the party, led by Phillip Van Patten, the national secretary, early expressing its opposition to the armed organizations, asserted that they misrepresented both the aims and policies of the socialist movement. In 1878, members of the S.L.P. were ordered to withdraw from the armed clubs, and all relationship between the latter and the party was disavowed. The Chicago section of the party protested sharply against what it regarded as a high-handed action of the executive committee. Through the two Chicago party organs, the *Vorbote* and the *Arbeiter-Zeitung,* a running polemic was carried on with those representing the position of the executive committee. In the Alleghany convention of the party in 1879, advocates of the armed groups secured enough adherents to censure the action of the committee, but the majority of the party agreed with the executive committee on the question. Even at the Alleghany convention, the moderate elements of the S.L.P. maintained control except on the vote of censure.[11]

By 1878, a split in the ranks of the S.L.P. over the question of armed groups was apparent; and this break anticipated the irreconcilable internal division of organized Socialism in the United States two years later. This schism did not result from differences of fundamental ideology. It sprang rather from divergent views upon the method of achieving the socialist goal. A growing element within the S.L.P., largely German, showed increasing concern over the *Bewaffnungsfrage,—* the "question of arming." They displayed a willingness to abandon orderly political action in favor of physical force as the mechanism of the social revolution. This meant the substitution of force for the ballot, and, in its most extreme form, the supplementing of educational "propaganda by word" by illegal acts,—"propaganda by deed."[12] It likewise implied an antagonistic attitude towards pure trade-unionism. Proponents of this extremist position were active at the Alleghany convention of the party, but the moderate forces had their way.

A prominent feature of the European revolutionary movement at this time was the broadening of the physical force tendency.[13] Contact between the revolutionaries of the two hemispheres was close and this development was shortly reflected in America. The passage of the German "exceptional laws" in October, 1878, designed to destroy the socialist movement in Bismarck's recently formed national State, and placing heavy penalties upon active socialists, led to the emigration of many embittered social-democrats to the United States.[14]

At the same time the treatment received by American workers at the hands of police and militia fostered a sullen anger among American socialists and caused them to turn to force, at least for defensive purposes. Furthermore, the political scene, which had seemed bright until 1880, now began to lose its encouraging aspects to socialists. On the eve of the presidential election of 1880, the S.L.P. split over the mode of participation in the election. One wing desired to fuse with the Greenbackers, while another insisted upon running an independent socialist candidate. The majority was in favor of fusion, and the S.L.P. participated as a party in the Greenback convention which nominated James B. Weaver. A number of the German members and many English-speaking socialists in Chicago bolted, and nominated their own local ticket. This wing, headed by Albert R. Parsons and Paul Grottkau, lost some of its taste for politics when their own venture turned out badly.

Meanwhile the spring elections of 1880 in Chicago had resulted in an occurrence which, as George Schilling says, "did more, perhaps, than all the other things combined to destroy the faith of the Socialists in Chicago in the efficiency of the ballot." The socialist candidate for alderman in the Fourteenth Ward, Frank A. Stauber, after winning a close victory over his opponent, was fraudulently deprived of his seat by the election judges. Long-drawn litigation, which cost the workers some $2,000, finally gave Mr. Stauber his seat in the spring of the following year. When the election judges, who had stuffed a ballot-box and forged a tally-sheet in order to return his opponent, were tried for these offences, they were found not guilty. This episode produced a wide-spread conviction that successful socialist candidates would be deprived of office without compunction by the entrenched parties. It followed, therefore, that little hope was to be placed in political action as a method of ultimately reconstructing the social order.[15]

The extremist members of the S.L.P. who abandoned the ballot and accepted force are distinguished by the term "social-revolutionaries." With reference to ultimate aim, they were no more "revolutionary" than the social-democrats. But in method they went far beyond their erstwhile comrades. It was not to be expected that both moderates and social-revolutionaries could be successfully contained within a single organization, and the first formal break came with the withdrawal of a number of New York members from the S.L.P. at the close of 1880.

As early as July of that year the first New York section of the party declared itself opposed to the tactics of the Van Patten wing. It proposed the calling of a convention to oust the old-line leaders and revise the constitution of the party. This suggestion fell flat, and members of the section established an independent club which raised money to publish socialist pamphlets for circulation in Germany. Out of this group there grew by November 15, 1880, the Social Revolutionary Club of New York. Its foundation was stimulated by the arrival of the German socialist and ex-deputy, Wilhelm Hasselmann. At first there were twenty-seven persons in the club, and the better known leaders, Justus Schwab and M. Bachman, were thoroughgoing Marxists, having been members of the S.L.P.[16] The source for its platform was the Gotha Program of the German Social-Democracy. It was, however, expressed in anti-authoritarian fashion, and an anarchist influence is suggested. The club shortly numbered sixty persons, and it resolved never to unite with the orthodox socialists. Its thoroughgoing opposition to parliamentary tactics cut it off completely from the S.L.P.

Late in 1880 and during the following year, social-revolutionary clubs appeared in Boston, Philadelphia, Milwaukee and Chicago. Though largely created by dissenting S.L.P. members, their ideological position was not always identic with that of the New York Club. The membership of the new organizations, overwhelmingly foreign, was drawn primarily from the ranks of the S.L.P. and immigrants recently arrived from Germany. In Chicago, the leading spirits in the bolt were men who had been active S.L.P. members, Paul Grottkau, Albert Parsons, and August Spies. The Chicago social-revolutionaries, it should be noted, had not made so clean a break with political action by 1881 as their New York comrades.[17]

The material on these early social-revolutionary clubs is so inadequate that it is not always safe to speak dogmatically about them. It can be said, however, that there is no convincing evidence that the groups had abandoned the fundamental elements of Marxism. A German student of the subject holds that the social-revolutionaries themselves split in turn into two factions, the anarchists in New York and the revolutionary communists in Chicago, which co-operated for the sake of agitation and propaganda.[18] There is probably no real basis for this distinction or for the assertion that there was a clearly defined anarchist element among the social-revolutionaries. Desire for autonomy on the part of the social-revolutionary groups and the presence of anti-authoritarian doctrines do not in themselves constitute a definite anarchist movement. The clubs, it can be said, were essentially Marxist. They had broken off from organized American Socialism over the question of method in revolutionary propaganda and tactics.[19]

What served to turn the extreme revolutionary movement in the United States from a socialist path and give it at least quasi-anarchist direction was a development in the radical movement of Europe,—the London Congress of 1881. This Congress was also largely responsible for the appearance of the International Working People's Association in America.

Following the split in the International Workingmen's Association and the expulsion of Bakunin in 1872, the anarchist wing of the International flourished for some half-dozen years. By 1877-78, however, the decline of the anarchist International was apparent, and its ninth, and what turned out to be its last Congress, was held in Verviers in 1877. This Congress was not strictly anarchistic in nature. Since non-anarchists were present, it is perhaps better described as a conference of anti-authoritarians. In March of the following year, the *Bulletin de la Fédération Jurassiènne,* the most important Bakuninist publication, made its final appearance. While the bonds among the different anarchist groups and sections had become rather tenuous, the tradition of the International had not disappeared. There existed both a Belgian and a Spanish Federation of the International Workingmen's Association in 1880, and the propaganda section of the International was still alive in Geneva, though it was not functioning actively.[20]

In 1880 a growing desire to revive the International was evident among anarchists in several countries. The need for some form of union, apparent to many, was enhanced by the growth of reactionary policies and activities on the part of European governments. Anarcho-communists of the type of Peter Kropotkin,[21] Élisée Reclus and Carlo Cafiero, who were now calling themselves "socialist revolutionaries," were eager to hold an international congress of anarchists, and Johann Most [22] was beginning to work tirelessly to transform the desire into an actuality. The initial step in this direction was really taken by the anarchist Belgian Federation of the International. At its Congress in December, 1880, it was decided to issue a call to revolutionaries throughout the world for the purpose of bringing a new International into existence by means of a congress. The proclamation of the Belgian Federation met with a lively response in revolutionary circles, and a special committee was set up in London, composed of Gustave Brocher, who was chairman, Errico Malatesta,[23] Trunk, and John Neve, to prepare the ground for the gathering of the revolutionaries.[24]

In March of 1881, this committee published an appeal to the revolutionaries of the "Old and New World" urging them to attend the Congress in London on July 14, 1881. This call was addressed both to anarchists and to anti-authoritarian socialists. An alliance of revolutionary elements was imperative to combat the "Holy Alliance of the reactionaries," and the strategy of the struggle with the "slave-holding society in which we live," was to be worked out. Further, the congress was to "lay the foundations of a fighting policy which has hitherto always been kept in the background." The appeal of the organization committee met with objection only from the Spanish Federation, and the revolutionary press, especially *Le Révolté*, the *Freiheit* and *La Révolution Sociale*, were most enthusiastic about the projected congress. The last named journal was at the time edited by "Citizen Serreau," an *agent provocateur* in the employ of the Parisian prefect of police, and was the most active and the least restrained in tone.[25]

The London Congress sat from July 14 to 20. It was reported that the forty-five delegates present represented sixty federations and fifty-nine groups and sections, enjoying a total membership of 50,000; but this estimate is much too generous.[26] Practically every European country was represented, as well as several anarchist groups in the United States. Among the outstanding participants were Peter Kropotkin, Emile Gautier, Louise Michel, Errico Malatesta, Saverio Merlino, Nikolai Tschaikowski, Frank Kitz, Gustave Brocher, Joseph Peukert, John Neve and Victor Dave. The character of the delegates suggests what the resolutions of the Congress make clear: that while the call was addressed to anarchists and anti-authoritarian socialists alike, the London Congress was essentially anarchistic. The American groups represented either directly or indirectly were the Social Revolutionary clubs of New York, the Social Revolutionary Group of Philadelphia, all German in membership, the German section of the Socialist Labor Party of New York, the Icarian Community of Iowa, and a revolutionary group of Boston.[27] In order to insure the future safety of the continental delegates, they were designated by number instead of name.

While anarcho-communist ideas colored the thought of a great number of the delegates, differences of opinion at the Congress were many and sharp, and among the delegates there were proponents of both extreme individualism and revolutionary dictatorship. Though all were favorably disposed to the resuscitation of the International, the problem of developing a form of organization that would give it potency and insure its life caused great difficulty. The majority of the delegates were firmly opposed to every practical step in the path of organization on the ground that it would limit individual liberty and curtail group autonomy. There was no positive solution for the problem of organization as such, and it was finally resolved to have the groups themselves accept or reject the recommendations of the Congress, whose decisions were in no way to be binding upon them. The groups belonging to the International were to have the right to correspond with one another; and to facilitate contact among them, an International Bureau of Correspondence, consisting of three members, was to be established to provide a connecting link for the various organizations.[28]

With reference to revolutionary theory, policy and action, the Congress made its stand clear on several important points, submitting these "propositions" to the member groups of the International for consideration. It asserted that the International Working People's Association recognized "the necessity of joining to spoken and written propaganda, propaganda by deed." Every possible effort must be made "to spread the idea of revolution and the spirit of revolt by deeds" among the great mass of the people not yet participating in the movement and still misled by illusions concerning the "morality and effectiveness of legal methods." Constitutional (i.e., legal) action must be abandoned, and illegality must be made "the sole path leading to the revolution. . . ." Such illegal propaganda would operate through a secret press, individual deeds, and a thorough study of such technical sciences as chemistry in so far as they can be of use to the cause of revolution. The Congress urged "the organizations and individuals belonging to the International Working People's Association to give great weight to the study and practical application of these sciences for offensive and defensive purposes." [29]

The frank advocacy of propaganda by deed by the Congress was to be expected. The increasing dependence upon illegal activity as a medium of propaganda and the theoretical justification of this tendency is one of the distinguishing characteristics of the revolutionary movement of the 'seventies and 'eighties. Propaganda by deed as a mode of revolutionary activity was first clearly enunciated at the Congress of Berne [30] in 1876. In the same year, a declaration of the Italian Federation signed by Malatesta and Carlo Cafiero affirmed that body's belief in the "insurrectional deed" as the "most effective and only medium of propaganda. . . ." Two years later, the Congress of the Jura Federation [31] flatly declared for insurrectional and revolutionary activity. In 1877, Malatesta, Carlo Cafiero and others, in the course of their ill-planned and aborted uprising, destroyed the records of the municipality of Benevento, an act which is sometimes regarded as the first significant step in propaganda by deed. From that time on, evidences of the practical application of the whole policy multiply. Even Peter Kropotkin, by temperament a pacific revolutionist, urged the adoption of propaganda by deed or action, declaring that "by insurrectional deeds the anarchists seek to awake in the people the popular sentiment and initiative for the double prospect of the violent expropriation of property and the disorganization of the State." Insurrectional deeds could and, in point of fact, did range from the destruction of records, symbolizing disrespect for property and constituted authority, to attacks upon representative individuals of the existing order. In some cases theft and murder, if they could aid the "cause," were regarded as valid forms of propaganda by deed. [32]

The acceptance of force both as a medium of propaganda and an instrument of reform was largely the result of the extreme anarchist conception that the individual was the proper judge of his grievances against society or its members and of the means of obtaining redress; of impatience with the achievements of peaceful, legal methods and constitutional action; the absence of a strong revolutionary movement among the "masses"; the influence of the Russian terrorists; the growing severity of the policy of repression and persecution adopted by most European governments; and the activities of *agents provocateurs*. This last factor is generally overlooked, but government agents were on many occasions responsible for inexcusable outrages. The purpose of provocative activities was to discredit all revolutionary movements by encouraging their violent elements and trapping their adherents.[33]

While the principles underlying anarchist and socialist thought do not necessarily imply the employment of insurrectional deeds as a means of realizing a new social order, they do not exclude violent methods. It easily and early became common to assume that some measure of force was absolutely essential in the destruction of an old and the creation of a new society. Many of the adherents of both revolutionary movements came to regard propaganda by deed as the only instrument that insured results.

It was by accretion rather than logical extension of basic theory that propaganda by deed became fixed in a large part of revolutionary thought. During the period under discussion, there was a tendency to transform the employment of force from a "social" to an "individual" manifestation. Even Bakunin, who completely accepted violence, held that the "social revolution" would be a spontaneous movement of the masses and had no place in his teachings, when he was not under Netchaev's influence, for insurrectional propaganda as such.[34] When propaganda by deed was approved at the close of the 'seventies and justified as necessary to arouse the masses, the term was understood to mean only acts of insurrectional nature performed by small minorities. But at the London Congress the conception was modified to include the acts of single individuals. In part, this final development in the meaning of propaganda by deed was forced by the repressive measures of the European governments. As police supervision became more rigorous, revolutionary activity was forced into underground channels, and the dependence placed upon individual action became greater. Propaganda by deed, theoretically, did not spring from individual hatred. However individually expressed, it always manifested an abhorrence of existing *social* institutions.

The delegates from the United States do not appear to have distinguished themselves at the London Congress. Carl Seelig, representing the Social Revolutionary Group of New York (and perhaps also the Philadelphia group), reported that the labor situation was the same in Europe and America, and, despite the difficulties that lay in the way of "socialistic" propaganda, it was altogether possible that the social revolution might come sooner in the United States than in any other country. He declared that the organizations for which he spoke were heartily in favor of a violent revolution. Thus far, however, the revolutionary groups were lamentably weak, and had failed to make use of several excellent opportunities to "overthrow the government" offered by major labor disturbances. He indicated that the groups whose sentiments he represented favored both open propaganda and secret organization.[35] Another American delegate naïvely informed the Congress that the tramps at home constituted "the most fully developed of all revolutionists in the States."[36]

Except for its stand on propaganda by deed, the Congress made no positive contributions to the revolutionary movement. It was by no means "an expression of the mass movement of the working classes," and extremely little in the way of international action followed it.[37] It did not, as *Le Révolté* anticipated, affect "the union of the socialist revolutionaries of both worlds. . . ."[38] Its influence, however, was felt in the United States in two ways. It stimulated an endeavor to organize the social revolutionary movement along national lines, and, by resuscitating it, made possible the introduction of the International Working People's Association into America.

In 1881, the New York Social Revolutionary Club, which had affiliated itself with the I.W.P.A., issued a call for a convention to achieve for the American revolutionary movement what the London Congress was designed to accomplish for the European. This appeal resulted in the gathering of representatives of social-revolutionary and other groups in the country in Chicago from October 21-23 of the same year.

When the conference—or "congress" as its participants preferred to designate it—formally opened in the North Side Turner Hall, one of its purposes was declared to be the adoption of measures "to inculcate in the minds of the working classes the necessity of organizing in a revolutionary way, so as to be ready for emergencies." Mention was also made of the use of force by the workers, who were deprived of any other means by which they could protect their rights.[39] Justus Schwab, representing the New York group, had announced in an interview a day earlier that the congress had been called "to found formidable organizations throughout the States of radical Socialists [that is, those who had broken away from the S.L.P] who desire a change of the social system." He hinted that the delegates were prepared to recommend the use of violence by workers in answer to violence.[40]

Only thirteen delegates were present when the congress was called to order by August Spies [41] of Chicago. All in all twenty-one delegates were listed, and, although it is very doubtful whether that number was ever in attendance at the same time, at least eighteen groups were represented. Among them were sections of the old and new Internationals, several social revolutionary clubs, at least one section of the S.L.P. from Jersey City, a "Socialistic Educational Society," the *Jägerverein* and *Lehr und Wehr Verein* of Chicago and the Liberty Club of Boston. Chicago was best represented with reference both to the number of groups and delegates. Of the former there were four and of the latter at least thirteen.[42] Groups or sections scattered through ten states—Massachusetts, New York, New Jersey, Pennsylvania, Kentucky, Iowa, Missouri, Illinois, Wisconsin and Nebraska—were represented in one way or another.[43]

At its inception, the congress was troubled by the question of open or closed sessions, and it was finally decided that the proceedings were to be public unless some issue for which publicity would be unwise came up for discussion. As soon as the delegates began to submit for consideration the instructions and recommendations of their respective groups, the absence of unanimity on any major question was thrown into striking relief. The Kansas City group demanded a centralized organization, agitation for direct legislation through the use of the referendum and recall, and the adoption of the rule that any candidate for office on a socialistic ticket must be a member of the party in good standing for at least a year. In contrast with this, the instructions of the Jersey City group endorsed the London Congress and called for the adoption of its program and platform. While the Philadelphia and Milwaukee groups requested a bold and uncompromising revolutionary platform and the use of violence, many Chicago "comrades" were represented as favoring the ballot. That a platform was finally elaborated and accepted is perhaps to be explained on the ground that all the delegates, irrespective of their views, were ardently anxious to avoid any suggestion of failure through disagreement. The numerical preponderance of the Chicagoans explains nothing, for there was great diversity of opinion among them.[44] It was inevitable, therefore, that sharp discussions should ensue before a body of principles could be adopted.

A primary point of disagreement was the question of the ballot. August Spies, Albert Parsons and Jacob Winnen (also of Chicago), among the more outstanding delegates, approved, for varying reasons, participation in politics. Spies suggested that election activities offered an excellent field for agitation. He argued that though the election of their own men and labor representatives to office might not result in much immediate gain, at least it enhanced the chances of favorable legislation, and, when such laws—as always—were ignored, there would be additional reason for agitation to make them effective. Parsons reminded the delegates that they were living in America, where people traditionally regarded the ballot-box as the mechanism for securing their demands. He advised that they could teach politically minded people the error of their ways through the usual instruments of propaganda without flatly repudiating political action, which might cause the loss of prospective adherents. He was in any case opposed to the complete abandonment of political activities. Winnen, commending Spies' stand, proposed the formation of an organization whose members were pledged to work for their ideas and ideals through the ballot.

Justus Schwab, supported chiefly by Blum and Peterson, led the opposition to these views. His argument was simple. Their task was "to enlighten the people," to prepare them for the coming social order, to make revolutionaries out of them.[45] That goal was best gained by propaganda by word and "other means," and not at all through political action. To this Spies objected that they could not "revolutionize the masses . . . with fine speeches. . . ." "Thinking people" can be converted in that way. But "we must convince the masses; we must prove, illustrate to the masses [the truth of] what we say! . . . .I am not a politician, but I regard participation in elections as . . . the most practical means of agitating and bringing our ideas to the masses. It is said that the coming crisis will bring out the revolution. That is true, but if we keep aloof from politics now, we will be *kept back then* by the [political] demagogues. . . ." Before a new social order can be established, the masses must be enlightened, not only in a general sense, but especially with reference to present conditions.[46]

Though the committee on platform stood four to two against political action (Schwab, Peterson, Blum and Swain against Spies and Parsons), it did not urge outright rejection of the ballot. It formulated instead a strange compromise in which participation in politics was recommended for the purpose of proving its inadvisability and inutility! [47]

The platform of the congress was expressed in a set of recommendations and a series of resolutions. The congress recommended: (1) the organization of those working men and women interested in solving the "social problem" into local, national and international associations in order to inform their members of the nature, condition and causes of their "slavery" and the means of abolishing the evils of society; (2) the encouragement and formation of trade-unions to prevent the further degradation of the workingman and the degeneration of society. It was also suggested that trade-unions were to be organized on "communistic" principles, and that aid and support were to be given only to those organizations which were "progressive" in character. Several speakers attacked this trade-union plank, and declared that they accepted it only because they recognized it was necessary to throw a "sop" to the trade-union element in order to win its support.[48] The Congress also urged: (3) the organization of the means of revolutionary propaganda in preparation for the "war-like attack" upon the present "system of exploitation" and its supporters which must take place if a new social and economic order is to replace it; and (4) independent participation in politics in order to demonstrate to the worker the iniquity of our political institutions and the futility of seeking to reconstruct society through the ballot. This peculiar compromise was a concession to the Chicago delegates, and the anti-political actionists succeeded in having the "vote" stigmatized as "an invention of the bourgeoisie to fool the workers." [49]

The Congress was surprisingly little concerned with economic theory, but a more definite economic note was sounded in the preamble to these resolutions. There it asserted that the appropriation, either by individuals or classes, of natural resources and all other goods necessary for the satisfaction of human needs is theft and an "encroachment upon human rights." To resist such appropriation is the "highest virtue. . . ." The institution of private property has reduced the working class to the status of "wage-slaves," and this class must strive "to acquire again its natural inheritance by all possible means."

Among the many resolutions adopted three were extremely important. One recognized political action in principle by asserting ". . . That under no circumstances our members are [to be] allowed to vote for any person or with any party which does not approve of our platform." Another resolved ". . . That the Congress assembled recognize the armed organizations of workingmen who stand ready with the gun to resist encroachment upon their rights, and recommend the formation of like organizations in all States." [50] The third, ratifying and indorsing the London Congress of the same year, declared that "acting upon its advice, we have organized ourselves in the United States in conformity with the conditions and circumstances surrounding us." This is a characteristic error, because the social revolutionaries of European origin only showed to what extent they were out of touch with the essential features of the American scene. It is apparent that on the basic question of the use of force the Chicago gathering was not prepared to go as far as the London Congress. True, the general principle of arming the workers was accepted, but apart from the blanket endorsement of the London Congress there was no positive recognition of insurrectional deeds.

Among other resolutions of the Chicago conference, one more deserves notice. This declared that in the future *Liberty,* published in Boston, the *Vorbote* and the *Nye Tid* in Chicago were to be recognized as "organs of the party." This offers further proof of the lack of definite direction among the social-revolutionaries. *Liberty,* edited by Benjamin Tucker was, from its establishment in August, 1881, strictly a philosophical anarchist publication. [51]

For a scheme of organization the Chicago gathering turned to the London Congress, and adopted a highly federative plan. The new organization, which was finally given the name Revolutionary Socialistic Party, was to consist of all organized groups accepting the "revolutionary principles adopted by this Congress." When it first convened, the gathering bore the name American Congress of the International Workingmen's Association. Then it was described as the National Socialistic Congress. Other names submitted, applied and finally discarded, were "International Working People's Association," "Communistic Revolutionary Association" and "Revolutionary Socialistic Labor Party."

A group could be formed by five persons, and all groups were to enjoy full autonomy. No coercive pressure could be brought to bear upon them. To co-ordinate their activities and provide a medium of common contact, an Information Bureau, with secretaries for different languages, was to be established at Chicago. This bureau, possessing no executive power, was to be supported by the voluntary contributions of the groups. Ten groups had the right to call a national convention. The federative body thus established was almost formless, and the extent to which the revolutionary groups were unified by it is illustrated by the fact that the Information Bureau did not come into existence until 1883.

It was hoped by the majority that the Chicago Congress would act as the catalyst creating unity along the revolutionary front. The *Vorbote,* of course, issued a strong plea for union, and complained of the disintegrating elements which always seemed to beset the movement. The English-language press of the city, however, refused to take the gathering of revolutionaries seriously. The Chicago *Tribune* declared, as might be expected, that socialistic beliefs were a menace to society and should be suppressed.[52] But when the congress was over, it dismissed its resolutions and recommendations as "a bombastic fulmination as harmless as the barking of a mangy and obnoxious cur, who would be summarily dealt with should he venture to show his teeth. The Revolutionary Socialists will not disturb anyone with their talk about guns." [53]

The Chicago gathering did not unify the revolutionary groups throughout the country or give them an unqualified anarchistic direction. Though the platform of the London Congress was approved, this action implied little more than the partial acceptance by socialists of the utility of force as a method of action. The adoption of a form of organization which was anarchistic in character may be explained on the ground that the groups were attracted by the federative principle because they feared that through an organization possessing real authority they might be brought back into the fold of orthodox Socialism. The vagueness of doctrine which is so typical of the movement of 1881 remains a notable characteristic for some years to come, and further indicates the lack of orientation. This may be ascribed to the desire to capture as many different revolutionary elements as possible. A careful enunciation of principles would defeat such a purpose. Having broken with the social-democrats over the related problems of constitutional, parliamentary action and violence, the social-revolutionaries remained nevertheless essentially socialists. Most of them were Germans, and the amount of basic anarchistic literature in their tongue available in America in 1880-1881 was small.[54] Several years were to elapse before a considerable body of European anarchist-communist thought found its way across the Atlantic in a form suitable for public consumption.[55] The relatively large body of anarchist literature produced by Americans during the course of the nineteenth century exerted an amazingly slight influence upon the social-revolutionaries.

Through the work of men like Josiah Warren, Stephen Pearl Andrews, Ezra Haywood, Lysander Spooner and, later, Benjamin R. Tucker, America made a distinct and characteristic contribution in the field of anarchist thought. These men, especially Josiah Warren, elaborated systems of individualistic or philosophic Anarchism, the roots of which are sunk deep in American soil. In their positive demand for complete individual liberty and their absolute opposition to the State and all other coercive or restrictive social institutions, these men were thoroughgoing anarchists. Their concern with individual sovereignty and their rejection of government sprang from eighteenth century concepts and the American environment. The thought of these Americans was diametrically opposed to Marxism. Their closest nineteenth century European counterpart is Proudhon, much of whose work was anticipated by Josiah Warren, who in many respects outstripped his famous French contemporary.

The doctrines of individual Anarchism had little attraction for the revolutionaries who had broken away from the S.L.P. Nor did they find a following of any consequence in the American labor movement. Only among intellectual circles were converts made. Not until the middle of the 'eighties and the following decade did a philosophic anarchistic movement of any significance flourish, and this was due largely to the labor of Tucker. When American social-revolutionaries finally turned to Anarchism, they found the teachings of quite another school more to their taste—that of Anarchist-communism. This, like Marxian Socialism, was carried over bodily to the United States from Europe.[56]

NOTES CHAPTER III

1. For the Utopian movement of the earlier portion of the century and the German socialist movement between the close of the 'forties and the Civil War, see Morris Hillquit, *History of Socialism in the United States*, fifth edition, New York, 1910, Part I and pp. 143-155; A. Sartorius Freehern von Waltershausen, *Der Moderne Sozialismus in den Vereinigten Staaten von Amerika*, Berlin, 1890, chap. II.
2. Herbert L. Osgood, "Scientific Anarchism," *Political Science Quarterly*, vol. 4, no. 1, March, 1889, pp. 31-32; Edmund J. James, "Socialists and Anarchists in the United States," *Our Day*, vol. 1, no. 2, February, 1888, pp. 88-94.
3. James C. Sylvis, *The Life, Speeches, Labors and Essays of William H. Sylvis*, Philadelphia, 1872; there is a dispute as to whether Uriah S. Stephens, founder of the Knights of Labor, was similarly influenced; he seems not to have been. Justus Ebert, *American Industrial Revolution. From the Frontier to the Factory; Its Social and Political Effects*, New York, 1907, p. 59; Commons,

op. cit., vol. 2, p. 197 and note; Ware, *op. cit.,* p. 27. On the "socialistic" aspects of the platform of the Knights of Labor, see Paul Frederick Brissenden, *The I.W.W. A Study of American Syndicalism* (Columbia *Studies in History, Economics and Public Law,* vol. 83), New York, 1919, chap. I; John Graham Brooks, *American Syndicalism. The I.W.W.,* New York, 1913, chap. I.

4. *Rep. of the Sen. Com. on Lab.,* vol. 1, p. 374.

5. *Ibid.,* vol. 1, p. 412. This was W. H. Foster.

6. *Ibid.,* vol. 1, p. 525; Hillquit, *op. cit.,* pp. 170, 172-173. The National Labor Union, 1866-1872, was the national expression of the post-Civil War labor movement. It was politically minded from its very inception.

7. Hillquit, *op. cit.,* pp. 168-170, 173, 177-181; Sartorius von Waltershausen, *op. cit.,* chap. III *passim;* Commons, *op. cit.,* vol. 2, pp. 206-212; *Report of the Fourth Annual Congress of the International Working Men's Association, Held at Basle, in Switzerland. From the 6th to the 11th September, 1869,* London (1869?), p. 23.

8. Michael Bakunin (1814-1876), like several other Russian revolutionaries, was of aristocratic birth. In the 1840's he came under Hegelian influences, and was also affected by Proudhonian and early Marxist thought. After becoming involved in the Dresden uprising of 1849, he was imprisoned in Siberia by the Russian government. He managed to escape, however, in 1861, and shortly afterwards he organized the secret International Alliance of Secret Democracy. He joined the First International in 1868, and his presence led to a sharp division between the Marxists and the advocates of his more uncompromising revolutionary theories which contributed to the decline of the International. He was in many respects a profound thinker, and the common appellation given to him, "Disciple of Violence," is neither correct nor representative of his significance. He was a thoroughgoing anti-authoritarian, directing his attack especially against the State and religion. He proposed the overthrow of the existing State by a mass uprising, inspired and led by small, secret groups, and the establishment of a voluntary, federalistic, collectivist (i.e., anarchist-collectivist) social order.

9. Hillquit, *op. cit.,* pp. 181-188; Commons, *op. cit.,* vol. 2, pp. 215-222; Ernest Ludlow Bogart and Charles Manfred Thompson, *The Industrial State, 1870-1893 (The Centennial History of Illinois,* vol. 4), Chicago, 1922, pp. 439-441; Sartorius von Waltershausen, *op. cit.,* chap. IV, *passim.*

10. Hillquit, *op. cit.,* pp. 188-192; Commons, *op. cit.,* vol. 2, pp. 269-277 *passim.*

11. This section on the *Lehr und Wehr Vereine* and the other armed societies is based upon: *Vorbote,* June 26, 1875; *Alarm,* January 9, 1885; Chicago *Inter Ocean,* August 6, 1900; John Ehlert, "Anarchists in Chicago," *America. A Journal of To-Day,* Chicago, vol. 1, no. 34, November 22, 1888, p. 2; Sartorius von Walters-

hausen, *op. cit.*, pp. 158-160; Hillquit, *op. cit.*, p. 213; Nathan Fine, *Labor and Farmer Parties in the United States, 1828-1928,* New York, 1928, pp. 106-109; Commons, *op. cit.*, vol. 2, pp. 280-281; Ebert, *op. cit.*, pp. 62-64 *passim.*

12. See below, pp. 65-67.
13. See below, pp. 66-67.
14. For the "exceptional laws" see William H. Dawson, *The German Empire, 1867-1914, and the Unity Movement,* 2 vols. London, 1919, vol. 1, chap. XII, *passim;* Commons, *op. cit.*, vol. 2, p. 288.
15. Ehlert, *loc. cit.*, p. 2; Edward B. Mittelman, "Chicago Labor in Politics 1877-96," *The Journal of Political Economy,* vol. 28, no. 5, May, 1920, pp. 415-417 *passim; Life of Albert R. Parsons* (George A. Schilling, "History of the Labor Movement in Chicago"), pp. xxviii-xxix; Sartorius von Waltershausen, *op. cit.*, pp. 162-164; Commons, *op. cit.*, vol. 2, pp. 287-288; Ebert, *op. cit.*, p. 63.
16. Knauer and Wytzca were also leading members in the club.
17. In Boston, there appeared in January, 1881, *The Anarchist,* designed to serve the revolutionary groups.
18. Sartorius von Waltershausen, *op. cit.*, p. 169.
19. For the social-revolutionary clubs see: *ibid.*, pp. 161-162, 169-175 *passim; Liberty,* vol. 4, no. 2, May 1, 1886 (Letter of M. Bachmann), p. 8; Max Nettlau, *Anarchisten und Sozial-Revolutionäre. Die historische Entwicklung des Anarchismus in den Jahren 1880-1886. (Beiträge zur Geschichte des Sozialismus, Syndikalismus, Anarchismus,* Band V), Berlin, 1931, pp. 376-377; Rudolph Rocker, *Johann Most, das Leben eines Rebellen,* Berlin, 1924, pp. 141-142; Ebert, *op. cit.*, pp. 62-63; Hillquit, *op. cit.*, pp. 213-214; Commons, *op. cit.*, vol. 2, p. 291; Fine, *op. cit.*, p. 110; Richard T. Ely, *Recent American Socialism (Johns Hopkins University Studies in Historical and Political Science,* Third Series, vol. 4), Baltimore, 1885, pp. 21-24.
20. Yu Steklov, *The History of the First International,* translated by Eden and Cedar Paul, New York, 1928, pp. 339, 349-350; Rocker, *op. cit.*, pp. 123-124. Steklov would have "the very name of the International . . . forgotten," while Rudolf Rocker states with more reason that its traditions were very much alive.
21. Peter Kropotkin (1842-1921), born Prince Peter Alexeyevich, was not only one of the leading anarchists of his day, but also made a mark for himself as a scientist and sociologist. He attempted to establish a theory of Anarchism upon a scientific basis, and conceived a communist-anarchist order of the future arising out of the voluntary association of groups and federations. An individual's co-operation in production would guarantee his right to existence. He left it to the individual to judge his own needs, and concluded that in the social order which he envisaged that the obligation to work would be spontaneous. The range of his interests was unusual, and his writings embrace noteworthy studies in geography,

anthropology, Russian literature, ethics, the French Revolution, political science, and, of course, anarchist doctrine. Jacques Elisée Reclus (1830-1905) was in close touch for several years with Kropotkin. He was a Frenchman, and throughout his life was connected with the revolutionary movement in Europe. He, too, was an anarchist, and did notable work in geography. He also dreamt of a social order based upon voluntary co-operation. Carlo Cafiero, who came from a rich aristocratic Italian family, dedicated his life and fortune to a revolutionary career. He was associated first with Bakunin and later with Malatesta, and participated in the anarchist uprisings in Italy in 1874 and 1877. He was an anarchist-communist. The strain of his life and its disappointments affected his mind, and he died in an asylum in the 'eighties.

22. See below, pp. 83-86.

23. Errico Malatesta (1853-1932), the Italian anarchist, is the best known and most important of this group of revolutionaries. His participation in a student demonstration led to his expulsion from medical school, and he took up the trade of electrician. In 1872 he became a member of the First International. After the death of Bakunin he was among the most influential anarchist agitators and conspirators. He toured extensively in the United States, South America and Europe. He differed fundamentally from Bakunin on the nature of the social order of the future in that he was an anarchist-communist. He received rough treatment at the hands of Italian Fascists shortly after the "March on Rome," but was little molested during the closing years of his life by the Blackshirts.

24. Steklov, *op. cit.*, pp. 350-351; Rocker, *op. cit.*, pp. 123-124.

25. Steklov, *op. cit.*, pp. 351-353; Rocker, *op. cit.*, pp. 124-125; *Le Révolté*, April 30, 1881.

26. *Le Révolté*, July 23, 1881. Steklov is probably justified in declaring that "In reality, with the exception of the Spanish Federation, not even one solid organization was numbered among those participating in the congress." *Op cit.*, p. 355.

27. *Le Révolté*, July 23, 1881; Nettlau, *op. cit.*, p. 376.

28. *Le Révolté*, July 23, 1881; Rocker, *op. cit.*, p. 357. The Pittsburgh Congress of 1883 was to come to a similar conclusion regarding the form of organization of the revolutionary bodies in the United States. See below, pp. 94, 108.

29. *Le Révolté*, July 23, 1881 (author's translation); Steklov, *op. cit.*, pp. 359-360.

30. The Congress of Berne was held by anarchists, October 26 to 29, 1876, who called it the "Eighth Congress of the International Workingmen's Association."

31. The Jura Federation, after the expulsion of Bakunin from the International, became a focal point of Bakuninist Anarchism and the center of revolutionary anarchist propaganda. It embraced the anarchist sections in the valley of the Rhone and Southern France.

It tended to regard itself as the successor of the disintegrated International.

32. Félix Dubois, *Le Péril anarchiste*, Paris, 1894, pp. 153, 155; E. V. Zenker, *Anarchism, A Criticism and History of the Anarchist Theory*, New York, 1897, pp. 273-274; *Alarm*, January 28, 1888; this contains Lefrancais' "Where Are the Anarchists Going?" translated by J. F. Kelly; the rest of the pamphlet is in the *Alarm* of December 31, 1887 and January 14, 1888; R. Garraud, *L'anarchie et la répression*, Paris, 1895, pp. 10-11; Sartorius von Waltershausen, *op. cit.*, pp. 183-184.

33. See the comments on this point in Peter Kropotkin, *Memoirs of a Revolutionist*, Boston, 1899; Louise Michel, *Mémoires*, Paris, 1886; Rocker, *op. cit.*, p. 128.

34. Paul Eltzbacher, *Anarchism*, translated by Steven T. Byington, New York, 1908, pp. 132-138 *passim*.

35. *Le Révolté*, July 23, 1881.

36. Steklov, *op. cit.*, pp. 356-357.

37. *Ibid.*, p. 356; *cf.* Rocker, *op. cit.*, p. 129.

38. July 23, 1881.

39. Chicago *Tribune*, October 22, 1881.

40. *Ibid.*, October 21, 1881.

41. See below, pp. 330-331 for brief sketch of his life.

42. Perhaps one other delegate was also a Chicagoan. In some cases it is extremely difficult to determine the exact relationship between delegates and groups. At least three Chicagoans represented groups from other sections by proxy.

43. The cities were Chicago, Milwaukee, Kansas City, Omaha, St. Louis, Louisville, Ky., Jersey City Heights, Union Hill, Hoboken and Paterson, all in New Jersey, Philadelphia, Boston and New York. Iowa seems to have had a general delegate at large in E. C. Walker. If there were real social-revolutionary groups in all these urban centers, it could be assumed that the movement had grown since 1880. But these groups, strictly speaking, did not have a great deal in common, as it will later appear. The sources for this analysis of groups, delegates, etc., are Chicago *Tribune*, October 22, 1881 and *Vorbote*, October 29, 1881. The latter is the fullest source for the congress. Material is also to be found in the *Tribune* for the dates given and October 24, 1881; *Fackel*, October 30, 1881. For other accounts, frequently in disagreement with the one which follows, see: Nettlau, *op cit.*, pp. 376-377; Rocker, *op. cit.*, p. 129; Fine, *op. cit.*, p. 110; Commons, vol. 2, *op. cit.*, pp. 291-292; Hillquit, *op. cit.*, p. 214; Sartorius von Waltershausen, *op. cit.*, pp. 176-177.

44. The platform committee, for example, was composed of Albert R. Parsons, August Spies, William Blum and P. Peterson of Chicago, Justus Schwab of New York and Joseph H. Swain of Boston. Spies and Parsons were diametrically opposed to the other Chicagoans on the committee on several major points. Swain, an

American individualist anarchist, seemingly a follower of Warren and Tucker, appears to have been badly out of place in the Chicago gathering.

45. Another delegate spoke of "revolutionizing" the people.

46. These arguments are all to be found in the *Vorbote*. The quoted sections are the author's translation; certain sections of the arguments are simply paraphrased. Compare the utterances of Spies and Parsons with their attitude on the same question three years later. Swain, who also spoke, argued on different grounds against any political activity. As a thoroughgoing anti-authoritarian he seemed to favor the complete withdrawal of all people from all activities related to government "as long as the capitalistic system rules . . ."

47. See p. 73, however, for their theoretical approval of political action.

48. It is not without significance that the strength of the anti-trade-union wing is not indicated in the report in the *Vorbote*. The Chicago *Tribune*, October 24, 1881, contains material which it would have been unwise to print in the *Vorbote*.

49. This last has evidently led previous students to conclude that the political plank was completely rejected. *Cf.* Commons, *op. cit.*, vol. 2, p. 292.

50. August Spies was opposed to this resolution.

51. See below, pp. 75-76.

52. October 23, 1881.

53. October 25, 1881.

54. Rocker, *op. cit.*, p. 142.

55. See below, pp. 101-102.

56. See, William Bailie, *Josiah Warren, The First American Anarchist. A Sociological Study*, Boston, 1906; Josiah Warren, *Practical Details in Equitable Commerce*, New York, 1852; Stephen Pearl Andrews, *The Science of Society*, Boston, 1888; William B. Greene, *Mutual Banking*, New York, 1870. Benjamin R. Tucker, *Instead of a Book. By a Man Too Busy to Write One. A Fragmentary Exposition of Philosophical Anarchism*, New York, 1893; Eltzbacher, *op. cit.*, chaps. I, VIII, X; Zenker, *op. cit.*, chap. VI; Paul Ghio, *L'anarchisme aux Etats-Unis*, Paris, 1903; Eunice Minette Schuster, *Native American Anarchism. A Study of Left-Wing American Individualism* (Smith College Studies in History, vol. 17, nos. 1-4, October, 1931-July, 1932), Northampton, Mass.; files of *Liberty*, 1881-1893.

IV. THE PITTSBURGH CONGRESS

AFTER the Chicago convention the social-revolutionary movement displayed little vitality. It had no cohesion, and its members had not yet oriented themselves. Their tentative groping was reflected in their failure to carry out some of the recommendations and resolutions of the convention. The Social Revolutionary Club of New York, which had supplied the initial stimulus for national organization, now showed no eagerness to establish the Information Bureau. Within the group itself, differences were beginning to arise which caused an open split a little more than a year later. At the same time the Chicago social-revolutionaries could not deny themselves another try at politics.

In the spring of 1881, the two socialist factions in Chicago each nominated a candidate for mayor. Those who had sufficiently broken with the S.L.P. to be classed as social-revolutionaries supported Timothy O'Meara; the other candidate, George A. Schilling, was nominated by socialists who had earlier cooperated with the Greenback Party. Both factions were so occupied destroying one another that they forgot about the "common enemy," and their candidates were miserably beaten.

Labor and socialist elements, however, were by no means through with politics. In 1882, the Trades Assembly of Chicago, forerunner of the Chicago Federation of Labor, put up its own ticket for the legislature under the name of the United Labor Party. At the same time a local Anti-Monopoly Party made up of greenbackers, anti-monopolists, single-taxers, prohibitionists, women suffragists, Knights of Labor, and socialists also entered the field. The support which the socialists gave was in a sense unfortunate, for they simply brought into the Anti-Monopoly fold the division over political action which was splitting their own ranks. Nothing could bring the Trades Assembly to cooperate with the anti-monopolists, and failure was fore-ordained. The campaign lacked all life, and as it drew to a close, candidates of both parties began to withdraw their names. Thus Albert Parsons and George Schilling withdrew from the Trades Assembly and the Anti-Monopoly tickets respectively. The remaining candidates were of course badly defeated. The results of the 1881 and 1882 elections cured the socialist extremists, temporarily at least, of any remaining belief in the efficacy of political action even as an instrument of agitation. During the course of 1882, a central committee for the co-ordination of the radical groups was established in Chicago but it was given no real power. The strength of the trade union sentiment was indicated by the representation granted to labor organizations of radical character in the central committee.[1]

Not until Johann Most arrived in the United States from England in mid-December, 1882, did the social-revolutionary movement acquire real vitality and some measure of cohesiveness. When Most reached America he was thirty-six years old, and had already lived a full life. He had just completed sixteen months of imprisonment at hard labor in England for the publication of an editorial in praise of the assassination of Czar Alexander II in March, 1881. This was his fifth experience with European prisons. A series of occurrences had served to make his youth particularly unhappy. The early death of his mother and his father's remarriage brought him much unhappiness. Due to an early operation a swelling developed on the left side of his face which disfigured him, and made him the butt of cruel remarks. His sensitiveness heightened the suffering he experienced on this score. His *Wanderjahr,* instead of bringing relief, meant further misery. All of this produced an intensely embittered young man who remembered his child-hood as a "nightmare," his youth as a period of constant hu-miliation, and who was beginning to think of his existence as a martyrdom to society. Were it not for his crooked face and unhappy childhood, there might have been no Johann Most, the social rebel.

A short stay in Switzerland led to his introduction to the recently formed International. In 1868 he left for Vienna, and the following year served the first of his prison sentences for radical activities, a one month term for an incendiary address. In 1870, as a result of his participation in a monster demon-stration demanding free speech, press and assembly, he was sentenced to five years' imprisonment, but was soon released. Within a few months he was expelled from Austria, and by June of 1871 he was back in Germany engaged in editorial work. In this field he displayed decided talents, and most of his subsequent career was given over to editorial activities.

Most remained in Germany until 1878, and during those seven years became further acquainted with Marxian thought. Though he is frequently credited with being an able student of Marx, this judgment may be questioned. He was sufficiently active in the most extreme of the socialist factions to merit three encounters with the police and the law, and jail visits of varying lengths. During the same period, however, he was twice elected to the Reichstag, once in 1874 and then in 1877. His third arrest in 1878 was followed by his expulsion from Germany under the anti-socialist laws. Of the two European countries in which radicals enjoyed relative peace from police molestation, Switzerland and England, Most chose the latter. In London he soon published a German socialist weekly *Die Freiheit*. His extreme views were regarded with suspicion by the more orthodox socialists, and both he and his journal were expressly disavowed by Liebknecht on behalf of the German Social-Democracy.

In London he received his first initiation into anarchist thought. He had no solid grounding in anarchist philosophy, but was undoubtedly attracted by its general indictment of the State and the Church. As a youth he had had an unfortunate experience with a parish priest, and to this there may perhaps be traced, in part, his life-long hatred of the Church. At about the same time he came under the influence of that phase of Bakunin's thought which resulted from the latter's association with the psychopathic Sergei Netchaev.[2] He was probably acquainted with the brutal revolutionary ethics of the phrenetic "Revolutionary Catechism" which was either a product of Netchaev's mad pen or was written by Bakunin under the former's influence.[3] But if he was not directly acquainted with Netchaev's revolutionary philosophy, aptly called "political sadism," he must have been cognisant of its essentials through contact with Russian terrorists.

By 1880, Most was so much out of tune with "orthodox" socialist doctrine that he was expelled from the Social Democratic Party in its convention of that year. In the following year there appeared his editorial in praise of Alexander II's assassination, and he was once more imprisoned.[4] When Most was released at the close of October, 1882, he quickly accepted the invitation of the New York Social Revolutionary Club to undertake a tour of the United States. At the same time he arranged to have the *Freiheit* appear in New York. When he disembarked at that city on December 18, after an unusually long voyage on the *Wisconsin*, Justus Schwab had already put out two numbers of the *Freiheit* with material supplied by Most before his departure.[5]

The social-revolutionary movement in this country needed a man like Most. He was a vigorous writer, and whatever he lacked in polish was made up for by his uncompromising resoluteness. His true métier was the militant journalist. In controversy, he was exceedingly pugnacious, and treated his opponents without courtesy, not hesitating to descend to personalities. He himself was merciless, and his pen was stinging. As a speaker Most was very popular. His incisive energy, remarkable voice and quick sense of the dramatic made him a forceful figure on the platform. Amazingly self-centered, he was immediately distrustful of those who disagreed with him. He was almost always impatient of the slightest compromise. He could quarrel suddenly—and with great bitterness—with the closest of friends. People fell into two categories in Most's eyes: they were either supporters or enemies. He felt that he "Who is not with me is against me." Utterly convinced of the proximity of the social revolution, his very certainty carried conviction. At the time he arrived in America, Most was a whole-hearted advocate of individual insurrectional deeds. Later he began to doubt the efficacy of such revolutionary tactics, and even condemned Alexander Berkman's attempt on the life of H. C. Frick in 1892. He possessed the talent to become a revolutionary general, though, perhaps, a temperamental one, yet throughout his life he lacked a significant army of followers.

Most was never prepossessing in appearance. To a reporter of the New York *Tribune* who was present when he landed, he was simply "a small, slender man about five feet four inches in height, with light hair and a full beard and mustache." His hair already was slightly streaked with grey.[6] The reception committee at the pier was very small, but this was probably due to the uncertainty of the *Wisconsin's* arrival. Taken in tow by the faithful Justus Schwab, derisively labelled the "lager beer man" by the New York *Herald,* Most was first welcomed by socialist compatriots in Hoboken. The meeting held in his honor that night at the Cooper Union Institute was a striking success. The hall was jammed, and by eight o'clock there was no longer even standing-room available. The enthusiastic audience came prepared to cheer and applaud, and it did. After apologizing in broken English for his inability to use that language, Most spoke at length in German, informing his audience that he had come to organize the socialist movement in this country. He conveyed to them expressions of sympathy from the workers of Europe, and, in describing conditions abroad, reaffirmed his faith in the proximity of the

social revolution. Two days later he started for Chicago, the
first step of his lecture tour.[7]

Most's reception by the New York press is interesting.

"The influence of Socialists in this country," declared the
New York *Tribune,* "is plainly growing weaker. . . . It is
with difficulty that the Socialists of this city have been able
to keep themselves before the public, although they never lose
an opportunity to bring themselves into notice. Yesterday they
. . . paraded the streets flying red flags as if the public were
a wild bull to be goaded into madness. They excited, however,
only derision and laughter, even among the workmen. . . .
The occasion of the demonstration was the arrival of the German agitator John Most. This man's sole claim to notoriety
seems to be that he is a foreigner who has been in jail about
a dozen times. Probably if he had his deserts he would be there
still." [8]

A day later, undertaking to destroy completely Socialism and
Most, the *Tribune* announced that

"The average Socialist in certain respects presents a strong
likeness to the cuttlefish. When pressed with searching questions concerning his beliefs, he emits a discharge of dark and
mysterious generalities and indefinite platitudes under which
he makes good his retreat. A fair example of this is to be found
in the utterances of Herr Most. . . .

"As a cuttlefish with a natural talent for evasion and a
slimy coldbloodedness . . . Herr Most is a success."

Considering the weakness of the movement, Most's tour
of the country was successful. The gatherings he addressed
were well attended, converts were made and new groups were
formed. He gave, without question, a distinct impulse to the
extreme revolutionary movement, and many members of the
S.L.P. affiliated themselves with the social-revolutionary clubs.[9]

These groups are commonly described as anarchistic, and
an outspoken revolutionary anarchist movement in the United
States is usually dated from Most's arrival.[10] The justification

for these judgments appears to lie in the fact that Most spoke of himself as an anarchist, and some of the groups used the same term in self-description. There is no positive evidence, however, which points to a change in the rather poorly developed ideology of the social-revolutionary clubs or in the nature of their membership. In so far as some of the groups were anti-authoritarian, they were anarchistic. But there is no ground for assuming more than this. The mental confusion characteristic of this phase of the American radical movement will be discussed later, and it is sufficient here to warn against the tendency to regard this movement as a clear-cut anarchistic one at this date.[11]

Most's tour and the growing circulation of the *Freiheit* resulted in a broadening of the insurrectional tendency, in which respect the American movement was following in the path of the European. In March, 1883, a portion of the *Revolutionary Catechism* was reprinted in the *Freiheit* under the heading "Revolutionary Principles." "For him [the revolutionist]," reads one brief section, "there is only one pleasure, one comfort, one recompense: the success of the revolution. Day and night he may cherish only one thought, only one purpose, viz., inexorable destruction. While he pursues this purpose without rest and in cold blood, he must be ready to die, and equally ready to kill everyone with his own hands, who hinders him in the attainment of this purpose. . . ."[12] In the following month, an article titled *"Praktische Winke"* dealt with the preparation, handling and exploding of dynamite.[13] The May 5 number contained a typical article on violence which bears the heading *"Dynamit,"* and in June, the readers of the *Freiheit* were told how to manufacture nitroglycerine.[14] There can be no doubt about Most's work in encouraging the existing willingness to employ force.

Most was anxious to unite the groups throughout the country. More than this, he was eager to align all anti-authoritarians and all social-revolutionists for common action. The obvious mechanism for such an accomplishment was a national congress, and this was an early concern of his.[15] At the same time, however, his own forceful personality was capable of creating a division wherever he found himself, and within three months of his arrival he had caused a rupture in the New York Social Revolutionary Club, which broke into two factions.[16]

A partial step toward unifying the social-revolutionary elements came with the final establishment early in April, 1883, of the National Information Bureau so optimistically provided for at the Chicago gathering in 1881. The body was given the name Information Bureau of the Socialist Federation of North America, and secretaries were elected for the different languages.[17] In accordance with the conditions set in 1881 the bureau possessed no executive power. The event that brought it into being was a meeting of Chicago revolutionaries at which August Spies and Paul Grottkau, who had made a trip through the country, asserted that there was a strong feeling favoring its creation. They also reported the existence of groups in New York, Philadelphia, Roxborough, Alleghany City, Salenville, Omaha, Kansas City, St. Louis, Cincinnati, Cleveland, Baltimore, Louisville, Detroit, Buffalo, and other urban centers.[18]

As late as June, 1883, no decision had been made as to when a national congress would be held. Two months later, however, the recently formed Information Bureau of the American Federation of Socialists (as its title now ran) announced through all available channels the forthcoming "Congress of the Socialists of North America," scheduled to convene in Pittsburgh on October 14.[19] A circular addressed "To the Socialists of North America" issued from Chicago by the Information Bureau on August 15, declared that socialists, "who should be the pioneers of Labor in the great Social War," were doing very little to aid the people in their struggle against the "oligarchie" which was ruling the country. In the midst of conditions which were constantly becoming worse, the socialists

"seem to be only partially cognizant of their mission. Some look indifferently upon the development of things and live in obscurity, instead of grasping every opportunity that is offered for the furtherance and promulgation of our ideas and the formation of organizations to prepare that force which is destined to abolish the infamous institutions of oppression of today, and class-rule in whatever form it may appear.

"What is the cause of this indifference?

"COMRADES: It is the deplorable dissension of the elements, who are all working for the same end.

"Let us put an end to this state of affairs. Let all those who have the cause of their oppressed class at heart, and who are sincere and earnest about it, meet in counsel and agree upon a uniform, practical and effective organization and agitation."

The Congress at Pittsburgh was to remedy this condition, and therefore, its primary task was the creation of the greatest possible unity among all socialist forces.[20] Three major items were placed on the tentative agenda. First, a report on the existing condition of the revolutionary "party" throughout the land was to be submitted; second, the "best method for giving greater currency to the idea of revolutionary socialism in this country" and for insuring victory for the cause was to be determined; and third, the broad questions of organization, agitation and the "party-press" to be discussed. Most, Paul Grottkau, and the others who exerted themselves to make the Pittsburgh Congress more than a mere gesture, appear to have felt that all their labor would be fully repaid if it gave the revolutionary groups, existing on a purely local basis, greater effectiveness through some form of voluntary union.[21]

Among other features, the Pittsburgh Congress was characterized by the mediocrity of its delegates.[22] Of the twenty-six present when it opened at nine o'clock Sunday morning, October 14, only three, Johann Most, Albert Parsons and August Spies, possessed distinction, and of these, the fiery Most, despite his limitations, was the ablest. In all, twenty-six groups scattered through eleven states, New York, Connecticut, Massachusetts, New Jersey, Pennsylvania, Maryland, Ohio, Illinois, Missouri, Wisconsin and Nebraska, were unequally represented. Chicago and New York enjoyed the heaviest representation—the first by five and the second by four delegates. Several delegates were empowered to represent more than one group, submit their recommendations, and vote for them by proxy. With the exception of two (or at most three) the delegates were all German, and the proceedings were carried on in English and German.

It is impossible to estimate accurately the total membership of the revolutionary groups participating in the Congress. That there were far less than 7,000 members is certain, for that is the number claimed by Parsons in 1885 after two years of propaganda and organization. An examination of the groups represented indicates only a slight penetration of "revolutionary Socialism" in centers such as Cincinnati, Chicago, Pittsburgh, Philadelphia, Milwaukee, Paterson, Cleveland, St. Louis, and New York. Chicago apart, the only reason for its strength in the Middle West appears to lie in the heavy German population of that region.

Chicago and New York were the two foci of the social-revolutionary movement. In both cities there existed conditions which made possible the emergence and growth of such a movement. It is not surprising that it took extremely slight root elsewhere, while flourishing to the degree it did in Chicago and New York. New York City was not only an industrial center, but its working population was heterogeneous and relatively lacking in what might be called a traditional American ideology. The city offered a closer approximation to a European urban center than any other in the country. Its foreign population, recalling the abuses which had caused their migration from the Old World, were quick to resent the duplication of European conditions here. New York was likewise the first American home of Socialism and Internationalism. During the 'seventies and 'eighties, due to the police policies of the continental States, it received a steady stream of actual or potential revolutionaries. Finally, it was the headquarters of Johann Most and the *Freiheit*.

Chicago also had an unusually heavy foreign population. The German colony, both large and influential, was effective in giving the city a current of socialistic thought. Socialist doctrines had successfully penetrated the circles of organized labor, and unusually friendly relationships obtained even between conservative labor leaders and radicals. The early success of the Socialist Labor Party had served to attract many into the revolutionary camp. The heterogeneous wage-earning population of the city did not live under the best of conditions, and the antagonism between large sections of the working-class and police provided a fertile field for radical propaganda. The atmosphere of the city, as Willis J. Abbot has remarked, especially during the period under consideration, was "highly stimulative to radical economic thought. In some degree this is doubtless due to the rapidity with which some men have grown rich, their sudden rise to fortune awakening in the minds of the less fortunate observers jealousy, resentment, and doubt of the system under which such sudden wealth could be accumulated." Chicago also had had an extensive history of violence in industrial disturbances from the memorable troubles of 1877 on. These factors explain the leading part played by the Windy City in the social-revolutionary movement.[23]

It was early apparent that the delegates to the Congress were opposed to any method of spreading their revolutionary ideas that was colored, however slightly, by legitimate political action or willingness to compromise. The instructions of the different groups to their delegates were unanimous on this point. Firmly persuaded that it was a monstrous error to regard the ballot as a solution for social ills, the social-revolutionaries were convinced that the short-lived political parties with which they had flirted were false will-o'-the-wisps. "Compromise," as expressed in the minimum demands of workers' parties for shorter hours, higher wages, better working conditions and the like, in the arbitration of disputes between workers and employers, and in any affiliation of workingmen with capitalistic parties and press, they held to be pointless and ineffectual.

At best such demands, ignoring the heart of the social problem, were petty and superficial. They were merely illusions of palliative reform.[24]

The abandonment of legal methods implies a recognition of the class-struggle as a conflict essentially violent in nature. This point was pressed home by Most in an article titled *"Unsere Grundsätze"* ("Our Fundamentals") in the *Freiheit* the day before the Congress convened. The Congress was strongly influenced by the reasoning and conclusions of this article. Since any serious attempt on the part of the workers to better their condition meets with repression and consequent failure, wrote Most, "it is only self-evident that the struggle of the proletariat against the bourgeoisie must have a violent revolutionary character, and the wage struggle alone will not lead us to our goal."

Recommendations for the arming of the working class were presented in behalf of the Milwaukee, Chicago, Pittsburgh, Baltimore, Philadelphia, Paterson, and New York groups among others. Several groups, the Chicago *Jägerverein* among them, also urged that the proletariat be armed "with the most recent scientific knowledge, especially in the field of chemistry," in addition to rifles and revolvers. This note becomes increasingly common later, and its importance must be fully recognized. It was one thing for workers to arm in answer to what they regarded as capitalistic aggression manifested in the actions of the police and militia and the employment of Pinkertons. But the use of dynamite by the working class was quite another matter.

All the groups were so eager to protect their individual autonomy and to prevent the creation of any central body with executive powers that the only type of organization possible was a very loose federation. The general sense of the Congress was reflected in the memorandum of the New York Group No. 1, declaring that any organization which does not wish to have inbedded in it the seed of self-destruction must avoid "the poisoned tree of centralization." The organization must be federalistic in nature. "Every group should be free and independent!" [25] Johann Most was no less opposed to any form of organization which might infringe upon the individuality and independent action of the groups.

The committee on organization [26] brought in the following nine-point plan which was accepted after a rather long debate:

"1. The organization is to consist of federated groups holding to the principles to be contained in the forthcoming proclamation.

"2. Five persons are permitted to form a group.

"3. Every group is to be an autonomous (independent) unit, and is to carry on its agitation and propaganda according to its local needs and understanding, on condition that its agitation and propaganda do not run counter to the principles of the proclamation.

"4. It is recommended that each group take its name from its locality.

"5. Where there are several groups in one locality, it is recommended that they form, without giving it any executive power, a general committee for the purpose of common activity.

"6. An Information Bureau should be established, with secretaries for the different languages, to act as an intermediary for the foreign and domestic groups.

"7. Groups desiring to join the Federation must give to the Information Bureau the number of their members and the recommendation of a neighboring group, and should submit a report to that body every three months.

"8. The agreement of a majority of the groups is necessary for the calling of a Congress.

"9. The expenses of the Information Bureau are to be taken care of by voluntary contributions of the groups."

So carefully had the Congress preserved the autonomous nature of the groups in this frame of organization, that the resulting structure could be little more than amorphous. Had there been a conscious effort to prevent the fusion of the social-revolutionary forces in the country, the Pittsburgh Congress could hardly have been more successful. The model followed was the loose type of federation adopted by the London Congress and by several existing organizations on the Continent. In accordance with the recommendation, the Information Bureau was continued, centered for another year in Chicago.

Disagreement developed over the choice of a name for the new organization. The name International Working People's Association, however, was formally adopted, in spite of the protests of the Chicago delegates, including Spies and Parsons. A majority of the delegates were in agreement on the name even before the Congress convened.

The Chicago delegates proposed to make full use of the trade-unions in effecting the social revolution. Influencing the trade-unions, they would utilize them to "form the advance guard of the coming revolution." A resolution, proposed by Spies and accepted by the Congress with almost complete unanimity, reiterated and amplified this point. It declared that those trade-unions resting upon radical principles and desiring the abolition of wage-labor are to be regarded as the foundation-stones of the social order of the future. They constitute an "army of the oppressed and disinherited" which will be instrumental in destroying the present economic system and instituting a socialized economic order. Such trade-unions, therefore, would receive both the sympathy and support of the I.W.P.A. in their unabating struggle against the "despotism of private capital." At the same time, the I.W.P.A. was determined to oppose all labor organizations of "reactionary" principles, as enemies of labor and obstacles to progress.

This resolution was adopted with few dissenting votes. But it is doubtful whether it reflected the dominant sentiment of the Congress. Among the eastern delegates there were many who appear to have thought that the game of revolution was best played without any formal connection with labor organizations. In the instructions to its delegates, the New York Group No. 1 merely stated that only because the trade-unions made possible the mass organization of the proletariat it was not indifferent to them. But, the instructions continued, revolutionaries must always be extremely critical of labor organizations. They were to join them in order to implant their ideas in them,—"to bore from within." Under no circumstances were "comrades" to concern themselves solely with "petty" questions such as demands for shorter hours and increased wages.[27] Johann Most placed no faith in "trade-union action," but "he was willing to make concessions" in its favor. This resolution, which followed the Manifesto in point of time, was probably offered to the Chicago representatives to compensate for the omission of the trade-union question from the Manifesto.

The Manifesto, addressed "to the Workingmen of America," was the crowning work of the Congress.[28] Spies, Parsons, Drury, Most and Reifgraber composed the committee chosen to draw up the document. The first draft of the Manifesto submitted to the Congress for consideration was based upon Most's *"Unsere Grundsätze."* Changes and additions were recommended by the delegates, and those with the original draft were returned to the committee for revision and completion. When the revised Manifesto was reported to the Congress, it was quickly accepted, and it was voted to publish 100,000 copies of the document in English, 50,000 in German and 10,000 in French. The revision entailed no fundamental changes, and the Pittsburgh Manifesto remained substantially an elaboration of Most's article in the *Freiheit.*

Characteristically enough, the Pittsburgh Manifesto opens with a passage from the Declaration of Independence,—and then goes on to borrow heavily from Marx.

"Fellow Workmen:—The Declaration of Independence says:

" 'But when a long train of abuses and usurpations, pursuing invariably the same object, evinces a design to reduce them (the people), under absolute Despotism, it is *their right,* it is *their duty* to throw off such government and provide new guards for their future security.'

"This thought of Thomas Jefferson was the justification for armed resistance by our forefathers, which gave birth to our Republic, and do not the necessities of the present time compel us to re-assert their declaration?"

Then there follows an analysis of the existing social structure. "Our present society," declares the Manifesto, "is founded upon the exploitation of the propertyless class by the propertied." This exploitation of the working-class by the capitalists takes a form in which the former receive for their labor "the price of the mere cost of existence (wages)," while the latter "take for themselves, i.e., steal the amount of new values (products) which exceeds the prices, whereby wages are made to represent the necessities instead of the earnings of the wage-laborer." Furthermore, the constant increase of technical efficiency and the numbers of the working-class result in an ever sharper competition among workers in the disposal of their labor. This causes the wages of the workers to fall, or at best prevents them from ever rising "above the margin necessary for keeping intact their working ability." This condition creates an impassable gulf between the two classes. While

"the propertyless are entirely debarred from entering the ranks of the propertied, . . . the propertied by means of the ever-increasing plundering of the working class, are becoming richer day by day, without in any way being themselves productive.

"With the accumulation of individual wealth, the greed and power of the propertied grows. They use all the means for competing among themselves for the robbery of the people. In this struggle generally the less-propertied (middle-class) are overcome, while the great capitalists, par excellence, swell their wealth enormously, concentrate entire branches of production as well as trade and intercommunication into their hands and develope [sic] into monopolists. The increase of products, accompanied by simultaneous decrease of the average income of the working mass of the people, leads to so-called 'business' and 'commercial' crises, when the misery of the wage workers is forced to the extreme."

This system, which reduces a constantly growing portion of the working-class to poverty and consequently to " 'crime,' vagabondage, prostitution, suicide, starvation and general depravity," is clearly "unjust, insane and murderous." [29] There is only one cure, and that is "to totally destroy it with and by all means, and with the greatest energy on the part of everyone who suffers by it and who does not want to be made culpable for its continued existence by his inactivity."

The workers can free themselves from "their chains" by "Agitation for the purpose of Organization; organization for the purpose of rebellion." Since all vital working-class movements are met with repression, regardless of country or type of government, the class-struggle must form itself upon international lines. ". . . the victory in the decisive combat of the proletarians against their oppressors can only be gained by the simultaneous struggle along the whole line of the bourgeois (capitalistic) society, . . . therefore the international fraternity of people as expressed in the International Working People's Association presents itself a self-evident necessity."

And what is the true social order that is to be established on the ruins of capitalism? It is one based upon a socialized economic life, which can be established only "when implements of labor, the soil and other premises of production, in short, capital produced by labor, is changed into societary property. Only by this pre-supposition is destroyed every possibility of the future spoliation of man by man. Only by common, undivided capital can all be enabled to enjoy in their fullness the fruits of their common toil." [30]

Obviously, the most serious obstacle to the establishment of this ideal society is the State which is a product of capitalism and which "has no other purpose than the upholding of the present order." Law, the school and the Church, likewise, serve no other interests but those of the capitalist class, insuring its dominance. In his struggle against the existing system and its props, his own efforts are the worker's sole reliance. Because of the very nature of the situation his own efforts must express themselves in terms of force. To wait for the capitalist class to make concessions is ridiculous. Peaceful, legitimate agitation insures failure. And to place dependence upon reform is mere delusion. There is but one remedy,— force.

"If there ever could have been any question on this point it should long ago have been dispelled by the brutalities which the bourgeoisie of all countries—in America as well as in Europe—constantly commits as often as the proletariat anywhere energetically move to better their condition. It becomes, therefore, self-evident that the struggle of the proletariat with the bourgeoisie must have a violent, revolutionary character.

"We could show by scores of illustrations that all attempts in the past to reform this monstrous system by peaceable means, such as the ballot, have been futile, and all such efforts in the future must necessarily be so, for the following reasons:

"The political institutions of our time are the agencies of the propertied class; their mission is the upholding of the privileges of their masters; any reform in your own behalf would curtail these privileges. To this they will not and cannot consent, for it would be suicidal to themselves.

"That they will not resign their privileges voluntarily we know; that they will not make any concessions to us we likewise know. Since we must then rely upon the kindness of our masters for whatever redress we have, and knowing that from them no good may be expected, there remains but one recourse—FORCE! Our forefathers have not only told us that against despots force is justifiable, because it is the only means, but they themselves have set the immemorial example.

"By force our ancestors liberated themselves from political oppression, by force their children will have to liberate themselves from economic bondage. 'It is, therefore, your right, it is your duty,' says Jefferson—'to arm!'

"What we would achieve is, therefore, plainly and simply:

"*First*:—Destruction of the existing class rule, by all

means, i.e., by energetic, relentless, revolutionary and international action.

"*Second:*—Establishment of a free society based upon co-operative organization of production.

"*Third:*—Free exchange of equivalent products by and between the productive organizations without commerce and profit-mongery.

"*Fourth:*—Organization of education on a secular, scientific and equal basis for both sexes.

"*Fifth:*—Equal rights for all without distinction of sex or race.

"*Sixth:*—Regulation of all public affairs by free contracts between the autonomous (independent) communes and associations, resting on a federalistic basis."

The Manifesto closes with a typical exhortation:

"The day has come for solidarity. Join our ranks! Let the drum beat defiantly the roll of battle: 'Workmen of all countries unite! You have nothing to lose but your chains; you have a world to win!'

"Tremble oppressors of the world! Not far beyond your purblind sight there dawns the scarlet and sable lights of the JUDGMENT DAY!"

The Pittsburgh Manifesto occupies a prominent place in the history of American radicalism even though it is in itself an unimpressive document. Its language is at best forceful and at worst distressingly slovenly. For the most part it is poorly written and suffers from obscurity and infelicity of expression. Its diagnosis of the ills of society—even from the viewpoint of a social-revolutionary—is incomplete and inaccurate, and its blueprint of the future is not always decipherable. It presents no lucid, comprehensive body of doctrine. It is not only baldly unoriginal in idea, but it gives evidence that the borrowed thought was incompletely digested and poorly synthesized and integrated. It shows, in short, that the leaders of the American social-revolutionary movement were swinging in pendulum-fashion between the extreme limits of Socialism and Anarchism, and were still groping toward an explicit theory of either Anarchist-communism or Collectivist-anarchism.

In its critical analysis of the existing society, in its assertions relative to the concentration of capital, the exploitation of the worker, the depression of his standard of living and the factors conditioning wages, in its reference to the nature of "business crises" and in its awkward presentation of the theory of surplus value,—in those and in other respects the Pittsburgh Manifesto borrows directly from Marxian Socialism. Its attack on the State and Church derives in large measure from Michael Bakunin. The proposal to regulate "all public affairs by free contracts between the autonomous . . . communes and associations . . ." is partly Proudhonian, partly Bakuninist and evidently partly the product of the influence of the Paris Commune. "The *régime of contracts* substituted for the *régime of laws*," wrote Pierre-Joseph Proudhon, "would constitute the true government of man and of the citizen. . . ." [31] Bakunin, too, would have rebuilt society upon a voluntary contractual basis. In the final stage of social evolution, he said, men will unite through contracts forming in turn a "free union of individuals into communes, of communes into provinces, of provinces into nations, and finally of nations into the United States of Europe and later of the whole world." [32] Bakunin's thought, as well as Marx's, is also apparent in the section on the economic basis of the new society. The Russian revolutionist wrote that the only method "which makes it impossible for anyone, whoever he may be, to exploit the labor of another, and permits each to share in the enjoyment of society's stock of goods . . . only so far as he has, by his labor, directly contributed to the production of this stock of goods," is to have "land, the instruments of labor, and all other capital, as the collective property of the whole of society. . . ." [33]

Kropotkin probably did not exert a significant influence upon those responsible for the Pittsburgh Manifesto. The superficial similarities which may be observed between the Manifesto and Kropotkin's teachings may not be taken as evidence of direct borrowing. His influence as a revolutionary thinker was not felt in the United States until the following decade, and no work of his appeared in America until 1887 when *Aux Jeunes Gens* was published in English and German translation.[34] Bakunin at that time was much better known to American revolutionaries by virtue of his brief visit to America and the rôle he played in the revolutionary movement of Europe. His *God and the State* appeared in English in the United States as early as 1883.[35]

The Pittsburgh Manifesto was an unintegrated product of various schools of revolutionary thought, and failed to present a consistent and well-rounded body of principles. It does not make clear, for example, whether those who drew it up contemplated a communistic or collectivistic society in the future. Collectivism, which derives to a major extent from Bakunin's thought, proposes the social ownership of the means of production, thus abolishing property which is individually hereditary, and the distribution of produced goods to the workers in proportion to the quantity and value of their labor. In this manner, only the means of production and not produced goods would be socialized, and private property would obtain in the means of consumption and consumptive goods. It also implies a federative voluntary organization of society. In Bakunin's words, it meant the "organization of society and of collective or social property from below upwards, by means of free association, and not from above downwards by means of some authority of some sort." Communism from this viewpoint is regarded as authoritarian, and involves the complete abolition of all forms of private ownership even in produced goods. The Manifesto failed to distinguish between these two tendencies which had been present in the revolutionary movement of Europe for some time, and were rather clearly apparent from 1869 on. Finally, the Manifesto contains only a hint of the anarchistic organization of the future ideal society.[36]

This is understandable. For the social-revolutionaries in America were not quite sure where they stood. Most, who was more than any other person responsible for the Manifesto and who possessed the most energetic mind of them all, had not yet thought his way clear on most of the fundamental problems. Introduced to anarchist thought by August Reinsdorf and Victor Dave, Most called himself an anarchist while he was still in England. But his views on Anarchism were exceedingly cloudy. It was not until the latter half of the 'nineties, as a result of Kropotkin's teachings, that Most's views crystallized and became unmistakably anarchist-communist.[37] Most himself admitted this in 1903. In 1883 he was sufficiently confused to defend the thought of the Manifesto as being "completely socialistic" in answer to some critical observations in *Le Révolté*.[38] As late as 1890 Most wrote, "The anarchists are socialists, because they too want a radical reform; and they are communists, because they too feel convinced that community of property must form the only basis of such a reform." Anarchists, however, are specially distinguished by their opposition to the State.[39] In the following year, Most wrote an article headed "Why I Am a Communist," in which he spoke of establishing "the collectivism of wealth," and of the new society to be founded upon "voluntary agreement, . . . need, . . . the virtues of a complete liberty. . . ." From this it would appear that Anarchism was the basis for Communism, yet Most declared that Communism was the necessary prerequisite for Anarchism.[40]

Mr. Hillquit and those who have followed him are wholly in error in asserting that the Pittsburgh Manifesto may be regarded as the "classic exposition" of Anarchist-communism.[41]

If it is vague in other respects, the Manifesto is unmistakably clear in its declaration that the new social order can be established only by force. Here it is obvious that the Pittsburgh Congress was heir to a characteristic phase of the European revolutionary movement which had already made its influence felt in the United States.

It has been seen that differences over the *"Bewaffnungs-frage"* forced a split in the American socialist movement, and that the social-revolutionary groups which were founded in 1880 and 1881 accepted the declaration on force made by the London Congress. The conception that force can be effectively used as an instrument of propaganda and of social reconstruction was not indigenous to the United States. The whole theory of insurrectional deeds was a product of a European *milieu*. This does not mean, of course, that under certain conditions Americans, whether workers or otherwise, were at all hesitant to resort to violence. In lynch law, the labor disturbances of the period, and the anti-Chinese movement on the Pacific Coast, Americans demonstrated that they were not distinguished by an unwillingness to employ violence. This is further confirmed by the rôle which violence has played in the history of the American frontier.

In the years after the Civil War, conflicts between labor and capital were frequently attended by circumstances which offered the worker considerable justification for the employment of force. Cautious Terence Powderly is reported to have said in 1880: "I am anxious that each of our lodges should be provided with powder and shot, bullets and Winchester rifles, when we intend to strike. If you strike, the troops are called out to put you down. You cannot fight with bare hands. You must consider the matter very seriously, and if we anticipate strikes, we must prepare to strike and use arms against the forces brought against us." [42] Powderly, it should be added, vigorously denied that he had ever said anything of this nature. Whether he gave expression to the sentiment or not, it was, nevertheless, one that was wholly understandable and, from the worker's viewpoint, defensible.

Yet American labor did not look with favor upon the employment of organized force through organizations of the *Lehr und Wehr Verein* type. Still more foreign to the psychology of the American worker was the entire theory of insurrectional deeds.[43] The *Lehr und Wehr Vereine* drew practically no members from the ranks of native born workingmen. When the Pittsburgh Congress declared for force, it was thinking essentially in terms of the European revolutionary movement. It thus sanctioned a policy and a method which had not been accepted in this country to any appreciable extent even in radical circles. The Manifesto of the I.W.P.A. did not specifically recommend insurrectional deeds, but a large number of the delegates at the Congress were unquestionably in full sympathy with propaganda by deed. Certainly Most and the eastern delegates were. Before the Congress had been called, many articles urging and teaching propaganda by deed had appeared in the *Freiheit*. During the three years following 1883, both the members and publications of the I.W.P.A. left no doubt concerning the positive position of the International on insurrectional acts.

NOTES CHAPTER IV

1. Mittelman, *loc. cit.*, pp. 415-417; Ehlert, *loc. cit.*, p. 2; *Life of Albert R. Parsons* ("History of the Labor Movement in Chicago"), pp. xxviii-xxx; Rocker, *op. cit.*, pp. 143-144; Commons, *op. cit.*, vol. 2, pp. 292-293.

2. Sergei Netchaev (or Nechayev) was born in 1847 and died in 1882 after ten years' imprisonment in the fortress of SS. Peter and Paul. The incredible life of this revolutionary is adequately sketched in English in Max Nomad, "Nechayev, 'The Possessed.' A Study," *Hound and Horn*, vol. 7, no. 1, October, December, 1933, pp. 69-114.

3. *Ibid.*, pp. 87-89; Max Nettlau, *Bibliographie de l'anarchie*, Paris, 1897, p. 45; Hélène Iswolsky, *La Vie de Bakounine*, Paris, 1930, pp. 233-234. Helene Iswolsky points out that the "Catechism" was so revolting and shocking that it was rejected by all sane revolutionists.

4. The best source for Most's life is Rocker, *op. cit.*, in which Chaps. I-VIII cover this portion of his career; see also, Emma Goldman, "Johann Most," *American Mercury*, vol. 8, no. 30, June, 1926, pp. 159-167; M[ax] B[aginski], "John Most," *Mother Earth*, vol. 1, no. 2, April, 1906, pp. 17-20; William Frederick Kamman, *Socialism in German American Literature* (*Americana Germanica*, no. 24), Philadelphia, 1917, pp. 31-32; Hippolyte Havel, "Anarchists: John Most—The Stormy Petrel," *Man!*, vol. 2, no. 1, January, 1934, p. 6; Hillquit, *op. cit.*, pp. 214-215.

5. Rocker, *op. cit.*, pp. 134-136, 143.

6. December 19, 1882.
7. New York *Tribune*, December 19, 1882.
8. *Idem.*
9. Rocker, *op. cit.*, p. 143; Ghio, *op. cit.*, p. 72; Hillquit, *op. cit.*, pp. 215-217 *passim;* Sartorius von Waltershausen, *op. cit.*, pp. 201-205, *passim.*
10. See the first three books cited in the previous note.
11. See below, pp. 102-103, 142-144.
12. *Freiheit*, March 18, 1883; quoted in English in Ely, *Recent American Socialism*, pp. 39-40.
13. April 14, 1883.
14. June 30, 1883.
15. Rocker, *op. cit.*, p. 145.
16. *Liberty*, vol. 4, no. 2, May 1, 1886.
17. Spies and William Blum served for the English section, Paul Grottkau and A. Hirschberger for the German, W. L. Rosenberg for the French, A. Mikolando for the Bohemian, and P. Livoni for the Scandinavian.
18. *Freiheit*, April 17, 1883.
19. *Ibid.*, June 9, August 11, 1883.
20. Photostat of this circular supplied by Miss Agnes Inglis in charge of the Labadie Collection, University of Michigan.
21. *Freiheit*, August 11, October 20, 1883.
22. The best single source for the Congress is the *Freiheit*, October 20 and 27, 1883, upon which the following account is largely based. Additional material is found in *Le Révolté*, November 24, 1883; Nettlau, *op. cit.*, pp. 378-381; Rocker, *op. cit.*, p. 145; Sartorius von Waltershausen, *op. cit.*, 212-222. Short and inadequate accounts are in Commons, *op. cit.*, vol. 2, pp. 293-296 (which erroneously has the Congress open on October 19); and Hillquit, *op. cit.*, pp. 215-216. In Carl Nold, "Fifty Years Ago," *Man!*, vol. 2, no. 1, January, 1934, pp. 5, 8, there is translated into English some of the material originally reported in the *Freiheit* of October 20.
23. Willis J. Abbot, *Carter Henry Harrison. A Memoir*, New York, 1895, p. 140; Ehlert, *loc. cit.*, p. 1; Fine, *op. cit.*, p. 106.
24. *Freiheit*, September 8, 1883, the instructions of New York Group No. 1.
25. *Idem.*
26. The committee consisted of delegates Rau, Strumpen, Kehn, Frick and Christ.
27. *Idem.*
28. It is dated October 16, 1883, and is easily available. The quotations from it which follow are from one of the leaflet copies published by the Congress. It is reprinted in Ely, *American Labor Movement*, Appendix 1, no. 5, pp. 358-363.
29. In *"Unsere Grundsätze"* Most describes the present order as "ungerecht, wahnitzig, und raubmorderisch."
30. This comes almost word for word from *"Unsere Grundsätze."*

31. Quoted in Eltzbacher, *op. cit.*, p. 75.
32. Quoted in *ibid.*, pp. 126-127.
33. Quoted in *ibid.*, p. 131.
34. Nettlau, *Bibliographie*, pp. 72-86 *passim*.
35. *Ibid.*, pp. 46-47. It was translated and published by Benjamin Tucker. It appeared under that title only a year earlier.
36. George Plechanoff, *Anarchism and Socialism*, translated by Eleanor Marx Aveling, Chicago (1907?), pp. 79-83; Paul Leroy-Beaulieu, *Collectivism, A Study of Some of the Leading Social Questions of the Day*, translated and abridged by Sir Arthur Clay, London, 1908, pp. 3-6; Hubert Lagardelle, "Michel Bakounine," *Revue Politique et Parlementaire*, vol. 41, no. 182, August, 1909, pp. 317-324 *passim*.
37. Rocker, *op. cit.*, pp. 142-143.
38. *Freiheit*, February 3, 1883.
39. Johann Most, *The Social Monster*, New York, 1890, pp. 6-7.
40. John Most, "Why I Am a Communist," in *The "Why I Ams."* *An Economic Symposium*, second edition (no. 11, *Unsettled Questions*. Fortnightly, New York, August 30, 1891), New York, 1892, pp. 35-39, especially pp. 37-38.
41. Hillquit, *op. cit.*, p. 126.
42. Quoted in Henry Mayers Hyndman, *The Chicago Riots and the Class War in the United States*, London, 1886, p. 3.
43. See, however, below, pp. 149-151.

V. SOCIAL REVOLUTION—CHICAGO STYLE

T HE efforts made by the social-revolutionaries to unite their forces in the United States were so fumbling that they may be described as an experiment in planned futility. Errors committed in Chicago in 1881, were repeated in Pittsburgh two years later. Except for the establishment of the I.W.P.A. in which the constituent groups were to enjoy— and actually possessed—full autonomy, the setting up of the National Information Bureau in Chicago, and the recognition or founding of certain publications as representative organs, the success of the Pittsburgh Congress in forming a united, national movement was slight. The plan of organization of the I.W.P.A., personal ambitions and antipathies, the fluidity of doctrine and loose nomenclature militated against unity. The movement itself, because of the American scene and its own character, did not acquire national scope.

After the Pittsburgh Congress, leading members of the badly shattered S.L.P.[1] made an offer of affiliation to the Chicago groups of the I.W.P.A. This was in line somewhat with the invitation to the members of the S.L.P. "to join us upon the principles laid down in our manifesto for uniform and effective propaganda" tendered by the Information Bureau. Though the Information Bureau had asserted that "there is no great difference between the aspirations of the 'I.W.P.A.' and the 'socialistic Labor Party,'" Spies responded to the plea for unity with the weak suggestion that the S.L.P. break up into autonomous groups which could then join the International. This actually meant a rejection of the offer of the S.L.P. members. Spies' counter-proposal makes it clear that union between the two wings of the radical movement could not take place. Unity would only follow with the complete surrender of one of them.[2]

The strength of the social-revolutionary movement was still concentrated—and was to remain centered—in its two focal points, Chicago and New York. In the latter city, the dictatorial figure of Johann Most continued to dominate the movement between 1883-1886. During those years there was little deviation either in organizing activity or ideology from the ground plan for both sketched in the Pittsburgh Manifesto. There was a further elaboration of the theory of violence marked by the amazing measure of attention given to the purely practical aspects of insurrectional methods. For this development Most appears to have been largely responsible. He once mounted the lecture platform with a rifle and explained its mechanism and operation to the audience. He even found employment at an explosives factory in 1884, where he obtained a practical knowledge of the manufacture and use of explosives. While he was employed at the factory he occasionally took some explosives to send to Europe, and he tried to inspire terroristic acts in Germany. Commenting upon the accomplishments of the revolutionary movement during 1885, Most asserted that considerable strides had been taken in "the arming of the American proletariat. . . ." During the years 1883-1886, there was greater stress upon anarchistic elements in the principles advocated by the *Freiheit,* but a more clearly defined theory of Anarchist-communism did not become apparent until after 1886.[3]

At this point, Most and the New York movement recede into the background, and Chicago, the second center of the social-revolutionary movement, dominates the remaining pages of this study. For the revolutionary movement of that city is inextricably, though not necessarily causally, linked to the Haymarket bomb which took so heavy a toll in lives, bitterness and tragic misunderstanding. Apart from this, the

Chicago movement during the years 1883-1886 was imbued with much greater vitality than that of New York. Not only was the Information Bureau centered in Chicago, but much stronger ties bound the revolutionary and labor elements than was the case in New York. The New York movement never matched the organizing activities, either in extent or in intensity, of their comrades in the Windy City. The movement in Chicago was alive and forceful, and despite the disparity in size of the two cities, the I.W.P.A. had a larger membership in that city than it did in New York.

There can be no doubt that the revolutionary movement grew with considerable rapidity in Chicago after 1883. While accurate statistics are lacking, the general indications are unmistakable. At the close of 1884, there were not less than six groups in the city affiliated with the I.W.P.A. By the midsummer of 1885, the number of groups had jumped to seventeen. This increase, as well as a growth in membership of the old groups, was in part the accomplishment of the American Group of the I.W.P.A. which held free, public meetings throughout the city at which labor issues were discussed.[4] Through meetings of this type and other gatherings arranged specially for the workers it was hoped that the proletariat would be drawn into the movement. Lake Front meetings were frequent and were especially successful on Sundays, sometimes attracting an audience of a thousand or more. On some Sundays,[5] as many as half a dozen labor meetings, arranged by I.W.P.A. members or groups, were scheduled. The speakers at these gatherings invariably included the leaders among the social-revolutionaries such as C. S. Griffin, Michael Schwab, Parsons, Spies, Sam Fielden, William Holmes, J. P. Dusey, and lesser figures such as John Waller, John Keegan and J. C. Goodden.[6]

When the moment seemed propitious, demonstrations of greater scope were arranged by members of the I.W.P.A. These served as splendid occasions for the spread of propaganda, and they also identified the movement with labor interests. They likewise gave the I.W.P.A. an appearance of a strength it never really possessed. The dedication of the Chicago Board of Trade building on April 28, 1885, called forth a demonstration and parade with the customary vituperative addresses denouncing the "capitalists" and the "system." [7] A mass protest meeting on Thanksgiving Day of 1884, in answer to the Governor's Thanksgiving proclamation is characteristic enough to warrant consideration.

Some three thousand people turned out despite severe weather and heard the speeches of Parsons, Griffin, Fielden, Spies and Schwab. Trenchant resolutions against the right of property were voted, and an ironic "Thanksgiving" resolution was adopted which declared "that we are thankful because we have learned the true cause of poverty and knew [sic] the remedy, and can only be more thankful when the principles are put in force." When the addresses were over, most of those in attendance formed a line of march and paraded through the city to the offices of the *Arbeiter-Zeitung*. Here, speakers urged them to organize in preparation "for the inevitable conflict which the capitalistic class would force upon them." Cheers were given for revolutionaries of every stamp in the Old World and for the Hocking Valley strikers. [8] Then the parade once more got under way, marched through the wealthier section of the city, past the Palmer House, and by the residence of ex-Minister Washburne, who was roundly jeered. [9] Black and red flags were carried by paraders as well as placards, some of which announced: "Private capital is the reward of robbery." "Our capitalistic robbers may well thank *their* Lord, we their victims have not yet strangled them." "The proletariate must be their own liberator." [10]

How effective such demonstrations were in winning converts to the I.W.P.A., it cannot be said. They did, however, serve to spread the gospel of the revolution. A more "respectable" medium of propaganda was the debates arranged by the I.W.P.A. between its leaders and its opponents. At one debate held with representatives of the Trades Assembly, Albert

Parsons declared that the only basic difference between the two bodies was the acceptance of peaceful means by the Trades Assembly. This was a conscious misstatement of fact since they disagreed on many other points.[11] Meetings were also called to correct current misconceptions of Socialism, Communism and Anarchism to which editors, clergymen, business people —in short, all bitter critics of these theories—were invited, and which of course they never attended.[12] Occasionally one of the leaders in the movement addressed an eminently "respectable" group, such as the Liberal League of Chicago.[13]

Limited in their work by lack of funds, the Chicago radicals nevertheless sent out organizers to found branches of the I.W.P.A. outside of the city. Frequently these organizers, among whom Sam Fielden, W. J. Gorsuch, Griffin, Spies and Parsons were outstanding, succeeded in establishing organizations where none had existed before. In many instances they merely founded additional ones. As a result of this activity new or additional sections appeared in Cincinnati, Cleveland and Canton in Ohio, and Louisville, Covington and Newport in Kentucky. Attention was obviously centered upon industrial centers not too far removed from Chicago.[14] The strenuous efforts to found American rather than foreign groups brought little return, and German and to a lesser extent Bohemian organizations multiplied more rapidly.

There was constant fluctuation in the number of groups affiliated with the I.W.P.A., but there were probably never more than eighty. Throughout most of 1885, the International claimed over seventy groups.[15] Only nine persons, however, were necessary to form a group! While the leaders of the I.W.P.A. claimed the meaningless "many thousand members," and Parsons once spoke of the 20,000 anarchists and socialists in Chicago alone, it is doubtful if there ever were more than 5,000 real members. In view of the fact that one of the most active groups, the American, in existence since 1883, had only ninety-five members at the close of April, 1885, this number does not appear to be too small.[16] Chicago

and its environs, with about one-quarter of the groups of the
I.W.P.A., had almost half of the membership. New York
ran Chicago a poor second with a membership smaller by
two-thirds.

After October 4, 1884, when the first number of the
Alarm appeared, five of the eight official organs of the International
were published in Chicago. In the *Alarm* the Chicago
movement possessed the only English publication. The *Arbeiter-Zeitung,*
which came out on week days, the *Vorbote,*
which appeared on Saturday, the *Fackel,* published on Sunday,
and *Boudoucnost,* a Bohemian paper, also appeared in Chicago.
Of the remaining three, two, the *Freiheit* and *Proletar,*
a Bohemian weekly, were published in New York, and the
Parole, a German weekly, in St. Louis. Wholly in sympathy
with the aims of the I.W.P.A., though not regarded as an
official publication, was *Nemesis,* an English journal, which
appeared in Baltimore in the summer of 1884 and which
existed no more than a year. Circulation figures for most of
these publications are not always reliable. It was asserted that
the *Alarm* had an average edition of 3,000 copies early in
1886. For the years 1883-1886, the circulation of the *Arbeiter-Zeitung*
never dropped below 5,000 and never reached 6,000.
The *Vorbote* laid claim to a circulation of 7,000 for the first
two years of that period, and to 8,000 for the last two. The
Fackel evidently enjoyed a wider and steadily growing reading
public during the same years. Its 1886 circulation of 12,200
was almost 3,000 above its 1883 circulation.[17]

The editorial work for the Chicago German publications
fell chiefly upon August Spies, while Albert Parsons carried
the burden of getting out the *Alarm.* The former was considerably
aided by Michael Schwab, and the latter had a prolific
assistant in Mrs. Lizzie M. Holmes who first wrote under the
pseudonym of May Huntley and later used her maiden name,
Lizzie M. Swank. C. S. Griffin and Dyer D. Lum [18] contributed
liberally to the *Alarm,* and Parsons' wife, Lucy, offered

an occasional article. The financial problem, always critical in the case of the *Alarm,* was partially solved for a while by the formation of a publishing society in which "comrades" purchased shares.[19] Picnics and benefits to raise funds, however, were always part and parcel of the movement.

With reference to doctrine, the Pittsburgh Manifesto served the social-revolutionaries in Chicago both as a summary of their fundamental beliefs and a point of departure for further elaboration. The brief platform of the I.W.P.A. which closed the Manifesto was reprinted time and again in the *Alarm* and *Arbeiter-Zeitung.* In general, nothing was added to the analysis of the economic structure of capitalism in the Manifesto, and frequently that section of the Pittsburgh document was slavishly followed.[20]

The attack on private property was constant. Private ownership, the greatest of crimes, was the source from which flowed the evils of capitalism. "No man," said the *Alarm,* "has the right to be the owner of anything. . . ." From this it followed that "no man should be paid for what he produces. . . . The moment you pay a man for what he produces he will take that pay and then spend his energies in taking advantage of somebody with it." [21] This attack upon the wage-system received frequent exposition with slight modifications. Thus the *Alarm* announced:

"We now have all the humanity, and all the events and conditions of humanity, all the tools thus far discovered, all the means of communication thus far known, all organization, and science and inducement to organize thus far known. And having all these things has created in us a love and ambition for more of them. . . . But we know that the wage system that requires a person to pay for a large percentage of what he receives, and consequently receive pay for a majority of the things he produces, is an ancient system that we have outlived, and is now a barrier in the way of our development of all other things that we have. Therefore we require the abolition of this . . . wage system. We call upon all men to refuse to pay for anything. We know that this course will make it impossible for them to receive pay for anything." [22]

From the criticism of private property to the attack upon statutory law which protected that institution was only a short step. Special classes acquired privileges first "by force and chicane," argued the *Alarm,* and their continued domination in society was made possible by the enactment of these privileges "into statute law" and constitutions. "Through this process, the means of existence . . . have been made into *private property* . . . until only a few privileged persons in society possess the right to live in liberty." Since those who possess no property are thus dependent upon those who do, the latter enjoy a virtual dictatorship where private property exists. The chief function of the State (which was never clearly defined), and its laws is the perpetuation of that dictatorship by the propertied.[23] The State, an instrument of economic injustice, making possible the continuance of the present order, was a chief target for attack. It was also assaulted because it was in itself the denial of liberty,—it was compulsion, coercive force crystallized. Despite the apparent similarity to Bakuninist thought in their bitter criticism of the State, the resemblance between the words of the Chicago social-revolutionaries and of the Russian revolutionist seems one of phraseology rather than one of basic concept.[24]

The problem of statutory law was also approached with eighteenth century phraseology and attitudes. The only valid and necessary law in existence, wrote Parsons, is natural law. "A statute is always used to oppose some natural law or sustain some other equally vicious statute." [25] Just what natural law means was never made clear. It sometimes appears as a "law" inherent in the nature of man. Sometimes it seems to be a "law" inherent in life, and occasionally it was further confused by being equated to "natural necessity." In any case, it was regarded as superior to any other form of law. In an editorial explaining the goal toward which he and his comrades were striving, Parsons wrote:

"Anarchists would . . . abolish statute law and all law manufacturers and thus permit the laws of nature to have full sway. That would be in accordance with natural law which is only another phrase for natural necessity. This would remove the barriers which make and keep the producer poor. . . . We would then have a free system, with science for its guide and necessity for its compelling force. It would then follow that all human beings freely producing and freely consuming, none could be denied any reasonable or natural demand. Free to unite and *dis*-unite, free to produce and to consume; poverty would vanish; ignorance, its offspring, would disappear, and peace and plenty would abound. This is the goal, the end aim of Anarchy." [26]

In a previous issue of the *Alarm,* Parsons wrote that in an anarchistic society "Reason and common sense, based upon natural law, takes [*sic*] the place of statute law, with its compulsion and arbitrary rules." [27]

Still another criticism of law was developed in terms of "rights." "One person," declared the *Alarm,* "has no right to interfere with another to take any advantage of him, and this being the foundation of justice, the best way to sustain it is to take away all restraint, and then it will not be safe to offend anyone. . . . Every person ought to have an untrammeled right to dispose of his life, person and talents, at his own discretion. . . ." [28]

The employment of typical eighteenth century terms and phrases is found with great frequency in the *Alarm.* Together with the stress placed upon "justice" and "fraternity," it gives a distinctly French socialistic cast to the doctrines Parsons was advocating. [29] The first number of the *Alarm* appealed to the working-classes "in the name of 'Liberty, Fraternity, and Equality.' . . ." [30] The ownership of the means of production by the working-class was also defended in terms of "rights" and "freedom."

"Capital, being a *thing,* can have no rights. Persons alone have rights. The existing system bestows all capital upon one class and all labor upon the other; hence the conflict is irrepressible. The time has now arrived when the laborers must possess the right to the free use of the capital with which they work, or the capitalists will own the laborers body and soul. No compromise is possible. We must choose between freedom and slavery. The International defiantly unfurls the banner of liberty, fraternity, equality, and beneath its scarlet folds beckons the disinherited of the earth to assemble and strike down the property beast which feasts upon the life-blood of the people." [31]

An eighteenth century attitude is found in the assertion that "the evil in man only appears when some natural law or natural right of that man has been violated," or interfered with by statutory law,[32] which implies that "artificial" human institutions are responsible for evil, and that man is by nature good. One of the members of the American group announced "that the first step in Socialism is a realization of the truth that man is naturally honest," and urged the "recovery" of man's "natural rights." [33]

As with "natural law," there was no attempt to define "natural rights." Thus, "natural rights" were taken to be "original" rights of man since lost. They were regarded as rights inherent in the nature of things, a reflection of natural law, and were even defined in the Hobbesian sense where rights are equated to sovereign powers for the satisfaction of desire. On the whole, it seems that these "rights" were held to be entirely individual, lifted clear of all social context, since it was not suggested that they are limited with reference to social function and social interest. Common welfare, it apparently was assumed, would result from the complete enjoyment of individual rights and the fulfillment of individual self-interest.

Quotations from the writings of Henry David Thoreau and Benjamin R. Tucker, whose entire approach was diametrically opposed to that of the social-revolutionaries, also appeared in the *Alarm*. There is liberal borrowing from Tucker's *Liberty* in the issue of October 11, for example, and the author of the editorial which bears the title "Rights of the People" in the January 24 number was probably well acquainted with Thoreau's essay "On the Duty of Civil Disobedience." [34] "Disobedience," he wrote, "is the true foundation of liberty. The obedient must be slaves."

How was society to be freed of its ills and evils? It was necessary to attack the problem at its very roots,—private property. Destroy private property, the cause of social evil, and with it will go its products,—wage-slavery, poverty, misery, crime, ignorance, injustice, war and every other ill of the existing order. The abolition of private property, therefore, "is the first and paramount aim of Anarchy, and for its accomplishment a resort to any and all means becomes not only a duty but a necessity." [35] "The capitalistic system must be overthrown. . . . To achieve our liberation we are not only justified, but we are in duty bound to employ all means." [36]

The use of the words "all means," however, is in a sense misleading, for political action was expressly excepted. After 1883 it is almost impossible to find anything but the most mordant criticism directed against political action. Those who still adhered to that method suffered from "politicophobia." [37]

Although it was sometimes proposed that the private-property "beast" might be destroyed by passive measures, the real meaning of the term "all and every means" is best taken as "any and every type of force." For a short while, some of the leaders insisted that if everybody refused to receive and give pay for goods and services, the capitalist system would collapse, and they seriously advocated such action.[38] At the Thanksgiving Day demonstration in 1884,[39] a resolution was adopted to the effect that no man shall either pay or receive pay for anything, and that no man should deprive himself of what he desires if the object of his desire is useful and not being utilized.[40] At the same time, however, a resolution was adopted which recommended the use of force and all types of arms and explosives to wipe out the existing system. Evidently little faith was placed in the first method, for it was quickly abandoned.

"Down with pay," exclaimed the *Alarm,* "and dynamite the man who claims it; and hang him who will not let his energies produce something. This," concluded the writer, "is Socialism." [41] "Workingmen of America, learn the manufacture and use of dynamite," advised the *Alarm.* "It will be your most powerful weapon; a weapon of the weak against the strong. . . . Then use it unstintingly, unsparingly. The battle for bread is the battle for life. . . . Death and destruction to the system and its upholders, which plunders and enslaves the men, women and children of toil." [42]

One I.W.P.A. group in the course of discussing the question "How can the idle obtain employment?" proposed that the "unemployed should attack the life and property of those who have robbed them of their labor products and so turn them adrift to starve." [43] Again and again it was asserted that only when the workers "arm themselves and by force acquire the right to life, liberty and happiness" will they secure their "stolen birthright." [44] "Each workingman ought to have been armed long ago," declared the *Arbeiter-Zeitung.* "Daggers and revolvers are easily to be gotten. Hand grenades are cheaply . . . produced; explosives, too, can be obtained. . . ." [45] "A number of strikers in Quincy . . . ," observed the same paper, "fired upon their bosses, and not upon the scabs. This is recommended most emphatically for imitation." [46] It was suggested at mass meetings that "If we would achieve our liberation from economic bondage and acquire our natural right to life and liberty, every man must lay by a part of his wages, buy a Colt's navy revolver . . . , a Winchester rifle . . . , and learn how to make and use dynamite. . . . Then raise the flag of rebellion. . . ." [47]

The conviction that force was the sole infallible means

to destroy the existing order and inaugurate the glorious new society, together with the consequent constant appeal to and encouragement of its use, was marked by four very general characteristics. No real appreciation of the difference between individual deeds and expressions of mass violence was evident, and both were advised. The use of force was encouraged both for defensive—in resistance to the police, militia, Pinkertons and the like—and aggressive purposes. While every type of violence and every method of destruction was accepted, the use of dynamite and similar explosives was especially encouraged. Finally, unusual stress was placed upon the purely practical aspects of the employment of force.

Thus, the *Alarm* and the *Arbeiter-Zeitung,* frequently following the lead of and reproducing items from the *Freiheit,* published articles on the manufacture of dynamite, gun-cotton, nitro-glycerine, mercury and silver fulminates and bombs. They also offered instruction in the use of dangerous explosives. One article in the *Alarm* bore the heading "A Practical Lesson in Popular Chemistry—The Manufacture of Dynamite Made Easy." [48] Another on the manufacture of bombs was subtitled, "The Weapon of the Social Revolutionist Placed within the Reach of All." [49] The files of both papers are liberally studded with such items. [50] The *Arbeiter-Zeitung* ran a notice through December, 1885, and the first three months of 1886, which offered free instruction in the handling of arms to workers "at No. 58 Clybourn Avenue. . . ." And the *Alarm* urged its readers who desired additional information on the manufacture and use of bombs to communicate with it. [51] Sometimes the mad "Revolutionary Catechism" of Netchaev was quoted. Lengthy discussions were frequently published on plans and methods of street-fighting, means of combating the militia, the preparation necessary for revolutionary action, the perpetration of the individual deed, the danger of discovery, and the like. [52]

Upon explosives, and upon dynamite in particular, the greatest emphasis was placed. Dynamite was the great social solvent,—it was the "emancipator." [53] The "right of property" could be destroyed, asserted the *Alarm*, and a glorious "free" society inaugurated "simply by making ourselves masters of the use of dynamite, then declaring we will make no further claims to ownership in anything, and deny every . . . person's right to be owner of anything, and administer instant death, by any and all means, to any and every person who attempts to claim personal ownership of anything. This method, and this alone, can relieve the world of this infernal monster called the 'right of property.' " [54]

No article lauding the admirable qualities of dynamite or editorial hymn praising its revolutionary virtues compares with the fantastic and unbelievable contribution of one T. Lizius [55] which was published in the *Alarm* as a letter to the editor:

"Dynamite! Of all the good stuff, this is the stuff. Stuff several pounds of this sublime stuff into an inch pipe (gas or water-pipe), plug up both ends, insert a cap with a fuse attached, place this in the immediate neighborhood of a lot of rich loafers who live by the sweat of other people's brows, and light the fuse. A most cheerful and gratifying result will follow. In giving dynamite to the down-trodden millions of the globe, science has done its best work. The dear stuff can be carried around in the pocket without danger, while it is a formidable weapon against any force of militia, police or detectives that may want to stifle the cry for justice that goes forth from the plundered slaves. It is something not very ornamental but exceedingly useful. It can be used against persons and things, it is better to use it against the former than against bricks and masonry. It is a genuine boon for the disinherited, while it brings terror and fear to the robbers. It brings terror only to the guilty, and consequently the Senator who introduced a bill in congress to stop its manufacture and use, must be guilty of something. He fears the wrath of an outraged people that has been duped and swindled by him and his like. The same must be the case with the 'servant' of the people who introduced a like measure in the senate of the Indiana legislature. All the good this will do. Like every-thing else, the more you prohibit it, the more it will be done. Dynamite is like Banquo's ghost, it keeps on fooling around somewhere or other in spite of his satanic majesty. A pound of this good stuff beats a bushel of ballots all hollow, and don't you forget it. Our law makers might as well try to sit down on a crater of a volcano or a bayonet as to endeavor to stop the manufacture or use of dynamite. It takes more justice and right than is contained in laws to quiet the spirit of un-rest. If workingmen would be truly free, they must learn to know why they are slaves. They must rise above petty preju-dice and learn to think. From thought to action is not far, and when the worker has seen the chains, he need but look a little closer to find near at hand, the sledge with which to shatter every link. The sledge is dynamite." [56]

The campaign of violence included items which ranged from Mrs. Parsons' pointed advice to tramps to learn to use explosives so that they could annoy the rich during hard times,[57] to C. S. Griffin's article on assassination. In the latter, which patently reflects the influence of Netchaev and Russian terrorism, Mr. Griffin declared that

"The moment the abolition of a government is suggested, the mind pictures the uprising of a hundred little despotic governments on every hand, quarrelling among themselves and domineering over the unorganized people. This fact suggests the idea that the present governments must be destroyed, only in a manner that will prevent the organization or rise of any and all other governments, whether it be a government of three men or three hundred millions. No government can exist with-out a head, and by assassinating the head just as fast as a gov-ernment head appears, the government can be destroyed, and by the same process all other governments can be kept out of exist-ence. . . . Those governments least offensive to the people should be destroyed last. . . . He alone is free who submits to no government. All governments are domineering powers, and any domineering power is a natural enemy to all mankind, and ought to be treated as such. Assassination will remove the evil from the face of the earth." [58]

The author himself observed that this was the policy of the Nihilists, and in closing said that "Assassination properly applied is wise, just, humane, and brave. For freedom all things are just."

In the last analysis, justification for the means—the use of force—was found in the validity of the end to be achieved—the creation of a new social order. But there were also attempts to support the doctrine of force on other grounds. Since capitalists specifically recommended the use of violence, said the revolutionaries, they were justified in doing likewise. In proof, statements made at the time of the 1877 strike were reprinted. "Tom" Scott, [59] for example, was credited with saying: "Give them [the workers] the rifle diet for a few days and see how they like that kind of bread." The Chicago *Times* was charged with asserting that "Hand-grenades should be thrown among those union sailors who are striving to obtain higher wages, as by such treatment they would be taught a valuable lesson, and other strikers could take warning from their fate." [60] The most carefully planned defense of the theory of violence came from one of the least violent of the revolutionaries, Dyer D. Lum, [61] who approached the problem historically, and carefully avoided specific, practical suggestions. He appealed to the "wage slaves of America" to arm themselves because it provided the only way out of their misery. [62] In a rather long article Lum marshalled the usual body of facts to prove that those in power yield only to those who wield even greater power. The conclusion was obvious: force alone could bring about the necessary changes in society.

The social-revolutionaries were far from being bloodthirsty cutthroats, and they felt it incumbent upon themselves to distinguish between their advocacy of violence and the cruelty implicit in it. Though it is said that "force is cruel," wrote C. S. Griffin, ". . . this is only true when the opposition is less cruel. If the opposition is a relentless power that is starving, freezing and exposing and depriving tens of thousands, and the application of force will require less suffering while removing the old cause, then the force is humane. Seeing the amount of needless suffering all about us, we say a vigorous use of dynamite is both humane and economical. . . ." [63]

The *Alarm*, in refuting the charge that socialists were "bloodthirsty," pointed out that socialists, "like all other thinking people, know that revolution must come. . . . Whether the . . . uprooting of a bad principle will require bloodshed depends, first, on how old it is, and how much the people are receiving it as second nature, and how much its supporters are interested in keeping it a-going. And, secondly, how strong, clear and determined the opposition is when it begins to oppose. This is why the communist and anarchist urges the people to study their school-books on chemistry . . . , and make themselves too strong to be opposed with deadly weapons. This alone can insure against bloodshed." [64]

In justice to the leaders of the movement it must be said that they repeatedly made it clear that the purpose of force was not to cause injury to individuals. Parsons, commenting upon the suggestion in *Lucifer* [65] that a remedy for bad times could be found in depriving a few hundred capitalists of their heads, declared:

"Hold on, comrade, not so fast please. Anarchists propose to 'crop off the head' of the *private* property beast. . . . It is more than probable, however, that in the effort to slay this 'monster' it will be necessary to 'crop off' the heads of a large number of its progeny (capitalists) who will stoutly defend the life of their parent." [66] They insisted that "Our war is not against men, but against systems; yet we must prepare to kill men who try to defeat our cause, or we will strive in vain." [67]

In an open letter to Powderly written at the close of August, 1886, [68] Parsons challenged

"Mr. Powderly to find a man who can truthfully say that I, as a socialist or anarchist, have advocated or countenanced 'the destruction of life and property.' Whoever says so," he continued, "lies.

"The foundation principle of socialism, or anarchy is the same as the Knights of Labor, viz., 'The abolition of the wages system' [69] and the substitution in its stead of an industrial system of universal cooperation. . . . If this be 'destruction of life and property,' then is Mr. Powderly equally criminal with the anarchists. The assertion that we use and advise the use of force is gratuitous and untrue. But we have declared that the existing social order is founded upon force and maintained by force, and we have and do still predict a social revolt of the working people against this force system; that they (the wage-workers) will be driven into open rebellion against class rule and class domination. This result will follow from cause to effect and not from anything that Mr. Powderly, myself, or anyone else may say or do. The more general and intelligent the diffusion of this truth the less violent and destructive will the period of transition be." [70]

While it may be true that the leaders of the Chicago movement never used force and while Parsons' presentation of the social revolution as an inevitable mass-movement was what the leaders had in mind, his statement that its employment was never advised is pure falsification.[71] His most successful justification of the theory of violence found expression in this letter, but it can in no sense be taken as an accurate reflection of what the social-revolutionaries actually advocated.

Though the propaganda of violence was evidently never taken with great seriousness by the press at large, there were, nevertheless, spasmodic "scares" in anticipation of terroristic acts.

"The latest scare about the Terrorist Socialists," *John Swinton's Paper* observed early in 1886, "is in Chicago, where the police have discovered that they are trying to destroy the city by infernal machines, dynamite bombs and electricity. A month ago, there was a similar scare in San Francisco. . . . A few months ago, the scare was in Pittsburgh. . . . Just before that Denver was agog on the same account. . . .

"These tremendous revelations and scares occur periodically in one place or another. . . .

"The capitalists are terrorized by their own crimes. To the thief, every bush is an officer. . . ." [72]

Except in 1886, there was no real expectation that this advocacy of violence would result in grave disturbances either in New York or Chicago.

The fact that the social-revolutionaries were not taken very seriously by the majority of the newspapers and the attitude of the man who dominated Chicago politically, Carter H. Harrison, explain why the radicals were not checked in their propagandist activities. Carter Harrison possessed most of the trade marks of the typical political boss and mastered the arts of the demagogue. Yet he resisted the pressure of the propertied classes for measures of suppression. When first inaugurated as mayor in April, 1879, he touched upon the presence of the radical organizations and the *Lehr und Wehr Verein* in Chicago in the following words:

"The constitution of the land guarantees to all citizens the right to peaceably assemble, the petition for redress of grievances. This carries the right to free discussion. It also guarantees the people the right to keep and bear arms. But it does not give to anyone the right to threaten or to resist lawful authority. The genius of our institutions rests on Law. To it and to its officers all good citizens should appeal for protection. I will protect all in their lawful rights. Some fear an organized resistance to authority. I do not. I do not believe that there is in our midst any considerable body of men mad enough to attempt any such folly, for they must know that they would be as chaff, compared to the solid masses who love our institutions and are determined that law and order shall reign." [73]

To his willingness to permit the radicals to carry on their propaganda until they actually violated the law, Harrison added political astuteness by later winning over the more "respectable" socialistic elements into the ranks of the Democratic party.

The offer of municipal jobs could not be resisted by some socialists, and their acceptance accelerated formation of factions within the party. Even after the Haymarket bomb was thrown Harrison did not give way to unrestrained condemnation of the radical elements in the city.[74] If Chicago had had a less indulgent mayor, the revolutionaries in the city probably would have been badgered and hounded long before the summer of 1886.

A guess at the probable consequences of the propaganda spread by the extremists in Chicago and elsewhere was hazarded by Professor Ely in his *Recent American Socialism*. Describing this propaganda as "European," Prof. Ely warned that though it had seen no practical application in America, the social-revolutionaries "themselves claim that our respite is a short one, since they are waiting for an opportune moment to begin the tactics of violence, and the favorable time is expected in a very near future." [75] He himself, however, foresaw no immediate danger to the Republic or its institutions.

"What we have to fear then is large loss of life, estrangement of classes, incalculable destruction of property and a shock to the social body which will be a serious check to our economic growth for years to come." [76] In the light of Prof. Ely's knowledge of the labor and radical movements and his training, his inaccurate prophecy is extremely interesting.

With the psychology characteristic of the ardent revolutionary, the Chicago leaders—as well as their "comrades" throughout the country—were convinced of the immediacy of the social revolution. It was not only inevitable but it was also proximate; it was perennially just around the corner. The *Arbeiter-Zeitung* spoke of the "already approaching revolution" which "promises to be much grander than that at the close of the last century, which only broke out in one country." [77] Prophetic utterances on its immediacy occur with frequency in the columns of the *Alarm*.[78] The sentences "We see it [the social revolution] coming. We predict it, we hail it with joy!" best sum up the attitude of the social-revolutionaries on this point.[79]

The nature—or the mode of manifestation—of this very definite social revolution was very frequently treated with annoying vagueness. Parsons took it to mean "the time when the wage-laborers of this and other countries will assert their rights—natural rights—and maintain them by force of arms. The social revolution means the expropriation of the means of production and the resources of life. . . ." [80] Sometimes the concept of the social revolution was developed in thorough-going Marxian terms. Arguing from the basic assumption of the class-struggle and the diminishing return to labor, it was concluded that the continuation of capitalism would inevitably result in an uprising of the people "as the last and only recourse to relief from oppression. The people will then trample the law under foot, they will destroy government." This social revolt will be precipitated by some apparently inconsequential occurrence.[81] Such assertions imply that the social revolution was viewed as a mass phenomenon engineered by and with force, in which leadership was taken by the workers, resulting in the destruction of capitalism and the introduction of a new social order. A fuller and more precise statement than this is unwarranted by disturbing inconsistencies in the available evidence. It rarely occurred to the leaders of the movement to clarify the meaning of the term "social revolution" for the benefit of themselves and their followers.

NOTES CHAPTER V

1. Alexander Jonas, Henry Emrich, George Lehr, H. Molkenbuhr.
2. *Plan of Organization, Method of Propaganda and Resolutions, Adopted by the Pittsburgh Congress of the "International Working Peoples' Association"* . . . , p. 4 (photostat of this pamphlet supplied by Miss Inglis); Hillquit, *op. cit.*, p. 218.
3. Files of the *Freiheit*, 1883-1886, particularly issues of April 14, May 5, June 30, 1883, December 26, 1885, and May 1, 1886; Nettlau, *op. cit.*, p. 382.
4. *Alarm*, October 11, 1884, August 8, 1885, November 15, 22, 1886.
5. November 23, 1884, for example.

6. *Ibid.,* November 22, 1884.
7. *Alarm,* May 2, 1885.
8. Wage reductions caused this bitterly fought and unsuccessful strike in Hocking Valley, Ohio. The strike involved some 4,000 coal miners, and lasted for six months.
9. He had been Minister to France during the Paris Commune.
10. *Ibid.,* November 29, 1884.
11. *Ibid.,* February 7, 1885.
12. *Ibid.,* January 15, 1885.
13. *Ibid.,* February 7, 1885.
14. *Cf., ibid.,* February 21, March 7, 1885.
15. *Ibid.,* March 7, 1885. There were frequent listings of the groups in the *Alarm; cf., ibid.,* October 17, 1885.
16. *Ibid.,* March 7, May 16, 1885; Sartorius von Waltershausen, *op. cit.,* p. 236 gives 7,000 members for 1887.
17. The circulation figures for the *Arbeiter-Zeitung* are: 1883, 5,200; 1884, 5,326; 1885, 5,110; 1886, 5,780. The number for 1883 was estimated; the figures for the other years were claimed by the publishers. The circulation of the *Vorbote* rose above the number given to 7,115 in 1884. The circulation of the *Factel* for 1884 and 1885 was 10,035 and 10,000 respectively. Both figures are those of the publishers. The *Freiheit* appeared as a weekly in 1882. *Die Parole* and *Proletar* both appeared in 1884. The *Alarm* appeared both fortnightly and monthly during its hectic life. It suspended publication in May, 1886, and was not revived until November 5, 1887 under the editorship of Dyer D. Lum. The *Vorbote* appeared as early as 1874 as a weekly, and so it remained. It was at first an organ of the Labor Party of Illinois. In 1876 is became an organ of the S.L.P. The *Factel,* a Sunday weekly, appeared in 1878. The first number of the *Arbeiter-Zeitung* came out June 1, 1876. George Engel and others started to publish *Der Anarchist,* a monthly, in Chicago in January, 1886. It gave up the ghost after four or at most five numbers. See below, p. 142. All the publications listed above were appearing in 1886. Nettlau, *op. cit.,* p. 376; Nettlau, *Bibliographie,* pp. 179-185; Kamman, *op. cit.,* pp. 47-49; Hillquit, *op. cit.,* p. 191; *N. W. Ayer and Son's American Newspaper Annual,* Philadelphia, 1883-1886; *Truth,* June, July, 1886.
18. See below, p. 131, n. 61.
19. *Alarm,* May 30, 1885.
20. *Cf., ibid.,* October 11, 1884, "Enslaved Labor."
21. November 29, 1884.
22. December 6, 1886.
23. March 7, 1885.
24. While it is true that for Bakunin the criticism of the State was the point of departure in his political thought, and that he regarded it as a "monstrous growth which nourished itself upon and oppressed society," his view of the State was also conditioned by a somewhat mystical conception of the nature of the proletariat. He

did not think of the proletariat in terms of class, but as "a sort of moving ocean," "une lave informe qui devait inonder l'univers, mais qui renoncerait toujours à prendre un moule rigide." Thus he always spoke of "masses" and not classes. The State was the principal obstacle to the happiness of the masses. It put an end to the "obscure agitation of the masses which was expressing the very idea of humanity." The State is thus the negation of humanity. To save humanity—not merely a class—it is necessary to destroy all political power, which is, after all, a crystallized manifestation of the State. Iswolsky, *op. cit.,* pp. 220-222; Lagardelle, *loc. cit.,* p. 322.

25. *Alarm,* January 13, 1885.
26. *Alarm,* April 4, 1885.
27. March 7, 1885.
28. November 22, 1884. Though the approach, as well as the final conclusions, in each case is markedly different, it is interesting to compare this with William Godwin, *An Enquiry Concerning Political Justice and Its Influence on General Virtue and Happiness,* edited and abridged by Raymond A. Preston, New York, 1926, vol. 1, pp. 70-71.
29. Samuel Bernstein, *The Beginnings of Marxian Socialism in France,* New York, 1933, pp. 92-93; Charles Gide and Charles Rist, *A History of Economic Doctrines from the Time of the Physiocrats to the Present Day,* translated from the second revised edition by William Smart, New York, n.d., p. 468; Jessica Peixotto, *The French Revolution and Modern French Socialism. A Comparative Study of the French Revolution and the Doctrines of Modern French Socialism,* New York, 1901, pp. vii-viii, 314 *ff.*
30. October 4, 1884.
31. *Ibid.,* March 7, 1885.
32. *Ibid.,* November 1, 1884.
33. *Ibid.,* November 14, 1885.
34. Henry David Thoreau, "On the Duty of Civil Disobedience," in *Man or the State?* compiled and edited by Waldo R. Browne, New York, 1919, pp. 70-89.
35. *Alarm,* March 7, 1887.
36. *Ibid.,* November 8, 1884.
37. *Ibid.,* March 7, 1885; *cf.* Parsons' communication in *Truth,* June, 1884, pp. 39, 41.
38. *Alarm,* November 29, December 13, 1884.
39. See above, p. 111.
40. *Ibid.,* November 29, 1884.
41. *Idem.*
42. November 8, 1884.
43. *Ibid.,* October 11, 1884.
44. *Ibid.,* March 7, 1885; Parsons' communication in *Journal of United Labor,* July, 1883, pp. 531-532.
45. March 23, 1885.

46. April 8, 1885.
47. *Alarm*, May 2, 1885. Samuel Fielden was speaking, and these remarks are typical of hundreds of similar exhortations.
48. April 4, 1885.
49. May 2, 1885.
50. *Cf., ibid.*, April 18, May 16, June 27, 1885. The issue of March 21, 1885, carried the announcement that following numbers would contain articles on the manufacture and use of dynamite bombs.
51. June 27, 1885.
52. *Cf., ibid.*, June 27, July 25, December 26, 1885; *Arbeiter-Zeitung*, March 15, 1885.
53. *Alarm*, November 15, 1884.
54. *Ibid.*, November 1, 1884.
55. He was a member of the I.W.P.A., living in Indianapolis.
56. February 21, 1885. This appeared on the third page of the *Alarm*, and is signed T. Lizius. The first section is very frequently quoted as if it were an expression of editorial opinion.
57. *Ibid.*, October 4, 1884.
58. *Ibid.*, April 18, 1885.
59. Thomas A. Scott, president of the Pennsylvania R. R.
60. *Ibid.*, November 1, 1884.
61. Lum, born in 1840, died April 6, 1893. He dedicated much of his life to the cause after seeing service in the Civil War. In 1876 he was a candidate for Lieutenant-Governor in Massachusetts, and served as secretary to a congressional commission in 1877. He was a man of decided intellectual ability.
62. *Ibid.*, June 13, 1885.
63. *Ibid.*, January 13, 1885.
64. October 25, 1884.
65. This lively anarchist periodical published in Valley Falls, Kansas, was not regarded as an organ of the I.W.P.A.
66. *Ibid.*, August 8, 1885.
67. *Ibid.*, November 1, 1884.
68. This was immediately after the death sentence had been imposed upon Parsons in connection with the Haymarket bomb. See below, chap. XV.
69. At the fourth session of the General Assembly of the K. of L. (September 7-11, 1880), Powderly urged the abolition of the "curse of modern civilization—wage-slavery." McNeill, *op. cit.*, pp. 410-411.
70. Entire letter quoted in *The Labor Leaf*, September 1, 1886.
71. There can be no real dispute on this point.
72. January 24, 1886.
73. Abbot, *op. cit.*, p. 97. For Harrison, see also Johnson, *op. cit., passim;* Lloyd Lewis and Henry Justin Smith, *Chicago, The History of Its Reputation*, New York, 1929, pp. 158-159.
74. Abbot, *op. cit.*, pp. 140, 142-143.
75. *Op. cit.*, p. 44. He cites the *Freiheit*, February 18, 1884, in proof.

76. *Ibid.,* p. 63.
77. February 23, 1885.
78. *Cf.,* August 8, 22, 1885.
79. These words are Parsons' and they were used in his letter to Powderly cited above, pp. 124-125, and in his address to the court, see below, pp. 342-343.
80. Quoted in *Life of Albert R. Parsons,* p. 101.
81. This is as well put as it ever was in the *Alarm* in *Anarchism: Its Philosophy and Scientific Basis as Defined by Some of Its Apostles,* Chicago, 1887, pp. 164-166. Authorship is credited to Parsons but only a portion of the book is his; his wife did the editing.

VI. UTOPIA—CHICAGO STYLE

NOWHERE is the lack of consistent and systematic thinking more striking or the language more carelessly employed than in the discussions of the nature of the new social order. It might even be said that to systematize the "doctrines" of the Chicago leaders during this period deprives their thought of an essential trait.

To the Chicago revolutionaries the glorious commonwealth of the future continued to be known as the "free society." [1] "This free society would be purely economic in its character. . . ." Economically it rests upon the principle "that the means of life—all things necessary to sustain existence—must belong to the whole people." This point is emphasized time and again in various ways. "We would make capital common property, indivisible and inalienable." "Free land, air, light and water. Free access to all the productive and distributive forces. . . ."

In so far as the "free society" rests economically upon the socialization of the means of production, it is unmistakably socialistic. In contrast to Marx, however, it seems to be assumed that the establishment of a socialist economy follows immediately on the heels of the destruction of capitalism. No transition period is provided for by way of the dictatorship of the proletariat. [2] This idea could not be accepted since it was believed that the State *and every coercive institution must first* be destroyed before the "free society" could be brought into existence. The idea of the domination of one class in place of another—the proletariat in place of the bourgeoisie—was out of tune with the insistence of the Chicago revolutionaries upon a completely classless society free from all marks of privilege which would follow the destruction or abolition—not the gradual disappearance—of the State and law. Thus they would even probably reject Engels' view of the transition to the new social order which, superficially at least, seems much closer to what they vaguely had in mind.

"The proletariate seizes the State power," wrote Engels, *"and transforms the means of production in the first instance into State property.* But in doing this, it puts an end to itself as the proletariate, it puts an end to all class differences and class antagonisms, it puts an end also to the state as state. . . . When . . . [the State] becomes really representative of society as a whole, it makes itself superfluous. . . . The first act in which the state really comes forward as the representative of society as a whole—the taking possession of the means of production in the name of society—is at the same time its last independent act as a state. . . . The state is not 'abolished,' *it withers away."* [3]

The Chicago revolutionaries never realized the necessity of providing for a transition period, probably because they were never impelled to examine thoroughly the process by which a capitalist society was to be transformed into a socialized one. Instead they visualized a total and immediate replacement of one social order by the other—a change depending on and consisting in the abolition of the State and the socialization of the means of production—rather than a process of transformation.

With these two steps taken, presumably simultaneously, the essentially economic "free society," "dealing only with the production and distribution of wealth," is established. The "free society" operates as "one grand corporation, or what seems to express it better, one grand co-operation." If this appears ambiguous, further descriptions of the "free society" do not shed much more light. It is "A uniting of all men and all private and incorporated enterprises in one grand corporation, that this mighty engine may be wielded for the benefit of each man, and against no man." The following, too, attempts to convey the same idea: "We would substitute co-operative labor for the present system of private enterprise with its hired labor. This would make the wage laborers their own masters, instead of the hirelings and serfs they are now." Here there is suggested a completely unified economic order, free from any single regulatory or controlling body, in which every "human being" is sovereign and is "freely producing and freely consuming," in which money and prices do not exist. There will be no buying and selling which "is but another name for robbing and killing." Whether the producers will get equal returns for their labor or whether the return will be determined by their needs is never made altogether clear. There is a slight hint that the Chicago leaders had the latter in mind in the equivocal statement that when the "free society" will be instituted no person "could be denied any reasonable or natural demand."

The corollary to the absence of all coercive elements in the "free society" is voluntary association. This is implied in the term "co-operative," which was so frequently employed. What units, however, were to be linked together voluntarily? They were the "autonomous communes" mentioned in the Pittsburgh Manifesto. These "communes" in turn obviously had to result from the free association of individuals.[4] In considering the problem of free association and the associative units, however, the Chicago leaders, notably Parsons and Spies introduced something which was not present in the Pittsburgh Manifesto.[5]

As a purely economic society the new order would deal "only with the production and distribution of wealth," and it was planned that "The various occupations and individuals would voluntarily associate to conduct the processes of distribution and production. The shoemakers, carpenters, farmers, printers, moulders and others would form autonomous or independent groups or communities, regulating all affairs to suit their pleasure. The Trades' Union, Assemblies and other labor organizations are but the initial groups of the free society." [6] This statement is significant. The Pittsburgh Manifesto was completely silent on the question of the trade-union, though the Congress itself was not. That document did not even remotely hint that labor organizations were to be the unit cells of the future commonwealth. In this statement lies the first real evidence of anything resembling the syndicalist tendency with which the Chicago movement has usually been credited.

Despite the labor affiliations of the Chicago revolutionaries and the effect of their movement upon local labor organizations,[7] there are few definite suggestions before March, 1885, that the trade-union (or any comparable labor organization) is to be regarded as the primary unit in the coming society. Thus, even if the strong syndicalist coloring of the movement, recognized by Prof. Selig Perlman, be admitted, it cannot be said to be present throughout the entire period 1883-1886. Furthermore, the Chicago "doctrinaires"—if the word can be applied with justice to Spies and Parsons—were patently driven to giving the trade-union a more prominent place in their scheme of things by criticism from organized labor.

The *Labor Enquirer* charged that the I.W.P.A. was not only opposed to the trade-unions but would wage a war to the death upon them. If Johann Most's utterances represented the views of the International on the question, the assertion was justifiable. Parsons, however, undertaking to defend the I.W.P.A. from this accusation, bluntly declared that the statement was wholly incorrect. In proof he submitted the labor resolution adopted by the Pittsburgh Congress, which, he declared, represented the official attitude of the International on the trade-union question. Either because of his own trade-union sentiments, or because he felt that the censorious accusation of the *Labor Enquirer* might jeopardize the movement in trade-union circles if it went unanswered, Parsons went even further. "The International," he wrote, "recognizes in the Trades Union the embryonic group of the future 'free society.'

Every Trade Union is, *nolens volens,* an autonomous commune in process of incubation. The Trades Union is a necessity of capitalistic production, and will yet take its [capitalistic production's] place by superseding it under the system of universal free co-operation." The I.W.P.A. is not at odds with the trade-union as such. Quite the contrary. It is with "the methods which some of them employ . . . which the International finds fault, and as indifferently as it may be considered by some, the development of capitalism is hastening the day when all Trades Unions and Anarchists will of necessity become one and the same." [8]

Largely on the basis of this statement, Prof. Perlman argues that the significant rôle thus given to the trade-unions made the doctrines of Spies and Parsons "distinctly 'syndicalistic' . . ." [9] He finds that in Chicago there took place a "blending of anarchism and trade unionism" which "produced a kind of 'syndicalism' which was not dissimilar from the French 'syndicalism' of to-day." The views of Spies and Parsons on the "ideal society, trade union action (or direct action), political action, and the use of violence in strikes," in Prof. Perlman's eyes warrant this conclusion. He holds that this early "syndicalism" was present in 1883. [10]

In a later number of the *Alarm,* Parsons qualified his blanket acceptance of the trade-union. Not every trade-union in existence, he wrote, operates to destroy capitalism. ". . . the union which says 'there is no occasion for war between employer and employe,' and can see nothing wrong in the wage system, which places the worker's life and liberty at the disposal of any and every employer, cannot be expected to do justice with each other and among themselves. Such a union is no union at all. . . ." [11] This merely echoed the gist of Spies' resolution on the union question adopted by the Pittsburgh Congress. In the face of his previous declaration, it indicated Parsons' distrust of—if not his thorough-going opposition to—every labor organization which was disinclined to accept the class-struggle theory and was not militantly dedicated to the destruction of the wage system. If only those trade-unions which subscribed to these points both in theory *and practise* could be designated as "true" unions, then the vast majority of American labor organizations would have to be ruled out. Those not falling into the first class actually served, in Parsons' view, as props of the capitalistic order.[12] This is inferentially admitted in an editorial in the *Alarm* on "Socialistic Trade Unions," where the need for labor organizations to constitute an advance guard in the struggle against capitalism is shown and their formation urged.

"In their [employers'] minds all workers are more or less anarchistic, and during a strike intimidation and physical force are in various ways resorted to in order to prevent other persons from taking the places of those . . . on . . . strike. . . . Physical force and armed interference keep the workers in subjection . . . therefore, in self-defense must every worker be ready to strike back, and the socialistic labor movement has necessarily reached the stage when every trades union and mixed group is also a military organization. . . . The principles and practises of the socialistic labor movement furnish the only safe and reliable foundations for keeping the working people within trades unions . . . and therefore must we without delay go to work and organize socialistic trade unions, who will unite, discipline, arm and lead the workers in the fight against capitalistic spoliation." [13]

There is a definite syndicalist ring to the concluding sentence. But in order to decide whether the Chicago revolutionaries may be credited with elaborating "a full-blown program of revolutionary syndicalism in all but the name itself" some twenty years before it appeared on the Continent, the nature of European Syndicalism must be first briefly examined.

Syndicalism, as it has developed in France and to a lesser extent in Italy after the opening of the present century, springs essentially from Marxian sources. In it there are, however, definite anarchistic and Blanquist [14] influences, and it must be considered in the light of the history of the French labor movement. Accepting the class-struggle idea as well as other elements from Marxism, Syndicalism rejects all political and parliamentary action. The great change is to be wrought not through political action but through direct action of the working class organized in *syndicats* (trade-unions) which must be free from all middle-class spirit or ideals. The *syndicat* should be industrial rather than craft in nature. Through the *syndicat* the workers are enabled to engage in a direct struggle with their employers. The workers must display a heightened class-consciousness, reject all compromise, and labor unceasingly in their own interests. The revolution will not come "inevitably." It must be *made* by the proletariat. The key to the emancipation of the working-class lies in "direct action" by the working-class itself. Direct action, which is not necessarily violent action, is not only a manifestation of the will of the proletariat, but it provides the sole real means of exerting pressure in attaining its end. The best expression of direct action is the strike, especially the general strike, since it strengthens the "will to revolution" and sharpens the antagonism between classes. The general strike thus appears as a necessary preliminary of the revolution. In addition to the strike, direct action may also find expression in the boycott, sabotage and the label. Force, in the last analysis, is the lever by which the present order will be overturned. The social revolution will abolish the State, and in the new social order the unit cell will be the trade union (*syndicat*). Property will be socially owned. The workers will control industry through the *syndicats,* all of which will be linked together in a voluntary, federated system. Thus, Syndicalism proposes in a sense "an economic pluralism, a feudalism within the industrial organization." [15]

Undoubtedly the doctrines of the European syndicalists and the thought of the Chicago revolutionaries—especially that of Parsons and Spies—contain common elements. With reference to certain questions such as political action, reform measures, compromise with employers and the like, there are strong resemblances between the two. But despite such striking similarities, there are several considerations which offer ground for questioning whether the Chicago movement can be credited with a "full-blown program of revolutionary syndicalism in everything but the name itself. . . ." [16]

There is contained in the writings of the Chicago leaders much that is utterly foreign to the nature of modern Syndicalism—witness their eighteenth century phrases and ideas. So inconsistent is the body of their teaching, that careful pruning and selection are necessary to make the syndicalist strain stand out sharply. They never understood direct action in the same terms as do the syndicalists. Nor did they elaborate a comparable theory of the general strike. Had they done this, their first response to the eight-hour day movement could never have been a negative one. Its value in the light of a general labor strike would have been seized immediately. [17] Their assumption, however short-lived, that the capitalist order might be brought to ruin simply by the voluntary cessation of buying and selling, or, with equal ease, by a liberal application of dynamite is, on its face, wholly unsyndicalist.

Then there is the undeniable fact that those utterances of the Chicago leaders which smack most strongly of modern Syndicalism appeared in answer to the sharp criticism of the International from the ranks of organized labor. The looseness which marks the enunciation of principles by the social revolutionaries in 1883 was in part caused by their desire to attract as many radical or revolutionary factions in the country as possible. Probably the position of the Chicago leaders in the spring and summer of 1885 on the revolutionary rôle of the trade-union was produced by a similar motive. At any rate, the known facts do not exclude the hypothesis that the importance then given to the trade-union was designed to identify the interests of organized labor with the revolutionaries. The Chicago leaders, interestingly enough, did not press the points announced in the spring and summer of 1885. Between that date and May 1886, there were few if any utterances of the same views. [18]

To what extent the distinctive position given to the trade-union by some of the Chicago leaders was commonly accepted by the mass of the members of the I.W.P.A.—or even of the Chicago groups—cannot be determined. C. S. Griffin, Sam Fielden, Gorsuch, Engel and others who were active at the time or later, did not—at least positive evidence that they did is lacking—regard the trade-union as the unit cell of the future commonwealth. Among others, Louis Fischer, concerning whom a great deal will be said later,[19] makes no mention of a free, associative society built upon the labor union in a letter in which he summarizes his views.[20] Dyer D. Lum, a frequent contributor to the columns of the *Alarm* and intellectually head and shoulders above most of the Chicago revolutionaries, never pointedly wrote of the trade-union as the co-operative unit of the free society.[21]

"Liberty . . . is the basis upon which true co-operation rests," wrote Lum. "To remove the shackles from individual activity in order that co-operative activity may have natural genesis is the mission of anarchy. It looks to the state only to abolish privilege; it looks to the freeman for the co-operative unit." In an article discussing the nature of the "productive group" in the future society which appears to have been written by Spies' close associate, Michael Schwab, the trade-union concept is lacking.[22]

There was also among the social-revolutionaries of the city a small group of extremists, in which George Engel was a leading figure. It is almost impossible to find an adequate exposition of the views of this group except on the question of violence. One of the members of the group of whom much will be said later, Louis Lingg, in a statement of "principles," declared that in the "free society" of the future, there was to be neither coercion nor authority. Production and distribution were to be communistic and "co-operative." "Men can organize," he wrote, "into groups of production in accord with their individual inclinations. . . ." This was to be done voluntarily; there was to be no centralized direction of production or distribution. Commodities were to be exchanged mutually by equating them in terms of labor time. This ideal society, which could function without authority because men were naturally good, was to be introduced by violence. Lingg certainly did not visualize the trade-union as the basic cell of the coming social order.[23] Nor did the extremist group to which he belonged, as far as it can be seen. George Engel had no real grasp of the revolutionary principles he discussed in the columns of the *Anarchist*. He proposed no special plan for the organization of the social-revolutionary utopia, distinguishing himself largely by his brutal version of the anarchist position on government and the State.[24]

As a matter of fact, and this should have been long evident, the various doctrines validly associated with the Chicago movement resist almost entirely being pressed into one of the familiar categories of revolutionary theory. In their bottling of the social panacea, the social-revolutionaries were extremely careless both with label and ingredients. They used the terms Anarchism, Socialism and Communism interchangeably, as if to imply that there was no essential difference among them.[25] "We are called by some Communists, or Socialists, or Anarchists," announced Parsons. "We accept all three of the terms." [26] At one moment Anarchism and Socialism are bluntly declared to be identic.[27] At another it is asserted "We are Socialists, pure and simple, where all titles are simple possessions, with no schemes for perpetuating unions, or preventing them." [28] Spies, classed as a socialist in March, 1885, lectures as an anarchist in February of the following year, and points out that the economic goals of Anarchism and Marxian Communism are indistinguishable.[29] Engel sees no difference between Socialism and Anarchism except in tactics.[30] In the summer of 1885 the leaders commonly describe their doctrines as Communism. In January of the following year they call themselves "Anarchistic Socialists." [31] The only fairly definite tendencies in nomenclature that may be observed are the increasing frequency with which the word "Anarchy" and its derivatives are employed after the spring of 1885, and the greater use of combination terms such as "Communist Anarchism," "Socialist Anarchism," and the like.[32]

This loose use of terminology sorely distressed the strict social-democrats in Chicago who took pains to point out that Socialism was not Communism and was severely at odds with Anarchism. They, therefore, guarded themselves from confusing the three conceptions in their propaganda.[33] After the Haymarket bomb was thrown, the Executive Committee of the S.L.P. issued a pamphlet in which the differences between Socialism, Communism and "nihilism" were more strongly emphasized, and in which the "revolutionary anarchists" were stigmatized as the worst enemies of true Socialism.[34]

The very confusion of terms, the mixed doctrines, lack of clear thinking and inadequate knowledge, all indicate that the leaders of the Chicago movement were groping towards the formulation of a social philosophy essentially communistic in its economic aspects and anarchistic in its "political" implications. Though they declared that the future commonwealth was to be primarily economic in nature, they were most intensely concerned with a negative characteristic of the "free society," the complete absence of all governmental and coercive institutions. This they regarded as an absolute prerequisite to the existence of the new society. With Bakunin they would declare: ". . . we reject all legislation, all authority, and all privileged, licensed, official and legal influence, even though arising from universal suffrage. . . ."[35] They never tired talking of the sovereign individual and the substitution of "equal rights and equal duties" for "law."[36] This point was succinctly presented by Dyer D. Lum. "Anarchy, or the total cessation of force government," he wrote, "is the fundamental principle upon which all our arguments are based. Communism is a question of administration in the future, and hence must be subordinate to and in accordance with the principles of Anarchy and all its logical deductions."[37]

The attempted reconciliation of anarchistic and socialistic

or communistic elements was neither complete nor free from major contradictions. As far as it went, however, it produced a species of anti-authoritarian Socialism (or Communism) to which there was added the theory of propaganda by deed, and violent, forceful revolution. The underlying contradiction between anti-authoritarianism and the employment of force was generally minimized. In any case, the employment of coercive measures in the face of a blanket condemnation of all coercion could always be justified on the ground that force was the chief prop of the existing order.

The condemnation of governmental authority—the chief source of anti-authoritarianism—was accompanied by the repudiation of all forms of authority. Thus, there was the usual assault upon the Church, social custom and sometimes the "bourgeois" family. Criticism of these, however, was never as significant in the eyes of the Chicago revolutionaries as it was to Most and his followers.[38] In this sense the former concerned themselves far more strictly with essentials. Their general attitude is well represented by those passages in the Pittsburgh Manifesto which touch upon the Church.

Even a superficial examination of the "revolutionary spirit" of those who constituted the Chicago movement shows several marked psychological traits. These may be said to be broadly similar to those commonly ascribed to most extremists, whether classed as implacable revolutionaries or religious fanatics.[39] Especially is one struck by their violent love of liberty —the obvious corollary to their equally intense hatred of authority. This went far beyond a demand for specific liberties. Liberty loomed in their minds as a glorious, absolute ideal, however vague or ill-defined. So strong was this love of liberty, in some instances, that it led some of them to thoroughly authoritarian words, if not deeds. A passionateness and aggressiveness marked nearly every utterance of theirs. Equally evident was their righteousness, the natural concomitant of an unshakable conviction that their beliefs were wholly "true." They were highly impressionable and emotionally easily excited. One seems to sense in them a constant nervous tension. That they should exhibit a certain measure of illogicality is not strange. It seems unwarranted to infer, as has been done, from the emphasis which they gave to the words "reason," "logic" and "science" that a well developed "sense of logic" was one of their primary traits.[40]

Their sensitiveness to "social injustice" was extremely keen. It was with a sort of impatient, sharpened and exaggerated humanitarianism that they responded to the iniquities of capitalism. This led them, in part, to urge violence and recommend the destruction of life, without hesitation. The tender letter on the social injustices of a capitalistic society written by T. Lizius, who produced the tribute to dynamite published in the *Alarm,* illustrates this.[41] Their sensitiveness led their cordial enemies, the social-democrats, to assert that the "revolutionary Anarchists" were not only a product of the injustices of the existing social order, but that they were "rendered crazy" by it.[42] This characteristic perhaps sprang from an unconscious identification of the individual self with society at large. Despite their dominant individualism, which was at once egoistic and self-sufficient, they were capable of assuming in turn, the woes of the world upon their shoulders, a social spleen and, in consequence, a broad altruism.

The revolutionary spirit, of course, expressed itself in a fervor of proselytizing activity. There were men in the movement who were born missionaries, many of whom, like many missionaries of the Church, were apparently ready to suffer martyrdom. How much of this complete "dedication to the cause" was mere lip-service, and how much was profoundly sincere, can never be known. Nor can one say how many of those urging violent deeds were actually capable of them. Perhaps the vast majority would have found the execution of what they advised wholly impossible. By temperament they were not fitted for the acts they so energetically encouraged. It may be said—with more truth than cynicism—that the Chicago revolutionaries fell into two groups: one, consisting of but a handful, really contemplated violent action; the second contemplated nothing more dangerous than violent accusation and denunciation.

In the fall of 1885, there was much talk of the union of the I.W.P.A., especially the Chicago wing, with another International, the International Workingmen's Association, founded in San Francisco, July 15, 1881. This organization owed its birth and existence largely to Burnette G. Haskell, a young American lawyer who detested his profession and who was well grounded in revolutionary doctrines and labor problems.[43] Haskell's unquestionably brilliant mind was unfortunately affected with an erratic streak which caused many people to lose confidence in him. Though it looked to the defunct Marxist International as its intellectual parent, the I.W.A was also affiliated with the International re-established by the London Congress of 1881, from which it borrowed much in the way of organization.

Though unmistakably socialistic, the doctrines of the I.W.A. were marked by several distinctive traits. Among the most outstanding may be noted the unusual stress placed upon education, the definite "natural rights" strain,[44] the complete opposition to political action in juxtaposition with the rejection of propaganda by deed, and the willingness to unite with other "revolutionary" bodies.

"The cause of all misery, vice, poverty and crime," announced the I.W.A., "is the system which denies to each worker the full value of what the worker produces." In place of the present capitalistic order, it looked forward to a "scientific system of governmental co-operation of the working-people." Here, too, a "Co-operative Commonwealth" is to replace a competitive capitalistic order. Only one barrier stands in the way of the inauguration of that ideal—the ignorance of the working-class. Therefore, "The only way to remove that barrier is the way of EDUCATION." Ultimately, as a result of the proper educational campaign, a stage will be reached where the ruling class will become thoroughly frightened. In consequence there will be precipitated "a universal revolution from the throes of which the NEW WORLD will be born." Political action was to be absolutely excluded as a means of education. It was more than pointless. It was pernicious, since political activity served only to degrade a people. The inevitable social revolution may be accompanied by violence, but violence must not precede it. Forceful action before it breaks, is suicidal, traitorous to the cause.[45]

Propaganda by deed, where the means for oral and written propaganda exist, as in the United States, wrote Haskell, is wholly unnecessary. "And I should be sorry," he continued, "to see any steps taken to spread our doctrines here by the indiscriminate use of dynamite. We want dynamite collectively for the revolution when it comes. We can applaud its use by individuals . . . to right their private wrongs; but its whole-sale use merely for propaganda does not the slightest good and those who . . . advocate it are no real friends of the social revolution." Reaction in one form or another would result and the great upheaval would only be postponed.[46]

Completely public in its methods of propaganda, its doctrines and aims, the I.W.A. was partly secret in organization. Its smallest divisions were groups consisting of only nine members, which met when and where they pleased. Each member, to whom the division executive issued a red card, was under obligation to form another group, but not more than one. Theoretically, the members of the I.W.A. were thus individually acquainted with only sixteen fellow members. Both groups and members were designated by numbers and letters rather than by names. The groups made up the divisions of which there never were more than two,—the Pacific Coast Division and the Rocky Mountain Division. Haskell was division executive of the first and "Joe" Buchanan of Denver, who had already played an active rôle in the labor movement in the mid-West, headed the second, which he founded in 1883. The I.W.A. was always strongest on the Pacific Coast, where out of a total claimed membership of 6,000 in 1887, 3,800 were to be found in California, Oregon and Washington Territory alone. The remainder were scattered through the Rocky Mountain Division and in the South and East. The chief organ of the I.W.A., founded as a weekly in 1882, Haskell's *Truth,* was also much concerned with the Chinese problem. By the summer of 1884, *Truth* was appearing as a monthly, and at the end of the year went out of existence. Much of the burden of propaganda was then carried by Buchanan's interesting Denver *Labor Enquirer.*[47] The columns of *Truth* were always open to revolutionists of all stripes, and Parsons, Mrs. Holmes and others of the Chicago movement were occasional contributors. Whatever evidence there is indicates that the I.W.A. was more successful in winning converts from labor ranks than was the I.W.P.A. A great many local labor leaders were captured for the cause, and large numbers of Knights of Labor became members of the I.W.A.[48] The two organizations, the I.W.P.A. and the I.W.A., were popularly distinguished from one another by the terms "Black" International and "Red" International respectively.

After allowing several suggestions for the affiliation of the "Red" and "Black" Internationals to go unanswered,[49] the *Alarm* finally announced that it saw no good reason why the proposal should not be accepted.

"The 'Black' and 'Red' International may differ upon the constructive side, but both believe in the final overthrow of the property beast by revolutionary action.[50] The members of both are thoroughly and permanently divorced from the bourgeoisie world around them. They have nothing in common with existing societary regulations. . . . Neither branch believes in the possibility of obtaining labor's emancipation by peaceable methods, and both know that industrial slaves have no political power; all are brothers; comrades in the same underlying cause, and all internationalists look forward with eager anticipation to the universal social revolution." [51]

To the plea for harmony and union which followed this statement W. C. Owen, secretary of the central committee of the I.W.A., replied by urging that the two bodies sink their differences. He asserted that the members of his organization were of the "opinion that *every* available weapon" should be used to overthrow the existing social order.

The union, as might be expected, was never consummated, but it cannot be said which of the two organizations was responsible. The I.W.P.A. had given every indication in the past that it would not compromise on major differences and perhaps lose its own identity for the sake of uniting with any other revolutionary body. After reaching its height in 1886-1887, the I.W.A. experienced a sharp decline, and soon went out of existence as a distinct organization. Alliance with the S.L.P. was contemplated but never carried through. Many I.W.A. members, however, finally were found in the ranks of that party.

To what extent did the blurred principles of the social-revolutionaries of Chicago and their doctrines of violence affect the workers of the city? It was only natural that the American Group decided, on May 14, 1885, "to arm and organize into a company and become part of the military organization now forming throughout the city . . . [and] to establish a school on chemistry, where the manufacture and use of explosives would be taught." [52] There is, however, no evidence which shows that such a school was founded, or that the ninety-five members of the group joined one of the *Lehr und Wehr Vereine* already in existence. On the contrary, it is known that not all the members of the American Group were *Lehr und Wehr* members.[53] As a result of the intensive propaganda campaign waged between 1883 and 1886, an increase in the membership of the *Lehr und Wehr Vereine* should have taken place. The files of the *Alarm* give the impression that this actually occurred, but so inadequate are the data on this point, that reliable statistics on the growth in membership cannot be compiled.

Outside of Chicago, there were after 1884, armed groups in Detroit (The Detroit Rifles), in Cincinnati (The Rifle

Union), in St. Louis (two *Lehr und Wehr Vereine*), in Omaha (The International Guards), in Newark *(Lehr und Wehr Vereine)*, in New York (*Lehr und Wehr Verein* and International Guards Association), in San Francisco (an armed branch of the Shriners), in Denver, and other cities.[54]

Early in 1886, the armed associations in Chicago received a severe blow. On January 4, the United States Supreme Court in the case of *Presser* v. *the State of Illinois*[55] held that the Illinois "statute prohibiting all bodies of armed men excepting the regular State militia and United States troops from associating, drilling or parading with arms in any city" without having a license from the governor, is valid. Association in military groups in the face of State law to the contrary was not a right which a citizen of the United States could claim.[56] This decision put an end to public drilling and parading with weapons by the armed groups in Chicago. Though they continued to exist, their activities were carried on quasi-secretly.[57]

The efforts to "educate" the worker in the employment of force and in revolutionary ideology did bring some positive results, but the return did not compare favorably with the energy expended. In the spring of 1884, under the leadership of the Progressive Cigar Makers Union No. 15, the Central Labor Union of Chicago was formed. This body was made up of delegates from butchers', metal workers', painters', cigarmakers', printers', cabinet-makers', and other trade-unions composed largely of foreigners. Many of the affiliated unions were frankly radical or had radical leanings. A good number of the unions were clearly under socialist or I.W.P.A. influence. When it was about a year old, the Central Labor Union claimed a membership of some 12,000. In the spring of 1885, it recommended that the workers arm in answer to the employment of Pinkertons, police and militia by their employers.[58] At the same time some extremists among the cigar-makers found the existing organizations too tame, and accordingly organized the Revolutionary Cigar Makers Association, which appears to have been affiliated with the I.W.P.A., and which actively carried on the propaganda of the "Black" International.

Many metal workers appear to have been extremely receptive to propaganda urging the use of force. After their participation in a successful strike at the McCormick Harvester plant in April, 1885, which was marked by bitter clashes between strikers, Pinkerton agents and strike breakers, the metal workers' union resolved to arm its members, and an armed section of the union seems to have been established. The Metal Workers' Federation Union of Chicago, formed in 1885, announced that the working-class could be emancipated only by "the entire abolition of the present system of society," and proposed a co-operative free commonwealth as the ideal social order. This is a clear reflection of the influence of the Chicago social-revolutionaries, as is the decentralized plan of trade-union organization which was recommended. It was also strenuously opposed to participation in politics, and placed dependence upon education of and direct action by the workers. Beyond these evidences, however, the activities of the social-revolutionaries apparently made little impression upon the labor movement of Chicago.[59]

Industrial disputes during this period, especially those in the southwest involving railroads, were sometimes accompanied by sabotage on the part of the workers. In the course of the strike on the Denver and Rio Grande in 1885, even dynamite was several times employed. Dynamite may have been also used in and around New York City in the course of labor disputes between 1883 and 1886. These activities, however, are not to be ascribed to the propaganda of the I.W.P.A. In the case of the southwestern railroad strikes the workers resorted to sabotage without the slightest influence of the "Black" International.[60]

Though Chicago did not take the talk of arming the workers with oppressive seriousness, the city nevertheless did not regard it with benign amusement. Dispatches from Chicago dated February 8, 1885, assert that the presence of armed groups in the city resulted in the formation of military bodies on the part of business men, the organization of armed bands by employees in wholesale houses, and the enlargement of the national guard. It was reported that "Although the fact is not generally known even in this city, in one large business house alone there is an organization of 150 young men who have been armed with Remington breech-loading rifles and pursue a regular course of drilling. . . . This is by no means an isolated case."[61] On Thanksgiving Day of the same year, the militia held a street-riot drill in Chicago which had all the earmarks of a warning not very subtly given.[62]

NOTES CHAPTER VI

1. See the Pittsburgh Manifesto.
2. In his letter to Weydemeyer in 1852 and in his criticism of the Gotha program, Marx pointed out that the transition from capitalism to Communism is made possible by the dictatorship of the proletariat. Cited in Sidney Hook, *Toward the Understanding of Karl Marx*, New York, 1933, pp. 299, 304; Werner Sombart, *Socialism and the Social Movement*, translated by M. Epstein, London, 1909, pp. 69-71.
3. Friedrich Engels, *Herr Eugen Dühring's Revolution in Science (Anti-Dühring)*, (*Marxist Library, Works of Marxism, Leninism*, vol. 18), translated by Emile Burns, New York, n.d., pp. 314-315.
4. Free production and consumption by individuals, the freedom to unite and "dis-unite" which the individual is to enjoy, and the concept of individual sovereignty all permit no other possibility but this.
5. This entire preceding section is based upon files of the *Alarm*, especially the numbers of October 11, November 1, 22, December 6, 1884; January 24, March 7, April 4, August 22, September 5, 1885; February 20, March 6, 1886. *Cf.*, Parsons' letter to Powderly in *Labor Leaf*, September 1, 1886; Parsons, *Anarchism;* August Spies, *Autobiography; His Speech in Court, Notes, Letters, etc.*, edited by Nina Van Zandt, Chicago, 1887.
6. *Alarm*, March 7, 1885.
7. See below, pp. 149-151.
8. *Ibid.*, April 4, 1885.
9. In Commons, *op. cit.*, vol. 2, p. 297.
10. *Ibid.*, p. 296; Selig Perlman, *A Theory of the Labor Movement*, New York, 1928, p. 159; Selig Perlman, *A History of Trade Unionism in the United States*, New York, 1929, pp. 91-92. Fred E. Haynes, *Social Politics in the United States*, Boston, 1924, p. 65,

follows Prof. Perlman completely. Nathan Fine, *op. cit.*, pp.
110-111 sees the existence of syndicalists in the West as early as
1881; labels the Pittsburgh Manifesto a "clear-cut anarchist program . . ."; and speaks of the Chicago revolutionaries as
"anarchist trade unionists . . ." thus evidently suggesting Syndicalism but avoiding the use of the term. It is surprising that Prof.
Perlman fails to cite the numbers of the *Alarm* quoted below, for
they support his thesis more strongly than the material he gives as
evidence.

11. June 13, 1885.
12. Even in those cases where the labor organizations were theoretically
in favor of the destruction of the wage system, as in the case of
the Knights of Labor, they did not function to that end, but exerted themselves to secure better working conditions, shorter hours
and higher wages.
13. September 19, 1885.
14. Louis Auguste Blanqui (1805-1881) was a French revolutionist
who urged in one form or another through his long life a revolution through the use of force. Towards the close of his life he
gave more and more stress to the arming of the workers who were
to capture the government and establish a proletarian dictatorship.
He exerted a considerable influence upon Most and indirectly upon
the Chicago revolutionaries. See, Michel Raléa, *L'idée de révolution dans les doctrines socialistes. Étude sur l'évolution de la
tactique révolutionaire*, Paris, 1923, pp. 208-231.
15. Louis Levine, *Syndicalism in France* (Columbia University
Studies in History, Economics and Public Law, vol. 46, no. 3),
second edition, New York, 1914, especially chap. V; George Sorel,
Reflections on Violence, translated by T. E. Hulme, third edition,
New York, 1912; Sombart, *op. cit.*, pp. 100-107; Sir Arthur Clay,
*Syndicalism and Labour, Notes upon Some Aspects of Social and
Industrial Questions of the Day*, New York, 1911, chaps. I-II;
Rodney L. Mott, "The Political Theory of Syndicalism," *Political
Science Quarterly*, vol. 37, no. 1, March, 1922, pp. 25-40; Raléa,
op. cit., pp. 371-388; Kung Chuan Hsiao, *Political Pluralism. A
Study in Contemporary Political Theory*, New York, 1927, pp.
111-113.
16. Perlman, *A Theory of the Labor Movement*, p. 159.
17. See below, pp. 167-170.
18. Nor do they appear in selected writings of Parsons published after
his death; see Parsons, *Anarchism*. Mrs. Parsons, however, in
that volume does repeat the idea. "We hold that the granges,
trade-unions, Knights of Labor assemblies, etc., are the embryonic
groups of the ideal anarchistic society. Under anarchy the different
groups, including all the industrial trades, . . . will maintain themselves apart and distinct from the whole. We ask for the decentrali-
zation of power from the central government into the groups or

classes." (P. 110.) The trade-union idea does not appear in the speeches made in court.

19. See below, pp. 336-337 for sketch of his life.

20. This letter from Fischer to Dyer D. Lum, dated February 1, 1887, is quoted in full in *Liberty,* February 26, 1887.

21. *Cf., Alarm,* March 6, 1886; Parsons, *Anarchism,* chap. VI, especially pp. 156-158.

22. *Freiheit,* August 1, 1885. Schwab—if the article is his—writes that the "productive groups," the product of free association, consist of individuals who have complete liberty to join and secede.

23. *Alarm,* December 17, 1887. Lingg's article was translated by Fischer.

24. Sartorius von Waltershausen, *op. cit.,* p. 311.

25. *Alarm,* January 13, February 7, 1885.

26. *Ibid.,* April 18, 1885.

27. *Ibid.,* March 21, 1885.

28. *Ibid.,* November 22, 1885.

29. *Ibid.,* March 21, 1885, February 6, 20, 1886.

30. Sartorius von Waltershausen, *op. cit.,* p. 311.

31. *Alarm,* August 22, 1885, January 9, 1886.

32. *Cf., ibid.,* August 8, 1885.

33. *Freiheit,* April 17, 1886, Most's comment on their strictures is characteristic and revealing. "Is there no whip," it may be freely translated, "with which to lash these dogs?"

34. *Socialism and Anarchism. Antagonistic Opposites, Socialistic Library,* no. 6, June 1, 1886, New York.

35. *Freiheit,* February 13, 1886 (in English).

36. *Alarm,* November 8, 1884.

37. *Ibid.,* March 6, 1886.

38. See files of the *Freiheit;* Ely, *American Labor Movement,* pp. 242-245.

39. What follows makes no pretense at being a psychological study. For a suggestive but inadequate treatment of revolutionary psychology see A. Hamon, *Psychologie de l'anarchiste-socialiste,* Paris, 1895. How true the following is of all of those drawn into the movement it is impossible to say. The conclusions reached are based upon all the pertinent material examined in connection with this study. See also, the very poor study by Cesare Lombroso, *Études de sociologie. Les anarchistes,* translated by A. Hamel and A. Marie, Paris, n.d.

40. Hamon, *op. cit.,* chap. VII, where Hamon credits them with this.

41. *Freiheit,* August 8, 1885.

42. *Socialism and Anarchism,* pp. 7-8.

43. Haskell's co-founders were Americans with the exception of an Englishman who had been a member of the First International.

44. This is pertinently illustrated by the following: "Wanted for Mme. Tussaud's Curiosity Wax-Works in London, a man who

understands his natural rights and is not a Socialist." *Truth,* July, 1884 (Old Series, no. 114, New Series, vol. 1, no. 2), p. 89.

45. *Ibid.,* June, 1884 (Old Series, no. 113; New Series, vol. 1, no. 1), p. 64.

46. *Ibid.,* January 26, 1884. Prof. Ely unfortunately does not distinguish between communications to *Truth* and expressions of editorial opinion. He thus gives the impression that Haskell accepted propaganda by deed, *Labor Movement in America,* chap. X, *passim.* Prof. Cross (see note 49) also fails to draw the line between propaganda by deed and the use of force to effect the revolution, in which Haskell believed. Haskell wrote the above in answer to a proclamation published in the same number of the "Black Hand" an "International Organization" which was never more than a figment of someone's imagination. Most was said to be responsible for the proclamation. Prof. Ely quotes part of it in *ibid.,* pp. 260-261. Much of the violence in the columns of *Truth* can be ascribed to pure bravado. The remainder is found in translations from the works of European revolutionaries or in contributions from non-members of the I.W.A. Members of the I.W.P.A. were frequent contributors.

47. Two other journals also appeared on the coast after *Truth* went under.

48. *Commonweal,* September, 1885, p. 85, April, 1886, p. 32. Other sources for the I.W.A. apart from those cited are: *Truth,* for 1883; June, 1884, pp. 30-35, July, 1884, pp. 90-92, 122-124; Joseph R. Buchanan, *The Story of a Labor Agitator,* New York, 1903, pp. 264-273; McNeill, *The Labor Movement,* pp. 615-616; Sartorius von Waltershausen, *op. cit.,* pp. 249-254; Ely, *Labor Movement in America,* pp. 251-253; Ira B. Cross, *A History of the Labor Movement in California,* Berkeley, 1935, chap. X; Hillquit, *op. cit.,* pp. 230-232; Commons, *op. cit.,* vol. 2, pp. 298-300.

49. *Alarm,* October 17, 31, 1885.

50. This ignored the fact that they defined "revolutionary action" differently.

51. *Ibid.,* November 28, 1885.

52. *Ibid.,* May 16, 1885.

53. See below, chap. XIII *passim.*

54. Sartorius von Waltershausen, *op. cit.,* p. 243; Buchanan, *op. cit.,* p. 183.

55. 116 U. S. 252. Lyman Trumbull argued before the Court in behalf of Presser.

56. *Cf., Albany Law Journal,* April 10, 1886, pp. 297-298.

57. Ehlert, *loc. cit.,* p. 2, Chicago *Inter Ocean,* August 6, 1900.

58. It is interesting to note that at a meeting of the Central Labor Union of New York City, October 14, 1883, a motion presented by the Advance Labor Club "to form militia companies" was discussed and tabled. New York *Tribune,* October 15, 1883.

59. *Alarm*, April 18, May 2, June 13, June 27, October 17, 1885; Bogart and Thompson, *op. cit.*, pp. 463-466; Commons, *op. cit.*, vol. 2, pp. 297-298.
60. Buchanan, *op. cit.*, chaps. V-VI *passim;* Brissenden, *op. cit.*, p. 34; Commons, *op. cit.*, vol. 2, pp. 367-369; *Free Society*, November 6, 1898, p. 8.
61. *Alarm*, February 21, 1885.
62. *Ibid.*, December 12, 1885.

VII. THE EIGHT-HOUR MOVEMENT

T HOUGH the Haymarket bomb and the eight-hour movement are always linked together, the two are only indirectly related. The gathering at which the bomb was thrown did not grow out of the eight-hour strikes in Chicago. Nevertheless, an examination of the eight-hour movement is essential to a correct understanding of the Haymarket Affair.

The quest for a shorter working day has marked American labor history almost as much as the struggle for higher wages. As early as 1825, demands for a ten-hour day were heard, and in every decade from the 'forties to the 'eighties shorter working-day movements appeared. The local or sectional ten-hour movements of the 'forties and 'fifties and the more nearly national eight-hour movement of the following decade, in which Ira Steward played so vital a rôle, were characterized either by humanitarianism, the appeal to public sentiment, the reliance placed upon legislation to secure the shorter day, or the limited and local use of industrial action to reduce hours. The movement of the later 'sixties completely accepted the method of political action and legislation,[1] although it was in no way free from several major strikes, some of which were accompanied by violence. This eight-hour agitation coincided with a vigorous revival of the trade-union movement and widespread organization, and prepared the ground for the extensive shorter hour strike movement in 1872.

In this year, the attempt to reduce working-hours by direct industrial action, though still subordinated to the efforts to secure legislation, reached its height. The movement was still definitely local in character. In New York City alone, however, almost 100,000 workers, belonging largely to the building trades, went out on strike. In some instances the struggle for the eight-hour day lasted three months. But the movement was at best only partially successful.[2] With the advent of the industrial depression in 1873, the drive for shorter hours ceased. When labor resorted to militant action during the six long years of the depression, it was, almost without exception, to prevent wage cuts.[3]

Though the movement for shorter hours up to the close of the 'seventies cannot be called successful, some gains were made. The first national legislation affecting hours of government employees came in 1840 with the signing of the ten-hour law by President Van Buren. In 1868, three years after the first bill on the subject had been introduced in Congress and after a similar measure had once been passed by the House, an eight-hour law for federal employees was enacted June 25. This measure met the hostility of government officials, and raised troublesome questions as to the scope of its application and the rates of wages. Many federal departments cut wages when hours were reduced, and, under a ruling of the Attorney-General, the law was held to apply only to direct employees of the government. President Grant, to clarify the wage question, issued a proclamation May 19, 1869, ordering that wages should remain at the same level despite the reductions in hours. This was so largely ignored that a second proclamation followed May 11, 1872. The law, unfortunately, lacked provisions for enforcement, and apart from Grant's proclamations, no real efforts were made to give it effect. In 1878, an attempt was made to provide for enforcement by joint resolution of Congress, but only the House acted favorably. As late as 1886, President Cleveland declared that he thought the law was a good one and that it should be enforced.[4]

The act of 1868 was an exceedingly small return for the energies expended during the period to secure federal legislalation. More important were the statutes passed by the States.

By engaging in local politics, labor could bring greater pressure upon the State legislatures than it could upon Congress. As a result, a considerable body of legislation defining a legal day's work in hours, regulating the hours of labor for State and municipal employees and limiting the working hours of women and children was secured. By 1886, nineteen States and one territory had passed laws affecting hours of labor. But the wording of the statutes and the lack of enforcement destroyed much of the value of this legislation.[5] The Chicago *Knights of Labor,* discussing in 1886 the Illinois law passed nineteen years earlier, remarked that "the eight-hour law as it now stands . . . is a dead letter. There is not one person in a thousand who knows there is such a law."[6] The same statement could have been made of the eight- and ten-hour laws of other States.

Political and legislative action had not proved successful. Nor was there much cause for rejoicing over the gains made by labor organizations. National labor organizations had taken little part in any of the more extensive strike movements for reduction of hours in 1868 and 1872. For American industry at large, the eight-hour day was still as far from attainment early in the 'eighties. There were exceptional instances where employees could boast of an eight-hour day or a forty-eight hour week. It was also true that the length of the working day had been much reduced from the fourteen and fifteen hours of factory toil common earlier in the century. In 1883 most New England textile mill workers had an average working day of slightly more than ten hours, with a shorter Saturday balancing longer week-day hours.[7] Organized cigar-makers in the same year generally worked between fifty-five and sixty hours a week, while the hours of the unorganized ranged from sixty-six to ninety hours a week.[8]

Full statistics for the first part of 1886 indicate that no major change in hours of labor had taken place since 1883. The length of the average working day for forty selected industries in twenty-eight States, embracing 552 establishments and 139,143 workers was a trifle over ten hours. The ten-hour day or sixty-hour week was the most common working time.[9] An examination of the hours of labor in 434 industrial establishments in Illinois in 1886 gives the same result.[10] The average working week of 177,810 workers throughout the country, who engaged in strikes for a shorter day in 1886, was 61.81 hours before they went on strike, with the ten-hour day the most common single working time.[11] In certain occupations working hours ranged far above this average. New York City bakers worked from eighty-four to 120 hours a week. Transportation workers in most urban centers rarely put in less than eighty-four hours a week. Ninety hours a week was not uncommon, and in many cases they averaged well over 100.[12]

The resurgence of the eight-hour movement in 1886 was in large measure responsible for making that year an epochal one in working-class history. In that year labor made a spirited—though not well organized—attempt to win the eight-hour, or at least a shorter day, through a concerted strike movement theoretically national in scope and affecting all industries. It constitutes the first, vague approximation of a national general strike in American labor annals.[13]

Probably the first call for the establishment of the eight-hour day by mass labor action was announced by the Industrial Congress [14] when it resolved at its final convention in 1875 that the eight-hour system would be inaugurated "by a united movement on the part of the working masses of the United States" on July 4, 1876.[15] Exactly what the Congress had in mind is not clear. The declaration implied a wide strike movement, but, as Prof. Ware observes, "it might have involved nothing more than a general request for the eight-hour day, which might, or might not result in success, compromise or strikes." [16] The Congress went out of existence the same year, and the depression prevented a strike movement from materializing.

Labor was not through with legislative action. In 1880

a national committee was formed consisting of Richard F. Trevellick, chairman, John G. Mills, secretary, Charles H. Litchman, then Grand Secretary of the K. of L., Albert Parsons and Dyer D. Lum, to secure the recognition of the eight-hour principle by Congressional legislation. Some members of the committee, notably Parsons, worked assiduously. Congressmen were energetically canvassed, but nothing was accomplished.[17] Parsons' activities at this time are especially noteworthy in the light of his later career.[18] At the General Assembly of the K. of L. in 1880, Litchman appealed for funds to support a delegation at Washington to work for a strict eight-hour law. He continued to lobby at his own expense at the national capitol for another six years.[19]

In the years 1880-1885, organized labor expended far less energy than it did after 1865 in wrenching eight-hour statutes from unwilling State legislatures. Nor did labor, both organized and unorganized, spend its forces in strikes to secure reductions in hours. Its efforts during these years were primarily directed to win wage increases and, as the effects of the industrial depression which started in 1882 became more marked, to prevent wage reductions. In 1883, for example, 70.09 per cent of the strikes were for increase of wages and against wage reductions. In 1884 these causes were responsible for 65.01 per cent of the strikes. In 1883, only 1.26 per cent of the strikes were for reduction of hours and against increase in hours. In 1884, these reasons caused 2.03 per cent of the strikes.[20]

In the midst of depression a struggle for shorter hours was out of the question. Only with an improvement in industrial conditions and with greater security in employment could labor attempt to reduce hours. The first evidences of a quickening in industrial activity always brings a demand for a shorter and fixed working day.[21] By coincidence, a weak labor organization of national scope in 1884, a year distinguished by the large number of strikes against wage cuts, set a future date for the inauguration of the eight-hour day,—a date which found industry recovering from the depression.

The Federation of Organized Trades and Labor Unions of the United States and Canada, founded at Pittsburgh in 1881 was experiencing a loss in membership and strength in 1884. This decline was not typical of the labor movement at large, for many organizations were increasing their membership. Largely to inject new vitality into the organization, it was decided to have it take the lead in a national movement for the eight-hour day. By a vote almost unanimous, the 1884 convention of the Federation "*Resolved* . . . that eight hours shall constitute a legal day's labor from and after May 1, 1886, and that we recommend to labor organizations throughout this jurisdiction that they so direct their laws as to conform to this resolution by the time named." [22]

This resolution did not explicitly designate the strike as the method of winning the eight-hour day. In the light of the Federation's earlier demand for the eight-hour day by union action, however, and the attitude of the convention on legislative action in general, it may be concluded that the Federation accepted the strike without actually saying so. This conclusion, however, may well be the product of reading the nature of the 1886 movement back into the proposal from which it resulted. The resolution itself contains no provision for inaugurating the eight-hour day. It simply recommended that the unions affiliated with it consider the question. The Federation itself did little to prepare the ground for a mass movement, and even later suggested that the strike be used only when peaceful efforts to secure shorter hours had failed. In view of this and the small membership of the unions united with the Federation,[23] the eight-hour resolution might have been nothing more than an optimistic, if not chance, effort designed to give it new life. Some good might come of it, and it could never do the Federation harm. If the Federation really planned to lead a national eight-hour strike movement, it was undertaking a task far too grandiose for its own capacities. The idea of inaugurating the eight-hour day on a fixed date by general strike had, it may be observed, been proposed as early as 1873 by the California Eight-Hour League.[24]

Even its affiliated unions showed no enthusiasm over the eight-hour proposal. Only a small portion of the membership actively considered the question. Many unions were unquestionably in favor of the shorter day, but the wisdom and probable success of the May 1 movement were widely doubted. Organized labor in California, already enjoying a nine-hour day, was quite disinterested in an eight-hour movement. Yet the small convention of the Federation in 1885 repeated the declaration that the eight-hour system was to go into effect on May 1, 1886. It requested that member unions which did not propose to strike for the shorter day should aid financially those which would.[25] The strike is here unconditionally accepted as the weapon for gaining the eight-hour day. The trade-unions were apathetic, and only two national trade-unions took up and voted favorably upon the introduction of the eight-hour day.[26]

Officers of the Federation, however, proceeded to establish machinery by which the eight-hour day could be gained through peaceful negotiation with employers. The latter were circularized and a form agreement was drawn up to be signed at conferences between the unions and employers. The unions were meanwhile to agitate for the eight-hour day through mass-meetings and other means. If peaceful negotiation proved barren, then the unions were to resort to the strike. This program was submitted to the Knights of Labor, which was asked to co-operate.[27]

This was not the first time that the Federation had approached the Knights with the eight-hour project. After the passage of the 1884 resolution, the K. of L. was invited to co-operate but the Order, or at least its officials, was unsympathetic to the May 1 plan. At the General Assembly of the Order in 1885, a resolution proposing that it support the

Federation in 1886 was almost ignored. This boded ill for the eight-hour struggle, for the active assistance of the Knights was essential if it was to succeed.

It has already been seen that the Order favored securing the eight-hour day through legislative action.[28] As early as 1871, Uriah S. Stephens urged a reduction of hours by the cessation of work at five o'clock on Saturdays. Its original platform, silent on the method of gaining the eight-hour day, did declare for a decrease in the number of working hours to that number to provide greater leisure and enable labor to share in the advantages created by labor-saving machinery. In 1879, Stephens came out for legislative action, and this view prevailed among many of the officials of the Order. Successively in 1881, 1882, and 1883, proposals were made at the General Assemblies to set aside a specific day upon which the workers of the country were to demand that eight hours constitute a legal day's labor. In 1884, a change in the preamble of the constitution of the Knights of Labor replaced the old shorter hour plank (Art. XIV) with Article XXI, which declared it the aim of the Order "To shorten the hours of labor by a general refusal to work for more than eight hours." [29]

This did not mean that the Order was willing to engage in a general strike movement for the eight-hour day. Its later policies and the failure to specify a date for labor's "general refusal to work for more than eight hours" show this clearly. The rank and file of the Order was ready for militant methods, but its leaders were far too peace-loving to resort to widespread industrial action. It is true, of course, that the Order was drawn into the 1883 strike of the telegraphers, in which the eight-hour day was one of the issues involved. The strike was a bitter failure. The support which the Knights gave to the telegraphers was open to much criticism, and left the latter disgruntled with the Order.[30] Powderly, who shied from the idea of a general strike was not even pleased with Article XXI as it stood. Unfortunately, both for the movement and the Order, he was able to determine the official stand of the

Knights. In discussing the problem in a secret circular of December 15, 1884, he wrote—with an eye to rebuffing the radicals—that he "wished to see a revolution; I wish to see some killing done; I wish to see the systems by which the worker is oppressed killed off; and I long to see a revolution in the working time of those who toil." He requested "that all assemblies and district assemblies take up for discussion Section XXI of the preamble; discuss it thoroughly during the winter, first in the privacy of the assembly, then in the public press and before the people." [31] A campaign of education and agitation was necessary, he declared, to prepare both worker and employer for the eight-hour day. Members of the Order were to write essays on the question, and he called for a concerted assault upon the press with eight-hour propaganda on Washington's Birthday. An article of his urging that the movement should be national in scope, "and should have the hearty co-operation of all men," appeared in the April number of the *North American Review.*[32]

That Powderly thought of the eight-hour issue in terms of legislative action and was opposed to the May 1 plan of the Federation was made clear by his annual address to the General Assembly of 1885. He asserted that "the eight-hour question . . . is a political one," and recommended "that the proposition to inaugurate a general strike for the establishment of the short-hour plan on the first of May, 1886, should be discountenanced by this body. The people most interested in the project are not as yet educated in the movement, and a strike under such conditions must prove abortive. The date fixed is not a suitable one; the plan suggested to establish the system is not the proper one." [33]

Resolutions by new assemblies requesting the next General Assembly to fix May 1 "as the day on which to strike for eight hours," only intensified Powderly's opposition. Fear that the Order would become involved in a movement which would do it irreparable injury, because it was not prepared to carry the burden of the eight-hour strike alone; the mushroom growth of the Knights in 1885-1886; his undervaluation of the strength of the Order; his native caution; his approach to the eight-hour question in terms of legislation; the thought that the Federation might capitalize a movement for which it was doing extremely little; the feeling that revolutionary elements might utilize the movement for their own purposes; his refusal to regard an eight-hour day as a solution for all social ills,—these factors led to Powderly's order against participation in the May 1 movement in his famous secret circular of March 13, 1886.[34]

"It is evident," he wrote, "that our members are not properly instructed, else we would not find them passing resolutions 'approving of the action of our executive officers in fixing the first of May as the day to strike for eight hours.'[35] The executive officers of the Knights of Labor have never fixed upon the first of May for a strike of any kind, and they will not do so until the proper time arrives and the word goes forth from the General Assembly. No assembly of the Knights of Labor must strike for the eight-hour system on May first under the impression that they are obeying orders from headquarters, for such an order was not, and will not, be given. Neither employer or [sic] employe are educated to the needs and necessities for the short hour plan."[36]

Powderly's secret circular, it will be seen, did not prevent the rank and file of the Order from welcoming with open arms the eight-hour day issue, and many assemblies participated in the May 1 movement. It did, however, rob the movement of a good measure of the concerted action which it so sorely needed. Had the trade-unions early united on the eight-hour issue, the defection of the leadership of the Knights would not have been so keenly felt, even though the membership of the Order reached the astounding figure of 700,000 in 1886.[37] Many trade-unions were not eager to engage in a struggle for the eight-hour day, and some, without much hesitation, quickly substituted a nine-hour goal.[38] The Federation, on its last legs in 1886, did little to further the movement beyond circularizing organized labor and urging a determined drive on May 1.[39] Its weakness threw the burden of carrying the movement upon the local unions.

Had there not been an improvement in industrial conditions in the spring of 1886; had there not been a long preparatory period of agitation for a shorter day; had there not been a tremendous growth in the membership of labor organizations in 1885-1886; had not the eight-hour day assumed the proportions of a cure-all; had public sentiment not supported the demand for a shorter working day; and, finally, had not the radical element in at least one industrial center, Chicago, energetically fought for the eight-hour day, the movement would have been a ludicrous fiasco. The first three factors need no further examination, but the others do. The last point, though of secondary importance in its influence on the scope of the movement, is nevertheless of major significance.

When the movement for a shorter day was first discussed, the leaders of the I.W.P.A., including those in Chicago, turned a deaf ear. Parsons published in the *Alarm* of August 5, 1885, a circular letter of the Federation requesting co-operation in the impending struggle and explaining the importance of securing the eight-hour day through industrial action, and then commented upon it in extremely unfavorable terms. He held that the entire movement was a huge error. As long as machinery is privately owned, he argued, the workingman can never reduce his hours of labor,—"those who are in economic bondage and wage-slavery," can control neither wages nor hours. Capitalists could, if they wished, reduce the hours of toil, but they will do nothing of the sort. Since labor could only determine its hours when it controlled capital, the whole movement was a waste of precious time and effort.[40] Albert Parsons had travelled a long way since 1880, when he was buttonholing Congressmen for the sake of an eight-hour law. The Federation did not let this go unanswered, and in reply the *Alarm* declared that it did "not antagonize the eight-hour movement; . . . it simply points out that it is a lost battle, and . . . though the eight-hour system should be established the wage workers would gain nothing." [41]

To the Chicago social-revolutionaries, the eight-hour movement meant a compromise with the wage-system which they were struggling to abolish. Even if successful, it could result only in a temporary readjustment in that system. It was fruitless to dissipate the energies of the working-class to gain a measure of relief which might aid in perpetuating their bondage as wage-slaves. Johann Most was in complete agreement with this argument, and, in contrast with his Chicago comrades, did not later change his views on the futility of the eight-hour strikes. On April 23, 1886, in an address at Germania Hall, he brushed aside the whole movement as inconsequential, and warned that the workers would gain absolutely nothing from it. When they were ready to march forth with rifle on shoulder and expropriate their exploiters they would improve their condition. To struggle for shorter hours and higher pay was equivalent to fighting "for a little more butter on their bread." [42]

Most published, in the *Freiheit* of January 23 and 30, 1886, a long, critical communication from Chicago on the entire eight-hour question. The correspondent—whose identity is hidden under the initial "H"—after weighing all the pertinent factors, concluded that the movement would probably fail because of the poor economic condition of the workers, the inadequacies and weakness of their organizations, and the presence of a surplus labor supply. He asserted that the workingmen of the city and the country at large were not keen on joining in the eight-hour strikes. If the shorter day were not successfully inaugurated on the first, he warned, then the entire movement would fail. The employers would reject the demand of the workers, and even use force against them. Unless the workers were jarred out of their indifference and lethargy, their cause was doomed to defeat. If they wished to win they would have to arm and prepare to use their weapons. Otherwise they would simply be shot down like wild dogs by the authorities. Why, queried the writer, should labor ask for a mere pittance? If it was ready to engage in a struggle, why not attempt to do away with capitalism? It was possible that a "real revolution" might arise from the eight-hour strikes, and the correspondent hoped that the May 1 movement would culminate in a thorough-going social upheaval.

These views are representative of the attitude of the leaders of the I.W.P.A. in Chicago. Johann Most, however, never recognized the possibility that the movement might end in an uprising. The Chicago leaders evidently did, and this in part accounts for the change in their stand. Many of the radical leaders had been active in the labor movement and in the earlier eight-hour movement, while strong ties bound the labor and radical movements in general in the city. These two factors were also in part responsible for the abandonment of their early position. On October 11, 1885, the Central Labor Union of Chicago called a meeting to discuss the eight-hour issue, and August Spies introduced several resolutions to the effect that it was too much to expect the employers to grant voluntarily the shorter day. They would do everything to prevent its inauguration, calling upon the police, militia and Pinkertons for assistance. The workers were, therefore, urged to procure arms before May 1, in order to meet force with force. It was also announced at this meeting that the radicals were "sceptical in regard to the benefits that will accrue to the wage-workers" as a result of the eight-hour contest, but since it was a class-struggle, they would aid in it as long as the workers would show an "open" and united front to their common enemy.[48] In short, the eight-hour movement as such won the sympathy of the social-revolutionaries in so far as it was a specific manifestation of the class-struggle.

For several months after this date, the radicals remained merely interested observers of the movement. They reminded the workers that unless they armed, it would collapse,[44] and asserted that they could not give it active support because it meant "compromise," and recognition that the "wage-system is right." [45] By the opening of 1886, this position was abandoned. In January, the *Alarm* announced that the I.W.P.A. was "extremely" active in the eight-hour movement. Labor was still, of course, urged to arm.[46] In the following month, the movement had become an absolute "necessity," a great protest against capital. "It is," declared the *Alarm,* "a historical unfoldment of the great idea contained in the rights of man. . . ." [47] In April, the I.W.P.A. was a forceful factor in preparing for the great May 1 strikes, and its leaders were busily engaged in organizing the unorganized workers. Parsons at this date "thought [that] the attempt to inaugurate the eight-hour system would break down the capitalist system and bring about such disorder and hardship that the Social Revolution would become a necessity." [48]

Thus, the Chicago social-revolutionaries finally ended by entering whole-heartedly into the eight-hour movement. Their labors were extensive, and were to some degree responsible for the scope and vigor of the movement in Chicago.

By 1885-1886, the various theoretical bases for an eight-hour day had been fully formulated. For a good portion of the American working-class it took shape as a more vital issue than ever before. It was regarded as a major stride towards emancipation from industrial slavery,—as a promise of greater things to come. Many of its proponents held it would cure America's industrial ills. The earlier arguments for a shorter day had been based primarily upon what might be called "moral" grounds. Since Ira Steward's time, greater stress had been placed upon economic reasons which were sometimes sound and frequently fallacious. In the 'eighties, the advocates of the eight-hour day utilized every possible contention which served their purpose, although they generally demanded the shorter day in the name of economic necessity and well-being.

It was argued that a reduction in working hours would cure industrial depressions caused by overproduction, in turn the product of long hours and improved machinery. The shorter day would decrease the amount of goods produced.

Unemployment, due to long hours, machinery, and industrial depressions would be reduced. It was assumed that a twenty per cent reduction in the total hours of labor, would create employment for twenty per cent more workers. This would mean an increase in the number of active consumers, and would necessitate greater production. This would be to the advantage of both employer and worker. Ira Steward's theory was revived to demonstrate that an eight-hour day would result in increased wants, which would bring about higher pay and greater production of goods through the wider use of machines. A shorter day would benefit the employer because it would step up, rather than diminish the productive capacity of his employees. Evidence was presented to prove that under the Massachusetts ten-hour law both production and wages in that State had mounted.

The eight-hour day, in short, would remedy many industrial ills, make possible a more equitable distribution of wealth, and would confer valuable social, intellectual, physical and moral benefits upon the worker by giving him greater leisure. The workingman's home life would be improved, his physical well-being guarded, his intellectual level lifted. "Long hours," remarked James Redpath, "make shoddy Americans;" he preferred "dear goods" to "cheap men." [49] There was no reason to fear, it was argued, that the shorter day would result in greater idleness, drunkenness, and crime.[50]

United upon its desirability, the advocates of the eight-hour day were not in agreement on the question of wages. One group, drawn essentially from labor circles proposed that wages for a day's labor remain the same though hours be reduced. Practically speaking, they wanted ten hours' pay for eight hours' labor. The second group, coming largely but not wholly, from outside the labor movement, were opposed to paying a ten-hour wage for an eight-hour day. This was equivalent to retaining the same hourly rate and decreasing the daily wage of labor. Labor's insistence upon the same daily wage later, when the strike movement got under way, served to alienate a large number of sympathizers, and caused a division in labor ranks.

Though some employers looked with favor upon a shorter day, capital interests were in general bitterly opposed. To the employer and the average business man, the form that the demand for the eight-hour day was taking, rather than the number of hours of labor, constituted a dangerous threat. Thus, the New York *Tribune* approved the eight-hour day in principle, but only on condition that it be instituted without disturbances, without strikes, without any effort on the part of organized labor. The *Tribune* desired to have each workingman gain an eight-hour day for himself by individual bargaining.[51] The New York *Evening Post* had no serious objections to an eight-hour day for eight hours' pay, but it was critical of an organized movement to reduce hours. If it were successful, warned the *Post,* the consequences would be disastrous, because a worker might then be compelled to labor no more than eight hours despite his own intense desire to work nine, ten or twelve.[52] This would destroy individual freedom. Edward Atkinson, a typical economic liberal, based his opposition to the eight-hour day on the same ground: it involved the denial of freedom.[53] Mr. Atkinson also found himself a foe of limiting hours by law, because such legislation would be class legislation pure and simple, directed *only against capitalists and factory employees.*[54]

The *Commercial and Financial Chronicle* showed a similar regard for the well-being of labor. Admitting that "it is a legitimate question for labor to settle for itself, whether it will work ten, one or no hours," the *Chronicle* declared that to limit hours to eight was "clearly a less wise use of an industrious man's liberty [than] can . . . be imagined. If the earnings of labor come out of the profits of capital—its share of the product, whatever that product be—it scarcely needs to be said that no man can earn as much in one hour as in ten or as much in nine as in ten. Under pressure, such a demand may be enforced, yet the arrangement, if concluded, cannot but readjust itself, and to the disadvantage of the ambitious, industrious laborer in the end. . . ." [55] Later, the *Commercial and Financial Chronicle* reiterated its contention that "every man is at liberty to fix the duration of his own labor," but that such settlements must be the product of individual agreement.[56] *The Independent,* a religious publication, spoke out even more decisively against the eight-hour day, declaring "that the whole eight-hour movement is senseless and useless agitation of mistaken men, fraught with no good to anybody, and that it would only work harm by being successful." [57] It demonstrated that it was economically unwise, unnecessary on the ground of physical fatigue, and devoid of benefit to the workingman. It was "A charitable scheme for the benefit of saloon keepers." [58] With this view P. M. Arthur, Grand Chief Engineer of the Brotherhood of Locomotive Engineers, was in thorough accord. He opposed the eight-hour day because "two hours less work means two hours more loafing about the corners and two hours more for drink." [59]

In general, the daily press of the country disapproved of the eight-hour movement, and expressed its opinions in terms ranging from mild contempt to extreme distaste. It was argued that labor was prodigal with its energies, for if it would only wait, it would have the eight-hour day sooner or later. There was no sense in hurrying the inevitable.[60] Fortified with weighty statistics and faulty economics, newspaper editors were ready to prove that a shorter day must have unfortunate results, among which the inevitable decrease in the quantity of goods produced loomed extremely large. A heavy barrage of ridicule was also directed against the movement.[61]

Yet it is incorrect to speak of "the universal condemnation of the eight-hour demand by the general press during the months preceding May 1, 1886. . . ." [62] Scattered through the country a number of papers gave support, frequently qualified, to the idea. These included the Boston *Advertiser,* the Troy *Telegram,* the Philadelphia *Press,* the Detroit *Tribune,* and the Cleveland *Plain Dealer.*[63] Even the *Banker's Magazine and*

Statistical Register presently announced that it favored the reduction of working hours, even by law, but was opposed to ten hours' pay for eight hours' work.[64]

By 1886, the eight-hour day had made a large number of converts among men of some prominence in many fields, though not all were agreed upon the way it was to be achieved. Many still placed complete faith in legislative action, and an even greater number were utterly against paying ten hours' wages for eight hours' work. They did, however, align themselves in support of the eight-hour principle, and this body of opinion was not without its effect. James B. Weaver, Senator William Mahone of Virginia, Representatives William D. Kelly and Thomas M. Bayne of Pennsylvania, Representative Frank Lawler of Michigan, Senator Henry M. Teller of Colorado, and Senator Henry L. Dawes of Massachusetts were in favor of an eight-hour working day and an eight-hour law passed either by the States, Congress or both.[65] It was noted by the eight-hour advocates that President Cleveland had spoken highly of the Federal eight-hour law, saying he believed "that the law is a sound and good one, and that it should be enforced to the letter . . . the government cannot afford to set the example of non-enforcement and non-observance of its own enactments."[66]

Labor leaders, with the exception of Powderly and a handful of others, were actively advocating the shorter day. Samuel Gompers, John Swinton, Thomas A. Armstrong, editor of the *National Labor Tribune,* John J. Jarrett, formerly president of the Amalgamated Association of Iron and Steel Workers, John Costello, president of the Monongahela River and Railroad Miners' Association, Richard Davis, secretary of the Pennsylvania Miners' Amalgamated Association, Joseph Gruenhut, Chicago labor reformer and Recorder of Statistics in the Health Department of that city, and a great many others, regarded the eight-hour day as an extremely vital issue.[67] Henry George declared that in the "attempt to limit the working day to eight hours, the labor associations

are taking the most hopeful step they have yet attempted." [68]
George Gunton was an early advocate of the shorter day and
an eight-hour law. Converts were found among the clergy.
With several, such as the Rev. Heber Newton and Rev. Robert
Collyer, approval of the eight-hour day was almost unqualified.
Others, the Rev. Edward Everett Hale, for example, only gave
the movement their half-hearted approbation, and Lyman Abbott, generally very sympathetic to labor, was only vaguely in
favor of the shorter day. Most of the churchmen of the period,
however, did not take a decisive stand on the question.[69]

The eight-hour movement, then, was not without the support of public sentiment outside of labor ranks. The organized
workers seized upon it with eagerness, even where their officials were antagonistic or at best disinterested. Thus, in spite
of Powderly, paid organizers of the K. of L. utilized the eight-
hour issue to establish new assemblies.[70]

With the Federation impotent and the Knights officially
opposed after the issuance of Powderly's secret circular, the
eight-hour movement became in organization and direction
essentially local. That is to say, the task of agitating for the
shorter day was left to the local labor organizations, except in
the case of the cigar makers.[71]

In so far as it affected industrial centers throughout the
entire country, however, the eight-hour movement was national in scope. Preparatory agitation for the May 1 strikes
reached major proportions in March, and came to a head in
April. In that month a considerable number of shorter hour
strikes either had already begun, or the eight-hour issue had
been injected into labor struggles for increased wages and
other causes. The May 1 movement was, therefore, to some
extent anticipated by developments during April.[72]

It was obvious that the movement would attain intensity
only in a limited number of industrial centers, and that it
would be turned by practical considerations into a demand
simply for a shorter day. By the close of April it was apparent that it would show its greatest strength in Chicago, New

York, Cincinnati, Baltimore, and Milwaukee. Boston, Pittsburgh, St. Louis and Washington were also being affected to a lesser degree.

By the last week in April, *Bradstreet's* estimated that 62,000 workers in Chicago, among whom were included 35,000 packing yard employees, were prepared to strike if their demand for the eight-hour day were not granted. By Friday, April 30, another 25,000 men in that city had requested the shorter day without threatening to strike, and 20,000, had already won the eight-hour day. Several thousand were already out on strike in Chicago. In no other city did the movement arouse the same enthusiasm or sweep along so great a number of workers either before or after May 1. Among the workers already drawn into the struggle in Chicago were furniture makers, machinists, gas-fitters and plumbers, iron-moulders, brick-makers, freight-handlers, stock-yard employees, hod-carriers and plasterers, butchers' employees (asking for a ten-hour day), toy-makers, boot and shoe workers, dry goods clerks and printers. Employees in other trades joined these on or after May 1.

In and around New York City, some 20,000 foundrymen and metal workers announced that they would strike if they were not granted a nine-hour working day. Before May 1, employers seemed willing to concede to the demands of the cigar and furniture workers for the shorter day. The furriers expected to compromise without much difficulty on a nine-hour day. In general, there was no wide-spread effort to raise wages and reduce hours at the same time in New York City. Concessions had already been won by the workers before May 1 in St. Louis, Philadelphia, and Louisville. In many cases, employers were extremely reluctant to match strength with the workers. Strikes were frequently avoided by compromising on ten hours' pay for a nine-hour day. A large number of workers, too, were willing to accept nine-hours in preference to engaging in long, costly struggles. Some 12,000 skilled workers in Pennsylvania, ostensibly demanding the eight-hour day, were ready to compromise on nine hours. In Philadelphia labor was ready to accept a slight decrease in hours together with a slight gain in pay. Throughout New England, the movement was practically without strength except in Boston. Even there the threat of a general strike if the eight-hour demand was refused, commonly made ten days before May 1, was rarely heard as that date drew near. In Boston, too, labor was eager to compromise. In Paterson, New Jersey, the effect of Powderly's secret circular of March was early observed, and there was a definite division in working-class ranks. Knights of Labor members, generally regarding the eight-hour movement as premature, were unwilling to engage in it. Nevertheless, some 10,000 masons, bricklayers, boiler-makers, and silk workers strongly favored participation.[73]

Even before May 1, almost a quarter of a million industrial workers throughout the country were more or less vitally interested in the eight-hour movement. Some thirty thousand had already been granted an eight or at least a shorter hour day, and at least 6,000 were on strike during the last week of April. It was currently estimated that not less than 100,000 workingmen were prepared to resort to the strike to secure their demand, and of this number almost eighty per cent were determined to win the eight-hour day.

On May 1 and the days following, the movement acquired a greater scope and intensity than contemporaries had anticipated. Especially in Chicago did it attain unusual proportions. By the close of the second week in May, some 340,000 workingmen had participated in the movement, and of this number about 190,000 were reported as having gone out on strike. Chicago with 80,000 participants and strikers, had a larger number than any other industrial center.[74]

But if Chicago witnessed the most aggressive effort to win the eight-hour day, it was also the scene of an entirely unforeseen development which did not grow out of that struggle and which had unfortunate consequences for the movement and for labor in general.

NOTES CHAPTER VII

1. See the declaration of the Boston Eight-Hour League, formed in the spring of 1869, which called "once again as we have and shall continue to call, for the concentration of the whole power and forces of the labor movement upon the simple and single issue of the legislation necessary to secure the eight-hour system, first, for all the labor employed at public expense, whether by contract or by the day." Quoted in *Fourth Biennial Report of the Bureau of Labor Statistics of Illinois*, p. 471.

2. In New York City, bricklayers, paper-hangers, plasterers, painters, stone-cutters, stone masons, masons' laborers, and plate-printers, are credited with having won the eight-hour day.

3. For the foregoing material see, *Fourth Biennial Report of the Bureau of Labor Statistics of Illinois*, pp. 466-472; McNeill, *op. cit.*, pp. 122, 124, 125, 133-136 *passim*, 138, 139, 142-143, 349-350; Marion Cotter Cahill, *Shorter Hours. A Study of the Movement Since the Civil War (Studies in History, Economics and Public Law,* edited by the Faculty of Political Science of Columbia University, no. 380), New York, 1932, pp. 11-12, 31-40 *passim;* Ware, *op. cit.*, pp. 4-6, 299; Commons, *op. cit.*, vol. 1, pp. 536-546, vol. 2, pp. 87-103 *passim*, 151-152; *Labor: Its Rights and Wrongs*, pp. 34-36; Sidney Webb and Harold Cox, *The Eight Hours Day*, London, 1891, pp. 47-51; Robert Donald, "The Eight Hours Movement in the United States," *The Economic Journal*, vol. 2, London, March, 1892, pp. 550-552.

4. *House of Representatives, 51st Congress, 1st Session, Report no. 489, Adjustment of Accounts, Eight Hours Law*, pp. 1-9; Cahill, *op. cit.*, pp. 66-72; *Labor: Its Rights and Wrongs*, pp. 36-38; *Fourth Biennial Report of the Bureau of Labor Statistics of Illinois*, pp. 469-470; Commons, *op. cit.*, vol. 2, pp. 103-105, 124-125; Terence Vincent Powderly, *Thirty Years of Labor, 1859 to 1889*, Columbus, Ohio, 1889, pp. 472, 474-475.

5. Commons, *op. cit.*, vol. 2, pp. 105-110; Cahill, pp. 94-116 *passim;* *Fourth Biennial Report of the Bureau of Labor Statistics of Illinois*, pp. 473-474; Webb and Cox, *op. cit.*, pp. 47-51 *passim.*

6. July 10, 1886, quoted in Beckner, *op. cit.*, p. 180 footnote.

7. *Rep. of the Sen. Com. on Lab.*, vol. 3, pp. 6, 28, 75. The following working scheme is typical: on week days the hours ran from 6:30 to 12 o'clock, and from 1 to 6:45; on Saturday work ceased at four.

8. *Ibid.*, vol. 1, p. 450 (according to Adolph Strasser).

9. *First Annual Report of the Commissioner of Labor*, table, p. 226.

10. *Fourth Biennial Report of the Bureau of Labor Statistics of Illinois*, table II, pp. 482-490.

11. *Third Annual Report of the Commissioner of Labor*, table I, pp. 36-615.

12. *Idem.* In at least one case, they worked 119 hours a week.
13. Syndicalists and industrial unionists like to regard the eight-hour strikes of 1886 as a true general strike movement. Thus, Siegfried Nacht wrote that when the American workingmen "were preparing to conquer the eight-hour day from capitalism, they did not think of the roundabout way of political action, but decided to make an attempt to achieve it directly in the whole United States thru the general strike. . . ." *Free Society,* April 24, 1904, pp. 1-2.
14. The Industrial Congress, which lasted from 1873-75, was an attempt to revive the National Labor Union without its political aspects. It was dominantly trade-union in character.
15. Ware, *op. cit.,* pp. 17-18, 300; *Fourth Biennial Report of the Bureau of Labor Statistics of Illinois,* p. 472.
16. Ware, *op. cit.,* p. 300.
17. *Alarm,* December 3, 1887; Powderly, *op. cit.,* p. 477; John J. Flinn, *History of the Chicago Police, From the Settlement of the Community to the Present Time, under Authority of the Mayor and Superintendent of the Force,* Chicago, 1887, p. 256.
18. See above, chaps. V-VI *passim.*
19. Powderly, *op. cit.,* p. 478; Cahill, *op. cit.,* p. 41.
20. *Twenty-First Annual Report of the Commissioner of Labor, Strikes and Lockouts, 1906,* Washington, 1907, compiled from tables, pp. 56-57, 60, 61.
21. Mittelman, *loc. cit.,* p. 407.
22. Quoted in Commons, *op. cit.,* vol. 2, p. 376; see for this material and the following paragraph, *ibid.,* pp. 375-377; Cahill, *op. cit.,* pp. 153-154; Ware, *op. cit.,* pp. 250-253 *passim;* McNeill, *op. cit.,* p. 170.
23. Well under 50,000 at this time according to Commons, *op. cit.,* vol. 2, p. 377.
24. Cited in Cahill, *op. cit.,* p. 153.
25. Such financial aid was to be conditional on the fact that those unions which struck did not also demand an increase in wages.
26. The Cigar Makers and the German-American Typographia.
27. *Ibid.,* pp. 154-155; Ware, *op. cit.,* pp. 252-255 *passim;* Commons, *op. cit.,* vol. 2, p. 377.
28. See above, p. 161.
29. Ware, *op. cit.,* pp. 300-301; Commons, *op. cit.,* vol. 2, p. 378; Cahill, *op. cit.,* pp. 41-42; T. V. Powderly, "The Organization of Labor," *North American Review,* vol. 135, July, 1882, p. 125.
30. Ware, *op. cit.,* pp. 128-130; Cahill, *op. cit.,* pp. 149-150.
31. Powderly, *op. cit.,* p. 483.
32. Quoted in *ibid.,* pp. 483-492.
33. *Record of the Proceedings of the Ninth Regular Session of the General Assembly, Held at Hamilton, Ont., October 5-13, 1885,* n.p., 1885, p. 15; also quoted in Powderly, *op. cit.,* p. 493.
34. Powderly, *op. cit.,* pp. 495-496; Ware, *op. cit.,* pp. 310-313 *passim;*

Commons, *op. cit.*, vol. 2, pp. 378-379; *Labor: Its Rights and Wrongs*, p. 71.

35. Powderly here was not altogether honest. The resolutions, as he himself says (see above, p. 165), asked the next General Assembly—i.e., of 1886—to fix May 1 as the day on which to strike.

36. Powderly, *op. cit.*, p. 496.

37. Douglas, *loc. cit.*, p. 873, gives the following membership figures:

    1883— 52,000
    1884— 61,000
    1885—105,000
    1886—710,000

   According to the records of the proceedings of the General Assemblies for these years (pp. 527, 796, 174, 38 in the volumes for 1883, 1884, 1885, and 1886 respectively) the official membership for the Order was:

    1883— 51,914
    1884— 71,326
    1885—111,388
    1886—729,677.

38. Ware, *op. cit.*, pp. 311-312.

39. *John Swinton's Paper*, January 24, 1886.

40. *Alarm*, August 5, 1885.

41. *Ibid.*, September 5, 1885; *cf.*, Dyer D. Lum, *A Concise History of the Great Trial of the Chicago Anarchists in 1886. Condensed from the Official Record*, Chicago (1886?), p. 17.

42. *Freiheit*, May 1, 1886; *cf.*, *ibid.*, January 2, 1886.

43. *Alarm*, October 17, 1885. These resolutions were carried. The Central Labor Union, it will be remembered, was made up of unions of radical temper or affiliation.

44. *Ibid.*, November 14, 1885.

45. *Ibid.*, December 12, 1885.

46. January 23, 1886.

47. February 20, 1886.

48. *Ibid.*, April 3, 1886.

49. *Labor: Its Rights and Wrongs*, p. 46.

50. For contemporary arguments for the shorter day see: *Rep. of the Sen. Com. on Lab.*, vol. 2, pp. 219-222 (contains reprint of William J. Noble, "Eight Hours as the Standard Day's Work.— An Appeal in Behalf of the Same to the Workingmen of America."); *Fourth Biennial Report of the Bureau of Labor Statistics of Illinois*, pp. 474-475, 477-478; *Labor: Its Rights and Wrongs*, pp. 42-76 *passim;* Charles E. Endicott, *Capital and Labor. Address Before the Central Trades Union . . . at Boston, March 28, 1886*, n.p., n.d., pp. 11-12; *John Swinton's Paper*, May 2, 1886; Lum, *op. cit.*, p. 13; Ware, *op. cit.*, p. 5 notes; Commons, *op. cit.*, vol. 2, pp. 89-90; Cahill, *op. cit.*, pp. 13-20; Lemuel Danryid, *History and Philosophy of the Eight-Hour Movement*, fourth edition, Washington, 1899, pp. 8-15.

51. April 23, 1886.
52. April 23, 1886.
53. Edward Atkinson, "The Hours of Labor," *North American Review*, vol. 142, May, 1886, p. 512 *ff*.
54. Letter in *Bradstreet's*, April 24, 1886, pp. 260-262.
55. Vol. 42, no. 1088, May 1, 1886, p. 529.
56. Vol. 42, no. 1089, May 8, 1886, p. 558.
57. Vol. 38, no. 1953, May 6, 1886, p. 568.
58. Vol. 38, no. 1958, June 10, 1886, p. 733.
59. Quoted in Endicott, *op. cit.*, p. 11.
60. This point was made frequently. Edward Atkinson stresses this in his letter to *Bradstreet's* cited above. The eight-hour day, he said, will come when it will; it cannot be stopped.
61. See the representative opinions for different sections of the country reproduced in *Public Opinion*, vol. 1, no. 3, May 1, 1886, pp. 50-52.
62. Commons, *op. cit.*, vol. 2, p. 379.
63. *Public Opinion*, vol. 1, no. 3, May 1, 1886, pp. 50-52.
64. Vol. 40, no. 12, June, 1886, pp. 890-891.
65. *Labor: Its Rights and Wrongs*, pp. 42, 43, 43-44, 49-50, 51-52, 58, 61.
66. *John Swinton's Paper*, January 31, 1886; *H. of R. 51st Con. 1st Sess., Report no. 489*, p. 5.
67. *Labor: Its Rights and Wrongs*, pp. 44, 45-46, 52-53, 55, 55-60; *Public Opinion*, vol. 1, no. 4, May 8, 1886, pp. 69-75 *passim*.
68. *Labor: Its Rights and Wrongs*, p. 76; *cf.*, pp. 74-76.
69. *Ibid.*, pp. 48, 53-55, 63-65 *passim*; *Public Opinion*, vol. 1, no. 4, May 8, 1886, pp. 67-69. See the answer from members of the clergy in *Public Opinion* to the question: "What is the proper relation of the pulpit to the Labor Question?" The response for the most part begged the issue in moral, platitudinous generalizations.
70. Commons, *op. cit.*, vol. 2, pp. 379-380.
71. *Ibid.*, p. 384.
72. This was especially true of the situation in Chicago. See *Fourth Biennial Report of the Bureau of Labor Statistics of Illinois*, p. 479.
73. *Bradstreet's*, May 1, 1886, p. 274; New York *Times*, May 1, 1886; *John Swinton's Paper*, April 25, 1886.
74. *Bradstreet's*, May 8, p. 290, May 15, p. 306, June 12, 1886, p. 394; *Fourth Biennial Report of the Bureau of Labor Statistics of Illinois*, table II, pp. 482-490; *Third Annual Report of the Commissioner of Labor*, table 1, pp. 36-615. The contemporary estimates in *Bradstreet's* are surprisingly accurate, as an examination of the strike statistics for 1886 in the last citation indicates. From the latter it can be computed that there were almost 180,000 workers who struck for shorter hours during the entire year. Since the bulk of these went out on strike during April and May, the figures in *Bradstreet's* may be taken to be wholly representative. The question of the results is considered below.

VIII. CHICAGO—MAY 1

A CTIVE preparation for the May 1 movement and agitation for the eight-hour day began in Chicago near the close of 1885. In November of that year, the National Eight-Hour Association of Chicago was founded largely through the efforts of George Schilling, William Gleason, and Joseph Gruenhut. A manifesto issued by the Association developed the usual arguments in favor of the shorter day, and declared that the curtailment of working hours without proportionate reductions in wages would eliminate unemployment, competition in the labor market which made for low wages, and overproduction.[1] Trade-unions and labor associations were sympathetic to the program of the Eight-Hour Association,—especially those organized since the opening of 1885 and those in process of establishment after January, 1886. Before long, the Trade and Labor Assembly of the city and the Central Labor Union supported the Eight-Hour Association, and the labor organizations of Chicago and vicinity were urged to enter militantly into the impending struggle.[2] By the close of the winter of 1886, the leaders of the I.W.P.A. had also allied their organization with the movement.

By April, the eight-hour day had won such staunch support from the rank and file and generated so much enthusiasm that Chicago seemed "afire" with the movement. A monster demonstration on April 17 in the Cavalry Armory, called by the Knights of Labor and the Trades and Labor Assembly, drew 7,000 people inside the hall, and perhaps twice that number outside.[3] Eight days later, on a Sunday, there was a huge eight-hour demonstration arranged by the Central Labor Union in which members of the I.W.P.A. were active. Some three or four thousand workers, representing twenty-five unions, carrying banners and flags, paraded with music to the Lake Front, where they were addressed from two speaker's platforms by John A. Henry, Parsons, Schwab, Spies, Fielden and others. Perhaps as many as 25,000 persons witnessed this demonstration.[4]

Nearly everyone was certain that with this display of spirit and the excellent organization of the Chicago workers, the movement would succeed. The seeming willingness of many employers, especially small manufacturers, to meet the demands of their men rather than risk a strike when orders were coming in, enhanced the reigning optimism. The determined stand of most of the larger manufacturers against granting reductions in hours together with wage increases, however, boded ill for the future of the movement. They raised the cry that they could afford to concede nothing to their employees unless the eastern manufacturers, their competitors, would also grant the demands.

Members of the Eight-Hour Association early recognized that the question of wages would create great difficulty, and soon abandoned all talk of wage increases with reductions in hours. The Association clearly was concentrating solely on the eight-hour issue. An address which it issued in March, urged eight hours' pay for eight hours' work.[5] A short time before May 1, the Association issued another address to labor organizations in which it announced that the workers "are ready to make sacrifices in wages, in order that more people may find employment, and for the general good of the whole community. Surely such a self-sacrificing spirit should meet with a cordial response from the employing classes."[6] George Schilling pointed out in the *Eight Hour Day,* published by the Trades and Labor Assembly of Chicago, that it was an error to confuse the question of wages with the eight-hour issue; it was patently impossible for Chicago employers to grant ten hours' pay for an eight-hour day unless eastern manufacturers did likewise. He further warned against rash action by the workingmen of the city which might jeopardize the entire movement, pleading for peaceful settlement of the questions involved. Strikes, he urged, were to be avoided and prevented wherever possible.[7]

Such utterances were in part designed to counteract the militant agitation carried on by the I.W.P.A., which, having finally entered the eight-hour struggle, was determined to make the most of it. It is understandable that the pure trade-union elements and leaders of the Eight-Hour Association felt that the work of the social-revolutionaries was prejudicial to their cause. The revolutionary tone and fervor of Spies' editorial in the *Arbeiter-Zeitung* on May 1, for example, could hardly be expected to induce employers to look with sympathy upon the demands of the workers. "The dies are cast!" exclaimed Spies, "the first of May, whose historical significance will be understood and appreciated only in later years is here." For two decades, Spies declared, the working class had "begged their extortionists and legislators to introduce an eight-hour system" with no results. Finally a major movement was instituted as a result of the action of the Federation. The employers, he warned, would not give way to the demands of the workers without a bitter struggle. They would first attempt to starve their employees into submission. Would the workers permit that to happen?[8]

At the same time the press was willing to utilize the pronouncements of the radicals to attack them and indirectly cast reflection on the eight-hour issue.

"The socialistic agitators," inaccurately announced the Chicago *Inter Ocean* on May 1, "have boasted that they would turn the demonstration in favor of the eight-hour rule to good account. They have boasted that it was in their power to direct, or . . . to influence any agitation set on foot by the wage workers of this country. It is intimated that there will be in Chicago to-day some of the shrewdest wire-pullers of the socialistic movement. If they are here there is one standing admonition that the wage workers should keep always in mind—'Kick them out.'" The Chicago *Mail* in a scathing editorial singled out Parsons and Spies and exhorted the city to place in advance upon their shoulders responsibility for any untoward occurrence.

"There are two dangerous ruffians at large in this city; two sneaking cowards who are trying to create trouble. One of them is named Parsons; the other is named Spies. Should trouble come they would be the first to skulk away from the scene of danger, . . . the first to shirk responsibility.

"These two fellows have been at work fomenting disorder for the past ten years. They should have been driven out of the city long ago. They would not be tolerated in any other community on earth.

"Parsons and Spies have been engaged for the past six months [*sic*] for the precipitation to-day. They have taken advantage of the excitement to bring about a series of strikes [*sic*] and to work injury to capital and to honest labor in every possible way. They have no love for the eight-hour movement, and are doing all they can to hamper it and prevent its success. These fellows do not want any reasonable concession. They are looking for riot and plunder. They haven't got one honest aim nor one honorable end in view.

"Mark them for to-day. Keep them in view. Hold them personally responsible for any trouble that occurs. *Make an example of them if trouble does occur.*" [9]

Labor leaders like George Schilling were urging the workers to keep "sober" and avoid all disorder, but the city authorities, while issuing reassuring statements that no serious disturbances were expected, were preparing for anything May 1 might bring. The police force was ready for emergency action from May 1 on, and the militia, numbering 1,350 men, was equipped for instant participation in street disorders.[10] Leading business men were also prepared, through a committee of the Citizens' Association of Chicago, to observe intently whatever developments might follow May 1. This committee had almost continuous sessions from the first on "for the purpose of agreeing upon a plan of action in case the necessities of the situation should demand [its] intervention in any way. . . ." [11]

Early in the year, the press of Chicago was not unsympathetic to the eight-hour idea. But, when the cry grew for ten hours' pay for eight hours' work, when radicals of all shades threw themselves into the movement, and when it appeared that an aroused working-class, if victorious in one venture might make further demands, it regarded it less kindly.[12] With the approach of the first of May, inquietude grew in Chicago, and the press withdrew whatever support it had at first extended. As the agitation gained in strength during the last week in April, the tension in Chicago increased. Though city authorities declared that no serious trouble was expected— and announced that if disturbances did occur the city was well prepared to handle them [13]—there were signs of danger.

Clashes between police and workers had been frequent since the beginning of the year. Between them the sharpest animosity had developed. The rather small, overworked police department, long used as if it were a private force in the service of the employers, was detested by the working-class. During March and April, disturbances occurred repeatedly, and it was a common sight to see patrol-wagons filled with armed policemen dashing through the city. The force was busy dispersing gatherings of workingmen, regardless of their nature, and, on occasion, the workers retaliated, attacking patrol-wagons or assaulting the police. Charles Edward Russell, then a young Chicago newspaperman, recalls that the police "sometimes blundered, and dispersed gatherings that were perfectly orderly and unobjectionable. . . ." [14] The wide employment of Pinkerton operatives by employers augmented the ill-feeling.

Many of the conflicts arose in connection with a labor dispute at the McCormick Harvester factory. This plant had frequently been the scene of grave labor troubles. To those acquainted with Chicago's industrial history, another dispute there must have been an extremely unhappy omen. Into this quarrel the question of hours did not even enter. It arose over the issue of unionization, and the discharge of a number of men engaged in union activities. Particularly irritating was the fact that the men had been discharged in violation of a promise the previous April that such activities would not be ground for dismissal. While the matter was still being discussed, on February 16, the plant was shut down and 1,400 employees locked out.

Two days after the lock-out a strike was called. McCormick explained that he would not give up his right to hire and fire as he pleased; he would not be "dictated to" by his employees. He had ordered the shops to be closed, he specifically stated, to avoid trouble. By the end of the month, however, he announced that his factory would open the first week in March, and gave notice that he would need between 800 and 1,000 men. Extensive preparations were made, and the Chicago *Tribune* queried on March 1: "Will Blood Be Shed?" The company employed a large number of "Pinkertons," and the city placed between 350 and 500 police at its disposal. On March 2, 300 men reported for work. A mass meeting of the locked-out employees on the same day, at which Parsons and Schwab spoke, registered a protest against the use of police and "Pinks" and the employment of "scabs." Before it was over, it was attacked by the police and broken up. During the rest of the month, Black Road, near which the McCormick plant was situated, was frequently the scene of disturbances. All was quiet there immediately before the May 1 movement, but the McCormick factory still remained a danger spot as the strike and lock-out continued.[15]

Chicago, too concerned with what May 1 might bring, did not await that day with composure. A despatch of April 30 was headed "Anxiety in Chicago." Already railroad and gas company employees, iron mill workers, meat packers and plumbers were out on strike for shorter hours. "The police are preparing for any disorder that may occur. An order has been issued to keep all the reserve police ready for a call, and it is known that preparations have been made for any outbreak." [16] On May 1, the *Illinois State Register* reported that "The supreme officers of the police department have ceased in the attempt to smooth over the fears of the last few weeks regarding the labor movement. Their sole idea now is that . . . there will be a great deal of trouble. It was decided last night to place the entire police on reserve early Saturday morning . . . many hundreds of additional men can be pressed into service as special policemen as soon as any serious outbreak should occur." [17]

The dreaded May 1 came, passed and left Chicago altogether unmarked. Despite the excitement which pervaded the city, the "apprehension of serious trouble," and the parades and demonstrations, the day passed in utter peace. No less than 30,000 men struck, some two-thirds of them demanding ten hours' pay for eight hours' work. Perhaps twice that number were out on the streets participating in or witnessing the various demonstrations. An immense and successful ball, held under the auspices of the Trades and Labor Assembly, closed the peaceful demonstrations. Apparently somewhat reassured, the Chicago *Tribune* flippantly described what had occurred during the day.

Successful demonstrations, however, do not mean victories. Despite many gains for labor, it quickly became apparent that a large number of employers were determined to resist stubbornly. The lock-out was immediately brought into play in answer to the eight-hour demand and strikes.[18]

May 2, Sunday, passed even more quietly than the first. There were few additions to the ranks of the strikers, and the excitement which had marked the previous day had largely vanished. The streets were not crowded, there were no parades, and "compared with the surging crowd of yesterday," the numbers gathered around the radical headquarters on West

Lake Street were small. The *Inter Ocean* warned that unruly demonstrations and violence would cause the loss of the eight-hour strikes,[19] and it seemed as if the workers would take the advice to heart. The police considered the "fact that Saturday and Sunday passed without serious violence" most encouraging, but they did not abandon their "preparations for suppressing outbreaks. . . ." The nervous expectancy earlier present, was largely dissipated at the close of the second, and it was generally thought that the attempt to win a shorter day would not be marked by serious trouble. Optimism among the workers ran high. The movement had developed unusual strength. Many workers had already gained major concessions, and a large number of firms led their employees to believe that their demands would be satisfactorily met.[20]

It was not Chicago's fortune, however, to escape without a serious clash between workers and police on the following day, a product of the long, drawn-out McCormick dispute. May 3 opened quietly, even though additional workers struck, and there was a repetition of the first with its many parades and meetings. Among the gatherings was one arranged by the officials of the Lumber Shovers' Union, whose members were striking for a reduction in hours, for that afternoon on Black Road, near the McCormick factory.[21] On the previous morning, Sunday, delegates of the Lumber Shovers' Union at a meeting of the Central Labor Union requested that a good speaker be sent to address the strikers. At a second meeting of the Central Labor Union that same afternoon, August Spies was present in the capacity of a reporter, and when he was asked to speak at the lumber shovers' demonstration, he readily consented.

He arrived at the appointed place on Black Road Monday afternoon, to find some 6,000 strikers already assembled.[22] Some at first refused to let him speak because he was known as a "socialist." Not until the secretary of their union, who presented Spies, told the the strikers that he was sent by the Central Labor Union, did the heckling cease. Spies' address, dealing with the question of shorter hours, was free from revolutionary propaganda and inflammatory utterances. He urged the workers to stand together and not give way before their employers or they would court defeat. Shortly before he concluded, the bell of the McCormick plant, some three or four blocks away, rang, and about five hundred members of the assemblage made for the workers leaving the factory. Spies vainly exhorted them to remain, declaring that they were in no way concerned with McCormick's employees. Five or ten minutes after this interruption his address was over and the gathering elected him a member of the committee to treat with the lumber bosses.

Those who had broken away from the lumber shovers' meeting were striking McCormick workers. They at once attacked the strike-breakers, and pitching into them with sticks and stones, they drove the "scabs" to the factory for safety. The few police stationed there fired their revolvers in a vain attempt to disperse the crowd, which was smashing the windows of the factory. Some shots were also fired by the strikers in answer to those of the police. A telephone call for aid brought first a patrol-wagon with eleven officers, and then a police detail of almost two hundred men which followed on foot at a double-quick. The police reenforcement, making good use of club and revolver, charged the workers, whose resistance crumpled immediately.

When Spies came upon the scene the police were hotly pursuing the fleeing strikers. Several dropped before his eyes from blows and bullets. An excited eye-witness wildly cried out that he had seen a number of workers killed by the police. Spies hurried back to Black Road. There he passionately harangued the lumber shovers, pleading with them to aid their fellow-workers. But his appeals were met with stolid indifference, and he rushed in great haste to the *Arbeiter-Zeitung* to write up the episode.

The affray was costly. One striker was killed outright, five or six were seriously wounded by bullets, and an undetermined number were otherwise injured. The police suffered less severely. Two or three were badly manhandled before the larger body of police appeared, six in all were injured, but none was shot.

Spies, however, did not know this. Incised upon his mind was the picture of workingmen scattering before the charge of armed police. His belief that a large number of strikers had been killed and injured was reenforced by an inaccurate account of the clash in a late edition of the Chicago *Daily News,* which reported six men dead. Fired to fever heat by the day's developments, he set himself to write. After completing an account of the episode for the columns of the *Arbeiter-Zeitung,* he composed an indignant, bitter and fervid circular. Through no wish of his it came to be called, because of its heading, the "Revenge Circular," the unfortunate word "Revenge" being inserted independently by a compositor of the *Arbeiter-Zeitung.*[23] It reads:

"REVENGE! WORKINGMEN! TO ARMS!

"Your masters sent out their bloodhounds—the police— they killed six of your brothers at McCormick's this afternoon. They killed the poor wretches, because they, like you, had courage to disobey the supreme will of your bosses. They killed them because they dared ask for the shortening of the hours of toil. They killed them to show you 'free American citizens' that you must be satisfied and contented with whatever your bosses condescend to allow you, or you will get killed!

"You have for years endured the most abject humiliations; you have for years suffered immeasurable iniquities; you have worked yourselves to death; you have endured the pangs of want and hunger; your children you have sacrificed to the factory lords—in short, you have been miserable and obedient slaves all these years. Why? To satisfy the insatiable greed and fill the coffers of your lazy thieving masters! When you ask him now to lessen your burden, he sends his bloodhounds out to shoot you, to kill you!

"If you are men, if you are the sons of your grandsires,

who have shed their blood to free you, then you will rise in your might Hercules, and destroy the hideous monster that seeks to destroy you.

"To arms, we call you, to arms!

"YOUR BROTHERS."

This circular appeared both in English and German.[24] Spies detained six compositors of the *Arbeiter-Zeitung* staff after quitting-time to set it up. Of the 2,500 copies printed, only about half were distributed, most of them at the many labor meetings held that night. Spies disclaimed authorship of the heading, and later insisted that the word "Revenge" was inserted without his knowledge. Had he been aware of it in good time, he asserted, he would have had it removed.[25]

The Chicago newspapers saw in the riot at McCormick's a critical stage in the eight-hour movement and the work of the "anarchist" agitators. Reports of the disturbance were neither impartial nor accurate. It was spoken of as a "conflict between the police and the anarchists," and the mob was described as "liquor-crazed. . . ." Blame for the disturbance was specifically placed upon the speakers.[26] Yet the clash was not taken seriously, and the opinion was expressed that the city was amply protected against further disorders by its police. Nevertheless, additional precautions were taken. Several army companies were reported to be drilling in preparation for conflicts with strikers.[27] Police Captain Bonfield, whose prowess as a skull-cracker was fully recognized, announced that evening: "We have perfected arrangements for prompt and decisive action in all cases. I believe we are strong enough to suppress any uprising. I do not believe it will be necessary to call out the militia, because I do not anticipate any serious trouble. There will be more or less rioting, a few sanguinary conflicts, some blood spilling perhaps, but I do not anticipate anything like a repetition of the riot of 1877." [28]

The lessons drawn from the Black Road conflict by the press were not unexpected. "Two things were made so clear yesterday," declared the *Inter Ocean* on May 4, "that there is no chance for misunderstanding. It was demonstrated that the men who follow the lead of Spies and Parsons are a menace to society. . . . It was also demonstrated that the city police is well . . . able to disperse or destroy any mob that may gather under such leadership." Neither the Chicago disturbance nor a much more serious clash between unarmed strikers and militia in Milwaukee, with disastrous consequences to the former,[29] caused alarm throughout the country. "Indeed, considering the number of men who are idle," commented the New York *Tribune,* "exceptional order has been maintained, except in one or two instances in Chicago and Milwaukee." [30]

Those who hoped that there would be no further disorders were disappointed on the following day. Tuesday morning workers throughout the city were in an ugly temper, and clashes with the police were endemic the entire day. The animosity of the workers against the police was bitter. There was no mistaking that. At nine in the morning a mob attacked and, in spite of the efforts of the police, later practically destroyed a drug store. The owner's telephone had been used by the police to send messages to headquarters, and the mob took this to mean that the proprietor was a police spy. A saloon was shortly afterwards the scene of another clash. In the afternoon a large crowd congregated around the McCormick plant, and engaged in a bloody battle with the police. At seven in the evening another clash between workers and police occurred. In addition, there were minor scraps between individual officers and workingmen.[31]

In the meantime, arrangements had been made by delegates of labor unions for a demonstration meeting to be held the evening of the fourth in Haymarket Square in protest against police brutality. When August Spies came, as usual, to the office of the *Arbeiter-Zeitung* on Tuesday morning, Adolph Fischer, a fellow-member of the I.W.P.A. and employed by the paper, asked him to address that gathering.

After Spies had readily consented, there came to his notice the circular announcing the meeting. Fischer had attended to the printing and subsequent distribution of the handbills, and up to that moment Spies was entirely ignorant of their existence. Printed in both English and German, they announced:

"ATTENTION WORKINGMEN!

GREAT
MASS-MEETING
TO-NIGHT AT 7 O'CLOCK
AT THE
HAYMARKET
RANDOLPH STREET, BETWEEN DESPLAINES & HALSTED

Good speakers will be present to denounce the latest atrocious act of the police, the shooting of our fellow-workmen yesterday afternoon.

WORKINGMEN ARM YOURSELVES AND APPEAR IN FULL FORCE!
THE EXECUTIVE COMMITTEE"

When Spies read the circular he immediately demanded that the line "Workingmen arm yourselves and appear in full force!" be stricken out. Unless that were done, he would not only refuse to speak, but he would not even attend the meeting. "I objected to that [line]," he later explained, "principally because I thought it was ridiculous to put in a phrase which would prevent people from attending the meeting; another reason was [that] there was some excitement at the time, and a call for arms like that might have caused trouble between the police and the attendants of that meeting." Fischer, evidently convinced by these reasons, quickly went over to the printer to make the correction. Some of the notices had already been printed, but the press was stopped and the objectionable line cut out. Of the 20,000 handbills distributed, only two or three hundred contained the words to which Spies took exception. The columns of the *Arbeiter-Zeitung* also carried a notice of the meeting.[32]

Of the many labor gatherings scheduled for the night of the fourth, no other was called in a place which could hold so large a crowd as the Haymarket. No other was announced by the distribution of so many handbills. It was expected that at least several thousand workers would turn out to hear the police assailed for acts still fresh in everyone's mind.

NOTES CHAPTER VIII

1. Lum, *op. cit.*, p. 13; Flinn, *op. cit.*, p. 258; Pierre Ramus (Rudolph Grossman), *Der Justizmord von Chicago. In Memoriam 11. November, 1887. Nach urkundlichen Dokumenten und historischen Quellen dargesteelt . . . bearbeitet . . . von Pierre Ramus,* Zurich, 1912, p. 11; Spies, *op. cit.*, pp. 35-39 *passim.*
2. *Freiheit,* May 22, 1886, communication from Chicago titled "The Happenings in Chicago," and signed "Ahasverus"; Lum, *op. cit.*, pp. 14-15.
3. *John Swinton's Paper,* April 18, 1886; Freiheit, May 22, 1886.
4. Chicago *Tribune,* April 26, 1886; New York *Times,* April 26, 1886; *Freiheit,* May 1, 1886; Flinn, *op. cit.*, p. 265.
5. *Eight Hours for a Day's Labor. Address No. 2 by the National Eight-Hour Association of Chicago. Liberty Library,* vol. 1, no. 2, Chicago, March 13, 1886, p. 4.
6. Quoted in Flinn, *op. cit.*, p. 258.
7. Quoted in *ibid.*, p. 268; Chicago *Inter Ocean,* May 1, 1886.
8. See also Flinn, *op. cit.*, pp. 265-266, for the translation followed here.
9. May 1, 1886, quoted in Flinn, *op. cit.*, pp. 266-267. Flinn at the time was editor of the *Mail* and wrote the editorial.
10. Chicago *Inter Ocean,* May 1, 1886; Flinn, *op. cit.*, p. 270.
11. *Annual Report of the Citizens' Association of Chicago. October, 1886.* Chicago, 1886, pp. 33-34.
12. Bogart and Thompson, *op. cit.*, pp. 166-167.
13. Chicago *Inter Ocean,* May 1, 1886.
14. Charles Edward Russell, "The Haymarket and Afterwards. Some Personal Recollections," *Appleton's Magazine,* vol. 10, no. 4, October, 1907, pp. 401-402; *Acht Opfer des Klassenhasses (Nach den Berichten der New Yorker Volkszeitung),* New York, 1890, p. 4; Bogart and Thompson, pp. 167-168.
15. Chicago *Tribune,* February 19, 20, March 1, 2, 1886; Flinn, *op. cit.*, pp. 260-264, 271; *Acht Opfer des Klassenhasses,* p. 3; Bogart and Thompson, *op. cit.*, p. 166.
16. New York *Tribune,* May 1, 1886.
17. Quoted in Bogart and Thompson, *op. cit.*, p. 168.
18. Chicago *Tribune,* May 1, 2, 1886; Chicago *Inter Ocean,* May 2, 1886; New York *Tribune,* May 2, 1886; *Bradstreet's,* May 8,

1886, p. 290; Flinn, *op. cit.*, pp. 265, 269, 270; Bogart and Thompson, *op. cit.*, pp. 168-169.

19. May 2, 1886.

20. Chicago *Inter Ocean*, May 2, 3, 1886; Chicago *Tribune*, May 3, 1886; New York *Tribune*, May 3, 1886 (Chicago dispatch); *Nation*, vol. 42, no. 1,088, May 6, 1886, p. 374; Flinn, *op. cit.*, p. 270.

21. For what follows, see *In the Supreme Court of Illinois, Northern Grand Division. March Term, A. D. 1887. August Spies et al., vs. The People of the State of Illinois, Abstract of Record*, 2 vols., Chicago, 1887, vol. 2, pp. 251-255, 297-298 (hereafter cited as *Abstract of Record*); *In the Supreme Court of Illinois, Northern Grand Division. March Term, A. D. 1887. August Spies et al., vs. The People of the State of Illinois. Brief on the Facts for Defendants in Error*, Chicago, 1887, pp. 137-140, 147-157 (hereafter cited as *Brief on the Facts for the State*); *In the Supreme Court of Illinois, Northern Grand Division, March Term, A. D. 1887. August Spies et al., vs. The People of the State of Illinois. Brief and Argument for Plaintiffs in Error*, Chicago, 1887, pp. 40-45 (hereafter cited as *Brief and Argument*); Lum, *op. cit.*, pp. 129-130, 134-139; less valuable are Spies, *op. cit.*, pp. 40-45; Sigmund Zeisler, *Reminiscences of the Anarchist Case*, Chicago, 1927, p. 6; Flinn, *op. cit.*, pp. 271-278.

22. Spies claimed an attendance of 10,000, Spies, *op. cit.*, p. 40.

23. The man's name was Herman Podeva. *Abstract of Record*, vol. 2, pp. 90-91; Lum, *op. cit.*, p. 86.

24. The German version, differing in many respects from the English reads:

"Revenge! Revenge! Workingmen! To Arms!

"Working people, this afternoon the bloodhounds, your exploiters, murdered six of your brothers at McCormick's. Why did they murder them? Because they dared to be dissatisfied with the lot which your exploiters made for them. They asked for bread, and were answered with lead, mindful of the fact that the people thus can be most effectively brought to silence. For many, many years you have submitted to all humiliations without a murmur, have slaved from early morning till late in the evening, have suffered privations of every kind, have sacrificed even your children,—all in order to fill the coffers of your masters, all for them! And now, when you go before them and ask them to lessen your burden, they send their bloodhounds, the police, against you, in gratitude for your services, to cure you of your discontent by means of leaden balls. Slaves, we ask and entreat you, in the name of all that is dear and sacred to you, to avenge this horrible murder that was perpetrated against your brothers, and that may be perpetrated against you tomorrow. Working people, Hercules, you are at the parting of the ways! Which is your choice? Slavery and hunger, or liberty and bread? If you choose the latter, and do not delay a moment; then, people, to arms! Destruction upon the human beasts who call themselves your masters! Reckless destruction,—that must be your watchword. Think of the heroes whose blood has enriched the path of progress, of liberty, and of humanity—and strive to prove yourselves worthy of them.

"YOUR BROTHERS."

Given in English translation in John Henry Mackay, *"The Anarchists," A Picture of Civilization at the Close of the Nineteenth Century,* translated by George Schumm, Boston, 1891, pp. 199-200.

25. *Abstract of Record,* vol. 2, pp. 298-299; *Brief on the Facts for the State,* pp. 157-162; Spies, *op. cit.,* p. 42.
26. Chicago *Inter Ocean* and Chicago *Tribune,* May 4, 1886.
27. *Idem.*
28. Quoted in Flinn, *op. cit.,* p. 278.
29. The militia fired upon the strikers without provocation.
30. May 4, 1886.
31. Flinn, *op. cit.,* pp. 285-290.
32. *Abstract of Record,* vol. 2, pp. 299-301 *passim; Brief and Argument,* pp. 49-50, 82; Lum, *op. cit.,* 134-139 *passim;* Spies, *op. cit.,* p. 43.

IX. THE BOMB

ALTHOUGH Spies knew that the meeting was scheduled to start at half-past seven, it was later than that when he first set out for the Haymarket. He expected to address the crowd in German, and, as it was customary for the German speakers to appear last, he saw no reason for hurrying. He stopped on his way to leave the revolver he usually carried in the care of a German friend. Sometime between eight-fifteen and eight-thirty he arrived at Haymarket Square accompanied by his brother Henry.[1]

The old Haymarket, which no longer exists, was a long, oblong space, formed by the widening of Randolph Street, running East and West, between Desplaines and Halsted Streets. The space was in great part enclosed by rather large buildings of the factory and warehouse types. One end of the oblong was formed by Desplaines Street running North and South. If an observer were to stand at the intersection of the Square and Desplaines, face South and walk down the west side of the street, he would come almost immediately upon the Desplaines Street Police Station. An even shorter walk North on the east side of Desplaines Street from the same point would bring him to a narrow blind alley adjacent to Crane Brothers' large manufacturing establishment.[2]

It is said that the Square could accommodate some twenty thousand people. Since a gathering of impressive size was anticipated, the Haymarket was chosen. When Spies arrived, however, no meeting was in progress and no speakers were present. Knots of men standing disinterestedly about the South

corner of Desplaines Street offered the only indication that a
gathering had been contemplated. Spies called them together
and opened the meeting. The Haymarket proper was no place
for so small a crowd, and looking about for a suitable rostrum,
he decided to use a truck wagon in front of Crane Brothers'
factory six or eight feet North of the alley. He mounted the
improvised platform, and inquired for Parsons. Twice he
called out, "Is Parsons here?" When someone volunteered the
information that Parsons was addressing another meeting at
Halsted and Randolph Streets, Spies announced, "Never mind,
I will go and find him myself." Someone else then suggested,
"Let's pull the wagon around on Randolph Street and hold
the meeting there." Spies objected to the proposal with "We
may stop the street-cars." [3]

He then descended from the wagon, and, accompanied
by his brother and two young men, Ernest Legner and Rudolph Schnaubelt, set off in search of Parsons. He returned
without him, however, having been gone no more than ten
minutes. Finally, one Balthasar Rau was sent to find Parsons,
Spies mounted the wagon again, and the "great" Haymarket
mass-meeting inauspiciously opened.

"Gentlemen and fellow workmen:" Spies began, "Mr.
Parsons and Mr. Fielden will be here in a very short time to
address you. I will say, however, first, this meeting was called
for the purpose of discussing the general situation of the eight-
hour strike, and the events which have taken place in the last
forty-eight hours. It seems to have been the opinion of the
authorities that this meeting was called for the purpose of
raising a little row and disturbance. This, however, was not
the intention of the committee that called the meeting. The
committee that called the meeting wanted to tell you certain
facts of which you are probably aware."

He pointed out that the "capitalistic press" was "mis-
representing the cause of labor. . . ." Blame for the violence
which sometimes accompanied strikes was to be laid primarily

at the door of the employers and the police. It was "the natural outcome of the degradation . . . to which the working people are subjected." Then he referred to his experiences of the day before. "I was addressing a meeting of ten thousand wage slaves yesterday afternoon in the neighborhood of McCormick's. They did not want me to speak. The most of them were good church-going people. . . . I spoke to them and told them they must stick together. . . ." Then the police came and blood was shed.

"It was said that I inspired the attack on McCormick's. That is a lie. The fight is going on. Now is the chance to strike for the existence of the oppressed classes. The oppressors want us to be content. They will kill us. The thought of liberty which inspired your sires to fight for freedom ought to animate you today. The day is not far distant when we will resort to hanging these men. (Applause and cries of 'Hang them now.') McCormick is the man who created the row Monday, and he must be held responsible for the murder of our brothers. (Cries of 'Hang him!') Don't make any threats, they are of no avail. Whenever you get ready to do something, do it and don't make any threats beforehand. There are in the city today between forty and fifty thousand men locked out because they refuse to obey the supreme will . . . of a small number of men. The families of twenty-five or thirty thousand men are starving because their husbands and fathers are not men enough to withstand and resist the dictation of few thieves on a grand scale. . . . You place your lives, your happiness, everything [in] the arbitrary power of a few rascals who have been raised in idleness and luxury upon the fruits of your labor. Will you stand that? (Cries of 'No') The press say . . . that there are no Americans among us. That is a lie. Every honest American is with us. Those who are not unworthy of their tradition and their forefathers."

Such was the subject matter and the tenor of Spies' address. It lasted some twenty minutes, and throughout it, there were no remarks more inflammatory or violent than those quoted.[4] When Spies was informed of the arrival of Parsons and Samuel Fielden, he brought his remarks to a close and presented Parsons to the crowd.

It was fully nine o'clock when Parsons faced his audience. He was a successful spell-binder of the old school. That evening his speech consumed between forty-five minutes and an hour. It was in the main a review of conditions in the world of labor, and contained much statistical material. He had a reputation as a blood-and-thunder orator, but his Haymarket address cannot be regarded as incendiary.

In the distribution of wealth under capitalism, said Parsons, the worker only received fifteen cents out of every dollar and the remainder went to the capitalist. In Socialism lay the remedy for the wrongs which the worker suffered. The most violent portion of his speech was an attempt to make his audience conscious of the worker's plight.

"It is time to raise a note of warning," he declared. "There is nothing in the eight-hour movement to excite the capitalists. Do you know that the military are under arms, and a Gatling gun is ready to mow you down? Is this Germany or Russia or Spain? (A voice: 'It looks like it.') Whenever you make a demand for . . . an increase in pay, the militia and the deputy sheriff and the Pinkerton men are called out and you are shot and clubbed and murdered in the streets. I am not here for the purpose of inciting anybody, but to speak out, to tell the facts as they exist, even though it shall cost me my life before morning. . . . It behooves you, as you love your wife and children, if you don't want to see them perish with hunger, killed or cut down like dogs in the street, Americans, in the interest of your liberty and your independence, to arm, to arm yourselves. (Applause and cries of: 'We will do it, we are ready now.') You are not."

The remainder of his address was aptly described by a newspaper man as "wind-up." It is worth noting that when Parsons mentioned Jay Gould and someone cried "Hang him!"—he deprecated such sentiments. It was reliably reported that his words "to arm" were uttered without undue emphasis.

It was not much before ten o'clock when Parsons introduced Samuel Fielden, who took as his chief theme a statement of Congressman Foran of Ohio that the workingman could expect no relief or aid from legislation. He also touched upon the insecurity of the working class, the concentration of the means of production in the hands of a few, the necessity of staunch opposition by the worker if he were not to be crushed by the capitalist. But the strongest portion of his speech revolved about the relationship between the workingman and the law.

"There is no security for the working class under the present social system," he declared. ". . . Congressman Foran says the laborer can get nothing from legislation. He also said that the laborers can get some relief from their present condition when the rich man knew it was unsafe for him to live in a community where there are dissatisfied workingmen, for they would solve the labor problem. I don't know whether you are Democrats or Republicans, but whichever you are, you worship at the shrine of heaven . . . the law is your enemy. We are rebels against it. The law is only framed for those that are your enslavers. (A voice: 'That is true.') Men in their blind rage attacked the McCormick factory and were shot down in cold blood. . . . Those men were going to do some damage to a certain person's interest who was a large property owner, therefore the law came to his defense; and when McCormick undertook to do some injury to the interest of those who had no property the law also came to his. . . . and not to the workingman's defense when McCormick attacked him and his living. (Cries of 'No.') There is the difference. . . . You have nothing more to do with the law except to lay hands on it and throttle it until it makes its last kick. It turns your brothers out on the wayside, and has degraded them until they have lost the last vestige of humanity, and they are mere things and animals. Keep your eye upon it, throttle it, kill it, stab it, do everything you can to wound

it—to impede its progress. Remember, before trusting them
to do anything for yourself, prepare to do it yourself. Don't
turn over your business to anybody else. No man deserves
anything unless he is man enough to make an effort to lift
himself from oppression."

Fielden had not spoken more than ten minutes when a
biting wind swept up and rain clouds blackened the sky. The
drizzle that began to fall caused many of the 1,200 or 1,300
people to leave for shelter. At this point Parsons interrupted
to propose that the meeting adjourn to Zepf's Hall, half a
block away. Someone offered the information that the hall
was already occupied. Fielden announced that he needed only
a few minutes to complete his speech, and the meeting would
be over. The crowd meanwhile had dwindled to about one-
fourth of its former size. Fielden, little disconcerted by the
fact that he had lost most of his audience, continued:

"Is it not a fact that we have no choice as to our existence, for we can't dictate what our labor is worth? He that
has to obey the will of another is a slave. Can we do anything except by the strong arm of resistance? The socialists
are not going to declare war; but I tell you war has been declared upon us; and I ask you to get hold of anything that will
help to resist the onslaught of the enemy and the usurper. The
skirmish lines have met. People have been shot. Men, women
and children have not been spared by the capitalists and the
minions of private capital. It has no mercy—so ought you.
You are called upon to defend yourselves, your lives, your
futures. What matters it whether you kill yourselves with
work to get a little relief, or die on the battle field resisting the
enemy? What is the difference? Any animal, however loathsome, will resist when stepped upon. Are men less than snails
and worms? I have some resistance in me; I know that you
have, too; you have been robbed, and you will be starved into
a worse condition."

At about twenty minutes past ten, Fielden was almost
through. He began, "In conclusion". . . But the sentence was

never completed. To everyone's amazement a large body of police suddenly appeared and made for the wagon. Fielden, taken aback, stopped in bewilderment. The small crowd, no less startled, could only wonder and wait.

Led by Captains Bonfield and Ward, the head of the police column of 180 men halted about three or four paces from the end of the wagon. Without hesitation Captain Ward turned to the handful of people present. "In the name of the people of the State of Illinois," he directed, "I command this meeting immediately and peaceably to disperse." He waited a moment, and repeated the order, this time adding, "And I call upon you and you [here he turned and pointed to bystanders] to assist." Fielden, as if he had anticipated the command, immediately replied, "We are peaceable." At the same time, he, Spies, and others on the wagon began to descend.

Abruptly, and with no other warning than the dimly glowing light and slight sputtering of its fuse, a dynamite bomb hurtled through the air. It struck the ground, and with a fearful detonation exploded near the first rank of the police. For a breathless moment there was the frigid stillness of sudden horror.

Quickly the police reformed their ranks. They opened fire on the still stunned spectators. There was a feeble response from the crowd. But even before the police charged, its members were wildly fleeing for safety, from the enraged police.[5] In the mad dash people fell right and left, struck by bullets or clubbed down. A matter of seconds, and it was all over. Except for the injured the meeting place was clear, and but for their moans and cries, quiet.[6]

The Haymarket "Riot" was over. . . . And the Haymarket Affair had begun.

NOTES CHAPTER IX

1. For Spies' movements and activities before and after the meeting, see *Abstract of Record*, vol. 2, pp. 120-125 *passim*, 238-243 *passim*, 299-301; *Brief and Argument*, pp. 32-35, 54-74 *passim*, 113-114;

Lum, *op. cit.*, pp. 134-139 *passim*. Spies, *op. cit.*, pp. 43-44; also see below chap. XIII, for additional citations.

2. It was called Crane's alley.

3. These quotations are from the uncontradicted testimony of Police Officer McKeough.

4. The best source for Spies' speech and those of Parsons and Fielden is *Abstract of Record*, vol. 2, pp. 129-134; for additional material on all three speeches, *ibid.*, 105-108 *passim*, 116-120 *passim*, 126-127, 176-182 *passim*, 186-188 *passim*, 190-194 *passim*, 264-275 *passim*, 301-302, 315-320. Other sources which contain reports of the addresses, most of them based on the above are: *Brief on the Facts for the State*, pp. 206-217; *Brief and Argument*, pp. 5-6, 21-23, 54-57; Lum, *op. cit.*, pp. 89-90, 93-94, 142; Flinn, *op. cit.*, pp. 305-308. See also, below, chap. XIII. The first citation is the testimony of Mr. English of the *Tribune*, whose assignment included securing the most violent portions of the speeches. His notes sometimes garble the speeches, are not full enough, but nevertheless constitute the best source.

5. Chicago *Tribune*, May 5, 1886, for the temper of the police.

6. For the developments at the meeting after Fielden began to speak see below, pp. 277 *et seq. Brief and Argument*, pp. 7-20, 24-25, 118-120; Spies, *op. cit.*, p. 44; Zeisler, *op. cit.*, p. 9.

X. REPERCUSSIONS

CHICAGO and the entire country were momentarily stunned. One policeman killed, almost seventy officers wounded,—it was ₁inconceivable. The casualties for which the police were responsible were overlooked. It was officially reported that they had killed one and wounded twelve persons, but it was said that the injured really came to five or six times that number.[1]

Public opinion quickly decided that the bomb was the work of the motley crew of socialists, anarchists and communists infesting Chicago. Immediately there arose a vindictive cry for vengeance. There was no thought of suspending judgment until the available facts were gathered and weighed, no attempt to be just. With the blast of the bomb, the press lost every vestige of objective accuracy. News accounts of the Haymarket meeting were so highly colored that they could not be distinguished from expressions of editorial opinion.[2]

A characteristic headline screamed: "NOW IT IS BLOOD! . . . A Bomb Thrown into [Police] Ranks Inaugurates The Work of Death."[3] The earliest news reports had no doubts as to who was responsible for the bomb.

"The anarchists of Chicago inaugurated in earnest last night the reign of lawlessness which they have threatened and endeavored to incite for years. They threw a bomb into the midst of a line of 200 police officers, and it exploded with fearful effect, mowing down men like cattle. Almost before the missile of death had exploded the anarchists directed a murderous fire from revolvers upon the police as if their action were prearranged, and as the latter were hemmed in on every side—ambuscaded—the effect of the fire upon the ranks of the officers was fearful. . . . The collision between the police and the anarchists was brought about by the leaders of the latter, August Spies, Sam Fielden, and A. R. Parsons, endeavoring to incite a large mass-meeting to riot and bloodshed." [4]

Reports in other Chicago dailies were generally written with greater heat than this excerpt, and accounts which appeared on May 5 are in many respects more trustworthy than those of later date. The Chicago *Tribune,* for example, first reported that the police fired immediately after the bomb exploded. Later it was widely assumed that the bomb served as a signal for a fusillade from the crowd.[5] Newspapers of other cities were no more accurate as to fact and no less venomous in tone. Thus, the New York *Tribune* reported:

"A squad of officers marched up close to the speaker's stand. Some one shouted: 'Kill the . . .'

"Almost as soon as the words had been uttered, three bombs were thrown from near the stand into the midst of the squad of officers. . . . The explosion of the bombs was terrific, and they were instantly followed with a volley from the revolvers of the policemen. The rioters answered with theirs, which . . . they were well provided with. The mob appeared crazed with a frantic desire for blood and holding its ground poured volley after volley into the midst of the officers." [6]

On the morning of the fifth the effects of the previous night's tragedy were quickly sensed. "I passed many groups of people . . . whose excited conversations about the events of the preceding night, I could not fail to overhear," writes a Chicagoan. "Everybody assumed that the speakers at the meeting and other labor agitators were the perpetrators of the horrible crime. 'Hang them first and try them afterwards' was an expression which I heard repeatedly. . . . The air was charged with anger, fear and hatred." [7]

Beneath the rage which shook the city there ran a definite current of fear. It was no time for calm, dispassionate reflection before the passing of judgment, and "good men forgot reason and clamored for revenge." [8] In this mood, they were readily convinced that they, their government, and the social and economic system under which they lived were in danger of immediate destruction. The bomb sounded a note of terror, and people no longer reflected or thought. If the newspapers may be believed, it appears that a temporary madness swept Chicago. The First Infantry Regiment was kept in readiness. Substantial citizens prepared to organize groups of vigilantes. Preposterously wild and vague rumors circulated like wildfire. New "uprisings" were breathlessly awaited.[9] Instead of allaying these fears, the press fostered them. "After the violent outbreak of the anarchists Tuesday night, their slaughter of police officers in one portion of the city, and their work of pillage and ruin in another, it is little wonder that the law-and-order element woke up frightened yesterday," asserted the *Inter Ocean*. "The cowardly tactics of the curs were discussed on every hand. Business men were fearful. . . ." [10] In view of the unrest, Mayor Carter H. Harrison issued a proclamation which declared that, since crowds, processions and the like were "dangerous" with conditions as they were, he had ordered the police to break up all such gatherings. He further urged "all law-abiding people to quietly attend to their own affairs and not to meet in crowds." [11]

So absorbed was Chicago in the Haymarket "Riot" that other disturbances in the city on the night of the fourth were completely overlooked, even though they resulted in casualties among police and civilians.[12] The "Riot" remained front page news for weeks. For once the press of the country spoke in one voice. Newspapers whose viewpoints and interests clashed, pro- and anti-Cleveland papers, "gold" and "silver" papers, protectionist and anti-protectionist,—all were in agreement. Radicals, regardless of their affiliations, were anathematized. The cry for vengeance was universal. The bomb-thrower must be punished with death, and, no less important, radicalism must be suppressed and all radicals punished. Because the "anarchist" and socialist groups were composed largely of foreigners, aliens were indiscriminately damned. Especially severe was the literary castigation of the Germans.

Denouncing "anarchists" and their like as "vipers," "ungrateful hyenas" and "serpents," the Chicago *Tribune* characterized the "toleration" which had been accorded them "excessive, ill-considered." Unless Anarchism and Communism were quickly and thoroughly crushed, the *Tribune* continued, the people of Chicago "must expect an era of anarchy and the loss of their property, if not their lives." The bomb had at least served to awaken Chicago to the danger of the situation.[13] Taking much the same view, the Chicago *Herald* announced that the anarchist movement, composed of the "offscourings of Europe," menaced the very foundations of American society. To protect that society, the "fangs" of the anarchists "must be drawn."[14] The Chicago *Journal* called for "sharp, decisive measures" and "prompt justice," while the Chicago *Times* urged a "speedy trial" to wipe out the stigma of the Haymarket meeting upon the fair city of Chicago.[15] Almost every newspaper held that the anarchists and socialists had "violated every law of God and man, and neither courtesy, leniency, nor mercy should be extended to them."[16] Two days after the bombing, the *Inter Ocean* editorially outlined the legal ground for convicting the men who were popularly regarded as responsible for the events of May 4.

"It is now seen that the deadly bomb of Tuesday night was the logical and legitimate result of the red flag of a few days previous. How far are such men as Spies, Parsons, Fielden, Schwab and their class responsible for the uprising, explosion, shots and slaughter of Tuesday evening? They are guilty of homicide. The law is clear on that point. *They were accessories before the fact.* What does that mean? Just this in plain words: Spies, Parsons and Fielden made incendiary speeches on Tuesday night to men all too ready to put into practise the inflammatory harangues of their leaders. . . . For months and years these pestiferous fellows have uttered their seditious and dangerous doctrines. Even if they had not opened their lips on Tuesday night, their very presence, with their well-known and destructive views, would have been an invitation to the mob . . . to commit acts of lawlessness. . . .

"These men are accessories before the fact to the murder of Officer Joseph M. Degan . . . and to the murder of every other man, woman, or child who may die within a year and a day from the date of receiving their injuries." [17]

Letters to the newspapers by the ever alert *Vox Populi* and his associate *Pro Bono Publico* cried to the skies for justice and revenge which, for the moment, were synonymous.[18] Mayor Harrison was frequently and roundly criticized for having permitted the activities of anarchists and communists to go unchecked. Had he set limits upon their propaganda and organization, it was argued, the bombing would not have occurred.[19] The disaster served as a text for preachers throughout Chicago on Sunday, and clergymen were no less denunciatory than laymen. The Rev. J. Coleman Adams, reflecting the popular attitude, declared that the socialists should be stamped out and the supremacy of the "land" maintained.[20] Some members of the Baptist clergy, however, assumed a far more reasonable attitude.[21]

Organized labor joined in the universal condemnation of radicalism. Because radicals had been associated with the labor movement, it was felt that the "respectable" workers had to make it clear that they had not been contaminated. This the Knights of Labor element was quick to do in a smashing editorial in their Chicago organ.

"Let it be understood by all the world that the Knights of Labor have no affiliation, association, sympathy or respect for the band of cowardly murderers, cutthroats and robbers, known as anarchists, who sneak through the country like midnight assassins, stirring up the passions of ignorant foreigners, unfurling the red flag of anarchy and causing riot and bloodshed. . . . They are entitled to no more consideration than wild beasts." [22]

These expressions echoed the sentiments of General Master Workman Terence V. Powderly, who was prompt to castigate the "anarchists."

"The scenes of bloodshed and disorder," he declared, "which have occurred in Chicago are disgraceful, uncalled for, and deserving of the severest condemnation and punishment. Honest labor is not to be found in the ranks of those who march under the red flag of anarchy, which is the emblem of blood and destruction. . . . There is not a Trade-Union in America that will uphold those men in Chicago who have been engaged in the destruction of life and property. . . . The anarchist idea is unAmerican, and has no business in this country." [23]

Most labor leaders aligned themselves with Powderly immediately after the bomb was thrown, though they did not all press for punishment as strongly as he did. But none was backward in condemning, for one reason or another, the methods advanced in the *Alarm* and *Arbeiter-Zeitung*.[24] "Mr. Powderly . . . and other gentlemen authorized to speak for other labor organizations," reported the *Inter Ocean*, vehemently and earnestly denounced the methods employed by the "socialists" of Chicago.

At a meeting of the Typographical Union No. 16 of Chicago held on the third day after the bomb was thrown, three significant resolutions were adopted. In unmeasured terms the Union condemned the deed and stigmatized those responsible for it as "the greatest enemy the laboring man has." A reward of $100 was offered for the "apprehension and conviction of the scoundrel" who threw the bomb. The delegates to the Trade and Labor Assembly of the city were instructed to present these recommendations at the next meeting of the Assembly for indorsement.[25] Illuminating, likewise, is a resolution of the Chicago Furniture Manufacturers' Association, whose members pledged themselves not to employ knowingly "any communist, anarchist, nihilist, or socialist, or any other person denying the right of private property or recommending destruction or bloodshed as remedies for existing evils." [26]

Every part of the country let itself be heard. The New York *Times* declared on the fifth that the Chicago anarchists were guilty of the bomb-throwing. These men were patently "cut-throats," and "the promptest and sternest way of dealing" with them was also the "wisest and most merciful." On the following day, the *Times* announced:

"No disturbance of the peace that has occurred in the United States since the war of the rebellion has excited public sentiment through the Union it is excited by the Anarchist's murder of policemen in Chicago on Tuesday night. We say murder with the fullest consciousness of what that word means. It is silly to speak of the crime as a riot. All the evidence goes to show that it was concerted, deliberately planned, and coolly executed murder." The *Times* fervently hoped that the "cowardly savages who plotted and carried out this murder shall suffer the death they deserve."

Echoing the *Times,* the New York *Tribune* asserted that the disturbances in Chicago and elsewhere were indisputably the work of foreign anarchists and socialists. No American workingmen were implicated. For this "anarchist illness" there was but one cure,—force.

"It is mobs of irrational but deliberate rioters," said the *Tribune,* "bent on doing as much mischief as possible, eager to take life and destroy property, and hostile in the intensest way to the social system which they have been admitted to. Only the sharpest and sternest application of force can be employed against them, therefore. . . . The anarchists are not honest workingmen, but pirates . . . and as such they must be dealt with." [27]

Deportation should also be employed to rid the country

of this element. Since they were no better than wild beasts, anarchists could be sent to inhabit some wild jungle or lonely Pacific isle, and the *Tribune* proposed a law for the enforced deportation of every confessed anarchist.[28] The New York *Sun* concurred, and was convinced that a carefully restricted immigration would do much to keep "foreign savages, with their dynamite bombs and anarchic purposes" from American shores.[29] Pleading for a swift trial and the proper verdict, the New York *Commercial-Advertiser* asserted that "These men were criminals and outlaws at home, and in changing their skies they have not changed their minds." [30] The New York *Herald* declaring, on May 8, "that there are times when mercy to the guilty is cruelty to the innocent," exhorted Chicago to exert itself to punish the guilty.[31]

There was little to choose between the editorial comments of the daily press and that of so typical a business publication as *Bradstreet's*.

"This week's happenings at Chicago go to show that the threats of the anarchists against the existing order of society are not merely idle vaporings. There are . . . individuals in the United States prepared to act upon the teachings of the anarchist leaders, and to destroy life and property in pursuance of those teachings. . . . In a time of disturbance like the present desperate men have a power for evil out of proportion to their numbers. It is, at such a time, of the highest importance that disorder of every kind should be suppressed in the incipient stage. As regards the anarchists themselves the time has gone by for regarding their proceedings as a source of amusement. They are desperate fanatics who . . . are opposed to all laws. When . . . their principles . . . find issue in overt acts, they must be repressed, swiftly, sternly and without parley. There is no room for anarchy in the political system of the United States." [32]

The impersonal *Commercial and Financial Chronicle* also commented, and incidentally threw light on the effect of the bomb in business circles.

"The socialist outbreak in Chicago this week and the cowardly murder of several policemen by means of hand grenades or bombs thrown in their midst, has been the engrossing subject of the week. Though the labor disputes are used as the cover and cause for this violence, there is no evidence to show and much to disprove that such methods have to any considerable extent the sympathy of the striking employees there or elsewhere. Yet as an influence on trade it has been quite impossible to disassociate the two, business at Chicago and at our own produce exchange being almost paralyzed on Wednesday and greatly interefered with since then, as a result of the fears which the outbreak excited—fears less [sic] in the disturbed state of labor everywhere violence might become epidemic . . . but the general horror and indignation which the Chicago affair excited and the stern measures which followed it have served in good measure to re-assure or at least quiet the public mind." [33]

Harper's Weekly exploited the bomb-throwing editorially and pictorially, running a two page imaginative drawing of the explosion which was matched in its inaccuraccy by its news reports.[34] Editorially, *Harper's Weekly* described the occurrence as "an outburst of anarchy; the deliberate crime of men who openly advocate massacre and the overthrow of intelligent and orderly society." It urged "the most complete and summary methods of repression. . . ." [35]

Of the entire New York English press, only lively, little *John Swinton's Paper* retained some measure of sanity. Making clear its unalterable opposition to the use of force, this labor journal dared place much of the blame for the Haymarket bomb upon the police. "If the armed squad had not been placed upon the outskirts of the assemblage as a menace," it declared, "if they had refrained from any attempt to break up the meeting as long as it was free from tumult, there is no reason to doubt that the diatribes of the speakers would have ended in silence and peace about the usual hour of ten o'clock." It added that "the police had carried provocation and intimidation to an extent never before known outside of New York." [36] Later, the point was hammered home that however unspeakable an act the bomb-throwing was, it in no way offered proof that the demands of the workers were unwarranted, that the eight-hour day was undesirable, that capital should be permitted to continue to fleece labor, that all workers were criminals, or "that the gulf now being fixed between the rich and the poor is a cheerful" one. The bomb, said *John Swinton's Paper,* was "a godsend to the enemies of the labor movement. They have used it as an explosive against all the objects that the working people are bent upon accomplishing, and in defense of all the evils that capital is bent upon maintaining." [37]

A critical note also appeared in the columns of the *Labor Enquirer* and the *Topeka Citizen.* "Twice as many honest men may be murdered in a coal mine," observed the first, "as have been killed in Chicago, and there isn't any noise at all about it. The American press is a wonderfully lopsided affair." The *Topeka Citizen* searching below the surface, declared:

"Now they are using dynamite, these discontented workingmen. For they are workingmen, whether they are foreigners or not. We do not say they are in the right, but are they wholly to blame? Is there not some reason for these outbreaks? To cure an evil it is necessary to eradicate the cause. The killing of a few rioters . . . does little or nothing toward stopping the spread of Anarchistic ideas. The proper way would seem to be to lay all prejudice aside and inquire into the cause of this growth of Anarchism . . . It is not right to condemn ideas without first inquiring into the causes which produce them." [38]

Two labor periodicals also suspended judgment temporarily. With the passage of little more than a month, these journals, the *Labor Leaf* and the *Workmen's Advocate,* were more than sympathetic to the men held responsible for the Haymarket bomb.[39] But such attitudes were highly exceptional. Throughout the country the press sounded again and again the already familiar major theme and variations.

No Quaker gentleness marked the opinions of the Philadelphia *Press:* "The stain of this bloody crime in Chicago does not rest upon any American name or inspiration. . . ." "It springs rather from a pestilent brood of socialist vipers . . . the enemies of general society." Even if it entails the use of the bayonet this element must be exterminated.[40]

"Give the bullet to the disorderly agitators," the *Press* urged, "so long as their hands are uplifted against the law, the iron bars to the convicted fomentors of disturbance, and the halter to the depraved conspirators who plot and perpetrate assassination."[41] Such sentiments were robustly applauded throughout the country. In the West the analogy between the anarchist and robber bands was quickly drawn, and the methods employed to wipe the latter out of existence were suggested for the suppression of the former. The note of force occurs time and again.

"What to do with the anarchists is the question. The most reasonable answer is to meet force with force. Since they wish to try bombs, give them all the war they need. But discrimination should be made as to leaders. Firing into a promiscuous crowd is a bad thing, it is always the innocent bystander who gets killed. The attempt should be made to kill or capture the leaders. This done, the gang will be broken, and innocent people can sleep safely in their beds."[42] An old frontier expression was paraphrased by the St. Louis *Globe-Democrat* to read: "There are no good anarchists except dead anarchists," and the Columbus, Ohio *Journal* announced that "There are too many unhung anarchists and rebels."[43] The Cleveland *Leader* frightened its readers with a nightmarish picture of the anarchist peril: "The anarchist wolf—unwisely permitted to take up its abode and propagate its bloodthirsty species in this country—has fastened its hideous, poisonous fangs in the body corporate of the American people."[44]

These views were echoed in the press of the national capital. To the Washington *Post* the anarchists were a "horde of foreigners, representing almost the lowest stratum found

in humanity's formation." The Washington *Sunday Herald,*
asserting that America had no room for such "incendiary
scum," urged that they "should be disposed of as quickly as
possible," and that those who were "amusing themselves by
killing Chicago policemen should be promptly hanged." [45] The
Washington *Star* saw in the bomb-throwing "a turning point
in the progress of the labor troubles in that city." No longer
would "imprudent acts" of workingmen be overlooked or
"charged to the account of excitement and quick temper." The
dynamite bomb had put another face on the situation. The
distinction between the "honest" worker and the man who desires disturbances would no longer be made. Repressive legislation, perhaps even the use of the bayonet, was now to be
expected.[46]

Throughout the country the conviction prevailed that the
radical groups had been given excessive leeway. For the well-
being of society they now had to be suppressed. Anarchists
and socialists could no longer be regarded as harmless eccen-
trics. They had already given warning of their dangerous
nature, and it was a warning which the municipal and State
governments would do well not to ignore.[47] The occurences
in Chicago and Milwaukee, declared the *Albany Law Journal*
on May 15,

"have revived very strongly in us several desires long vaguely
entertained, such as for a check upon immigration, a power
of deportation, a better equipment of the police, a prompter
and severer dealing with disorder in its first overt acts.
It is a serious thought that the lives of good and brave men,
the safety of innocent women and children, and immunity
of property should be, even for one hour, in a great city, at
the mercy of a few long-haired, wild-eyed, bad-smelling, athe-
istic, reckless foreign wretches, who never did an honest hour's
work in their lives, but who, driven half crazy with years of
oppression and mad with envy of the rich, think to level society and its distinctions with a few bombs. There ought to
be some law . . . to enable society to crush such snakes when

they raise their heads before they have time to bite. This riot in Chicago has been predicted for a year. These wretches have been boasting of their diabolical weapons and preparations for at least that time. . . . Haters of the human race [i.e., the anarchists] . . . a few scores of men presume on the weakness or patience of the authorities, publicly boast of their designs for months, execute them, and then boast on. This state of thing almost justifies the resort to the vigilance committee and lynch law. . . . It seems that the penal law of Illinois would warrant treating all these godless fiends as murderers, and we hope they will be so treated and extirpated from the face of the earth."

The noise of the bomb reached beyond the United States. Canada was shocked, and the tone of its press was hardly distinguishable from that of the States. Europe, no less amazed, found it difficult to believe that such an occurrence had taken place in the "Land of Liberty." Both the deed and all radicals were bitterly denounced. In England some newspapers blundered in charging the Irish revolutionists with the deed, and were twitted by Americans for their error.[48]

European revolutionaries, hesitating between the patent facts and their hopes, did not know whether to accept the bomb as an announcement of the dawn of the "Social Revolution." Le Révolté, in a mordant editorial, expressed the belief that the Chicago catastrophe and the resulting police activities meant open warfare.

"Blood flows in the United States. Tired of leading a life which is not even a mere existence, the worker makes a final effort to struggle against the beast of prey which is devouring him. And this beast of prey, ordering other miserable creatures who have sold him their arms in return for a secure morsel of bread, turns its slaves loose upon the worker. The repeating rifle and the bayonet are at work. Man, woman or child—it matters little which!—they will be assassinated in the street to insure the triumph of the exploiter. . . .

"It is in no way an accident that blood flows; it is a system. It is open war."[49]

NOTES CHAPTER X

1. Lum, *op. cit.*, pp. 33-34; Chicago *Tribune*, August 21, 1886. Another civilian casualty died later. See below, pp. 225, 234, n. 20, for police casualties.
2. Nearly all available newspaper files in New York City and Chicago have been consulted.
3. Chicago *Inter Ocean*, May 5, 1886.
4. *Idem.* See also the accounts in the columns of the following days.
5. May 5 and *ff.*
6. May 5, 1886.
7. Zeisler, *op. cit.*, p. 10.
8. Russell, *loc. cit.*, p. 404; Bogart and Thompson, *op. cit.*, p. 170.
9. Chicago *Tribune* and Chicago *Inter Ocean*, May 5 and 6, 1886.
10. May 6, 1886.
11. Chicago *Tribune*, Chicago *Times*, Chicago *Inter Ocean*, May 6, 1886.
12. *Freiheit*, May 22, 1886. This contains a long and interesting communication from Chicago dated May 9, and headed "The Happenings in Chicago."
13. May 5 and 6, 1886.
14. May 6, 1886.
15. May 7, 1886.
16. Chicago *Inter Ocean*, May 6, 1886.
17. May 6, 1886. The *Tribune* of the same date also suggested that Spies "and company" could be punished as accessories before the fact.
18. See the Chicago *Inter Ocean*, May 7, 1886, for example.
19. See the Chicago papers especially for May 6 and 7.
20. Chicago *Inter Ocean*, May 10, 1886.
21. *John Swinton's Paper*, May 16, 1886.
22. Chicago *Knights of Labor*, May 8, 1886.
23. Chicago *Inter Ocean*, May 6, 1886.
24. *Ibid.*, May 7, 1886.
25. Chicago *Tribune*, May 8, 1886.
26. Chicago *Herald*, Chicago *Times*, May 9, 1886.
27. May 6, 1886.
28. May 7, 1886.
29. May 9, 1886.
30. May 6, 1886.
31. Indicative of the interest the Haymarket episode aroused in New York City is the fact that the New York *Enquirer* devoted an entire page to it on May 8, 1886.
32. May 8, 1886.
33. Vol. 42, no. 1,089, May 8, 1886, p. 558.
34. May 15, 1886, pp. 312-313.
35. *Ibid.*, p. 306; *ibid.*, May 8, 1886, p. 290.

36. May 9, 1886.
37. May 16, 1886.
38. Quoted in the *Commonweal* (London), June 19, 1886, p. 95, no date given for either excerpt.
39. See the files for June, 1886.
40. May 6, 1886.
41. May 8, 1886.
42. Atchison *Champion*, May, 1886, in volume of clippings, Columbia University Library.
43. No date, quoted in *Public Opinion*, vol. 1, no. 5, May 15, 1886, p. 86.
44. May 6, 1886, quoted in *ibid.*, p. 84.
45. Issues of May 6 and 7 respectively, quoted in *ibid.*, p. 83.
46. May 5, 1886, quoted in *Labor: Its Rights and Wrongs*, pp. 77-80.
47. Albany *Evening Journal*, May 5, 1886.
48. *Public Opinion*, vol. 1, no. 5, May 15, 1886, pp. 86-87; *Statist*, London, May 8, 1886, pp. 503-504.
49. May 15-21, 1886; author's translation.

XI. THE POLICE GET TO WORK

URING the weeks which followed the fatal fourth of May, Chicago offered a perfect example of communal irrationality and hysteria. For this state of affairs the bomb itself was only in part responsible. Between the police, who carried on as if they were possessed, and the press, which abandoned every vestige of restraint, the nervous tension of the city was stretched to the breaking point.[1]

Like that of most American municipalities at the time, the police department of Chicago was far from efficient. For what it lacked in intelligence and skill it attempted to compensate by a raging fury of activity. Never was the drag-net worked so earnestly, so extensively, so incessantly. And never did it bring so rich a return. Pursuing obvious tactics, the police gathered in as many of the radical leaders as they could at once. Within two days after the fourth, no less than fifty supposed "hang-outs" of socialists and anarchists had been raided. Steadily the number of arrests mounted. Even the slightest suspicion of radical affiliation might mean a visit to police headquarters if not a stay in jail. On the seventh it was reported that "The principal police stations are filled with anarchists and men who were arrested out of the mobs Tuesday night. At Desplaines Street alone there are over fifty, at the Armory nearly seventy-five, and about twenty-five at Twelfth Street Station." All in all, well over two hundred suspects or witnesses passed through the hands of the police, and in several cases the examinations were rumored to be exceedingly "rigorous." [2] The police were aided in their investigations—and in the manufacturing of incredible tales—by Pinkerton agents. Immediately after the bomb was thrown, Melville E. Stone, editor of the Chicago *Daily News* and a leading figure in the Citizens' Association, communicated with William Pinkerton, and a number of reliable operatives were put on the trail of "leading anarchists." Whether this was done for the Association or was purely a personal act of Mr. Stone's does not appear.[3]

August Spies, Samuel Fielden, and Michael Schwab were arrested on the fifth, and the newspapers rejoiced. "Peace Reigns. The Howling Assassins of Tuesday Night Captured or in Hiding," screamed the headlines.[4] Adolph Fischer, the young compositor on the staff of the *Arbeiter-Zeitung,* was soon also in the hands of the police. Parsons, however, had vanished, and despite a great show of energy could not be found. Within a short time, Gottfried Waller, George Engel, Oscar Neebe, William Seliger and Louis Lingg were also gathered by the police net. Of these men, only George Engel was well known as an active anarchist. Lingg turned out to be a precious find. The police had been completely ignorant of his existence, and he was arrested on May 14 probably as a result of information supplied by one of his associates. When he was captured the police mistakenly announced that they held the bomb-thrower and that Lingg had "squealed." It later appeared that both statements were false.[5] Most of those arrested were taken without warrants, and until the evening of the fifth no specific charges were booked against them.

The task of operating the police drag-net and "the sorting of the fish therein fell to Michael J. Schaack."[6] Captain Schaack was blessed with boundless energy, an immodest belief in his own talents, a flair for the dramatic, and an immoderate appetite for fame. Houses were searched upon the slightest suspicion. Bombs were discovered all over Chicago. The newspapers published details of impossible plots and conspiracies which Schaack, the master-detective, had uncovered. Most of the bombs were either non-existent or had been planted by the police, and the conspiracies were manifestly the product of the heroic captain's imagination. Tales, which at any other time would have been laughed down as preposterous, gained credence.[7]

"I have often wondered," comments one who observed Schaack closely, "whether his delusions resulted from a kind of self-hypnotism or from mere mania; but certainly he saw more anarchists than vast hell could hold. Bombs, dynamite, daggers, and pistols seemed ever before him; in the end, there was no society, however innocent or even laudable, among the foreign born population that was not to his mind an object of grave suspicion."[8] None of the blunders which Captain Schaack made at the time, however, compare with one he committed later—he wrote a book. This fat volume, *Anarchy and Anarchists,* which purported to be a history of Anarchism and the Haymarket Affair, reveals that the Captain was primarily concerned with proclaiming and impressing others with his own genius. Stories of strange encounters with masked men, of mysterious meetings with fascinating ladies veiled in black, of anonymous notes and warnings which came in the nick of time, of astute "sleuthing"—in short, all the standard appurtenances of the detective thriller—crowd upon each others' heels in *Anarchy and Anarchists.*[9]

By far the strongest indictment of Schaack's activities came from a fellow police officer. In his literary effort the Captain was free with praise and blame for other members of the department, and immediately after the volume appeared charges and counter-charges filled the air. Among those who received critical attention in the book was Chief of Police Ebersold, who had been Schaack's superior in 1886. In addition to denying Schaack's accusations of stupidity and incompetence, Ebersold also declared that

"It was my policy to quiet matters down as soon as possible after the 4th of May. The general unsettled state of things was an injury to Chicago.

"On the other hand, Captain Schaack wanted to keep things stirring. He wanted bombs to be found here, there, all around, everywhere. I thought people would lie down to sleep better if they were not afraid their homes would be blown to pieces any minute. But this man, Schaack, . . . wanted none of that policy. Now, here is something the public does not know. After we got the anarchist societies broken up, Schaack wanted to send out men to organize new societies right away. You see what this would do. He wanted to keep the thing boiling, keep himself prominent before the public. Well, I sat down on that . . . and, of course, Schaack didn't like it.

"After I heard all that, I began to think there was perhaps not so much to all this anarchist business as they claimed, and I believe I was right."

To Schaack's charge that Ebersold had been responsible for releasing Rudolph Schnaubelt, later charged with having thrown the bomb,[10] Ebersold replied that the police "had nothing" on Schnaubelt when he was arrested and were forced to release him.[11]

There is reason to believe that the police were more interested in securing incriminating evidence against the "anarchists" in their possession than in discovering the bomb-thrower as such. To do this they pursued practises that have since become commonplace. For example, on May 7 and 8 two men, Jacob Mikolando and Vaclav Djmek, were arrested and thrown into jail. The police had no shred of evidence connecting them with the bombing. Mikolando, however, had been active in the I.W.P.A. The police promised both of them money and jobs (they were out of work) if they would become witnesses for the State. They were threatened with dire misfortune if they refused to repeat in court what the police told them. Despite this form of terrorization, the two did refuse, and after several days' incarceration were finally released.[12]

Lively accounts of the effects of police activities upon radical circles are given in two contemporary letters. In a letter to William Morris, the English socialist, a Chicago socialist tersely reported his impressions of the moment:

"All the world has by this time heard of last Tuesday night's affair. Who knows? Perhaps it is the opening of the Social Revolution! Be this as it may, it certainly has produced astonishing effects. One week ago freedom of speech and of the press was a right unquestioned by the bitterest anti-Socialist. . . . Today all this is changed. . . . Socialists are hunted like wolves. . . . The Chicago papers are loud and unceasing in their demand for the lives of all prominent Socialists. To proclaim one's-self a Socialist in Chicago now is to invite immediate arrest. . . . All the *attachés* of all the Socialist papers have been seized and the papers broken up. Twenty-three printers, writers, and *attachés* of the *Arbeiter-Zeitung* . . . have been imprisoned and booked on a charge of murder, my wife among the number. . . . Everybody connected with the *Alarm* and *Arbeiter* are to be prosecuted—and persecuted—so I have little hope of escaping the general deluge. Matters are in such a state now, however, that no one can tell what the outcome will be." [13]

The writer was mistaken in assuming that the arrested members of the *Arbeiter-Zeitung* staff were all charged with murder. The paper itself, suppressed on the fifth, was set up by newly secured compositors on Thursday, and was ready to go to press. No firm in the city, however, was willing to print it. It finally appeared on the eighth in smaller format with the understanding that it would be suppressed by the mayor if it carried any inflammatory articles. The last number of the *Alarm* had appeared on April 24, and the paper was not published again until November 5, 1887.[14]

The second letter, evidently written by a Chicagoan interested in the labor movement, reported that

"the newspapers have taken advantage of the trouble to lump the socialists, anarchists, and strikers all together, making no distinction between them, and the consequence is that the labor cause will have to suffer. There will be a lull, and then a terrible reaction. Mrs. Swank,[15] Mrs. Parsons, Mrs. Schwab and Mrs. Ames were also arrested. . . . The authorities are making a point against them that they do not believe in God. The police are principally Irish Catholics, and were glad to have a pretext to make the attack.[16]

"Public sentiment is against the anarchists overwhelmingly. Once in a while a cool-headed individual understands the situation, and sees the advantage being taken to crush out everything liberal or progressive in regard to labor or religion. . . . The public is too stupid to discriminate. Poor Fielden, to read the description of him, one would think he was a fiend incarnate. They have had their pictures taken and placed in the rogues' gallery, but the pictures in the newspapers are villainous caricatures." [17]

Lest it be thought that contemporaries exaggerated the mood in which Chicago found herself it should be observed that the color red—symbolic of revolution—was cut out of street advertisements and replaced with a less suggestive color. No less interesting was the response to a call for money to raise a fund for distribution among the police and the dependents of those officers who were victims of the bombing. By May 7, $44,358 had been subscribed, and on May 10 alone, the contributions came to $8,125. Eight days later the fund had mounted to $67,445.[18] The city at large was conscious of a genuine debt to the police force.[19]

Those officers who had been fatally wounded died as the days passed, and this tragic consequence of the Haymarket meeting was thus kept prominently before the public eye. All in all, the bomb accounted for the lives of six officers in addition to Policeman Degan who had been killed almost instantly.[20]

In the meantime, the law was moving swiftly. On May 5 the coroner's jury held an inquest over Policeman Degan, and returned a verdict charging all the prisoners then in the hands of the police with responsibility for his murder.[21] The fact that the bomb-thrower had not been identified proved troublesome for a moment, but Melville E. Stone suggested the way out of the difficulty. Called in consultation on the morning of the fifth, he proposed to the coroner, the City Attorney, Fred S. Winston, and the State's Attorney, Julius S. Grinnell, that the question of identification be ignored. He sketched in the following words the basis for the verdict finally rendered: ". . . that Mathias J. Degan had come to his death from a bomb thrown by a person or persons unknown, but acting in conspiracy with August Spies, Albert Parsons, Samuel J. Fielden, and others unknown." [22]

Not quite so rapidly was the legal defense of those accused of the bombing prepared. It was disturbingly apparent from the outset that it would involve a thankless and difficult task. The Central Labor Union of Chicago, however, retained its attorney, Mr. Salomon and his associate Mr. Sigismund Zeisler, to defend the radical leaders who were arrested. Both were young men recently admitted to the bar.[23] Since their clients had been arrested without warrants and held incommunicado, the lawyers immediately prepared a petition for a writ of *habeas corpus*.[24]

On May 17, with Judge John G. Rogers presiding, the grand jury was impanelled, and two days later it began its investigation. At the time, the accused protested that Judge Rogers' charge to the jury was biased. In view of the fact that it was founded upon newspaper records, however, it appears to have been eminently fair. The accused likewise felt that the grand jury, obtained by a special venire and composed of outstanding business men, "was plainly hand-picked." [25] But any jury chosen at that time would have struck an impartial observer as "hand-picked." There probably were not twenty-four "reputable" men in Chicago who were not convinced that the bombing had been planned and executed by those radicals either in the hands of or wanted by the police. The taking of evidence completed, the grand jury presented a batch of indictments to Judge Rogers on May 27.

Thirty-one persons in all were indicted. Of this number,

August Spies, Michael Schwab, Samuel Fielden, Adolph Fischer, George Engel, Louis Lingg, Albert R. Parsons, Rudolph Schnaubelt, William Seliger, and Oscar Neebe were the most important. They were charged with the following: with being accessories before the fact to the murder of Policeman Mathias J. Degan by means of a bomb; with murder by pistol shots; with being accessories to one another in the murder of Degan; and with a general conspiracy to murder. The other men were variously indicted for conspiracy, murder and riot. All in all, the indictments contained sixty-nine counts.[26]

The sections of the Illinois statute upon which the indictments rested are important. They read:

"An accessory is one who stands by, and aids, abets, or assists, or who, not being present aiding, abetting, or assisting, hath advised, encouraged, aided or abetted the perpetration of the crime. He who thus aids, abets, advises or encourages, shall be considered as principal and punished accordingly.

"Every such accessory . . . may be indicted and convicted at the same time as the principal or before or after his conviction, and whether principal is convicted or amenable to justice or not, and punished as principal." [27]

Of those indicted, only eight actually stood trial for murder. Several purchased immunity by becoming witnesses for the State. Rudolph Schnaubelt was never found, and most of the rest were released on bail to await the outcome of the trial of the more important individuals.[28] Two remained in jail until the trial of the eight was completed.[29]

The fate of the accused, while determined in the last analysis by the magnitude of the crime and unrelenting public sentiment, rested legally upon the judicial interpretation given to the conspiracy statute. The grand jury indictments, therefore, fore-shadowed the course of the trial, and struck the first blow in the attempt of the State to secure "atonement" for the Haymarket bomb.

On June 5 the grand jury rendered its final report which,

as it was expected, stated that the body of evidence heard and the investigations pursued made it clear that an anarchist conspiracy had existed, and that the Haymarket bombing was a deliberate act directly related to that conspiracy. The grand jury declared that

"We have endeavored . . . to be guided strictly by the instruction delivered to us by the court, in regard to the liability of a citizen under the law for the abuse of the privilege of free speech. We have in this connection . . . found true bills only against such persons as had in their abuse of this right been more or less instrumental in causing the riot and bloodshed at the Haymarket square. . . .

"It is a satisfaction for us to be able to state, as the result of a careful examination of a large number of witnesses, that in our opinion the danger has been imminent and serious, but it has been in the popular mind largely magnified and the number of these enemies of law and order overestimated. The evidence . . . produced was conclusive as to the fact that the anarchist conspiracy had no real connection with the strike or labor trouble, but that it simply made use of the excitement incident to those troubles. . . . By those in the best position to know we have been assured that the total number of anarchists in this country from whom danger need be apprehended is less than one hundred, and probably does not exceed from forty to fifty men.

"Associating with them and partly subject to their malign influence, there are perhaps a few hundred who would be dangerous in exact proportion to the extent that they are made to believe in the power of their leaders and in the weakness of the law.

"Then again, there are perhaps from two to three thousand men variously classed as socialists, communists, etc., . . . but who are not necessarily dangerous . . . to the peace and welfare of society so long as the law is enforced in such a manner as to entitle it to their wholesome respect.

"We find that the attack on the police of May 4 was the result of a deliberate conspiracy, the full details of which are now in the possession of the officers of the law. . . .

"We find that this force of disorganizers had a very perfect force of organizers of its own, and that it was chiefly under the control of the coterie of men who were connected with the publication of . . . the *Alarm* and *Arbeiter-Zeitung.* . . ."[30]

While the grand jury hearings were going on, a legal defense committee was organized to aid the accused radicals. At its head was Dr. Ernest Schmidt, a man who could lend dignity to any cause he supported. Dr. Schmidt, an outstanding physician in Chicago, was a socialist who had been candidate for the office of mayor and a staunch opponent of the use of violence. For a man of his position, his activities on the legal defense committee jeopardized an excellent reputation. Associated with him was George Schilling, in every sense a splendid person. Active in labor circles, Schilling was a socialist strongly opposed to violence who was soon attracted by single-tax doctrines. Money was needed to cover the many expenses which would arise in connection with the coming trial. Legal fees, printing, court reporting and investigating expenses all had to be met. The necessary funds were secured by the legal defense committee largely through appeals to workers. Before many months had passed the committee had several more active members, and, under the circumstances, was very successful in raising money.[31]

No less difficult than the task of raising money for lawyer's fees was the problem of securing an able counsellor. Since Salomon and Zeisler were lacking in years and experience, it was imperative that at least one lawyer of reputation and ability be associated with the case. Luther Laflin Mills, former State's Attorney for Cook County and a well known criminal lawyer, was approached, and, with his future career in mind, gave a blank refusal. William S. Forrest, also a recognized criminal lawyer, was then appealed to, but the fee he demanded was one that the defense committee was not prepared to meet.[32]

Only one lawyer was willing to be retained by the defense.

He was Captain William Perkins Black, to whom George Schilling had earnestly appealed for aid. Black, said to be related to Jeremiah S. Black, had already won a reputation as a successful corporation attorney. He had earlier taken an intellectual interest in Socialism, and had tried his hand at politics. A man of liberal tendencies, sturdy sincerity and impregnable honesty, he fervidly believed in an ideal justice. He made an impressive appearance with his majestic stature and his expressive bearded face, crowned by a head of white hair. During the trial he had occasion to prove that he was more than ordinarily gifted as an orator. Though he could see that his participation would probably severely injure his practise, he threw himself whole-heartedly into it. He was not cut of the same cloth from which ordinary men are fashioned. Recognizing his own shortcomings as a criminal lawyer, Black spent three unsuccessful days searching Chicago for someone to aid him.[33] Finally, William A. Foster of Iowa was retained as the fourth defense counsel. Foster "was a likeable, level-headed fellow, who, however, relied more upon his native wit and talent than upon close application and study." [34] His natural intelligence, an ability to distinguish and focus attention upon essentials, and an honesty of speech were worth a great deal during the trial.

It was immediately assumed by the newspapers that all four members of the defense counsel were affected in varying degrees with the virus of Anarchism. What other reason could prompt them to engage in such a case if this were not true? Black especially was subjected to much annoying comment and unwelcome observation.[35] It was even a bit distressing to some people that the prisoners were to enjoy a formal trial.[36]

Since the prisoners insisted that Judge Rogers, who had presided at the grand jury hearings, was strongly prejudiced against them, Captain Black applied for a change of venue, arguing that his charge to the grand jury showed bias. Black was anxious to get the trial transferred to the court of Judge

Murray F. Tuley, known to be an able and fair jurist. The State's Attorney objected, however, and it was finally decided to try the case before Joseph E. Gary who enjoyed an enviable reputation for impartiality.[37]

On the tenth of June, the lawyers for both prosecution and defense made their first appearance before Judge Gary. On behalf of the State, Mr. Grinnell suggested that the trial should open on June 21. He preferred an earlier date, but did not wish to appear to be hurrying the defense. Counsel for the defense and Captain Schaack strongly opposed the fixing of the trial at so early a date. Black, arguing for a postponement, declared that all possibility of a just verdict would be precluded if the case were tried so close to the event. The defense also charged that prisoners and witnesses alike had been intimidated by the police. Judge Gary remarked that it did not lie in the discretion of the court at this time to set a date for the trial. It was the right and duty of the State's Attorney to do that and the function of the trial judge to acquiesce. On the day fixed for the trial, however, counsel for the defense could file affidavits showing cause why the trial should be postponed, and at that time the court could grant a postponement. The date for the trial was, therefore, that suggested by Mr. Grinnell,—June 21, six and a half weeks after the fatal Haymarket meeting and five days after the death of the seventh policeman.[38]

NOTES CHAPTER XI

1. It is interesting that in Robert Herrick's biographical novel, *The Memoirs of an American Citizen*, New York, 1905, the leading character observes:

"The morning after the fourth of May the city was sizzling with excitement. From what the papers said you might think there was an anarchist or two skulking in every alley in Chicago with a basket of bombs under his arm. The men on the street seemed to rub their eyes and stare up at the buildings in surprise to find them standing. There was every kind of rumor floating about. . . . It was all a parcel of lies, of course, but the people were crazy to be lied to, and the police, having nothing better, fed them lies." (P. 82.)

2. Chicago *Inter Ocean*, May 7, 1886; Chicago *Times*, May 9 and 10, 1886; Chicago *Tribune*, May 6 and 7, 1886; *Liberty*, vol. 4, no. 3, May 22, 1886, p. 4; Russell, *loc. cit.*, p. 404. See also the two letters cited below, notes 13, 17.

3. Melville E. Stone, *Fifty Years a Journalist*, New York, 1921, p. 172; Charles A. Siringo, *Two Evil Isms. Pinkertonism and Anarchism*, Chicago, 1915, pp. 3-4.

4. *Inter Ocean*, May 5, 1886.

5. Chicago *Inter Ocean* and Chicago *Tribune*, May 7-15, 1886. For Lingg's capture, Chicago *Inter Ocean*, May 15. He was taken only after a demoniacal struggle with Herman Schuettler, reputed one of the bravest men on the police force; see also Russell, *loc. cit.*, p. 405.

6. Russell, *loc. cit.*, p. 405.

7. It was currently believed that a conspiracy was in existence involving the destruction of Chicago, the annihilation of the government and the assassination of prominent citizens.

8. Russell, *loc. cit.*, p. 405.

9. The volume is generously illustrated, and it has been rather aptly described as a "big picture-book for grown-up children . . ." (Mackay, *op. cit.*, p. viii.)

10. See below, chaps. XIII-XIV, XXIII, *passim*.

11. Interview in Chicago *Daily News*, May 10, 1889; see also Ebersold's statement in *ibid.*, May 11, 1889, where he said:
   "Another thing is, Schaack and some others were trying to make capital out of the anarchist business. They wanted to keep the people frightened for purposes of their own. I tried to calm the excitement. [?] I was satisfied that seven-eighths of this anarchist business was wind. He wanted to hire men to organize anarchist groups. I put my foot on that."

12. Affidavits which these men made are reproduced in John P. Altgeld, *Reasons for Pardoning Fielden, Neebe, and Schwab*, Springfield, Ill., 1896, pp. 24-25 (cited hereafter as Altgeld, *Pardon Message*).

13. *Commonweal*, London, May 29, 1887, p. 71. The author of this letter was probably William Holmes, the only one of the Chicago radicals who regularly corresponded with William Morris.

14. *Freiheit*, May 22, 1886; *John Swinton's Paper*, June 20, 1886. There were claims that the circulation of the *Arbeiter-Zeitung* increased after the bombing. Both journals were milder in tone when they resumed publication.

15. He means here Mrs. Holmes.

16. This point is made nowhere else. Perhaps this element may explain some of the police brutality. It is at best a remote possibility.

17. This private letter, addressed to Mr. E. A. Stevens, is reprinted in the *Labor Leaf* (Detroit, Mich.) May 12, 1886. The last paragraph of the letter in which George Schilling is accused of washing his

hands of Fielden, has no basis in fact. Schilling did what he could—which was a great deal—for Fielden and the others, although he disagreed with them on the question of violence. Mr. Schilling reaffirmed this point in an interview with the author.

18. Chicago *Inter Ocean*, May 7, 18, 1886; Chicago *Tribune*, May 11, 1886.

19. Chicago *Inter Ocean*, May 7, 1886.

20. They were officers Mueller, Barrett, Flavin, Sheehan, Reddin and Hansen. They died in the order in which their names are listed. Hansen died on June 14, a week before the trial opened.

21. Chicago *Tribune*, May 6, 1886; Zeisler, *op. cit.*, p. 12.

22. Stone, *op. cit.*, p. 173.

23. Zeisler, an Austrian by birth, had arrived in the United States in 1883, and was twenty-six years old. The year of his arrival he had received the degree of Doctor Juris at the University of Vienna, and in 1884 he graduated from the Northwestern University Law School.

24. Zeisler, *op. cit.*, p. 12.

25. *Ibid.*, p. 15.

26. *Idem;* Chicago *Inter Ocean*, May 28 and 29, 1886; Chicago *Times*, May 28, 1886; Chicago *Tribune*, August 21, 1886; *Abstract of Record*, vol. 1, pp. 1-2; John D. Lawson, editor, *American State Trials. A Collection of the Important and Interesting Criminal Trials which have taken place in the United States, from the beginning of our Government to the Present Day*, 13 vols., St. Louis, 1919, vol. 12, pp. 12-14 (cited hereafter as *Amer. St. Tr.*, vol. 12).

27. *Amer. St. Tr.*, vol. 12, p. 17.

28. The bond was small, only $400.

29. There was much talk later of bringing most of those indicted to trial because of the success of the prosecution. One was released August 20, 1886.

30. Chicago, *Inter Ocean*, June 6, 1886.

31. Zeisler, *op. cit.*, pp. 16-17; *Labor Leaf*, September 8, 1886. Charles F. Seib was one of those who labored unceasingly throughout the length of the case.

32. Zeisler, *op. cit.*, p. 17.

33. *Ibid.*, p. 18; Edward Aveling, *An American Journey*, New York, n.d., p. 128; Caro Lloyd, *Henry Demarest Lloyd (1847-1903), A Biography*, 2 vols., New York, 1912, vol. 1, p. 85; *Social Science*, vol. 1, no. 15, October 12, 1887, pp. 2-3.

34. Zeisler, *op. cit.*, p. 18.

35. *Workmen's Advocate*, October 1, 1887.

36. That the men "were not lynched but were to be tried under the forms of orderly legal procedure aroused the wrath of editors and was taken by them as a personal insult." So writes Zeisler, *op. cit.*, p. 16. This seems an exaggeration.

37. *Ibid.*, p. 19; Chicago *Inter Ocean*, June 11, 1886. Were it not for

the Haymarket Affair, Joseph Eaton Gary's only claim to distinction, might perhaps rest upon the fact that he sat as a judge in Chicago for no less than forty-three years. By birth a rural New Yorker—he was born in 1821 and died in 1906—Judge Gary had practised law in Missouri, New Mexico, California and Wisconsin. He finally settled in Chicago where he was elected to the Cook County Superior Court in 1863. In 1888 he was promoted to the Appellate Court, and later became its chief justice. He is supposed to have been highly regarded both as lawyer and judge.

38. Chicago *Inter Ocean*, June 11, 1886; Zeisler, *op. cit.*, p. 19 is in error here.

XII. "TWELVE GOOD MEN AND TRUE"

WHEN the trial formally began on the twenty-first, the intensity of public feeling had not notably diminished. The desire for retaliation for the bombing had become an *idée fixe*. To make an "example" of these men would at once demonstrate the strength of American institutions and constitute a decisive step in the suppression of all revolutionary tendencies. It was in such an atmosphere of unreasoning but understandable emotion that "justice" was to be done.

During the early days of the trial, the rather small, exceedingly plain court room of the Cook County Criminal Court, where Judge Gary sat, was only partially filled because many restrictions had been placed upon admission. The room was distinguished only by the large number of lawyers, officials, reporters and police in attendance, and the presence of "several richly dressed ladies. . . ."[1] Before long, however, the court room was so jammed day after day with avidly interested and curious spectators during the oppressively hot summer, that it became uncomfortably crowded. As counsel for the State there were Julius S. Grinnell, State's Attorney, Francis W. Walker and Edmund Furthman, his regular assistants, and George C. Ingham, special assistant.[2] In the prisoner's dock sat Spies, Schwab, Engel, Fielden, Fischer, Lingg, and Neebe.

Parsons and Schnaubelt were still missing. The former had left Chicago the night of the fourth for the home of William Holmes in Geneva, Wisconsin. After a short stay he went to Waukesha in the same State. His small stature, clean-cut features, flowing mustache, and jet-black hair made him easy to recognize. To prevent this, he affected a simple disguise by wearing ill-fitting clothes, shaving off his mustache, and ceasing to use the dye long employed to color his prematurely gray hair. He was thus transformed into an undistinguished, oldish man. Mrs. Parsons and defense counsel were soon made aware of Parsons' hiding place and his disguise. They were puzzled as to what Parsons was to do. Black believed that if Parsons were to make a dramatic entry into court, his surrender would win public sympathy for the defendants, but Foster, with greater common sense, argued that while such a gesture might have momentary value it would in the end cost Parsons his life. Black, however, winning Mrs. Parsons over to his view, finally carried his point. It was decided that he and Parsons were to appear together in court where the latter was to surrender himself.[3] This was an unfortunate decision. If Parsons had waited until the jury was impanelled before he gave himself up, he would have had a separate trial. It is questionable whether his absence up to that time would have affected the other prisoners adversely.

Parsons, either eager to wear the martyr's cloak or feeling that his absence would prejudice the case of those on trial, was anxious to give himself up. William Holmes later declared:

"When I heard that he [Parsons] had gone to Chicago to stand trial, I hastened . . . to the jail. I said to him: 'Do you know what you have done?' and he said: 'Yes, thoroughly. I never expect while I live to be a free man again. They will kill me, but I could not bear to be at liberty, knowing that my comrades were here and were to suffer for something of which they were as innocent as I. . . .' "[4]

Whatever the determining motive, Parsons—his hair jet-black again—appeared in court with Capt. Black about half past two in the afternoon of the twenty-first. Mr. Furthman recognized him immediately, and leaned over to whisper his discovery to Mr. Grinnell, who in turn addressed Judge Gary: "Your Honor, I see Albert R. Parsons in the courtroom. I move that he be placed in the custody of the sheriff." Capt. Black, the whole point of his little game thus destroyed, angrily ejaculated: "Your motion, Mr. Grinnell, is not only most ungracious and cruel, it is also gratuitous. You see that Mr. Parsons is here to surrender himself." Here Judge Gary broke in with "Mr. Parsons will take his seat with the other prisoners." [5]

Far more important than this episode, sensationally reported by the press, were the unsuccessful attempts of the defense to withdraw the plea of not guilty entered for each of the defendants and quash the indictment, and to secure a separate trial for Spies, Schwab, Fielden and Neebe. [6] While no one seriously expected that Judge Gary would rule favorably on the motion to quash the indictment, there was some hope that separate trials for some of the defendants might be granted. Defense counsel argued that if the eight accused were tried together, testimony applicable only to some of the defendants would bear against all—that the evidence against each as an individual would in fact avail against the entire eight. Judge Gary, within whose power it lay to have the prisoners tried separately, refused the request of the defense. [7]

When the task of picking a jury began, it became apparent that the trial was going to be long and wearing. Twenty-one out of the forty-nine days which it lasted were consumed in choosing the twelve jurors, no less than 981 talesmen being examined. [8] So rapidly was the regular panel exhausted, that on June 29, a special bailiff was appointed by the court, both State and defense agreeing, to summon the necessary venire-men. Though not commonly resorted to, this procedure was entirely legal. [9] Where the special bailiff labored under a marked prejudice, this practise might have unfortunate consequences, and in this instance the special bailiff, Henry L. Ryce, was not the man to execute his task properly. On more than one occasion he is said to have remarked: "I am managing this case, and know what I am about. Those fellows are going to be hanged as certain as death. I am calling such men as the defendants will have to challenge peremptorily and waste their time and challenges. Then they will have to take such men as the prosecution wants." [10]

The defense fully recognized how difficult it would be to secure an unbiased jury, and in the eyes of Black and his associates it appeared that Judge Gary's rulings were making the task altogether impossible. The court at that time and since has been criticized for adding burdens to the labors of the defense and lightening those of the prosecution. To determine the validity of this charge its rulings on the qualifications of jurors must be considered.

John Johnson, talesman, stated under examination that he had heard and read about the Haymarket "Riot" and had also discussed it. Believing in substance what he read, he had already formed and expressed an opinion which he still entertained. That opinion, however, might possibly be removed by contrary evidence, and he felt that he could try the case fairly. When Mr. Johnson was asked by defense counsel whether his opinion was of such a nature as to demand strong evidence to modify or remove it, Judge Gary interrupted and refused to allow him to answer the question. The court, in overruling the challenge for cause, held him qualified to serve as a juror, and the defense had to challenge peremptorily.[11] A peremptory challenge, it may be noted, is one that may be exercised without assigning any cause, in order to get rid of an objectionable talesman qualified by the court.

Clarence H. Hill also declared that he had formed and expressed an opinion on the basis of what he had read and heard. In addition, he entertained a definite prejudice against all anarchists. When asked, "You have no opinions, biases, or prejudices which it would require testimony to overcome?" he frankly answered, "Yes, sir; I have." Here again the court overruled the challenge for cause.[12] In the course of the examination of W. N. Upham, who made admissions similar to those of Johnson and Hill, the court asked: "The question is whether you have ever formed or expressed an opinion as to the guilt or innocence of any one of these eight men of the murder of Officer Degan?" "I can't say what I have expressed in words," answered Mr. Upham, "but my opinion was that some of them are guilty." Since Mr. Upham also stated that he "believed" he could render a fair verdict on the evidence, Judge Gary overruled the challenge for cause with the comment, "That is not any ground of challenge under the law." [13] William Neil admitted that he had a very strong opinion, that he doubted whether he could lay aside the impression of the moment during the trial, and that "it would take pretty strong evidence" to affect his opinion. Yet the court did not disqualify him for jury service. Once Mr. Neil stated that he would give a verdict on the evidence heard, the challenge for cause was overruled. [14]

After two days marked by such ruling, Parsons passed the following note to Mr. Zeisler: "In taking a change of venue from Judge Rogers to Lord Jeffries, did not the defendants jump from the frying pan into the fire? Parsons." [15]

It could be argued that in the strictest legal sense, each of these rulings by Judge Gary was justifiable, since Chapter 78, section 14 of the Illinois Statutes relating to "Jurors," after being amended in March, 1874, reads:

". . . *Provided further,* that it shall not be a cause of challenge that a juror has read in the newspapers an account of the commission of the crime with which the prisoner is charged, if such juror shall state on oath that he believes he can render an impartial verdict, according to the law and the evidence: and *provided further,* that in the trial of any criminal cause, the fact that a person called as a juror has formed an opinion or impression, based upon rumor or upon newspaper statements (about the truth of which he has expressed no opinion) shall not disqualify him to serve as a juror in such case, if he shall upon oath state that he believes he can fairly and impartially render a verdict therein in accordance with the law and the evidence, and the court shall be satisfied of the truth of such statement." [16]

This plainly places vast discretionary powers in the hands of the trial judge. If the court is willing to press the implication of the statute to the point where a statement of belief in the ability to "render an impartial verdict, according to the law and the evidence" becomes almost the sole measure of competence, it is clear that grave injustice may be done. This possibility appears to be the source for the admonition laid down in *Plummer* v. *People,* a case in which the principle enunciated in the amended statute is followed. An opinion or an impression formed by a juror on the basis of rumors or newspaper statements, about which he has expressed no opinion, said the court, does not disqualify him "if it shall appear from his statement, under oath, that he believes he can render an impartial verdict in accordance with the law and evidence." But, warned the court, "Where the juror has been exposed to influences, the probable effect of which is to create a prejudice in his mind against the defendant, which it would require evidence to overcome, to render him competent, it should clearly appear that he can, when in the jury box, entirely disregard those influences, and try the case without, in any degree, being affected by them." [17] Had Judge Gary heeded this warning, he would have escaped the reproach and criticism later directed against him.

In no sense were Judge Gary's rulings defensible. While the law placed the power of determining the qualifications of a juror in the hands of the trial judge, it can hardly be argued that it was designed to enable him to qualify jurors who were patently not competent. In a later case, *Coughlin* v. *People,* the Supreme Court of Illinois, after reviewing precedents on the qualifications of jurors, declared that

"It is plain that the rule in this State, except so far as it is modified by the statute, is perfectly well settled, that if a juror has made up a decided opinion upon the merits of the case, either from personal knowledge of the facts, or from the statements of witnesses, or from the relations of the parties, or from either of them, or from rumor, and that opinion is positive and not hypothetical, and is such as will prevent him from giving an impartial verdict, he is disqualified. No case can be found where a juror, after admitting the existence in his mind of an opinion of that character, has been permitted to establish his own competency by testifying that, notwithstanding his opinion, he can or will render a fair and impartial verdict. Such opinion has uniformly been held to be a disqualification per se, and is incapable of being removed by testimony of the juror or other evidence tending to show that it will not affect his verdict. A decided and positive opinion as to the merits of the case, raises such manifest presumption of partiality as at common law would constitute a principal cause of challenge. The incompetency of the juror follows as a necessary legal consequence which is incapable of being rebutted. And so . . . where such fixed and positive opinion is shown, and the juror testified that, he could nevertheless render a fair and impartial verdict, such testimony of the juror has been wholly disregarded, and he has been held to be incompetent, in spite of his own assertion of his impartiality." [18]

Obviously it rested with the court to determine which opinion is fixed and which is only hypothetical. Therefore, if the court took decided opinions, which put in question the impartiality of talesmen, as Judge Gary did, and assumed that these opinions were hypothetical, it followed that an assertion of belief in the ability to render a fair and impartial verdict in accordance with the law and the evidence was sufficient to establish competency. In Judge Gary's case, it suggests that the court was either unable to distinguish between positive and hypothetical opinions, or that he was so prejudiced that he refused to see the difference between the two. In any case, the defendants suffered.

Judge Gary was extremely anxious to secure from the talesmen an admission of belief in their ability to give a fair and impartial verdict in accord with the law and the evidence, regardless of their prior opinions. That anxiety and its consequences offer the key to the determination of his impartiality or his partiality. Judge Gary apparently argued backward from the statement of the venireman's belief in his ability to render an impartial verdict to the conclusion that he had no fixed and positive opinions, and was, therefore, qualified to serve as a juror. To secure such an assertion, he lectured, coaxed, cajoled, argued, and even pleaded. In *Coughlin* v. *People* the court expressly condemned this type of "argumentative cross-examination by the court."

The examination of Leonard Gould offers an excellent, but not exceptional, instance in point. Mr. Gould had already declared that he had formed and expressed an opinion as to the guilt or innocence of the defendants, that this opinion was based on what he read, that he believed what he had read to be true, and that he was prejudiced against socialists. Then Judge Gary took him in hand, and the following exchange of question and answer—not unlike some of the conversations in "Alice in Wonderland"—ensued:

"Question [by Judge Gary]. I want to ask you whether you believe you can listen to the testimony and other proofs that may be here introduced in court, and the charge of the judge, and render an absolutely impartial verdict in this case, notwithstanding your present opinion, bias, or any prejudices that you may have?

"Answer [by Mr. Gould]. Well that is the same question over again.

"Q. Do you say that you can't answer it?

"A. Well, I answered it as far as I could answer it. . . .

"Q. You say you don't know that you can answer that either yes or no?

"A. No, I don't know that I can."

At this point Mr. Gould was challenged for cause by the defense. But Judge Gary once more asked Mr. Gould if he could render a fair and impartial verdict in accordance with the law and the evidence.

"A. Well, in a general way, I think I could listen to the law and the evidence and form my verdict from that. . . .

"Q. Now, do you believe that you can, that you sufficiently reflected upon it so as to examine your own state of mind, when you say yes or no?

"A. It is a difficult question for me to answer.

"Q. Well, make up your mind as to whether you believe you can fairly and impartially render a verdict in accordance with the law and the evidence. Most men in business possibly have not gone through metaphysical investigations of this sort, so as to be prepared to answer off hand without some reflection?

"A. Judge, I don't believe I can answer the question.

"Q. Can't you answer whether you believe you know?

"A. I should try. If I had to do it I should do the best I could.

"Q. The question is whether you believe you can or not. I suppose, Mr. Gould, you know the law is that no man is to be convicted of any offense with which he is charged unless the evidence proves that he is guilty beyond a reasonable doubt?

"A. That is true.

"Q. The evidence heard in this case in court?

"A. Yes.

"Q. Do you believe that you can render a verdict in accordance with that law?

"A. Well, I don't know that I could.

"Q. Do you believe that you can; if you don't know of any reason why you cannot, do you believe you can?

"A. I could not answer that question. . . .

"Q. Have you a belief one way or another whether you can or cannot?

"A. If I were to sit on the case I should get just as near to it as possible, but when it comes to laying aside all bias and all prejudice, and making it up in that way, it is a pretty fine point to them.

"Q. Not whether you are going to do it, but what you do believe you can—that is the only thing. You are not required to state what is going to happen next week, or the week after, but what do you believe about yourself, whether you can or cannot?

"A. I am just about where I was when I started."

Perseverance had its reward, and in the end Judge Gary won his point. Once again he asked: "This question, naked and simple of itself, is, do you believe that you can fairly and impartially render a verdict in the case with the law and the evidence?" Mr. Gould, probably close to exhaustion, at last responded with the proper formula: "I believe I could." The challenge for cause was, of course, promptly overruled, and the defense challenged Mr. Gould peremptorily.[19]

Judge Gary was responsible for other amazing rulings. He overruled a challenge for cause where a venireman admitted not only prejudice against all anarchists, but also kinship to one of the policemen fatally wounded by the bomb. He qualified a talesman who was acquainted with the leading police officers of the city, a close friend of one of the policemen killed by the bomb, and whose opinion on the case was based upon information given him by police officers. He overruled challenge for cause where a venireman frankly stated, "I hardly think you could bring proof enough to change my opinion." Another venireman who declared that "I have a very decided opinion in this case; it will take a good deal of evidence to overcome the opinion I have formed to convince me," was also found qualified to serve.[20] When one venireman informed the court that his opinion at the moment was of such a nature that it would affect his conclusions even after listening to the evidence, Judge Gary remarked: "It is incomprehensible to me." [21] Another venireman admitted that he had formed and expressed an opinion as to the guilt of the defendants, and that that opinion would handicap him in his judgment. Coaxed by the court, he stated that he thought he could render a fair and impartial verdict, but that he still felt that he would be handicapped. "Well," Judge Gary was inspired to remark, "that is a sufficient qualification for a juror in the case. Of course, the more a man feels he is handicapped, the more he will be guarded against it." [22]

By law, every defendant in a murder trial in Illinois was entitled to twenty peremptory challenges. With the court constantly overruling challenges for cause, the peremptory challenges of the defense—160 in all—were being rapidly consumed. It was wise for the defense to accept talesmen qualified by the court who were not hopelessly prejudiced so that the peremptory challenges might be employed when the occasion was vital. By the time eleven jurors had been selected, forty-three peremptory challenges remained to the defense. At this point counsel for the defense were faced with an important consideration. In a recent case, *Wilson* v. *People*,[23] the State Supreme Court held that erroneous rulings of the trial judge did not constitute ground for a reversal unless all the peremptory challenges had been first consumed.[24]

The first talesman to appear for examination after the defense had exhausted its peremptory challenges was Mr. H. T. Sanford. He admitted that he had already formed and expressed an opinion as to the guilt of the accused, and declared that he was prejudiced against the defendants. Under the persuasive questioning of the court, however, Mr. Sanford stated that he "believed" he could render a fair and impartial verdict. He was, of course, challenged for cause, but Judge Gary promptly overruled the challenge, and Mr. Sanford became the twelfth juror.[25]

The completion of the jury brought cheers from the press. It had taken from June 21 to July 15 to pick "twelve good men and true." The delay had been annoying. Now that the irksome job was over, the trial proper could proceed with dispatch. It was frankly recognized that a more rapid movement of justice had thus far been impeded by the universal bias against the accused.

"The great anarchist trial," said the Chicago *Inter Ocean*, "is at last fairly under way. Nearly a month of time was consumed in securing a jury, during which the county was raked over pretty thoroughly for 'twelve good men and true' who could give the accused a fair trial. During those twenty-two days of search and research for unbiased jurors no less than 982 men were examined. The proportion of eligibility, according to this pointer, is about 1 to 82, and that probably represents public sentiment. Nearly everybody has formed an opinion which it would be very difficult to change. This much can certainly be said on that point without any violation of the proprieties which hedge about a case on trial." [26]

What was this jury like? It clearly did not possess an open mind either on the crime or on the men it was about to try. It would have been miraculous had the jury been absolutely free from all preconception and bias. Its twelve members were H. Cole, S. G. Randall, T. E. Denker, C. B. Todd, F. S. Osborne, A. Hamilton, J. H. Brayton, C. A. Ludwig, A. H. Reed, J. B. Greiner, G. W. Adams and H. T. Sanford. Only one of the twelve was born on foreign soil.

Mr. Sanford, the twelfth juror, was twenty-four years old and was in the employ of the Chicago and Northwestern Railroad. Mr. Adams, twenty-seven years old, was a commercial agent. Under examination he had admitted to having formed an opinion, but since he declared he did not hold it very strongly he was accepted. Later, when the motion for a new trial was argued, an affidavit was submitted to show that his opinion was, on the contrary, exceptionally firmly rooted and definite. He is supposed to have stated that "if I was on the jury I would hang all the damned buggars." Mr. Adams, however, filed an affidavit of complete denial at the time. Mr. Greiner, about the same age and in the employ of the Chicago and Northwestern, had likewise come to a decision as to the guilt or innocence of the defendants on the basis of what he had read. Mr. Greiner, it should be noted, naïvely believed that an accusation was in itself presumptive evidence of guilt!

Alanson H. Reed, approaching fifty, was a man of means, and was regarded as one of Chicago's leading citizens. The fact that he was a free-thinker might imply a degree of liberal-mindedness. He admitted to a prejudice against socialists, anarchists and communists, and asserted that he had already formed an opinion on the nature of the crime and on the guilt or innocence of the prisoners largely on the basis of newspaper sources. The foreman of the jury was Mr. Osborne, a head salesman in one of the departments of the Marshall Field Store Company. Nothing in the course of his examination indicated that he was not competent to serve as a juror. Apart from his admitted prejudice against socialists, anarchists and communists, Mr. Ludwig, a bookkeeper by profession, likewise appeared to be qualified for duty on the jury. Nothing worth noting was disclosed by the examination of Mr. Randall, a salesman by occupation.

There was sufficient reason to doubt the competence of Mr. Denker. This young shipping-clerk informed the court that he had already come to an opinion on the case, that he thought his opinion would make it difficult for him to make a fair decision, and that he believed what he had read and heard. He was challenged for cause, but since he firmly insisted that he believed that he could render an impartial verdict on the evidence, the challenge was overruled and he was accepted by the defense. At a later date two affidavits were submitted to prove his extreme bias. On the day following the bombing he is supposed to have declared that "He [Spies] and the whole damn crowd ought to be hung." [27] Mr. Denker in answer denied ever having made such a statement.

Of the remaining jurors, two, J. H. Cole, a railroad contractor and constructor past fifty, and J. H. Brayton, bore a prejudice against Socialism, Anarchism and Communism. The court did not permit Mr. Cole to state to what degree that bias would influence him in making his verdict. Mr. Brayton, in addition, had formed an opinion on the nature of the crime and the guilt or innocence of the defendants. C. B. Todd had also reached conclusions on these questions upon the basis of oral and written material. Mr. Andrew Hamilton, a hardware merchant, frankly admitted under examination that he had declared that someone should be made to serve as an "example" for the bombing, and, if the accused were connected with the affair, that they should be.

Of the twelve jurymen six were in their twenties. None could be strictly classed as an industrial worker, and seven, if the salesmen are included, may be regarded as white collar employees. Of the others, one was a commercial agent, one an employer of labor, and two were fairly well-to-do business men. All twelve had formed an opinion on the case. This could not have been otherwise, unless the jury were composed of individuals so unintelligent that they had failed to hear or read of the bombing, or, having done so, were unable to grasp its implications. Such a jury would be imbecilic rather than impartial. Four of the jurors were unmistakably prejudiced against Socialism, Anarchism and Communism, and the same bias was present in varying degrees in at least five more. At least four of the twelve should not have been qualified to serve in a case as serious as this. Nevertheless, on the whole, the jury was as good a one as could have been secured under the circumstances. It is important to note that eight of the jurors were accepted first by the defense and then tendered to the State, and that the defense raised objections to only two of the remaining four.[28] There is some evidence to show that the jury was very carefully watched to prevent the members from being "reached" by the defense through bribery or any other means.[29] It has also been charged that at least one of the jurors was directly influenced by a friend of the State's Attorney, Mr. Grinnell.[30]

It is extremely improbable that a less biased jury could have been selected under the circumstances. This, however, in no way exculpates Judge Gary from the charge of gross partiality which, with the passage of time, has been more and more frequently directed against him. This accusation is justified. It cannot be shown that Judge Gary was honestly interested in securing an impartial jury within the fullest meaning of the term. The court never sought to determine by the demeanor of a talesman whether he was equipped to serve as an unbiased juror. On the contrary, the record discloses the complete warping of the purpose of the statute relating to jurors by Judge Gary's unblushing efforts to qualify jurors through extended questioning designed to induce a talesman to state he could try the case fairly. There was no judicial reason for the court to coax and wheedle and plead for the magic "I believe." His procedure was indefensible and reprehensible.

To say that Judge Gary was partial, however, does not necessarily make him a *conscious* ally of the prosecution.

But there is no question that the whole body of his personal beliefs and attitudes militated against his affording the accused unbiased, judicial treatment.

NOTES CHAPTER XII

1. Chicago *Inter Ocean,* Chicago *Tribune,* June 22, 1886.
2. Mr. Grinnell, like Judge Gary, was a New Yorker by birth. He had become State's Attorney two years earlier. In 1887, he was promoted to a judgeship of the Superior Court. Four years later he resigned to become chief counsel for the Chicago City Railways.
3. *Life of Albert R. Parsons,* pp. 212-227; Zeisler, *op. cit.,* pp. 19-20; *Free Society,* November 29, 1899 (this number is incorrectly dated), William and Lizzie Holmes, "Reminiscences," pp. 2-3 *passim;* Samuel P. McConnell, "The Chicago Bomb Case. Personal Recollections of an American Tragedy," *Harper's Magazine,* vol. 168, no. 1,008, May, 1934, p. 736.
4. Quoted in Lloyd, *op. cit.,* vol. 1, p. 85.
5. Another version has it that Black's words were: "This man is in my charge and this demand is not only theatrical clap-trap, but an insult to me." Parsons is supposed to have said then: "I present myself for trial with my comrades, your honor." Zeisler, *op. cit.,* p. 22; *Am. St. Tr.,* vol. 12, p. 18; *Life of Albert R. Parsons,* pp. 221-222; Chicago *Inter Ocean,* June 22, 1886.
6. The defense motion to have the indictment quashed was based on the following grounds: (1) there was a multiplicity of counts in the indictment; (2) there was a misjoinder of counts in the indictment; (3) the indictment was uncertain and insufficient; (4) during the grand jury investigation, Furthman and Grinnell were present in the grand jury room and questioned witnesses then under examination by the grand jury; (5) the grand jury

were improperly drawn and impanelled; (6) Judge Rogers' charge
was improper and erroneous. *Abstract of Record*, vol. 1, pp. 2-4;
Chicago *Inter Ocean*, June 22, 1886.

7. *Abstract of Record*, vol. 1, pp. 2, 4-5; Zeisler, *op. cit.*, pp. 21-22.
Zeisler reports that the court did so "sarcastically."

8. Zeisler, *op. cit.*, p. 23; Joseph E. Gary, "The Chicago Anarchists
of 1886: The Crime, The Trial and the Punishment," *Century
Magazine*, vol. 45, no. 6, April, 1893, p. 804.

9. This was in full accord with the statutory law of Illinois, Act of
February 11, 1874, chapter 78, sec. 13 of the laws of Illinois.

10. *Abstract of Record*, vol. 1, pp. 26-27; Altgeld, *Pardon Message*,
pp. 4-6. All of this was made known later. Ryce, of course, denied
the accusation of bias.

11. *Abstract of Record*, vol. 1, p. 53; *Brief and Argument*, pp. 339-340.

12. *Brief and Argument*, p. 340; Lum, *op. cit.*, p. 50; *Abstract of
Record*, vol. 1, pp. 53-54.

13. *Brief and Argument*, pp. 340-341; Lum, *op. cit.*, pp. 50-51; *Abstract of Record*, vol. 1, pp. 36-37. This venireman also was
prejudiced against socialists, anarchists, and communists, holding
their influence to be pernicious, and was opposed to trade unions.

14. *Brief and Argument*, p. 343; Lum, *op. cit.*, p. 52; *Abstract of
Record*, vol. 1, pp. 57-58.

15. Zeisler, *op. cit.*, p. 24.

16. Quoted in *Spies* v. *Ill.*, 123 U. S. 131, at p. 133.

17. *Plummer* v. *People*, 74 Ill. 361, at p. 366.

18. *Coughlin* v. *People*, 144 Ill. 140, at p. 177.

19. *Brief and Argument*, pp. 353-356; *Abstract of Record*, vol. 1, pp.
97-100. For other examples of such coaxing by the court, see Lum,
op. cit., pp. 53-58 *passim*; *Abstract of Record*, vol. 1, pp. 75,
95-96, 102-104.

20. *Abstract of Record*, vol. 1, pp. 43, 69-70, 85, 102-104. The examples
cited here are in no way exceptional.

21. *Ibid.*, vol. 1, p. 75.

22. *Ibid.*, vol. 1, p. 105; Zeisler, *op. cit.*, p. 24.

23. 94 Ill. 299.

24. Zeisler, *op. cit.*, p. 25.

25. *Ibid.*, pp. 25-26; *Brief and Argument*, pp. 383-384; *Abstract of
Record*, vol. 1, pp. 139-140.

26. July 17, 1886. The figure 982 should be corrected to 981, and
twenty-one days, not twenty-two, were consumed in finding a jury.

27. One of the affiants is supposed to have been a well known opponent
of Anarchism.

28. *Abstract of Record*, vol. 1, pp. 34, 48-49, 51-52, 55, 79-80, 108,
121-122, 124, 139-140; *Brief and Argument*, pp. 380-384; Lum,
op. cit., pp. 60-64; Gen. M. M. Trumbull, *Was It a Fair Trial?
An Appeal to the Governor of Illinois*, Chicago, 1887, pp. 11-12;
Anarchy at an End. Lives, Trial and Conviction of the Eight

Chicago Anarchists. How They Killed and What They Killed With, etc., Chicago, 1886, pp. 4-5.

29. Siringo, *op. cit.,* p. 5.
30. George Schilling in an interview with the author. He claims that Frank Collier, then a prominent lawyer in the mid-West, brought pressure to bear upon the juror.

It might also be noted that in Robert Herrick's, *The Memoirs of an American Citizen,* the leading character, Harrington, is summoned for jury duty in the "anarchist" trial. He is unwilling to serve, but his employer urges him to, and in answer to the question why he himself does not serve, the employer says: "I haven't been drawn. Besides, it has been thought wiser not to give the jury too capitalistic a character." Harrington's employer makes it clear that the firm expects him to serve on the jury if he is selected, and that he would be properly rewarded in return (p. 86 *et seq.*).

XIII. THE EVIDENCE

O<small>N</small> the day the last juror was chosen, Mr. Grinnell rose to outline the case to the jury.[1] "Gentlemen," he began. "For the first time in the history of our country are people on trial for endeavoring to make anarchy the rule, and in that attempt for ruthlessly and awfully destroying human life. I hope that while the youngest of us lives this in memory will be the last and only time in our country when such a trial shall take place. It will or will not take place as this case is determined." This was in no sense, then, an ordinary murder trial.

Mr. Grinnell, making a special effort to drive home the fact that the prosecution would not play upon the prejudices of the jury, pleaded for a verdict based upon the "facts" and "reason." The State's Attorney followed this, however, with several statements which put in question either his sincerity or his understanding of these words. Americans, he informed the jury, have long advocated the principles of free speech and complete liberty, even though they permitted harsh criticism of our fundamental institutions. If, however, Americans were convinced that "our institutions, founded upon our Constitution, the Declaration of Independence, and our universal freedom, were above and beyond all Anarchy," they were miserably mistaken. "In the light of the 4th of May we now know that the preachings of Anarchy [by] . . . these defendants hourly and daily for years, have been sapping our institutions, and that where they have cried murder, bloodshed, Anarchy and dynamite, they have meant what they said, and proposed to do what they threatened." The existence of American government had been jeopardized by the defendants who were ringleaders in an active, widespread revolutionary movement. "The firing upon Fort Sumter was a terrible thing to our country," said Mr. Grinnell, "but it was open warfare. I think it was nothing compared with this insidious, infamous plot to ruin our laws and our country secretly and in this cowardly way. . . ."

The accusations made by the prosecutor were numerous. The defendants were not only murderers, they were enemies of the State, conspirators of the worst sort. The State was prepared to present proof that Spies had time and again asserted that only through force could the wrongs of man be adjusted; that he had used the eight-hour day issue as a blind for the introduction of anarchy; that he had stated that the revolutionists were ready for anarchy in Chicago. Spies, asserted Mr. Grinnell, as early as the previous January, had planned to precipitate matters at a gathering later to be held in the Haymarket. Spies had revealed this to a newspaper reporter to whom he also had given a dynamite bomb with the explanation: "These are the bombs that our men are making in the city of Chicago, and they are distributed from the *Arbeiter-Zeitung* office. . . ." The prosecution was prepared to show that the riot at the McCormick factory was deliberately provoked by Spies, and that his viciously false report of that occurrence as well as the lying "Revenge Circular" were composed with premeditated intent to incite the people. The German "Revenge Circular," Mr. Grinnell said, was "the most infamous thing that was ever in print. . . . It is not only treason and Anarchy but a bid to bloodshed and a bid to war."

The charges mounted. Parsons had encouraged and described the use of dynamite. All of the defendants had advised over a long period of time the employment of dynamite against capitalists and the police. The defendants had declared that workers must arm themselves. Mr. Grinnell likewise repeatedly insisted that the prosecution would show that the defendants were cowards. How this was pertinent to the charge that the defendants were responsible for the murder of Officer Degan is not immediately apparent. Mr. Grinnell asserted that the police and the prosecution had uncovered the existence of an appalling conspiracy which envisaged nothing less than the destruction of Chicago and American government!

Carried away by the magnitude of his revelations, the State's Attorney was not always unambiguous. No one, however, could mistake the essential nature of his charges. He was prepared to show that with the approach of May 4, "Everything was ripe with the Anarchists for ruining the town [Chicago]. Bombs were to be thrown in all parts of the city. . . . Everything was to be done that could be done to ruin law and order." On the night of the third, a group of anarchists held a meeting at which a formidable conspiracy, devised by one of the defendants, George Engel, was elaborated and adopted. "It meant destruction to this town absolutely," declared Mr. Grinnell, "if this plan had been carried out." According to the State's Attorney, Engel was in constant communication with Louis Lingg, who had been engaged in making bombs, and the bomb which exploded in the Haymarket was indisputably of Lingg's manufacture.

What of Engel's plan? It was perhaps not immediately grasped as Mr. Grinnell described it, but it undoubtedly impressed the attentive jury. When enough bombs had been manufactured they were to be left at Neff's Hall, a rendezvous of the anarchists, where the conspirators were to get them. Several bombs were to be brought to Haymarket Square, where it was hoped a monster gathering of some 25,000 workers would be in progress. Other

"individuals with the bombs were to distribate themselves in various parts of the city. They were to destroy the station houses; they were to throw bombs at every patrol wagon . . . going toward the Haymarket Square. . . . They expected there would be a row down there at the Haymarket

Square, of course. There was going to be one bomb thrown there at least, and perhaps more, and that would call the police down; but the police must be taken care of; . . . must not be permitted to go. . . . They were to be destroyed, absolutely wiped off the earth by bombs in other parts of the city. . . . And they were to build a fire up toward Wicker Park. . . . Others were to take other parts of the city and burn them so that they would be destroyed."

Mr. Grinnell concluded this recital with a perfect anti-climax. "It is not necessary for me," he unblushingly declared, "to go into any more of the details of that conspiracy. It was carried out to the letter."

The State possessed the facts to show that each defendant was implicated in this grim plot to wipe out Chicago. It was the greatest good fortune that the police interfered when they did. The Haymarket meeting was disorderly, the speeches most inflammatory. Only the providential action of Captain Bonfield served to prevent the social revolution. In his attempt to explain the late arrival of the police, however, the State's Attorney blundered. It would have been wiser to remain silent on that point.

The prosecution would attempt to show who threw the bomb. Though the State's Attorney mentioned no one by name, he probably had the missing Rudolph Schnaubelt in mind. "The indictment in this case," he stated, "is for murder. . . . Now it is not necessary in a case of this kind, nor in any case of murder . . . that the individual who commits the . . . particular offense—for instance, the man who threw the bomb—should be in court at all. He need not even be indicted. The question for you to determine is, having ascertained that a murder was committed, not only who did it, but who is responsible for it, who abetted it, or encouraged it? There is no question of law in the case."

From Mr. Grinnell's presentation of the evidence, it appeared that the prosecution would attempt to show that the accused were implicated both directly and indirectly in the crime of May 4. Had they not been members of a specific conspiracy which was carried out? Had they not urged, through their press and by word of mouth, violence, bloodshed and the use of dynamite?[2] He emphasized their direct relationship to the Haymarket bomb, and virtually promised to offer evidence disclosing the identity of the bomb-thrower. Furthermore, he never once implied that the defendants had aided and abetted an unknown principal, for he had said that the jury, "having ascertained that a murder was committed," must determine *"not only who did it,* but who is responsible for it, who abetted it, assisted it, or encouraged it?"[3] These points should be kept in mind, because the theory upon which the case was prosecuted and the tactics employed by the State saw several radical changes before the trial was over.

The testimony introduced during the course of the trial was voluminous.[4] With the court meeting on week days for two three-hour sessions, the presentation of evidence and the cross-examination of witnesses lasted from July 16 to August 10. This mass of evidence may be considered under four general categories: (1) that touching upon the immediate background of the Haymarket meeting; (2) that relating to the meeting proper, including the nature of the gathering, the tone of the addresses, the arrival of the police, the throwing of the bomb and the like; (3) that concerning the particular activities of the accused prior to and during the day and night of May 4; and (4) that dealing with the remote background of the bomb in terms of the radical movement in Chicago. This classification, neither very sharp nor all-inclusive, may serve as an aid in recalling the pertinent evidence.

The grand jury indictment permitted the prosecution to introduce testimony in substantiation of two distinct hypotheses. One held that Rudolph Schnaubelt was the actual principal acting in accordance with a conspiracy in which the defendants participated and of which the bombing was the intended result. The second assumed that the accused were accessories to an unknown principal. It was upon the first hypothesis that the State built its initial attack.

I. THE MONDAY NIGHT CONSPIRACY

As preparation for showing that Schnaubelt was the bomb-thrower, the State submitted what at first glance appeared to be indisputable proof of the existence of a specific conspiracy which resulted in the Haymarket bomb. Evidence for this plot, which quickly became known as the "Monday night conspiracy," was given chiefly by Gottfried Waller and Bernard Schrade, two social-revolutionaries who had turned State's witness.[5]

Up to the time of his arrest,[6] Waller had been a member in good standing of an I.W.P.A. group. This group had an armed section to which he likewise belonged which usually met at Grief's Hall.[7] On Monday night, May 3, the members of the group came there in response to the cryptic announcement "Y—Come Monday Night" in the *Fackel,* the usual form in which a notice for a meeting of the armed section appeared. Because all the rooms in the building were occupied, the forty or more members who responded gathered in the basement. Waller, presiding as chairman, called the meeting to order about eight-thirty. Naturally enough, the first topics to be discussed were the affray at the McCormick plant that afternoon and the "Revenge Circular."

Then George Engel rose and presented a plan, already adopted by a group in the northwest side of the city, designed to co-ordinate the movements of the armed sections in times of disturbances. Stripped of its ambiguity, this provided that when the word *Ruhe* appeared in the *Arbeiter-Zeitung* under the heading *Brief-Kasten* (Letter-Box), it would be a signal for the armed men to gather at a pre-determined spot. The northwest side group had already chosen Wicker Park as its meeting place. As soon as the armed men were assembled, a committee was to "observe" the state of affairs in the city. If any serious conflict between workers and police came to its notice, it was to report immediately to the armed men. The latter were then to aid the workers by storming police stations and engaging in other similar ambitious enterprises. This plan which Engel originated and proposed had already been accepted by the northwest side group. After several points were clarified through discussion, it was also adopted by the group meeting in Grief's Hall.

On careful examination, it is plain that Engel's scheme needed greater explicitness before it could be considered workable. It left unsettled several pertinent questions. Was the plan general or specific in nature? Was it to operate in any clash between workers and police, or only in the contingency of a "revolutionary" uprising? Did it contemplate any particular time and place of action? Was it the mechanism by which a revolution was to be engineered, or was it merely a means of aiding workers in unequal combat with the police?

During the discussion on Monday night an effort was apparently made to secure definite answers to these and other questions. It was decided that the signal *Ruhe* was to be inserted in the *Arbeiter-Zeitung only in the event that a revolution had broken out.* Yet Engel declared that his plan was designed to operate solely in the event of a police attack. He may, of course, have contemplated a police attack brought on by a general uprising of workers. In such an eventuality, his scheme would probably provide a *modus operandi* by which the armed sections could co-operate with the workingmen. It was made clear in any case that if a "revolution" or conflict occurred at night, the armed men were to receive personal notification. There is good reason to believe that Engel's plan was understood to be general in nature, in that it prescribed a general mode of conduct to be followed by the armed sections whenever certain conditions were present. But exactly what these conditions were still remained unsettled. The testimony introduced on this point was contradictory.[8] Undoubtedly some of those present at the meeting believed that the plan would go into effect only if a proletarian uprising materialized. Some seem to have felt it would operate in the eventuality of police aggression; still others thought it would be employed if the police took action in answer to an uprising. The plan, obviously, was neither fully articulated nor clearly understood. Waller himself declared that there was no mention at the meeting of a place where dynamite, arms, or bombs could be obtained.

After the group in Grief's Hall had accepted this scheme, Waller suggested that a meeting be called for the following day to protest against the activities of the police on that afternoon (May 3). Adolph Fischer then proposed that such a meeting be held on the following night (Tuesday) in the spacious Haymarket. It was understood that the armed men were not to attend it. Beyond this the projected Haymarket meeting was not discussed.[9]

An exceedingly interesting question arose during the cross-examination of Waller. When he was asked by the State whether he ever possessed bombs, Mr. Foster objected for the defense on the ground "that the witness was not on trial and . . . the fact that *he* might have had bombs was no evidence against the defendants on *their trial* for murder." Replying for the State, Mr. Ingham pointed out that the prosecution based its case on the theory that the accused had been the leaders of a gigantic conspiracy extending over a period of several years against law and order as such, and that the Monday night meeting was only one phase of this conspiracy. "If you show," pertinently asked Mr. Foster, "that some man threw one of these bombs without the knowledge or authority, or approval of any of these defendants, is that murder?" Mr. Ingham, his response virtually sustained by the court, answered: "Under the law of the State of Illinois *it is* murder. The law of this State is strong enough to hang *every one* of these men." [10] This brief exchange between the two was pregnant with significance in view of later developments, and may also indicate a partial modification of the prosecution's initial hypothesis,[11] as well as the opening of a new line of attack.

The presence of the word *Ruhe* under the heading *Brief-Kasten* in the *Arbeiter-Zeitung* of May 4, lent support to the State's contention that the bomb was connected with the Monday night meeting. Spies, as editor, had made a note for its insertion. But the defense was able to show, without contradiction, that Spies was ignorant of the significance of the word. He merely ordered its insertion in pursuance to a note in German he received which read: "Mr. Editor, Please insert in the letter-box the word 'Ruhe' in prominent letters." When Spies learned on the afternoon of May 4 its meaning, he asked someone connected with the armed groups "to go and tell them that the word was put in by mistake." [12] About five o'clock in the afternoon, Spies was informed that this had been done. Waller asserted that he and other members of the armed group failed to understand why the word had been inserted, since it was to appear only if a "downright revolution had occurred." [13]

The "Monday night conspiracy" was a pivotal point in the State's case. Could the prosecution prove its hypothesis that the Haymarket bombing was a direct product of the gathering in Grief's Hall, the case against the defendants would be clinched. It must be admitted, however, that no such causal connection was shown. "There was nothing said about the [Haymarket] meeting," said Waller on the witness stand. "There was nothing [*sic*] expected that the police would get to the Haymarket." Benjamin Schrade, testifying for the State, and George Engel, both of whom were present, corroborated Waller's statement. Since police interference was unforeseen, it was deemed unnecessary to have members of the armed sections present. "They [those in attendance at Grief's Hall]," declared Engel, "did not think that the police would come to the Haymarket; no preparations were made for meeting any police attack there."

The publication of the signal *Ruhe* in the *Arbeiter-Zeitung* dented the armor of the defense. It has been seen, however, that its meaning was unknown to Spies, who did what he could to inform the interested parties that it was printed in error. Waller himself admitted that he did not understand why the word appeared on the fourth. Furthermore, no shred of uncontroverted evidence was introduced to demonstrate a connection between the signal and the Tuesday night meeting. Who sent the request for its insertion to Spies? And what was the motive? These questions are no more answerable today than they were in the dingy courtroom where Judge Gary presided in 1886.

No direct evidence was presented by the State to show that the Haymarket bomb was thrown by a participant in the "Monday night conspiracy." Of the eight defendants, only George Engel and Adolph Fischer attended the meeting in Grief's Hall. Fischer, present at the Haymarket meeting for a short while, was absent when the bomb was thrown. Engel was not there at all. The State never contended that either Engel, Fischer or any other person who participated in the Monday night meeting actually threw the bomb, and its attempt to prove that Schnaubelt was present at the meeting was not crowned with success.

If, as the State argued, the Haymarket bomb was the result of the "Monday night conspiracy," it logically follows that the throwing of that missile was foreign to the original design of the "conspiracy." Engel's plan was not aggressive in nature. It would function only under certain conditions. The State argued that it was to operate in the event of a "general uprising." Since there was no "general uprising," the bomb did not fit in with the "conspiracy" which the State sketched. On the other hand, the bomb was not an answer to a police attack since it served to precipitate one. It is, of course, possible that the missile was thrown in anticipation of an assault by the police. This possibility, however, was neglected by the State.

The State, obviously, desired to construct as damaging a case against the defendants as possible. The story of the "Monday night conspiracy" was revealed by a man who moved in the same circle with most of the defendants. He was well acquainted with Engel and Fischer, knew Neebe slightly and Spies by sight. He had been arrested and indicted together with them. By becoming a witness for the prosecution Gottfried Waller had escaped trial. He had been closely examined by the police and the prosecution. He gave no sign of reluctance when testifying. There is no reason to believe that Waller was in possession of pertinent knowledge which he consciously withheld out of consideration for the defendants. Had he been in a position to assert that the Haymarket bombing was a direct consequence of the Monday night meeting, he would have done so. Under cross-examination he frankly admitted his relations with the prosecution.

"I know that I am indicted for conspiracy;" he said, "I was arrested about two weeks after the 4th of May, by two detectives, Swift and Whalen, and taken to East Chicago Avenue Station; I saw there, Captain Schaack, and in the evening Mr. Furthman; I was released about half past eight of the same day. No warrant was shown to me; I was never arrested since my indictment; I was ordered to come to the station four or five times; at every occasion I had conversations with Furthman about the statements made here in court. . . . Captain Schaack gave me $6.50 for . . . rent; whenever I used my time sitting in the station, I was paid for it; once we had to sit all day and we were paid two dollars; he gave me twice before five dollars each time. I have been at work for the last two weeks. . . . Captain Schaack helped me get the job." [14]

Subsequently Waller's sister and sister-in-law prepared affidavits in which these admissions were confirmed. The affidavits also asserted that Waller had been a nightly visitor at the police station from the time he was arrested to the opening of the trial; that Captain Schaack had promised him immunity if he testified properly during the trial, threatening him with death if he did not; that the portions of Waller's testimony injurious to the defendants were dictated to him by the police. The affidavits likewise disclosed that Waller was sent to Hamburg, Germany, after the trial, where he assumed, with the advice of the police, the name of Miller.[15]

II. RUDOLPH SCHNAUBELT, "BOMB-THROWER"

After endeavoring to show a causal connection between the bomb and the "Monday night conspiracy," the prosecution attacked the problem of the actual bomb-thrower. The State first attempted to prove that it was hurled by Rudolph Schnaubelt, the young German radical who had been twice arrested and released, with the aid of the defendants. Testimony supporting this contention was supplied by two witnesses for the State, Harry L. Gilmer and M. M. Thompson.[16]

Earlier in the evening of May 4, Gilmer—so his story ran—had visited the Palmer House to see Judge Cole and ex-Governor Merrill of Des Moines, who, he understood, were then in Chicago. Failing to find them, he stopped on his way home at the Haymarket at about a quarter to ten to look for a friend whom he expected to find there.[17] The meeting was in progress, and he paused in Crane's alley to listen to Fielden. Suddenly, someone in the crowd shouted, "Here come the police!" Immediately after the cry rang out, a man stepped down from the wagon used by the speakers, and joined a small group of people standing on the south side of the alley. This man had a bomb, and somebody else lit a match and touched off its fuse. He then took two steps forward and tossed it into the street.

Gilmer, testifying that he knew the bomb-thrower by sight but not by name, described him as being five feet, ten inches in height, broad-chested, full-faced with deep-set eyes and a light, sandy beard. He judged the weight of the bomb-thrower to be about 180 pounds. Shown a photograph of Schnaubelt in court, Gilmer dramatically asserted that Schnaubelt was the man who had thrown the dynamite bomb. Spies, according to Gilmer, had supplied the match with which the fuse was lit, and Adolph Fischer was among the small group from whose position the missile was hurled.[18]

If Gilmer was correct, the guilt of Spies and Schnaubelt was unmistakable. It was soon made evident, however, that his testimony could not be taken at face value.

He had related a markedly different version of his experience to a reporter of the Chicago *Times* on the fifth.[19] The latter [20] declared on the witness stand that "He said to me in that conversation . . . that he saw the man light the fuse *and throw* the bomb, and added, 'I think I could identify *him* if I saw him.' I asked what kind of looking man he was, and Gilmer said: 'he was a man of medium height, and I think he had whiskers, and wore a soft slouch hat, but his back was turned to me.' " Gilmer also thought the man wore dark clothes. In this version Spies was not mentioned, and the man who threw the bomb also lit its fuse. Furthermore, according to this account, Gilmer was not in a position to discern the face of the bomb-thrower.[21]

During his cross-examination it was shown that Gilmer was not called to testify either before the coroner or the grand jury, although he was already in touch with the police and had even conferred with Mr. Grinnell about a week after the fourth. Since it was unlikely that a witness for the State would be intimidated, this demanded explanation. None was ever given. The inference may be made that the prosecution deemed it wise to save Gilmer's testimony for the trial proper, where, even though it might be shown to have no validity, it would nevertheless have effect. Gilmer also received extremely small sums of money from Detective James Bonfield, —sometimes as much as a quarter at once.

To proceed with an examination of Mr. Gilmer's testimony. According to his own information he was six feet, three inches tall, and could easily look over the head of the bomb-thrower. Schnaubelt was exactly the same height. Therefore, either the witness for the State made an error of five inches in estimating Schnaubelt's height, or the man who threw the bomb was not Schnaubelt. Gilmer swore that Spies lit the bomb. No other evidence was offered to support this statement. On the other hand, thirteen witnesses—contradicted only by Gilmer—agreed that Spies did *not* leave the wagon when the police came on the scene. He remained there until the order to disperse was given. When he did step down, aided by his brother Henry and someone else, he did not enter the alley. As Spies was descending, someone attempted to shoot him, and his brother, in warding off the assailant, was badly wounded. Thus, Gilmer's testimony describing Spies' movements was shown to be inaccurate in every important respect by witnesses for the State and the defense. This "star" witness for the State blundered again in asserting that Adolph Fischer was present when the bomb exploded. It was conclusively established that Fischer was at Zepf's Hall, where he had gone some time before.

The question of the exact spot whence the bomb came was both vital and perplexing. Gilmer testified that the bomb-thrower stood *within* Crane's alley, on its south side. Choice of this position was dictated by his contention that Spies had descended from the wagon, joined a knot of people near it, and lit the fuse of the bomb. Other evidence proves that Gilmer's assertions were the product either of unconscious error or wilful misstatement. Sixteen witnesses swore that the bomb was not thrown from the alley proper, *but from a spot south of it.* Of these sixteen, three, a policeman and two newspaper reporters had been summoned by the State. Though there was agreement that the bomb had *not* been hurled from the alley proper, there was sharp disagreement over the distance south of the alley from which it came. Careful consideration of the evidence leads to the conclusion that the bomb was probably thrown from a point some fifteen paces south of Crane's alley.

A Mr. John Bernett told an arresting story on the witness stand which further discredits Gilmer. Bernett disclaimed acquaintance with the men on trial and sympathy with their beliefs. He swore that he was standing some thirty-eight feet south of Crane's alley during the course of the meeting. While he was there the man who threw the bomb stood directly in front of him. According to Bernett, the bomb-thrower wore a mustache, but no beard, and was his own height, five feet, nine inches. Shown Schnaubelt's photograph, and asked if he recognized him as the bomb-thrower, Mr. Bernett emphatically answered "no." He also informed the jury that he had made the same response when shown the photograph two weeks before by Mr. Furthman.

Were it not for the nature of the case and the psychological atmosphere of Chicago, it would have been unwise of the prosecution to call Gilmer to the stand. His testimony was not only unsupported, but was contradicted in all its essentials. Gilmer was either merely an unreliable witness because of faulty memory, or his story was largely pure fabrication in which the prosecution had a hand. The last is the more likely.

The character witnesses summoned first by the defense and then by the State probably provided much amusement for those who had no personal stake in the trial. Witnesses for the State, of course, gave Gilmer a clean bill of health. They were willing to believe him under oath. Unfortunately for Gilmer, however, the eighteen witnesses who appeared in his behalf were not very well acquainted with him. Some were old army associates, several had employed him briefly from time to time. None had any knowledge of his reputation for truth among his friends, and none moved in his "social circle." Ex-Judge Chester C. Cole and ex-Governor Samuel Merrill, who were summoned from Des Moines, had employed Gilmer there as a house painter. Judge Cole knew nothing of him since 1879, and the Governor had lost sight of him since 1875-1876. So far as they knew, there was no reason for not believing him under oath. Neither was in Chicago on May 4, nor had they informed anyone that they might be there at that date.[22] The nine men and women summoned by the defense were either neighbors of Mr. Gilmer or acquainted with people who knew him. They roundly agreed that Mr. Gilmer "was not to be believed under oath." One of them rather reluctantly declared: "I think I know his general reputation for truth and veracity among his neighbors. It is bad. I don't think I could believe him under oath. . . . It was a kind of general thing to discuss Gilmer's truthfulness and veracity." [23] There is a story current to the effect that in 1893, when Gilmer lay ill in a Chicago hospital with a broken leg, he called in several people who were interested in the "anarchist" case and confessed that his testimony at the trial had been largely perjured. It is impossible to say exactly how valid this "confession" is.[24]

Through Mr. Thompson, its second "star" witness, the prosecution hoped to support its initial thesis—that Schnaubelt actually hurled the bomb—and to implicate Michael Schwab and August Spies in the deed. Thompson, too, had attended the Haymarket meeting.[25] Between seven-thirty and seven-fifty P.M. he was standing on the corner of Desplaines and Randolph Streets engaged in conversation with Mr. Brazelton of the *Inter Ocean*. During the course of the chat, the latter had occasion to point out Schwab, whom Thompson had never before seen, hurrying along Desplaines Street. After taking a short stroll, Thompson returned to the Haymarket in time to see Spies mount the wagon and hear him call out for Parsons. Spies descended when he was informed that Parsons was not present, and, accompanied by Schwab, the witness affirmed, walked into the alley south of Crane Brothers' building. Thompson alleged that he could overhear Spies and Schwab in conversation, and took oath that the word "pistol" was used once and the word "police" twice. Then Thompson drew near enough (his reason for moving closer to them was not made clear) to catch Spies' question: "Do you think one is enough or hadn't we better go and get more?" This, Thompson took to be a reference to bombs. Schwab failed to reply to the query. Schwab and Spies then left the alley, and, said Thompson, "walked south on Desplaines Street to Randolph, west on the north side of Randolph to Halsted, crossed Halsted diagonally to the southwest corner of the street intersection," stopping there for about three minutes. Then, leaving this corner and the crowd gathered there, they made their way back to the wagon. The witness was in close proximity all the while, and heard the word "police" mentioned as the pair approached Union Street.[26] He came abreast with them at the moment Schwab said, "Now, if they come, we will give it to them." Thompson, continuing to shadow Spies and Schwab, observed a "third man," who suddenly "stepped out of the wall of a building," and joined them. Spies, Schwab and the newcomer were closely grouped. Thompson said they went into a "huddle." Something was passed by Spies to the "third man," which the latter placed in his right hand coat pocket. All three then returned to the wagon, which Spies and the "third man" mounted. Thompson evidently gave this person the closest attention, for he testified that the gentleman never once removed his right hand from his pocket throughout the meeting. When shown a photo of Schnaubelt in court, Thompson stated that he believed it a likeness of the "third man."

As it stands, Thompson's narrative fails to carry conviction. There are too many objections which spring from the testimony itself. He admitted that he had never seen Spies or Schwab before the night of the fourth, and consequently had never heard either of them speak. He did not understand German, and insisted that the conversaton on which he eavesdropped was in English. He was unable to indicate the subject of that talk or to connect it as a whole with those sections which he reproduced in court. Spies and Schwab, many witnesses asserted, always used their mother tongue when together. Was it likely that they would converse in English—an acquired language—if they were conspiring to use a bomb against the police? Was it probable that they would be careless enough to discuss such a subject without being certain that they were alone? Would they speak so loudly that their words carried to a person standing several feet away, and at one time around the corner of a building? Furthermore, in his description of the meeting of Spies, Schwab and the third man, Thompson asserted that the positions of the three were such that Spies faced him while the third man stood opposite Spies. He was able, nevertheless, to recognize this man's face, watch him throughout the meeting, and then, in court two months later, identify him as Schnaubelt.

Other testimony, both for the defense and the prosecution, riddled Thompson's tale.[27] It was fully demonstrated that Schwab, though present in the Haymarket on the night of May 4, did not meet Spies. The former's account of his movements on that night was so convincingly substantiated by unrefuted evidence, that it cannot be questioned. On Tuesday evening Schwab left his home about seven-forty, and arrived at the office of the *Arbeiter-Zeitung* some ten minutes later. He remained there less than a quarter of an hour, and answered a telephone call requesting Spies to address a meeting at Deering. Schwab, accordingly, set out for the Haymarket to acquaint Spies with this message. Failing to find Spies at the Square, he went on to Deering, intending to speak there. While on his way he met Schnaubelt north of Desplaines and Randolph Streets, and mentioned the Deering meeting. After this brief stop, he continued with a friend whom he had met.[28] Schwab spoke at the Deering meeting, and, stopping only to enjoy a glass of beer, returned to his home about eleven o'clock.

Testimony of police officers gave full reason for believing that Thompson's description of Spies' movements was inaccurate. "When Spies got on the wagon first," said one officer,[29] "he called out twice if Parsons was there, and told somebody in the crowd to go and find Parsons and said Fielden would be here later. Then he said that he would get down from the wagon and find Parsons himself. He got down and went in a southwesterly direction." He was followed by two policemen who failed to see the meeting of the three men described by Mr. Thompson.[30] "There was a man with him," said one officer, "who I think was Schwab, but I am not sure of that. . . ." Testimony offered by Mr. English, a reporter on the staff of the *Tribune,* also upheld the defense in its contention that Schwab did not meet and speak with Spies and a third man.

So overwhelming is the evidence on these points, that one must conclude that while Schwab was present in the Haymarket before the meeting really began, he did not meet and converse with Spies and Schnaubelt, and he was not there when the bomb was thrown. Nor can there be any question that Fischer was absent from the Haymarket when the bomb was thrown.[31] There is also good reason to believe that Schnaubelt, who attended the meeting, left Haymarket Square at or shortly before ten o'clock.

One who reads the records of the court today cannot place great dependence upon the testimony of Gilmer and Thompson. Apart from the points where they confirmed each other, their testimony was practically unsupported. There were glaring contradictions between their testimony and that of other witnesses for the State. Schnaubelt cannot be regarded as the bomb-thrower on the basis of such evidence. Schnaubelt, however, disappeared, and this was regarded at the time, and has been since, as a confession of guilt. But it can in no sense stand as proof that he was the actual bomb-thrower.[32] It has been justifiably charged that through Gilmer and Thompson the prosecution wittingly presented perjured evidence. Such tactics, however, were really unnecessary. One who had his finger at the pulse of Chicago should have known that the verdict would be "guilty" regardless of the evidence adduced in court.

III. LOUIS LINGG, "BOMB-MAKER"

The police were well rewarded when they seized Louis Lingg. Between him and the other men on trial there was little in common. He was not popularly known in radical circles, and the authorities had evidently been unconscious of his existence up to the time the bomb was thrown. In many respects Louis Lingg's personality and his actions previous to the trial did as much as any other set of circumstances to determine the fate of all eight defendants. He approached in type the fanatical revolutionist of the Netchaev type. Louis Lingg did not throw the Haymarket bomb, but he was engaged in manufacturing dynamite bombs. He alone among the eight men on trial possessed the temperament necessary for the perpetration of such a deed.

Lingg's singular activities were revealed by William Seliger, who had been indicted for murder together with those on trial.[33] Lingg occupied a room in the house in which Seliger resided, and the latter could observe much that his unusual tenant did. As a matter of fact, his own testimony indicates that he was dominated by Lingg's forceful personality.

Seliger was aware that his tenant had been making bombs for some five or six weeks prior to May 4, for he had been helping Lingg. Early on the fourth he informed Lingg that he wanted the bombs and materials removed from the house without delay. Lingg's answer indicated that he was accustomed to giving Seliger orders and having them obeyed. "He told me," Seliger recalled in court, "to work diligently at those bombs and they would be taken away that day . . ." After breakfast Seliger set to work, and when Lingg, who had been out to a meeting, returned about one o'clock in the afternoon, he upbraided Seliger for having accomplished so little. Ignoring Seliger's protest that he found no pleasure in the task, Lingg simply remarked, "Well, we will have to work very diligently this afternoon."

With Lingg, Seliger and at least three other German comrades working at different times during the afternoon, some fifty bombs—round and pipe-shaped dynamite contrivances with caps attached—were completed. At about eight-thirty in the evening, Lingg and Seliger left the house. They carried between them, by means of a stick through the handle, a small trunk filled with these bombs. The trunk weighed some thirty to fifty pounds. What followed is best related in Seliger's own words:

"That is the way we were carrying the trunk which was taken to Neff's Hall [another well known meeting place of the radicals], 58 Clybourn Avenue. On the way to Neff's Hall, Nunsenberg [He had helped Seliger and Lingg make bombs during the afternoon.] met us. We took the package into the building, and through the saloon on the side into the hallway that led to the rear. After the bombs were put down in the passage way, there were different ones [i.e., several people] there, three or four, who took bombs out for themselves. I took two pipe bombs myself. Carried them in my pocket. We went away from Neff's Hall, Thielen and Gustav Lehman were with me. Later two large men of the *Lehr and Wehr Verein* came to us; I believe they all had bombs. We went on to Clybourn Avenue, north, toward Lincoln Avenue, to the Larrabee Street [police] station, where we halted. Lingg and myself halted there. I don't know what had become of the others. . . . In front of the Larrabee Street station, Lingg said it might be a beautiful thing if we would walk over and throw one or two bombs into the station. . . . Then we went further north to Lincoln Avenue and Larrabee Street where we took a glass of beer. Webster Avenue station is near there. After we left the saloon we went a few blocks north, then turned about and came back to North Avenue and Larrabee Street. While we stood there the patrol wagon passed. . . . Lingg said he was going to throw a bomb, and I said 'It would not have any purpose.' Then he became quite wild, excited, said I should give him a light. I was smoking a cigar, and I jumped into the front opening before a store and lighted a match, as if I intended to light a cigar, so I could not give him a light. When I had lighted my cigar, the patrol wagon was just passing. Lingg said he was going to see what had happened, saying that something had certainly happened on the west side. . . . [Because of the patrol wagon Lingg took it for granted that something had occurred.] The patrol wagon was completely manned. . . . Then we went toward home. First Lingg wanted to wait until the patrol wagon would come back, but I importuned him to go home with me. We go home shortly before eleven, I cannot tell exactly. . . . After that talk [about the 54 West Lake Street meeting and the word *Ruhe*] we went away; Lingg wanted to go to the west side, and I talked with him to go with me to 58 Clybourn Avenue. Lingg and I went there; there were several persons present at Neff's Hall. I did not speak with Lingg at Neff's Hall; a certain Herman said to him in an energetic tone of voice: 'You are the fault of it.' I did not hear what Lingg said to that; they spoke in a subdued tone. . . . On the way home Lingg said that he was even now scolded, chided for the work he had done; we got home shortly after twelve. We laid the bombs of our own on Sigel Street between Sedgwick and Hurlbut, under an elevated sidewalk. I laid two pipe bombs there; I saw Lingg put some bombs there; I don't know what kind."

As in the case of Waller, it may be assumed that William Seliger did not consciously withhold any evidence out of consideration for the defendants. By his own admission, Seliger was also guilty of manufacturing bombs. He, too, had been faced with trial. The more he revealed to the detriment of the defendants, the less precarious his own position became. It is not likely that Seliger concealed any vital information further implicating his late accomplice.[34]

On the basis of all the testimony bearing on Lingg, certain definite conclusions can be drawn. He did manufacture bombs. On the night of May 4, they were placed in the passage-way of a saloon. How many people had access to them is not known. At least ten persons, including Seliger, and Lingg, procured bombs from the trunk. How many others did likewise is an open question. Lingg had also given bombs and fuses and caps to someone else on the fourth. Lingg did not hurl the Haymarket bomb. He was not present at the meeting, in fact was not within two miles of Haymarket Square that evening. He knew nothing of the "Monday night meeting" and of the signal *Ruhe* until the night of the fourth and presumably not until the bomb went off. The evidence does not reveal that he was aware of any specific plan to explode a bomb. Nor does it appear in the record that he knowingly gave one of his own bombs to any individual to be used in the Haymarket that night.[35]

Was the Haymarket bomb made by Lingg? This was a vital question. The State submitted expert testimony[36] to prove that the bomb was similar in composition to those manufactured by Lingg. This rested on the chemical analysis of those portions of the bomb which were recovered, of which there were only three tiny fragments, and of bombs manufactured by Lingg. It was shown that similar metal was used in both, and that a nut from the Haymarket bomb which supposedly struck a bystander corresponded with the nuts found on the Lingg bombs. The expert witnesses summoned by the State, however, never went beyond the statement that there were similarities between the Haymarket bomb and Lingg's missiles. No other evidence was produced to prove that one of Lingg's bombs had been thrown on the fourth.

No effort was made by the prosecution to show that any of the other defendants not considered at length thus far —Parsons, Fischer, Fielden, Neebe and Engel—threw the bomb or directly aided the actual bomb-thrower, whoever he was. Their activities, prior to and during the Haymarket meeting, were reconstructed with ease. Only in connection with certain alleged acts of Fielden did controversy develop.

IV. GEORGE ENGEL

The case of George Engel offered no difficulties.[37] At the time of the meeting he was at home with Mrs. Engel and some friends drinking a glass of beer. He first learned of the bomb when Waller, on his way home from the Haymarket, stopped and informed him of what had occurred. Waller also said, "We ought to go down there and do something," a suggestion which he deprecated. Engel had told Waller that the individual who committed the deed did a foolish thing,— that he had no sympathy with such nonsensical butchery. Then came an observation foreign to his usual attitude. He believed that policemen were "just as good as people,"—a serious breach of revolutionary orthodoxy and not in conformity with his oft-expressed views. Advising Waller to go home as quickly as possible, he remarked that the "social revolution" must grow out of the "people." When that occurs, the police and militia, throwing down their arms, will join the masses. Though Waller denied the statement attributed to him, his testimony corroborated in every other respect the defense's version of Engel's activities on the night of the fourth.

Obviously, the only direct link between Engel and the Haymarket bomb was the "Monday night conspiracy;" and it would be necessary to give full credence to the prosecution's interpretation of that "conspiracy" to establish that. Ultimately, the State concentrated its efforts upon a different line of attack to implicate not only Engel but all the defendants in the murder of Degan.[38]

V. ADOLPH FISCHER

The evidence against Adolph Fischer can be quickly summarized.[39] This young man was on the staff of the *Arbeiter-Zeitung;* he had attended the "Monday night conspiracy" meeting; he had been instrumental in calling the gathering in the Haymarket; he was armed with a revolver and sharpened file, and wore a belt, the buckle of which bore the letters "L. U. W. V." when he was arrested. He was not, as Thompson testified, present at the Haymarket meeting when the bomb exploded. He attended it for a trifle less than an hour, and then left for Zepf's Hall where he was when the bomb exploded. Apart from testimony to show his general activities in the radical movement, this was the sum total of evidence presented against Adolph Fischer.[40]

VI. SAMUEL FIELDEN

Samuel Fielden cannot be treated so summarily.[41] On Sunday (May 2), he had arranged to address a labor gathering scheduled at 368 or 378 West 12th Street for Tuesday night. When he returned home from work on the evening of the fourth, his eye was caught by a notice in the *Daily News* announcing a meeting of the American group of the I.W.P.A. for 8 o'clock that night at 157—5th Avenue, at which "important business" was to be discussed. Fielden was treasurer of the group, and decided to forego the pleasure of speaking in order to attend. It was almost eight o'clock when he arrived, and found about fifteen present, among them Parsons. The "important business" was the organization of the sewing women of Chicago for the eight-hour movement.

Fielden's first knowledge of the Haymarket meeting came with the arrival of Balthazar Rau—sent by Spies to find Parsons—who announced the need for speakers in the Haymarket. Most of those present went over to the Haymarket. There, Parsons, Fielden and two other men of the American group mounted the wagon. What occurred after this has already been related.

It was shown that Fielden was entirely ignorant of the Monday night meeting and the "conspiracy" concocted at it. He declared that he first discovered the significance of the word *Ruhe* after he was in jail. It was never claimed that he aided the actual bomb-thrower at the scene of the crime. The prosecution did assert, however, that Fielden threatened the police when they appeared, and fired a revolver at them.

Testifying for the State, Police Lieutenant Quinn swore that as the police were approaching, Fielden cried, "Here they come now, the bloodhounds! Do your duty men, and I'll do mine!" or some similar expression. Several police officers claimed they heard something to that effect, but were not certain that Fielden uttered the cry. The witnesses for the prosecution did not concur on this point, for Captains Bonfield and Ward and three newspaper reporters all admitted that they failed to hear Fielden or anyone else give voice to such a threat. At the same time, Lieutenant Quinn and a number of others also heard Fielden remark, "We are peaceable." This is in itself contradictory because both expressions, according to police testimony, had to come at almost the same moment.

In addition, fifteen witnesses for the defense testified that Fielden did not cry out against the police. Yet the State, arguing that references to the police as bloodhounds were exceedingly common among radicals, insinuated that the remark attributed to Fielden implied preparation to meet the police with force.

Lieutenant Quinn also contended that Fielden, while descending from the wagon, fired a shot in the general direction of the head of the police column. This cannot be taken seriously, since the testimony pointed overwhelmingly to the fact that there was no firing before the bomb exploded. Nor does it appear from a careful examination of the evidence for the State alone that Fielden used a revolver during the Haymarket meeting. Several witnesses for the prosecution, admirably situated to observe Fielden, failed to see him fire, and those who supported Lieutenant Quinn were in frequent contradiction with his testimony and with one another's. Testimony for the defense, of course, cleared Fielden of this accusation. It appears that Fielden, like everybody else, made a headlong dash for safety immediately after the bomb exploded. But he did not escape without injury. While running toward the intersection of Randolph and Desplaines Streets, he was struck by a bullet above the knee. Fielden declared under oath that he not only did not fire a revolver, but that he never carried arms, and had never in his life used a gun against any person.

Related to this problem was the question whether the police or the crowd fired first after the bomb was thrown. The prosecution presented evidence to show that the bomb served as a signal for a concerted attack upon the police. Most of the officers called to the stand held that they were fired upon immediately after the bomb burst and before they had an opportunity to employ their revolvers.[42] Not all the policemen, however, offered testimony to support the contention that the bomb was the signal for a fusillade of pistol shots. Some did not know whether the police or members of the crowd employed revolvers first. This was the gist of Lieutenant Stanton's testimony, although he admitted that he himself fired immediately after the bomb exploded. Witnesses to the number of twenty-two swore that persons in the crowd did not open fire upon the police, but that the reverse occurred. An eye-witness to the entire meeting, testifying for the defense, declared that he revisited Haymarket Square the following morning and observed that the walls of the surrounding buildings were bullet-marked in a fashion which indicated that the police were responsible for most of the firing. The wall back of the space where the police had been aligned was untouched.[43]

There would be little need to deal with this point, had not the prosecution insisted that members of the crowd opened fire first. At a later date the State declared that the "fact" that this occurred was "almost conclusive evidence that the throwing of the bomb that night was the result of a conspiracy."[44] How a controverted "fact" can serve as conclusive evidence is not altogether clear.

VII. ALBERT R. PARSONS

Albert R. Parsons, like Fielden, was also totally unaware that a meeting had been arranged in the Haymarket for the night of the fourth.[45] He had been in Cincinnati from May 2 through to the morning of the fourth. When he returned to Chicago he inserted the announcement of the meeting of the American group in the *Daily News*. On the way to that meeting on the evening of the fourth, together with his wife, their two children and Lizzie Holmes, Parsons met two newspaper reporters. One of them, Mr. Owen, in testifying for the State, said:

"I saw Parsons at the corner of Halsted and Randolph Streets shortly before eight o'clock. I asked him where the [Haymarket] meeting was to be held; he said he didn't know anything about the meeting. I asked him whether he was going to speak. He said, no, he was going over to the South side. Mrs. Parsons and some children came up just then, and Parsons stopped an Indiana street car, slapped me familiarly on the back, and asked me if I was armed, and I said, 'No, have you any dynamite about you.' He laughed, and Mrs. Parsons said, 'He is a very dangerous looking man, isn't he?' and they got on the car and went east."

What happened after that—how Parsons left the meeting of the American group with Fielden at Rau's request, spoke at the Haymarket, and suggested an adjournment to Zepf's Hall when it started to rain—has already been described. During Fielden's address, Parsons went over to his wife, children and Mrs. Holmes who were seated in another wagon a few feet away from the one that was used as a rostrum, and left with them for Zepf's Hall. It was while he was there he heard the bomb explode. He thought at first that the noise was due to a Gatling gun used by the police, but he quickly discovered what had actually occurred. The thought of leaving the city must have flashed immediately into his mind, for within a few minutes he asked a comrade's advice on the problem, and borrowed five dollars from him.

This is all the evidence directly relating Parsons to the Haymarket meeting and to the bomb.

VIII. OSCAR NEEBE

Oscar Neebe, the last of the eight defendants, offers a puzzling case. Neebe was on trial for murder, yet, all the evidence presented by the prosecution to prove him guilty of that crime consists in: (1) he held stock to the value of two dollars in the organization which owned the *Arbeiter-Zeitung*; (2) on the evening of May 3, he was in Franz Heun's saloon, showed the latter the "Revenge Circular," conversed with him about the McCormick disturbance, and remarked, "It's a shame that the police act that way, but maybe the time comes when it gives the other way—that they [the workers] get a chance too;" (3) he was in the *Arbeiter-Zeitung* office in the absence of Spies and Schwab on May 5; (4) he was a member of the

I.W.P.A.; (5) when his home was searched without a warrant on May 7, a pistol, a sword, a breech-loading gun and a red flag were found.[46]

Were Neebe's plight free from tragic implications, the evidence submitted to show that he was a dangerous man and that society was safer with him behind prison walls would be thoroughly ridiculous. Even at that time Neebe's arrest and indictment caused amazement.[47] "It seems hardly credible," it was said shortly afterwards, "yet it is true that all the testimony against Neebe would not justify a five dollar fine." [48]

IX. WHY THE POLICE APPEARED

One question vital to the entire case has not yet been considered. Why did the police appear to disperse the meeting? The prosecution contended that the tenor of the meeting was such that the responsible police officer, Captain Bonfield, was certain it would terminate in a violent disturbance. So incendiary were the speeches, claimed the State, that they would have incited the crowd to mass violence had not the police interfered. In short, its consequences would have been even more tragic if it had not been dispersed.

In addition to Captain Bonfield, whose testimony was based on verbal reports of police officers detailed to the meeting, three newspaper reporters appearing as witnesses for the State swore that the meeting was "noisy" and "turbulent," and that the speeches were inflammatory in nature.[49] Of the latter, however, one testified that only about a quarter of those in attendance were in any way excited, while the rest of the auditors were largely indifferent. Another divided the members of the crowd into two groups, those hostile to the speakers and those even more enthusiastic than the speakers. This reporter averred that the crowd was in no way different in its demonstrations from that at any political gathering.

Two other witnesses for the State, both newspaper reporters, asserted that the crowd was very quiet. One, Mr. G. P. English, of the Chicago *Tribune*, described the gathering as "peaceable and quiet for an outdoor meeting. I didn't see any turbulence." It was his impression that the speeches, which were silent about employing force that night, were set addresses and were milder than usual. Mr. English had been instructed to make notes especially of the more violent portions of the speeches. At first he took them in his coat pocket to escape observation. During Spies' address, he explained, they became so confused that "I took another position in the face of the speaker, took out my paper, and reported openly during the rest of the meeting." [50]

Together with this there must be considered the defense testimony of Mayor Carter H. Harrison.[51] He had first arranged for police reserves at the Desplaines station to be kept in readiness to disperse the Haymarket gathering if it threatened to result in another McCormick riot. After making these preparations, he concluded that it would be better were he present to order its dispersal in person if it became necessary. He was at the meeting from its faltering inception until near the close of Parsons' address, except for the time he left to speak to Captain Bonfield at the police station.

"I did, in fact," he testified, "take no action at the meeting about dispersing it. There were occasional replies from the audience, as 'Shoot him,' 'Hang him,' or the like, but I don't think, from the directions in which they came, here and there and around, that there were more than two or three hundred actual sympathizers with the speakers. Several times cries of 'Hang him' would come from a boy in the outskirts, and the crowd would laugh. I felt that the majority of the crowd were idle spectators, and the replies nearly as much what might be called 'guying' as absolute applause. Some of the replies were evidently bitter; they came from immediately around the stand. The audience numbered from 800 to 1,000. The people in attendance, so far as I could see during the half hour before the speaking commenced, were apparently laborers or mechanics, and the majority of them not English-speaking people, mostly Germans. There was no suggestion made by either of the speakers looking toward calling for the immediate use of force or violence towards any person that night; if there had been, I should have dispersed them at once. After I came back from the station [i.e., when he reported to Bonfield at the station house] Parsons was still speaking, but evidently approaching a close. It was becoming cloudy and looked like threatening rain, and I thought the thing was about over. There was not one-fourth of the crowd that had been there during the evening, listening to the speakers at that time. In the crowd I heard a great many Germans use expressions of their being dissatisfied with bringing them there for this speaking. When I went to the station during Parsons' speech, I stated to Captain Bonfield that I thought the speeches were about over; that nothing had occurred yet, or looked likely to occur, to require interference, and that he had better issue orders to his reserves at the other stations to go home. Bonfield replied that he had reached the same conclusion from reports brought to him, but he thought it would be best to retain the men in the station until the meeting broke up, and then referred to a rumor that he had heard that night, which he thought would make it necessary for him to keep his men there, which I concurred in. During my attendance of the meeting I saw no weapons at all upon any person."

The gist of the rumor to which Captain Bonfield referred was that some or all the people at the meeting would go over to the Milwaukee and St. Paul freight houses, then filled with "scabs," and blow them up. The mayor had also been privately apprehensive that the Haymarket meeting was designed as a blind to mask a real attack on McCormick's.

Mayor Harrison left the meeting just as Parsons reached the conclusion of his peroration. Now the critical question is, did the character of the meeting change after his departure? The tenor of the evidence presented by the defense showed that there was no apparent change.[52] The change in weather materially reduced the size of the crowd, and those who remained appeared anxious to get away. What was regarded as the most incendiary portion of Fielden's speech had no appreciable effect upon his auditors, who were not perceptibly aroused when he urged them to "kill" and "stab" the law. The rain had thoroughly dampened their enthusiasm. Since Captain Bonfield asserted that he was continuously receiving information on the nature and progress of the meeting, he must have been fully cognizant of all this. It cannot be argued that the Captain, knowing that the crowd was in an ugly temper, decided that police were needed to prevent the destruction of life and property. Nor can it be argued that Fielden's excoriation of the law itself—a verbal attack upon an institution—was a threat of personal violence against officers of the law, warranting the dispersal of the gathering by force.

It is significant that the order to the police to "fall in" was given very suddenly. Not once did the police column halt until it stood before the wagon. The men in the front ranks, led by Captain Bonfield, set so rapid a pace that those who left the police station last had to travel almost at a double-quick to get into line. Lieutenant Stanton stated that the police "stepped off pretty lively. . . ." [53] Was Captain Bonfield eager to disperse a meeting dispersing of itself, near completion, and attended only by some three hundred unresponsive people? The evidence suggests that this question is correctly answered in the affirmative. In this connection the testimony of a Mr. Barton Simonson, who appeared for the defense, is illuminating. Mr. Simonson, absolutely unconnected with the defendants, swore that Captain Bonfield in conversation with him on the night of May 3, indicated that he would enjoy using force against a gathering of socialists or strikers. He recalled the police captain's words on the witness-stand: " 'The trouble there is that these'—whether he [Bonfield] used the word Socialists or strikers, I don't know—'get their women and children mixed up with them and around them and in front of them, and we can't get at them. I would like to get 3,000 of them in a crowd without their women and children'—and to the best of my recollection he added—'and I will make short work of them.' " [54]

If it is true that Captain Bonfield ordered the police to

disperse the meeting for reasons which were primarily personal, then upon his shoulders must rest part of the culpability for the Haymarket tragedy.

NOTES CHAPTER XIII

1. *Amer. St. Tr.*, vol. 12, pp. 24-46; for a short summary see *Anarchy at an End*, p. 6.
2. It has been claimed that Grinnell argued that the defendants were directly and *not* indirectly responsible for the bombing. (Frederick Trevor Hill, *Decisive Battles of the Law*, New York, 1907, p. 252.) It seems more accurate in view of his own statement to admit that he also made a point of their indirect relationship to the throwing of the bomb. *Amer. St. Tr.*, vol. 12, p. 34.
3. Author's italics.
4. The stenographic record of the court filled some 8,000 typewritten pages, between a million and a half and two million words.
5. For the "Monday night conspiracy" see *Abstract of Record*, vol. 2, pp. 3-9, 9-12, 24-25, 73-76; Lum, *op. cit.*, pp. 68-73; *Brief and Argument*, pp. 83-89; *Brief on the Facts for the State*, pp. 140-143, 162-176; Zeisler, *op. cit.*, pp. 13-14.
6. See above, p. 222.
7. At 54 West Lake Street.
8. Waller and Schrade differed on this point.
9. This is according to the testimony introduced by the State. Waller made this statement.
10. Lum, *op. cit.*, pp. 72-73.
11. That sketched in Grinnell's opening address for the State.
12. Balthazar Rau did this.
13. For the signal *Ruhe* in addition to the last citation see *Brief and Argument*, pp. 50-53; *Brief on the Facts for the State*, pp. 201-203; *Abstract of Record*, vol. 2, p. 306.
14. *The Chicago Martyrs; Their Speeches in Court. With a Preface and Extract of Record prepared for the Supreme Court of Illinois to which is added the Reasons for Pardoning Fielden, Neebe and Schwab, by John Altgeld, Governor of Illinois,* Glasgow (1893?), p. 101.
15. *Alarm*, December 3, 1887; Ramus, *op. cit.*, pp. 31-32.
16. It seemed to be generally agreed during the trial that Schnaubelt was not present at the Monday night meeting.
17. For Gilmer's testimony see, *Abstract of Record*, vol. 2, pp. 141-147; Lum, *op. cit.*, pp. 97-98; *Brief and Argument*, pp. 57-58; *Brief on the Facts for the State*, pp. 318-324.
18. He also testified that Spies was not on the wagon when the bomb was thrown, but that he stood on the street talking to Schwab.
19. The conversation took place in front of police headquarters.
20. W. A. S. Graham.

21. *Abstract of Record*, vol. 2, pp. 321-322; Lum, *op. cit.*, p. 142. For the following material in rebuttal of Gilmer's testimony see, *Abstract of Record*, vol. 2, pp. 176-182, 186-188, 188-190, 190-194, 209-215, 217-218, 233-235, 238-240, 240-243, 243-244, 261-264, 279-284, 292-294, 302-303 (this is not all in direct refutation; but among the pages given there are to be found the different versions of the episodes Gilmer described); Lum, *op. cit.*, pp. 133 *et seq.; Brief and Argument*, pp. 58-77.

22. *Abstract of Record*, vol. 2, pp. 324-337.

23. *Ibid.*, pp. 194-195, 195-196, 199-200, 200-201, 227, 250, 258, 259, 292; Lum, *op. cit.*, pp. 120-122.

24. This was told to the author by George Schilling and Clarence Darrow. But Mr. Darrow's memory was very uncertain on a number of important points, and the author became sceptical of the whole "confession." Mr. Schilling evidently had heard the story from another source. He did not claim, as Darrow did, that he was present when Gilmer made the admission. It is true that Gilmer was in a Chicago hospital at the time suffering from a broken leg.

25. For his testimony see, *Abstract of Record*, vol. 2, pp. 134-137; Lum, *op. cit.*, pp. 95-96; *Brief on the Facts for the State*, pp. 310-318; *Brief and Argument*, pp. 26-28.

26. Union Street runs north and south across the Square between Halsted and Desplaines Streets.

27. For this see, *Abstract of Record*, vol. 2, pp. 120-125, 129-134 *passim*, 186-190, 205-206, 215-217, 233-244 *passim*, 247-250, 261-275 *passim*, 286-296, 300-301, 315; *Brief and Argument*, pp. 27-39 *passim;* Lum, *op. cit.*, pp. 95-96, 117, 135-136.

28. Mr. Preusser.

29. Officer Cosgrave.

30. Testimony of Officer McKeough who, together with Officer Myers, followed Spies.

31. See below, p. 276.

32. See below, chap. XXIII.

33. For the pertinent evidence concerning Lingg, see, *Abstract of Record*, vol. 2, pp. 44-53, 73-76, 82-83, 276; *Brief on the Facts for the State*, pp. 143-145, 176-201; *Brief and Argument*, 99-104; Lum, *op. cit.*, pp. 79-80, 83-85.

34. Seliger's wife also received money for rent and living expenses from Captain Schaack.

35. It is questionable whether the accusing remark presumably made by Herman was ever addressed to Lingg. This bit of Seliger's testimony was flatly contradicted. Other sections of his testimony also suffered contradiction, but without seriously invalidating the general tenor of his evidence. Those contradictions have been accounted for in the summary on Lingg's activities. If it is granted that Herman did upbraid Lingg, it does not necessarily imply the existence of some definite connection between Lingg and the

Haymarket bomb. Herman might have meant that the bombing was the inevitable outcome of the activities pursued by Lingg.

36. *Abstract of Record*, vol. 2, pp. 166-168; *Brief on the Facts for the State*, pp. 233-240; Lum, *op. cit.*, pp. 100-101.

37. *Abstract of Record*, vol. 2, pp. 3-9 *passim*, 243-244; *Brief and Argument*, pp. 96-99; Lum, *op. cit.*, pp. 166-167.

38. See below, pp. 289 *et seq.*

39. *Abstract of Record*, vol. 2, pp. 26-30 *passim*, 39-40, 224-227, 238-240 *passim*, 247-248; Lum, *op. cit.*, pp. 86, 165-166; *Brief and Argument*, pp. 66-67.

40. It was said that the assistant foreman of the *Arbeiter-Zeitung* shop requested Fischer to take away the belt and revolver found on him when he was arrested, lest the foreman get into trouble if the premises were searched by the police.

41. *Abstract of Record*, vol. 2, pp. 1-3 *passim*, 12-20 *passim*, 22-23, 26, 36-38, 105-108 *passim*, 127-128, 129-134 *passim*, 176-182 *passim*, 190-194 *passim*, 196-198, 208-209, 215-217, 222-223, 235-240, 246-247, 261-264, 264-275, 313; Lum, *op. cit.*, pp. 73-77, 90, 95, 113, 118-122, 122-124, 126-127, 132-133; *Brief and Argument*, pp. 3-4, 10-11, 13-20 *passim*, 119-122; *Brief on the Facts for the State*, pp. 268-310. These citations cover all the points in the text up to the section on Parsons.

42. Captain Bonfield swore that seventy-five to one hundred shots came from the crowd before the police replied.

43. This witness, Dr. Taylor, was a member of the American group of the I.W.P.A.

44. *Brief on the Facts for the State*, p. 286.

45. *Abstract of Record*, vol. 2, pp. 105-108 *passim*, 116-119 *passim*, 124-127, 129-134 *passim*, 224-227, 227-229, 235-240 *passim*, 245-246, 261-264, 313-321; *Brief and Argument*, pp. 21-22, 24-25; Lum, *op. cit.*, pp. 92-93, 140-142. Mrs. Parsons also gave the author a vivid description of her husband's activities on the fourth which checks fully with all other accounts.

46. The evidence against him is best summarized in *In the Supreme Court of Illinois. The Anarchists' Cases. Brief for the Defendants*, Leonard Swett, Chicago, 1887; M. M. Trumbull, *The Trial of the Judgment*, Chicago, 1888, p. 11.

47. Zeisler, *op. cit.*, p. 19.

48. Trumbull, *The Trial of the Judgment*, p. 11.

49. *Abstract of Record*, vol. 2, pp. 1-3, 116-119, 120, 122-125; *Brief on the Facts for the State*, pp. 206-217.

50. *Abstract of Record*, vol. 2, pp. 105-108 *passim*, 129-134 *passim;* *Brief and Argument*, pp. 55-56, 114; Lum, *op. cit.*, p. 95.

51. *Abstract of Record*, vol. 2, pp. 174-176; *Brief and Argument*, pp. 114-116; Lum, *op. cit.*, pp. 111-112.

52. *Cf.*, *Abstract of Record*, vol. 2, pp. 186-188 (especially), 190-194 *passim*, 238-243 *passim*, 264-275 *passim*, 279-292 *passim*.

53. *Ibid.*, vol. 2, pp. 15-17; *Brief and Argument*, p. 117.

288 HISTORY OF THE HAYMARKET AFFAIR

54. *Abstract of Record,* vol. 2, pp. 176-182 *passim;* Lum, *op. cit.,* p. 114. Bonfield's alleged statement is paraphrased in Sarah E. Ames, *An Open Letter to Judge Joseph E. Gary, who in 1893, seeks to justify his participation (in 1887) in the lynching, under the hypocritical guise of the law, of men who entertained and expressed unpopular opinions,* Chicago, 1893, p. 8.

XIV. "GENTLEMEN OF THE JURY"

THE bulk of the evidence considered up to this point is related, in varying degrees, to the hypothesis that Schnaubelt was the bomb-thrower, that those on trial aided him to perpetrate the deed, and that the bomb was made by one of the defendants. In addition to this and other evidence already examined, the State introduced, over the objections of the defense, a mass of testimony drawn with admirable care from the public and private activities of all eight defendants during the three years prior to 1886. Their writings, speeches, associations, organizing activities, personal friendships, and correspondence were gone over with a fine comb to provide this material. Though not related directly to the bomb-throwing and the circumstances of the crime, it was skilfully employed by the prosecution, and its effect was greater than that of more pertinent evidence.

To justify the introduction of this testimony, it was necessary for the prosecution to fashion a new hypothesis for the bombing which left unconsidered the determination of the actual criminal agent. This hypothesis assumed that a "general conspiracy" existed in Cook County over a number of years which had a dual object: the overthrow of the existing social order, and the destruction of the "legal authorities of the State and county. . . ." Thoroughly organized and unmistakable in intent, this subversive conspiracy adopted force to accomplish its ends. Among the large number of persons whom it embraced were the defendants. The connection between the bomb and the conspiracy was, in the eyes of the prosecution, plain.

The bomb was thrown by a member of the conspiracy in pursuance of its object, and was thus "the opening-shot" in the inception of the social revolution. Since each defendant was an active participant in the conspiracy, it followed that each was responsible for its results. Therefore, concluded the prosecution, if the person who actually threw the bomb was instigated by the defendants acting in pursuance of the design of the conspiracy, the defendants were accessories to the deed. As accessories, they were equally guilty with the principal, whoever he might be.[1]

The development of this peculiarly broad hypothesis, which ignored the significant question of the actual bomb-thrower, was facilitated by two factors. One was the Illinois accessory statute which makes all the parties to a conspiracy confederates to one another and wipes out the distinctions between first and second degree principals and between principal and accessory.[2] The other lay in the "unsettled state" of the law of conspiracy itself. "The offense of conspiracy," it has been said, "is more difficult to be ascertained precisely than any other for which indictment lies; and is, indeed, rather to be considered as governed by positive decisions than by any consistent and intelligible principles of law."[3]

The prosecution encountered no difficulty in showing by an oppressive number of citations from the *Alarm,* the *Arbeiter-Zeitung,* the *Fackel* and the *Anarchist* what everyone already knew: that some of the defendants had constantly and openly expressed their unequivocal opposition to the existing social order; that all of them, regarding that order as evil, labored to replace it with a totally different social system; that all of the defendants had apparently accepted violence as the mechanism by which this change was to be made; and that most of them had publicly advocated the use of force, even encouraging violence against representatives of the present order. Furthermore, some of the defendants had been teaching how to manufacture and utilize certain instruments of destruction. They had thus furnished information on the preparation of dynamite and nitroglycerine, the manufacture of bombs, on the use of weapons in general, and on the general tactics of street fighting. The journals of the movement with which the defendants were affiliated made constant reference to the violent expropriation of property which would accompany the social revolution, and to the loss of life of defenders of the old order. The nature of the excerpts from the organs of the I.W.P.A. which the prosecution monotonously read into the record of the trial has been sufficiently illustrated by extracts given in a previous chapter and needs no further attention.[4]

In speeches made by some of the defendants, notably by Spies, Parsons and Fielden, the use of force had been encouraged, and dynamite bombs and various arms had been specifically mentioned. Frequently, the prosecution held, Spies, Parsons and Fielden had pointedly recommended the use of arms against the police. In 1885, for example, Spies urged the workers to rise in armed revolt, for force alone could destroy wage-slavery. On the Chicago Lake Front in 1885, Parsons advised his audience to arm, because only with force could the working-class defend itself against the violence of the police and other governmental agencies. On another occasion he was reported to have said that "The only way to convince these capitalists and robbers is to use the gun and dynamite." A week before the Haymarket meeting, Schwab declared, "Everywhere police and murderers are employed to grind down workingmen. For every workingman who has died through the pistol of a deputy sheriff, let ten of those executioners fall."[5]

With equal ease the prosecution showed that some of the defendants had been or still were active members of armed societies which indorsed the use of force. All of them were members of the International Working Peoples' Association, an organization dedicated to the extirpation of the existing social order through a violent social revolution. Their membership in the I.W.P.A. meant that they accepted its platform—

and the closing section of the Pittsburgh Manifesto was read to the jury.

One of the defendants, Lingg, engaged in the manufacture of bombs, and, asserted the prosecution, at least one other, Spies, had bombs and dynamite in his possession over a period of time. Testimony was adduced to show that Spies had declared in 1885 that the revolutionaries in Chicago had 9,000 dynamite bombs. The State also contended that most of those involved in the "general conspiracy" to destroy existing institutions were armed in one way or another. At least two of the defendants, Parsons and Engel, were shown to have made inquiries concerning the prices of revolvers and rifles purchased in large quantities, but they never bought the weapons.[6]

By reading into the record a letter and a post card found in the offices of the *Arbeiter-Zeitung,* the prosecution proved that Spies was in touch with Most, the high-priest of the revolutionary movement in America. The letter probably contained a disguised reference to dynamite, while the card was beyond question a thoroughly harmless message. In the eyes of the State, this correspondence between a "local" leader and the commanding general of the social revolution was additional confirmation of the existence of the far-reaching "general conspiracy."

Not only was the jury bombarded with a mass of newspaper extracts, but the prosecution also compelled it to listen to an English translation of Most's notorious *Science of Revolutionary Warfare,* the lengthy German title of which reads: *Revolutionäre Kriegswissenschaft. Ein Handbuchlein zur Einleitung betreffend Gebrauches und Herstellung von Nitroglycerin, Dynamit, Schieszbaumwolle, Knallquecksilber, Bomben, Brandsätzen, Pisten u. s. w., u. s. w.*[7] It was argued that since this vicious little volume was sold at gatherings and picnics of groups which accepted the doctrines of the defendants, the latter were in agreement with what it contained, and were engaged in its distribution. In point of fact, it was never shown that any of the defendants sold the pamphlet. Nor was there even proof that any of them had really read it through.

The last link in the new hypothetical chain forged by the State was the introduction of evidence to show that a specific date, May 1, 1886, had been set for the inauguration of the social revolution.[8] For proof, the prosecution presented the undenied fact that the defendants regarded the eight-hour struggle as vital, and encouraged the workers to arm in answer to police aggression. On this point, a resolution proposed by Spies at a meeting the previous October was read into the record. Since it was certain that employers would, in resisting the eight-hour day, utilize police, militia, and Pinkertons, asserted the resolution, "we urge upon all wage-workers the necessity of procuring arms before the inauguration of the proposed eight-hour strike in order to be in a position of meeting our foe with his own argument—force." On January 22, 1886, the *Arbeiter-Zeitung,* declared that the eight-hour day could be brought about only "with armed force. . . ." On the following day that journal concluded similar advice with the words: "Therefore, comrades, armed to the teeth, we want to demand our rights on the first of May. In the other case there are only blows of the club for you." May 1, frequently described as "the eventful day," "the decisive day," was generally expected to inaugurate, beyond the question of shorter hours, a general conflict between capital and labor. That the radicals capitalized the eight-hour issue there is no question, and that many of them hoped—perhaps with grave doubts— that it might be the first of a series of major struggles, may be believed. It is also true that after the first show of critical disinterest, they offered the eight-hour movement exciting encouragement as a leading editorial in the *Arbeiter-Zeitung* of May 1, illustrates:

"Bravely forward. The conflict has begun. . . . Workmen, let your watchword be: No compromise! Cowards to the rear! Men to the front. . . . The first of May is come. For twenty years the working people have been begging extortioners to introduce the eight-hour system. . . .

"That the laborers might energetically insist upon the eight-hour movement, never occurred to the employers. . . . Workmen, insist upon the eight-hour movement. . . . The extortioners are determined to bring their laborers back to servitude by starvation. It is a question whether the workmen will submit, or will impart to their would-be murderers an appreciation of modern views. We hope the latter."

Apart from this, there was not the slightest shred of evidence—and none has come to light since—to support the contention that the social revolution was "scheduled to begin" on May 1. Only an infantile mind could take the sentiments of the radicals with reference to the eight-hour issue and their utterances concerning the first of May as confirmatory evidence that the alleged "general conspiracy" to destroy the existing social order had established a precise day for the social revolution.

It can easily be imagined with what tenacity the defense objected to the introduction of all this testimony—the newspaper excerpts, the addresses of the defendants, Most's book, post-card and letter, etc. The object of the trial, argued the defense, was the determination of the defendants' guilt or innocence in the murder of Degan. The trial was not designed to prove that the accused ascribed to a given set of revolutionary doctrines. Since the bulk of this evidence was clearly unrelated to the question of Degan's death, it was irrelevant to the case and, therefore, inadmissible. To this the State replied that any testimony offering proof of the existence of a conspiracy or the connection of the accused with it was admissible. Therefore, evidence touching neither on the murder nor the defendants was relevant.

Despite this argument it still did not appear that there was any connection between the "general conspiracy" which the State outlined and the specific crime of murder for which the defendants were being tried. To introduce evidence to prove the existence of the "general conspiracy," and then *to assume* that the specific crime of murder was related to it, was to befog the issue. The court, however, accepted the argument of the prosecution, and held that evidence admissible. In ruling on the introduction of Most's booklet and the platform of the I.W.P.A., Judge Gary said:

"I have no doubt but what it is competent. The circumstances may be significant or not, depending on the surroundings; whether it is significant or not it is for the jury to determine. . . . Whether the defendants or any of them were intending to have a mob kill people, and were teaching them how to kill people, is a question which this jury is to find out from the evidence. And [the platform of the I.W.P.A. and Most's pamphlet] are admissible upon the investigation of that question." [9]

The effectiveness of this type of evidence became clear when the attorneys addressed their closing arguments to the jury. By the State it was employed to play upon the emotions and biases of the jurymen. The defense was compelled to expend much energy and time minimizing it. While testimony for the State was still being taken, the defense could only register its objections. It did submit, however, four very moderate extracts from the *Alarm,* two of which contained quotations from the writings of Mill and Victor Hugo.[10] It also demonstrated through the cross-examination of State witnesses that no secrecy attended any phase of the revolutionary movement in Chicago.[11]

On Tuesday, August 10, the submission of evidence came to an end. On the following day, counsel for State and defense began their closing arguments. Despite the length of the addresses—they were not completed until the nineteenth—and days of intense heat, the tiny courtroom was packed. For the first time during the trial, Judge Gary ordered the galleries of the court opened on the eighteenth. Eager throngs struggled for admission. The fortunate ones who jammed the courtroom were attentive and well behaved. A surprisingly large number of observers were women and during the afternoons they outnumbered the men four to one.[12]

In cold print, the closing addresses do not strike one as distinguished examples of courtroom oratory. Delivered, however, with the inevitable table-thumping, displays of passionate righteousness, and the other stock devices of the trial lawyer, they won the unflagging attention of the auditors.

Counsel for the State spared no pains to impress the jury with the magnitude of the case and the peculiar responsibility it imposed upon them. "Gentlemen of the jury:" declaimed Mr. Ingham, "There are verdicts which make history. Your verdict in this case will make history. It is of great importance —greater than any of us can begin to appreciate—that your verdict be right."[13] ". . . I think I exaggerate nothing," he continued, "when I say that never since the jury system was instituted . . . has there been elevated and placed upon the shoulders of any twelve men the responsibility that rests upon you today. For, if I appreciate this case correctly . . . the very question . . . is whether organized government shall perish from the face of the earth. . . ."[14]

In these words the *leitmotif* of the State's argument was announced. It was a theme that was endlessly embroidered. This was no mere trial for murder. It was a contest between absolutes of right and wrong—between the good of a well-ordered society and the evil of anarchy. Upon its outcome rested the fate of the United States. Mr. Walker declared at the close of his argument:

"You stand now, for the first time in this country, between anarchy and law, between the absolute overthrow of the present system of society and government, by force and dynamite, and constitutional law. . . . The foundation stone of the great edifice of justice has been attacked. Shall it stand erect? Gentlemen, that rests with you. The police have done their duty. . . . Let the jury have the same courage, the same spirit and the same fortitude under its responsibility. They (the police) can, indeed, rest in peace. The flowers of spring shall bloom upon their graves, moistened by the tears of a great city. Outraged and violated law shall be redeemed, and in their martyrdom anarchy shall be buried forever." [15]

Mr. Grinnell, too, vigorously hammered away at the same theme. He was convinced that "we are making history." [16] The United States passed through the fire of the Civil War, only to be faced with the threat of anarchy. "As I said," Mr. Grinnell declared, "there is only one step from republicanism to anarchy. Let us never take that step. And, gentlemen, the great responsibility which has developed upon you in this case is greater than any jury in the history of the world ever before undertook. . . . You are to say whether that step shall be taken." [17] His final words were awesome: "You stand between the living and the dead. You stand between law and violated law. Do your duty courageously, even if that duty is an unpleasant and a severe one." [18]

The jury was urged to put away all thought of leniency. It was not to withhold a verdict of guilty because it would bring death to the defendants. To acquit for fear of the consequences of a verdict of guilty was dangerous. "Such a verdict," warned Mr. Walker, "shocks the public and tends to a demoralization of the law." [19] Mr. Ingham uttered a similar warning, and urged the jury not to concern itself too much with "reasonable doubts." [20] Mr. Grinnell prophetically gave notice that an acquittal would permit the anarchist movement to regain its rudely shattered strength.[21] He pleaded with the jury not to disagree. "You have been importuned . . . to disagree. Don't do that; don't do that. . . ." [22]

From the arguments pursued by Mr. Grinnell and his associates it appears that the charge of murder was only incidental to the whole case. The defendants were faced with a far more weighty accusation. "Don't try, gentlemen, to shirk the issue," thundered the State's Attorney. "Anarchy is on trial; the defendants are on trial for treason and murder." [23]

Immediately there came a query from Capt. Black: "The indictment does not charge treason; does it, Mr. Grinnell?"

In summarizing the evidence in the case, counsel for the State skilfully played the spotlight upon those points which were most damaging, the "general conspiracy" hypothesis being given the greatest emphasis. It occupied the prosecution far more than any evidence which could be regarded as directly implicating the defendants in the murder of Officer Degan. Rudolph Schnaubelt was almost forgotten.

For years, the defendants had been planning the destruction of "law and order." Finally a bomb was thrown on the night of May 4, in furtherance of that conspiracy. "Yes," exclaimed Mr. Walker, "this bomb was thrown in furtherance of the social revolution—in furtherance of the plot to annihilate the police." [24] From this it followed that the accused were as guilty as the actual bomb-thrower, whoever he was. Once again the jury heard extracts from the revolutionary journals which "were full, from the very first number to the last, of revolutionary, inflammatory articles, declarations that the Anarchists would arm themselves, and threats to force their doctrines down the throats of American citizens, even if blood had to be spilled." [25] Could it be denied that a widespread conspiracy had been in existence for several years? Or that the common object of this conspiracy was the subversion of the government of Illinois and of the United States? Could there be any doubt that the bomb was thrown in furtherance of that common design? "If there were a common design," declared Mr. Walker with distressing logic, "it made no difference who threw the bomb. All the parties connected with the conspiracy were guilty, no matter who committed the deed." [26] At the cost of interrupting Mr. Walker's flow of eloquence, the question must be raised: "If there were a common design" to do what? Throw a bomb, kill a police officer, or overturn the social order? Furthermore, did Mr. Walker really mean that the defendants, as parties to a conspiracy, were guilty regardless of who threw the bomb? Were they not guilty only if a member of the conspiracy had committed the crime?

Chicago, said Mr. Walker, had come close to being the chosen spot where the "social revolution" would break, and whence it would spread throughout the land. Bonfield alone "stood in the way of the social revolution." He even discovered in Balthazar Rau its "Paul Revere." [27]

The prosecution tried to bolster the "general conspiracy" hypothesis by presenting a "special" conspiracy which flowed from it. Thus, the Monday night meeting, Lingg's bombs, and other facts adduced during the examination of witnesses were once more paraded before the jury *to prove the existence of a specific conspiracy embraced in the larger plot.* Furthermore, there was the Haymarket meeting, "an unlawful assembly," [28] convoked for the purpose of committing riot. Incendiary addresses had been made which warranted police interference, and which in themselves were sufficient to convict the speakers of a misdemeanor! [29]

Troublesome indeed was the question of the bomb-thrower. If the State placed any weight at all upon Gilmer's testimony then it was ridiculous to insist upon an "unknown" bomb-thrower at the same time. But the attorneys for the State held with equal fervor to his testimony and to the theory that the bomb-thrower was an unknown individual. Counsel for the State was outraged at the thought that the defense had attempted "to disqualify Harry Gilmer, the old soldier, and [that] they [had] asked the jury to discredit this man who had defended law and order under the American flag." [30]

"An attack was made upon Gilmer," thundered Mr. Ingham, "and witnesses were brought to asperse his character who were busy putting up their cent per cent shanties while he was baring his breast to the bullets of the enemies of the country . . ." [31] If Gilmer was unimpeachable and his story was to be taken at face value, as the prosecution insisted, [32] why did not a single one of the attorneys for the State flatly name Schnaubelt as the bomb-thrower? [33] Why the constant escape into the phrase "no matter who committed the deed?" Mr. Grinnell even dealt very gingerly with the veracity of Harry Gilmer. He mentioned Schnaubelt only very briefly in connection with the testimony of Gilmer and Thompson, and spoke of his disappearance. He said nothing more about him.[34]

Mr. Grinnell gave the problem of the actual bomb-thrower a great deal of attention. His reply to the argument offered by the defense, that a visible connection must be shown between the defendants and the bomb-thrower, was significant.

"We have not got to say to you that this man was actually seen throwing that bomb," he asserted, "and that he was part of the conspiracy; not at all. We have a right to say . . . that the circumstances of this case point to a man, whatever his name may be, or if it is unknown, and that these circumstances show to you that that man was a member of the conspiracy, then they are all guilty.

"We have not got the bomb-thrower here," he continued. "We have got the accessories, the conspirators, the individuals who framed the plan . . . , who advised and encouraged it, and if we never knew who did it, if there was not a syllable of proof in this case designating the name of a single representative who perpetrated that offense . . . still the defendants are guilty. We have been trying this case under the rulings of this court upon that hypothesis. If that is not so, then the gentlemen can take advantage of the numerous exceptions in the Supreme Court." [35]

In short, so thoroughly did the bomb fit in with the avowed doctrines and demonstrated activities of the accused, that no question remained of their original responsibility in the death of Policeman Degan. Thus, the problem of the bomb-thrower was merely incidental to the question of the existence of a plot to initiate the social revolution. It will be recalled, however, that Mr. Grinnell pointedly declared in his opening address to the jury that the State knew and would produce the bomb-thrower either by name or identification. This evidently plagued him, for in attempting to explain that earlier statement he admitted that an error had been made. ". . . I said in that opening that we would show that the man left the wagon, lighted the match and threw the bomb. That was not absolutely correct. I should have said that the man that came from the wagon . . . was in that group, assisted, and that the bomb was thrown by the man whom we would show to you." [36] If this was clarification, then the jury was having a neat trick played upon it.

Since this made no sense, it perhaps did no damage. Mr. Grinnell dealt his heaviest blows with his open appeal to the prejudices of the jury:

"The proof has been submitted," he declared; "everything has been done for the defense that could be done. Gentlemen, it is time in all conscience that you did have a judgment; and if you have now prejudice against the defendants under the law as the Court will give it to you, you have a right to it. Prejudice! Men, organized assassins, can preach murder in our own city for years; you deliberately hear the proof and then say that you have no prejudice!"

Capt. Black took exception to this description of his clients, but had to remain content with Judge Gary's "Very well, save the point upon it." [37] Even more inexcusable was a statement made very shortly afterwards by Mr. Grinnell: "We stand here, gentlemen, as I told you . . . , already with the verdict in our favor. I mean in favor of the prosecution as to the conduct of this case . . ." Capt. Black was immediately on his feet "to note an exception to that statement . . . that there has been given a verdict already in favor of the prosecution."

From the Court there curtly came, "Save the point upon it."

Capt. Black persisted: "It is an outrageous statement." [38]

Counsel for the State naturally urged the fullest penalty for all eight defendants. Yet, when Mr. Grinnell spoke of Oscar Neebe, he declared: "The testimony has been analyzed . . . in regard to his connection with the *Arbeiter-Zeitung* office, his connection with these people from time to time . . . and he circulated not two circulars but a lot of them. Gentlemen, I am not here to ask you to take the life of Oscar Neebe on this proof. I shall ask you to do nothing in this case that I feel I would not do myself were I seated in your chairs." [39] He then listed for the jury the varying degrees of guilt of the defendants. "Spies, Fischer, Lingg, Engel, Fielden, Parsons, Schwab, Neebe, in my opinion . . . is the order of punishment."

The attorneys for the prosecution were handsomely applauded by the daily press for their efforts, and Grinnell and Ingham were singled out for special praise. It was proposed that both be rewarded with higher offices. Counsel for the defense were treated less kindly. Mr. Zeisler's address put "the jury to sleep," and Mr. Foster's arguments were waved aside with the tag "sophistry." [40]

Mr. Foster charged the State with playing upon the prejudices of the jury and with introducing totally irrelevant material.[41] He bluntly accused the prosecution of deliberate manufacture of testimony.[42] He insisted that this was not a case that would "make history," establish the validity of Anarchism, or determine the existence of Socialism in the United States. The question at issue, he and his colleagues pointed out, was the guilt or innocence of the defendants in the death of Degan, even though the prosecution was trying them for their social and economic beliefs.[43] "The prosecution demand," Mr. Foster declared, "that the defendants should be convicted and strangled to death because they believe in the principles of Socialism and Anarchy." [44] And again, "If these men are to be tried on general principles for advocating doctrines opposed to our ideas of propriety, there is no use for me to argue the case. Let the sheriff go and erect the scaffold; . . . let us stop this farce now if the verdict and conviction is to be upon prejudice and general principles." [45]

All three men devoted considerable time to a thorough examination of the evidence. Two-thirds of Capt. Black's address was given over to this, and he naturally concluded that the evidence before the court demonstrated the innocence and not the guilt of the defendants. Furthermore, he insisted upon the necessity of proof which actually showed some connection between the criminal agent and the men on trial.[46] Mr. Zeisler also skilfully summarized the pertinent testimony. He asserted that no special conspiracy resulted from the Monday night meeting, that Spies was not responsible for the fracas at McCormick's, that the Haymarket meeting was both lawful and peaceable, and that Mr. Gilmer was, under no circumstances, to be believed.[47]

Mr. Foster covered much the same ground, but more caustically. He attacked Gilmer and Thompson, labelling the former a "most gigantic and colossal liar. . . ."[48] Of the Monday night conspiracy, he declared that "it was absurd to think that thirty or forty men hid away in a basement and passing resolutions, could strike at the foundations of government and social order. It reminds us of the three tailors of Tooley Street posing as 'We the people of England.' If these men had such an object in view, murder was not the offense they should be tried for; a jury should be impanelled to test their sanity."[49]

Counsel for the defense hammered away at the structure of conspiracy erected by the State. Mr. Zeisler opened the attack in his first words to the jury:

"Gentlemen:" he said, "It is not only necessary to establish that the defendants were parties to a conspiracy, but it is also necessary to show that somebody who was a party to that conspiracy had committed an act in pursuance of that conspiracy. Besides, it is essential that the State should identify the principal. . . . If the principal is not identified, then no one could be held as accessory. Upon this theory the case must stand or fall, and it was for this reason that the defense impeached the testimony of Harry L. Gilmer, as that testimony is vital for the case."[50]

To demonstrate how childish it was to assert that a conspiracy was on foot to inaugurate the "social revolution" on

May 1, he discussed the term.[51] A revolution, he said, cannot be made. It "is a thing which develops itself, but no single man, nor a dozen of men can control the inauguration of a revolution. The social revolution was fixed for the 1st of May! . . . The social revolution by which the present state of proprietary conditions should be changed all over the world, was to be inaugurated by Mr. Spies and by Mr. Parsons and Mr. Fielden on the first day of May! Has ever a ridiculous statement like that been made to an intelligent jury?" [52]

One of the characteristics of a conspiracy is secrecy. Yet, the principles and activities of the defendants, Zeisler reminded the jury, were well known to the authorities of Chicago for three years. Why were they never arrested and prosecuted for conspiracy? If they were not arrested because they did not commit an overt act, and the State's Attorney, therefore, had no reason to interfere, then, declared Mr. Zeisler, "there was no conspiracy." This was an erroneous argument—and Mr. Zeisler probably knew it—since "the conspiring together itself constitutes an overt act which may well furnish the basis of criminal liability." [53] In closing his argument, Zeisler pointed to the morass of inconsistencies into which the prosecution had fallen as a result of attempting to support two distinct conspiracy hypotheses.[54]

Mr. Foster reduced the whole question of conspiracy to a single problem. Did the defendants enter upon a conspiracy to commit murder on the night of May 4? Anything unconnected with the death of Degan had nothing to do with the case. If they were also involved in another conspiracy, to destroy existing institutions, they could be tried another time. At the moment they were on trial solely for the murder of Degan.[55] Capt. Black was emphatically clear on this point:

"The sole question before the jury," he said, "[is], who threw the bomb, for the doctrine of accessory before the fact, under which it was sought to hold defendants, was nothing but the application to the criminal law of the civil or common law doctrine that what a man does by another he does himself.

When the prosecution charged that the defendants threw it, their charge involved that the bomb was thrown by the procurement of these men, by their advice, direction, aid, counsel or encouragement, and that the man who threw it acted not only for himself, or upon his own responsibility, but as a result of the encouragement or procurement of these men. The State must show that the agent of the defendants did the deed, and it is not sufficient to show that the defendants favored such deeds." [56]

Precluded from appealing to their economic and social prejudices, counsel for the defense pleaded for the exercise of reasoned mercy by the "twelve good men." They urged the jury to put aside all bias in determining the fate of the defendants, and to think of the case solely as a trial for murder. The jurors were entreated to keep the following in mind to guide them in their deliberations: "What I would that others would do unto me, if I were situated in the place of these defendants, even that I am now ready to do unto them." [57]

The lengthy trial was almost over. It only remained for the court to charge the jury and for the jury to render its verdict.

The nature and effect of the instructions demanded, given and refused by Judge Gary are critically important.[58] There were six instructions requested by the State and granted by the court which the defense regarded as especially pernicious. More than one contemporary felt that through these instructions Judge Gary "greatly facilitated the conviction of the prisoners." [59]

Instruction four was based directly upon the prosecution's theory of conspiracy.

"The Court further instructs the jury," it reads, "as a matter of law, that if they believe from the evidence in this case, beyond a reasonable doubt, that the defendants, or any of them, conspired and agreed together, or with others, to overthrow the law by force, or to unlawfully resist the officers of the law, and if they further believe from the evidence, beyond a reasonable doubt, that in pursuance of such conspiracy, and in furtherance of the common object, a bomb was thrown by a member of such a conspiracy at the time, and that Mathias J. Degan was killed, then such of the defendants that the jury believe from the evidence, beyond a reasonable doubt, to have been parties to such conspiracy are guilty of murder, whether present at the killing or not, and whether the identity of the person throwing the bomb has been established or not." [60]

In non-legal language, this means that the court asserted that persons, not present when the crime was committed, can be held for murder, *though the actual criminal agent be unproduced and unidentified, on the ground of prior confederacy.* But how was the jury to believe that the bomb was thrown by a member of the conspiracy if the identity of the thrower was not established?

This instruction implied that the State had abandoned the hypothesis that Schnaubelt threw the bomb. Its assumption that accessoryship may be proven even though the identity of the bomb-thrower is not established and no causal or even casual relationship between bomb-thrower and accessories is indicated, was patently vicious. The question of how an unknown, unindividuated person may be shown "beyond a reasonable doubt," to be a member of the type of conspiracy here assumed makes fascinating speculation.

The defense also found the fifth instruction dangerous because it presumed an hypothesis which was entirely unsupported by any evidence before the court. This instruction reads:

"If the jury believe from the evidence beyond a reasonable doubt, that there was in existence in this county and State a conspiracy to overthrow the existing order of society, and to bring about social revolution by force, or to destroy the legal authorities . . . by force, and that the defendants, or any of them, were parties to such conspiracy, and that Degan was killed . . . by a bomb . . . thrown by a party to the conspiracy, and in furtherance of the objects of the conspiracy, then any of the defendants who were members of such conspiracy at that time are in this case guilty of murder, . . . although the jury may further believe from the evidence that the time and place for the bringing about of such revolution . . . had not been definitely agreed upon by the conspirators, but was left to them and the exigencies of time, or to the judgment of any of the co-conspirators." [61]

Yet it was the prosecution which introduced evidence to prove that the "social revolution" was planned for May 1, and made an effort to show that there actually was a careful plan in existence.

But this instruction caused the defense far less trouble than instruction five and one-half, characterized by the defense as thoroughly "vicious" and perhaps the most important instruction given for the people.

"If these defendants," it reads, "or any two or more of them, conspired together with or not with any person or persons to excite the people or classes of the people of this city to sedition, tumult, and riot . . . to take the lives of other persons, as a means to carry their designs and purposes into effect, and in pursuance of such conspiracy, and in furtherance of its objects, any of the persons so conspiring publicly, by print or speech, advised or encouraged the commission of murder without designating time, place or occasion at which it should be done, and in pursuance of, and induced by such advice or encouragement, murder was committed, then all of such conspirators are guilty of such murder, whether the person who perpetrated such murder can be identified or not. If such murder was committed in pursuance of such advice or encouragement, and was induced thereby, it does not matter what change, if any, in the order or condition of society, or what, if any, advantage to themselves or others, the conspirators proposed as the result of their conspiracy, nor does it matter whether such advice and encouragement had been frequent and long-continued or not, except in determining whether the perpetrator was or was not acting in pursuance of such advice and encouragement, and was or was not induced thereby to commit the murder. If there was such conspiracy as in this instruction is recited, such advice or encouragement was given, and murder committed in pursuance of and induced thereby, then all such conspirators are guilty of murder. Nor does it matter, if there was such a conspiracy, how impracticable or impossible of success its ends and aims were, nor how foolish or ill-managed were the plans for its execution, except as bearing upon the question whether there was or was not such conspiracy." [62]

This instruction even broadened the grounds on which the defendants could be held guilty as accessories. It assumes that general advice to the public to commit deeds of violence, without reference to the object or a particular crime, or the time, place or manner of the crime, makes for responsibility in its commission. According to this, if A, in an address to the public at large, urges the destruction of the Republican Party, and B murders the members of the National Committee of the party, then A is equally responsible in the crime even though it cannot be shown that B heard the speech, or was in any way influenced by it. In the light of such an instruction, the defense pointed out, Horace Greeley, Wendell Phillips and William Lloyd Garrison were equally guilty with John Brown in the crime at Harpers Ferry. If the instruction were followed very rigorously, it meant that the defendants could be held guilty of murder solely by virtue of being parties to a conspiracy designed to "excite" the people. The instruction paradoxically makes the defendants responsible as accessories to an act of an "unknown" who was not a member of their conspiracy, as accessories to an act which went beyond the common design of the conspiracy which was "the excitement of the people to crime" and not the commission of any act of violence.

Three instructions which the court gave on behalf of the people with reference to "reasonable doubt" provoked the charge that Judge Gary was working hand in hand with the prosecution. A thoroughly impartial judge, it was argued, would never grant instructions [63] so patently designed to minimize the possibility of acquittal on the ground of reasonable doubt. "A doubt, to justify an acquittal," Judge Gary informed the jury, "must be reasonable, and it must arise from a candid and impartial investigation of all the evidence in the case, and unless it is such that, were the same kind of doubt interposed in the graver transactions of life, it would cause a reasonable and prudent man to hesitate and pause, it is insufficient to authorize a verdict of not guilty. If, after considering all the evidence, you can say you have an abiding conviction of the truth of the charge, you are satisfied beyond a reasonable doubt." [64] This implies that a reasonable doubt may arise only from the evidence considered and not from a lack of evidence. In another instruction, the court limited even more, and unjustifiably, the conditions under which a doubt in a juror's mind would be "reasonable" and warrant an acquittal.

"The Court further instructs the jury," said Judge Gary, "as a matter of law, that the doubt which the juror is allowed to retain on his own mind, and under the influence of which he should frame a verdict of not guilty, must always be a reasonable one. A doubt produced by undue sensibility in the mind of any juror, in view of the consequences of his verdict is not a reasonable doubt, and a juror is not allowed to create sources or materials of doubt by resorting to trivial and fanciful suppositions and remote conjectures as to possible states of fact differing from that established by the evidence. You are not at liberty to disbelieve as jurors, if from the evidence you believe as men; your oath imposes upon you no obligation to doubt where no doubt would exist if no oath had been administered." [65]

The United States Supreme Court, however, has held that a "reasonable doubt" is an "actual doubt."

Perhaps no outcry concerning his impartiality or lack of it would have been raised had not Judge Gary already given cause for serious misgivings on that score during the trial.

When the jury was being selected his rulings, remarks, and demeanor all gave evidence of definite bias.

"I know, or the Court judicially," he observed, "what are the objects of communists, socialists and anarchists. . . . You must presume that I know, because it has been decided that for a man to say that he is prejudiced against horse thieves is no ground for imputing to him any misconduct as a juror. Now you must assume that I know either that anarchists, socialists and communists are a worthy, a praiseworthy class of people, having worthy objects, or else I cannot say that a prejudice against them is wrong." [66]

During the trial his rulings consistently favored the prosecution. He permitted liberties to counsel for the prosecution which should have been curtly checked. During the closing arguments he virtually gave Mr. Grinnell and his associates *carte blanche*. Those associated with the defense, therefore, saw in the instructions he granted to the State and those he refused to the defense additional indication of the hostility already displayed during the course of the trial. A contemporary, who later held a judgeship in Chicago, has since indicted Judge Gary for his behavior.

"From the first we were critical of Judge Gary," writes Samuel P. McConnell. "Neither Judge Rogers nor I liked his rulings nor [*sic*] his conduct. I never was in the courtroom during the trial when he did not have on the bench sitting with him, or near him, three to five women. He seemed to treat the affair as a Roman holiday. . . . One day my wife sat on the bench and Gary showed her a puzzle. When I heard this I was shocked at his levity, with eight men sitting there in dire peril of their lives, certain to die if he continued to rule every motion against them as he did. Judge Rogers agreed with me that Gary was making new law and ignoring every rule of law which was designed to assure a fair trial for a defendant on trial for his life." [67]

Also injurious to the defendants were the instructions which the court refused to give for the defense. These may be summarized as follows: (1) To convict a defendant of a crime as accessory, the evidence must prove that the criminal agent acted with the aid of the defendant. (2) Though one person may urge the commission of a certain criminal act, if that act is committed by someone else of his own volition, completely uninfluenced by the first party, the latter is not responsible. (3) If the jury believes that the bomb was not a direct consequence of the Monday night meeting and its objects, but was thrown by some person acting upon his own responsibility, the defendants are not guilty. (4) To convict the defendants, the jury must find, beyond a reasonable doubt, that they entered into an illegal conspiracy, that the Haymarket meeting, related to that conspiracy was an unlawful assembly, and that the bomb was thrown either by a member of the conspiracy or by some other person aided by the conspirators in furtherance of its design. (5) Unless the jury can find that the bomb was thrown by a member of the conspiracy whose object was the overthrow of the present government, or by someone outside of the conspiracy knowingly aided or advised by one or more of the defendants, the latter must be acquitted. (6) Only those defendants who, in the opinion of the jury, actually aided, abetted or advised the perpetration of the crime, whether present or not, should be convicted. (7) If the jury believes that the Haymarket gathering was legal, orderly, peaceable, and free from criminal purpose, that the police order to disperse was, therefore, unwarranted and illegal, and that when the order to disperse was given somebody for some highly personal motive, without the knowledge or aid of the defendants threw the bomb, then the verdict should be not guilty. (8) Under the laws of the State of Illinois, "no person can be legally convicted . . . on account of any opinion or principle entertained by him," and the doctrines of the defendants are not material to the case. (9) The evidence introduced against Neebe leaves "not guilty" as the only possible verdict.[68]

With the instructions read, the penultimate act of the tragedy of errors popularly called the "great anarchist trial" was over.

NOTES CHAPTER XIV

1. The hypothesis of a general conspiracy was intimated by the type of evidence introduced, but not until the closing addresses of the attorneys was it very carefully formulated. See below, pp. 296 *et seq*. It was well presented by the prosecution in the brief submitted when the case went to the State Supreme Court, *Brief on the Facts for the State*, pp. 1-3.
2. See above, p. 228.
3. Quoted in Francis B. Sayre, "Criminal Conspiracy," *Harvard Law Review*, vol. 35, no. 4, February, 1922, p. 393 note, see also, p. 405.
4. See above, chap. V. This published material is to be found in *Abstract of Record*, vol. 1, pp. 154-201; *Brief on the Facts for the State*, pp. 3-130 *passim*. Much of it was reproduced in the decision of the State Supreme Court.
5. *Abstract of Record*, vol. 2, pp. 20-21, 23-24, 54-58, 67-81 *passim*, 94-105 *passim*, *Brief on the Facts for the State*, pp. 3-130 *passim*.
6. *Abstract of Record*, vol. 2, pp. 54-58, 67-71; *Brief on the Facts for the State*, pp. 3-130 *passim;* Lum, *op. cit.*, pp. 82, 100.
7. Published in New York by the Internationale Zeitung Verein. For a condensed English version see *Abstract of Record*, vol. 1, pp. 142-154.
8. *Brief on the Facts for the State*, pp. 131-137.
9. Lum, *op. cit.*, p. 82.
10. *Abstract of Record*, vol. 1, pp. 201-204.
11. *Abstract of Record*, vol. 2, pp. 94-105 *passim*.
12. Chicago *Inter Ocean*, Chicago *Tribune*, August 12-20, 1886. Mr. Walker, who opened for the prosecution, was followed in turn by Mr. Zeisler, Mr. Ingham, Mr. Foster, Capt. Black and Mr. Grinnell.
13. *Am. St. Tr.*, vol. 12, p. 174; for Ingham's entire address, *ibid.*, pp. 174-197. The addresses can also be found in full in the issues of the Chicago *Inter Ocean* and Chicago *Tribune;* and newspaper summaries with verbatim quotations of varying length are in *Anarchy at an End:* Walker's argument, pp. 7-13, Zeisler's, pp. 13-18, Ingham's, pp. 18-30, Foster's, pp. 30-44, Black's, pp. 44-52, Grinnell's, pp. 52-64.
14. *Am. St. Tr.*, vol. 12, p. 175.
15. *Ibid.*, p. 165; for Walker's whole address, *ibid.*, pp. 154-165.
16. *Ibid.*, p. 239; for his entire argument, *ibid.*, pp. 238-260.
17. *Ibid.*, p. 241.
18. *Ibid.*, pp. 259-260.
19. *Ibid.*, p. 155.
20. *Ibid.*, pp. 176-178.

21. *Ibid.*, p. 248.
22. *Ibid.*, pp. 258-259.
23. *Ibid.*, p. 252.
24. *Ibid.*, p. 157.
25. *Ibid.*, p. 180.
26. *Ibid.*, p. 164.
27. *Ibid.*, pp. 161, 162.
28. *Ibid.*, p. 157.
29. *Ibid.*, p. 188.
30. *Ibid.*, pp. 158-159.
31. *Ibid.*, pp. 191-192.
32. *Ibid.*, p. 164.
33. *Ibid.*, pp. 164, 191-192, 257-258.
34. *Ibid.*, pp. 257-258.
35. *Ibid.*, pp. 244, 246.
36. *Ibid.*, pp. 251-252.
37. *Ibid.*, pp. 248-249.
38. *Ibid.*, p. 250.
39. *Ibid.*, p. 258.
40. Chicago *Inter Ocean* and Chicago *Tribune*, August 13 *ff.*, 1886.
41. *Am. St. Tr.*, vol. 12, pp. 198-199; for his whole address, *ibid.*, pp. 199-223.
42. *Ibid.*, p. 211.
43. *Ibid.*, pp. 206, 225-226.
44. *Ibid.*, p. 203.
45. *Ibid.*, p. 200.
46. *Ibid.*, pp. 226-236.
47. *Ibid.*, pp. 171, 173-174.
48. *Ibid.*, pp. 217-218.
49. *Ibid.*, p. 213.
50. *Ibid.*, pp. 165-166.
51. *Ibid.*, pp. 166-167.
52. *Ibid.*, p. 168.
53. Sayre, *loc. cit.*, p. 399.
54. *Am. St. Tr.*, vol. 12, pp. 170-171, 174.
55. *Ibid.*, pp. 201-202.
56. *Ibid.*, pp. 225-226.
57. *Ibid.*, p. 223; *cf.*, p. 238.
58. All the instructions both given and refused are to be found in *Abstract of Record*, vol. 1, for the defense, pp. 11-23, for the State, pp. 6-11; and in *Am. St. Tr.*, vol. 12, for the defense, pp. 268-282 *passim*, for the prosecution, pp. 261-268.
59. *Appleton's Annual Cyclopaedia*, 1886, p. 13; the writer of this comment was very pleased with the verdict.
60. *Am. St. Tr.*, vol. 12, p. 262.
61. *Ibid.*, p. 263.
62. *Ibid.*, p. 264.
63. Instructions twelve, thirteen, and thirteen and a half.

64. *Ibid.*, p. 267.
65. *Ibid.*, pp. 267-268.
66. *Brief and Argument*, p. 400.
67. McConnell, *loc. cit.*, p. 733.
68. *Am. St. Tr.*, vol. 12, pp. 271-275, 282.

XV. THE VERDICT

O N Thursday, the nineteenth, the fate of eight men was placed into the hands of the twelve jurors. With a phrase they could cause eight lives to be snuffed out.

As early as eight-thirty in the morning of the twentieth, more than a thousand people thronged the sidewalks in front of the Criminal Court Building. The entrance was blocked by a cordon of police. All police stations were carefully guarded, and police reserves were kept in readiness throughout the city. The police, it was later learned, had already been notified on Thursday night of the verdict, and these measures were taken in anticipation of an unfavorable reaction to it. Admission to the courtroom itself was limited to the immediate relatives of the defendants, reporters and a fortunate few who satisfied the scrutiny of the police. The presence of Mrs. Schwab, Mrs. Parsons, Spies' mother and sister and other female relatives of the prisoners served to inject another dark note into the impending tragedy.

Every juror's face was solemn and determined as he passed into the building. Capt. Black appeared in court at nine-thirty, shocked by the rapidity with which the jury had reached a verdict. Already he had consulted with the defendants, and prepared them for the worst. His sensitive countenance was paler than usual when reporters questioned him. ". . . they stand it like heroes—they are prepared to laugh at death," he said.

Within a few moments the prisoners were brought in and seated. They were guarded with extreme care, and members of the squad of forty-eight policemen within the court permitted none of the spectators to approach too closely.

Now the jury was filing in. The defendants, sharply on edge, kept their seats with difficulty. Only Schwab, Engel and Parsons were able to simulate calmness. The faces of all eight were drained of color. Their bloodshot eyes were intent upon the jurors. They seemed to know what the verdict was. The solemn suspense of the moment was like a sharp pain. Then, almost on the stroke of ten, there came the anticipated verdict.[1]

"We the jury find the defendants, Adolph Spies, Michael Schwab, Samuel Fielden, Albert R. Parsons, Adolph Fischer, George Engel, and Louis Lingg guilty of murder in the manner and form as charged in the indictment, and fix the penalty at death. We find the defendant Oscar E. Neebe guilty of murder in the manner and form as charged in the indictment, and fix the penalty at imprisonment in the penitentiary for fifteen years." [2]

Within the courtroom a brittle silence quickly shattered by an excited current of staccato discussion, but exceptional order. Outside—where the news had been instantly transmitted—jubilation and three rousing cheers for the jury which had performed its duty so nobly.[3]

Immediately after the verdict was read the prisoners were led back to jail. It had been a soul-shaking morning. Fielden could not walk without support. Schwab almost tottered. Lingg and Engel, walking with firm tread, gave no outward sign of strain. Spies and Fischer, ghostly pale, seemed carried along by an inner strength. Parsons' staunch erectness radiated defiance. Neebe, for the moment, was a broken man. For him the blow was a crushing one. When asked the previous night, "What will you take right now as a compromise sentence?" he stoutly replied, "Not one hour." [4]

There was good reason for Neebe's optimism. The prosecution really had no case against him. Even Mr. Grinnell indicated that his guilt was less than that of the others. There is good reason to believe that the State came close to giving up the case against him. Mayor Harrison later wrote:

"I was present in the courtroom when the State closed its case. The attorney for Neebe moved his discharge on the ground that there was no evidence to hold him on. The State's attorney, Mr. Julius S. Grinnell, and Mr. Fred S. Winston, corporation counsel for the city, and myself were in earnest conversation when the motion was made. Mr. Grinnell stated to us that he did not think there was sufficient testimony to convict Neebe. I thereupon earnestly advised him, as a representative of the State, to dismiss the case as to Neebe and if I remember rightly, he was seriously thinking of doing so, but on consultation with his assistants and on their advice he determined not to do so lest it would have an injurious effect on the case as against the other prisoners." [5]

Mr. Winston, supporting Carter Harrison's statements, added, "I never believed there was enough evidence to convict Mr. Neebe, and so stated during the trial." [6] It would be unfair to stamp Mr. Grinnell as a prosecutor willing to sacrifice Neebe to the questionable mercy of a biased jury to secure the conviction of the other defendants, without noting that in a letter to Gov. Fifer in 1890 he bluntly denied Mayor Harrison's version of the episode. Insisting upon his own sincere belief in Neebe's guilt, he asserted that he thought that the "jury might not think the testimony presented in the case sufficient to convict Neebe, but that it was in their province to pass on it." [7] Mayor Harrison's statement, however, was confirmed by Mr. Winston. Mr. Grinnell could not very well admit its accuracy without indicting himself.

How long did it take the jury to pass sentence of death upon seven men and place another behind bars for fifteen years? Despite the seriousness of the verdict, the length and complexity of the trial, the mass of evidence which needed sifting, and some very moot points of law, only three hours were spent in deliberation. And perhaps more than two-thirds of this time was consumed in discussing the fate of Neebe. [8]

The jury's verdict was both swift and popular. What wonder, then, that it was cheered, and that proposals multiplied for rewarding the jurors for their services with cold cash? Before the verdict was given suggestions were made through letters to the Chicago *Tribune* to raise a fund, ranging from $10,000 to $100,000 in which each of the twelve men was to share equally. The *Tribune* made the same generous gesture editorially. There is no evidence, however, that these proposals ever bore fruit.[9]

Interviewed after the verdict, one of the jurors, Mr. Todd, said that he and his fellows had already come to a decision before they heard the closing arguments. Another juror made it clear that the arguments of defense counsel had had no effect upon them. "We had made up our minds," he declared, "if Waller's testimony was corroborated by independent testimony to convict every one of the prisoners." He also observed that Juror Brayton "was the most forcible advocate of the verdict rendered. He noted the evidence from day to day . . . Juror Reed remarked to him that he appeared to have a brief in the case." [10]

Prepared as they were for the verdict, all four attorneys for the defense were visibly affected.[11] They had hoped against hope for the acquittal of at least some of the defendants. Later in the day Capt. Black expressed their reactions to the verdict:

"I was never so shocked in all my experience as I was this morning. I should not have been more horrified had I myself received the death sentence. I had expected a conviction, of course. But seven men convicted to hang! We did not expect an acquittal from a jury so prejudiced, but such a verdict as this destroys a good deal of my faith in human nature. Mr. Grinnell had in his closing argument placed the defendants in the order in which he considered them guilty, beginning with Spies and ending with Neebe, and any ordinary jury would have seen from that that he did not expect a conviction in all cases." [12]

Upset as he was, Black gave little indication of emotion when he formally moved, immediately after the verdict, for a new trial. He conferred briefly with Mr. Grinnell and the court, and it was agreed to argue the motion during the September term.

The cheers from the crowd in front of the court-house on the morning of the twentieth represented the intense satisfaction which swept Chicago when news of the verdict spread.[13] Judge Gary had good reason to recall that "The verdict was received by the friends of social order . . . with a roar of almost universal approval." [14] The business men of Chicago made no effort to hide their joy. One of them movingly announced, "I was nervous lest the jury should not hang them all. I regard it as a just and righteous verdict." [15]

Chicago was happy. Gone was the nervous tension, the psychopathic fear of a few months ago. The anarchist menace had been laid low by the virtuous arm of justice. Law and order had triumphed over evil and anarchy. "[The] Anarchists Must Go!" shouted the headlines. "Seven of the Indicted Found Guilty of Murder and Worthy of Death. . . . Chicago, the Nation and the Civilized World Rejoice. . . ." [16] With joy they screamed: "The Scaffold Waits—Seven Dangling Nooses for the Dynamite Fiends. . . ." [17]

"The long strain of suspense and anxiety is over," observed the *Inter Ocean*. "Not since the [beginning of the] century has there been any trial . . . in this or any other country the verdict of which has been awaited with such profound interest. . . .

"Anarchism has been on trial ever since May 4; and it has now got its verdict. . . . The verdict . . . is unquestionably the voice of justice, the solemn verdict of the world's best civilization. . . .

"Another of the important results of the trial is the plainness with which it now comes to be understood that such isms as anarchism . . . are of the nature of treason, and that, in order to secure the public safety, it is necessary that those who seek to propagate them be treated accordingly and summarily." [18]

This thought was repeated the following day by the *Inter Ocean.* "Anarchism is treason and when any undertake to substitute it in place of law, it becomes a crime of the deepest dye. Death is the only fitting penalty." Anarchism was now doomed in this country, asserted the *Inter Ocean.*

The Chicago *Times,* editorially reviewing the case, declared that the defendants had "been fairly prosecuted and ably defended under the processes of the law which they would have throttled, and twelve good and true men have doomed them all save one to death. Instead of throttling the law, the law has, as Fielden predicted, 'throttled' them." [19] The Chicago *Tribune* felt that the

"universal satisfaction with which the verdict of the jury was received was based upon this very point—namely: that the law had been vindicated and had shown itself amply able to cope with Anarchism and strangle it. Every law-abiding person breathed more freely and felt more secure when it was decided that the official executors of the law could be protected and its penalties could be enforced. The verdict of the jury was tantamount to a declaration that American law is powerful enough to protect society against the conspiracies of organized foreign assassins and to insure the blessings of a good and free government to all classes of people. It was a notice to the Anarchistic organizations that their conspiracies for unlawful violence, for murder and destruction of property, and for assaults upon the authority of law and government must and will be put down. . . .

"The bearings of this verdict," continued the *Tribune,* "however, extend far beyond local limits. It has killed Anarchism in Chicago, and those who sympathize with its horrible doctrines will speedily emigrate from her borders or at least never again make a sign of their sentiments. It goes still further than this. It is a warning to the whole brood of vipers in the Old World—to the Communists . . . , the Socialists . . . , the Anarchists . . . , the Nihilists . . . , — that they cannot come to this country and abuse its hospitality and its right of free speech . . . without encountering the stern decrees of American law. The verdict of the Chicago jury will, therefore, check the emigration of organized assassins in this country." [20].

The *Tribune* saw only one cause for regret. The "murderous, communistic conspirators who sought to throttle the constitution and laws," still possessed the right to appeal their case.[21]

Every Chicago newspaper testified that the convicted men had been treated with magnanimous fairness, and that "the prisoners . . . had the very best protection the law could afford them." [22]

From the New York press there came the same applause. "All honor to Chicago for her example!" exclaimed the New York *Sun*. "She deserves the thanks and the gratitude of every community in the country and she has them in the fullest measure." [23] "Let the great Western community be congratulated upon the wholesome example she has set," echoed the Brooklyn *Eagle*. "The precedent will be faithfully observed." [24] The entire country rejoiced over the outcome of the trial: ". . . the people that fought each other four years . . . in order to settle conflicting ideas as to the best way in which to perpetuate our institutions, are back of these Chicago verdicts—in Chicago, in New York, in Boston, in New Orleans, and everywhere else." [25]

The New York *Commercial Advertiser,* having expressed its gratitude to the jury, advised that "Now the duty of the municipal authorities of Chicago should be . . . to guard against any anarchist outbreak . . . [or, in the event that it occurred,] to punish such an outbreak so severely that the last remnant of anarchy will be forever quieted." [26] Worried by current rumors to the effect that if the sentence were carried out the revolutionaries in Chicago would retaliate, the New York *World* declared that "Society cannot afford to let these men escape." Were five thousand rather than seven men involved, the verdict would have to be carried out. "It would be mistaken mercy to swerve a hair's breadth from the decree of the court. The louder the threats of vengeance, the more certain should be the doom." [27]

In *Harper's Weekly*, Nast's pen translated editorial comments into merciless illustrations. The "Union" crushed struggling anarchists in a powerful fist over the caption, "Liberty is not Anarchy." Another cartoon showed seven nooses dangling from a stark scaffold labelled "The Law." The caption reads: "Equal to the Anarchists. They will have all the rope they want, and more, too." [28]

From the South there came an altogether priceless editorial.

"All the chapters in that dramatic and horrible Haymarket tragedy have been written save one," said the New Orleans *Times-Democrat;* "all the acts finished but the last. It was a drama attended by saturnalian lights and scenes. Act I, represented the conspirators gathered in the ill-lighted gloom of their secret halls . . . among heaps of deadly bombs. Act II showed a wild mob turned loose on the streets, with murder in their flaming eyes, and the terrible weapons of assassins in their hands . . . Act III represents Justice standing as a Nemesis before a group of cowering criminals . . . When the curtain rolls up again with a nation as spectators, to show the final tableau in Act IV, it will disclose a row of gibbetted felons, with haltered throats and fettered hands and feet, swinging slowly to and fro, in the air; then it will be rung down again, and the people will breathe freer, feeling that anarchism, nihilism, socialism, communism are forever dead in America!" [29]

Less dramatic was the comment of the Birmingham, Alabama, *Age:* "The result at Chicago is cheering. The law is equal to the preservation of order." [30] The Augusta, Georgia, *Chronicle* succinctly advised: "Let the Chicago anarchists hang, decently, speedily and in order." [31] The feeling of safety and security which the conviction created was touched upon by the Louisville *Courier-Journal.* "The safety of every home, the well-being of every family, the very existence of social order were involved in these trials, and now . . . there is everywhere a feeling of greater security." [32] Rarely was it admitted that the "fate" of the "anarchists" was "a hard one." [33] On the contrary, "the severe punishment of these anarchists" was a "healthful and refreshing tonic" for "the people of this country, excited already too long by fears of murderous outbreaks." [34]

Not a daily newspaper of standing in the entire country had a word to say in criticism of the conduct of the trial or the verdict. "We do not believe that there was ever, with the single exception of President Garfield's murderer," said the St. Paul *Press,* "a verdict that was received by the millions with such sincere approval." [35] Much of the approbation which greeted the verdict can be traced to the conviction—sometimes the hope—that it meant the death of Anarchism and its associate evils. It was prophetically announced that the "same scaffold that bears" the "dangling forms" of the anarchists, "will also hold the dead body of Anarchism in America." [36] The same thought was differently expressed by the Pittsburgh *Commercial Gazette.* "If the hanging of the seven wretched men who have been condemned will rid the country of pestilent anarchists, or hold them in wholesome dread of the law, their lives will not have been wholly wasted." [37]

In agreement with the daily press, the weekly *Nation* expressed keen pleasure at the outcome of the trial, and urged that anarchists be sternly suppressed at all times. For reasons not readily apparent, the *Nation* asserted that there had been such active agitation and pressure brought to bear in favor of the men, that only the sturdy righteousness of the jury had prevented a miscarriage of justice! [38]

However unanimous the chorus of approval, dissenting voices could be heard. The *Arbeiter-Zeitung* attacked the verdict without compunction and charged the jury with prejudice. [39] The New York *Volks-Zeitung* was equally incensed. Another small German paper also ventured to criticize the verdict as "judicial murder." [40] The attitude now taken by labor periodicals indicates that a major shift in sentiment had occurred in labor ranks. The *Labor Leaf,* sympathetic to the defendants from the time of their arrest, assailed both the trial and the verdict as legal outrages. Holding the police responsible for the entire affair, it declared that the eight men were railroaded.

"That someone threw a bomb is certain;" said the *Labor Leaf,* "that it killed and wounded a large number of police is also certain; that the police were there without just cause, and for the express purpose of attacking the crowd, is certain; but that the eight men now under sentence had done a single act which justified their arrest and conviction has not been proven by any evidence yet produced.

"In this sense the verdict is an outrage." [41] Equally outspoken was the *Workmen's Advocate,* a journal of much larger circulation.

"Look at the case in the light of Truth and Reason:" it urged, "200 policemen raid a peaceable company which had gathered to exercise the right of free assembly and free speech; these policemen are treated to the contents of a bomb thrown by an unknown personage, as likely as not a Pinkerton 'detective'; thereupon begins a reign of terror for the Anarchists; no man or woman whose honest convictions have tended toward Anarchy, and who has expressed those convictions, is safe from arrest. . . . So the play goes on, until the curtain rises upon a new scene—the 'trial.' The prosecution puts upon the stand every professional perjurer in Chicago, with the exception of a few 'journalists'—God save the mark!—who are encouraged to do their share of the lying in making reports of the case; [in] spite of all this, it is proven that none of the defendants had any hand in the bomb-throwing; that Parsons, Schwab and Fischer were nowhere near the police at the time . . . and that not a shot was fired except by the police themselves! And the conclusion of the whole matter is that—not for breaking any law, but—for daring to denounce the usurpations of the robber rulers of our Satanic society, these Anarchists must die!" [42]

Two small journals of labor or liberal affiliation, the *Anti-Monopolist* and the *Cloud County Critic*, were sympathetic to the eight men. The former suggested that the witnesses for the State had been given cash for their services, and the latter suggested that the bomb might have been thrown by an *agent provocateur* with results more serious than had been intended.[43]

Other signs indicate the drift in labor opinion since the opening of the trial. At the General Assembly of the Knights of Labor held in Richmond in October, 1886, a resolution framed by Victor Drury was offered by James E. Quinn of New York to the effect that the gathering regarded with deep sorrow "the intended execution of seven workingmen in Chicago," and pleaded "for mercy in behalf of the condemned." The conservatives in the Order were solidly opposed to it. General Master Workman Powderly, who was presiding, left the chair, and fought against the resolution as it stood tooth and nail. He pointed out that the condemned were not workers, that their act was imbecilic, that the resolution identified the Knights with anarchists, and, finally, that labor owed the anarchists not sympathy but "a debt of hatred for the unwarrantable interference at a time when labor had all it could do to weather the storm. . . ." The General Assembly ultimately did adopt the following resolution almost unanimously:

"*Resolved,* That while asking for mercy for the condemned men, we are not in sympathy with the acts of the anarchists, nor with any attempts of individuals or associated bodies that teach or practise violent infractions of the law, believing that peaceful methods are the surest and best means to secure necessary reforms." [44]

During the following month, Local Assembly 1,307 of the K. of L. published an open letter in protest against the death sentence of Parsons, a Knight, in which the trial was described as "a travesty on justice" and the verdict an outrage.[45]

Labor, however, had not yet solidly aligned itself behind the condemned men. According to William Holmes most of the trade-unions in Chicago either openly indorsed the verdict or refused to condemn it, although many workers objected to the punishment as too severe. The unions probably feared that a public expression of sympathy would do them harm. For some puzzling reason "few people, *and no Socialists* [in Chicago], believe the verdict will be carried out. There is a surprising unanimity of opinion that in some way the terrible fate which menaces these men will be averted." Few of the prisoners, however, shared this optimism.[46]

Judging by the daily press, it appears that most Americans had been living in mortal fear of anarchists, communists and socialists. If this were true, it would explain the robust applause which greeted the announcement of the verdict. Thus it struck Judge Gary, who later wrote that "from this fear" of the radical "sprung approval of anything which tended to the extirpation of the anarchists." [47] Yet, one cannot readily believe that an overwhelmingly large number of Americans were convinced that their entire social and economic fabric was in real danger of destruction, or, more specifically, that a plot had been fomented to overthrow their government.

It is much more likely that while the public at large was immediately antagonistic to a handful of revolutionaries whose beliefs it assumed to be represented by the eight men on trial, it was not moved by any conscious fear of the radicals. Bankers, business men, manufacturers, property owners, small tradesmen, and the like perhaps really quaked at the bogey of revolution. When the anarchist spoke about the evils of the present order, he pointed to the rich man as an example. When the communist asked for the equal division of wealth, it was the man of property whom he assailed. When the socialist proposed to socialize all industry, it was the railroad magnate and the coal baron whom he would expropriate. Capitalists and bourgeoisie might well have felt that when the right of private property was denied, and the entire existing economic system was questioned, they were being attacked as individuals.

When the newspapers portrayed the American people trembling in dread of the horrors of the "social revolution," it was the apprehension, perhaps even the panic, of these groups that was expressed. And since the thought of the "man on the street" was conditioned by the press, his reactions to the "raw and bloody bones" of revolution were generally indistinguishable from those of his wealthier fellow-citizens.

NOTES CHAPTER XV

1. This descriptive material is drawn from the Chicago daily papers for August 21, especially the Chicago *Tribune* and Chicago *Inter Ocean*.
2. This can also be found in Gary, *loc. cit.*, p. 807.
3. It is related in Aveling, *op. cit.*, pp. 123-124, that "unimpeachable witnesses" declared that after the verdict Judge Gary "went out to his wife, who was waiting for the result, and said: 'All is well, mother. Seven to be hanged, and one fifteen years. All is well.'" There is no other evidence that Judge Gary actually said this.
4. Chicago *Tribune*, August 21, 1886. Whether Bailiff Selden asked this question out of curiosity or as an official attempt at reaching a compromise sentence, does not appear.
5. Quoted in Altgeld, *Pardon Message*, p. 27.
6. *Idem.*
7. *Idem.*
8. *Labor Leaf*, September 1, 1886.
9. Chicago *Tribune*, *August* 18-21, 1886; *John Swinton's Paper*, September 12, 1886; *Life of Albert R. Parsons*, pp. 200-201 note.
10. Chicago *Tribune*, August 21, 1886.
11. Chicago *Inter Ocean*, August 21, 1886.
12. Chicago *Tribune*, August 21, 1886.
13. *Appleton's Annual Cyclopaedia, 1886*, p. 15.
14. Gary, *loc. cit.*, p. 87.
15. Chicago *Tribune*, August 21, 1886.
16. Chicago *Inter Ocean*, August 21, 1886.
17. Chicago *Tribune*, August 21, 1886.
18. August 21, 1886.
19. August 21, 1886.
20. August 21, 1886.
21. *Ibid.*, August 22, 1886.
22. Chicago *Mail*, August 21, 1886. See also the long editorial in the *Inter Ocean*, August 20 on this theme, and the Chicago *News*, August 21, 1886.
23. August 21, 1886.
24. August 21, 1886.
25. *Idem.*
26. August 21, 1886.
27. August 24, 1886.

28. September 4, 1886, pp. 564, 571; for editorial, p. 562.
29. New Orleans *Times-Democrat*, August 21, 1886, quoted in *Public Opinion*, vol. 1, no. 20, August 28, 1886, p. 381.
30. August 21, 1886, quoted in *ibid.*, p. 382.
31. August 21, 1886, quoted in *ibid.*, p. 384.
32. August 21, 1886, quoted in *ibid.*, p. 383.
33. Memphis *Appeal*, August 21, 1886, quoted in *ibid.*, p. 384.
34. Richmond *State Democrat*, August 21, 1886, quoted in *ibid.*, p. 383.
35. August 21, 1886, quoted in *ibid.*, p. 382.
36. Albany *Journal*, August 21, 1886, quoted in *ibid.*, p. 383.
37. August 21, 1886, quoted in *ibid.*, p. 383.
38. Vol. 43, no. 1,104, August 26, 1886, p. 167.
39. See the issues at the time of and after the verdict.
40. Oregon *Staats-Zeitung*, cited in *Arbeiter-Zeitung*, November 1, 1886.
41. August 20, 1886.
42. August 29, 1886.
43. Cited in *Labor Leaf*, September 15, 1886.
44. Powderly, *op. cit.*, pp. 544-545; *Free Society*, November 6, 1898 (T. P. Quinn, "Some Recollections"), pp. 7-8.
45. Date of the letter, November 17, 1886; cited in *Commonweal*, December 4, 1886, p. 287.
46. *Ibid.*, October 2, 1886, p. 211. Holmes' assertion is supported by a statement of one of the leaders of the Cleveland radicals, Chris Saam. He did not think that the men would hang, but, should the sentence be carried out, he was certain that the seven doomed men would be considered martyrs to the "cause," and Anarchism would receive a new impetus. Chicago *Tribune*, August 23, 1886.
47. Gary, *loc. cit.*, p. 87.

XVI. THE ACCUSED THE ACCUSERS

O N October 1, the defense began to argue its hopeless
motion for a new trial before Judge Gary. A new
trial was requested on the ground that the jury was
not impartial; that the convicted men had not been proven
guilty of murder; that there had been no conspiracy in existence to commit the bombing in the Haymarket; that those
who had preached violence had done so only in answer to the
illegal use of force against workingmen; and, finally, that the
prosecuting attorney was guilty of serious improprieties. On
the seventh, Judge Gary denied the motion.[1] He declared that
the newspaper writings and the speeches of the condemned
men "furnish an answer to the argument . . . that what they
proposed was they should . . . arm . . . to resist any unlawful attacks which the militia or the police might make upon
them." Since 1884, he said, the anarchists had been conspiring
to overthrow the existing social order and the government.
The eight-hour issue had been utilized as a means to that end.
It was immaterial, said the court, whether any of the defendants anticipated or expected the bomb-throwing. To set aside
the verdict, Judge Gary warned, would lead to the introduction
of anarchy.

Capt. Black immediately took exception to the court's
ruling. He requested that the verdict be delayed until a bill of
exceptions could be prepared and presented. For this, some
three weeks would be necessary. The court, eager to finish with
the trial completely, declared that sentence would be pronounced

at once, but that he would grant a three-week delay after November 11. Black again gave notice of an exception.[2]

As the Chicago *Tribune* pointed out editorially,[3] Judge Gary's denial of the motion for a new trial could surprise nobody. It was absurd to expect that he would turn a legal somersault and reverse his previous rulings. The defense merely requested a new trial to prepare the ground for an appeal to the State Supreme Court.

As is customary, the court, before condemning the seven men to death and Neebe to fifteen years' imprisonment, asked the defendants if there were reasons why sentence should not be pronounced. The prisoners did have "reasons why sentence should not be pronounced," and it took them three days, from October 7 to 9, to present them. For those three days the court was virtually theirs. They sketched their lives, expounded their beliefs, analyzed the evidence, castigated the prosecution, and pilloried the verdict. For three days the court was their forum. They were the accusers.

August Spies was the first to address the court. Though rather short in stature, he was well-built and sufficiently attractive in face and body to strike others as a handsome man. A fine forehead, an intelligent, strong countenance with good features, a heavy mustache in the American style, and an enviable poise and assurance made him extremely prepossessing. Born in Central Germany in December, 1855, of a family of moderate means—his father was a minor government official—he enjoyed a pleasant childhood and youth and a fair education. The death of his father led to his departure at seventeen for America. The next year found him in Chicago. Not until 1875, did he acquire any knowledge of Socialism. Then he began to read widely in socialist literature, and he became more than a passable student of Marx. His active mind soon led him to extended reading in other associated fields. Two years later he became a member of the S.L.P., and then joined a *Lehr und Wehr Verein*. His radicalism was, thus, a product of his stay in the United States. The labor struggles of 1877 and of the following years, led him to accept the doctrine of violence. His belief in the validity of political action died very slowly, as it has been shown, and he himself stood as a candidate for office several times. By 1880, he was one of the leading figures in the radical movement in the West, and in that year assumed the editorship of the *Arbeiter-Zeitung*. He wrote with great ease and a certain literary flavor in English and German, and spoke both languages fluently. Contemporaries who viewed Spies under trying circumstances found much to admire in his ardent sincerity, affability, and freedom from "false pride." His cynicism was, curiously enough, balanced by a strain of sentimentality.[4]

Spies spoke at great length (his address fills sixteen pages of close print), and fully expounded his doctrines. Considered in the light of the circumstances under which it was delivered, it is quite good. In protesting his innocence, he attacked the prosecution and the police.

"I have been indicted," he said, "on a charge of murder, as an accomplice or accessory. Upon this indictment I have been convicted. There was no evidence produced by the State to show or even indicate that I had any knowledge of the man who threw the bomb, or that I, myself had anything to do with the throwing of the missile. . . . If there was no evidence to show that I was legally responsible for the deed, then my conviction and the execution of the sentence is nothing less than willful, malicious and deliberate murder. . . . Before this court, and before the public, which is supposed to be the State, I charge the State's Attorney and Bonfield with the heinous conspiracy to commit murder." [5]

He averred that a young man who attended the Haymarket meeting, Legner by name, was spirited away to Buffalo, New York, after spurning a bribe offered by the State, because his testimony would prove Spies' innocence and brand the star witnesses for the State as perjurers.[6] Spies claimed that the articles in the *Alarm* and the *Arbeiter-Zeitung* dealing with the manufacture and use of explosives were largely modeled upon or translated from articles which had first appeared in the Chicago *Tribune,* Chicago *Times* and Chicago *News.* He made special reference to one in the *Tribune* of February 23, 1885, and to the contributions of Generals Molineux and Fitz John Porter "in which the use of dynamite bombs against striking workingmen is advocated as the most effective weapon against them." [7]

It was not murder for which he was being tried, declared Spies, but for his belief in Anarchism. The State's Attorney, he said,

"has intimated to us that Anarchism was on trial. . . . There was not a syllable said about Anarchism at the Haymarket meeting. At that meeting the very popular theme of reducing the hours of toil was discussed. But, 'Anarchism is on trial!' foams Mr. Grinnell. If that is the case, your Honor, very well; you may sentence me for I am an Anarchist. I believe . . . that the State of castes and classes—the state where one class dominates over and lives upon the labor of another class . . . —is doomed to die, and make room for a free society, voluntary association, or universal brotherhood, if you like. You may pronounce the sentence upon me, honorable judge, but let the world know that in A.D. 1886, in the State of Illinois, eight men were sentenced to death because they believed in a better future. . . ." [8]

Spies never denied that he and his comrades had advocated the use of dynamite, and he found justification for this in the fact that the ruling class employed force to prevent all reform and progress. But he denied absolutely the charge that he and his comrades deliberately planned the violent destruction of the existing social order on a specific date.

"To charge us with an attempt to overthrow the present system on or about May 4, by force," he declared, "and then establish Anarchy, is too absurd a statement, I think, even for a political office-holder to make. If Grinnell believed that we attempted such a thing, why did he not . . . make an inquiry as to our sanity? Only mad men could have planned such a brilliant scheme, and mad people cannot be indicted or convicted for murder. If there had existed anything like a conspiracy . . . , does your honor believe that events would not have taken a different course than they did on that evening and later?" [9] In another portion of his address, he touched again upon the conspiracy outlined by the State:

"It has been charged that we (the eight here) constituted a conspiracy," he said. "I would reply, to that, that my friend Lingg, I had seen but twice at meetings of the Central Labor Union, where I went as reporter; before I was arrested, I had never spoken to him. With Engel, I have not been on speaking terms for at least a year. And Fischer, my lieutenant (?), used to go around and make speeches against me. So much for that." [10]

Spies took special pains to present Anarchism or Socialism—he used the terms interchangeably—in the most favorable light. Anarchism was not all violence and destruction. It was, on the contrary, a philosophy which implied freedom from all force and coercion. Under no circumstances would he deny his anarchistic beliefs.

"I cannot divest myself of them," he said in his concluding words, "nor would I, if I could. And if you think that you can crush . . . these ideas . . . by sending us to the gallows; if you would once more have people to suffer the penalty of death because they have dared to tell the truth—and I defy you to show us where we have told a lie—I say if death is the penalty for proclaiming the truth, then I will proudly and defiantly pay the costly price! Call your hangman! Truth crucified in Socrates, in Christ, in Giordano Bruno, in Huss, Galileo, still lives—they and others whose number is legion have preceded us on this path. We are ready to follow!" [11]

Even the Chicago *Tribune* grudgingly admitted that Spies' address was not as bad as it had expected, and undertook to answer his defense of Anarchism in a lengthy editorial. The *Tribune* insisted that Anarchism meant chaos, confusion, disorder, and "wherever and whenever it comes to the surface from its slimy depths it takes the form of violence, of riots, of assaults upon the police and of attacks on the rights of private citizens." [12] All the succeeding speeches reproduced in full in the news columns, were also deemed worthy of critical editorial comment by the *Tribune*.

Michael Schwab, who followed Spies, possessed neither the fluency nor polish of the latter as a speaker. Though born only two years before Spies, he looked considerably older. His height and his thin angular body made him appear gaunt. The length of his face was accentuated by long hair and a long black beard. His deep-set eyes looked through scholarly spectacles, and it was easy to see why he struck Charles Edward Russell as "the ideal of a German university professor."

Schwab came to America from Bavaria when he was twenty-six. He had received fairly good schooling up to the age of sixteen, when he was apprenticed as a book-binder. When he reached Chicago in 1879, he was already an avowed socialist. After a short stay in Milwaukee and the West, he returned to Chicago in 1882, where he became a reporter and shortly afterwards joined the editorial staff of the *Arbeiter-Zeitung*. His appearance was more scholarly, but he was not as thorough a student of Socialism as Spies. [13]

Schwab's address was in the main deadly earnest in tone, and its occasional satirical sallies were ponderously dull. Yet his honesty and directness gave his words a certain impressiveness. With bitterness he protested his complete innocence of the crime for which he was convicted. "I am condemned to die," he said, "for writing newspaper articles and making speeches." [14] "Justice has not been done, more than this, could not be done. If one class is arrayed against the other, it is idle and hypocritical to think about justice. Anarchy was on trial, as the State's attorney put it in his closing speech." [15] To talk about a "gigantic conspiracy" is childish. "A movement is not a conspiracy. All we did was done in open daylight." [16] They had to spread their doctrines, he said. Someone had to bring light to the working masses. "If we had kept silent stones would have cried out." [17]

He, too, seized the opportunity to explain his doctrines, and, it may be noted, employed the words Communism, Anarchism, and Socialism as if they were synonymous. Never for a moment would he admit that his utopian vision lay beyond the reach of mankind. "Anarchy is a dream," he declared, "but only in the present. It will be realized. . . . Who is the man that has the cheek to tell us that human development has already reached its culminating point? I know that our ideal will not be accomplished this or next year, but I know that it will be accomplished as near as possible, some day in the future." Schwab likewise made it clear that anarchy was not to be identified with violence. "In the present state of society," he said, "violence is used on all sides, and, therefore, we advocated the use of violence against violence, but against violence only as a necessary means of defense." [18]

In certain respects, the short address of Oscar Neebe, the least intellectual and interesting of all eight men, is the most moving. Unassuming, simple, direct, its very poverty of expression is an asset, conveying, as it does, bewilderment and pathetic dignity. Neebe was not an outstanding figure in the revolutionary movement. He had been active chiefly in trade-union circles, and in his breast there burned little of the fire of the fanatical idealist. He was thirty-six at the time, and, though of German descent, was born in New York City. He came to Chicago when fifteen, went East, and then returned in 1875, entering the labor movement. By trade a tinsmith, at the time the bomb was thrown he had developed a fairly successful yeast business. His slightly halting speech belied his appearance, for physically he was an extremely powerful man. His huge body was crowned by a large and rather good-looking head, graced with a beard and mustache in the style of Louis Napoleon. In mind and personality, however, he was a "colorless creature. . . ." He was a simple soul, and he knew very little about Anarchism and Socialism. [19]

Briefly he reviewed his activities in behalf of labor, weakly criticized the capitalists, spoke of the better conditions that would come with the advent of a socialistic society, and summarized the evidence that had been adduced against him.

"Well, these are the crimes I have committed," he declared in closing. "They found a revolver in my house and a red flag there. I organized Trade Unions. I was for reduction of the hours of labor, and the education of the laboring man, and the re-establishment of the *Arbeiter-Zeitung*—the workingmen's newspaper. There is no evidence to show that I was connected with the bomb-throwing, or that I was near it, or anything of that kind. So I am only sorry, your honor—that is, if you can stop it or help it—I will ask you to do it—that is, to hang me, too; for I think it is more honorable to die suddenly than to be killed by inches. I have a family and children; and if they know their father is dead, they will bury him. They can go to the grave and kneel down by the side of it; but they can't go to the penitentiary and see their father, who was convicted of a crime that he hasn't had anything to do with. That is all I have got to say. Your honor, I am sorry I am not to be hung with the rest of the men." [20]

Adolph Fischer, born in Bremen, left Germany for America when he was fifteen, and at the time of the trial had been in the country some thirteen years. He had become interested in Socialism during the last years of his German schooling as a result of an instructor's attack upon it. He learned his trade in the United States, and from 1883 on, when he arrived in Chicago, he had worked as a compositor for the *Arbeiter-Zeitung*. Intellectually, he was wholly undistinguished. Physically, however, he was tall and well-built. Though a suggestion of weakness marked his pleasant face with its well-kept mustache, there was nothing weak about the man. He was a zealot who would not hesitate to sacrifice his life for the "cause." Parsons and Spies were too mild for him, and he had aided Engel in founding the short-lived *Anarchist* to provide the extremists with a medium of expression. He had spurned an offer by Grinnell, Furthman and the police to purchase immunity by testifying for the State.[21]

Fischer failed to rise to the occasion as some of his comrades did. Brief and to the point, he dealt sharply with the prosecution; denied that he was guilty of murder; and summarized his part in the Haymarket meeting to prove his innocence. ". . . I protest against my being sentenced to death," he proclaimed, "because I have committed no crime. I was tried . . . for murder, and I was convicted of anarchy. I protest against being sentenced to death, because I have not been found guilty of murder. However, if I am to die on account of being an Anarchist . . . I will not remonstrate. . . ."[22]

As a result of the trial Fischer expected a rapid spread of Anarchism in America, rather than its extirpation. In rendering a verdict of guilty, the jury had "done more for the furtherance of Anarchism than the convicted would have accomplished in a generation."[23]

Louis Lingg followed Fischer, and the contrast between the two must have been striking. Though he spoke in German, he dominated the courtroom. He was an uncompromising prosecutor, and the court was on trial. Only twenty-two, Lingg was the youngest of the eight prisoners. He was little known in Chicago until the time of the trial, and there rapidly grew up about him a host of stories, most of which are apocryphal. It was said—and generally believed—that he was the illegitimate son of a nobleman and that this fact was instrumental in warping his life. In the brief autobiographical sketch which he wrote, however, there is no mention of this. Born in Mannheim, Baden, he lived, according to his own account, an extremely poor life after the death of his father, a laborer, in 1877, when Lingg was seven years old. He was apprenticed to a carpenter, and after joining a Workingmen's Educational Society came in contact with socialist thought. In 1883, he went to Switzerland where he became a social-revolutionary in that he accepted propaganda by deed. Largely to escape military service, he came to America in the summer of 1885, going directly from New York to Chicago. In that city he quickly became active in trade-union circles, joined a carpenter's union, and was elected as its delegate to the Central Labor Union. Though not sympathetic with the trade-union ideal as such, he organized the International Carpenters' and Joiners' Union. He felt that the sooner the workers perceived the inadequacy of trade-unionism, the sooner they would become revolutionists.

Lingg was an attractive man with his extraordinarily well-shaped head, heavy crop of hair and handsome bearded face with fascinating steel gray eyes. Despite his small stature, his compact body was powerful. His faith, marked by a rare religious earnestness, was unquenchable. His revolutionary fanaticism was revealed in his address to the court and in a letter which he subsequently wrote explaining that he had "advocated . . . propaganda by deeds with the intention that it shall not only be a slight return for the exploitation, suppression and murder of my fellow workmen, but principally that it may challenge our exploiters and their legal tools to vigorous persecution, because I feel confident that the inevitable and also forcible revolution must come soon, when we may be successful." [24] His opening words set the key for his entire address:

"Court of Justice!" he began. "With the same irony with which you have regarded my efforts to win, in this 'free land of America,' a livelihood such as humankind is worthy to enjoy, do you now, after condemning me to death, concede me the liberty of making a final speech.

"I accept your concession; but it is only for the purpose of exposing the injustice, the calumnies, and the outrages which have been heaped upon me." [25]

Briefly analyzing the pertinent evidence introduced against him, he scornfully announced his innocence of the charge of murder. He was not convicted of murder, Lingg continued. "The Judge has stated that much only this morning in his *résumé* of the case, and Grinnell has repeatedly asserted that we were being tried, not for murder, but for Anarchy, so that the condemnation is—that I am an Anarchist!" [26] Defiantly he denounced the police, the attorneys for the State, the judge. "I do not recognize your law, jumbled together as it is by the nobodies of bygone centuries," he exclaimed, "and I do not recognize the decision of the court." [27] His closing words revealed Lingg's temperament and personality completely.

"I repeat," he thundered, "that I am the enemy of the 'order' of today, and I repeat that, with all my powers, so long as breath remains in me, I shall combat it. I declare again, frankly and openly, that I am in favor of using force. I have told Captain Schaack, and I stand by it, 'If you cannonade us, we shall dynamite you.' You laugh! Perhaps you think, 'You'll throw no more bombs'; but let me assure you that I die happy on the gallows, so confident am I that the hundreds and thousands to whom I have spoken will remember my words; and when you shall have hanged us, then, mark my words, they will do the bomb-throwing! In this hope I say to you: I despise you. I despise your order, your laws, your force-propped authority. Hang me for it!" [28]

Heavy in build, plain of face, and phlegmatic in movement, George Engel immediately brought to mind the typical German bartender. There was nothing in his appearance to suggest the revolutionist. Yet he was a leader in the small group of extremists who found the *Alarm* and the *Arbeiter-Zeitung* too moderate. His fifty years made him considerably older than most of his fellow prisoners. Engel's life follows a fairly familiar pattern. Of German birth, he came to the United States in 1873 after a year's stay in England. He lived in Philadelphia for a year and then went on to Chicago. Here he first became acquainted with socialist thought through the *Vorbote,* and joined in turn a section of the First International, the S.L.P., and finally the I.W.P.A. The modern psychologist would probably trace his brutal conception of Anarchism and revolution to an unhappy childhood, a temporary eye affliction which almost cost him his sight, and many years of dire poverty.[29]

His address, which was in no way distinguished, was in part autobiographical and in part a defense of his doctrines. His only crime, he asserted, was the fact that he was a member of the International. Of his own part in the Haymarket bombing, he declared that "On the night on which the first bomb in this country was thrown, I was in my apartments at home. I knew nothing of the conspiracy which the State's attorney pretends to have discovered." [30]

"It is true," he continued, "I am acquainted with several of my fellow defendants; with most of them, however, but slightly, through seeing them at meetings and hearing them speak. Nor do I deny, that I, too, have spoken at meetings, saying that, if every workingman had a bomb in his pocket, capitalistic rule would soon come to an end.

"That is my opinion, and my wish. . . .

"Can anyone feel any respect for a government that accords rights only to the privileged classes and none to the workers? . . .

"For such a government . . . I can feel no respect, and [I] will combat it despite its power, despite its police, despite its spies.

"I hate and combat, not the individual capitalist, but the system that gives him those privileges. My greatest wish is that workingmen may recognize who are their friends and who are their enemies.

"As to my conviction, brought about as it was, through capitalistic influence, I have not one word to say." [31]

Samuel Fielden, a hard-working teamster, was, with the exception of Parsons, the only one neither of German birth nor descent. He was a Lancashire Englishman who came to the United States in 1868, and who, at the time of the trial, was close to forty years old. A workingman all his life, he was drawn into the radical movement by the "iniquities" of capitalism. His knowledge of Socialism and Anarchism was not profound, and his criticism of the existing order sprang from ethical and humanitarian convictions perhaps produced by his early religious background. Despite the blood and thunder of his street-corner and Lake Front orations, he was personally the most mild-mannered individual. Charles Edward Russell correctly observed that "to conceive of him as in any way a dangerous person seemed a suggestion of humor." Peculiarly enough, his flowing black beard gave him a striking facial resemblance to Bakunin.[32]

Fielden spoke at great length. His address, notable in few respects, fills over twenty-five pages of small print. In it he touched in turn upon his life, his activities in labor and radical circles, the nature of the doctrines he professed, the evils of capitalism, his rôle in the Haymarket episode, and his innocence of any crime.[33]

If Fielden's address was long, Parsons' was interminable. He spoke for two hours on October 8 and six on the following day. Though his address was well-prepared and excellently delivered, it bored the courtroom audience. But Parsons realized that this was to be his last appearance as a speaker, and he was determined to make the most of it.[34]

Tremendous interest centered in Parsons. Not only was he a recognized leader of the revolutionary movement, but he was the only "real" American among the eight men. Had he desired, he could have boasted of ancestors who came over on the second voyage of the Mayflower, and of a family which counted among its members Major-General Samuel Parsons of the Revolutionary army, Theophilus Parsons, the American jurist, and W. H. Parsons, a brother, major-general in the Confederate Army. Parsons' parents were transplanted northerners, and he was born in Alabama. When the Civil War broke, he joined the Confederate forces although only thirteen. He had already been apprenticed as a printer, and three years after the close of the War he founded and edited the Waco *Spectator*. This venture had to be given up because he turned scalawag in politics and lost caste and support. His Republican affiliations, however, brought his appointment as Assistant Assessor of U. S. Internal Revenue in 1870. About a year later, he was elected a secretary of the Texas State Senate. He was advanced in the Internal Revenue service to chief deputy collector at Austin, which post he held until 1873.

In that year he moved to Chicago, where he found employment as a compositor. He immediately joined a typographical union, and, before long held official posts in labor organizations. He was soon led to an examination of socialist doctrines, and by 1876 he was a professed socialist. The same year found him a member of the Knights of Labor. During the great strike of 1877, he was blacklisted by employers for addressing a gathering of workers, and for two years could not secure work as a printer. His experiences during the exciting days of 1877 provided whatever stimulus his nascent radicalism needed. In the succeeding years he was active in politics, and was nominated on socialistic labor tickets twice for county clerk, once for Sheriff, thrice for alderman, and once for Congress. In 1879 he declined the nomination for president on the S.L.P. ticket voted him by the Alleghany City convention of the party on the ground that he was not of constitutional age. Shifting steadily to the left, he broke with the Socialism of the S.L.P. and became increasingly critical of political action. In 1884 he became editor of the *Alarm*. His work in the labor movement, however, did not cease. In build and size Parsons resembled Spies, A well-modeled head and clean-cut features were distinguished by long black hair, keen, intelligent dark eyes, and a long but carefully-kept mustache.[35]

Parsons was easily the most fluent and polished speaker of the eight. His first words dealt with the trial and the verdict.

"Your honor:" he began, "If there is one distinguishing characteristic which has made itself prominent in the conduct of this trial, it has been the passion, the heat, and the anger, the violence both to sentiment and to person, of everything connected with this case. You ask me why sentence of death should not be pronounced upon me, or, what is tantamount to the same thing, you ask me why you should give me a new trial in order that I might establish my innocence and the ends of justice be subserved. I answer you and say that this verdict is the verdict of passion, born in passion, nurtured in passion and is the sum total of the organized passion of the City of Chicago." [36]

To present himself and his ideas to best advantage, Parsons went on to recount the history of the working-classes in America, sketched his life, attacked the economics of capitalism, and made clear what he understood by Anarchism and Socialism. With reference to the verdict, he maintained "that our execution, as the matter stands just now, would be a judicial murder. . . ." [37] The case itself was simply another manifestation of the fundamental alignment of capital against labor, and the verdict was clearly an attempt to suppress the voice of the working masses.[38] The prisoners had violated no laws. They merely had exercised rights guaranteed to Americans—the rights of free speech, press and public assemblage. There was no evidence to connect himself or his fellows with the death of Degan. True, Parsons advocated the use of dynamite because

"today dynamite comes as the emancipator of man from the domination and enslavement of his fellow men. . . . It is democratic; it makes everybody equal. . . . It is a peacemaker; it is man's best and last friend; it emancipates the world from the domineering and the few over the many. . . . Force is the law of the universe . . . , and this newly discovered force makes all men equal and therefore free. . . .

"Now, I speak plainly. Does it follow, because I hold these views, that I committed or had anything to do with the commission of that act at the Haymarket?" [39]

Because he was wholly innocent of any crime, he had given himself up for trial. It was his duty to share whatever fate might be visited upon his comrades.

The restlessness which had pervaded the courtroom during Parsons' address gave way to a frigid quiet when he concluded. Judge Gary rose to pronounce sentence, and a sob momentarily pierced the silence. He spoke very quietly. As he proceeded his voice grew weaker, and at the very last it was hardly audible.[40] In his lengthy address to the prisoners Judge Gary almost directly answered their remarks. To their plea for Anarchism, he countered with a lecture upon the American system of government. There need be noted here only the closing words of what was in great part a moralistic discourse.

"The existing order of society," he said, "can be changed only by the will of the majority. Each man has the full right to entertain and advance, by speech and print, such opinions as suit himself; and the great body of the people will usually care little what he says. But if he proposes murder as a means of enforcing them he puts his own life at stake. And no clamor about free speech or the evils to be cured or the wrongs to be redressed will shield him from the consequences of his crime. His liberty is not a license to destroy. The toleration that he enjoys he must extend to others, and he must not arrogantly assume that the great majority are wrong and that they may rightfully be coerced by terror or removed by dynamite.

"It only remains that for the crime you have committed —and of which you have been convicted after a trial unexampled in the patience with which an outraged people have extended you every protection and privilege of the law which you derided and defied—the sentence of that law be now given."

Once more the prisoners listened to their sentence. They gave no sign of being disturbed.

"In form and detail," said Judge Gary, "that sentence will appear upon the records of the court. In substance and effect it is that the defendant Neebe be imprisoned in the State Penitentiary at Joliet at hard labor for the term of fifteen years.

"And that each of the other defendants, between the hours of ten o'clock in the forenoon and two o'clock in the afternoon of the third day of December next, in the manner provided by the statute of this State be hung by the neck until he is dead. Remove the prisoners." [41]

NOTES CHAPTER XVI

1. Chicago *Tribune,* October 2-8, 1886; Gary, *loc. cit.,* pp. 834-835.
2. Chicago *Tribune,* October 8, 1886.
3. *Idem.*
4. Spies, *op. cit., passim; Life of Albert R. Parsons,* pp. 265-274; *Social Science,* vol. 1, no. 18, November 5, 1887, pp. 1-2; *Alarm,* December 31, 1887; *Liberty,* vol. 4, no. 15, February 12, 1887, p. 1; Russell, *loc. cit.,* p. 407; Art Young, *On My Way,* New York, 1928, p. 121. Art Young, who was then a young reporter and sketched the men during the trial, said, in conversation with the author, that he remembered Spies as the most impressive of all eight men.
5. *The Chicago Martyrs. The Famous Speeches of the Eight Anarchists in Judge Gary's Court, October 7, 1886, and Reasons for Pardoning Fielden, Neebe and Schwab, by John P. Altgeld,* San Francisco, 1899, p. 1. There are many editions of the speeches of the men in court. The first edition, Chicago, 1886, has been examined.
6. *Ibid.,* pp. 1-2.
7. *Ibid.,* p. 3.
8. *Ibid.,* p. 4.
9. *Ibid.,* p. 5.
10. *Ibid.,* p. 15.
11. *Ibid.,* p. 16.
12. October 9, 1886.
13. Russell, *loc. cit.,* p. 407; Aveling, *op. cit.,* p. 119; *Commonweal,* vol. 4, no. 106, January 21, 1886, p. 19; *Liberty,* vol. 4, no. 15, February 12, 1887, p. 1; *Social Science,* vol. 1, no. 18, November 5, 1887, pp. 7-8.
14. *Chicago Martyrs,* p. 17.
15. *Idem.*
16. *Idem.*
17. *Ibid.,* p. 18.
18. *Ibid.,* p. 20.

19. *Social Science*, vol. 1, no. 18, November 5, 1887, pp. 15-16; *Liberty*, vol. 4, no. 15, February 12, 1887, p. 1; *Commonweal*, February 18, 1886, p. 51; Russell, *loc. cit.*, p. 408; Aveling, *op. cit.*, p. 120.
20. *Chicago Martyrs*, p. 25.
21. *Social Science*, vol. 1, no. 18, November 5, 1887, pp. 9-10; *Liberty*, vol. 4, no. 15, February 12, 1887, p. 1; *Alarm*, January 4, 1888; Russell, *loc. cit.*, p. 408; Aveling, *op. cit.*, p. 120; *Life of Albert R. Parsons*, pp. 275-279.
22. *Chicago Martyrs*, p. 26
23. *Ibid.*, p. 27.
24. *Alarm*, December 17, 1887; *Social Science*, vol. 1, no. 18, November 5, 1887, pp. 12-13; *Social Science Review*, vol. 1, no. 20 November 19, 1887, pp. 10-11; *Liberty*, vol. 4, no. 15, February 12, 1887, p. 1; Russell, *loc. cit.*, p. 409; *Commonweal*, February 11, 1888, p. 45.
25. *Chicago Martyrs*, p. 28.
26. *Idem.*
27. *Ibid.*, p. 30.
28. *Idem.*
29. *Life of Albert R. Parsons*, pp. 279-282; *Liberty*, vol. 4, no. 15 February 12, 1887, p. 1; *Social Science*, vol. 1, no. 18, November 5, 1887, pp. 11-12; Sartorius von Waltershausen, *op. cit.*, p. 311; *Commonweal*, February 4, 1888, p. 37.
30. *Chicago Martyrs*, p. 34.
31. *Idem.*
32. Russell, *loc. cit.*, p. 408; *Commonweal*, January 7, 1888, p. 5; *Liberty*, vol. 4, no. 15, February 12, 1887; *Social Science*, vol. 1, no. 18, November 5, 1887, pp. 5-6; interview with George A. Schilling.
33. *Chicago Martyrs*, pp. 34-62.
34. Chicago *Tribune*, October 10, 1886.
35. *Life of Albert R. Parsons*, pp. 1-4, 12-26; *Social Science*, vol. 1, no. 18, November 5, 1887, pp. 3-4; *Alarm*, December 3, 1887; *Liberty*, vol. 4, no. 15, February 12, 1887, p. 1.
36. *Chicago Martyrs*, p. 64.
37. *Ibid.*, p. 66.
38. *Idem.*
39. *Ibid.*, p. 83.
40. Chicago *Tribune*, October 10, 1886.
41. Michael J. Schaack, *Anarchy and Anarchists*, Chicago, 1889, pp. 606-607.

XVII. THE APPEAL

A<small>N</small> appeal to the State Supreme Court was decided upon as soon as the verdict in the lower court was announced. After Judge Gary had pronounced sentence, Capt. Black informed the Court: "Your Honor knows that we intend to take an appeal to the Supreme Court in behalf of all the defendants. I ask that there be a stay of execution in the case of Mr. Neebe until the third day of December." Mr. Grinnell agreed, and the stay was granted.[1] December 3, 1886 had been set for the execution of the sentence, and a stay of execution had to be first secured to argue the appeal. The desired *supersedeas* was granted on November 25, after Capt. Black and Leonard Swett appeared for the prisoners before Chief Justice Scott of the State Supreme Court.

The personnel of the defense counsel was strengthened by the acquisition of Leonard Swett, Lincoln's friend and law associate, who replaced William Foster. The latter had withdrawn from the case when the trial closed in the lower court to the accompaniment of criticism by some Chicago radicals. Foster's services had been both valuable and intelligent. But he had never quite regarded his clients as martyrs, and his lack of sympathy with their ideals was unmistakable. With Swett a member of counsel and the drift in public opinion in favor of the condemned men,[2] there was some basis for the slight optimism displayed by those associated with the defense.

Nearly everyone welcomed the appeal to the State Supreme Court. It was not widely feared that the Court would upset the verdict, and no harm was seen in carrying the case to the higher court. There were few, however, who were disturbed by the possibility of a reversal. They felt, as did Judge Gary, that if this occurred major disturbances, perhaps even "anarchy," would follow.[3] Carter Harrison, Chicago's perennial mayor, who was running for office when the case was being argued before the higher court in March, 1887, appeared disturbed on this score.

"My fear is," he announced to his constituents, "that we will have some terrible trouble in this city in the next two years if the Supreme Court gives the anarchists a new trial. Judge Gary has told me that they could never have a new trial; they could not get a jury. . . . I have been successful in being able to quell all disturbances with the police. The future may develop something different. If I should be elected mayor again I should feel that I would not dare to be away from Chicago where a half day's ride could not bring me home." [4]

Mayor Harrison, it should be observed in this connection, had declared, in September of the previous year, his opposition to the execution of the "anarchists" because it would produce a serious wave of resentment and make martyrs of them. At the same time, he asserted that to obtain evidence, he had "utilized the extreme force of my office in a way which, if done by police in London would have upset the throne of Victoria and which could be done in no monarchical country with safety." Yet, a few moments earlier, he had said: "I do not believe that there was any intention on the part of Spies and those men to have bombs thrown that night." [5] Nevertheless, if the Supreme Court reversed the decision the well-being of the municipality which Carter Harrison served would be jeopardized.

On March 13, 1887, at nine in the morning, six elderly men representing the legal wisdom of the State of Illinois entered the small chamber where the Supreme Court sat at Ottawa, a town almost due west of Chicago and near the

Illinois River. The prim dignity of their manner was unaffected by the respect with which they were greeted by those in the courtroom. Justice Schofield presided in place of Chief Justice Scott who was ill. With the court called to order, it was announced that "No. 1, People's docket, August Spies and others versus the People of the State of Illinois, is marked as ready." [6]

For three days the attorneys on both sides argued before the court and the largest attendance in its history. Leonard Swett, opening for the defendants, was followed in turn by Ingham, Zeisler, Grinnell, Attorney-General Hunt, and Capt. Black. The arguments, each limited to two hours, were given the closest attention. They were fully reported and commented upon in the daily press, which bestowed upon Black a few unwilling words of commendation.[7] When he had concluded, Black made a motion that the defense be allowed to amend their brief in answer to the authorities cited in the brief of the State. This was denied by the court on the ground that the motion "was inadmissable after oral argument." [8]

The oral arguments were based, of course, upon the briefs submitted to the Court. The State presented two briefs, one on the law and the second on the facts.[9] Two briefs were likewise submitted in behalf of the defendants, one prepared by Leonard Swett,[10] the other drawn up by Black, Salomé and Zeisler.[11] The defense based their arguments for a reversal on the following grounds: (1) that some of the instructions of the court, both given and refused, were in error; (2) that some of the remarks of the court were sufficiently improper to be considered erroneous; (3) that errors obtained in connection with the impanelling of the jury; (4) that the improprieties of the closing argument of the State's Attorney were ground for a complaint of error; (5) that the State's theory of conspiracy, upon which the whole case rested was untenable in the light of the facts and the law; (6) that illegal evidence had been brought to bear against the defendants; and (7) that errors had obtained after the verdict when the petition for a new trial had been rejected.

Leonard Swett argued that there was no evidence to show that the defendants were guilty under the law and the indictment. He conceded that some of the defendants had been foolish, intemperate, and extravagant in their speeches and writings. But for this they could not be hanged. There was no evidence to justify Neebe's conviction, and at least a "reasonable doubt" existed as to the guilt of the others. Granted that Lingg, for some "crazy" reason, made bombs, it could not be proved that he had thrown or given one to some other person to be thrown. He was, therefore, not guilty. The State's theory of conspiracy, declared Swett, was a meaningless "jumble." In conspiracy trials, he observed,

"it is necessary to prove the union of the minds conspiring or the conspiracy first, and then, that union once being established, the acts and declarations of each become the acts and declarations of all. This case seems to have proceeded upon a sort of jumble of all doctrines, and particularly, the law of conspiracy was reversed and the acts and declarations of each person caught in the drag-net of this prosecution were used to prove a conspiracy of the parties, and the guilt of all of the particular crime charged. The case ought to be reversed for the jumble alone." [12]

Swett reminded the court that the defendants had been tried at a time of great excitement. If they were hung it would be in answer to the wave of hysteria which followed the Haymarket tragedy. Public opinion clamored for their execution because they had threatened to disturb "the fixed order of things. . . ." [13]

Capt. Black's oral argument was a skilful presentation of the defendants' case. "I say in all sincerity," he began, "that the Plaintiffs in error whom I represent are here asking for justice. We claim that upon a fair consideration of the evidence adduced in this record, under the rules of law properly applicable thereto, these defendants . . . are shown to be innocent of the crime of which they stand charged, and of the commission of which they have been convicted." [14] In concluding, Black stressed the importance of the instructions given by Judge Gary for the State.

"The instructions," he said, "embody the erroneous rulings which were applied to the introduction of evidence.[15] They permit the finding of these men guilty, when for ought that appears in this record, your Honors, . . . will be compelled to say that bomb may have been thrown by somebody in no way connected with those defendants, directly or indirectly. It may have been done by an enemy of theirs. . . . It was thrown outside of the purpose of the Haymarket meeting. It was thrown in disregard of the arrangement and understanding for that meeting. It was thrown to the overthrow of the labor and the effort that these men were then giving their lives to, namely, the establishment of the eight-hour day. It brought to an end their efforts. It disappointed their hopes. It was not of their devising. The record shows it.

"The record fails to show who threw the bomb. And the question is, whether upon the barbaric *lex talionis,* that whenever a man was slain a man of the opposing faction must be slain, these seven men shall die, because seven policemen, whom they did not like as a class, and who certainly did not love them, have died?" [16]

The defense supported its contentions with an analysis of the evidence and an appeal to precedent. An accessory could be tried and convicted as principal independently of the principal under the Illinois statute. But an Illinois decision which affirmed this, also asserted that "in such case the guilt of the principal must be alleged and proved." [17] A Virginia case of 1882 offered some support for the argument that there can be no conviction of an accessory without at least the identification of the principal by proof.[18] The defense held that general advice to perpetrate violent deeds" without reference to the particular crime charged, and without specifying object, manner, time or place," [19] did not constitute responsibility for murder. Accessoryship could only be established by evidence of special counsel, and such evidence was lacking. In support of this argument the defense cited a North Carolina conspiracy case in which the defendants had been originally indicted on three counts: (1) for conspiracy to commit rape upon "F"; (2) for the same offense upon "E"; and (3) for the same offense upon "certain female persons to the [grand] jurors unknown." The Court held erroneous the instruction of the trial judge to the effect that the jury might convict upon the first two counts, though evidence was lacking, if they thought that the defendants were guilty under the third count.[20] In the same connection the defense cited a New York ruling which declared that it is erroneous, in charging a jury, to suggest a motive for a crime not warranted by the evidence, thus prejudicing the jurors against the prisoner. "A motive for the commission of a crime cannot be imagined; but the facts from which such motive may be inferred must be proven." [21]

To show that the lower court was in error in permitting the submission of evidence not related to the defendants, the defense cited *People* v. *Kennedy* which held that where circumstantial evidence is introduced to connect defendants with a criminal act, those circumstantial facts are not competent as evidence if they are unrelated to the defendants.[22] Chief Justice Denio observed in his decision that circumstantial evidence "consists in reasoning from facts which are known or proved, to establish such as are conjectured to exist, but the process is fatally vicious if the circumstances from which we seek to deduce the conclusion depends itself upon conjecture." [23] Two cases cited by the defense appeared to sustain the argument that circumstantial evidence had been improperly used and that the charge of the court to the jury on the evidence was not competent. One [24] lay down the rule that circumstantial evidence should be acted upon cautiously, especially when public feeling might lead to misuse of the facts and the drawing of false inferences. In the second, the Supreme Court of Illinois concluded that when "the facts are not proved, or are controverted, and the evidence is conflicting, the court, in instructing the jury cannot assume them to be true without usurping the province of the jury, and it is error to do so. . . . Neither is it proper that an instruction should, even hypothetically, give a one-sided or partial view of the facts." [25]

During the trial in the lower court, the defense had objected to certain remarks of the prosecuting attorney. It contended that these remarks were improper, offered legitimate ground for a complaint of error, and, finally, that it was the duty of the court to prevent the prejudicing of the jury by such conduct. In a previous case the Supreme Court of Illinois had decided that it was the duty of the presiding judge to check the State's Attorney when, in his closing address, he argues for a conviction upon the basis of assumed, unproved facts. Such conduct, when carried to extremes in a doubtful case, justifies a reversal of the judgment of conviction.[26] The Supreme Court had also held it highly improper for the prosecutor "to inflame the passions or arouse the prejudices of the jury" to the injury of those on trial for a grave crime. The court should prevent this from occurring.[27]

The points raised by the defense on the mode of impanelling the jury have already been discussed,[28] and there is no need to consider them again here. It is clear enough that both the spirit and the letter of the law had been violated by Judge Gary.[29] It is worth noting that a large number of the cases cited by the defense do not support the contentions made in the appeal.

Credit must be given to the State for the skilful manner in which it conducted its case. It committed no blunders as it did during the trial in the lower court. In refuting the arguments of the defense, the State's theory of conspiracy was improved in manner of presentation and buttressed with the appeal to legal precedent.

The State held, it will be recalled, that where a conspiracy existed to do an unlawful act involving force, the act of each conspirator in furtherance of the common design is the act of all. When murder results, all are guilty of murder, though the conspirator responsible for the deed cannot be identified, and even though the particular act was not arranged for, as long as it was the natural result of the conspiracy, and perpetrated in furtherance of the common design. "Whether the act was the act of a member of the conspiracy," asserted the State, "whether it was done in furtherance of the common design, is a question of proof." [30] Everything in proof of the conspiracy or the connection of the defendants with it constituted, said the State, competent evidence. The State also argued that the court was to determine whether a conspiracy had been established *prima facie*. Once it had been established *prima facie* in the opinion of the trial judge, it followed as a matter of "elementary" law that "any act or declaration of any member of the conspiracy, though he may not be a party defendant, in furtherance of the conspiracy, is evidence against all the conspirators on trial." [31]

As with the defense, many of the citations offered by the State are of extremely doubtful authority.[32] An Indiana case, for example, which was supposed to confirm the theory that the defendants could be found guilty of the act of an unknown principal, clearly does not apply. In this case the court observed that where the evidence had established beyond a reasonable doubt that the crime of larceny with which the defendants were charged was committed by one of them in pursuance of a common purpose, the jury could find each of them guilty even though the evidence left the identity of the particular defendant who took the property in doubt.[33] Here, however, the principal was identified as a member of the conspiracy. In the case at issue it was never asserted that the principal was one of the defendants,—that is, that one of the accused threw the bomb. It remained to be proved that the unknown bomb-thrower was a member of the conspiracy.

In the contention that the Illinois Court recognized no distinction between principal and accessory, at least with reference to trial and punishment, the State was eminently correct. In 1868 the Supreme Court of the State asserted that in two earlier decisive cases [34] "this court held that an accessory before the fact might be indicted, tried, and convicted as a principal." [35] This upholds the statutory declaration that an accessory may be punished as principal. But does it support the contention that an accessory may be found guilty even if the principal is unidentified and in fact unknown? If the defendants were accessories to an unknown principal because the particular deed *fitted in with their general advice,* then they could be guilty as conspirators, even if the bomb had been thrown by an *agent provocateur.* The State was entirely willing to grant that the failure to identify the principal "increases the difficulty of proving that, whoever he was, he was actuated by the advice of the accessory." (!) But this, concluded the State, was a difficulty that was one of fact and not of law. [36] This argument, however, provides no solution. Prof. Thayer has pointed out that it is a major task to determine what is a matter of fact and what is a matter of law. He observes that "the allotment of facts to the jury, even in the strict sense of fact, is not exact. The judges have always answered a multitude of questions of ultimate fact involved in the issue." [37]

On the questions concerning the establishment of a conspiracy *prima facie* in the eyes of the trial judge and the type of evidence which could be properly submitted, the State argued more successfully. *Greenleaf on Evidence* asserts that

"A foundation must first be laid by proof sufficient, in the opinion of the judge, to establish prima facie the fact of conspiracy between the parties, or proper to be laid before the jury as tending to establish such fact. The connection of the individuals in the unlawful enterprise being thus shown, every act and declaration of each member of the confederacy, in pursuance of the original concerted plan and with reference to the common object, is, in contemplation of law, the act and declaration of them all and is therefore original evidence against each of them. It makes no difference at what time any-one entered into the conspiracy. . . ." [38]

The State could further show that it was an accepted legal doctrine that

"The evidence in proof of a conspiracy will generally, from the nature of the case, be *circumstantial*. Though the common design is the essence of the charge, it is not neces-sary to prove that the defendants came together and actually . . . [conspired] to have that design, and to pursue it by com-mon means. If it be proved that the defendants pursued by their acts the same object, often by the same means . . . the jury will be justified in the conclusion, that they were engaged in a conspiracy to effect the object. Nor is it necessary to prove that the conspiracy originated with the defendants; or that they met during the process of its concoction; for every person, entering into a conspiracy or common design already formed, is deemed in law a party to all acts done by any of the other parties before or afterwards, in furtherance of the com-mon design." [39]

The very nature of a conspiracy, the State pointed out, made it almost impossible to prove it except by circumstantial evi-dence, unless one of the accused conspirators testifies against his co-conspirators. To justify the unusual dependence upon circumstantial evidence, the State cited *United States* v. *Cole* [40] where the Court said: "A conspiracy is rarely, if ever, proved by positive testimony. . . . Unless one of the orig-inal conspirators betray his companions . . . their guilt can be proved only by circumstantial evidence. . . . But in such a case the circumstances must be so strong as to be inconsistent with the innocence of the accused. It is said by some writers on evidence that such circumstances are stronger than positive proof. A witness swearing positively, it is said, may misappre-hend the facts or swear falsely, but that circumstances cannot lie."

The decision from the higher court of Pennsylvania in

the famous Molly Maguires case offered a precedent for the introduction of evidence relating to organizations of which the defendants were members. "To show the motive for murder and to explain the prisoners' connection therewith," said the court, "it is competent for the commonwealth to give evidence of the purposes, practises and objects of a society organized for the commission of crime, and to prove that those who committed the murder were members of said organization, and that through its instrumentality it was committed." [41] It was never for a moment suggested, however, that the I.W.P.A. was "a society organized for the commission of crime," or that the *Lehr und Wehr Vereine* were in themselves criminal organizations. Nor was it ever argued that the crime at the Haymarket was committed directly through these societies.

The State depended heavily upon a statement in a contemporary English text on criminal law to support its theory of conspiracy. "If persons are assembled together to the number of three or more," it reads, "and speeches are made to those persons to excite and inflame them, with a view to incite them to acts of violence, and if that same meeting is so connected, in point of circumstances, with a subsequent riot that you cannot reasonably sever the latter from the incitement that was used, those who incited are guilty of the riot, although they are not present when it occurs." [42] This deals with incitement to riot, and the extension of the incitement to riot theory to the "anarchist" case is unwarranted by the facts. It offers no clarification or affirmation of the State's theory of conspiracy, and as an argument by analogy it befogs the issue. The evidence does not justify the conclusion that the speeches of *some* of the defendants at the Haymarket meeting were inextricably connected with the bombing.

The Supreme Court did not hurry its decision. Not until September 14, did Judge Benjamin D. Magruder, noticeably pale, read the opinion of the Court, in which the full bench concurred. In practically every particular it sustained both

the rulings and the verdict of the lower court.[43] The decision
was a complete victory for the State. But there was a slight
note of dissent. One of the members of the Court, Justice
Mulkey, declared:

"Not intending to file a separate opinion, as I should
have done had health permitted, I desire to avail myself of
this occasion to say from the bench, that while I concur in
the conclusion reached, and also in the general view presented
in the opinion filed, I do not wish to be understood as holding that the record is free from error, for I do not think it
is. I am nevertheless of opinion that none of the errors complained of are of so serious a character as to require a reversal
of the judgment.

"In view of the number of defendants on trial, the great
length of time it was in progress, the vast amount of testimony
offered and passed upon by the court, and the almost number-
less rulings the court was required to make, the wonder with
me is that the errors were not more numerous and more serious
than they are.

"In short, after having carefully examined the record,
and given all the questions arising from it my very best
thought, with an earnest and conscientious desire to faithfully discharge my whole duty, I am fully satisfied that the
conclusion reached vindicates the law, does complete justice
between the prisoners and the State, and that it is fully warranted by the law and the evidence." [44]

Since the case was so grave, it is unfortunate, that Justice Mulkey failed to list these minor errors.

No phase of the case was left untouched by the opinion
of the Court.[45] Not only were the points of law reviewed, but
the evidence was meticulously sifted and considered. In the
eyes of the Court, several questions were fundamental to the
entire case. "Did the defendants have a common purpose or
design to advise, encourage, aid or abet the murder of the
police? Did they combine together and with others with a view
to carrying that purpose or design into effect? Did they or

. . . any of them do such acts or make such declarations in furtherance of the common purpose or design, as did actually have the effect of encouraging, aiding or abetting the crime in question?"[46] Only by a thorough review of the evidence, declared the Court, could these questions be answered.

The bomb which exploded in the Haymarket, said the court, was a round bomb, consisting of two semi-globes fastened by bolts or solder, the metal being an alloy of tin and lead with traces of zinc, iron and antimony. A projecting fuse which had to be ignited, was necessary to set the bomb off. Many of the bombs manufactured by Louis Lingg, who had declared his intention to make bombs at least six weeks before May 1, and had transported dynamite to his room around the middle of March, were spherical in shape and had projecting fuses. Shells of bombs demonstrated to have been of Lingg's manufacture, were shown to be of the same composition by chemical analysis. Dissimilarities between the Haymarket bomb and those made by Lingg could easily be explained by the crude materials and tools employed by the latter. Furthermore, a nut taken from the body of Policeman Hahn on May 5 was not only similar to the nuts on Lingg's bombs, but, in fact, fitted the thread of the bolts which held the two halves together.[47] In view of this evidence, the Court observed that "we think the jury were warranted in believing . . . that the bomb, which killed Degan, was one of the bombs made by the defendant Lingg."[48]

Lingg made bombs, proceeded the court, because he was a member of the I.W.P.A. which urged the destruction of the existing order by force and the communization of capital. Groups and a number of armed sections belonging to this organization existed in Chicago. There was a general committee which met in the building housing the offices of the *Arbeiter-Zeitung* to which all the Chicago groups but one, the North-West Side Group, sent delegates. The I.W.P.A. had its press and its Bureau of Information.[49] The Court concluded that the "branch of the International Workingmen's [*sic*] Association which existed in Chicago . . . was a compact, well disciplined organization." [50] This organization was in itself an unlawful conspiracy. "Its *purpose* was unlawful," declared the Court. "It designed to bring about a social revolution," which meant the destruction of the right of private property. "The police and the militia were looked upon as protectors and guardians of the form of ownership in property objected to. Hence, 'social revolution' meant war upon the police and militia." [51] As unlawful as its purpose were the methods employed by the International, for these involved the arming and drilling of groups of men in direct violation of the militia law of Illinois. [52]

The defendants, stated the Court, shaped the policy of the International. They attempted to increase its membership, and they openly preached the social revolution by word and print. They urged the use of force and advised violence. [53] "The time, when the war against the police was to be inaugurated," the Court further declared, "was not an indefinite period in the future. The evidence shows, that the date fixed for the inauguration of the social revolution, was the 1st of May, 1886." [54] The court thus decided that the eight-hour movement, because *some* of the defendants participated in it was to initiate the social revolution. [55] The defendants manufactured and handled bombs; they purchased or planned to acquire firearms; they bought quantities of dynamite. This was all done in behalf of the International in preparation for the social revolution. [56] The Court concluded that Lingg constructed bombs "under the auspices of the International Association, and in furtherance of its objects and purposes. What he did was merely a part of the general preparation, which the other defendants and the groups . . . , were making for the conflict expected to take place in the early part of May, 1886." [57] From this it followed, in the words of the Court, that "the jury were warranted in believing from the evidence, that the bomb, which exploded at the Haymarket, was made by the defendant Lingg in furtherance of the conspiracy already described." [58]

Was the bomb thrown by a member of the conspiracy? Did those who helped themselves to bombs in Neff's Hall expect to find them there? Was their delivery to that Hall part of a pre-conceived scheme within the general conspiracy? To each of these vital questions the Court answered in the affirmative, and offered as proof the Monday night meeting and the acceptance of Engel's plan. The court declared that "the jury were justified in finding that the actors upon the stage of Tuesday night's tragedy were playing the parts assigned to them in the conspiracy of the previous night, and that the death of Degan occurred as a part of the execution of that conspiracy, and while the parties to it were engaged in carrying it out." [59] The police, therefore, had acted properly in breaking up the Haymarket meeting. The Court also concluded that the bomb served as the signal for a fusillade of revolver shots from those who attended the meeting. In observing that "The mode of attack, as made, corresponded with the mode of attack, as planned," the Court showed that it had completely accepted the theory of the State.[60] Much space in the opinion was consumed in arguing away the discrepancies in the evidence,[61] and the Court, while recognizing the existence of the evidence introduced by the defense, depended wholly upon the evidence for the State. It remarked, of course, that the jury could draw whatever conclusions it pleased from the evidence.[62]

The offhand manner in which the Court ignored defense testimony is illustrated by the following comment:

"Counsel for the defense claim, that there is no proof showing the bomb to have been thrown by any one of the members of the organization for whose use Lingg may have made it; that the bomb may have been thrown by some person outside of that organization and having a private grievance of his own against the police; in other words, that the bomb-thrower has not been identified as a member of the conspiracy or as a person employed by it or acting in its interest.

"We think, however, that the jury were justified in believing from the evidence, that the man who threw the bomb, was either a member of the conspiracy, or an agent employed by it. . . . Three circumstances especially served to identify him as being connected with the conspiracy. First, the bomb, that exploded, was one of the bombs made by Lingg; second, the bombs made by Lingg were finished and distributed so short a time before the explosion, that they could hardly have been obtained elsewhere than from his possession; third, the throwing of the bomb occurred almost at the same time with the firing of the shots; the latter followed so closely upon the former, that the two cannot be regarded as otherwise than as parts of a joint attack showing that the man, who threw the bomb, and the men, who fired the shots, were acting in unison with each other; this negatives the idea of independent action by an outside individual having a private grudge; the character of the attack as a joint one and the concert of action between those making it identify it as that kind of attack, which the conspirators planned to make." [63]

A careful analysis was made by the Court of the evidence against each of the defendants in turn. Engel and Fischer, it declared, were involved in the Monday night plan. "They advised and induced a band of 70 or 80 armed and drilled men to enter into a plot to murder the police in a certain contingency. . . . The murder of Degan took place as the legitimate consequence of an attempt to accomplish the objects of the conspiracy originated and planned by themselves. Therefore they aided, abetted, advised and encouraged the commission of that murder." [64] The fact that both Engel and Fischer were absent when the bomb was thrown was immaterial. [65] The Court found great significance in the fact that when Fischer was arrested on the morning of the fifth, he carried a loaded revolver, a ground file, cartridges, a fulminating cap, and that he wore a belt buckle bearing the insignia "L. & W.V." [66]

Spies' offenses were much more serious. He had inserted the word *Ruhe*. If he was cognizant of its meaning, he was aiding in the execution of the conspiracy. If he was not, it was immaterial. He had issued the "Revenge Circular." He had announced the Haymarket meeting, called it to order and addressed it. Over a number of years he had appealed to the workers to arm, and had urged them to employ force. The McCormick disturbance was laid completely at his door. Finally, he was a party (in some mysterious fashion) to the Monday night plan because some of those attending that gathering were present at the offices of the *Arbeiter-Zeitung* on Monday afternoon, when the meeting for the *following night* was discussed.[67]

Schwab, the Court pointed out, had written an article which appeared in the *Arbeiter-Zeitung* on May 4, in which he announced the existence of the class struggle, and declared that since peaceful action was fruitless the worker must defend himself with force. Since the members of the I.W.P.A. read the *Arbeiter-Zeitung,* said the Court, and since the evidence shows that Degan met his death at the hands of the International, it remained for the jury to determine whether the attack upon the police in the Haymarket was causally connected with the inflammatory language used in this and other newspaper articles. The Court itself left no doubt as to the manner in which it would answer this question.[68] Inciting to riot through the spoken or written word by an individual without his actual presence or participation at the riot, remarked the Court, is perfectly good legal theory. The fact that "Schwab went to Deering and there addressed some of the workingmen, who were expected at the Haymarket,[?] but failed to come, would in no wise lessen his responsibility for the death of Degan, if his acts and declarations . . . helped to cause that death. If he belonged to the same conspiracy with Degan's murderer and the murder of Degan was perpetrated in furtherance of that conspiracy, then the act of the murderer was his act." [69]

Did the court realize quite how significant those two "ifs" were?

Both Schwab and Spies, held the Court, were connected with the conspiracy resulting in Degan's death by the testimony of Thompson, apart from all the other evidence submitted. Laboring to render Thompson's story refutation-proof,[70] the Court declared that "Thompson's testimony is positive in its character and he is unimpeached as a witness, while that of the defense upon this subject is, for the most part, negative in character."[71] Gilmer's testimony though not unqualifiedly approved by the court, was not rejected. The court was generally willing to pass judgment on the evidence in other instances, either directly or by implication. Here it contented itself with remarking that there was a mass of testimony

"in reference to the statements made by Thompson and Gilmer. Some of this testimony sustains those statements and some of it discredits them. Any further review of it . . . will be impossible in this opinion. It is sufficient to say that it is very conflicting. It was the province of the jury to pass upon it. . . .

"It is not necessary for us to pass any opinion upon it, as we think there is enough evidence in the record to sustain the findings of the jury independently of the testimony given by Thompson and Gilmer."[72]

Though Fielden was not present at the Monday night meeting, he became a member of the conspiracy by joining those engaged in its execution on Tuesday. This conclusion, the Court felt, was called for by the evidence introduced during the trial.[73] His conduct at the Haymarket, "considered in connection with his acts prior thereto and with all the other facts . . . certainly warranted the jury in finding that he was one of the conspirators."[74] The Court similarly implicated Parsons. On the basis of his acts, declarations and affiliations prior to the Haymarket meeting and his presence and speech at that gathering,[75] it concluded that "The jury were warranted in believing that . . . Parsons was associated with the man, who threw the bomb and the men, who fired the shots . . . in a conspiracy to bring about a social revolution in Chicago by force on or about May 1, 1886. . . ." [76] His speech at the Haymarket was incendiary, and "he joined the others in their execution of the conspiracy and thereby became a party to it." [77]

Nothing throughout the lengthy opinion compares with the solemn statement of the Court concerning Oscar Neebe's guilt. All the evidence submitted against Neebe showed that he was a member of the International, that he had been active in the labor movement, that he had distributed copies of the "Revenge Circular," that he had held stock to the value of two dollars in the organization which published the *Arbeiter-Zeitung,* and that a pistol, sword, breech-loading gun, and red flag were found in his home. [78] The Court asserted that when someone

"as prominently connected as Neebe was with the International organization and its organ and leaders, was proven to have been engaged late on the night before the Haymarket murder in distributing an inflammatory circular calling upon ignorant workingmen to arm themselves and avenge the act of the police in quelling a riotous disturbance, we cannot say that the jury were not justified in holding him responsible, along with his confederates, for the murder of Tuesday night of one of the very policemen, whose death he was urging on Monday night. We do not think that the trial court erred in refusing the instructions asked on his behalf." [79]

The Court may be charged with failing in presenting the facts in the case, to consider properly any evidence except that which had been introduced by the State. Sometimes it dismissed evidence for the defense in the most perfunctory manner. Thus, it ignored Mayor Harrison's testimony and described the Haymarket meeting as disorderly, turbulent, and extremely dangerous. [80] It concluded that Spies incited the lumber-shovers to attack McCormick's plant, and interpreted Fielden's remark, "We are peaceable," as a signal for the bombing.[81]

In its rulings on points of law, the Court completely upheld the State. Upon the questions concerning the jury, the court held that (1) since eleven members of the jury were accepted when the defense still had not exhausted its peremptory challenges, the defense had no ground for complaint; (2) that where challenges for cause were overruled before the last juror was taken and talesmen had to be challenged peremptorily the defense had no complaint because they did not sit upon the jury; (3) that the only question the Supreme Court could properly consider was "Did the trial court err in overruling the challenge for cause of Sanford, the twelfth juror, or, in other words, was he a competent juror?" in answer to which the Court declared that he was competent; (4) that the trial judge did not err because Sanford's opinions were not so "strong and deep" that they could not easily be removed; (5) that the statutory law on jurors is not unconstitutional; (6) and that a prejudice against Anarchism, Socialism and Communism cannot be said to disqualify a juror.[82] A prejudice against socialists, communists and anarchists, said the Court, is merely a prejudice against crime. This would not force a jury to prejudge an innocent and honest man, and would not, therefore, disqualify a juror.[83] It could be argued from this that when a man admits he is an anarchist, he automatically confesses he is a criminal, and the presumption of guilt against him is strengthened. A related question involved the charge of bias on the part of the special bailiff, Ryce.[84] The affidavits testifying to his prejudice, asserted the Court, were mere hearsay, and, even if Ryce did make the statement attributed to him, it does not appear that the defendants were harmed by it.[85]

The most important questions of law arose in connection with instructions given by Judge Gary for the State and those which he refused to the defense. To the fourth instruction the defense had objected vigorously. "The theory of the fourth instruction," wrote the Court, "was that the bomb-thrower was sufficiently identified, if he belonged to the conspiracy and if he threw the bomb to carry out the conspiracy and further its designs, even though his name and personal description were not known. We do not think that this theory was an erroneous one." [86] This statement is deceptively ingenious. How is it possible to identify "sufficiently" an unknown man merely by assuming that he belonged to the conspiracy and threw the bomb? In effect the Court said that if the unknown man belonged to the conspiracy and if he threw the bomb, he was the bomb-thrower who belonged to the conspiracy! Thus an unknown bomb-thrower was "sufficiently identified" by assuming *without real evidence* that he belonged to the conspiracy.

In further answer to the contention of the defense that membership in a conspiracy could only be proved by some identification, the Court pointed out that some of the counts in the indictment charged that Rudolph Schnaubelt threw the bomb, while other counts in the indictment charged an unknown with the deed. Evidence had been presented in proof of both contentions. The jury was at liberty to believe either set of testimony. The defense was neatly pinned not upon one, but upon both horns of the dilemma. The burden of proof was thrown upon the defense and not upon the prosecution. If the defense showed that Schnaubelt was not the bomb-thrower, it proved that an "unknown" was.

"Counsel for plaintiffs in error," said the Court, "say that 'membership in the supposed conspiracy could not be proved without some evidence of identification.' In the first place some of the counts in the indictment charged that Rudolph Schnaubelt threw the bomb. Evidence was introduced tending to support this count. If the jury believed it, they must have found that the crime was committed by a member of the conspiracy, the proof as to Schnaubelt's membership in it being uncontradicted.

"In the next place, some of the counts in the indictment charged that the bomb was thrown by an unknown person. All the proof introduced by the defendants themselves, tending to show that Schnaubelt did not throw the bomb, tended also to prove that an unknown person threw it. If the jury believed the evidence of the defense upon this subject, they had before them other testimony from which they were justified in believing that the bomb-thrower though unknown by name or personal description, was a member of the conspiracy, and acting in furtherance of its objects." [87]

Strong exception had been taken by the defense to the last sentence of the fifth instruction,[88] on the score that there was no evidence in the record to support the hypothesis upon which it rested. To this the Court answered:

"We think there was such evidence. The hypothesis is, that the time and place for bringing about the destruction of the authorities was left to the judgment of some of the conspirators, instead of being definitely agreed upon by all of them. The publication of the word 'Ruhe'. . . was to indicate the *time* for the social revolution to begin and for the armed men to gather at their meeting places. Its publication was left to the judgment and discretion of a committee appointed by the conspirators. This committee was also to report to the armed men at what *place* the conflict with the police had occurred." [89]

Only a willful misreading of the evidence could make this conclusion possible.

Instruction number five and one-half had been regarded as particularly pernicious by the defense. It urged that the instruction "assumes that mere *general advice* . . . to commit deeds of violence, as contained in speeches or publications, without reference to the particular crime charged and without specifying object, manner, time or place, works responsibility as for murder," and further that it did not refer to the evidence. The court declared that ground for the second objection was removed by the instruction of the trial judge *sua motu,* to which the defense had separately objected. With reference to the first objection, the Court asserted that the interpretation given to it by the defense was mistaken, and that the instruction itself was corrected in the light of the restrictions and limitations of all the other instructions. Taken with all the others, said the Court, instruction five and one-half could not be misleading.[90] Despite this assurance, the defense and the court were in violent conflict over its meaning. This is what it meant to the Court:

"If the defendants, as a means of bringing about the social revolution and as a part of the larger conspiracy to effect such revolution, also conspired to excite classes of workingmen in Chicago into sedition, tumult and riot and to use of deadly weapons and the taking of human life, and for [such purposes] advised and encouraged such classes by newspaper articles and speeches to murder the authorities of the city, and a murder of a policeman resulted from such advice and encouragement, the defendants are responsible therefor." [91]

All the exceptions taken by the defense to the remarks of the State's attorney went for nought. The Court could "not see that the remarks of the State's attorney in his arguments to the jury were marked by any such improprieties, as require a reversal of the judgment." [92] The other objections of the defense to certain instructions given in behalf of the State were decisively negatived by the Court. To the complaint that the trial judge had improperly refused several vital instructions to the defense, the court answered that none of these instructions was improperly rejected. The arguments in support of this general conclusion were similar to those employed in the affirmation of the correctness of the instructions granted to the State.[93]

Those sections of the opinion dealing with the question of conspiracy constitute its salient feature. In them the court held that the State's conspiracy theory was good law. In the light of this, the following facts call for attention. Shortly before the spring of 1887, a "conspiracy bill," sponsored by Mr. Merritt, was introduced in the Illinois legislature. By March 8, the House Committee on Judiciary was considering the measure. It was passed and became law during the same session of the legislature, before the decision of the State Supreme Court was rendered. This stringent measure was designed to cope with such cases as the present one. It incorporated in every particular the theory of conspiracy which the State had formulated during the trial in the lower court, and which it followed upon appeal.

"If any person shall," the law reads, "by speaking to any public or private assemblage of people or in any public place, or shall, by writing, printing or publishing or by causing to be written, printed, published or circulated any written or printed matter, advise, encourage, aid, abet, or incite a local revolution, or the overthrowing or destruction of the existing order of society by force or violence, or the resistance to, and destruction of, the lawful power and authority of the legal authorities of this State, or of any of the towns, cities or counties of this State or by any of the means aforesaid shall advise, abet, encourage, or incite the disturbance of the public peace, and by such disturbance an attempt at revolution or destruction of public order, or resistance to such authorities shall therefore ensue, and human life is taken, or any person injured or property destroyed, every person so aiding, etc., shall be deemed as having conspired with the person or persons who actually commit the crime, and shall be deemed a principal in the perpetration of the same, *and shall be punished accordingly, and it shall not be necessary for the prosecution to show that the speaking was heard or the written or printed matter was read or communicated to the person or persons actually committing the crime, if such speaking, writing, etc., is shown to have been done in a public manner.*

"If two or more persons," the law further provided, "conspire to overthrow the existing order of society by force and violence . . . , and a human being is killed, or person injured, or property destroyed by any of the persons engaged in such conspiracy, or by anyone who may participate with them, . . . then all of the persons who may have conspired together as aforesaid, together with all persons who may participate in carrying into effect their common design, shall be deemed guilty of the crime committed by ony one or more of such persons, . . . and shall be punished accordingly; notwithstanding the time and place for the bringing about [of] such revolution . . . had not been definitely agreed upon by such conspirators, but was left to the exigencies of the time or of the judgment of co-conspirators, or some one or more of them."

Still another section of the same law facilitated conviction by making it unnecessary for the State to prove that those charged with conspiracy ever came together and entered into some agreement. It would be sufficient if it simply appeared that those charged with the crime were actually in concert, regardless of whether they acted separately or together, as long as the acts of each one knowingly made for the same unlawful result.[94]

If the men were "legally" convicted under the existing statutes, why was it necessary to formulate a new conspiracy law? If the theory of conspiracy under which they were convicted was warranted by the old law, why a new statute which followed it letter for letter? If under the old law, it was not "necessary for the prosecution to show that the speaking was heard or the written or printed matter was read or communicated to the person or persons actually committing the crime," providing it was "done in a public manner," why should the new statute specifically provide for this?

Was the Merritt "Conspiracy Law" an attempt to legalize a theory of conspiracy which was employed during the trial and which had no solid basis in law?

NOTES CHAPTER XVII

1. *Ibid.*, p. 607; Chicago *Tribune,* October 10, 1886.
2. See below, chap. XIX *passim.*
3. Chicago *Tribune,* October 8, 1886.

4. *Workmen's Advocate,* March 29, 1887.
5. Interview reported in *John Swinton's Paper,* September 26, 1886.
6. Under the Illinois procedure, the defendants became the plaintiffs. To avoid confusion this change in terminology will not be followed.
7. "It [Black's oral argument] was an able presentation of the smaller flaws of the prosecution, but was really technical in its character." Chicago *Inter Ocean,* March 19, 1887.
8. *Ibid.,* Chicago *Tribune,* March 18 and 19, 1887.
9. *In the Supreme Court of Illinois, Northern Grand Division, March Term, A. D. 1887. August Spies et al., vs. The People of the State of Illinois. Brief on the Law for Defendants in Error,* Chicago, 1887 (hereafter cited as *Brief on the Law for the State*). The second brief has already been cited as *Brief on the Facts for the State.*
10. *In the Supreme Court of Illinois. The Anarchists' Cases. Brief for the Defendants.* [*sic*] *Leonard Swett,* Chicago, 1887. Bound with this there is a synopsis of Swett's oral argument before the court with separate title: *In the Supreme Court of Illinois. The Anarchists' Cases, Synopsis of Mr. Swett's Oral Argument.*
11. This brief has already been cited as *Brief and Argument.*
12. His analysis of the nature of conspiracy is found in his brief, pp. 83-93.
13. This summary is based upon his brief, oral argument and Chicago *Tribune,* March 13, 1887.
14. *In the Supreme Court of Illinois, Northern Grand Division, March Term, A. D. 1887. August Spies et al., vs. The People of the State of Illinois, Argument of W. P. Black, for Plaintiffs in Error,* Chicago, 1887, p. 1.
15. The defense complained especially against the introduction of Most's book, the exhibition before the jury of the bloody clothes worn by officers other than Degan, the letter and postcard from Most to Spies, testimony concerning the "bombs" found in Chicago after the Haymarket, and the introduction of the flags, mottoes and insignia of the I.W.P.A. See *Swett's Brief,* pp. 68-79.
16. *Ibid.,* pp. 37.
17. *Yoe* v. *The People,* 49 Ill. 410.
18. "An accessory to a felony cannot be prosecuted for a substantive offense, but only as an accessory to the crime perpetrated by the principal felon, and in order to his conviction although it is not necessary now to show that the principal felon has been convicted, [which had formerly been the rule under the English Common Law] it is necessary to show that the substantive offense, to which he is charged as having been accessory, has been committed by the principal felon." *Hatchett* v. *Commonwealth,* 75 Va., 925 (Jan. Term, 1882), at p. 932.
19. See instruction no. 5½, pp. 307-308.
20. *State* vs. *Trice,* 88 N. C., 627.

21. *People* vs. *Bennett*, 49 N. Y., 137 (1872).
22. *People* v. *Kennedy*, 32 N. Y., 141 (1865).
23. *Ibid.*, p. 146.
24. *Petts* v. *The State*, 43 Miss., 472.
25. *Chambers* v. *The People*, 105 Ill., 409 (Jan., 1883).
26. *Fox* v. *The People*, 95 Ill., 71.
27. *Earle* v. *The People*, 99 Ill., 123. Other citations were in agreement with these general conclusions; *cf.*, *State* v. *Williams*, 65 N. C., 505 at p. 506; *Tucker* v. *Hennecker*, 41 N. H., 317, at p. 318.
28. See above, pp. 239-247.
29. Other points raised by the defense in the appeal, minor in nature, will be touched upon in connection with the decision of the Supreme Court. See below, chap. XVIII.
30. *Brief on the Law for the State*, p. 2.
31. *Ibid.*, p. 11.
32. *Cf.*, the English cases cited and *State* v. *Green* (15 So. Car. Rep. 67).
33. *Nevill* v. *The State*, 60 Ind., 308.
34. *Baxter* v. *The People*, 8 Ill., 568 (1846), and *Brennan* v. *The People*, 15 Ill., 511.
35. *Dempsey* v. *The People*, 47 Ill., 323 at p. 326 (1868).
36. *Brief on the Law for the State*, p. 43, *cf.*, pp. 46-47.
37. James B. Thayer, "'Law and Fact' in Jury Trials," *Harvard Law Review*, vol. 4, no. 4, November 15, 1890, pp. 147-175 *passim*, quoted section, p. 159.
38. *Greenleaf on Evidence*, sec. 3; *cf.*, *State* v. *Winner*, 17 Kan., 298.
39. *Greenleaf on Evidence*, sec. 93.
40. McLean, 513, at p. 601.
41. *Campell* v. *The Commonwealth*, 84 Penn. St., 187.
42. *Cox Criminal Law Cases*, p. 288.
43. Chicago *Tribune* and Chicago *Inter Ocean*, September 15, 1887.
44. *Anarchist Case. Advance Sheets of the Illinois Reporter, Comprising Pages 1 to 267, Inclusive of Volume 122, November 5, 1887*, Springfield, 1887 (cited hereafter as *Advance Sheets*), pp. 266-267; Chicago *Inter Ocean*, September 15, 1887. The wording in these sources is not identic.
45. For the opinion in full see either *Spies* v. *The People*, 122 Ill. 1, or *North Eastern Reporter*, vol. 12, pp. 865-996 or *Advance Sheets*, pp. 1-267; the latter is followed for reasons of convenience; most of the Chicago papers carried full summaries of the decision, *cf.*, *Inter Ocean*, September 15, 1887.
46. *Advance Sheets*, p. 102.
47. *Ibid.*, pp. 102-111.
48. *Ibid.*, p. 111.
49. *Ibid.*, pp. 112-119.
50. *Ibid.*, p. 199.
51. *Idem.*
52. *Ibid.*, p. 120. See above, p. 150.

53. *Ibid.*, pp. 120-126.
54. *Ibid.*, p. 127.
55. *Ibid.*, pp. 127-131 *passim.*
56. *Ibid.*, pp. 132-135.
57. *Ibid.*, p. 135.
58. *Ibid.*, p. 139.
59. *Ibid.*, p. 169.
60. *Ibid.*, p. 158.
61. *Ibid.*, pp. 139-169 *passim.*
62. *Cf. ibid.*, pp. 173-174.
63. *Ibid.*, pp. 175-176.
64. *Ibid.*, p. 176.
65. *Ibid.*, pp. 177-178.
66. *Ibid.*, p. 178.
67. *Ibid.*, pp. 178-191.
68. *Ibid.*, pp. 191-198.
69. *Ibid.*, p. 191.
70. *Ibid.*, pp. 201-207.
71. *Ibid.*, p. 207.
72. *Ibid.*, p. 212.
73. *Ibid.*, pp. 213-218.
74. *Ibid.*, p. 218.
75. *Ibid.*, pp. 218-224.
76. *Ibid.*, p. 224.
77. *Ibid.*, p. 225.
78. *Ibid.*, pp. 226-227; and see above, pp. 280-281.
79. *Ibid.*, p. 227.
80. *Ibid.*, pp. 155-156.
81. *Idem.*
82. *Ibid.*, pp. 256-264.
83. *Ibid.*, p. 263.
84. See above, pp. 238-239.
85. *Ibid.*, pp. 256-266.
86. *Ibid.*, p. 240.
87. *Idem; cf.*, pp. 241-243.
88. See above, pp. 306-307.
89. *Ibid.*, pp. 243-244.
90. *Ibid.*, pp. 244-249.
91. *Ibid.*, p. 251.
92. *Ibid.*, p. 266.
93. *Ibid.*, pp. 253-255.
94. Chicago *Tribune*, ʼarch 8-10, 1887; *Appleton's Annual Cyclopaedia, 1887*, pp. 374-375; see below, pp. 537-538.

XVIII. TO THE UNITED STATES SUPREME COURT

T HE opinion of the State Supreme Court, which the
Nation described as "an admirable example of terse,
clear, cogent statement of fact and of legal argument
based thereon," [1] left only two recourses open. The case could
be carried before the United States Supreme Court, and, if that
failed, the governor could be appealed to for a commutation of
sentence or pardon. Capt. Black and his fellow attorneys were
rudely shocked and keenly disappointed by the decision of the
State Supreme Court. "If that decision is correct," said Black,
"there is nothing to prevent the arrest, trial, conviction and
execution of any man who can be proved an anarchist." [2]

Meanwhile, the prisoners, though they had harsh words
for the decision, accepted defeat with equanimity. Spies sarcastically remarked that "it is now time for the British government to hang Gladstone and his associates for inciting the
riot at Mitchellstown [*sic*].[3] . . . If the people of this great
country are satisfied that free speech should be strangled, then
what use for me to complain." Parsons announced in the
grand manner that "I am sure our dear friends on the outside are more shocked by this decision than we are, and my
heart bleeds for them and for the insulted principles and traditions of my country. I have done my duty to myself and the
people [,] and I shall fearlessly stand the consequences. How
can I do otherwise when I know that I have not committed
a single crime against my fellow men or violated one clause

of the constitution?" Fielden and Schwab were in complete agreement with these sentiments. Fischer's comment was laconic: "I never expected anything else, and am not surprised at the result." [4]

All eight men kept themselves well in hand. Perhaps much of their self-possession was due to their failure to comprehend how much closer they had come to death. However great their individual courage, the seven who were faced with the gallows were still too young to await death with tranquility. And if by chance the governor were to commute their sentences and they escaped the hangman's noose, was there much choice between that and the living death of life imprisonment? [5]

Popular feeling in Chicago against the condemned men still ran high. The "respectable elements" of the city made no perceptible effort to hide the joy with which they received the decision. "Phil" Armour said: "It is a righteous verdict." [6] The firm of Peter Van Schaack and Sons declared that they had never received a piece of news which pleased them equally. George P. Bay, a banker, curtly commented, "I say carry out the law," and another outstanding business man felt that the case and the men should have been disposed of by "May 6 of last year. . . ." [7] Business interests perceived in the case an opportunity for injuring not only radicalism but the cause of labor, and the satisfaction with which they greeted the Supreme Court decision is understandable. [8] A statement attributed to a partner in a large Chicago clothing firm shows that it was felt that the case would irreparably injure the cause of labor. "No, I don't consider those people to have been found guilty of any offense, but *they must be hanged*," he is reported to have said. "I'm not afraid of anarchy; oh, no; it's the utopian scheme of a few, a *very* few, philosophizing cranks, who are amiable withal, but I do consider that the *labor movement should be crushed!* The Knights of Labor will never dare to create discontent again if these men are hanged." [9]

The daily press paid high tribute to the opinion of the Supreme Court. The Chicago *Tribune* was convinced that no person without bias "can read the invincible reasoning of the court without being convinced that the judges have performed a duty which they could not escape under the obligations of their oaths of office. . . . The decision rendered is in every sense an honor to the court and it will live in history as a timely, just, noble and fearless vindication of the supremacy of law." [10] The Chicago *Inter Ocean* was certain that the decision would rank as a "classic" in the future. Those who had feared a reversal no longer had cause to be disturbed. "The whole country," it said, "rests more easily now that the judgment of the Supreme Court . . . is made public." Society was deeply in debt to the Court. "The Nation was threatened with the development of a new phase of crime," which the decision averted for all time. [11]

From the "legal press" there came vigorous commendation. The *Albany Law Journal* declared that

"the opinion of the Illinois Supreme Court in the anarchists' case ought to convince any lawyer that the defendants had a fair trial, as free from error as possible in judicial proceedings, and that they are all guilty and richly deserve extirpation. A more depraved set of scoundrels never infested the earth, and society will be safer for their permanent absence. . . . Society will get no peace until it makes a few examples of these socialistic firebrands, haters of mankind, spoilers of property, defiers of God and judgment. We recommend to every lawyer to read Judge Magruder's opinion. A more masterly and convincing one was never uttered. . . . Every good American ought to read this case. . . . Then the community will wake up to a realization of what a volcano they have been sleeping on; what a viper this free and hospitable land has taken to its hearth. . . . The might of Law for Dynamite! say we." [12]

The *Columbia Law Times* observed that the Supreme Court decision was one "destined to be as wide reaching in its effect as any ever before delivered in this country." [13] It declared that "no person can read the able opinion of the Supreme Court without feeling convinced that the verdict of the jury was legal, just and right. The decision itself deserves an honorable place in history as a 'timely, noble and fearless vindication of the law.' " [14]

Comments of this nature filled the columns of the daily press throughout the country. The St. Louis *Globe-Democrat,* persuaded that the men should have been hanged a year earlier, was willing to forgive the delay, if the "ceremony" were postponed no longer.[15] The Kansas City *Journal* saw in the men "now awaiting execution in Chicago . . . a solemn announcement to all the world that this nation will not tolerate the methods of anarchy, and that the American people can and will save themselves from despotism by strangling the agents of anarchy at the very inception of their bloody business." [16] Regardless of the section of the country or the locality to which one turns, the same opinions are to be found. Only in intensity do the expressions of gratification over the Supreme Court decision vary.[17] The religious press also urged that the men should not escape the death penalty.[18]

But, as it will be seen, since the opening of the trial in Judge Gary's court, the dissenting voices had grown greatly. They were no longer few in number; they no longer represented a tiny minority. After the Supreme Court of the United States had played its relatively small but important part in the case, the note of dissent increased tremendously.

Even before the State Supreme Court rendered its decision, counsel for the defense had worked out the basis for an appeal to the highest court of the land.[19] Among the minor tasks involved was the preparation of a two-million word transcript of the record of the trial in the lower court, at a cost of $4,000 to the defense.[20]

Again there was a change in the legal staff of the defense. Of the original counsel only Mr. Salomon and Capt. Black appeared before the Supreme Court. Associated with them now were men of national reputation,—Benjamin F. Butler, Roger A. Pryor and J. Randolph Tucker. Either Capt.

Black or George Schilling, probably the latter, was responsible for securing the services of Roger A. Pryor, who was practising law in New York City with much success. Before the Civil War he had been an ardent advocate of States' rights and an extreme southern "fire-eater." When his service in the Confederate army was cut short by capture in 1864, he had already reached the rank of general. At the close of the War he established himself in New York City. He had been retained by Theodore Tilton in the latter's notorious suit against Henry Ward Beecher, and participated in other outstanding cases.[21] Pryor appears to have sincerely believed that the eight men had not received a fair trial. "I have not the least doubt," he is reported to have said, "that our application for a writ of error will be granted. . . . Indeed, the records show so many errors in the ruling and in the trial that I cannot see how our application can be denied."[22]

It is difficult to say what brought Ben Butler into the case. He probably entered it at Pryor's request, but Butler's unsavory career makes one suspicious of his every act. Perhaps his self-confessed weakness for taking the part of the "underdog" was the motive for Butler's participation. It has been charged, and with reason, that the quick-witted general sometimes limited the aid he rendered the "under-dog" to mere vocal encouragement, avoiding all personal participation in a fray.[23] Butler's association with the defense probably strengthened the case of the condemned in the public eye. It did not, however, strengthen their legal staff, for he was a skilful and cunning courtroom pleader rather than a profound student of the law.[24]

The acquisition of Butler and Pryor occasioned relatively little surprise. But Randolph Tucker's association with the defense brought the puzzled query: "Randolph Tucker—orator, scholar, statesman—what has he to do in such a case?"[25] The son of an eminent Virginia jurist, John Randolph Tucker had been professor of equity and public law at Washington and Lee, and had served in Congress from 1874-1887. He ranked as a leading constitutional lawyer, and was shortly to become dean of the Law School at Washington and Lee.[26] Though not sanguine over the outcome of the appeal, Tucker, of course, hoped that the Supreme Court would act favorably upon the petition of error which had to be presented in behalf of the condemned so that the case could be brought up for review.[27]

On the morning of October 21, counsel for the condemned men appeared in Washington before Justice Harlan. Though it was not customary, the public was admitted, with Justice Harlan's consent, to the small audience chamber. The striking differences in personal appearance of the five lawyers did not fail to attract attention. There was little, bustling Salomon; tall, handsome Capt. Black; General Butler of familiar form and countenance and distinguished dress; grayheaded and scholarly Tucker; and angular General Pryor with massive, granite-like jaw, coal-black eyes and long, black hair.

Shortly after entering the chamber and without even waiting for a formal motion from counsel for the prisoners, Justice Harlan announced that since there was "an application for a writ of error to bring up for review by the Supreme Court of the United States a judgment of the Supreme Court of the State of Illinois," and since the date fixed for the execution of the sentence was November 11, he felt it his duty "to facilitate an early decision of any question in the case of which the Supreme Court . . . may properly take cognizance. If I should allow a writ of error," he continued, "it is quite certain that counsel would have to repeat before that court the argument which they propose now to make before me. On the other hand, if I should refuse the writ, the defendants would be at liberty to renew their application before any other Justice of the Supreme Court; and, as human life and liberty are involved, that Justice might feel obliged . . . to look into the case and determine for himself whether a writ of error should be allowed." Thus the application might be made to each member of the bench, and much valuable time might be wasted. Justice Harlan, therefore, ordered that the counsel for the defense make their application before the full bench of the Supreme Court at its regular session that same day "to the end that early and final action may be had upon the question whether that court has jurisdiction to review the judgment in this case." [28]

The Supreme Court of the United States, of course, possesses limited jurisdiction. To have jurisdiction for such a writ of error, it must appear upon the record of a case "that a federal question was raised, and that the State court decided it adversely to the right claimed. . . ." Under these conditions the Supreme Court may re-examine the judgment of the State court and either affirm or reverse the decision of the latter.[29] The Supreme Court is limited strictly to federal questions. Regardless of the errors in the record, as long as the federal questions are rightly determined, the Court is bound to affirm the judgment of the lower court.[30]

The long petition submitted by the defense counsel averred "that the Supreme Court of Illinois had erred in its judgment, and had deprived [the petitioners] of their rights, privileges and immunities, and that in the proceedings at their trial there was drawn in question the validity of certain statutes of the State of Illinois as being repugnant to the Constitution of the United States, which nevertheless had been judged by the court to be valid." [31] When Roger A. Pryor, shortly after noon, addressed the full bench in support of this petition, he relied upon two points to demonstrate the federal questions involved in the case. The first was that the Illinois statute governing jurors had, by the action of the lower court, "been made to deprive the accused of the right of trial by an impartial jury, had abridged their privileges as citizens of the United States, and [was] about to deprive them of life, etc., without due process of law." The second point was that the prisoners, in violation of rights secured to them by the Constitution, were compelled to be witnesses against themselves over the protests of their counsel. In developing these two points, Pryor briefly surveyed the history of the case. Chief Justice Waite then ordered the printing and submission of the pertinent parts of the record to the Court, and announced that the Court would indicate on the 24th what was further to be done.

On that day Chief Justice Waite said that the Court had decided to hear the arguments of counsel in support of the petition for a writ of error "not only upon the point whether any Federal questions were actually made and decided in the Supreme Court of the State, but also upon the character of those questions, so that we may determine whether they are such as to make it proper for us to bring the case here for review." [32] This decision satisfied even those who were most anxious that the case be brought to an end. It was widely felt that the case, as the Chicago *Inter Ocean* observed "should be tested by every court, State or National, up to that of final appeal." [33]

Ten o'clock on the morning of October 27, two hours before the Court assembled, standing-room was at a premium in the narrow and stuffy Supreme Court chamber. Members of the bar and government officials arrived early to secure seats in the reserved section. The courtroom had not been so crowded in years. The hearing on the following day was equally well attended. From the comments of those present it seemed that a surprisingly large number were sympathetic with the prisoners.

A total of six hours, shared equally by defense and State, was granted for argument. To Randolph Tucker was assigned the task of opening, and he was followed in turn by Attorney General Hunt, Grinnell and Ben Butler, who appeared only in behalf of Spies and Fielden. [34] There is no need to consider here the constitutional arguments of the four attorneys before the Court. Their gist can be adequately presented through an examination of the opinion of the Court. For this, the interested parties did not have long to wait.

On November 2, Chief Justice Waite delivered the opinion, concurred in by the full bench,[35] which denied the writ of error. Chief Justice Waite pointed out that "the writ ought not to be allowed by the court, if it appears from the face of the record that the decision of the Federal question which is complained of was so plainly right as not to require argument. . . ."[36] Quoting from the brief of the defense, the Chief Justice listed the Federal questions there raised:

"'First. Petitioners challenged the validity of the statute of Illinois, under and pursuant to which the trial jury was selected and empanelled, on the ground of repugnancy to the Constitution of the United States, and the state court sustained the validity of the statute.

"'Second. Petitioners asserted and claimed, under the Constitution of the United States, the right, privilege, and immunity of trial by an impartial jury, and the decision of the state court was against the right, privilege, and immunity so asserted and claimed.

"'Third. The State of Illinois made, and the state court enforced against petitioners, a law (the aforesaid statute) whereby the privileges and immunities of petitioners as citizens of the United States, were abridged, contrary to the Fourteenth Amendment of the Federal Constitution.

"'Fourth. Upon their trial for a capital offense, petitioners were compelled . . . to be witnesses against themselves, contrary to the provisions of the Constitution . . . which declare that "no person shall be compelled in any criminal case to be a witness against himself," and that "no person shall be deprived of life or liberty without due process of law."[37]

"'Fifth. That by the action of the state court . . . the petitioners were denied "the equal protection of the laws," contrary to the guaranty of the . . . Fourteenth Amendment of the Federal Constitution.'"[38]

The defense relied heavily upon the "due process" clause of the Fourteenth Amendment and upon the Fifth and Sixth Amendments.[39] Three of the points here considered turn upon the nature of the jury and the statute governing jurors. Other reasons were also advanced in support of the petition for the writ of error. Ben Butler argued that the defendants had been "sentenced to death in their absence. . . ." [40] He also speciously contended that Spies and Fielden, of German and British birth, had been denied the equal protection of the laws of the country guaranteed by the treaties between their native lands and the United States. They had not received a trial by an impartial jury, and Spies had been subjected to unwarranted search and seizure. Under the treaties the prisoners were entitled "to all the rights and privileges at the time such treaties were made. A State had no power to try these men by one of its own laws which was not the law of the land at the time the treaties were ratified." [41] The privileges here violated, he said, were guaranteed by the Fourteenth, Sixth and Fourth Amendments, the last of which offers protection against unreasonable search and seizure.

For more than half a century before 1887, it was agreed that the first ten amendments "were not intended to limit the powers of the state governments in respect to their own people," but operated only upon the Federal government. Thus the defense found it necessary to argue that "while the ten Amendments as limitations on power only apply to the Federal Government, and not to the States, yet in so far as they declare or recognize rights of persons, these rights are theirs, as citizens of the United States, and the Fourteenth Amendment as to such rights limits State power, as the ten Amendments had limited Federal power." [42] In this the defense developed a constitutional theory and argument that appeared frequently in later years. [43]

The Supreme Court denied that the statute governing jurors was in any way unconstitutional, and declared that it "is not repugnant . . . to the constitution of" Illinois or to the Constitution of the United States. [44] Similar statutes elsewhere had already been sustained by the Court. [45] Furthermore the Court found that the constitutional rights of the defendants had not been impaired or violated "in the actual administration of the rule of the statute by the court. . . ." The Court, lim-

ited to a consideration of only two jurors, Denker and Sanford, concluded that the record disclosed no error in the administration of the actual rule of statute so gross as to constitute denial of a trial by an impartial jury.[46]

To the charge that Spies had been forced to testify against
himself, the Court responded that the defendant "voluntarily
offered himself as a witness in his own behalf, and by so doing
he became bound to submit to a proper cross-examination
under the law and practise in the jurisdiction where he was
being tried." If, as it was contended, he was submitted to improper cross-examination on a subject unrelated to the issue
at trial (the Most letter), it was "a question of state law as
administered in the courts of the State, and not of Federal
law." With that the Supreme Court had no concern.[47] Since
no objection was made in the trial court to the introduction
of Most's letter on the ground of unreasonable search and seizure, the Supreme Court had no jurisdiction. "To be review-
able here," declared the Court, "the decision [of a court denying a constitutional right, privilege or immunity] must be
against the right so *set up or claimed*. . . . If the right was
not set up or claimed in the proper court below, the judgment
of the highest court of the State in the action is conclusive, so
far as the right of review here is concerned." [48]

On the same grounds Butler's arguments with reference
to the violation of rights guaranteed to Spies and Fielden by
treaties between their native countries and the United States
were dismissed.[49] Nor could the Court take cognizance of the
presumed absence of the defendants when sentence was pronounced because the record showed the contrary.[50]

"Being of opinion, therefore," concluded the Court, "that
the Federal questions presented by the counsel for the petitioners, and which they say they desire to argue, are not involved in the determination of the case as it appears on the
face of the record, we deny the writ." [51]

To the press throughout the country the highest court of
the land definitively answered those who censured or even ques-

tioned the legality of the first trial and the opinion of the State Supreme Court. "No candid, thinking person," observed the Chicago *Tribune,* "can read the opinion of the Supreme Court and doubt the legality of the conviction of the anarchists." The *Tribune* noted that if the Court

"had followed its usual procedure the application for a writ of error in the Anarchists' case would have been dismissed as a matter of course and without any argument before the full bench. That a contrary course was taken was most fortunate. . . . By calling for argument not only on the technical preliminary question but on the merits of the case itself, the Court without granting a writ of error gave the Anarchists the extraordinary privilege of a full hearing even when it was not shown that the court had jurisdiction. Such unusual action was justified because human life was at stake and the legal questions involved were of paramount importance." [52]

The *Albany Law Journal* was pleased that "The last legal hope of the anarchists has been dispelled. The Supreme Court of the United States have denied their writ of error. . . . All that is left to these murderers is an appeal to the favor and leniency of that society which they have outraged, defied and sought to destroy. To use their own words, 'The law will throttle them' because they did not succeed in 'throttling the law.' " [53]

"Law and order" had won its victory in the courts. Nothing must interfere with the execution of the sentence; to this end the press marshalled public opinion. The newspaper reader was not permitted to forget that the condemned were "monsters" comparable only to "rattlesnakes," [54] and that they were boldly impenitent. "Not one word," asserted the Chicago *Times,* "containing or suggesting a feeling of grief for their crime or an indication of the nature of humanity with relation to the victims of it, has any one of them uttered." On the contrary, the prisoners "manifested the spirit of the creature without a soul, but with a heart of stone and a spirit of the archdemon, who glories in the human blood he has spilled, and in the agony and woe and grief unknowable his wickedness has caused." [55]

The State authorities were repeatedly warned against exhibiting the slightest compunction in hanging the condemned. "The sentences must be executed" became a slogan. There was no need to fear that the men would be transformed into martyrs. "Whatever may become of the convicted anarchists . . . there is no danger that they will ever be remembered by the American people other than as conspirators against the public peace." [56] To the New York *Tribune* the whole case demonstrated "that the friends of social order are in a vast majority and that they are able to vindicate the laws which they have made." [57] The "friends of social order" urged: "Now, with no more trouble and expense, let those seven anarchists hang at the legally appointed time." [58] The impending hanging of seven men sometimes failed to satisfy the voracious appetite of newspaper editors. The Cleveland *Leader* warned that anarchists and other revolutionaries would disturb the land until "The might of the law should be asserted in some way even more awe-inspiring and bloody than in the execution of the seven men now standing under the shadows of the gallows." [59]

When it became evident that a shift in public sentiment might make possible the commutation of the sentences to life imprisonment, Governor Oglesby of Illinois was tirelessly exhorted to let the sentences stand unchanged. He was warned not to let "sentimentalists" prevail.[60] The New York *Tribune* apparently thought that the slightest indication of timidity or delay in the execution of the sentence—let alone its modification—would mean that "our civilization is a failure." [61]

However satisfactory the opinion of the Supreme Court was to the friends of "law and order," the latter were not justified in regarding it as a definitive statement on the questions of law involved in the case or on the fairness of the trial in the lower court. Limited to a consideration of Federal questions as they appeared on the record, the Court only said that such questions either had not been raised in the lower courts, or that they had been correctly ruled upon. In the light of its field of proper jurisdiction and constitutional precedent, the opinion of the Supreme Court dismissing the petition for error, is not open to purely legal criticism.[62]

But this does not mean that criticism of the Supreme Court's action was not forthcoming. The Court was upbraided, not so much for what it did, but for what it failed to do. Nothing is more to the point than the sincere and moving letter which William Dean Howells dispatched to the New York *Tribune* on November 4.

"As I have petitioned the Governor of Illinois to commute the death penalty of the anarchists to imprisonment," he wrote, "and have also personally written him in their behalf, I ask your leave to express here the hope that those who are inclined to do either will not lose faith in themselves because the Supreme Court has denied the condemned a writ of error. That court simply affirmed the legality of the forms under which the Chicago Court proceeded; it did not affirm the propriety of trying for murder men fairly indictable for conspiracy alone; and it by no means approved the principle of punishing them because of their frantic opinions, for a crime which they were not shown to have committed. The justice or injustice of their sentence was not before the highest tribunal of our law and unhappily could not be got there. That question must remain for history, which judges the judgment of courts to deal with, and I, for one, cannot doubt what the judgment of history will be.

"But the worst is still for a very few days reparable; the men sentenced to death are still alive, and their lives may be finally saved through the clemency of the Governor, whose prerogative is now the supreme law in their case. I conjure all those who believe that it would be either injustice or impolicy to put them to death to join in urging him by petition, by letter or through the press and from the pulpit and the platform to use his power, in the only direction where it can never be misused, for the mitigation of their punishment." [63]

NOTES CHAPTER XVIII

1. *Nation,* vol. 45, no. 1,161, September 29, 1887, p. 241.
2. Chicago *Inter Ocean,* September 15, 1887; Chicago *Tribune.* September 16, 1887.
3. In September, 1887, there was a riot at Mitchelstown, County Cork, caused by the police attempt to force an official note-taker through the throng at a meeting addressed by Mr. Dillon. R. H. Gretton, *A Modern History of the English People, 1880-1922,* New York, 1930, p. 216.
4. *Advance and Labor Leaf,* September 24, 1887. Joseph Buchanan called on the men shortly after the decision, and asked them what they thought of it. The quotations are from their replies. In the Detroit *Journal,* October 14, 1887, there is a long article by Jo Labadie, based upon an interview with the men in which Spies' comments on the decision are reproduced at length.
5. Interview with George Schilling who was in close touch with the men during those trying days.
6. Chicago *Inter Ocean,* September 15, 1887.
7. Chicago *Tribune,* September 15, 1887.
8. This is in part illustrated by a conversation—supposedly reliably reported—between Capt. Black's wife and a certain George Emery. The latter, described as an "eminent Christian" citizen of Chicago, and a wealthy man, was an active member of the Citizen's Association.

    "Well," Mr. Emery remarked to Mrs. Black, "your husband's clients are going to be hung."

    "Not lawfully," replied the latter.

    "Law! I care nothing for law!" exclaimed Emery, "they shall be hung whether it's lawful or not!"

    "Stay," said Mrs. Black, "you do admit, then, that there's no law by which they can be convicted?"

    "Oh, yes," came the reply, "I'll admit that, but will say that it won't affect the issue; they must be hung anyhow!" *Workmen's Advocate,* September 24, 1887; *Social Science,* vol. 1, no. 17, October 29, 1887; *The Anarchist* (London), November 1, 1887, p. 7; the story also appeared in the New Haven *Advocate* and probably in other publications.
9. Detroit *Journal,* October 14, 1887. This statement appears in the course of a long article by Jo Labadie to whom it was related by a friend of the man who is supposed to have made it, Mr. Hill, the New York partner of the firm of Willoughby, Hill and Co.
10. September 15, 1887.
11. September 15, 1887.
12. October 29, 1887, p. 341.
13. "The Anarchists' Cases," *Columbia Law Times,* vol. 1, no. 1, October, 1887, p. 17. Though unsigned, an ink notation shows that this was written by T. Gold Frost, one of the editors.

14. *Ibid.,* p. 19.
15. Cited in Chicago *Tribune,* September 15, 1887.
16. *Idem;* and undated clipping in Columbia University Library scrapbooks.
17. See Chicago *Tribune,* September 15, 1887, for comments of the Boston *Post,* Boston *Journal,* Minneapolis *Post,* Omaha *Bee,* Omaha *Republican,* Omaha *Herald,* San Francisco *Bulletin,* San Francisco *Chronicle,* San Francisco *Alta,* Kansas City *Star,* New Orleans *Picayune,* Joliet *Express;* for other localities, Chicago *Tribune,* September 16, 1887; New York *Times,* New York *Tribune* and New York *World* for September 15 *ff.,* 1887.
18. *Open Court,* vol. 1, no. 17, September 29, 1887, p. 466.
19. *Workmen's Advocate,* September 17, 1887. Salomon announced that if necessary, the case would be carried to the Federal Court on the following grounds: ". . . 1. On the exercise of the unreasonable search and seizure. 2. On compelling the defendants to give evidence against themselves. 3. On the lower court's denial of the right of free speech. 4. On the lower court's denial of the right of peaceable assemblage. 5. On the lower court's denial of the right of free belief. 6. On the denial of an impartial jury. 7. On the want of proper information of the nature and cause of the accusation." The actual appeal was taken on different grounds.
20. (New York?) *Sun,* October 2, 1887, clipping, Labadie scrap-book.
21. Among them were the Sprague estate litigation, *Ames* v. *Miss.,* the Morley letter case, and the trial of O'Donnell for the killing of the informer Carney. Subsequently he was appointed judge of the Court of Common Pleas of New York by Gov. Hill (in 1890), was elected to that post, and then in 1894 by the revision of the Constitution of New York State was transferred to the State Supreme Court. *The National Cyclopaedia of American Biography,* New York, 1907, vol. 9, p. 147; interview with George Schilling.
22. *Commonweal,* October 15, 1887, p. 331. This is in a letter probably from William Holmes to William Morris.
23. Gamaliel Bradford, *Damaged Souls,* Boston, 1923, pp. 224, 248.
24. Had Ben Butler not virtually retired from active politics at this date, one would suspect that he was making political capital of the case in labor ranks.
25. Quoted in Chicago *Inter Ocean,* October 28, 1887.
26. *The National Cyclopaedia of American Biography,* vol. 7, p. 487.
27. Chicago *Inter Ocean,* October 21, 1887.
28. *Ibid.,* October 22, 1887; *Spies* v. *Illinois,* 123 U. S. 131, at p. 142.
29. William H. Dunbar, "The Anarchists' Case," *Harvard Law Review,* vol. 1, no. 7, February 15, 1888, p. 308. What constituted a federal question was defined in the words of the Revised Statutes, section 709, quoted in *idem.*
30. *Ibid.,* pp. 309-310; Chicago *Inter Ocean,* October 22, 1887.
31. 123 U. S. 131, at pp. 132-133. For the entire petition see *ibid.,* pp. 132-141.

32. *Ibid.*, p. 143.
33. October 22, 1887.
34. For the arguments of Tucker and Butler, see 123 U. S. 131, at pp. 143-155 and pp. 157-163 respectively; for Hunt and Grinnell, Chicago *Inter Ocean,* October 28 and 29, 1887. Pryor submitted a separate brief, in addition to the general brief signed by him with the others. 123 U. S. 131, at pp. 155-156.
35. There were only eight members of the Supreme Court at this time, since Justice William Burnham Woods who died on May 14 was not yet replaced. The seven associate justices were S. F. Miller, S. J. Field, J. P. Bradley, J. M. Harlan, S. Matthews, H. Gray, S. Blatchford.
36. *Ibid.*, p. 164.
37. The quotations are from the Fifth and Fourteenth Amendments. Spies, Parsons and Fielden, it was claimed, were forced to testify against themselves.
38. *Ibid.*, p. 165.
39. The sixth amendment reads: "In all criminal prosecutions the accused shall enjoy the right to a speedy and public trial by an impartial jury. . . ."
40. *Ibid.*, pp. 162-163.
41. *Ibid.*, pp. 157-162 *passim.*
42. *Ibid.*, p. 166.
43. Andrew C. McLaughlin, *A Constitutional History of the United States,* New York, 1935, pp. 729-731.
44. 123 U. S. 131, at p. 170.
45. *Ibid.*, pp. 168-170. A notable case in which the Court sustained this type of statute was *Hopt* v. *Utah,* 120 U. S. 430.
46. *Ibid.*, pp. 170, 179-180.
47. *Ibid.*, p. 180.
48. *Ibid.*, p. 181.
49. *Ibid.*, p. 182.
50. "If this is not in accordance with the fact, the record must be corrected below, not here. It will be time enough to consider whether the objection presents a Federal question when the correction has been made." *Idem.*
51. *Idem.*
52. November 3, 1887.
53. November 12, 1887 (written before the execution).
54. New York *Times,* November 8, 1887.
55. *Ibid.*, November 3, 1887.
56. Chicago *Inter Ocean,* November 6, 1887.
57. November 3, 1887.
58. Nashville *American,* Nov. 3, 1887, quoted in *Public Opinion,* vol. 4, no. 31, November 12, 1887, p. 101; see also the Florida *Times-Union,* Nov. 3, 1887, quoted in *ibid.*, p. 101; Atlanta *Constitution,* Nov. 8, 1887, quoted in *ibid.*, p. 100.
59. November 7, 1887, quoted in *ibid.*, p. 100.

60. Pittsburgh *Times*, November 7, 1887, quoted in *ibid.*, p. 99.
61. November 8, 1887.
62. The Court was criticized on other legal grounds, however, relating to the proper interpretation of the Fourteenth Amendment. Dunbar, *loc. cit.*, pp. 307-326 *passim*.
63. New York *Tribune*, November 6, 1887.

XIX. DISSENTING VOICES

As the weeks rolled by after May 4, changes were taking place in the character of the multiple group and class attitudes and sentiments—simplified as "public opinion"—toward the eight men charged with responsibility for the Haymarket bomb. Immediately after the bomb-throwing, the country at large interpreted the occurrences of May 4 with an amazing unanimity of opinion. The occurrence had generated a hysteria which destroyed reasoned judgment. With the passing of time, individuals and groups shook off this hysteria. People remained blinded by prejudice and fear, even after the victims of their mass emotions had been sacrificed on the gallows. But there were those who valiantly raised their voices against the execution, who denounced the conduct of the first trial, censured the higher courts for their decisions, and labored to save the men from death. The first week of November, 1887, witnessed the culmination of the sentiment in favor of the condemned men. The transformation of a once wholly hostile attitude to one partly sympathetic, was the product of many factors. Different currents fused to make up the stream of opinion which came to the support, in one way or another, of the condemned.

They had, of course, tireless defenders in their own associates. The organs of the I.W.P.A. were never circumspect in affirming their position. When the verdict was rendered in the lower court, Johann Most thundered in the *Freiheit:* "On the twentieth of August, 1886, twelve carefully selected bribed scoundrels, directed by the lowest servitors of the pride of the ruling moneyed class, under pressure of the demoniacal, degenerate roaring of the motley rabble of outcasts of the press of the world, committed in Chicago a monstrous crime, the atrocity of which has never been surpassed in the record of judicial murder throughout the annals of crime." [1] To the "Anarchists of the entire world!" Most appealed: "Imprint well on your minds what has just happened in Chicago. Close your ranks tighter than they have ever been; and swear by everything that is holy to you, to accept the gauntlet so audaciously thrown in your face. . . ." [2] When the decision of the State Supreme Court became known, the *Freiheit* declared:

"The unbelievable has happened. That which no man, regardless of his shade of opinion would hold as credible has now become a fact.

"The beast of capitalism wants blood. . . ." [3]

In similar vein the *Arbeiter-Zeitung* exclaimed:

"The sentence affirmed! The unheard of and apparently impossible has come about. Our breath stops in pronouncing it, and the ink refuses to flow from the pen to write it down.

"The class malice of the Citizens' Association has vanquished the most evident demands of humanity. The Supreme Court at Ottawa, the legal instrument of the rule of capital, this morning affirmed the disgraceful sentence of the court of first resort, which orders that seven of our comrades shall die a martyr's death for the cause of the laboring people, and condemns the eighth to fifteen years in the penitentiary.

"What they are to suffer . . . is not for the death of the police officers who fell on the Haymarket. The spirit of the new times is to be strangled on the gallows." [4]

That the "martyrs" should receive the support of their own comrades was only natural. They were also sustained, however, by Ben Tucker and his fellow philosophical anarchists, although the latter could not stomach the doctrines and methods of the I.W.P.A. [5] When the State Supreme Court rendered its decision, *Liberty* observed that the "judges say that Spies and his comrades must hang, though they cannot prove them guilty of murder. It is for the people now to say that the judges must go, there being no doubt as to their guilt." [6] Tucker himself appealed for funds to continue the fight to save the men. [7] However great the folly of the bomb-thrower, *Liberty* found that of the law still greater. The men were sentenced for what they thought and said, and not because they were connected with the bomb. [8] Another radical publication, *Lucifer,* fully agreed with *Liberty.* [9] The working-class journals of socialist leaning and the socialist organs of distinct working-class appeal also defended the condemned as innocent individuals who were being "railroaded" to the gallows. [10]

The cause of the eight men was also espoused by some intellectuals of liberal bent. Robert Ingersoll, for example, publicly declared that the "men were tried during a period of great excitement," when a fair trial was an impossibility. Without charging Judge Gary with partiality, he made it clear that he regarded the court's ruling as "wrong." Under the instructions given, he said, any man who spoke in favor of a change of government could have been convicted of murder. "I am satisfied," Ingersoll declared, "that the defendant Fielden never intended to harm a human being." [11]

George Francis Train, whose remarkable talent for eccentricity obscured his liberalism, broke a long period of silence to take up the cudgels for the eight men. Train, whose incredible life had already embraced such diverse activities as railroad building, the organization of the Credit Mobilier, participation in the 1870 Marseilles Commune, a presidential candidacy, an entanglement with the Claflin sisters, and a period in an asylum, set out to make people conscious of a miscarriage of justice. His medium was the lecture platform. As a public speaker he was arresting, to say the least, and, even though he made people laugh by his extravagant eccentricities, he was able to say things in public which were taboo for anyone else.

Train understood the value of the sensational, and he advertised the plight of the condemned men in his unique, racy, provocative manner. In 1874, he had given up public speaking, but he was sufficiently affected by the case to lecture on September 18, 1887 on the "Anarchist Trial." [12] He dared tell his audiences that if it were absolutely essential that seven men hang, the American people could better afford to sacrifice the seven judges of the Illinois Supreme Court than the condemned! [13] Though his inimitable style does not stand translation into printer's ink, something of his manner can be gathered from the following excerpt from his lecture in the Princess Skating Rink in Chicago shortly before the date set for the execution.

" 'Being born on the mountain top,' said Mr. Train, 'I saw you couldn't hang seven men in Chicago for committing no crime.' (Great applause.) . . .

" 'You hang those seven men if you dare, and I will head twenty million workingmen to cut the throats of everybody in Chicago. . . .

" 'How can you convict men of being accessories to a crime for which there is no principal?' he suddenly shouted. 'Furthermore, how are these seven men accessories and why should they hang? By similar reasoning Jeff Davis and Robert E. Lee ought to have hanged for the firing on Sumter; . . . and Mayor Harrison and the chiefs of police who permitted the anarchist leaders to incite the Haymarket massacres during years of inflammatory speeches should hang.' (Cheers of evidently earnest endorsement.) . . .

" 'What do they want to hang those men for? Are they afraid of them?' " [14]

During the hectic days following the decision of the United States Supreme Court, Train continued to do what he could to save the men from death.

Of entirely different stamp and intellectual caliber was Henry Demarest Lloyd. Sincere, honest, forthright, Lloyd was in many respects one of the most able and admirable men of his time. Sensitive to social and economic injustice, Lloyd was

outraged by the Haymarket Affair, which influenced profoundly his later economic and social thought. Passage after
passage in his private note-books reveal the anguish he suffered when the men were found guilty. He regarded the verdict as inexcusable and cruelly unjust,[15] and "he was unlike
himself," wrote a friend, "in denouncing Judge Gary for acting as prosecuting attorney on the bench." [16] Certain that the
condemned men were innocent, he doubted whether anyone in
the social-revolutionary movement was responsible for the
bomb. In 1893, he wrote in a personal letter, "I want to say
to you here and now, for reasons which are cogent with me,
I have always had a great doubt as to whether the bomb was
thrown by an anarchist at all; as to whether it was not thrown
by a police minion for the purpose of breaking up the eight-
hour movement." [17] Sacrificing respectability and reputation,
he labored unceasingly to save the condemned from the gallows.

Not all liberals were equally courageous. Many gave way
before the pressure of the press and the hysteria of fear. In
many, their property sense dulled their social conscience, and
they slipped behind the comforting wall of legality which the
courts had erected. To his everlasting credit William Dean
Howells cannot be counted among these. He spoke his mind
when the United States Supreme Court refused to interfere
with the case, and long before that, his sympathies were with
the condemned. He attempted to induce John Greenleaf
Whittier, once a reformer and still a Quaker opposed to capital punishment, to use his influence in behalf of the condemned
men. On November 1, 1887, Howells wrote to Whittier:

"I enclose a paper on the anarchists by a very good and
able minister of Chicago. The conclusions reached there I
reached many weeks and even months ago. The fact is that
those men were sentenced for murder when they ought to have
been indicted for conspiracy. [Sic]

"I believe the mind of the Governor of Illinois is turning
towards clemency; several things indicate this. A letter from

you would have great weight with him. I beseech you to write it, and do what one great and blameless man may do to arrest the greatest wrong that ever threatened our fame as a nation. Even if these men had done the crime which our barbarous laws punish with enormitude, should a plea for mercy be wanting from you?" [18]

Whittier flatly rejected Howells' plea for a letter of mercy to the governor. The latter's request that he sign a petition for clemency was also not granted. Whittier as much as told Howells to write the letter himself, "giving as an excuse for his refusal," remarks the former's biographer, "that Howells could do it better. He added that though he did not believe in capital punishment, he was not disposed to interfere with these criminals, because they were more dangerous than other murderers." [19] John Greenleaf Whittier, the Quaker, more closely approached Theodore Roosevelt's stand on the Haymarket case than that of Howells. The bomb threw Roosevelt into a frenzy. He wrote from his ranch in the West that he would have shot down the rioters. In an address during the summer of 1887, in which he attacked Henry George, he declared that "it was to the common interest of all Americans that the 'Chicago dynamiters be hung.' " [20]

Another liberal upon whom the Haymarket Affair was to have a marked effect before it ran its course was Dr. William M. Salter, a leader of the Ethical Culture Society of Chicago. During the days immediately before the execution, Salter worked tirelessly to save the men. Many years later he wrote that it was an error to combat anarchistic propaganda with force, and that he was certain that the Chicago anarchists urged the use of force only to repel force.[21] Before he reached these conclusions Salter experienced a disturbing inner struggle from the clash of his ethical culture ideas, his desire to see justice done, his predisposition to side with the underdog, and his conviction that the men as anarchists threatened the existence of the State and society, and, therefore, should be punished. On October 23, 1887, in the Grand Opera House in

Chicago, Salter lectured before the Ethical Culture Society on "What Shall Be Done with the Anarchists?" [22] After summarizing the evidence, he concluded that although the bomb-thrower was unknown, Lingg, Fischer and Engel were guilty as accessories; that Fielden's violent harangue was responsible for the appearance of the police; and that if the police had not arrived, the bomb would not have been thrown. The evidence against Spies, Schwab, Fielden and Parsons, he felt, "is not such as to convince any fairminded, unprejudiced man beyond reasonable doubt." This assertion, however, he immediately qualified. "I do not say because the four I have mentioned are not guilty, they are therefore guiltless of any connection whatever with the Haymarket crime. They are simply not guilty of the *crime with which they were charged*. They were not accessories to the murder of Degan. . . . *If not guilty of the crime with which they were charged, of what are they guilty?*

". . . They are guilty of sedition, of stirring up insurrection. They were all members of a conspiracy against the State."

What was to be done with the men? Salter proposed that Spies, Schwab, Fielden and Parsons "should not be punished as equally guilty with Engel and Fischer and Lingg. . . ." For the first four he recommended imprisonment for several years. It would be a "public crime" to hang them. For the others life imprisonment would be fitting. The State could be magnanimous and spare their lives.[23] Salter's position was a peculiar one. The men were responsible for the crime, he said, but not guilty of it, and nevertheless deserved punishment. This stand, which he later abandoned, brought immediate criticism from Chicago radicals and labor circles. Lizzie M. Holmes, for example, quickly showed the weaknesses in his argument and conclusion.[24]

Not all of Salter's associates were willing to go as far as he did. Mr. B. F. Underwood in a signed editorial, "Anarchy and the Anarchists," in the fortnightly *Open Court*, Chicago's liberal, quasi-philosophical journal, declared that those who advocate violence should be treated as criminals. Those who were expressing sympathy with the condemned men, he wrote, were giving "no thought now to the fate of the guardians of the law who were cruelly murdered by a dynamite bomb . . . , or of the widowhood, orphanage, and anguish caused by that terrible tragedy. While sympathy is felt and expressed for the anarchists . . . , those who died in defense of law and order . . . should not be forgotten." [25]

The advanced social reformist element in New York City, if their representative journal, *Social Science,* accurately reflects their sentiments, were definitely sympathetic to the condemned. For this periodical, the impending execution was "judicial murder." [26] The free-thinking element also appears to have offered what support it could to the eight men. Their organ, The *Truth Seeker,* observed, less than two weeks after the bomb exploded, that "the police were in the beginning the unjustifiable aggressors. . . ." [27] When the trial was over, The *Truth Seeker* declared that it reflected "no credit upon either the police or state's attorneys of Chicago, and the verdict is the result of popular prejudice against the Anarchists. It is a monstrous verdict, and unless reversed by the Supreme Court of Illinois will end in judicial murder." [28]

One American who championed the cause of the working-class and who had discovered how society might be refashioned without a "social revolution," assumed a position on the case which bitterly disappointed many of his followers. He was Henry George. On January 15, 1887, George wrote in his New York *Standard:*

"Spies and his associates were convicted by a jury chosen in a manner so shamelessly illegal that it would be charity to suspect the judge of incompetency.

"The accusation was murder, by an explosive thrown by an unknown person between whom and the defendants no connection was shown. The meeting at which it was thrown was peaceable and lawful. The mayor so declared it; and although the chief of police agreed with him, hardly was the mayor out of sight when the chief, at the head of a squad of policemen, ordered it to disperse; then the bomb was thrown.

"The only evidence against the defendants in connection with this meeting was that they were present and that some of them spoke. Yet this jury, many of whom confessed to fixed opinions against the accused, found a verdict of murder." [29]

When the State Supreme Court handed down its decision the *Standard* was silent. On October 8, 1887, *Liberty* remarked that it "seems to be the only labor paper which has found no word of indignant protest and condemnation in reference to the Illinois Supreme Court decision. . . ." [30] The *Standard's* silence also amazed the Chicago *Labor Enquirer*.[31] Finally on October 8, 1887, the following paragraphs appeared on the first page of the *Standard* over Henry George's name:

"There is no ground for asking executive clemency in behalf of the Chicago Anarchists as a matter of right. An unlawful and murderous deed was committed in Chicago the penalty of which, by the laws of the State of Illinois, is death. Seven [*sic*] men were tried on the charge of being accessory to the crime, and, after a long trial, were convicted. The case was appealed to the supreme court of the State of Illinois, and that body, composed of seven judges, removed both in time and place, from the excitement which may have been supposed to have affected public opinion in Chicago during the first trial, have, after an elaborate examination of the evidence and the law, unanimously confirmed this sentence.

"That seven judges of the highest court of Illinois, men accustomed to weigh evidence and to pass upon judicial rulings, should, after a full examination of the testimony and the record, and with the responsibility of life and death resting upon them, unanimously sustain the verdict and the sentence, is inconsistent with the idea that the Chicago Anarchists were condemned on insufficient evidence." [32]

On January 15, George wrote, "No well-informed lawyer can defend the convictions upon legal grounds." On October 8, he declared, "It was proved beyond a doubt that these men were engaged in a conspiracy as a result of which the bomb was thrown, and were therefore under the laws of Illinois as guilty as though they themselves had done the act." [33] Early in July, 1887, he had asked Joe Buchanan to "assure the boys in jail that I am in full sympathy with them, and that they can count on me to do all in my power to set them free." Later he refused to sign a petition of clemency addressed to Governor Oglesby of Illinois.[34]

What had happened to Henry George? Had a careful reading of the Illinois Supreme Court opinion convinced him of the guilt of the accused, as he asserted in the *Standard* of November 19, 1887? Yet his son suggests that if he had read the decision of the Supreme Court in full or the record of the first trial, he would never have reached that conclusion.[35] Henry George himself later explained that he did not "oppose the hanging of the anarchists . . . because force was no remedy for the evils they complained of." [36] Nevertheless, he did send a letter to Governor Oglesby pleading that imprisonment be substituted for the death sentence.

Henry George was sharply castigated for his change of front, and William Morris was among the many who branded him "Traitor." [37] The criticism he received was deserved. It cannot be argued that Henry George's stand was the product of honest conviction. He had no abiding faith in the eternal "rightness" of the courts. He probably never gave the Supreme Court opinion a thorough examination. A letter from Judge Maguire dealing with the case could not have influenced him because it was dated November 2, 1887. George's switch seems to have been primarily dictated by political motives. In September, 1887, he was engaged in a lively campaign for the office of Secretary of State of New York, and he apparently simply traded in his earlier sympathy with the condemned men for votes.[38] He may also have been moved by another motive. He had been fighting the New York socialists, and the latter were supporting the condemned. George may have hoped to indict them in the mind of the average worker by identifying them with the Chicago revolutionaries.[39] Whatever the deciding factor was, Henry George enjoyed the unenviable distinction of being the only person of note who *first* condemned the conviction of the eight men, and *later* discovered that the verdict was defensible on legal grounds.[40]

From all sides there came indications that the entire case was being considered in a new light. Surprising sympathy, for instance, was expressed for Neebe when his wife died in March, 1887. A well-known Chicago lawyer and real-estate dealer wrote to Oscar Neebe that the latter was a "victim of one of the most senseless panics that ever seized a community." [41] Another Chicago lawyer announced, after the State Supreme Court decision, "I now propose to burn my law books." [42] Even the Chicago *Legal Adviser* later pointed out that in view of the testimony upon which the men were convicted, commutation of the sentences would be generally viewed "as an act of clemency which will be everywhere respected, and do more to quiet the fear expressed than any other mode that could be pursued." [43]

Lyman Trumbull of Illinois, who twenty years earlier displayed a commendable integrity during the impeachment of Andrew Johnson, declared that he

"was not altogether satisfied with the manner in which the trial of the anarchists was conducted. It took place at a time of great public excitement, when it was about impossible that they should have a fair and impartial trial. A terrible crime had been committed which was attributed to the anarchists, and in some respects the trial had the appearance of a trial of an organization known as anarchists, rather than of persons indicted for the murder of Degan. . . . The condemned men claim . . . to be the advocates of a principle, and to execute them would, in my judgment, be bad policy. It will be claimed for them that they were executed as martyrs to a cause, while if put in prison they will soon be forgotten." [44]

Another "Trumbull," unrelated to the more famous Lyman, energetically fought in defense of the condemned men.

He was Gen. M. M. Trumbull, a native of England who had come to the United States when he was twenty. After seeing service in the Mexican and Civil Wars, he held high office in Iowa, and, at the time of the trial, was successfully practising law in Chicago. Trumbull's unqualified opposition to all theories of revolutionary violence did not prevent him from following the trial in the lower court and the appeal with minute care. After the State Supreme Court decision, he published the first of two able pamphlets on the case. It bears the title, *Was It a Fair Trial? An Appeal to the Governor of Illinois.* In it he roundly charged that "the trial was unfair, the rulings of the court illegal, and the sentence unjust." [45] He appealed to the governor on the ground that "the record shows that none of the condemned were [*sic*] fairly proven guilty, while some of them were fairly proven innocent; not innocent of sedition and inflammatory speech, but innocent of murder." [46]

It cannot be said to what extent this pamphlet circulated, but it appears to have been fairly widely read. On November 3, 1887, Mrs. Parsons sold five thousand copies of *Was It a Fair Trial?* on the streets of Chicago at five cents each.[47] Trumbull's second pamphlet, *The Trial of the Judgment. A Review of the Anarchist Case,* a much fuller study, did not appear until 1888.

The opinion of the State Supreme Court led to the publication of another pamphlet which administered an energetic thumping to the machinery of "law and order." This brochure from the pen of Leon Lewis, who wrote pot-boilers for Beadle's Dime Library, bears the title *The Ides of November, An Appeal for the Seven Condemned Leaders and a Protest against their Judicial Assassination.*[48]

"A handful of judicial conspirators in Chicago," he wrote, "incited by police bullies and irresponsible newspaper hirelings, and backed by a mob of scared and feeble-minded egotists, have contrived THE JUDICIAL ASSASSINATION OF SEVEN INNOCENT MEN, under a flimsy pretext and coloring of legal process, for an act with which they have had no proved connection, and of which the real author is still unknown, as is also the fact whether he belonged to the police or the workingmen, or was merely some solitary criminal acting SOLELY upon his own volition." [49]

Several clerics likewise refused to accept the dominant version of the Haymarket episode, objected to the conduct of the trial, and opposed the execution of the condemned. Among them were the Rev. J. M. L. Babcock, a co-worker of Wendell Phillipps and Garrison, John C. Kimball, and Hugh Pentecost, minister of a Congregational Church in Newark.[50] Mr. Babcock delivered on October 23, 1887, an address in Boston's historic Faneuil Hall in which he excoriated the "disgraceful judicial proceedings" of the lower court, and charged that the judges of the State Supreme Court had surrendered to public feeling.[51]

Nothing has yet been said of the views of one large class which was thoroughly interested in the entire Haymarket case. What stand did labor—and this, practically speaking, means *organized* labor—take? Immediately after May 4, as it has been seen, labor hastened not only to condemn the bombing, but to cast blame upon the Chicago radicals and demand their punishment. Where the labor press did not unite in the universal chorus, it was silent. It ignored the Haymarket episode completely. There were, of course, exceptions to these generalizations, as it has been seen.[52]

Why did the K. of L. Assemblies and other labor organizations strongly denounce "the Chicago dynamiters?" [53] Why did they rush to disavow any sympathy with radical organizations or principles? [54] Why was there not one reference to the Haymarket episode in the *Locomotive Firemen's Magazine,* with which Eugene Debs was then connected, between June, 1886, and December, 1887? Why was the *Boycotter* almost as silent? Why did it proudly parade its patriotism, and insist that "American Labor" could in no way be connected with "the anarchy, disorder and bloodshed in Chicago . . . ?" [55]

Why was the *Journal of United Labor,* the official national publication of the K. of L., mute on the Haymarket episode until September 25, 1886?

It takes no profound searching to discover the answers to these questions. The American workingman was just as shocked and distressed by the bomb as anyone else. On the whole the American working-class had no use for revolutionary "isms." The disavowal of the bomb and of the social-revolutionaries was, therefore, quite normal. Furthermore the bomb was at least coincidentally connected with the eight-hour movement. It was, therefore, necessary for labor to insist that the bomb and those responsible for it, were foreign to the eight-hour movement and inimical to the interests of the worker. Finally, labor sensed that the entire episode could be used by capital to injure the working-class. Capital could and actually did strike at organized labor through the Haymarket Affair. It was an ideal blind behind which the employers could operate. It was all very well to urge, as the *Craftsman* did, that "while the red-handed dynamiters of Chicago are being denounced on all sides, let us not forget those who are morally responsible for these deeds." [56] But this was not enough. It was essential to demonstrate that labor was opposed to lawlessness, that it was the sworn enemy of the communist and the anarchist, and that it was a pillar of strength in the perpetuation of the Constitution and the flag. Patriotic gestures were the obvious defense to accusations of lack of patriotism. Thus, the second annual assembly of the Knights of Labor of Michigan adopted "A resolution condemning anarchy and revolutionary schemes, and declaring the stars and stripes as the flag of the order. . . ." [57] For this reason, the *American Labor Budget,* an organ of the K. of L., editorially declared:

"Socialism, anarchism, and murder find no defenders in the K. of L. If a conflict should ever occur as the results of communism, the Knights of Labor will be found upholding the constitution of the United States and laws of the country against all transgressors.

"The Knights of Labor are the stoutest opponents yet placed against socialism and anarchy. They are friends of the law and of order. They believe in order, and are determined that the laws shall be obeyed. Down with socialism and anarchy. Up with education and equality." [58]

Organized labor, especially the K. of L. worked assiduously to keep radicals and workers distinct in the public mind. "How often," complained the Chicago *Knights of Labor* in August, 1886, "must the working men as a class deny their connection or sympathy with anarchy?" [59] The considerations which moulded organized labor's stand are to be seen in operation at the Convention of the Illinois State Federation of Labor which met a month after the bomb was thrown. This body refused to deliberate upon a resolution which condemned anarchists, capitalists and corporations. The committee on resolutions deemed it "unwise to pass or even discuss any such resolution on account of the already excited state of the public mind. . . ." It later substituted a resolution attacking inflammatory speech-making which, despite the efforts of George Schilling, was quickly adopted. [60] At the convention of the Federation early in the following year, a resolution branding the verdict as a product of "class hatred" and demanding a new trial was still judged impolitic, and was not permitted to come to a vote. It was not until 1889 that the Illinois State Federation of Labor thought it safe to declare publicly that the men had not received a fair trial. [61]

Similar considerations and the conviction that the radicals were making serious inroads among the Knights on the Pacific Coast [62] account for Terence V. Powderly's determined though not always unequivocal position. Later he justified his stand on the ground that the bomb "did more injury to the good name of labor than all the strikes of that year, and turned public sentiment against labor organizations. . . ." [63] Addressing the 1886 General Assembly of the K. of L. which convened in Richmond in October, Powderly declared: "While I condemn and denounce the deeds of violence committed in the name of labor during the present year, I am proud to say that the Knights of Labor as an organization are not in any way responsible for such conduct. He is the true Knight of Labor who with one hand clutches anarchy by the throat and with the other strangles monopoly!" [64] This theme reappeared in Powderly's "Independence Day Proclamation," in which he exclaimed, "The watchword of the people should be *neither monopoly nor anarchy shall rule in this country—both must go*." [65] Elsewhere he bluntly asserted, "The Knights of Labor respect the law. I hate Anarchy and I hate Anarchists." [66] Powderly instructed the Knights in Chicago at the close of '86 to cease collecting money for the legal defense of the condemned men, and to return what had already been collected. [67] Commenting upon a statement in the Chicago *Times*, "published by the grace of Armour," that a "true remedy" for strikes lay in the employment of "Gatling guns, with brave men behind them," he wrote that to advise "the use of Gatling guns is dangerous; it is un-American, and will never work in these United States. Besides, the wrong fellow always gets hit. The Pinkerton Anarchist aims at a striker and hits an innocent child. The Chicago Anarchist throws a bomb at a capitalist and hits a poor policeman. The striker lives, the capitalist lives, and no good has been accomplished." [68]

Before the autumn of 1886, a new note was apparent in the same labor press which had shortly before unqualifiedly condemned the men. The Chicago *Knights of Labor* as early as the middle of July observed that "from recent developments it looks as though Inspector Bonfield is the man who . . . appears to be primarily responsible for the riot . . ." [69] Between October and the close of 1886, a large portion of the labor press and a good number of labor organizations had shifted their position on the "anarchist" case. In December, the Chicago *Knights of Labor* remarked that "public opinion has turned completely around regarding the eight convicted anarchists . . . within the past few months." [70] A bitter opponent of organized labor pointed out in November, 1886, that the Knights, the trade-unions, and the single-taxers "have been brought to take a lively interest in averting punishment from the anarchists who advised and contrived [the bomb-throwing]." [71] After the State Supreme Court decision, the conviction that a grave miscarriage of justice had occurred was intensified in working-class circles.[72] By that date there was a clear-cut division in labor ranks on the case,[73] and the condemned had a steadily mounting number of sympathizers among workingmen.

When *John Swinton's Paper* declared on August 22, 1886, that it could "not see how any jury could convict the prisoners of the crime for which they were indicted, upon the flimsy and perjured evidence of the spies and informers who were the principal witnesses against them," few journals openly concurred.[74] But, when the *Workmen's Advocate* spoke of the "shocking, though not surprising news that reaches us just before we go to press, [of] the acquiescence of the Supreme Court of Illinois in the proposed judicial murder of Messrs. Parsons, Fielden, Spies, Fischer, Engel, Lingg, and Schwab, and the consignment to prison of Oscar Neebe, for no other reason than to gratify a frightened bourgeoisie in the first stages of disintegration," [75]—it was voicing the sentiments of a large number of labor organs.

The *Workmen's Advocate* was as mordant as the Chicago *Tribune*. It cried out against the work of a "murderous plutocracy"; it raged against the complacent acceptance of the impending execution in an editorial called "Chicago's Shame"; it spoke of "The dastardly attempt to murder seven citizens of Chicago . . . ;" it asserted that the men were victims of a gigantic conspiracy "to throttle free speech." [76] These expressions were echoed in the columns of labor publications such as the *Advance and Labor Leaf*,[77] the New York *Leader*, the Paterson *Labor Standard*, the Cincinnati *Unionist*, the Troy *Ray*,[78] the Chicago *Labor Enquirer*, the Lonaconing (Maryland) *Review*,[79] the *Labor Tribune*,[80] and the Lansing *Sentinel*.[81]

Labor made its sentiments known in still other ways. On September 14, 1887, at a meeting of the Progressive Labor Party in New York City, resolutions were adopted condemning "the sentence as judicial murder," urging "Organized Labor all over the country to protest in mass meetings against this infamous action," and pledging assistance to the condemned. The United German Trade Unions of New York passed a similar resolution, and District Assembly 49 of the K. of L. resolved, "That we emphatically condemn the judicial powers that condemned those men to death," and extend to them "our moral and financial aid." [82] D. A. 49 of New York did this despite the threat of the general executive board of the K. of L. to suspend or even expel a District Assembly taking such action.[83] This District Assembly endorsed jointly with the Central Labor Union of New York, a public appeal to the working-class, dated September 16, 1887, and signed by fourteen well-known labor leaders.

"You are aware," it begins, "of the decision rendered by the Supreme Court of Illinois confirming the verdict of the lower court . . . and fixing the day of execution of the prisoners of November 11th of this year.

"As citizens who stand united on the broad platform of human rights and equal justice to all, irrespective of political or social opinions, we now appeal to you to do all in your power to secure a modification of the above-mentioned decision.

"Liberty, free speech and justice impartially and fearlessly meted out to friend and foe, are the only safe-guards and the primary conditions of a peaceable social development in this country.

"Under the misguiding and corrupting influence of prejudice and class-hatred, those men have been condemned without any conclusive evidence, as accessories to a crime, the principals of which, as well as the motive which may have actuated the same, are unknown.

"The execution of this sentence would be a disgrace to

the honor of our nation, and would strengthen the very doctrines it is ostensibly directed against.

"The undersigned appeal, therefore, to you, as representatives of Organized Labor, the foremost champions of our rights and liberties, to immediately take such steps as may save our country from the disgrace of an act that can be considered in no other light than as a judicial murder, prompted by the basest and most un-American motives. . . .

"Leaving to you to decide as to the most efficient method to be adopted, we would suggest that a call should be issued by all the representative labor organizations of this country for a great public demonstration to be held simultaneously in this [New York] and in all other cities of the Union on or about the 20th of October. . . .

"Yours in the cause of Justice and Humanity,

"SAMUEL GOMPERS,	TOM O'REILLY,
"JAS. E. QUINN,	JOHN D. DUNN,
"MARTIN A. HANLY,	GEO. H. MCVEY,
"FRANK FERRELL,	A. G. JOHNSON, JR.
"EDWARD KING,	MATTHEW BARR,
"EVERETT GLACKIN,	FRED HALLER, and
"HENRY EMRICH,	MICHAEL J. KELLY." [84]

Resolutions, dated October 8, 1887, protesting against the verdict and petitioning the governor of the State to spare the lives of the men were unanimously adopted by two Chicago assemblies of the K. of L., the Sons of Liberty Assembly, No. 1,307 and the Women's Assembly, No. 1,789, and were published in the form of appeals asking for aid to save the men. The Chicago daily papers, to which the resolutions of the Women's Assembly were sent, refused with one exception to publish them even as news matter.

Following the suggestion of D. A. 49 and the Central Labor Union, meetings were held on October 20, attended by large numbers of workingmen. In Chicago, some five thousand people were present under the auspices of the Amnesty Association.[85] In New York City the mass-meeting protesting against the death sentence was held in Cooper Union, and was a stirring affair. Despite a heavy rainstorm the hall was packed with an enthusiastic crowd of three or four thousand. P. J. McGuire, James E. Quinn and Samuel Gompers were among the labor leaders who spoke.

McGuire pointed out that the execution of seven men would not destroy anarchy in the United States. On the contrary, he said, it would serve to pour oil on the flames of revolution. Gompers asserted that the meeting was not held to sanctify a crime, but rather to urge the State not to commit one. Mr. T. B. Wakeman, a lawyer, Mr. McGregor, president of the Humane Society, and Daniel De Leon, then a lecturer at Columbia University and far from the fiery socialist of later years, also joined in the plea for justice and mercy. De Leon, who was aware of the possible consequences of his appearance to his career, declared, "I come here deliberately and for the good name of our beloved country that its proud record shall not be bloodstained by a judicial crime as the one contemplated in Chicago." The partisan audience, which punctuated the remarks of the speakers with cheers and applause, adopted resolutions disavowing sympathy with Anarchism, and protesting against the denial of a fair trial and the violation of the right of free speech. Similar mass-meetings were held in a large hall in Sulzer's Harlem Park and in Hoboken.[86]

A significant indication of the sympathies of the American working-class is furnished by the generosity with which labor contributed to the fund of the legal defense committee. This had been organized, it will be recalled, during the grand jury investigation with Dr. Ernst Schmidt as its able head. Legal expenses and the support of the dependents of those arrested were estimated at about $100 a day, a huge sum for the time and for those involved. During and shortly after the trial in the lower court, some 30,000 Chicago workingmen are reported to have contributed to the fund.[87] It took some urging, but the money came in. Early in September, 1886, an appeal in the form of a letter signed by George Schilling, Charles F. Seib and others was circulated. It asked for contributions, and suggested the purchase of a copy of Parsons' Haymarket address by every Knight and trade unionist to show that organized labor was protesting against the outrageous "corruption" that made the verdict possible.[88] Shortly before the case was argued in the State Supreme Court, the defense fund committee again pleaded for money. It announced that of the $20,000 collected, only $2,000 would be left when the expenses for the first trial and the appeal were met.[89] If a new trial were granted, at least another $15,000 would be necessary.[90] Not less than $50,000 were raised in all, and a large portion of that sum, certainly more than half, came out of the pockets of American workers.[91] The remainder came from the radical movement, which gave heavily, and from other quarters. The Boston Turn Verein, for example, whose members included influential German citizens, sent $100.[92]

It is impossible to say to what extent the "Chicago anarchists" had won the sympathies of the working-class. The Haymarket case did, however, split the ranks of labor wide open. Nowhere can this division be studied to greater advantage than in the Knights of Labor, where it coincided with a struggle for control of the offices of the order, and where it sowed further dissension.

It has been seen that at the Richmond General Assembly of the K. of L. in October, 1886, a resolution "asking for mercy for the condemned" was adopted after a stirring battle.[93] This was a victory for the sympathizers of the accused, for at the special convention of the order which had met earlier in Cleveland (May 25), the bomb-throwing and those arrested for it were condemned.[94] Before the General Assembly of the order convened in Minneapolis, October 4-19, 1887, for its eleventh regular session, it was recognized that the Haymarket question would be widely discussed. Delegates, interviewed before the assembly formally convened, were concerned with the plight of the "anarchists." "Do you know," said one, "that I think it is dead wrong to hang these fellows. I believe that those men are innocent. . . . I don't favor anarchy or anything of that kind, but I believe in giving the devil his due." [95] Powderly always linked the bomb with Anarchism and Socialism, and Jo Labadie, taking advantage of this, proposed to embarrass the General Master Workman by raising an open debate on Socialism, and demanding why Powderly, "who for years was a member of the Socialistic Party, has abandoned his socialistic principles." [96]

The administration machine of the order, aware of the coming conflict in the Assembly, took the offensive. Through the credentials committee it tried to exclude certain delegates who were championing the cause of the condemned or who were themselves of radical affiliation. An unsuccessful attempt was made to reject the credentials of George Schilling and Charles Seib. Joe Buchanan, however, was denied his seat by the committee on the technical ground that his local assembly had been suspended for nonpayment of dues. Buchanan had with him the sum in arrears and offered to pay it. But the delegates sustained the report of the committee, and he lost his seat. [97]

In anticipation of the debate on the floor of the Assembly, Powderly dedicated a considerable portion of his address as General Master Workman to the question of "anarchy within the order" and his attitude toward the "Chicago anarchists." [98] He asserted that he had not said a word publicly about the seven men condemned to death up to the composition of this very address. [99] His matured opinion on the case was:

"If these men did not have a fair trial, such as is guaranteed every man in the United States, then they should be granted a new trial. If they have not been found guilty of murder, they should not be hanged. If they are to be hanged for the actions of others it is not just. The man who threw the bomb in Chicago should be hanged and his accomplices should receive the punishment allotted to such offenses by the laws of the State of Illinois. Before the public I have never said a word concerning these men. I have never felt called upon to say anything, for it is none of my business; yet some of their friends have put words of condemnation in my mouth in order to have me say something in their favor." [100]

Powderly informed the Assembly that he had received a letter, dated November 25, 1886, from a Chicago officer of the order, which asserted that Knights in Chicago were moving heaven and earth to aid the condemned, that D. A. 24 had passed resolutions of sympathy, that D. A. 57 had barely failed to appropriate $50 for the defense fund, and that both these district assemblies had roundly censured Powderly for his stand on the case. Powderly dispatched a reply to be read to the assemblies in which he denounced these activities, assailed Anarchism, and pointed out that as "individuals we may express our feelings as we please," but as Knights of Labor no sign of sympathy could be shown to anarchy or anarchists. A similar letter was also sent to the Master Workman of unruly D. A. 57.[101] During the early part of 1887, Powderly wrote several other letters to Knights in Chicago on the same question. These he read to the Assembly.[102] In all of them he stressed one point—no official action should be taken which might provide an excuse for identifying the K. of L. with Anarchism. Powderly's position, however, was not always consistent. Thus in a letter of January 16, 1887, he wrote:

"I believe that the men who are under sentence of death . . . were too hastily judged; I believe that passion has as much to do with the conviction as reason. . . . I believe that the man who threw the bomb should hang as high as ever murderer hung, yet . . . the Knights of Labor had nothing to do with the sending of these men to Haymarket Square. . . . I believe that these men should have a new trial, for if they do not . . . they will be held up as martyrs to a cause they did nothing to advance. If I were an anarchist I would be pleased to see them hanged, for that would give me something to point to in the future. . . . I am not in favor of capital punishment for any crime, and if I am ever drawn on a jury where the life of my fellow-man is at stake, I will never vote to strangle him." [103]

Yet he concluded that as long as the law provided for the death penalty, it was proper to hang a criminal to "vindicate" the law. [104]

When it was argued that justice dictated that the order—whose motto was "An Injury to One is the Concern of All"—should aid Parsons, a fellow-Knight, Powderly was obdurate. He knew nothing concerning Parsons. Whether guilty or innocent, Parsons did not act on May 4 as a member of the K. of L. Anyone as an individual might aid Parsons if he pleased. But the order could not. [105]

Powderly had brought the Haymarket case into the open. A number of documents dealing with various aspects of the questions it aroused had been submitted to the proper committees for consideration. [106] But the fireworks did not come until the afternoon of October 10, when James E. Quinn, representing D. A. 49 of New York, a veritable thorn in Powderly's side, moved the following carefully composed resolution:

"WHEREAS, Considering that the development of the human mind in the nineteenth century has reached a point expressed almost universally against capital punishment, or the taking of human life by judicial process, as a relic of barbarism: Therefore be it

"*Resolved,* That this convention express sorrow that the men in Chicago were doomed to death, and that it use every endeavor to secure the commutation of the sentence of death passed upon them." [107]

Though milder than that passed the previous year at Richmond, this resolution fell upon the Assembly like a bombshell. Before Quinn was half way through it, a score of delegates were on their feet in protest. When the motion was seconded, Powderly ruled it out of order. Obviously it was so drawn as to utilize Powderly's declared opposition to capital punishment for putting the order on record against the executions. But the General Master Workman was not to be budged. When a motion to suspend the rules was lost, George Schilling proposed that the question of the condemned anarchists be made the special order of business when the session opened the very next day. When this was likewise defeated, Joe Evans of Pittsburgh appealed from the decision of the chair. Powderly, however, was sustained by the Assembly 121 to fifty-three.[108] A motion to reconsider was followed by a sharp debate, in which Powderly, having called General Worthy Foreman Griffiths to the chair, participated. Speaking much longer than anyone else,[109] he made a passionate plea for the rejection of the resolution. He scored both it and the anarchists within the Order, and used every possible trick, even inventing two attempts upon his person by "anarchists," to keep the assembly in line. It was not an address of which he could have been proud; an opponent described it as "illogical, cowardly, brutal and violent. . . ." It served its purpose, however, for Powderly was sustained. The noise of the debate had penetrated beyond the walls of the hall in which the Assembly sat. Nevertheless, an effort was made to suppress the entire episode and hide every indication of disharmony at the session, which Powderly nullified.[110]

A revolt against Powderly was attempted by some thirty delegates drawn chiefly from D. A. 24 and D. A. 57, directed by Jo Labadie, Schilling and Charles Seib, who opposed the head of the order on other questions as well as on the Haymarket case. While the Assembly was in progress, this minority, dubbed "Kickers" withdrew to another hall and held a series of discussions.[111] In the Assembly they had even attempted to carry a measure making possible the display of red flags and banners in processions of the K. of L. They could muster only twenty-nine votes, and were defeated.[112] The majority responded to this by amending the constitution of the order to prohibit assemblies from displaying [113] any colors but those of the State or nation in a procession or parade.

When the "Kickers" on their way home from Minneapolis stopped at Chicago, they numbered thirty-five. There they elected a provisional committee of five with Charles Seib as secretary, drew up a sharp indictment of the K. of L. leadership, listed the abuses in the order, and demanded its complete reorganization. No mention, however, was made of the Haymarket or the condemned men.[114]

Powderly's success in controlling the official declarations of the Assembly, however, is no true index of the sentiments of the individual delegates. The representatives did not object to the circulation of a petition among them asking Governor Oglesby to commute the sentence to life imprisonment.[115] One who attended asserted that "Nearly all the delegates signed the petition asking for the pardon of the condemned 'anarchists,' but would not take such official action in the premises [of the convention hall] as would seem to commit their constituents to approval of such action." [116] Individual assemblies and district assemblies further indicated the leanings of rank and file Knights by condemning Powderly's "moral cowardice" and censuring the General Assembly for failing to pass the resolution Quinn had offered.[117]

The American Federation of Labor gave additional proof of the shift that had taken place in the sympathies of the working class when its convention passed a resolution pleading for mercy in behalf of the condemned and denouncing the employment of violence on principle.[118]

Further evidence of the change in working-class opinion need not be adduced. Before the case reached the Federal Supreme Court, an impressive section of the working-class had come to believe that the men had not been fairly tried, that the execution of the seven "anarchists" would be unjustifiable judicial murder, or, even if the men were in some degree responsible for the bomb, this extreme punishment would be impolitic and unwarranted. When the fate of the condemned finally rested in the hands of the chief executive of Illinois, labor brought pressure for a pardon or commutation of sentence.

What brought about this transformation in labor sentiment? Perhaps the primary factor was the very consideration which at first led labor to take the same stand as capital. Labor was afraid of being identified with extremists—socialists, anarchists and communists—lest capital be given a weapon with which to attack it. But capital interests did use the hysterical fear aroused by the bomb to assail labor. Its passionate disavowals of the three "isms" and strong disapproval of the deed did not avail. "It does seem," declared the Chicago *Knights of Labor,* "as though the press at large has taken upon itself the task of convicting workingmen of socialism, anarchism, communism, and all the other isms . . . regardless of their denials or protests, and it is high time that wholesale misrepresentation ceased." [119] It was easy to argue, a contemporary pointed out, that the prosecution hardly pretended "that their elect eight were any more guilty than a great number of other Socialists professing the same ideas, and [that] this criminating hospitality ought to extend to all strikers who have countenanced violence against the property of their employers. . . ." [120] When labor was attacked through an occurrence it had itself assailed, its normal reaction was to defend the persons involved against whom capital had raised its voice.

There were other reasons, too. It was felt that several of the Chicago "anarchists" were being punished for their labor activities. The *Workmen's Advocate* spoke of the seven "fellow citizens" who had been sentenced to death "for advocating the cause of labor. . . ." [121] Parsons, after all, was a Knight of ten years' standing, and his working-class endeavors were not immediately forgotten. As the worker continued to read accounts of the case in the daily press, he was supplied with material for questioning the fairness of the trial. When his own journals made him conscious of the gross partiality which had reigned during the trial, the conviction grew that the law had persecuted rather than prosecuted the condemned. [122]

The very unanimity of the capitalist press made him suspicious. He could see that every effort was made to send the men to the gallows.[123] Not unaware of the social and economic conditions in which he found himself, the worker could be convinced that the condemned had been silenced by the law because they had cried out against existing evils.[124] When opponents of Anarchism and Socialism aligned themselves with the "anarchists," many a worker was led to question the justice of the verdict. It is also very probable that the current labor conviction that the law was simply a tool of the capitalists served to shift the sympathies of many. One contemporary likewise felt that "the constant appeal to the sense of justice of the American people" was an instrumental, if lesser, factor in effecting the change in attitude.[125]

By November, 1887, the number of those who questioned the justice of the verdict had reached an impressive total. No class was wholly unrepresented in this group. No longer was there an unqualified roar of condemnation of the accused. When the United States Supreme Court refused to interfere, the protest against the execution of the verdict swelled to arresting proportions. The Governor of Illinois was deluged with pleas asking for commutation of the death sentences to life imprisonment and even for pardon. The dissenting voices were now heard.

NOTES CHAPTER XIX

1. August 28, 1886, author's translation.
2. *Idem,* author's translation.
3. September 17, 1887. Author's translation. See also *ibid.,* September 24, 1887.
4. September 14, 1887, quoted in *Advance and Labor Leaf,* September 24, 1887; for a slightly different version see Chicago *Inter Ocean,* September 15, 1887.
5. See above, chap. X; and *Liberty,* vol. 4, no. 8, July 31, 1886.
6. *Ibid.,* vol. 5, no. 4, September 24, 1887, p. 1.
7. *Ibid.,* p. 4.
8. *Cf., ibid.,* vol. 5, no. 6, October 22, 1886, p. 1.
9. Cited in *ibid.,* vol. 4, no. 8, August 21, p. 7, and no. 9, September 18, 1886, p. 4.

10. See below, pp. 408-409, 419-420.

11. These opinions which Ingersoll had long entertained privately, were made public November 3, 1887, in an interview in the New York *Mail and Express*, which is quoted in Robert G. Ingersoll, *Works*, 13 vols., New York, 1912, vol. 8, pp. 291-292.

12. For Train's life, see his autobiography, George Francis Train, *My Life in Many States and Foreign Lands, Dictated in my Seventy-Fourth Year*, New York, 1902, especially the preface, pp. ix-x; *Social Science*, vol. 1, no. 14, October 5, 1887, pp. 2-3.

13. Quoted in *Liberty*, vol. 5, no. 5, October 8, 1887, p. 1.

14. Quoted in *Liberty*, vol. 5, no. 7, November 5, 1887, p. 5, from a report of the speech in the Chicago *News;* see also *Social Science,* vol. 1, no. 15, October 12, 1887, p. 12.

15. Caro Lloyd, *op. cit.,* vol. 1, pp. 88-109 *passim.*

16. *Ibid.,* vol. 1, p. 86.

17. *Ibid.,* vol. 1, p. 106.

18. Quoted in Albert Mordell, *Quaker Militant. John Greenleaf Whittier,* New York, 1933, pp. 261-262.

19. *Ibid.,* p. 262. Howells did write the letter which was published in the *Tribune.* In the meantime a reporter questioned Whittier on the subject, and published the interview in the same paper. In it he made representations which almost brought the friendship of the two men to an end. Howells protested some of the statements in the interview, and Whittier replied later in a letter poorly defending his position. *Ibid.,* pp. 262-263.

20. Henry F. Pringle, *Theodore Roosevelt. A Biography,* New York, 1931, pp. 110-111, 116.

21. William M. Salter, "Second Thoughts on the Treatment of Anarchy," *The Atlantic Monthly,* vol. 89, no. 535, May, 1902, pp. 581, 585 ff. This article followed the assassination of President McKinley. Salter wrote: "I suspect that every one of them save possibly Lingg, would have reprobated the wanton murder of last September," p. 581.

22. This address is reprinted in The *Open Court,* vol. 1, no. 19, October 27, 1887, pp. 530-535.

23. *Ibid.,* pp. 531, 532, 534.

24. See the extremely able open letter in Chicago *Labor Enquirer,* October 29, 1887, signed "Lizzie M. Swank." This started an almost endless controversy over Salter's stand on anarchy between him and Mrs. Holmes and Gertrude Kelly, which continued through 1888 in the *Alarm.* One of Salter's best expositions of his position is in the issue of February 11, 1888.

25. Vol. 1, no. 17, September 29, 1887, p. 465; *cf.,* The *Open Court,* vol. 1, no. 18, October 13, 1887, p. 495, for a defense of private property and a bitter attack on extreme radicalism.

26. See for example, *Social Science,* vol. 1, no. 13, pp. 6, 8; no. 17, p. 13.

27. Vol. 13, no. 20, May 15, 1886, pp. 312-313.

28. Vol. 13, no. 35, August 28, 1886, p. 552. See the entire editorial "The Trial of Anarchy in Chicago," pp. 552-553, and the communication from Chicago signed "E. A. Stevens," *ibid.*, p. 551.
29. Quoted in Spies, *op. cit.*, pp. 71-72; see also *Workmen's Advocate*, October 15, 1887.
30. Vol. 5, no. 5, p. 1.
31. October 29, 1887.
32. Quoted in Benj. R. Tucker, *Henry George, Traitor*, New York, 1896, pp. 8-9. The italics in Tucker's pamphlet are here omitted.
33. Quoted in *Workmen's Advocate*, October 15, 1887.
34. Chicago *Labor Enquirer*, October 29, 1887.
35. Henry George, Jr., *The Life of Henry George*, 2 vols., Garden City, N. Y., 1911, vol. 2, p. 498 note.
36. Quoted in *Onward*, Detroit, January 1, 1889, from the *Manistee Broadaxe*, clipping, scrap-book, Labadie Collection.
37. Tucker, *Henry George, Traitor*, p. 9.
38. *Ibid.*, pp. 6-7.
39. *Workmen's Advocate*, October 15, 1887; *Alarm*, December 3, 1887.
40. For a pro-Henry George version of his position, see George, Jr., *op. cit.*, vol. 2, p. 498; for a thoroughgoing criticism of George containing extensive information, see *The Road to Freedom*, vol. 8, no. 3, November, 1931 (Emma Goldman's letter), p. 5; *Free Society*, May 8, 1898 (Alden S. Huling, "Henry George and the Chicago Case"), p. 2.
41. Mr. E. P. Hotchkiss. Chicago *Tribune*, March 12, 1887.
42. *Ibid.*, September 15, 1887.
43. Quoted in The *Open Court*, vol. 1, no. 20, November 10, 1887, p. 562.
44. Quoted in Trumbull, *The Trial of the Judgment*, pp. 57-58; and The *Open Court*, vol. 1, no. 20, November 10, 1887, p. 563. The versions in these sources differ slightly. The second is to be preferred.
45. P. 1.
46. *Idem.*
47. New York *Times*, November 4, 1887.
48. Greenpoint (N. Y.), 1887. It was published either in September or October.
49. *Ibid.*, p. 3.
50. See below, pp. 471-472.
51. *Social Science*, vol. 1, no. 18, November 5, 1887, p. 14.
52. See above, pp. 214-215.
53. *The Craftsman*, May 15, 1886, clipping, scrap-book, Labadie Collection.
54. Scudder, Jr., *The Labor-Value Fallacy*, p. 9 note.
55. May 8, 1886.
56. May 15, 1886, clipping, scrap-book, Labadie Collection.
57. *Advance and Labor Leaf*, August 6, 1887.
58. Quoted in *Liberty*, vol. 4, no. 5, July 3, 1886, p. 7.

59. Eugene Staley, *History of the Illinois State Federation of Labor* (*Social science studies directed by the Local Community Research Committee* of the University of Chicago, no. 15, [i.e., 16]), Chicago, 1930, p. 70.
60. *Ibid.*, pp. 67-68.
61. *Ibid.*, pp. 68-69.
62. Powderly, *op. cit.*, pp. 540 *et seq.*
63. *Ibid.*, p. 543
64. *Proceedings of G. A., K. of L., 1886*, p. 10.
65. T. V. Powderly, *Independence Day. Powderly's Proclamation*, May 7, 1887. The words in italics are in heavy red type in the original. The quotation was supplied by Miss Inglis.
66. Quoted in *Liberty*, vol. 5, no. 5, October 8, 1887, p. 5.
67. *Ibid.*, vol. 4, no. 13, January 1, 1887, p. 5.
68. *Journal of United Labor*, vol. 8, no. 9, September 3, 1887, p. 2,482. The statement was reprinted in the Lansing (Michigan), *Sentinel*, October 27, 1887.
69. Quoted in Staley, *op. cit.*, p. 68.
70. Quoted in *idem.*
71. Scudder, *op. cit.*, p. 9 note.
72. Aveling, *op. cit.*, p. 127.
73. This was recognized editorially in *The Epoch*, vol. 2, no. 34, September 30, 1887, p. 145.
74. *Cf., John Swinton's Paper*, May 23, August 29, 1886.
75. September 17, 1887.
76. *Idem.*, September 24, October 8, 22, 29, November 5, 1887.
77. See for example August 29, 1887.
78. See typical quotations from these journals in the *Advance and Labor Leaf*, September 24, 1887.
79. September 23, 1887.
80. Clippings, undated, scrap-book, Labadie Collection.
81. October 27, 1887.
82. *Advance and Labor Leaf*, September 24, 1887.
83. Chicago *Labor Enquirer*, clipping, scrap-book, Labadie Collection, probably September 10, 1887.
84. It was published in various labor papers, such as the Denver *Labor Enquirer*, October 22, 1887 and the Milwaukee *Labor Review*, October 22, 1887. Miss Inglis supplied a photostat of the appeal and photostats of the appeals mentioned in the following paragraph.
85. New York *Leader*, October 21, 1887; Chicago *Inter Ocean*, October 21, 1887.
86. The New York *Leader*, October 21, 1887; Chicago *Inter Ocean*, October 21, 1887.
87. *John Swinton's Paper*, October 10, 1886.
88. *Labor Leaf*, September 8, 1886. The other signers were William Gleeson, Fred W. Long, A. H. Simpson, William H. Jackson.
89. Actually the committee undercalculated.

90. Photostat of the appeal "To All Friends of an Impartial Administration of Justice!" provided by Miss Inglis. The committee was at this date composed of Frank Bielfeld, Albert Currlin, Edward Gottge, Julius Leon, Henry Linnemeyer, Sr., Peter Peterson, Dr. Ernst Schmidt, George Schilling, Charles F. Seib, Ferdinand Spies and Frank A. Stauber.

91. Ramus, *op. cit.*, p. 33.

92. Chicago *Labor Enquirer*, October 29, 1887.

93. See above, p. 325.

94. The proceedings of this gathering which sat until June 3, are printed in *Labor: Its Rights and Wrongs*, pp. 170-272.

95. Undated clipping, scrap-book of Minneapolis Assembly, compiled by Miss Inglis, Labadie Collection (cited hereafter as Minneapolis scrap-book).

96. Clipping in Minneapolis scrap-book, probably from Chicago *Tribune*, October 4, 1887. In a pencilled notation on this clipping, Labadie later wrote: "All there is to this is that I did have documents showing that Powderly was a member of the Socialist Labor Party in about 1881." It was also claimed that Powderly was at the Greenback-Labor Convention of 1880 as a delegate of the S.L.P. See *Advance and Labor Leaf*, September 17, 1887. Powderly, in his address to the Minneapolis Assembly as General Master Workman, explained the matter as follows: In 1880, when Philip Van Patten, national secretary of the S.L.P., was a member of the General Executive Board of the K. of L., he and Powderly became close friends. The latter was ignorant of Socialism, and Patten supplied him with reading matter on its principles. Powderly looked kindly upon the program of the S.L.P. In August, Patten sent him a membership card in the S.L.P. with dues paid up for three months. He regarded this as a complimentary gesture, and declared he "never cast a vote for the candidates of that party, was never a member of any of its sections, and had no connection with it except in the manner related above." *Proceedings of G. A., K. of L., 1887*, p. 1536.

97. Minneapolis *Evening Journal*, October 3, 6, 1887, Minneapolis scrap-book.

98. *Proceedings of G. A., K. of L., 1887*, pp. 1499-1505.

99. September 10, 1887.

100. *Ibid.*, p. 1500; also quoted in *Ohio Valley Budget* (Wheeling, West Virginia), November 5, 1887, clipping, Minneapolis scrap-book.

101. *Proceedings of G. A., K. of L., 1887*, pp. 1500-1501.

102. *Ibid.*, pp. 1503-1505 *passim*.

103. *Ibid.*, p. 1503.

104. *Idem.*

105. *Ibid.*, pp. 1503-1505.

106. See for example *ibid.*, pp. 1671, 1682, 1702, 1735, 1773, 1807, 1809, 1822.

107. *Ibid.*, p. 1723.
108. The actual sentiment of the Assembly was 120 to fifty-four, because Schilling voted in the affirmative so that he could move for a reconsideration.
109. It was charged that his address consumed a half-hour, while the other speakers were limited to five minutes each.
110. For this episode see: *ibid.*, pp. 1723-1726; *Ohio Valley Budget*, November 5, 1887; clipping in Minneapolis scrap-book (probably Minneapolis *Evening Journal*, October 10, 1887); Detroit *Evening News*, November 16, 1887 (contains Labadie's report of the Assembly to D. A. 50); *Advance and Labor Leaf*, November 19, 1887 (also contains Labadie's report); Powderly, *op. cit.*, pp. 548-555 *passim*.
111. *Alarm*, November 5, 1887.
112. *Journal of United Labor*, vol. 8, no. 17, October 29, 1887, p. 2514.
113. *Proceedings of G. A., K. of L., 1887*, pp. 1671, 1807.
114. Clippings dated October 24, 1887, Minneapolis scrap-book; Detroit *Evening News*, October 24, 1887.
115. Minneapolis *Evening Journal*, October 19, 1887.
116. Detroit *Evening News*, October 24, 1887. Statement of Mr. A. M. Dewey, who attended as an ex-delegate.
117. Chicago *Labor Enquirer*, October 29, 1887.
118. Commons, *op. cit.*, vol. 2, p. 394.
119. Quoted in Staley, *op. cit.*, p. 70.
120. Edgworth, "Scylla and Carybdis, Or Legality and Anarchy," *Social Science*, vol. 1, no. 17, October 29, 1887, p. 9.
121. November 5, 1887.
122. *Cf.*, the statement of C. G. Dixon in the Chicago *Tribune*, September 15, 1887.
123. *Workmen's Advocate*, September 24, 1887, editorial "Constitution Attacked."
124. *Cf.*, *idem*.
125. Aveling, *op. cit.*, p. 126.

XX. THE LAST WEEK

As early as October, 1887, Governor Oglesby received letters and petitions urging him to commute the sentence of death and to pardon the "anarchists." [1] Messages of this nature came even from Europe. Members of the extreme left of the French Chamber of Deputies, in "the name of humanity and of the solidarity between the two great Republics" and on the ground that "political" offenses should not be punished by capital punishment, telegraphed the governor on October 29, asking him to spare the lives of the "Anarchists now lying under sentence of death." [2] Most of the members of the Paris Municipal Council and the Council of the Department of the Seine had earlier forwarded a similar request to Governor Oglesby through the American minister. [3] London was the scene of an impressive mass-meeting on October 14, at which William Morris, Stepniak, the Russian revolutionary, George Standring, Peter Kropotkin, George Bernard Shaw and Annie Besant spoke in defense of the eight men. [4] On November 6, at forty-nine different meetings of socialist, secularist, and radical clubs, 16,405 English working-men voted in favor of "a protest against the murder of the labor leaders." [5] Other Englishmen who played an active part in the movement for clemency included Sir Walter Besant, Walter Crane, Stopford Brooke and Ford Madox Brown, the painter. [6]

As November 11 drew near, letters, petitions, memorials, and resolutions poured in upon the governor. Some protested against the impending executions, others against any executive act which would prevent them from taking place. Capt. Schaack, puzzled by the efforts to save the condemned from the gallows, later wrote that "it was surprising to note how many who had hitherto clamored for blood . . . now exerted themselves . . . to secure executive clemency." People who earlier de manded that they be strung up, were now talking of the "pooɪ innocent men; it is too bad to hang them." [7] The daily press and the leading periodicals of the country resented this "soft-headed" sentimentality. They exhorted the governor not to interfere. [8]

On November 7, twenty-nine Methodist ministers of Cleveland urged Governor Oglesby "in behalf of justice and in the protection of all the interests of our land, . . . to let the law take its course, severe though it may be. . . ." [9] Only one clergyman who was opposed to capital punishment voted against this resolution. Earlier, reports that the governor might react favorably to the pleas for clemency created dissatisfaction in parts of the State, and brought warnings that he would lose heavily among his Republican supporters. [10]

To the Amnesty Association, the Defense Committee, labor organizations, and a number of individuals, there fell the task of directing sentiment against the executions. The Amnesty Association had been formed immediately after the trial in the lower court to circulate petitions for pardon. When the case was appealed, the Association went out of existence, but with the adverse decision of the State Supreme Court it was re-vived. When it was resurrected with Lucian S. Oliver as president, it had about 150 members. [11] It was necessary for the Association to secure respectful requests for mercy from the prisoners to meet the legal forms. It was also understood that the governor would probably take no action unless the condemned also indicated that they had abjured their principles. This, obviously, would cause some difficulty, but it was essential. Grinnell and others apparently intimated that Fielden and Schwab might be saved from the gallows if they were sufficiently repentant. [12] The Chicago press hinted "that the condemned anarchists might secure a commutation from death to life imprisonment if they 'humbled themselves in a proper spirit'. . . ." [13]

It was no easy job to secure a confession of contrition. Despite the nerve-wracking hours which Dr. Ernst Schmidt, Frank Stauber, and Henry Linnemeyer spent to induce the men to sign a statement of penitence, they were successful only with Spies, Schwab, and Fielden. For all but Spies the decision, one way or the other, was easy. He joined Schwab and Fielden in their appeal with the greatest reluctance. The letter which the three of them addressed to Governor Oglesby deserves quotation.

"Sir:" they began, "in order that the truth may be known by you and the public you represent we desire to state that we never advocated the use of force, excepting in the case of self-defense. To accuse us of having attempted to overthrow law and government May 4, 1886, or at any other time is as false as it is absurd. Whatever we said or did, or said or did publicly, we have never supported, or plotted to commit, an unlawful act, and while we attack the present social arrangements, in writing and speech, and exposed their iniquities, we have never conspicuously broken any laws. So far from having planned the killing of anybody at the Haymarket, or anywhere else, the very object of that meeting was to protest against the commission of murder. We believe it to be our duty as friends of labor and liberty to oppose other use of force than that which is necessary in the defense of sacred rights against unlawful attacks. And our efforts have been in the direction of elevation of mankind, and to remove, as much as possible, the causes of crime in society. Our labor was unselfish. No motives of personal gain or ambition prompted us. Thousands and thousands will be testimony to this. We may have erred at times in our judgment. Yes; we may have loved mankind not wisely, but too well. If, in the excitement of propagating our views, we were led into expressions which caused workingmen to think that aggressive force was a proper instrument of reform, we regret it. We deplore the loss of life at the Haymarket, at McCormick's factory, at East St. Louis, and at the Chicago Stock Yards." [14]

This communication, said Henry Demarest Lloyd, was in the first place "a renunciation of the doctrine of reform by force. In the second place it is a suggestion to the working-men of the country to rely upon securing reform by constitutional means and the ballot, and, in the third place, it is the first [sic] expression which these men have given that they regret the loss of life at the Haymarket." [15] Salter, convinced that the men had a slight chance to save their lives, only if they appeared as supplicants, was distressed by the position assumed by Lingg, Fischer, Engel and Parsons. They refused point-blank to sign such a statement. Instead they had issued letters to the governor asserting that the circularizing of petitions for clemency did not have their sanction. They dramatically demanded the traditional "liberty or death." ". . . I regret the petition for my imprisonment, for I am innocent," wrote Parsons, "and I say to you that under no circumstances will I accept a commutation to imprisonment. In the name of the American people I demand my right . . . to liberty." "If I cannot obtain justice from the authorities and be restored to my family," declared Fischer, "then I prefer that the verdict be carried out as it stands." George Engel and Louis Lingg requested either unconditional release or death. [16]

The plea for mercy by Spies, Schwab and Fielden was bitterly attacked by many Chicago revolutionaries, to whom it was a sign of weakness and loss of revolutionary courage. Schwab and Fielden probably attached their signatures because they had been informed that it might save their lives. No such hopeful promise could have been extended to the others. Yet, if Spies was excluded from the bargain why did he sign the letter to Oglesby? Spies, who shortly regretted his act, was apparently influenced by two factors. He was evidently led to believe that if he, regarded as one of the leaders of the eight men, would partially repudiate his past activities, all seven would have a chance to escape the gallows. In the second place, he did not want to die, and he was beginning to realize how close he was to death. About this time, Spies asked Schilling if they would really be executed. He refused to believe that the hanging would actually take place, and expressed the conviction, born of hope, that "the people" would not let it happen. He was hurt when Schilling declared that if the State called for volunteers to hang the condemned, at least one hundred thousand men would come clamoring to the doors of the jail offering their services.[17]

While the men were being induced to "humble themselves in the proper spirit," the amnesty forces were actively circulating petitions. As a matter of expediency, talk of securing pardons was stopped. The petitions, almost without exception, begged the governor to commute the sentences of the seven men to life imprisonment. This alone held out hope for success. George Schilling, Dr. Ernst Schmidt, William Salter, Henry Demarest Lloyd, Cora L. V. Richmond, and a number of labor leaders were now among the chief amnesty workers. Tables were set up throughout Chicago by a committee of the Amnesty Association to facilitate the securing of signatures.[18] On November 3, Salter set a petition in circulation among the leading citizens of the city. By the following morning he had secured twenty signatures, including those of Judge Tuley, at this time Chief Justice of the Circuit Court, ex-Judge Booth, Julius Rosenthal, a well-known lawyer formerly president of the Chicago Law Institute and holder of a number of public offices, and William R. Manierre, an alderman.[19] Judge Tuley, who had studied the case from its very inception, declared that the men were "technically guilty," but he felt "that their actual complicity in the murder of" Degan had not been shown. The application of the extreme penalty he thought unwise. Public policy would be better served if the death sentences were changed to life imprisonment.[20]

The large number of lawyers who participated in the movement for executive clemency suggests dissatisfaction with the trial in the lower court. In addition to Tuley and Booth, Judges Thomas Moran of the Appellate Court, McAlister and Baker also signed a petition for commutation of sentence.[21] Other members of the legal profession in Chicago who followed suit included Whig Ewing, United States District Attorney, W. C. Goudy, leader of the Chicago Bar and a municipal office holder, Stephen S. Gregory, later elected president of the American Bar Association, Gen. M. M. Trumbull, F. S. Winston, Samuel P. McConnell, who within three years was elected a judge of the Circuit Court, and Lyman Trumbull, who had been a member of the State Supreme Court.[22]

S. P. McConnell, who together with Judge Rogers, his father-in-law, had followed the trial with painstaking care,[23] had been amazed and shocked by many of Judge Gary's rulings. He also drew up a petition. When he approached Lyman Trumbull, the latter "read the petition, then buried his face in his hands and said, 'I will sign. Those men did not have a fair trial.' "[24]

Petitions were also circulated among special groups. One was directed to pharmacists and physicians.[25] Members of the Illinois Legislature were individually reached by a committee of the United Labor Party.[26]

On November 9, the Chicago *Tribune* published the names of those "leading citizens" who signed clemency petitions. Most of the names carry no distinction today, but they impressed Chicagoans of that day. Among those who affixed their signatures to petitions asking that the sentences of *all seven* men be commuted, excluding those already mentioned, were: Lyman Gage, banker and later Secretary of the Treasury under McKinley, I. R. Boyesen, a son of H. H. Boyesen, Norwegian author and educator, Emil G. Hirsch, educator, editor, rabbinical scholar and professor of rabbinical literature and philosophy at the University of Chicago, B. F. Underwood, editor of the *Open Court,* and Marvin Hughitt of the Chicago and Northwestern Railroad.[27] A petition urging that the sentences of Spies, Fielden and Parsons be commuted was signed by other leading citizens.[28] Potter Palmer, wealthy real estate operator who had declined Grant's offer of the post of Secretary of the Interior, added his name to a petition in behalf of Spies, Schwab and Fielden. Gen. H. H. Thomas who saw service during the Civil War and afterward in the army, Eugene C. Preussing and A. M. Pence regarded only Fielden and Lingg as worthy of executive clemency. Others [29] favored clemency for all but Lingg.

"Leading" New Yorkers were similarly approached for signatures, and as early as November 4, a large number of representative citizens had signed a petition for commutation of the death sentences.[30] Members of the Society of Clergymen for the Advancement of Labor met in New York on November 3, and resolved to draft a petition for clemency to be circulated among the clergy. The Rev. Dr. B. F. De Costa and Father Huntington were especially active in this work.[31] The latter shortly after pleaded for clemency by letter and telegram.[32]

Interest in the "anarchist" case mounted as the date of the execution drew near. "Every movement of Governor Oglesby," it was reported, "is watched with fervid curiosity, and the rigid surveillance which he encounters on every side has become so irksome to him that he has deemed it best to enforce the strictest rules of secrecy in regard to all his actions." Besieged by indefatigable newspaper men, the governor was forced to adopt a policy of absolute silence in order, he explained, to avoid misunderstandings.[33] Speculation over the governor's final decision was animated. At the State capital, Springfield, it was first thought "that the governor will commute the sentence of one or two of the unfortunate beings who are doomed to die . . . [so] that the lawless may learn the wages of anarchy is death." [34] Then it was rumored that none of the condemned had a chance to escape death.[35] Friends of the governor in his home town, Lincoln, felt that either all seven would hang or that Schwab and Fielden alone might be favored by executive clemency.[36] Throughout Illinois and

Michigan, growing sympathy with the men was reflected in the hope that the death penalty would not be exacted.[37] A dispatch to the New York *Sun* showed that the same sentiment was observable in Chicago.[38] Many Chicagoans were sanguine that four of the prisoners would not be hanged.[39]

Meanwhile pressure continued to secure expressions of contrition from the condemned. If Governor Oglesby were disposed to be merciful it would facilitate his task. It is difficult to extend clemency to one who obdurately demands unconditional liberty or death. On November 5, Justus Schwab implored his comrades "to ask the Governor for commutation of sentence in behalf of your families, yourselves and the cause you have so nobly espoused. . . . History and the future will certainly find a different verdict. Give us contemporaries a chance to pause. . . . If you will live, liberty will live. Every man has a right to sacrifice his own life, but not those of his fellowmen." [40]

Governor Oglesby did not indicate publicly how he would ultimately dispose of the case. In private he made it clear to a small number of influential Chicagoans who favored clemency that his mind was still open. Lyman Gage received word from Springfield to the effect that the governor was willing to commute the sentences of Parsons, Spies, Neebe, and Schwab if the leading business men of the city would request it. Governor Oglesby apparently said that if the business interests of Chicago were opposed to executing the men they should meet, adopt a course of action, and inform him of their decision. On the basis of this information, Gage quickly arranged for a meeting attended by fifty of Chicago's foremost bankers, merchants, and manufacturers. Henry Demarest Lloyd was also present. Gage bluntly asserted that the question before the gathering was whether they should have the men "choked" or ask for a commutation of sentence. Arguing with great earnestness, he advanced three reasons which in his eyes justified the latter course. In the first place, the law had been sufficiently vindicated because the "anarchist" case had gone from the lower court to the highest in the land. In the second place, if the "anarchists" were imprisoned they would, in a sense, be hostages of society, and society would be far better protected by their incarceration than by their death. Finally, since labor widely believed that capitalists desired their death, it would be wise, magnanimous and expedient for the leading citizens of Chicago to petition for clemency.

For a moment it seemed as if Gage's plea would carry the conference. Had it not been for the efforts of two men it would have done so. But Marshall Field and Julius Grinnell prevented that. Grinnell had not been invited to the conference. Marshall Field brought him along to serve as his mouthpiece. When Mr. Field arose to address the gathering he made the excuse that he was not a public speaker, and introduced Julius Grinnell to present his side of the question. As soon as Marshall Field's strong opposition to commutation of the death sentence was known, the sense of the meeting changed. Grinnell's long and explosive harangue against action that might interfere with the scheduled executions was simply a lengthy and forceful presentation of Marshall Field's views. When Grinnell finished, those in attendance began to depart, and the meeting gradually evaporated. Marshall Field's wealth had defeated Lyman Gage's arguments.

Gage informed Henry Demarest Lloyd that "Afterwards many of the men present came around to me singly, and said that they had agreed with me in my views and would have been glad to join in such an appeal, but that in the face of the opposition of powerful men like Marshall Field they did not like to do so, as it might injure them in business or socially, etc." [41]

The authorities completely disregarded the movement for executive clemency in their arrangements to insure "the peaceful execution," as the Chicago *Tribune* put it, of the seven men.[42] Additional supplies of arms and ammunition were distributed among the police stations. Special precautions were taken to guard the water-works in case an attempt at jail delivery should be accompanied by incendiarism, which Capt. Schaack seriously expected. Unusual numbers of policemen were kept on reserve at strategic stations, where they engaged in extended rifle drills. At the jail in which the men were incarcerated "martial law" was virtually in effect. Business houses employed private watchmen to guard their premises until after November 11.[43] On November 4, a conference was held at the mayor's office attended by Mayor Roche, Ebersold, the commander of the First Brigade of the Illinois National Guard, and a representative of the military committee of the Citizens' Association. Plans were laid for preserving order until after the hangings. The military committee of the Citizens' Association promised to supply "fifty or more six-chamber repeating rifles" by Monday, the seventh, "for use if necessary on Friday [November 11]."[44] The Citizens' Association also turned over to the police 400 Springfield rifles, 12,000 rounds of cartridges, bayonets, and a Gatling gun.[45] Two companies of the United States Sixth Infantry Regiment (Companies F and K) entrained at Salt Lake City for Chicago and were expected to reach their destination by Monday night or Tuesday morning.[46] Arrangements were made for calling out the State troops. For an entire week these preparations continued.[47]

Rumors ran wild in the city. The "anarchists" were drilling for a forceful jail delivery. If the men were executed they were expected to take revenge upon Chicago. These tales were met by the promise that the police would deal summarily with any disturbance.[48]

As anticipation of an outbreak grew, the city again became as restive and nervous as it was immediately after May 4. In the light of the extensive precautions taken, it is interesting to note that Detective Jim Bonfield, brother of Capt. Bonfield, had earlier asserted that he expected no trouble. "It stands to reason," he pointed out, "that they [the 'anarchists'] won't attempt anything. They will hope up to the last minute the trap of the gallows is sprung, and any outbreak would lessen their chances . . ." The morale of the "anarchists," he said, was completely broken. Since they were naturally cowards there was no reason to fear a disturbance. He found proof of their lack of courage in the fact that they did not stand their ground when the police opened fire at the Haymarket meeting. He also explained that their speakers gained the necessary courage for making "their force speeches" by consuming huge quantities of beer! [49]

In the meantime an unexpected development gravely discouraged the friends of the prisoners. On Sunday, November 6, Lingg's cell was searched at about ten in the morning, and four bombs, each approximately six inches long and an inch in diameter, were found. These bombs were so small that they could only serve for self-destruction. Their discovery was attended by peculiar circumstances. Sheriff Matson, in charge of the jail, asserted that they had been found wholly by accident. He could offer no reason to explain why the cells of the men had been changed and searched. No other bombs or poison were found. Six hours passed after the finding of the bombs before newspaper reporters were informed, and the bombs were privately analyzed. Only Sheriff Matson knew the chemist who reported that they were filled with dynamite. Apart from the sheriff's statement, the bombs, it was said at the time, might have been filled with molasses. [50]

It was asserted that the police had a definite motive for placing and subsequently discovering the bombs in Lingg's cell. They were too small to be used for any purpose but suicide. If Lingg wanted to destroy himself, why, asked the Detroit *Evening News,* were there so many bombs? With the growth of public opinion in favor of the condemned, a feeling "of disappointment and resentment" apparently developed in police circles. There was even talk of giving this feeling some form of public expression. [51] The comment made by one of the jailers creates suspicion. "Merciful God," he exclaimed when he saw the bombs, "we have been on the brink of a volcano. What a revolution in public sentiment this will produce." [52]

Lingg insisted that he knew nothing about the missiles discovered in his cell. "I didn't know," he said, "that there was a bomb within ten miles of the jail." [53] The other prisoners likewise professed ignorance. It is, of course, possible that they were smuggled in by a friend of Lingg. The prisoners received fruit, flowers and other gifts from their sympathizers, and the bombs might have been sent in that fashion. They might also have been given to Lingg by another inmate of the jail acting as an intermediary.

Regardless of the manner in which the bombs got to Lingg's cell, they had an adverse effect upon the chances of the seven men to win a commutation of sentence. Dr. Salter admitted that the discovery of the bombs was a terrible "setback." "It's the worst thing that could have happened," he disconsolately declared. He had planned to go to Springfield to speak to the governor in behalf of the men, "but now," he said, "I have hardly enough courage to attempt the journey." [54] Salter hoped to minimize their effect by securing a denunciation of Lingg from the prisoners. Only Schwab, Fielden and Spies, however, were willing to fall in with his scheme. Speaking for all three, Spies claimed that he was absolutely ignorant of the bombs until he learned of their existence from Sheriff Matson. He had not spoken to Lingg for nine months, and he called the young German carpenter a monomaniac, suffering from a martyr complex. Spies criticized Lingg because the latter was not only determined to sacrifice his own life for the sake of the movement, but was also doing everything in his power to sacrifice those of his fellow-prisoners. "It's useless to condemn the action of an irresponsible man!" Spies wrote. "If anyone holds us, or any one of us, responsible for Lingg's deeds, then I can't see why we shouldn't be held responsible for any mischief, whatsoever, committed in the world." [55]

Fischer, thoroughly puzzled by the entire episode, was certain that Lingg had not intended taking the lives of any of the jail officials from whom the men had received decent treatment. Nor did he believe that Lingg was the type to commit suicide. He was too courageous for that.[56] Salter was so determined to prevent the episode from having injurious consequences, that he tried to suppress a letter which Parsons wrote for the occasion. This epistle, which was finally released, charged that the bombs had been planted by the police.

"It is a mare's nest," wrote Parsons, "a canard; a put-up job to create a sensation and manufacture public prejudice. How in the world could bombs get into Lingg's cell unknown to those whose sole business it is to see that no such things get there? . . . There is no aperture in the wire gratings through which such missiles could get in. Or have the obliging guards in the inspection room been passing up bombs to Lingg's cell? Remember, our cells were searched about three or four weeks ago and the scrutiny redoubled since. Nothing was found then. While it was impossible for bombs to get to Lingg without the knowledge of the officials, it was not impossible that some one of the many persons who have had ready access to his cell to put them there yesterday morning, [i.e., November 6] after he was taken out of his cell. There are those in this community who would not hesitate a moment to put up such a job on the Anarchists. Lingg could have no use for bombs in the jail. . . . Those bombs, if they were really found there, were put there by someone whose business it was to find them there. . . . This last 'find' of bombs is in keeping with the many other fakes lately thrown upon the community. The story is too thin. It won't wash. Now, I don't impute a 'conspiracy' to the jail officials. I believe both Folz [chief jailer] and Matson are honorable men." [57]

An examination of editorial comment shows that the episode affected public sentiment throughout the country. It offered additional confirmation of the basic viciousness of the "anarchists," and it strengthened the arguments of those who opposed clemency.[58]

"What little sympathy existed in Washington for the condemned Anarchists," a Washington news dispatch reads, "(which, however, was on the increase because of the signatures of so many prominent men at Chicago and elsewhere to petitions for clemency) received a peremptory check on the receipt of the intelligence that bombs had been discovered in Lingg's cell. A few persons were inclined to doubt that these bombs had been found as stated, but said that if it were clearly shown that the bombs had thus been smuggled and concealed, the question of clemency should no longer be considered." [59]

The *Universalist,* a religious publication, similarly pointed out that "The discovery of the bombs . . . has convinced many who inclined previously to the side of mercy that these are not fit subjects for clemency, and that the stern verdict of the law . . . should take its course." [60] The religious press, it should be noted, without major exception, urged the governor not to give way before the entreaties of mercy. "The pardon of the anarchists," declared the *Interior,* a Presbyterian publication, "would be a tacit surrender of the city." The *Advance,* a Congregational journal, observed that "Pity is good; mercy is divine; but justice must not be sacrificed to a one-sided and short-sided maudlin sentimentality." [61]

The discovery of the bombs disheartened the amnesty workers, but it did not disrupt their activities or plans. They marshalled their forces for a great concerted effort on November 9, which Governor Oglesby set aside for a public hearing. The governor's task was a difficult one. He had to acquaint himself with the "facts" of the case without reading the 8,000 page record of the trial for which he claimed he lacked time. He had to examine hundreds of letters and telegrams which poured in on him from all sections of the country. He was supposed to give due consideration to the petitions which came to his desk and to the character of their signers. On November 9 alone, he received almost five hundred letters.[62] About one-half of the communications urged him to stand firm and permit the execution of the sentences.[63] The governor, reported the press, was "doing all a mortal man can to arrive at such information as shall finally shape the character of his fateful decision." [64]

Chartered cars, from Chicago, which left Tuesday night, November 8, carried the leading sympathizers and relatives of the condemned to Springfield where they were joined, on the morning of the ninth, by others who came on their own and a large delegation from New York City.[65] Probably three hundred persons were present in Springfield that day ready to appear before the governor, and perhaps a third came from outside of the State.[66] When the "friends of the condemned anarchists" had "made their last stand," as the press put it,[67] Governor Oglesby had heard appeals from Captain Black, Gen. M. M. Trumbull, Cora L. V. Richmond, Elijah H. Haines, State Senator A. J. Streeter, Henry Demarest Lloyd, William Salter, George Schilling, L. S. Oliver, Samuel Gompers, S. P. McConnell, Joe Buchanan, and representatives of labor and other organizations. He also conferred privately with members of the families of the condemned before the day was over.

At nine-thirty in the morning, the governor, with Attorney-General Hunt at his side, seated himself before a table in a large, ornately decorated audience-room in the State capitol. The press, the petitioners and several officials found their places, and shortly afterward Black asked, "Shall I proceed, Governor?" It was the beginning of an arduous and critical day.

Black read a petition, signed by Spies, Schwab, and Fielden, which set forth the grounds for the plea for executive clemency. From time to time he interpolated comments and explanations. Occasionally the governor asked a question. Black followed this with a lengthy argument to show that the exercise of executive mercy would be both expedient and just, and concluded his moving appeal amid a profound silence. The governor was judicial deliberation itself. He gave no sign of what was passing through his mind.[68] Gen. Trumbull, who followed, addressed himself to the governor "as an old soldier, who has fought with you on the battlefields of the

Republic. . . ." His brief address closed on a note of earnest supplication: "In behalf of the families of these men," he said, "in behalf of the men themselves, in behalf of thousands and hundreds of thousands of people who sympathize with them in their misfortunes, I implore your Excellency to show mercy in this case." [69] Mrs. Cora L. V. Richmond, the well-known Chicago spiritualist, appeared for the Amnesty Association. She utilized every device to touch the governor's heart, and left the eyes of her auditors tear-stained. She tempted Governor Oglesby with the thought that if he were merciful his name would be inscribed upon "the scroll of humanity along with that of the martyred Abraham Lincoln," and reminded him that the Amnesty Association, representing "all classes of people," spoke in the name of "humanity." [70]

Three reasons prompted Elijah M. Haines, ex-Speaker of the Illinois House of Representatives, to attend. He was opposed to capital punishment; he was certain that the conspiracy, as members of which the men were convicted, had not been proven; and he felt that "the peculiar complications of this case would make the execution of these men hazardous to the best interests of society." [71] Another member of the State legislature, Senator A. J. Streeter, added his voice to that of Mr. Haines. He presented a petition of the United Labor representatives of the last legislature which was also signed by Democratic and Republican legislators. The document urged that the governor grant a thirty day reprieve "to permit developments in public feelings." Streeter likewise was convinced that the interests of society would best be served if the men were sent to the penitentiary. [72]

After a short recess in the early afternoon, the parade of petitioners before Governor Oglesby was resumed at two o'clock. George Schilling acted as a sort of master of ceremonies, introducing the speakers and hurrying things along. L. S. Oliver presented the great petition of the Amnesty Association. It bore 41,000 signatures gathered since November 2. A monster petition with no less than 150,000 names, said Mr.

Oliver, had been prepared in New York City. Before the close of the day, the Association received petitions with about 10,000 signatures from Cleveland and Kansas City.

Labor was well represented that afternoon. William Bailey and John Campbell in behalf of the Quincy Trade and Labor Assembly, submitted a petition and "told the governor . . . why they, as workingmen, believe[d] it best to commute the sentences of the condemned." The "anarchists" might have been "over-zealous," but they "meant no wrong." In the name of "humanity and common justice," they urged the governor to commute the sentences.[73] A petition, signed by 16,000 persons and drawn up by the Central Labor Union of Chicago, was presented by William Urban. P. S. Schulenberg of Detroit, representing forty-five societies, of which ten were labor organizations, also pleaded with the governor in the much-taken name of "justice and humanity." Encouraged by Governor Oglesby, Charles G. Dixon of Chicago, active in labor circles, added an oral argument to the petition he submitted. In behalf of militant D. A. 49 of New York, Edward King, Edward Farrell, a colored labor leader, and James E. Quinn appeared. King also represented the Central Labor Union of New York. George Schilling likewise addressed the governor. He emphasized the fact that the worker was gradually being brought to believe that the law was lenient to the rich and harsh to the poor. The implication was clear enough.[74]

Samuel Gompers and Joe Buchanan were labor leaders of greater note who hurried to Springfield to aid the condemned. Only Gompers, however, appealed publicly to the governor. Buchanan did his work in private conference after the open hearing. Gompers, always an able speaker, won the immediate attention of the governor who raised a number of pertinent questions.

"I have differed with these men in theory," declared Gompers. "I have differed with them in practise. I have differed with them in methods. Because . . . we may have been opponents . . . fighting for labor upon different sides of the house, I know of no reason why I should not raise my voice and ask you, sir, to interpose and save their lives from the gallows. The execution I think, would be an execution not of justice, not to the interests of the great State of Illinois, not to the interest of the country, not to the interest of our fellow men. I come to you," he pointed out, "as a representative of the Central Labor Union of New York, besides as President of the American Federation of Labor. . . ."

Gompers based his plea for executive clemency upon a strange ground. "If these men are executed," he argued, "it would simply give an impetus to the so-called revolutionary movement. . . . These men would . . . be looked upon as martyrs. Thousands and hundreds of thousands of laboring men all over this country would consider that those men had been executed because they were standing up for free speech and free assemblage. We ask you, sir, to interpose your great power and prevent so dire a calamity." [75] If it be charged that this was a specious argument, it can be said that Gompers probably used it because he felt it would have weight with the governor. In any case he did make a hurried trip from the East to appear in behalf of the men. His bitter rival, the histrionic Powderly, did not utter a word to aid them.

The public hearing showed that the amnesty movement had gained impressive strength. What it lacked in the way of human drama and surprise was supplied by the private audiences which the governor held. On November 9, it was disclosed that Judge Gary and Julius Grinnell petitioned Governor Oglesby by letter to commute the sentences of Fielden and Schwab! Judge Gary referred the governor to the decision of the Supreme Court for the history of the case and its legal aspects. Then he went on to point out that apart from what was "there shown," it should be noted that "there is in the nature and private character of" Samuel Fielden

" . . . a natural love of justice, an impatience at all undeserved suffering, an impulsive temper, and an intense love and thirst for the applause of his hearers made him an advocate of force as a heroic remedy for the hardship that the poor endure. In his own private life he was the honest, industrious, and peaceable laboring man.

"In what he said in court before sentence he was respectful and decorous. His language and conduct since have been irreproachable. As there is no evidence that he knew of any preparation to do the specific act of throwing the bomb that killed Degan, he does not understand even now that general advice to large masses to do violence makes him responsible for the violence done by reason of that advice, nor that by being joined by others in an effort to subvert law and order by force makes him responsible for the acts of those others tending to make that effort effectual.

"In short, he was more a misguided enthusiast than a criminal, conscious of the horrible nature and effect of his teachings, and of his responsibility therefore. What shall be done in his case is partly a question of humanity and partly a question of State policy. . . ."

Judge Gary concluded that *"action"* by the governor *"favorable to him is justifiable."* [76]

Fielden, evidently, was not quite the villain he had been painted during the trial. He was really not a "criminal," and presumably had been found guilty of murder and sentenced to death because he was "a misguided enthusiast" who loved "justice." He was "honest, industrious and peaceable" in private life. He had planned no crime. Was this the same Fielden who, according to the State, had given the signal for the bomb-throwing and fired at the police? How did his "respectful and decorous" attitude in court bear upon his request for a commutation of sentence?

Mr. Grinnell endorsed and approved the "recommendation by Judge Gary," and added

"thereto the suggestion, upon application of Mr. Foster, one of the attorneys who appeared for the defendants . . . that

Schwab's conduct during the trial and when addressing the court before sentence, like Fielden's, was decorous, respectful to the law, and commendable. I feel that you should know this fact which exists alone as to these two—Schwab and Fielden.

"It is my further desire to say that I believe that Schwab was the pliant, weak tool of a stronger will and more designing person. Schwab seems to be friendless."

Mr. Grinnell would not recommend mercy for any of the others, but as for Fielden and Schwab, he wrote, "I do not feel like putting any obstacle in the way of a commutation of their sentence to imprisonment for life, although I should have preferred to have received from Schwab a statement similar to that from Fielden, which is a great factor in his favor, in my opinion." [77]

Mr. Grinnell had but recently cried that if Fielden and Schwab remained alive, the government, nay, the nation itself, would be destroyed. He had stigmatized them as "rattlesnakes" and "traitors," worthy of no better end than the hangman's noose. Schwab the murderous menace to society, was now a "friendless," "pliant, weak tool of a stronger will and more designing person." What caused the metamorphosis? Was it his eating of humble pie? Or was Mr. Grinnell, in extending the boon of life, merely displaying the expansive magnanimity of the victor? Whatever the motive, he was not alone in his act, for Mr. Ingham, his special assistant, likewise wrote to the governor asking for executive clemency for Fielden and Schwab. [78]

Before the governor's private audiences had terminated, he also heard appeals from S. P. McConnell, Henry Demarest Lloyd, William Salter, Joe Buchanan, George Schilling, and members of the families of the condemned. [79] In keeping with the belief that an expression of contrition by the condemned [80] would increase the chances of commutation, the letter signed by Spies, Fielden and Schwab which has already been examined, and specially prepared petitions bearing the names of the last two were privately submitted to the governor. Fielden discussed his relations with the labor movement in his appeal, and declared that he was drawn into it and the radical movement because he became "intoxicated with the applause" of his audiences. He insisted that he had never been connected with any crime. "In view of these facts," concluded Fielden, "I respectfully submit that, while I confess with regret the use of extravagant and unjustifiable words, I am not a murderer. I have never had any murderous intent, and I humbly pray relief from the murderer's doom." Schwab confessed "that many utterances of mine . . . expressions made under intense excitement, and often sans deliberation, were injudicious. These I regret, believing that they must have had a tendency to incite to unnecessary violence oftentimes." He was insistent upon his innocence of the bomb-throwing, pointing out that he had not attended the Haymarket meeting and had "deplored" its results.[81]

Spies had reluctantly signed the petition to Governor Oglesby with the remark "I believe I am making a mistake." [82] The charges of cowardice which followed cut deep, and he was eager to prove to his fellow revolutionaries that he was not the weakling they painted him. Certain that nothing he could do would prevent his execution he addressed a letter to the governor withdrawing his earlier request for clemency. He entrusted it to Joe Buchanan on the promise that it would be read to the governor. Buchanan arranged for a private audience on the ninth to do this. In addition to himself and Governor Oglesby, only Lloyd, Salter, and five German radicals were present. In the midst of a silence broken only by his own voice and the sound of the nervous, swift pacing of the governor, Buchanan read Spies' unexpected communication.

"The fact some of us," it begins, "have appealed to you for justice (under the pardoning prerogative) while others have not, should not enter into consideration in the decision of our cases. Some of my friends have asked you for an absolute pardon. They feel the injustice done them so intensely that they cannot conciliate the idea of a commutation of sentence with the consciousness of innocence. The others (among them, my-self), while possessed of the same feeling of indignation, can perhaps more solemnly and dispassionately look upon the matter as it stands. They do not disregard the fact that through a systematic course of lying, perverting, distorting, and slandering, the press has succeeded in creating a sentiment of bitterness and a hatred among a great portion of the populace that one man, no matter how powerful, how courageous, and just he be, cannot possibly overcome. . . . Not wishing, therefore, to place your excellency in a still more embarrassing position between the blind fanaticism of a misinformed public on the one hand, and justice on the other, they concluded to submit their case to you unconditionally.

"I implore you not to let this difference of action have any weight with you in determining our fate. During our trial the desire of the prosecution to slaughter me and to let off my co-defendants with slighter punishment was quite apparent and manifest. It occurred to me then, and to a great many others, that the prosecution would be satisfied with one life—namely, mine. Grinnell in his argument intimated this very plainly.

"I care not to protest my innocence of any crime, and of the one I am accused of in particular. . . . But to you I wish to address myself now, as the alleged arch-conspirator (leaving the fact that I have never belonged to any kind of a conspiracy out of the question altogether); if a sacrifice of life must be, will not my life suffice? . . . Take this, then; take my life. I offer it to you that you may satisfy the fury of a semi-barbaric mob, and save the lives of my comrades. I know that every one of my comrades is as willing to die and perhaps more so than I. It is not for their sakes that I make this offer, but in the name of humanity and progress, in the interests of a peaceable, if possible, development of the social forces that are destined to lift our race upon a higher and better plane of civilization.

"In the name of the traditions of our country I beg you to prevent a sevenfold murder upon men whose only crime is that they are idealists. If legal murder there must be, let mine suffice." [83]

Why did Spies offer his life in sacrificial exchange for those of his comrades? He must have known that his extraordinary proposal would not be accepted. He could have cleared himself of the charges of cowardice without going to such lengths. Spies was utterly convinced that he did not have the shadow of a chance to escape the gallows. Parsons, Engel and Lingg had publicly repudiated any measure of executive clemency. But for these two considerations it is questionable whether this letter would ever have been written. It is highly probable that his message to the governor was inspired by Schilling, who asserts he told Spies that "since you are being considered the 'leader' in the sense of being the strong man of the lot and for misleading the others, why don't you request that your life be taken and the remainder of your comrades released." [84] The only real effect the letter had was to clear Spies' name among the revolutionaries.

It was Joe Buchanan's fate to undertake an even more distressing task before the private audience with the governor was over. Before entering the governor's chamber, he was given a note from Parsons by Capt. Black which he was also to read. Parsons' communication requested, in short, since he was found guilty of the murder of Degan, and was to be hanged because he was present at the Haymarket meeting, that a reprieve be granted him for a sufficient period of time so that his wife and two children, who also attended the gathering, could be indicted, tried, convicted, and put to death together with him! When he had heard this fantastic demand through, Governor Oglesby exclaimed, "My God, this is terrible!" [85]

Buchanan discharged one other task which, by contrast, was pleasant. He presented Governor Oglesby with a petition for clemency signed by almost fifty delegates to the General Assembly of the K. of L. held the previous month in Minneapolis. [86]

November 9 witnessed the greatest concerted effort to prevent the execution of the condemned, but it was not their "last stand." The day closed with the ultimate issue of the case as much in doubt as it had ever been. No hint was forthcoming from the governor of the nature of his decision. Thus far he had played a creditable rôle. He had received the scores who pleaded with him to commute the sentences with courteous dignity. He had patiently heard their appeals with every evidence of thoughtful interest. What would he do?

His position was an unenviable one. Thousands had asked him to be merciful. At least an equal number—and perhaps many more—were insistent that he do nothing to affect the decision of the courts. The conservative press recognized that his position was "embarrassing and distressing," and that there had "never before been a pardon application made in this country which has subjected a State Executive to such a terrible ordeal." [87] But there was no question that it would administer a sharp verbal drubbing to the governor if he were over-kind to the condemned. To commute the sentences of all seven men, to say nothing of pardoning one or more of them, might be the prelude to a speedy political suicide. In a survey of press opinion, on November 10, the Chicago *Herald* listed no less than twenty-two major papers from all sections of the country which held that the sentences should not be modified in any way. This in no sense reflected the full strength of the sentiment opposed to executive clemency. To refuse to interfere with the decision of the courts would bring bitter censure from liberal and labor elements. If labor developed a long memory, it might even be costly politically.

Even if, by some wild freak, Governor Oglesby had desired to pardon the condemned, the act would not be operative in every case, for some of the men rejected a pardon, and acceptance by the convicted person was necessary for its validity.[88]

Unless Governor Oglesby turned out to be a man of rare courage, he evidently would pursue a middle course to avoid antagonizing too many people. As the Chicago *Tribune* pointed out, one could hope at best only that he would act favorably upon the petitions of Fielden and Schwab.[89]

NOTES CHAPTER XX

1. Chicago *Inter Ocean,* October 28, 1887.
2. *Commonweal,* November 5, 1887, p. 358.
3. Spies, *op. cit.,* p. 95; *Commonweal,* December 4, 1886, p. 287.
4. *Commonweal,* October 22, 1887, p. 340.
5. *Freedom* (London), vol. 2, no. 15, December 18, 1887, p. 59; Lloyd, *op. cit.,* vol. 1, p. 87, gives a slightly different version.
6. Spies, *op. cit.,* p. 75. William Morris addressed an interesting letter to Robert Browning urging him to sign a petition for clemency. The letter is reproduced in facsimile in Zeisler, *op. cit.,* opposite pp. 36-37.
7. Schaack, *op. cit.,* p. 623.
8. *Cf., Nation,* vol. 45, no. 1167, November 10, 1887, p. 366, where it was prophetically announced that if the men did not meet with the death they deserved so well, they might be pardoned in the future. "No civilized community," concluded E. L. Godkin, "can afford to offer such a sight as this."
9. Chicago *Inter Ocean,* November 8, 1887; *The Truth Seeker,* vol. 14, no. 47, November 19, 1887, p. 744.
10. Chicago *Labor Enquirer,* October 29, 1887.
11. Chicago *Tribune,* September 5, 1887.
12. Dyer D. Lum later wrote that he was indirectly in touch with Grinnell, who asserted that Fielden and Schwab might be saved if they signed what was required of them. Grinnell had discussed Parsons' case with Gary, and had concluded that there was absolutely no chance for him. "It was an open secret," wrote Lum, "that in presenting the case to the jury Julius Grinnell meant to have excepted Parsons from the extreme penalty, but forgot it. Parsons' eight-hour speech of defiance when called up for sentence banished the last rays of hope." *Alarm,* June 16, 1888. There is no other evidence supporting these statements.
13. *Alarm,* November 15, 1887.
14. Chicago *Inter Ocean,* November 6, 1887; *cf., ibid.,* November 4 and 5, 1887.
15. *Ibid.,* November 6, 1887.
16. Parsons' letter was written as early as October 13. Fischer's is dated November 1. They were not published until after the re-cantation by Spies, Schwab and Fielden. The others were probably written for the occasion. All four are printed in the *Alarm,* November 5, 1887. The letters of Fischer, Lingg and Engel are also printed in *The Anarchist* (London), December, 1887, pp. 2-3; and in German in Ramus, *op. cit.,* pp. 40-43.
17. Interview with Schilling.
18. Chicago *Tribune,* Chicago *Inter Ocean,* New York *Times,* New York *Tribune,* November 7, 1887.
19. Chicago *Inter Ocean,* November 4, 1887.

20. New York *Times,* November 4, 1887.
21. Chicago *Tribune,* November 9, 1887; McConnell, *loc. cit.,* p. 735.
22. Chicago papers, November 5-9, 1887; McConnell, *loc. cit.,* p. 735.
23. Judge Rogers was Tuley's predecessor as Chief Justice of the Circuit Court, and had presided over the grand jury which indicted the men. He died before the case reached this point.
24. McConnell, *loc. cit.,* p. 735, 732-735 *passim.*
25. It was drawn up by George P. Englehardt, editor of the *Western Druggist,* and Dr. James Kiernan. Chicago *Inter Ocean,* November 6, 1887.
26. This circular letter was signed by R. M. Burke, C. G. Dixon, W. P. Wright, and George F. Rohrbach.
27. B. F. Ayer, H. D. Lowell, E. P. Schmidt, W. A. Johnson, Alex Clarke, William I. Pope, Edward Browne, Ernest Prussing, Dr. S. G. Jacobson, Julius Stern, Thomas G. Wendes, Daniel E. Shorey, A. W. Woodward, W. G. Erwin, and Eugene Hogue also signed this petition.
28. Including Joseph Kirkland, lawyer, author, and later literary editor of the Chicago *Tribune,* Alex S. Bradley, T. G. Kearns, John S. Sutherland, and John S. Healey.
29. Gustave Sues, P. H. Bolton and Jacob Brenner.
30. The signatures include the names of Courtlandt Palmer, Raymond S. Perrin, Francis B. Thurber, Moncure D. Conway, Robert G. Ingersoll, Thomas Davidson, James Redpath, the Rev. C. H. Eaton. New York *Times,* November 4, 1887.
31. *Idem.*
32. New York *Sun,* November 6, 1887.
33. Chicago *Inter Ocean,* November 6, 1887.
34. *Idem.*
35. Chicago *Herald,* November 8, 1887.
36. *Idem.*
37. New York *Times,* November 6, 1887.
38. New York *Sun,* November 6, 1887.
39. Chicago *Herald,* November 8, 1887.
40. Chicago *Inter Ocean;* New York *Tribune,* November 6, 1887.
41. This conference is described in Lloyd, *op. cit.,* vol. 1, p. 90, based upon Lloyd's note-book. Schilling gave the author an account of the conference which differs in only one or two respects from the above.
42. November 3, 1887.
43. *Idem; Alarm,* November 5, 1887.
44. New York *Times,* November 5, 1887.
45. *Ibid.,* November 6, 1887.
46. *Idem;* Chicago *Inter Ocean,* November 6, 1887.
47. Chicago *Inter Ocean,* November 8, 1887.
48. The Chicago newspapers, November 6-11, 1887; New York *Tribune,* November 8, 1887; Buchanan, *op. cit.,* pp. 416-417.
49. Chicago *Tribune,* November 3, 1887.

50. Chicago daily papers, November 7-9, 1887; New York *World*, New York *Sun*, New York *Times*, November 7-8, 1887; Detroit *Evening News*, November 7, 1887; Schaack, *op. cit.*, pp. 630-632.
51. Detroit *Evening News*, November 7, 1887.
52. Chicago *Herald*, November 7, 1887.
53. *Ibid.*, November 8, 1887.
54. *Idem.*
55. *Idem.*
56. *Idem.*
57. *Idem.*
58. See the press comments reproduced in Chicago *Herald*, November 10, 1887.
59. *Ibid.*, November 8, 1887; see also, New York *Sun*, November 9, 1887.
60. Quoted in Chicago *Inter Ocean*, November 11, 1887.
61. *Idem.*
62. *Ibid.*, November 10, 1887.
63. Lloyd, *op. cit.*, vol. 1, p. 93; Chicago *Evening Journal*, November 14, 1887.
64. Chicago *Inter Ocean*, November 10, 1887.
65. *Idem;* Chicago *Herald*, November 8, 1887.
66. Buchanan, *op. cit.*, p. 398.
67. Chicago *Inter Ocean*, November 10, 1887.
68. *Idem;* Schaack, *op. cit.*, pp. 624-625.
69. Chicago *Inter Ocean*, November 10, 1887; Schaack, *op. cit.*, pp. 625-626.
70. Chicago *Inter Ocean*, November 10, 1887; Schaack, *op. cit.*, p. 625.
71. Chicago *Inter Ocean*, November 10, 1887; Schaack, *op. cit.*, p. 626.
72. Chicago *Inter Ocean*, November 10, 1887; Schaack, *op. cit.*, p. 626; Lloyd, *op. cit.*, vol. 1, p. 93.
73. Chicago *Inter Ocean*, November 10, 1887; Schaack, *op. cit.*, p. 626.
74. Chicago *Inter Ocean*, November 10, 1887; Schaack, *op. cit.*, pp. 626-627.
75. Chicago *Inter Ocean*, November 10, 1887; Schaack, *op. cit.*, pp. 626-627; Samuel Gompers, *Seventy Years of Life and Labor*, 2 vols., New York, 1925, vol. 2, p. 180. Gompers' own version of his address is much more favorable to himself than the contemporary accounts.
76. Trumbull, *The Trial of the Judgment*, appendix, p. 73, author's italics.
77. *Ibid.*, appendix, pp. 73-74.
78. In connection with these letters, there may be noted a brief communication addressed to the Governor by Judge Richard S. Tuthill who wrote:
"In view of the above statements of Judges Gary and Grinnell and Mr. Ingham, touching Fielden and Schwab, and as well in consideration of what I myself know of the fact of the case as affecting those two men, I sincerely recommend and hope that

executive clemency may be extended to each of these men." *Ibid.*, appendix, p. 74.

79. Chicago *Inter Ocean*, November 10, 1887; Schaack, *op. cit.*, p. 727; Lloyd, *op. cit.*, vol. 1, p. 94; Buchanan, *op. cit.*, p. 395 *ff*. Among those counted as relatives of the condemned was Nina Van Zandt Spies. Nina Van Zandt, a handsome daughter of a well-to-do family had romantically fallen in love with Spies during the trial. She married him by proxy, probably at Schilling's suggestion, while Spies was incarcerated in jail. Her act won her, of course, a good deal of tasteless notoriety, and perhaps provided her, before the tragedy ran its course, with a sufficiency of enjoyable anguish and heart-break. It is difficult to tell how sincere the lovely-looking Nina was. Not very long after the execution of her husband she married a wealthy Italian, and departed for Italy. By 1892, she was back in Chicago. Four years later she was no longer living with her new husband, and planned to lecture for a livelihood. At this date she declared that she had married Spies at Capt. Black's request. The latter, she claimed, induced her to do it by the argument that the marriage would make it impossible for a jury to convict him. She probably meant to say that Spies would not go to the gallows if they were married. Her version of the entire affair places her in the position of the young, innocent school-girl, to whom a great wrong was done. Spies, *op. cit.*, preface, appendix, pp. 86-88; interview with Schilling; clippings, scrap-book, Labadie Collection.

80. "If we could conscientiously admit even that we had made mistakes in our propaganda," Fischer later wrote, they could expect some measure of executive clemency. Lloyd, *op. cit.*, vol. 1, p. 89.

81. Schaack, *op. cit.*, pp. 627-628. Mr. Edward Johnson, a slate and stone merchant of Chicago, submitted a petition signed by thirty-one of Fielden's employers in which they testified to his good character, and declared that his tragedy was that he "was cursed with a gift of rude eloquence" and a love of acclaim.

82. Buchanan, *op. cit.*, p. 382.

83. *Ibid.*, pp. 395-397; Schaack, *op. cit.*, p. 627; *Alarm*, November 19, 1887; Detroit *Evening Journal*, November 11, 1887.

84. Interview with Schilling. There is no other evidence that this actually occurred.

85. Buchanan, *op. cit.*, p. 399.

86. *Ibid.*, pp. 399-400.

87. Chicago *Tribune*, November 10, 1887.

88. *Harvard Law Review*, vol. 1, no. 5, December 15, 1887, p. 244.

89. November 10, 1887.

XXI. NOVEMBER 11, 1887

A SMALL number of amnesty workers remained in Springfield awaiting the governor's decision. They moved disconsolately about the city on the tenth, unable to learn how their cause was faring.[1] Before Governor Oglesby could take official action, sensational news rocked the State capital and Chicago. Louis Lingg had cheated the hangman.

Shortly before nine in the morning, a muffled explosion, originating in Lingg's cell, echoed through the County Jail. When guards entered, they encountered a horrible sight. The lower half of Lingg's face was partly blown away and shattered, yet he was still alive. Not until a quarter to three in the afternoon did he die, conscious almost to the very end. A short-lived rumor that he might survive raised the grim question of how healthy a man had to be—to be hanged.

How Lingg managed to commit suicide is not altogether clear. A fulminating cap was probably the agent of his destruction. These caps, used to explode dynamite, were, fuse and all, about an inch and a half in length. Presumably, he placed the cap in his mouth, lit the fuse by a candle-flame, and, lying on his cot, awaited his end. It is also possible that he employed a very small cigar-shaped bomb. It has been suggested that he killed himself with a bomb similar to those found in his cell, which was smuggled to him at the last moment by a prisoner in the jail.[2]

The "genuineness" of Lingg's suicide was questioned in some quarters. George Francis Train, for example, asserted that the jail authorities were responsible for his death.[3] There is, however, no real evidence for believing that Lingg did not kill himself. It is generally held in radical circles that Lingg wilfully put an end to his own life.[4] The *Alarm* of November 19, 1887, could offer no satisfactory explanation for "the tragical death of Louis Lingg. . . . Brave and rash even to a fault, fear never led him to suicide. Whether he sought to remove his life to render the fate of the rest less hazardous, or to prevent the officials from having the satisfaction of hanging him, or in fact, any of the details of the act itself, must be left entirely to conjecture." Whatever the motive, there is little reason for assuming that he did not kill himself.

A significant motive for Lingg's suicide may be found in the attempt by the defense to prevent his execution by having him declared legally insane. On the 9th, Mr. Vere V. Hunt appeared before Judge Richard J. Prendergast of the County Court and filed a petition, signed by a doctor and Lingg's friends, to try the sanity of Lingg. Judge Prendergast refused to grant the writ *de lunatico inquirendo* on the ground of lack of jurisdiction. Lingg might have thought that the scheme promised success, and, rather than be stamped a lunatic, preferred to kill himself. Mr. Hunt presented the same petition to Judge Baker on the tenth, and it was rejected once more.[5]

Lingg's death served to recall the quickly forgotten story that Engel had attempted suicide on November 6 by taking an overdose of a drug.[6] Engel apparently suffered some temporary ill-effects from taking too large a dose of a sleep-inducing drug. But he unquestionably did not attempt suicide.[7] Lingg's death was reported to have brought Mrs. Engel, to whom the care of the corpse was intrusted, an offer of $10,000 for the right to exhibit the body.[8]

Though it cannot be dogmatically asserted, it is most probable that Lingg's suicide did not affect the ultimate fate of his fellow-prisoners. For a moment it was thought that Lingg's death would make it easier for the governor to show mercy to the others,[9] but the manner in which the latter disposed of the case made it clear that this was an error. Yet there may be some significance in the fact that Governor Oglesby did not reach a final decision before the news of Lingg's death reached Springfield. At three o'clock, the capital received word of his death. An hour and a half later, it was announced that the governor would issue a statement to the press at seven that evening.[10]

Governor Oglesby's decision was not wholly unexpected. He commuted to life imprisonment the sentences of Fielden and Schwab only. In his official communication, the governor said that it would not be a proper "exercise of the constitutional power to grant reprieves, commutations, and pardons" unless he were convinced of the "entire innocence" of the seven men condemned to death. His "careful consideration of the evidence in the record . . . ," he declared, "as well as of all alleged and claimed for them outside of the record, has failed to produce upon my mind any impression tending to impeach the verdict of the jury or the judgment of the trial court or of the Supreme Court affirming the guilt of all these parties.

"Satisfied, therefore, as I am, of their guilt," he continued, "I am precluded from considering the question of commutation of the sentences of Albert R. Parsons, Adolph Fischer, George Engel, and Louis Lingg to imprisonment in the penitentiary, as they emphatically declare they will not accept such commutation." They on the contrary had demanded " 'unconditional release' or, as they express it, 'liberty or death'. . . ." Fielden, Schwab, and Spies had petitioned for executive clemency. "Fielden and Schwab," said the governor, "in addition present, separate and supplementary petitions for the commutation of their sentences. While . . . I am satisfied of the guilt of all of the parties . . . , a most careful consideration of the whole subject leads me to the conclusion that the sentence of the law as to Samuel Fielden and Michael Schwab may be modified . . . in the interest of humanity, and without doing violence to public justice." He regretted that "under the solemn sense of the obligations of my office" that he was "unable" to come to the same conclusion in regard to the sentences of the other defendants.[11]

Governor Oglesby's decision was obviously as much a compromise as the various factors involved permitted. While his official communication implies that executive clemency might also have been extended to the others had they appealed as contrite penitents, it can safely be said that this was only a remote possibility at best. Only the most incredible optimist could have hoped that Spies, Lingg, Fischer and Engel would be saved from the gallows by the governor. It has been said that Parsons possessed a bare chance, if he would retract his principles and beg for forgiveness.[12]

The governor, speaking off the record, explained why he could commute only the sentences of Fielden and Schwab. To James E. Quinn he "said that for every petition for mercy received from the friends of the condemned men, he could produce hundreds from business men and reputable law-abiding citizens all over the country requesting him to remain steadfast in supporting the decision of the courts." Those who pleaded for clemency were not in complete agreement. "But the business men were unanimous that the men should all be hanged. It was the best that the governor could do to commute the sentences of Fielden and Schwab. . . ."[13] To a reporter Governor Oglesby pointed out that he acted as he did because Schwab and Fielden were essentially "good" persons at heart. Further, they were really not anarchists, and they had expressed contrition and begged for mercy. Therefore, he could spare their lives, "and still the majesty of the law and supremacy of the government would be upheld."[14]

The commutation message produced varied reactions, but it was rather widely felt that the governor had acted with justice and mercy. His decision was regarded as essentially sound.[15] "The sober public opinion of the country," declared the New York *Sun*, "will approve Governor Oglesby's action in regard to the condemned Chicago Anarchists."[16] In the national capital popular sentiment seemed to be opposed to the governor's act. Lawyers in Washington, however, who had studied the case closely held that he had done the right thing.[17] In some quarters the governor was sharply assailed. "Governor Oglesby," commented *The American*, "for reasons which must be pronounced 'as weak as water,' saw fit to commute the sentence of . . . Fielden and Schwab, to imprisonment for life, i.e., until the popular indignation has cooled, and the sentimentalists get a Governor of Illinois on whose sympathies they can work." [18] The *Central Law Journal*, also disappointed, asserted that the governor had only "discharged two-thirds of his duty . . ." [19] The *Albany Law Journal*, opposed to the commutations, was especially critical of the leniency shown to "Fielden, the most violent of the crew. The government will get no thanks for its mercy." As a matter of general policy this journal felt that it was better "to make dead than living martyrs of" the men.[20] Hundreds of thousands throughout the country felt that the law had been cheated by the governor's show of mercy. The results of a poll conducted on November 8 in St. Louis, on the question of commutation, certainly indicates this. For every person voting for commutation of the sentences, there were five in favor of hanging all seven men.[21]

The amnesty workers were in turn surprised and downcast by the governor's act. While they did not hesitate to say that they had expected something better, they were prudent enough to avoid incisive criticism of the governor.[22] However badly they might have felt at not having accomplished more, they at least could pride themselves on the partial success which crowned their efforts.

Two unsuccessful eleventh hour attempts to postpone the execution were made on Friday, November 11. Mr. Salomon appeared before Judge Tuley to secure an order holding up the execution of Parsons on the ground that his death warrant was incorrectly drawn. His request was immediately turned down.[23] The second effort to prevent the hanging from taking place was made possible by the receipt of a telegram from New York by Capt. Black. On the tenth, he read this exciting message:

"I have proof showing Anarchists to be innocent. Guilty man in New York—located. Have telegraphed to Gov. Oglesby. Proof is under oath. How shall I communicate it?

"(Signed) AUGUST P. WAGENER,
"Counselor-at-law, 59 Second Ave." [24]

Disheartened by the magnitude and hopelessness of their task, many of the amnesty workers doubted if the telegram could be used to delay the executions. Joe Buchanan, however, was convinced that its message was genuine. He forcefully argued that it should be employed to induce the governor to grant a reprieve. After some discussion, it was decided that Black and Buchanan should hasten to Springfield to confer with the governor. A telegram was immediately dispatched to the latter to the effect that they would call upon him early Friday morning to discuss a new and important development in the case. Together with these two a New York newspaper man, William Fleron by name, left for Springfield early Thursday night. Mr. Fleron, who declared that he was well acquainted with New York City radicals, professed to know the sender of the telegram. He interpreted the message to mean that the actual bomb-thrower was in the hands of New York anarchists, who were waiting to be told what to do with him. [25]

At half-past eight Friday morning, the three men were conferring with the governor who, it transpired, had received a similar communication from New York. Mr. Fleron presented his version of the contents of the message and affirmed his belief in its authenticity. Black proposed that the governor grant a sixty or ninety day reprieve, during which efforts could be made to bring the alleged bomb-thrower to Illinois for examination. To this suggestion Governor Oglesby queried: "If I grant your request for sixty days' reprieve, will you deliver the man who threw the bomb to the authorities of the State?" Black's reply was a virtual promise that if the bomb-thrower were in their possession, every effort would be made to hand him over to the authorities within forty-eight hours.

"And if I refuse to interfere with the execution of the

sentence, what will you do with this man in New York?" further questioned the governor.

"In the event of your refusal," declared Black, "we can do nothing."

There was no other possible answer. With the excuse that he wished to consider the problem in private, Governor Oglesby withdrew from the room. Twenty minutes later he returned. His countenance gave his reply before his lips uttered it. There was to be no miraculous last minute reprieve. "I regret very much," he began, "that I must say to you I cannot interfere with the sentence of the court in the cases of your friends. . . . While my sympathies are with the condemned men, I must regard my obligations as governor of the State and must perform my duty." [26]

At ten-fifteen the conference with the governor came to an end.

Two hours later, Spies, Parsons, Fischer, and Engel stood upon the gallows.

Extensive preparations had already been made or were in progress to prevent a jail delivery, disorder at the time of the execution, or retaliation immediately after the hanging. Despite this, Chicago was tense and nervous on Thursday and Friday. The placing of police, militia, and Federal troops in and about the city [27] had only served to intensify its uneasiness. The constant reports that the police were discovering veritable caches of bombs throughout the city made for greater disquietude.[28] Citizens went about armed, expecting a savage outbreak.[29] Merchants who sold guns decided to lock up their stores on Thursday afternoon and to have the larger shops guarded lest an attempt at looting be made by the "anarchists." [30] "The dread of some catastrophe impending was not alone in men's talk but in their very faces and in the air." [31] A contemporary recalls that hundreds of citizens left Chicago for the suburbs and other cities.[32] Melville E. Stone recalls that when the "fateful Friday . . . arrived, threats of assassination were by no means infrequent. There was a widespread expectation that the jail would be destroyed by dynamite. A cloud of apprehension lowered over the city. There was a hush, and men spoke in whispers. Everyone awaited the hour for the execution of the dread mandate of the law with solicitude, indeed with fear. I have never experienced quite the like condition." [33]

By way of further precaution, a secret court session was held by Judge Baker on the afternoon of the tenth which restored indictments for conspiracy, which had earlier been struck off, against nineteen "anarchists." [34] The police were instructed to keep these men under the closest surveillance, and were armed with the necessary legal papers to arrest them for the slightest reason. This was done as a "precautionary measure so that if one of them showed their heads [sic] they could be put down summarily." [35] The jail in which the men were incarcerated took on the appearance of a fort prepared for attack. Ropes were stretched around it for a block in each direction, and all traffic was suspended. Some three hundred policemen armed with Winchesters and fixed bayonets guarded it. At strategic points in the vicinity and on roof-tops, additional police were stationed. [36]

Was there any real basis for Chicago's expectations of violent disorder? Actually there was very little. The "bombs" so fruitfully discovered were most probably police manufactured, and only for a brief moment did some social-revolutionaries seriously consider liberating their comrades by force. Much wild talk undoubtedly accompanied the equally desperate hope that in some inconceivable way a rescue might be effected. Some of the revolutionaries from other cities who hurried into Chicago immediately before the eleventh did have harebrained plans in mind. The condemned strongly discouraged all such schemes of which they were informed, and the realities of the situation quickly disillusioned those who dreamed of a dramatic jail-delivery. Thus, Robert Reitzel, the fiery and extremely able editor of *Der Arme Teufel* ("The Poor Devil"), who arrived in Chicago from Detroit a week before the eleventh quickly abandoned his suggestion of a forcible rescue when he saw that there was not the barest chance of success.[37]

The condemned faced their approaching doom with none of the perturbation that racked the city. They passed the last hours of their lives with an unfaltering stoic calm. The "fortitude they displayed," remarked the Chicago *Tribune,* "was worthy of a better cause. In a righteous contest . . . they might have been heroes. . . ." [38] There was no break in their perfect composure when Spies, Fischer, Parsons and Engel learned of the governor's decision. Early Thursday evening, some of them were permitted to meet friends and relatives for a last farewell. Then they returned to their cells, where they wrote letters and chatted with the death watch.[39] Their self-possession was uncanny. Parsons seemed to be in thorough good humor, and sang "Annie Laurie" before going to sleep two hours past midnight. Engel and Fischer were fully composed. "He is the peer of any hero in point of courage," said one of the jailers of Fischer. "He talks freely and calmly of his actions and their results. He will die a second John Brown. But never in my life do I want to spend with a condemned man his last night on earth." [40] Spies, temperamentally more highly-strung than his fellow-Germans, gave no sign of being upset.

No change in the men was apparent on the morning of the eleventh. They had passed what appeared to be a restful night, even though there could be heard throughout it the noise of the hammering which accompanied the erection of the gallows in the jail proper. They "saluted" one another "with firm voices," and then attacked their breakfast with relish. They read the morning papers. Some of them penned one or two brief letters. To Dyer D. Lum, Parsons wrote in part: "Well, my dear old comrade, the fatal hour draws near. Caesar kept me awake till late at night with the noise (music) of hammer and saw, erecting his throne, my scaffold. Refinement! Civilization! Matson (sheriff) tells me he refused to agree to let Caesar (State) secrete my body, and he has just got my wife's address to send her my remains. Magnanimous Caesar!" [41] The spiritual consolation offered to the four men—who were notoriously irreligious—was refused.

At eleven-thirty Sheriff Matson, Jailer Folz, the county physician, and several deputies, appeared before Spies' cell. In an uncertain voice the sheriff read the death warrant first to Spies and then to the other three men in turn. With their arms pinioned, their wrists handcuffed, and their bodies cloaked in white, muslin shrouds, the four men marched to the scaffold. Benches providing places for two hundred persons faced the gallows. With complete unconcern the four took their positions on the trap. The nooses were placed around their necks. Fischer helped to adjust his. Spies' was too tight. He smiled a "Thank you" when it was made more comfortable.

Suddenly, piercing the painful silence, there came Spies' voice from beneath the hood which covered his head:

"There will come a time when our silence will be more powerful than the voices you strangle today!"

And then from Fischer: "Hurrah for anarchy—" followed by the same exultant cry from Engel cutting into Fischer's concluding words, "This is the happiest moment of my life!"

Parsons' voice rang out: "Will I be allowed to speak, O men of America? Let me speak, Sheriff Matson! Let the voice of the people be heard!"

The trap had been sprung. [42] The State of Illinois had created four martyrs. It only remained to canonize them.

.   .   .   .

The executions passed without any untoward incidents. Chicago was, of course, agitated. People gathered on street corners and before newspaper offices and bulletin boards excitedly discussing the whole affair and the hangings. Bulletin boards in the principal business part of the city were surrounded by steadily growing crowds since nine o'clock in the morning. But there were no demonstrations. There was not a sign of the trouble which the authorities expected and for which they had prepared so assiduously. [43] Mrs. Parsons, and her two children and Mrs. Holmes, it is true, were arrested during the day, but this occurrence did not result in any undue excitement.[44] The crowds which scanned the bulletins so closely were not joyous when the news for which they were waiting appeared. Forceful expressions of approval were uncommon.[45] Newspaper reporters heard significant comments from members of the crowds. "The police have had their revenge today, and Bonfield has shot his mouth off a good deal oftener than Lingg did his, but if he don't look out he'll get it in the same way. The men haven't all forgotten the clubbing they got at the time of the West Side street-car strike, and it's my belief that the bomb was thrown by one of the men he had clubbed, and not by the anarchists themselves." [46] When the hangings were announced someone cried out: "The American people will be ashamed of it. It is the murder of four brave men." [47] Though the day seethed with perturbation, it passed with the utmost quiet. "Trade down town," remarked a business man, "was duller today than it has ever been." [48]

Nor did any unusual occurrence accompany the funeral on Sunday. The authorities turned over the four bodies to friends for burial, and this act was praised as a gracious gesture by the press.[49] Special conditions were laid down by Mayor Roche of Chicago under which the public funeral was to be conducted. The line of march was precisely delimited; no banners, flags, or arms were to be displayed; no music except dirges was to be played; no demonstration was to be made; no speeches were to be delivered. It was to be held between twelve and two o'clock. From beginning to end the funeral procession was subject to police regulation and surveillance.[50]

The funeral cortège followed the five caskets, including Lingg's, to beautiful Waldheim Cemetery, where they were laid in a temporary vault. It was, if not the "largest ever seen in Chicago," [51] as it has been said, certainly one of the most impressive. At least six thousand people marched to mournful music behind the five coffins. Only one banner was borne aloft throughout the length of the procession—an American flag proudly carried by a Civil War veteran. The streets were jammed with observers, but the city was unnaturally quiet.

How many watched the funeral, either out of sympathy or curiosity, cannot be exactly determined. The estimates ran from 150,000 to half a million. Probably a quarter of a million lined the route taken by the funeral cortège.[52]

At Waldheim there were over ten thousand people—perhaps as many as fifteen thousand—who observed the simple burial exercises. Here flags, red ribbons and flowers were in evidence. There were no religious services, but the occasion had a religious solemnity. Capt. Black, Thomas J. Morgan, the socialist labor leader, Albert Currlin, former editor of the *Arbeiter-Zeitung,* and Robert Reitzel delivered addresses which kept the vast throng at the cemetery until night-fall. Capt. Black eulogized the men he had served so well. He was not there, he told his listeners, "to speak to you any special word concerning the cause for which these men lived . . . , but . . . rather of themselves, to tell you their love for the cause which commanded their services, was sealed at last by their lives, not grudgingly, but given with unstinted measure. . . ." They were not "beside the caskets of felons consigned to an unglorious tomb. We are here by the bodies of men who were sublime in their self-sacrifice, and for whom the gibbet assumed the glory of a cross." [53]

The quiet tone which marked Capt. Black's address was lacking in the others. Black spoke as a friend; Morgan, Currlin and Reitzel as "comrades."

"Let the voice of the people be heard!" cried Morgan. "That has been the cry of suffering humanity all the world over. . . . And what has been the answer in the United States? The dead bodies now lying before us is the answer given by this glorious, free America. . . . There is no necessity for lamentation on account of the death of these men. . . . The survivors ought to begin work, and at once, that the public mind might be opened to the real meaning of the dead men's teachings. . . . Revenge? How shall we take it? By force directed against Grinnell, Judge Gary, Bonfield? No!"

Such measures would be pointless. The world must be taught the enormity of the wrong which had been committed in Chicago and the infamy of those who had made that wrong possible. To put Gary, Grinnell and Bonfield to everlasting shame would be revenge enough.[54]

Albert Currlin castigated the American working-class for not assisting those who had slaved in its interests. He urged those present to "Vow it by your man's honor that you will not rest till America, till the world knows how justice is dealt with by your oppressors. . . . Devote all your energies to the task of avenging the crime committed." [55]

Robert Reitzel's speech was delivered in German. He spoke as a revolutionary, out of great sorrow and an acid hate.

"Friends of freedom!" he began. "My first word over these coffins shall be an accusation, not against the moneyed rabble, who thanked God today . . . that He was again a righteous judge, but against the workers of Chicago. For you, the workers of Chicago, have permitted five of your best, most noble and consistent representatives of your cause, to be murdered in your midst. . . .

"There was a time when the workers could not conceive that only *complete* freedom could wipe out their slavery and insure their human dignity. . . . As at the time of the French Revolution, the bourgeoisie declared itself the Nation . . . , so now the time has come when the workers must declare themselves to be the ruling and lawgiving power. Here at the side of these coffins, it is only proper that all hearts take this vow: We will carry out what these people strove for, we will make a practical reality of the Rights of Man. . . .

"There is one thing we must say at the side of these coffins. . . . They died as men, as heroes! . . . These dead comrades will indeed live on. They were crucified on 'Good Friday.' This Sunday is 'Easter Sunday' and must become a day of resurrection for all times. . . .

"We have no cause to mourn for these dead comrades; . . . as the cross was once the symbol of love, so the gallows of the nineteenth century will become the symbol of Freedom. But we must mourn for our own shame. . . . Let us part from these graves with the words of Herwegh in our hearts:
"We have loved long enough,
At last we will hate!" [56]

A little more than a month later, on December 18, the caskets were placed in a permanent grave. Again peaceful Waldheim was visited by a vast crowd, and again there were speakers. With Joe Buchanan presiding, the great gathering was addressed by Paul Grottkau, Albert Currlin, and Capt. Black. Before half a dozen years had passed, a stately monument was placed over the graves.[57] Waldheim was soon to become almost a place of pilgrimage and the monument almost a shrine.

The executions acted like a tonic upon Chicago. They were like a beam of fresh sunlight cutting a bright path through massed black clouds, dispelling all fear of the impending storm. The apprehension and dread which had infected the city were dissipated. Four lives was the price of Chicago's catharsis. A Chicagoan recalls that on that "fateful Friday . . . four men were hanged . . . , and as if by the wind of the morning, the cloud lifted and the business of the great city moved on in its wonted way." [58] Charles Edward Russell confesses that "It sounds now a horrible and cruel thing to say, yet visibly, most visibly, all other men's hearts were lightened because these four men's hearts were stilled." [59] Those who were reasonably certain that no holocaust would descend upon the city experienced this same feeling of deliverance. Joe Buchanan later admitted that "a feeling of relief came to me, as I realized that the reign of terror, dreaded by so many had not come upon the city." [60] The crisis in the "acute paranoia from which Chicago had been suffering" [61] was passed, but entire recovery was a long way off. The period of convalescence was an extended one, and, there occurred periodic relapses.[62]

For the daily press, the four hangings wrote *finis* to the Haymarket case. "The Law Answers Anarchy," [63] screamed the headlines. "Justice Is Done," cried the Chicago *Inter Ocean,* "Destroying Factors of Republican Institutions Pay the Penalty with their Lives. . . . American Justice Deals Malignant Anarchy Its First and Final Death Blow." [64] The *Inter Ocean* declared that "Armed anarchy is dead in this city, and dead by force of law and reason." The curtain had fallen upon the last act of the tragedy, "and behind it are the dead. It was inevitable that it should end thus—'the wages of sin is death'; 'sin is the transgression of the law.' " [65] The Chicago *Tribune,* too, spoke of the tragedy which had just run its course to "a strange and solemn" end, and observed that if there was one element in "this long and thrilling drama more conspicuous than another, . . . it is the absolute certainty that those who seek to overthrow American law and social order by conspiring force and violence will only rush headlong to their own destruction. . . . Those who draw the sword against peace and law in this free country will perish by the sword." [66]

The same theme appeared in the editorial columns of the Chicago *Evening Journal.* Twenty years earlier the South had been taught the price of revolt. Now, "The Anarchists of Chicago, if not of the entire country, have . . . been taught that a rebellion of violence against law and authority will not only be . . . repelled but punished." [67]

For the New York *Herald,* the four-fold hanging was "An Impressive Moment in the History of the Republic" because the country had come to grips with and given its first lesson to anarchy. There could have been no other possible conclusion to the case, said the *Herald,* for those who threw the bomb and "who killed the policemen in the Haymarket did it deliberately and because those policemen represented the government of the United States. They struck, therefore, at the government itself and would have destroyed it if they could. . . . If they have been hurled into a traitor's grave by the inexorable decree of even handed and iron handed justice, it is because they conspired against the very existence of orderly society." [68] The New York *Times* insisted that the penalty paid by the "anarchists" was one exacted by the nation at large. [69]

The press did not tire of pointing out that anarchy had engaged in a combat with the law which established the supremacy of the latter. Whether the "execution was right or wrong" was of no consequence. [70] Anarchism had been given a body blow from which it would not readily recover. A method of dealing with a horrible scourge had been tested and found successful. To immunize society against the virus of Anarchism, Socialism, and Communism, however, the *Nation* suggested that it was necessary to go even further. Not only must "our police" be supported "in hunting . . . down" anarchists, socialists, and communists, but the latter must come to a more "shameful and terrible" end than the four just executed. [71] The hangings brought a sense of relief to the country at large as well as to Chicago. Freed from a non-existent terror, daily press and periodicals applauded the medium of their release— the death of four men. [72] The impersonal comment of the *Commercial and Financial Chronicle* is not without interest. "The elections this week and the execution of the anarchists have been events which drew off attention from the market, and now that these are past there is nothing in the way of more active business." [73]

The executions, however, were not universally cheered. The body of opinion which held them to be utterly indefensible was considerable. It needs little imagination to picture the response of the radical press. With its first page encased in heavy black borders, the *Freiheit* declared that though many people had up to the last moment thought that it would not occur, "The long prepared, cold-blooded, murderous massacre of our Chicago comrades has taken place." But the hangings would not destroy anarchy. On the contrary, they would give the movement greater force. Its soil would be fertilized by the blood of the martyrs. The *Freiheit* exhorted the revolutionaries "to emulate" Lingg, to "become what he was!"

"Our aims are great and noble," declared the *Freiheit,* "they are one with the aims of culture itself. Consciousness of this must steel and strengthen us to endure to the end, to struggle and fight.

"And when we become fatigued in this, then let the gallows of Chicago be the symbol which will spur us on anew. The 11th of November, 1887, will never be forgotten." [74]

The People, a short-lived labor and radical journal published in San Francisco, also appeared with its front page framed in mourning borders. It stamped the hanging of the four men as a "cold-blooded murder, a million times worse than that committed at the Haymarket, because of its being done in the name of the law and justice. . . ." [75] The *Arbeiter-Zeitung* likewise raged against the "quadruple judicial murder" that had taken place, and promised a "day of reckoning . . . to the capitalists." Though one battle had been lost in the open war with the ruling classes, the revolutionists must not lose heart and the struggle must continue.[76] The *Alarm,* too, urged that the fight must not cease for a moment. It must go on with greater vigor. There was no cause for mourning. The men had died bravely, and though their physical bodies had been destroyed, their spirit and ideals lived on.[77] The same thought was given poetic expression in *Liberty:*

> "They never fail who die
> In a great cause: the block may soak their gore;
> Their heads may sodden in the sun; their limbs
> Be strung to city gates and castle wall—
> But still their spirit walks abroad." [78]

"Of the tragedy just enacted in Chicago," queried *Liberty,* "what is there to say? Of a deed so foul perpetrated upon men so brave what words are not inadequate . . . ?" These men were "the John Browns of America's industrial

revolution. . . . The labor movement has had its Harpers'
Ferry; when will come the emancipation proclamation?" [79]

Equally moved by the executions were the radical organs
in England. Upon "our comrades," declared the *Commonweal,*
the bourgeoisie of Illinois, inspired by fear, had "wreaked" a
"cowardly vengeance. . . ." Throughout the world, continued
the *Commonweal,* "each socialist has before his eyes the image
of the gallows whereon the four have died, and the shadow
of the prison wherein their comrades are to linger out a death
in life." [80] *Freedom* pointed out that November 11 "hence-
forth be a red-letter day in the Socialist Calendar. Red, for it
is stained with the blood of some of the most earnest and
devoted men who have ever championed the cause of the
people. Memorable, because that quarter of an hour's legal
murder will do more to shake the blind faith of the masses in
law and authority than the eloquence of years." [81]

Journals which cannot be regarded as radical voiced their
protest against the execution. "It is not putting it too strongly,"
declared *The Truth Seeker,* "to say that these men were
sacrificed to public clamor, led by an unscrupulous press . . .
the real issue of whether these men were guilty of murder was
lost sight of." Within five years, said *The Truth Seeker,* everyone will be agreed that the men were convicted on "wholly
insufficient evidence. . . ." Their execution, "clearly a mistake,
from whatever point it be viewed," will serve to embitter the
worker against "those whom he regards as [his] capitalistic
enemies. . . ." [82] An article in the *Social Science Review* contended that when a government hanged four men "for being
anarchists, then it is time for everybody to be anarchists, so
far as that government is concerned." [83]

A small number of clergymen courageously spoke out
against the executions. They were A. A. Miner of Boston, John
C. Kimball of Hartford, John C. Collins of New Haven, and
Hugh O. Pentecost of Newark. [84] Mr. Pentecost of the Belle-
ville Avenue Congregational Church, took the executions for
the theme of his sermon on the Sunday after the execution. He

asserted that the men had not been proven guilty, that capital punishment was un-Christian, and that the real anarchists of the country were the great monopolists. In later years he attacked the execution in even sharper terms, stigmatizing it as "one of the most unjust and cruel acts ever perpetrated by an organized government—not only immoral but illegal." [85] Mr. Kimball of the Hartford Unity Church also preached his Sunday sermon on the same topic with such sympathy for the men that he lost his post in consequence. Later he explained that he was only one of a large number of "Sober, law-abiding citizens . . . who felt called upon to protest earnestly against the executions" on several grounds. He declared that the hangings did "not touch in any degree the real seat of our social troubles." [86]

A significant portion of the American working-class manifested its opposition to the hangings immediately before and after the eleventh. Three to five thousand persons, most of them workers, paraded in New York City on the night of the tenth in a peaceful, protest demonstration arranged by the radicals. Workers were also well represented among the two thousand so-called "Reds" who gathered on the same night in Cincinnati for the same purpose. Though they gave no cause, they were dispersed by the police.[87] The large crowd which gathered in New Era Hall in Boston, on the night of the eleventh, to do honor to the four men, was made up largely of workers, and was addressed by George E. McNeil, the labor leader.[88] In Providence, Rhode Island, the organized workers of the city condemned the executions, and held a demonstration meeting on November 13.[89]

Not even the most conservative labor organs saw cause for rejoicing in the hangings. The official journal of the Knights of Labor, completely dominated by Powderly, declared that while the law had "been vindicated and four men have been strangled as a warning to those who would 'throttle the law,'" the hangings would not give anarchy its death blow.[90] The officials of the K. of L. did not represent the sentiments of its rank and file members. The organ of the Knights in Chicago, which had earlier remarked that the men "were indicted for murder and conspiracy and convicted of anarchy," [91] now found the execution indefensible. It declared on November 12, that "they die as they lived, game to the backbone." [92] Individual assemblies went much further, and condemned the executions in ringing terms, as did the Karl Marx Assembly, No. 9,856.[93]

Another labor publication bitterly opposed to Anarchism nevertheless criticized the executions. ". . . we don't believe in hanging men for the mere advocacy of false principles that might result in murder," declared the Alena, Michigan, *Labor Journal*. "The agitator should be punished; but only the murderer should be hung. The fact that men can be legally hanged now, on general principles, to gratify the prejudices of public opinion against their doctrines, is not a good sign of the times." [94] Four men had met their end "on the gallows," declared still another paper, "for no cause except denouncing robbers. The State of Illinois has stained her name with a blot such as will call for retribution from outraged justice." [95]

Almost one-third of the November 19 issue of the *Workmen's Advocate* was given over to the executions, which its headlines described as "Foulest Murder." Here was "a crime of the kind that brings its perpetrators and abettors into the category of the most dangerous criminals and enemies of the masses—the working people." The *Advocate's* leading editorial on the hangings is worth quoting.

"Just after our last issue had gone to press," it reads, "came the news of the fate of the victims of capitalism.

"Five men murdered by authority of the people of Illinois. . . .

"Partial judges misconstrued the law to gratify their enemies.

"A prejudiced jury found them guilty.

"The constitution was trampled under foot, and the popular clamor for blood was catered to.

"One man was sentenced to prison for fifteen years; two for life; five condemned to death!

"What had they done? Conspired to murder their accusers. Conspired to expose and convict murder say we.

"Capitalism speaks of the legal murder of its victims as the last act in the tragedy. Fond fools!

"The history of the labor movement is not written yet."

This was a sharp indictment, and there is reason to believe that a large number of American workers were in agreement with it. But it did not represent the views of the American working-class as a whole, and had the American people been polled on the question, they probably would have voted for the execution of the "anarchists."

NOTES CHAPTER XXI

1. Chicago *Inter Ocean*, November 11, 1887.
2. Schaack, *op. cit.*, pp. 636-637. For Lingg's suicide see Chicago and New York papers, November 11, 1887; Schaack, *op. cit.*, pp. 634-636. There is a story that Dyer D. Lum gave Lingg, at the latter's request, a bomb in the shape of a cigar. Lum is supposed to have confided this in a letter to Voltairine de Cleyre. This has never been verified. In the light of Lum's general antipathy to violence, it is unlikely that he was a partner to such an act. The fact that Lum never questioned the suicide can hardly be taken as proof that he was aware of the precise manner in which Lingg met his death. The story that Lum gave Lingg a loaded cigar, was related to the author by Miss Inglis.
3. He rested his charge on the following: Lingg's death occurred on Thursday, the tenth. Up until the previous Sunday, the cells of the condemned had been illuminated by kerosene lamps. On Monday candles were substituted. No man who knew as much about explosives as Lingg did, would do such a bungling job if he wanted to commit suicide. Furthermore, the man who took care of the cells of the "anarchists," a prisoner named Otto Cottam, was discharged on Saturday. On Sunday, November 6, the bombs were found in Lingg's cell. Train spoke to Cottam who swore that the bombs were not in the cell Saturday night. Lingg had no visitors between that time and the finding of the bombs. Train took Cottam around to a number of newspaper offices where he repeated his story, and planned to take him to Springfield. But suddenly Cottam disappeared. Train asserted that he had been intimidated by the police. Therefore, concluded Train, the bombs

had been planted in Lingg's cell, and Lingg's death was brought about by the jail authorities. Interview in New York *World,* November 12, 1887.

4. *Cf.,* Ramus, *op. cit.,* pp. 44-47 *passim.*

5. Chicago *Inter Ocean,* November 10, 1887. New York *Sun,* and New York *Times,* November 10, 1887; Schaack, *op. cit.,* pp. 628-629; *Commonweal,* December 24, 1887, p. 417.

6. Either laudanum or opium.

7. Chicago *Inter Ocean,* November 7, 1887.

8. *Alarm,* November 19, 1887, in which the letter to Mrs. Engel containing this proposal is reproduced.

9. Chicago *Inter Ocean,* November 11, 1887.

10. *Idem.*

11. *Idem;* also to be found in the other Chicago papers of the same date and Schaack, *op. cit.,* p. 638.

12. According to an account in the *Alarm* of June 16, 1888, Melville E. Stone spent three hours with Parsons on the ninth pleading with him to beg for a commutation as an humble penitent. The implication is that Mr. Stone would not have done this had he not known that Governor Oglesby would act favorably on such an application. Mr. Stone's own version of this interview differs materially from this account. He claims that Parsons sent him a message requesting that he pay him a visit. The request came on the 6th, but Mr. Stone does not say that he saw Parsons on that day. They had a long talk during which Parsons—according to Mr. Stone—asked Mr. Stone to intercede in his behalf with the governor. Towards the close of their two to three hour talk, Stone claims that Parsons became very violent and, in a paroxysm of rage, attacked him. (Stone, *op. cit.,* pp. 175-176.) That Mr. Stone urged Parsons to petition for clemency is most probable. He himself writes that he told Fielden "precisely the things that I told Parsons, that penitence must precede pardon . . ." (*Ibid.,* pp. 176-177.)

13. New York *Sun,* November 14, 1887.

14. Chicago *Times,* November 12, 1887.

15. Chicago *Inter Ocean,* November 11, 1887.

16. Quoted in *idem; cf.,* the editorial stand of the New York *Star,* the New York *Times,* and the New York *Tribune* quoted in *idem.*

17. *Idem.*

18. Vol. 15, no. 38, November 19, 1887, p. 68.

19. Vol. 25, no. 20, November 18, 1887, p. 457.

20. November 19, 1887, p. 401.

21. New York *Tribune,* November 9, 1887.

22. Chicago *Inter Ocean,* November 11, 1887.

23. Schaack, *op. cit.,* p. 629.

24. Buchanan, *op. cit.,* p. 401.

25. *Ibid.,* p. 402; Chicago *Tribune,* November 11, 1887; Chicago *Inter Ocean,* November 11, 1887.

26. Buchanan, *op. cit.*, pp. 407-410; Detroit *Evening Journal*, November 11, 1887.
27. See above, pp. 434-435.
28. *Advance and Labor Leaf*, November 12, 1887.
29. Russell, *loc. cit.*, p. 410.
30. Chicago *Tribune*, November 9, 1887.
31. Russell, *loc. cit.*, p. 410.
32. Young, *op. cit.*, p. 122.
33. Stone, *op. cit.*, p. 177.
34. They were: Chris Spies, Schnaubelt, Seliger, S. S. Snyder, John Apel, Thomas Brown, Anton Hirschberger, Lorenz Herman, Victor Clermont, Bernhard Schrader, Waller, Herman Muenzberg, Otto Schuman, William Schubert, John Herlan, William Hagemann, Peter Huber, Ernest Buebner, Gruenwald.
35. *Alarm*, December 3, 1887.
36. Chicago papers of November 11-12; Schaack, *op. cit.*, pp. 643-644.
37. Carl Nold, "Anarchists: Robert Reitzel," *Man!* vol. 1, no. 7, July, 1933, p. 5; *Free Society*, November 4, 1900 (William Holmes, "Reminiscences of November 11"), pp. 2-3.
38. November 12, 1887.
39. For their last hours, see the daily papers, November 11 and 12; *Alarm*, November 19, 1887; *Harper's Weekly*, November 19, 1887, pp. 836-839; Schaack, *op. cit.*, pp. 642-643; *Life of Albert R. Parsons*, pp. 243-246.
40. *Alarm*, November 19, 1887.
41. Quoted in *Life of Albert R. Parsons*, p. 248.
42. For the morning of the execution and the hanging, see the daily press, November 11 and 12; *Life of Albert R. Parsons*, pp. 246-247; Schaack, *op. cit.*, pp. 644-648.
43. See the Chicago papers for November 11 and 12, 1887.
44. Their arrest was brought about by Mrs. Parsons' attempt to see her husband on the morning of the eleventh. The authorities had promised her this privilege, she claimed, but when she arrived with her children and Mrs. Holmes at the police lines at eight-thirty, Friday morning, she was denied entrance. She was shunted from one police officer to another. When she attempted to cross the police lines she was placed in a patrol wagon. Mrs. Holmes met similar treatment for protesting the actions of the police. They were later placed in a cell and searched, informed that the execution had taken place, and were finally released at three in the afternoon. The police claimed that the temporary arrests were for "persistent disobedience of the orders" in the case of Mrs. Parsons, and for "haranguing the people" in that of Mrs. Holmes. See *Life of Albert R. Parsons*, chap. IV, pp. 249-253, written by Mrs. Holmes; Chicago papers, November 11 and 12, 1887.
45. See the Chicago papers, November 11 and 12, 1887.
46. Chicago *Herald*, November 12, 1887.

47. Clipping (either of November 11 or 12), scrap-book, Labadie Collection.
48. Chicago *Herald,* November 12, 1887.
49. *Ibid.,* November 13, 1887.
50. Chicago papers, November 14, 1887; *Alarm,* November 19, 1887, June 16, 1888.
51. Buchanan, *op. cit.,* p. 423.
52. Chicago and New York papers, November 14, 1887; *Alarm,* November 19, 1887; Schaack, *op. cit.,* p. 649.
53. *Life of Albert R. Parsons,* p. 255. For his entire address, *ibid.,* pp. 254-260; Schaack, *op. cit.,* pp. 650-651; Ramus, *op. cit.,* pp. 67-68; Chicago papers, November 14, 1887.
54. *Alarm,* November 19, 1887; Chicago papers, November 14, 1887.
55. *Alarm,* November 19, 1887; Chicago papers, November 14, 1887.
56. Photostat supplied by Miss Inglis; also in Ramus, *op. cit.,* pp. 69-72; author's translation. An emasculated translation is in *Alarm,* November 19, 1887.
57. See below, p. 491.
58. Stone, *op. cit.,* p. 177; *cf.,* Chicago *Daily News,* November 12, 1887.
59. Russell, *loc. cit.,* p. 411.
60. Buchanan, *op. cit.,* p. 418.
61. Waldo E. Browne, *Altgeld of Illinois. A Record of His Life and Work,* New York, 1924, p. 84.
62. See below, pp. 479-485.
63. New York *Tribune,* November 12, 1887.
64. November 12, 1887.
65. *Idem.*
66. November 12, 1887.
67. November 12, 1887.
68. November 12, 1887.
69. November 12, 1887.
70. Detroit *Sun,* November 13, 1887, scrap-book, Labadie Collection.
71. November 17, 1887.
72. See *Harper's Weekly,* November 26, 1887, editorial, "The Lesson of Chicago," pp. 850-851; *Albany Law Journal,* November 26, 1887, p. 421; *American Law Review,* vol. 21, November-December, 1887 ("Notes—The Anarchist Case," pp. 988-991), p. 991.
73. Vol. 45, no. 1168, November 12, 1887, p. 634.
74. November 19, 1887. Author's translation. See also issue of November 12, 1887.
75. November 12, 1887.
76. *Cf.,* Chicago *Daily News,* November 12, 1887.
77. November 19, 1887. The *Alarm* editorially took the executions much more calmly than the other radical organs.
78. Vol. 5, no. 8, November 19, 1887; these are the opening lines of a poem which occupied the entire first page.
79. *Ibid.,* p. 4; see also p. 7.

80. November 19, 1887, p. 369.
81. Vol. 2, no. 15, December, 1887, p. 59.
82. Vol. 14, no. 47, November 19, 1887, pp. 744, 745.
83. Vol. 1, no. 21, November 30, 1887, p. 5 (E.F.B., "When Anarchism Is Justifiable").
84. *Workmen's Advocate,* November 19, 1887.
85. *Idem;* New York *Sun,* November 14, 1887; *Twentieth Century,* vol. 12, no. 12, January 11, 1894, p. 6; *cf., El Crimen de Chicago 11 de Novembre de 1887*), New York, 1889.
86. *Workmen's Advocate,* November 19, 1887; *Liberty,* December 17, 1887, pp. 1, 6-7; *Twentieth Century,* vol. 2, no. 17, May 4, 1889, pp. 151, 154-155 (here Kimball answers the question: "Why Did You Protest·Against the Hanging of the Anarchists?").
87. Chicago *Inter Ocean,* November 11, 1887; Detroit *Evening Journal,* November 11, 1887, clipping, scrap-book, Labadie Collection.
88. *Workmen's Advocate,* November 19, 1887.
89. *Idem.*
90. *Journal of United Labor,* vol. 8, no. 20, November 19, 1887, p. 2526. The conclusion drawn was obvious enough; "Sustain and strengthen the Knights of Labor as the surest antidote for anarchy."
91. Chicago *Knights of Labor,* September 17, 1887.
92. Compare this with the fierce condemnation of all radicals in the Chicago *Knights of Labor* immediately after the bomb-throwing, in which they were stigmatized as wild beasts and cut-throats.
93. *Alarm,* December 3, 1887. By resolution this Assembly arraigned the "judicial murder" of the men, and ordered that its charter be draped in black for thirty days. It also promised to commemorate November 11, every year, and to aid the families of the men.
94. November 11, 1887, clipping, scrap-book, Labadie Collection.
95. *Naugatuck Agitator,* quoted in *Workmen's Advocate,* November 19, 1887.

XXII. THE PARDON

CHICAGO had heaved a sigh of relief when the gallows wrote *finis* to the careers of Parsons, Fischer, Engel and Spies. Law and order had been vindicated; the final curtain had been rung down upon the Haymarket Affair and the radical movement. A "remedy" had been found for revolutionary agitation in the courts, the penitentiary, and the hangman. The city would have been happy to forget the whole affair and the wild rumors of "anarchist revenge." But the revolutionary movement failed to collapse in keeping with editorial prophecy. The police, tireless in revealing dreadful conspiracies, kept the movement in the public eye, and Illinois within half a dozen years found itself with a governor who refused to regard the Haymarket case as closed.

Less than a month after the execution, money was raised through public concerts and gatherings to support the families of the men involved,[1] ar.l the Pioneer Aid and Support Association[2] was formed to look after their interests. The revolutionary groups were not even driven underground, although their meetings were sometimes held under great difficulties.[3] The organization of I.W.P.A. groups continued,[4] and there was little appreciable decrease in propagandist activities. It was even claimed that they were markedly increased by the midsummer of 1888,[5] and this was attributed to the effect of the Haymarket bomb.[6] Large gatherings of Chicago radicals in the spring of 1888, brought threats from the police that they would shortly be prevented from meeting. The Chicago *News* queried: "Shall they again be allowed to publicly preach their doctrines?"[7] The revolutionaries were giving greater weight to educational work than ever,[8] and a number of so-called "anarchist Sunday schools" were to be found throughout the city, especially on the northwest side.[9]

The German revolutionary organs continued to be published, and experienced a gain in total circulation figures in 1889 over 1886 after a drop in 1888.[10] Revived on November 5, 1887, under the able editorship of Dyer D. Lum, the *Alarm* appeared to have at least as many readers as under the guidance of Parsons, and it was in no worse financial straits.[11] It was watched with the gravest suspicion by the ever alert Capt. Schaack, who announced that he was carefully reading each number, and it was thoroughly distrusted by the daily press. The journal appeared until April 22, 1888, when it suspended publication until June 16 of the same year.[12] Lum's stand on the whole question of force and propaganda by deed was not as extreme as Parsons', but the *Alarm* remained aggressive, militant, and revolutionary until its death in February, 1889.[13] It was a constant reminder that the revolutionary movement in Chicago was far from dead.

A dispatch from Chicago to the New York *Sun* of March 17, 1889, asserted that "anarchist" meetings occurred nightly; that five hundred "anarchists" were being faithfully shadowed by the police; and that there were some 75,000 radicals in the city. The figures are undoubtedly exaggerated, but there is no question that this report was correct in so far as it indicated that the Chicago movement possessed considerable vitality.

In the decade after 1887, Chicago witnessed a more active, widespread, and intelligent discussion of revolutionary doctrines and labor theories than ever before. This was, obviously, a product of the Haymarket bomb and the tragic dénouement of the case. It was a convincing demonstration that a body of thought cannot be killed by hangings.

The police and press working hand in glove, taught Chicago to believe that hundreds of dangerous revolutionaries roamed its streets. The police badgered the radicals, raided their groups, broke up meetings, stumbled upon hidden bombs, and divulged hair-raising plots. All this made grand newspaper copy, and the men of the Fourth Estate exploited such material. The police were stimulated by their success in the Haymarket case. They were acclaimed as the intrepid protectors of Chicago, and they were egged on by business interests. The harsh treatment afforded them by the radical and labor journals also served to spur them on. It was not unnatural that they took the law into their own hands.[14]

Fortified with the excuse that they were destroying the radical movement—which, in theory, had already been thoroughly smashed—the police let their zeal run riot. They were in large measure responsible for a host of incredible rumors which warned that Chicago would witness an attempt by "anarchists" to destroy the city within a short time.[15] In July, 1888, Lucy Parsons was arrested for selling a book containing her husband's writings.[16] That summer John Bonfield, now police inspector and chief of detectives, discovered the existence of a grave conspiracy, raided dwellings and meeting places for bombs, and made several arrests.[17] The *Alarm* suggested that Bonfield's ardor was inspired by talk of the appointment of a new chief of police, and that his exertions solidified his position in business circles.[18] Bonfield at this very time wrote someone in the South that while there were "cranks" in Chicago, they were not dangerous. He also informed his correspondent that "the reports which you refer to concerning dynamite are greatly exaggerated."[19] The newspapers made so much of Bonfield's masterly detective work that the Philadelphia *Record* observed:

"Whenever an enterprising journalist of Chicago is short of news he instructs one of his staff of ambitious reporters to go out and find an anarchist bomb. Another such deadly missile has been discovered concealed perilously near the foundations of the Chicago Historical society building."[20] As a result of Bonfield's labors, before 1888 had run its course, one Hronek was sentenced to the penitentiary for twelve years.

"The vicious anarchist has got to die," cried the Chicago *Times*. "The sooner he dies the better." [21] The hounding of the "anarchists" continued into 1889. Meetings were broken up, and individuals were molested.[22] So indefensible were the actions of the police, that Judge Tuley protested early in 1889, that "the Anarchists have the same rights as other citizens to assemble peaceably for the discussion of their views; . . . the police have no right to presume an intention on their part to break the laws; . . . their meetings must not be prohibited or interfered with until a breach of the law is actually committed; . . . in no other city of the United States except Chicago have the police officials attempted to prevent the right of free speech on such unwarranted pretenses and assumptions of power, and . . . it is time to call a halt." [23]

There was less "red-baiting" during the remainder of the year and in 1890. In 1891 and 1892, the police again became active when meetings were held to commemorate the hanging of the "four martyrs." These police exertions assumed comic opera proportions. On the night of November 12, 1891, the police descended upon a meeting of the stockholders of the *Arbeiter-Zeitung* in Grief's Hall, on the pretence that it was a gathering of "reds" plotting revenge upon Chicago for executing their comrades. This was too much for ex-Mayor Harrison, who criticized the defenders of law and order, and for some newspapers which were beginning to suspect that police officers were willing to injure the city merely to secure promotion.[24]

Early in January, 1892, the Chicago *Herald* carried a front page story which charged, on the word of a responsible informant, that the recent raid on Grief's Hall "was simply a scheme to show men who had been putting up money to keep down anarchist movements that the followers of Parsons and Spies were not yet dead." This accusation came from "an attorney of great prominence, whose only clients are of the wealthy class." According to this lawyer, two days after the bomb was thrown, a letter was addressed to three hundred leading capitalists of Chicago requesting them to attend four secret meetings scheduled for the night of May 7. The purpose of these gatherings was indicated in the opening words of the communication announcing the meetings:

"In view of the threatened crusade against interests that have been founded by men and builded into splendid structures it is believed to be necessary that we combine to aid the municipal government in the suppression of ideas which are antagonistic to those held by good citizens of this country."

At the four gatherings $115,000 were immediately raised, and each person pledged himself to contribute to "an annual fund of $100,000 until anarchy had been buried as deep as the graves of Spies, Parsons and their pals." Until the fall of 1891, the original participants in this venture responded without question to the assessments of the finance committee which was created. The only instructions given this committee were: "Use this money as you may find best, the object being to crush out anarchy." The committee paid out the money to the police, so that the officers of the law were actually drawing a salary in addition to the one paid by the city. At the close of October, 1891, a meeting of the contributors was held at which the finance committee reported that no money was expended during the year because it was believed that "anarchy was dead," and that $57,650 remained on hand in the treasury. Up to this time, the police had consumed from $50,000 to $140,000 annually for "wiping out" the revolutionary movement.

Before the raid on Grief's Hall, the police made several requests for money. "The committee refused to advance another penny. 'Anarchy no longer exists,' said the chairman, 'and we are about to close our books.'" Despite the fact that the meeting of the stockholders of the *Arbeiter-Zeitung* in Grief's Hall was well publicized, it was raided by the police to create the impression that the revolutionary movement was still dangerous and that the expenditure of more money was essential. The committee, however, saw through the game and refused to contribute another cent. A report it prepared "showed that $487,000 had been expended and all we had to show for it was the hanging of four men, the horrible self-murder of one, the imprisonment of three others and the unearthing of an alleged plot against Grinnell and Judge Gary."

The only well-known individuals prominent in this "citizens' movement" to destroy anarchy were J. Harley Bradley, manufacturer of agricultural implements, J. Irving Pearce, owner and manager of the Sherman House, and Murray Nelson, politician and business man.[25] Leading members of the Citizens' Association were probably active in this attempt to make Chicago safe for capitalism, and it is even possible that the entire enterprise was the work of the Association. Mr. Bradley had served as a member of the executive committee of the Association. Since additional evidence is lacking, however, this is no more than speculation.

These accusations made by the "attorney of great prominence" were never denied. They were not, however, so much as mentioned in any other major Chicago paper, and apart from an editorial note in the Chicago *Herald* of January 5, received no attention. They may be accepted as substantially valid.

Interference with a meeting commemorating November 11 in 1892 later led to bitter criticism of the police and city authorities by the radicals. The police responded by breaking up another meeting, and a Chicago paper declared that "after five years of quiet these alien plotters of sedition and destruction have begun again to raise their heads and talk and act in precisely the same style which preceded the murderous outbreak in the Haymarket . . . Since that time, however, the city has learned something and it does not propose to allow anarchy to spread and mature into assassination again." A bit of advice was added. "The aliens, therefore, if they are wise, should understand now that if they persist in their course, the result will be that some of them will be shot, some

will be hanged, and the rest of them will go to the penitentiary." [26]

The treatment of the radicals by the police, the charges
and counter-charges of bribery and graft, the accusations made
early in 1892, all served to cast suspicion upon the department.
In 1888-1889, leading officers of the department were accused
of corrupt practises, and in 1888 Ebersold was removed from
the force. A year later, three officers, Captains Bonfield and
Schaack included, were suspended. [27] When plans were discussed for honoring the policemen who lost their lives at the
Haymarket and it was proposed to erect a monument, labor
was critical. On May 11, 1889, the Chicago *Knights of Labor*
observed that "Human beings have been imprisoned and
hanged on evidence furnished by a police system which . . .
is the most corrupt and vicious that the country has ever
known. A monument has been erected and an early date is set
for the purpose of unveiling it in commemoration of an event
that ought to bring the blush of shame to the cheek of every
honest citizen of our community." The following inscription
was proposed: *"This monument is erected to commemorate the
brutality and unheard of infamy of the Chicago police force
in 1886."* [28]

Despite the efforts of the police and the sensationalism
of the press, the threat of the "anarchist peril" gradually lost
its power. The men and women who had been active or had
aided the Amnesty Association now looked forward to securing the release of Fielden, Schwab and Neebe from prison.
The hangings had been made possible by the irresistible sweep
of public opinion. The whole case showed, as Brand Whitlock
says, "the power of words, the force of phrases, the obdurate
and terrible tyranny of a term. The men who had been hanged
were called anarchists, when, as it happens, they were men,
just men. And out of that original error in terminology, there
was evolved that overmastering fear which raved and slew in
a frenzy of passion that decades hence will puzzle the psychologist who studies the mind of the crowd." [29] There had been

a reaction from the possessed state of 1886-1887. This was only natural. A friend of Henry Demarest Lloyd, wrote two years after the hangings, "I thought I found in Chicago much compunction of conscience on account of those unnecessary executions." [30] To that staunch handful who had earlier held the conviction of the men indefensible, the taking of four lives and the passage of time added a greater number. The case was now beginning to be examined rationally.

Those who felt that the Haymarket trial had resulted in a gross miscarriage of justice viewed the pardon of the three men as a partial rectification of a grave error. A larger group who had believed that the eight men were not guiltless, now also looked with keen favor upon a pardon. They felt that the sentences were unduly severe and did not adequately protect society. They regarded a policy of leniency as wholly worthwhile. Even among those who had cheered the sentences, there was a large number who argued that the demands of law and justice had been sufficiently answered; it would be a wise act of mercy to pardon the survivors. [31]

Among the many thousands who were soon to petition the governor of Illinois to pardon the men, the legal profession was well represented. "It was but a very few years after the execution," recalls Clarence Darrow, "until the bar in general throughout the State, and elsewhere, came to believe that the conviction was brought about through malice and hatred, and that the trial was unfair and the judgment of the court unsound. . . ." [32]

There was little reason to expect any further exercise of executive clemency from Governor Oglesby. No direct appeal for a pardon was made until his successor, Governor Fifer, came into office. When Ebersold charged Schaack in 1889 with manufacturing evidence against the "anarchists," [33] the Chicago *Knights of Labor* asked Governor Fifer: ". . . Don't you think, Governor, that the men who were saved from the gallows and who are now languishing in Joliet have been sufficiently punished especially as the man who furnished the principal evidence against them [i.e., Capt. Schaack] now admits that it was seven-eighths wind, or in other words, false?" [34]

In 1890, another Amnesty Association, in which the workers of three years earlier were members, came into existence. This made concerted action possible. By directing the demands of various organizations and individuals into a single channel, the Association wielded considerable pressure. Labor groups, Turner Vereine, other German societies, and printers' organizations worked hand in hand with the Amnesty Association. [35] Especially strong was the movement for the pardon of Neebe. Meanwhile it was reported that the three inmates of Joliet made ideal prisoners, and that Schwab looked upon his speeches and writings of the early 'eighties as immature and rash. [36] In 1891, Governor Fifer was seriously considering pardoning Oscar Neebe. The pressure brought upon him by opposition forces, however, was greater than that which the amnesty workers could muster, and in the end he did nothing. [37] Those working to secure pardons were forced to wait for the advent of a new chief magistrate more sympathetic to their cause.

Early in 1892, however, efforts were again made to secure another trial for Fielden and Schwab. On January 2, Salomon and Ben Butler submitted briefs to the United States Supreme Court designed to show that Fielden and Schwab were not physically present when the State Supreme Court passed judgment and sentence of death on them, and that this was in violation of the "due process" clause of the Federal Constitution. The case was argued [38] on January 21 and 26, and on February 29, the Supreme Court gave its decision. In the opinion delivered by Justice Harlan, it was held that due process of law did not require the presence of the accused in the appellate court when the judgment of the trial court was affirmed and a new date set for the execution. [39] Eight days after Salomon and Ben Butler submitted their briefs, Illinois inaugurated a new governor.

In a major over-turn in State politics, Governor Fifer,

the Republican candidate for re-election, was defeated, and the Democrats captured, for the first time in thirty years, the gubernatorial chair with John P. Altgeld.[40] This made possible the success of the amnesty movement. It also served to bury the name of John Peter Altgeld beneath a flood of odium and abuse from which the song of poets and the labors of admirers have not yet been able to rescue it.[41] It was not the least tragic phase of the Haymarket Affair that it involved John P. Altgeld.

In the march of post-Civil War history, Altgeld stands out as one of America's most independent figures. He had convictions and dared express them in public and private life.[42] He was scrupulously honest when corruption in State and local politics was almost the order of the day. He was an earnest, intelligent reformer when callous individualism was justified, and reform meant a bitter, usually a losing, struggle against the strongholds of indifference and privilege. He was not obedient to "Big Business" though he himself was successful in business ventures and had accumulated a comfortable fortune.[43] He was "at once a consummate politician, and a real friend of the people." [44] He had the spiritual courage to hold to his ideals despite the threat of political destruction and the certainty of private financial ruin.[45]

With such a man in the governor's chair, the hopes of those who sought the pardons ran high. Some of his close friends had been assured that if he were elected, he would carefully investigate the case.[46] They were certain that he would pardon Fielden, Neebe and Schwab and many even thought that this would be his first official act.[47] His victory gave new energy to the Amnesty Association, the labors of which had as yet brought no return apart from a growth in size. By the summer of 1893, the Association embraced 375 branch lodges, was affiliated with almost all the central labor bodies and Turner societies in the State, and had a membership of 100,000 in Chicago. It had among its members men of the standing of Lyman J. Gage, Lyman Trumbull, and William Penn Nixon, editor of the Chicago *Inter Ocean*.[48]

Early in 1893, shortly after Altgeld's inauguration, a petition for pardon bearing some sixty thousand signatures was submitted to the new governor. It carried the names of Chicago's leading citizens, and, it is said, was signed by "the president of every bank and every railroad in Chicago." [49] This group was probably drawn into the amnesty movement by the influence of Lyman J. Gage and Lyman Trumbull and the tireless efforts of Mr. E. S. Dreyer, a banker, who had served as foreman of the grand jury which indicted the "anarchists." Mr. Dreyer regarded Neebe as entirely innocent from the first, and was convinced that though Fielden and Schwab were guilty to some degree, they had suffered more than enough.[50] To the great petition there was added the personal pleas of individuals who "besieged" the governor in their eagerness to get him to act.[51]

Samuel P. McConnell, who appealed in person, said to Altgeld, "I hope you are going to pardon Neebe." To this Altgeld answered that he had been going over the record of the case. "If you go through that record," warned McConnell, "you will see that you ought to pardon all three of them, and I hope you will. If you do though it will be the end of your political career."

"If I decide they were innocent I will pardon them, by God, no matter what happens to my career!" Altgeld answered.[52]

To many of his friends and to those demanding pardons, Altgeld's failure to grant a pardon immediately was perplexing and disappointing. As early as January 21, 1893, *Liberty* criticized the governor for keeping the three men in jail, and in May the same journal sharply reprimanded him for not having pardoned them.[53] Some impatient friends nagged him with reminders to act, and did not conceal their displeasure with him. Several began to wonder whether they had not been "deceived" in him.[54] Though he had been "brooding" over the case from the time he took office,[55] he put off those who up-braided him for his inaction with the excuse that he had been too occupied with other matters.[56] To Darrow, who informed him of the views of his friends, and who urged that there was no reason for delay, Altgeld replied:

"Go tell your friends that when I am ready I will act. I don't know how I will act, but I will do what I think is right. . . . We have been friends for a long time. You seem impatient; of course I know how you feel; I don't want to offend you or lose your friendship, but this responsibility is mine, and I shall shoulder it. I have not yet examined the record. I have no opinion about it. It is a big job. When I do examine it I will do what I believe to be right, no matter what that is. But don't deceive yourself: If I conclude to pardon these men it will not meet with the approval you ex-pect; let me tell you that from that day I will be a dead man." [57]

Altgeld's conception of the nature of the pardoning power and his own temperament prevented him from merely grant-ing a routine pardon as a matter of mercy. He held that the pardoning power "was not so much a personal prerogative as a judicial responsibility, to be exercised in correction of those wrongs which are inseparable from the regular processes of the criminal law." [58] Altgeld, therefore, proposed to undertake a searching, objective examination of the entire case. If the men had been illegally convicted, then justice called for their release from prison. If they were found guilty fairly, then "no punishment under our laws could be too severe." [59]

To those who knew him well and had learned that "in-justice was never for long out of the mind of John P. Alt-geld," [60] it should have been evident that his decision would be more than a simple act of clemency. With his training and experience as a lawyer and judge he was well prepared to analyze the case. Honest to a fault and unhesitant in giving blunt expression to his convictions, it was safe to assume that he would not issue a pardon message on grounds of leniency and sweetened with moral platitudes.

When he confided to close political associates that he intended pardoning all three men, he was urged to reconsider his decision. He was warned that his act would end his own career and probably wreck his party. Altgeld, however, was adamant. "As for our party," he declared, "that must stand or fall by its principles and its policy. As for myself, no man has the right to allow his ambition to stand in the way of the performance of a simple act of justice." [61]

Before Altgeld issued the pardons, two occurrences transpired which seemed almost to anticipate his act. The first was the publication of a long article by Judge Gary in *Century Magazine*, in which he reviewed the whole case, and defended the conduct of the trial, its result, and the sentences. Whether consciously or not, Judge Gary was, in a sense, presenting in advance an argument against the pardon of the three men. Essentially his article was a defense of his own conduct, and as such was polemical in nature. It did not, of course, go unanswered, and both it and the author were soon mercilessly criticized. [62]

The second occurrence was the unveiling and dedication of the monument which marks the grave of the "martyrs" at Waldheim on Sunday, June 25. A gathering of 8,000 people witnessed the ceremonies arranged by the Pioneer Aid and Support Association, which was responsible for the erection of the monument. The monument itself, designed by Albert Weiner, portrays an heroic bronze figure of Justice crowning with a laurel wreath a fallen and dying worker. [63] It was a striking coincidence that its unveiling was followed the next day by Altgeld's pardon message.

The governor had evidently decided upon the form and content of his pardon message much earlier, and he knew it would create a furor. Probably to prepare the way he sent George Schilling, who now headed the State Bureau of Labor Statistics, to sound out some of the more important members of the Chicago bench. He was to secure, if possible, their support for the amnesty movement. Schilling was unsuccessful. When he reported his failure to Altgeld, he warned the governor that if he was not prepared to bear full responsibility alone, he could give up all hope of issuing the pardons in the manner contemplated. Altgeld paced the room the two were in when he heard this, and turning to Schilling quietly said, "We don't need them, we don't need them." [64]

Only one person appears to have been acquainted with the contents of the message before it was sent to the printer. He was Samuel P. McConnell, to whom Altgeld read the entire paper. The governor asked for comment, and McConnell replied that he was pleased with the pardons but not with the message. "There's too much Altgeld and not enough Governor in it," he said. "It ought to be in the third person. You are Governor now and not Altgeld." Altgeld paused and answered: "I believe you are right and I will rewrite it and follow your suggestions." When McConnell read the message after its publication not a word had been changed.[65]

Early on June 26, Altgeld informed the Secretary of State, William H. Hinrichsen, that he was "going to pardon Fielden, Schwab, and Neebe this morning," and suggested that Hinrichsen might want to sign the papers in person. The latter asked if Altgeld believed it "was good policy to pardon" the men, and added that he himself did not think so. Altgeld emphasized his answer by striking the desk with his fist: "It is right." [66]

Brand Whitlock, then employed in the State Department, was given the task of drawing up the pardons, which he did, he writes, "in the largest, roundest hand I could command . . . and took them over to the governor's office." [67] There he found with the governor Mr. E. S. Dreyer, whose every movement betrayed great nervous strain. Altgeld, after signing each of the papers, handed them to Dreyer. The latter began, "Governor, I hardly . . ." when his voice broke and he unashamedly wept. Altgeld almost brusquely reminded the banker that unless he hurried he would miss the train to Joliet where he was to give the pardons to Schwab, Neebe and Fielden in person.[68] By mid-afternoon Dreyer had completed his pleasurable task. That night the three men returned with him to Chicago, where they were jubilantly welcomed despite their plea, "We want to go quietly to our homes." [69]

Not until two o'clock in the afternoon was the news of the pardons publicly known, and about the same time Altgeld's long message,[70] which had been secretly printed, was released.[71] The pardons took even some of Altgeld's close political associates by surprise,[72] but the message itself left them and everyone else flabbergasted. On the twenty-seventh, there was but one topic of conversation—the pardons and the governor's document. Already the great roar of disapproval which Altgeld expected could be heard. Whitlock met him the morning after the men were released from prison. "I saw him," he writes, "as I was walking down to the Capitol. . . . There was, of course, but one subject then, and I said:

"'Well, the storm will break now.'

"'Oh, yes,' he replied, with a not wholly convincing air of throwing off a care, 'I was prepared for that. It was merely doing right.'

". . . And the storm did break, and the abuse it rained upon him broke his heart; but I never again heard him mention the anarchist case." [73]

Even a superficial reading of the pardon message [74] makes it evident why there was a "storm." Altgeld had not granted the pardons because the men had been sufficiently punished for their acts, or for reasons of expediency, or out of magnanimity. On the contrary, he was freeing Fielden, Neebe and Schwab because he believed that they were not legally convicted and because the available evidence unmistakably showed that they were innocent of the crime for which they had been tried. In short, Altgeld was publicly asserting that these three, as well as the five who were no longer alive, had been "railroaded." The jury which tried them was, in effect, a packed jury, he declared. The trial, therefore, was not a legal one.

Altgeld had carefully examined the record of the trial, and he quoted extensively from it. He also cited the recent opinion of the Supreme Court in the case of *Coughlin* v. *The People* in which the Court declared that "where it is once clearly shown that there exists in the mind of the juror, at the time he is called to the jury box, a fixed and positive opinion as to the merits of the case, or as to the guilt or innocence of the defendants he is called to try, his statement, that notwithstanding such opinion, he can render a fair and impartial verdict according to the law and evidence, has little, if any tendency to establish his impartiality." [75] Altgeld further observed that the trial judge in this case had been guided by the rule laid down in the "anarchist" case, and that the Supreme Court had reversed the verdict because two of the jurors were incompetent.[76]

The governor bluntly declared that the proof adduced at the trial did not show that the defendants were guilty. He attacked Judge Gary's ruling that it was not necessary for the State to identify the bomb-thrower or even prove that he came under the advice or influence of the accused. ". . . in all the centuries during which government has been maintained among men, and crime has been punished," he asserted, "no judge in a civilized country has ever laid down such a rule before." [77] He concluded that "until the State proves from whose hands the bomb came, it is impossible to show any connection between the man who threw it and these defendants." [78] Altgeld himself believed that the bomb-thrower was moved by consideration of personal revenge against the police.[79] The governor was convinced of Neebe's innocence. "I have examined all of the evidence against Neebe with care," he wrote, "and it utterly fails to prove even the shadow of a case against him." [80]

Altgeld concluded his message with an indirect criticism of Judge Gary that is probably unique in the history of the exercise of the pardoning power by State executives.

"It is . . . charged," he wrote, "with much bitterness, by those who speak for the prisoners [i.e., those petitioning for pardon] that the record of this case shows that the judge conducted the trial with malicious ferocity . . . ; also, that every ruling throughout the long trial on any contested point, was in favor of the State; and further, that page after page of the record contains insinuating remarks of the judge . . . with the evident intent of bringing the jury to his way of thinking . . . ; that the judge's magazine article recently published, although written nearly six years after the trial is yet full of venom. . . . It is urged that such ferocity of subserviency [i.e., to the interests of the State] is without a parallel in all history. . . .

"These charges are of a personal character, and while they seem to be sustained by the record of the trial and the papers before me, and tend to show the trial was not fair, I do not care to discuss this feature of the case any further, because it is not necessary." [81]

The pardon message was a notable State paper. There is no wonder that it raised a "storm." It is, of course, open to criticism. Altgeld invited trouble by unmercifully censuring Judge Gary. Even Clarence Darrow remarks, "Undoubtedly his [Gary's] rulings were biased and unfair, but where is the man, who under the lashings of the crowd, is not biased and unfair?" [82] Altgeld would have done better to direct his criticism against the State Supreme Court which considered the case a year later, and whose seven judges could easily divide the responsibility of a reversal. The message, in short, erred in lack of policy and tact, and undoubtedly was responsible for turning an act that in itself might have met with favor into one that was condemned. Many who were unreservedly pleased with the freeing of the three men, resented the tone of the State paper which accompanied their release. Even those who knew and loved Altgeld have found him at fault in attacking Judge Gary and permitting a personal note to appear in an otherwise outstanding message. [83] It may reflect credit on Altgeld that he spoke so boldly, but it was unwise, since it "put a most effective weapon into the hands of his opponents." [84]

The pardon message subjected Altgeld to a flood of personal abuse such as has been directed at few persons for similar reasons. He had his defenders, but they were relatively few. To most of Chicago's wealthy citizens, Altgeld at once became a socialist, and he was denounced as such.[85] The Chicago *Tribune* greeted the pardons with a scorching editorial which charged Altgeld with paying for the votes of "anarchists" and "socialists" with the three pardons. His act proved that he "was not merely an alien by birth, but an alien by temperament and sympathies. He has apparently not a drop of true American blood in his veins. He does not reason like an American, nor feel like one." He was a socialist in everything but name.[86] The myth was concocted that Altgeld, the foreigner, was trying to force alien ideals upon his American electorate. A Chicago dispatch to the New York *Times* declared that "It is Altgeld's un-Americanism which unfits him for the office which he holds or even for citizenship." Dominated by ideals which are alien, he "would have developed into an out-and-out Anarchist if his lucky real estate speculations had not turned the course of his natural tendencies." [87] This "foreigner," it may be noted, arrived in America when he was all of three months old.

The Chicago *Tribune* answered Altgeld's pardon message with ammunition drawn from the State Supreme Court opinion, attacked him in vitriolic editorials, and joined with other papers in flaying him through vicious cartoons.[88] The New York *World,* for example, spread across its front page a crude cartoon depicting Altgeld on his hands and knees before a black-robed figure of death, carrying a flaming torch in one hand and a bomb with burning fuse in the other; around both figures bombs are bursting on soil labelled "Illinois." The caption under this work of art reads, "Gov. Altgeld's Message contains 17,000 words, but the above is a fair synopsis of it." [89] The Philadelphia *Press* ran a front-page cartoon in which Altgeld is shown holding hands with long-haired, bomb-carrying anarchists, gleefully dancing about the statue which had been erected to the police victims of the Haymarket.[90] The *Press* made political capital out of the situation. "A sentence of sweeping and irresistible condemnation," it declared, "will be passed by the American people upon the act of this demagogical governor and upon the Democratic party which placed him in power and gave him this opportunity to show his sympathy with Anarchism." [91]

The New York *World* condemned both the pardons and the message. "Gov. Altgeld," it asserted, "is added to the list of men who will be remembered for something they ought not to have done." [92] The New York *Evening Post* stated that the "document" which accompanied the pardons "reads as if" Altgeld himself were "an anarchist." [93] To the New York *Times,* the message revealed Altgeld "either as an enemy to the safeguards of society, or as a reckless demagogue . . . incapable of understanding the spirit and temper of the" American people.[94] In thorough agreement with these expressions of editorial opinion were the New York *Herald* and the *Tribune.*[95] Carried away by the enormity of the governor's deed, the New York *Sun* published an apostrophe "To Anarchy" which ends with these inspiring lines:

"O wild Chicago, when the time
   Is ripe for ruin's deeds,
When constitutions, courts, and laws
   Go down midst crashing creeds,
Lift up your weak and guilty hands
   From out of the wreck of States,
And as the crumbling towers fall down
   Write ALTGELD on your gates!" [96]

Politics played a relatively small rôle in determining editorial comment on Governor Altgeld's action. He was attacked equally by Democratic and Republican papers. Republican journals, of course, made political capital of the situation, but both groups generally spoke with one mind and voice. Thus, the St. Louis *Globe-Democrat,* staunchly Republican, declared on June 30:

"There is practically but one opinion throughout the whole country as to the action of Governor Altgeld. . . . It is condemned everywhere as a gross abuse of the pardoning power, and not a word is said in its defense except by the enemies of society. . . . The use of the pardoning power to defeat the ends of justice in such a case cannot be too severely condemned." [97] The Louisville *Courier-Journal,* a Democratic newspaper, said on the same day:

"In his pardon of Neebe, Fielden and Schwab, Governor Altgeld has made a mistake . . . both in the manner and the occasion of his extension of executive grace . . . the Governor's arraignment of the justice of the sentences . . . is a proceeding of the most inopportune kind, to say the very least . . . , and it has inevitably brought upon its author a flood of universal condemnation . . . it is surely a piece of unwisdom closely resembling culpable indifference to consequences . . . to undertake to reopen and review the action of a court already passed upon by the Supreme tribunals, State and National, and thus to let slip, and . . . to encourage the passions of crazy agitators, already sufficiently inflamed and dangerous." [98]

With good reason *Appleton's Annual Cyclopaedia* recorded that "On June 27 the country was astonished by the news that Gov. Altgeld had granted pardons to the three anarchists . . ." [99] In some localities the inhabitants were evidently more than astonished. The Mayor of Racine demanded Altgeld's immediate resignation from office,[100] and the citizens of Naperville, a town near Chicago, hanged the governor in effigy. Across the main street there dangled a grotesque figure on which were painted two hands clasped in friendship. On one was printed the word "Anarchy," and on the other, "Altgeld." [101]

The press of New York City, Philadelphia, Detroit,[102] and other urban centers took greater offense at the pardons than did that of Chicago. Perhaps this was due to Chicago's fuller knowledge both of the Haymarket Affair and of the integrity and honesty of the governor. It was, therefore, readier to recognize the strength of his position. The Chicago *Globe* praised his act and asserted that, despite the contemporary condemnation of the governor, time would prove both its "righteousness" and "justice." [103] Carter H. Harrison, once more mayor of Chicago, and now owner of the Chicago *Times,* personally dictated an editorial in which Altgeld's action was applauded, although the language of the pardon message was criticized. "Gov. Altgeld," declared the *Times,* "has done no more than right in giving them freedom for the rest of their days." [104]

Chicago papers which in no sense praised the governor, were not as extreme in their utterances as the Chicago *Tribune.* The *Inter Ocean* attacked the governor's arraignment of Judge Gary and the police as "outrageous," but it recognized that he had acted within his constitutional rights.[105] The Chicago *Herald* found the pardons "excusable" because the men had been sufficiently punished, but it was not to be thought that they "removed the stain of guilt from the memories of the Anarchists who sleep at Waldheim." [106] The Chicago *Record* took a similar position.[107]

Members of the bench and bar in New York City professed to be shocked and amazed at his act, and objected vigorously to the governor's review of the judicial aspects of the case,[108] but many lawyers and judges in Chicago expressed satisfaction with what had occurred. They did, however, criticize the language of the pardon message.[109] Several Chicago office-holders publicly indicated that they were pleased with the release of the men.[110] United States District Attorney Milchrist said: "I am not at all sorry to see the men liberated, but I think that full justice all around demanded some other excuse for the pardon than that the Judge was moved by prejudice." [111] Mr. Grinnell and Judge Gary took refuge in dignified silence—they had "nothing to say." Judge Gary found it unbecoming to enter into a "controversy." [112]

Chicago was less distressed by the governor's act than one might expect, even though the first reports from the city represent the "American portion of" the "community" as feeling "outraged" by what Altgeld had done. "The only people who are pleased are those who are tinctured with Anarchistic sentiments." [113] In view of the large membership of the Amnesty Association, the accuracy of this report may well be questioned. The Association itself, pleased with the successful consummation of its work, was preparing to vote its thanks to the governor and then disband. [114]

To the abuse which descended upon his head, Altgeld offered no reply. It must have been difficult not to answer attacks which patently utilized the pardons for political purposes, and charged that the governor granted the pardons to fulfill a pre-election promise to the anarchists and socialists. [115] ". . . Governor Altgeld's pardon message," said one political pamphlet, "was an unfair, dishonest, pettifogging advocacy of the cause of anarchists and murderers, and a malignant, lawless and brutal attack upon the courts of the land." [116]

Altgeld loved a fight in a just cause, but he had decided, wisely or unwisely, upon complete silence. Immediately after granting the pardons he is reported to have said, "Let them pitch in and give me the devil if they want to. They could not cut through my hide in three weeks with an axe." [117] He did, however, suffer deeply from the abuse. His friend, Judge Edward Osgood Brown, wrote that Altgeld "used to say that he was not sensitive to the furious denunciation of his action and of himself which swept over the country; but I know that he *did* feel it and its injustice keenly. And he told me that sometimes the exhibition of fanatical hatred to him seemed almost 'sublime' like a fearful storm." [118] A friend could not understand his silence amid the "vile slanders heaped upon him by the press. . . ." Altgeld remarked: "Remember this about any slander. Denial only emphasizes, and gives added importance to falsehood. Let it alone and it will die for want of nourishment." [119]

The conviction that he had performed his duty and had done what was "right" was enough to sustain Altgeld in the face of the denunciation which descended upon him. Support also came from "a little scattered company of justice-loving men and women, who dared to applaud his act as 'a deed which struck deeper than the matter of freeing a few individuals to the fundamental rights of human beings.' " [120] Approval for the governor's action was not restricted to this select group. Radicals were, of course, highly pleased. "Justice to the living has come at last," said Johann Most, "but Gov. Altgeld cannot put life in the murdered dead." [121] *Liberty* sang Altgeld's praises for releasing the men and for proclaiming their innocence.[122] The *People,* a New York socialist weekly, similarly hailed the pardons.[123] The Eighth National Convention of the Socialist Labor Party unanimously passed a resolution commending Governor Altgeld's action in the highest terms.[124] *Twentieth Century,* an intellectually radical journal, declared that the governor had "taken a step which only a brave man could have taken . . . which only a man whose sense of justice outweighed all personal considerations would dare to take." [125]

Altgeld really needed no such support. He had done what was possible to wipe out a grave injustice, and that was enough. To one of his associates he once said: "You are younger than I and will live to see my pardon of the anarchists justified." [126] Today only those who are completely blinded by prejudice can object to his act. His name, however, still remains to be delivered in the popular mind from the odium which the pardons and his rôle during the famous Pullman Strike attached to it.[127]

Surprisingly enough, the pardons did not mean the end of Altgeld as a political figure of importance. He remained one of the foremost Democrats in the West, and was a leader of the silver forces. Despite his own earnest protestations that he was in "no condition to stand for re-election," he was renominated for governor in 1896, and was endorsed by the Populists. He played an influential part in determining the platform and policies adopted by the Democratic National Convention of 1896, and at the convention was an outstanding figure. An astute political observer, H. H. Kohlsaat, thought that he would have received the nomination if he were of American birth. Although he was ill, he played a vital rôle in the campaign of 1896. He almost ignored his own campaign to emphasize national issues, and he delivered a notable three hour address in New York City in Cooper Union. Though he failed to be re-elected, he polled 475,000 votes, 50,000 more than he received in 1892, and ran 10,000 ahead of Bryan's vote in Illinois.[128] During the campaign the Republicans lost no opportunity to stigmatize Altgeld with the term "anarchist" and to describe his and Bryan's principles as "anarchistic." This was made possible by the pardon message and his controversy with Cleveland during the Pullman Strike. Theodore Roosevelt, for example, in an address in Chicago, called. "The Menace of the Demagogue" spoke of "Mr. Altgeld's recipe of free riot and free pardon of those foulest of criminals," and declared that "Mr. Altgeld condones and encourages the most infamous of murders. . . ."[129] During the national campaign, he was constantly spoken of as Bryan's right hand man.

Altgeld had obviously erred when he prophesied that the pardons would mean his political demise. When he died in March, 1902, the Chicago *Inter Ocean,* never an ardent supporter, declared that "he left the governor's office the most influential Democrat in the West, and with his bitterest opponents conceding his personal honesty and his political strength."[130]

Fielden, Neebe and Schwab were almost entirely forgotten when they were released from prison. So furiously did the storm rage around Altgeld, that they were ignored. For them this was indeed fortunate. Provided with funds by the Pioneer Aid and Support Association, they were able to find private occupations, and they dropped out of the public eye and, for all practical purposes, out of the radical movement. Because of their own unwillingness or because of the consideration of their comrades, they were not exploited in the revolutionary cause as they might have been. Perhaps their six years in prison had robbed them of their revolutionary fervor. But remembered they were and are, together with their five comrades, by radicals in America and the world over on every November 11.

NOTES CHAPTER XXII

1. *Alarm,* December 17, 1887.
2. It was also called the Pioneer Aid and Relief Association and the Chicago Pioneer Benefit and Aid Society. *Alarm,* December 31, 1887.
3. *Idem.*
4. *Ibid.,* July 14, 1888.
5. *Ibid.,* August 4, 1888.
6. See below, pp. 531-532.
7. Quoted in *ibid.,* March 24, 1887.
8. New York *Sun,* March 17, 1889.
9. Addams, *op. cit.,* p. 91. Jane Addams thus describes her visit to a "Sunday-school" in the winter of 1889. "One Sunday afternoon . . . a reporter took me to visit a so-called anarchist Sunday-school . . . the young man in charge was of the German student type, and his face flushed with enthusiasm as he led the children singing one of Koerner's poems. The newspaper man, who did not understand German, asked me what abominable stuff they were singing, but he seemed dissatisfied with my translation of the simple words and darkly intimated that they were 'deep ones' and had probably 'fooled' me." *Ibid.,* pp. 91-92.
10. The total circulation figures for the *Arbeiter-Zeitung,* the *Fackel* and the *Vorbote* for 1886 was 25,980; for 1887 there are no figures; for 1888, 16,000; for 1889, 25,595; for 1890, 23,750. The *Arbeiter-Zeitung* about held its own for the years given. The *Vorbote* declined sharply in 1888-89, and the *Fackel* experienced a great increase over 1886.
11. See Chicago *Herald,* November 27, 1887, interview with Lum. There is evidence, including a letter from Spies, to the effect that the latter, Schwab, Fielden and Neebe were opposed to the revival of the *Alarm* in November, because they felt it would be a competitor with Joe Buchanan's Chicago *Labor Enquirer.* It was clear that the radical-labor movement could not support too many organs. *Alarm,* June 16, 1888.
12. When it resumed on the last date, it was as a weekly instead of a fortnightly publication and it bore a "Chicago and New York" dateline.

13. A monthly of the same name appeared in 1893-1894 in Dallas, Texas, edited by Ross Winn.
14. New York *Sun*, March 17, 1889.
15. Russell, *loc. cit.*, p. 412.
16. *Alarm*, July 14, 1888.
17. *Ibid.*, July 28, 1888.
18. *Ibid.*, August 4, 1888.
19. Quoted in *idem*, from the Memphis *Appeal*.
20. Quoted in *ibid.*, July 14, 1888.
21. Quoted in *ibid.*, December 8, 1888. Hronek's conviction was based presumably on his possession of dynamite.
22. *Ibid.*, December 22, 1888, January 5, 1889.
23. Quoted in *Twentieth Century*, vol. 2, no. 17, May 4, 1889, p. 154. *Alarm*, January 19, 1889.
24. Chicago *Times*, November 15, 1891, Chicago *Herald*, November 14 and 15, 1891, and undated Chicago papers, clippings, scrap-book, Labadie Collection.
25. Chicago *Herald*, January 4, 1892.
26. Chicago newspaper, November, 1892, clipping, scrap-book, Labadie Collection.
27. *Alarm*, February 25, 1888; *Ohio Valley Budget*, February 9, 1889, clipping, scrap-book, Labadie Collection.
28. Quoted in *The Haymarket Monument. What Is It Erected For?* Chicago, 1889. For the police monument, see, Chicago papers, May 30, 31, 1889; Franklin H. Head, *Studies in Medieval and Modern History*, Chicago, n.d. (photostatic copy in Public Library, N.Y.C.), pp. 85-99, "Heroism Commemorated"; there is the address delivered at the unveiling of the monument. The monument itself shows a policeman standing with upraised and menacing club.
29. Brand Whitlock, *Forty Years of It*, New York, 1925, p. 41.
30. Quoted in Lloyd, *op. cit.*, vol. 1, p. 103.
31. Browne, *op. cit.*, pp. 86-87.
32. Clarence Darrow, *The Story of My Life*, New York, 1932, p. 99; personal interview with Mr. Darrow.
33. See above, pp. 233-234.
34. Quoted in *The Haymarket Monument, What Is It Erected For?*
35. Browne, *op. cit.*, p. 87; interview with Schilling.
36. *Open Court*, vol. 4, September 25, 1890, p. 2538. This contains a report of Paul Carus' visit to Joliet and his interview with Neebe and Schwab. Carus was then editor of the *Open Court*.
37. New York *World*, June 27, 1893; Browne, *op. cit.*, p. 87.
38. With Fielden alone as the plaintiff.
39. New York *Tribune*, January 3, 1892; *Fielden* v. *Ill.*, 143 U. S. 452.
40. Browne, *op. cit.*, pp. 42-50 *passim;* Bogart and Thompson, *op. cit.*, pp. 182-186 *passim*.
41. See Vachel Lindsay's "The Eagle that Is Forgotten"; Edgar Lee

Masters, *Spoon River Anthology, passim;* Browne, *op. cit.;* Darrow, *op. cit.;* Whitlock, *op. cit.*

42. See his statement in Browne, *op. cit.,* p. 43. "The successful private individual, the man who has convictions and who dares to express them, is the most important factor in American society."

43. Later wiped out in connection with the failure of his ambitious Unity Building enterprise.

44. Bogart and Thompson, *op. cit.,* p. 183.

45. For Altgeld's life, see Browne, *op. cit.*

46. Statement of Mr. Darrow.

47. Darrow, *op. cit.,* p. 100.

48. Chicago *Tribune,* June 27, 1893.

49. Browne, *op. cit.,* p. 87 and note.

50. Chicago *Tribune,* June 27, 1893; Whitlock, *op. cit.,* p. 74. Brand Whitlock spells his name Dreier.

51. Browne, *op. cit.,* p. 87.

52. McConnell, *loc. cit.,* p. 738.

53. Vol. 9, no. 21, p. 2, no. 36, May 6, 1893, p. 1.

54. Darrow, *op. cit.,* p. 100.

55. Whitlock, *op. cit.,* pp. 72-73.

56. Browne, *op. cit.,* p. 88.

57. Darrow, *op. cit.,* pp. 100-101; *cf.* Bogart and Thompson, *op. cit.,* p. 187 note, and Browne, *op. cit.,* pp. 89-90.

58. Browne, *op. cit.,* p. 88.

59. Altgeld, *Pardon Message,* p. 3.

60. Whitlock, *op. cit.,* p. 72.

61. Unpublished article by Louis F. Post, quoted in Browne, *op. cit.,* p. 90.

62. See Ames, *An Open Letter to Judge Joseph E. Gary,* an able pamphlet; C. L. James, "Judge Gary on the Anarchists," *Twentieth Century,* vol. 10, no. 16, April 20, 1893, pp. 10-11, in which Gary's article is sharply attacked; William Salter, writing in the Philadelphia *Conservator* pointed out that Gary in his article pursued a line of reasoning altogether different from that followed by the State Supreme Court in its opinion (*Liberty,* vol. 9, no. 41, June 10, 1893, p. 1); *Liberty,* vol. 9, no. 38, May 20, 1893, p. 3; M. M. Trumbull, "Judge Gary and the Anarchists," *Arena,* vol. 8, no. 47, October, 1893, pp. 544-561, is an able answer to Gary.

63. Chicago *Tribune,* June 26, 1893. It was remarked that the monument was roughly of the same height and cost as the police monument in the Haymarket.

64. Interview with George Schilling.

65. McConnell, *loc. cit.,* p. 738.

66. Chicago *Inter Ocean,* March 3, 1902, article, Hon. Wm. H. Hinrichsen, "Illinois Giants I Have Known—John P. Altgeld."

67. Whitlock, *op. cit.,* pp. 73-74.

68. *Ibid.,* p. 74.

69. Chicago *Tribune*, Chicago *Inter Ocean*, New York *World*, June 27, 1893.
70. It contains about 17,000 words.
71. Chicago *Tribune*, June 28, 1893.
72. See Hinrichsen's statement in *Inter Ocean*, March 16, 1902.
73. Whitlock, *op. cit.*, p. 75.
74. The message has been extensively printed. The Chicago *Tribune* and other Chicago papers reproduced it in full on June 27, 1893; it has been printed over and over as a separate pamphlet; it has been appended to editions of the speeches of the men and the *Life of Albert R. Parsons* which have appeared since 1893.
75. *Pardon Message*, pp. 14-15; see above, pp. 241-242.
76. *Ibid.*, pp. 15-16.
77. *Ibid.*, p. 17.
78. *Idem.*
79. *Ibid.*, p. 23.
80. *Ibid.*, p. 28.
81. *Ibid.*, pp. 28-29, author's italics. It was immediately forgotten that Altgeld said that these were the charges laid against Judge Gary by the amnesty workers and that he thought they "seemed to be sustained" by the record. It was assumed, and with justice, that Altgeld was here speaking his own mind.
82. Darrow, *op. cit.*, p. 102.
83. Whitlock, *op. cit.*, pp. 74-75; Addams, *op. cit.*, p. 207; also quoted in Browne, *op. cit.*, p. 111.
84. Browne, *op. cit.*, p. 111.
85. New York *World*, June 27, 1893.
86. June 27, 1893.
87. June 28, 1893.
88. June 28, 1893.
89. June 27, 1893.
90. June 28, 1893.
91. *Idem.*
92. June 27, 1893.
93. June 27, 1893.
94. June 28, 1893.
95. See for June 27 and 28, 1893.
96. Quoted in Browne, *op. cit.*, pp. 107-108.
97. Quoted in *Public Opinion*, vol. 15, no. 14, July 8, 1893, p. 333.
98. Quoted in *idem*.
99. 1893, New York, 1894, p. 398.
100. Chicago *Tribune*, June 28, 1893.
101. New York *Times*, June 30, 1893.
102. See the Chicago *Tribune*, June 28, 1893, for the editorial position of the Detroit press.
103. June 27, 1893.
104. June 27, 1893; New York *Sun*, June 27, 1893; Chicago *Tribune*, June 27, 1893; Abbot, *op. cit.*, pp. 143-144.

105. June 27, 1893, quoted in New York *Sun*, June 27, 1893.
106. *Idem.*
107. *Idem.*
108. New York *Times*, June 28, 1893.
109. Chicago *Tribune*, June 27, 28, 1893; New York *World*, June 27, 28, 1893. There seems to have been only one more or less important New York attorney who fully supported Altgeld.
110. Chicago dispatch to the New York *Tribune*, June 27, 1893; Chicago *Tribune*, June 27, 1893.
111. New York *World*, June 27, 1893.
112. Chicago *Tribune*, June 27, 1893; New York *Times*, June 28, 1893.
113. Chicago dispatch to the New York *Times*, June 27, 1893.
114. Chicago *Tribune*, June 27, 1893; New York *World*, June 28, 1893.
115. *The Pardon of the Anarchists*, title page mutilated, probably published in Chicago, 1893 (?), p. 3.
116. *Ibid.*, pp. 4-5.
117. New York *World*, June 28, 1893.
118. Quoted in Browne, *op. cit.*, p. 114; *cf., idem*, note.
119. *Ibid.*, p. 115.
120. *Idem.*
121. New York *World*, June 27, 1893.
122. *Liberty*, vol. 15, no. 44, July 1, 1893, p. 2.
123. July 2, 1893, quoted in *Public Opinion*, vol. 15, no. 14, July 8, 1893, p. 333. "Though tardily and imperfectly," said *The People*, "justice is at last done to the martyrs of Chicago."
124. *Labor Library*, No. 12, New York, June, 1894, pp. 22-23.
125. Vol. 11, no. 1, July 6, 1893, p. 1.
126. Browne, *op. cit.*, p. 114.
127. See Browne, *op. cit.*, chaps. XII-XVI.
128. John R. Tanner, his opponent, ran 30,000 votes behind McKinley. Browne, *op. cit.*, chaps. XXIV-XXVI; McConnell, *loc. cit.*, p. 739; Francis F. Browne, "The Presidential Contest. I—Altgeld of Illinois," *The National Review* (London), vol. 38, no. 166, December, 1896, pp. 452-473 *passim;* H. H. Kohlsaat, *From McKinley to Harding. Personal Recollections of Our Presidents*, New York, 1923, pp. 42 *et seq.;* John D. Hicks, *The Populist Revolt*, Minneapolis, 1931, p. 354; James Ford Rhodes, *History of the United States from the Compromise of 1850 to the End of the Roosevelt Administration*, 9 vols., New York, 1929, vol. 9, 1896-1909, pp. 27-28; Allan Nevins, *Grover Cleveland. A Study in Courage*, New York, 1933, pp. 690-701; William Jennings and Mary Baird Bryan, *The Memoirs of William Jennings Bryan*, Chicago, 1925, p. 101.
129. Speech before the American Republican College League, October 15, 1896, *The Works of Theodore Roosevelt*, National Edition, New York, 1926, 20 vols., *Campaigns and Controversies*, vol. 14, pp. 265, 273; *cf.*, pp. 258-274 *passim*.
130. March 13, 1902.

XXIII. WHO THREW THE BOMB?

I F this were really the "best of possible worlds," as Voltaire's cheerless optimist, Doctor Pangloss, insisted, the question of who threw the bomb would be answered at this point. The guilty one could then be revealed with all the neat dispatch with which the magician pulls a somewhat bored rabbit from the inevitable top-hat. Unfortunately, this cannot be done. The bomb-thrower still remains unknown. In the mass of related evidence, rumor, and fancy which can be gathered there is no positive key to the troublesome problem. There are "clues" without limit, and enough suspects to delight even a Capt. Schaack.

The mere name of the bomb-thrower is, in a sense, relatively unimportant. It is meaningless to say that "John Jones," about whom nothing at all is known, threw the bomb. It is quite another thing to assert that "John Jones," the bomb-thrower, was a social-revolutionary, a Pinkerton agent, a bank president, a laborer, or a homicidal maniac. Without such identification, neither the motivation nor the relationship of the criminal agent to his deed can be made clear.

Rudolph Schnaubelt stands first in the long line of suspects. Police and prosecution accused this young man, who, after being examined by the police, disappeared. Two witnesses took oath that he had hurled the deadly missile.[1] In *The Bomb*, Frank Harris' mélange of fact and fancy and of class and sex struggle, Schnaubelt is cast for the rôle of the bomb-thrower.[2] Mr. Harris' tale, in which Louis Lingg is the hero, is told through the person of Schnaubelt, who, led to commit the deed by Lingg, declares, "I threw the bomb which killed eight policemen and wounded sixty in Chicago in 1886. Now I lie here in Reicholz, Bavaria, dying of consumption under a false name, in peace at last." [3] Mr. Harris credited himself with having made a careful study of the Haymarket catastrophe, [4] and his well-meaning story, therefore, has strengthened the common belief in Schnaubelt's guilt.

Many others, who suspect the evidence for the State hold that Schnaubelt threw the bomb. George Schilling, who fought so valiantly in behalf of the condemned, is of this opinion because of Schnaubelt's flight and his conviction that the deed was the work of someone in the Chicago movement. [5] Charles Edward Russell, later most sympathetic to the men involved, is likewise convinced of Schnaubelt's guilt. In 1886, he asserts, he had "inside information from persons familiar with the inside of the whole story" which led him to this belief. [6] Unfortunately, he can no longer recall that vital information. It should be noted that many who feel certain that the deed was done by a member of the Chicago movement, do not believe that Schnaubelt was the perpetrator. [7]

Schnaubelt's flight, without question, gives rise to more doubt about his innocence than any other single factor. Frank Harris' version must be rejected since it is not founded upon positive evidence. The testimony of Gilmer and Thompson merits no serious consideration, since it was unsupported and flatly and repeatedly contradicted. Positive evidence implicating Schnaubelt is lacking. There are only assumptions and rumors —and his flight. Did he vanish from Chicago because he was guilty? Or was it because he preferred to be an innocent fugitive charged with the bomb-throwing rather than run the risk of having his neck legally broken by Chicago justice?

After he disappeared from Chicago, the first public indication that Schnaubelt was alive came with the appearance of the following letter in *Die Autonomie* [8] of April 9, 1887:

"Christiania, March, 1887
"WORTHY COMRADES:

"Having found the opportunity to read your organ, 'die Autonomie,' and thus to come in contact again with fellow comrades, I feel moved to publish something about my part in the Chicago Haymarket Affair of May 4 of last year.

"Those perjurers bought by the police would have me seen in the alley 'as my friend Spies lit the fuse of the famous bomb which I then was supposed to have thrown amid the assassins (*Mordbuben*) [by this he means the police] of the Chicago Citizens' Association.' In truth, throughout the whole meeting I found myself on the wagon used as the speakers' platform, which I left only when the police appeared to disperse the gathering. When on the following day I was informed in my workshop of the arrest of my brother-in-law Schwab, I went to the police to get him out on bail, which, however, was refused me. Later I myself was taken from work and questioned, but I was again released. Only when I realized the frenzied bloodthirstiness with which the hounds of law and order persecuted the arrangers of the meeting, I deemed it advisable to place my person in safety. I knew too well the hatred and rascality of these 'heroes of order' to be able to foresee that nothing would keep them back from satisfying their blood-thirstiness. The farce of the trial has proven how right I was. Had I *really* thrown the bomb, I surely would have no cause to be ashamed. I have, however, thought of that more than once. So much for now, in my next letter, I will acquaint you with the experiences of my journey.

"With hearty regards,
"SCHNAUBELT." [9]

Michael Schwab, Schnaubelt's brother-in-law, cast immediate doubt upon the genuineness of this letter. He asserted in the *Vorbote* that "on stylistic grounds alone [it] does not appear to have been written" by Schnaubelt. In answer, the editors of *Die Autonomie* explained that this letter was a personal one. They desired to give its contents wide publicity so that Schnaubelt's innocence might be authoritatively affirmed. Subsequently, a letter designed for publication, it was said, was received. This was published in *Die Autonomie* of June 18, 1887.

Christiania, May, 1887

"WORTHY COMRADES:

"I feel myself called to tell openly my personal experiences of the past year.

"The comrades have either read or heard that a person threw the excellent bomb of May 4 and then vanished, and that this person is 'Rudolph Schnaubelt.'

"The following, however, is the truth: I was present at the meeting in question and was an eye-witness of what took place there. From there I went home, never thinking that this occurrence would have such fatal consequences for me. But man proposes, and police wickedness disposes! *(Aber der mensch denkt und die Polizeischurkerei lenkt!)*

"That our worships, the police, should have become excited, every comrade can believe for himself, but that these beasts should develop such a fury was beyond expectation. That they did not want justice is known, and therefore, I believed that it would be better for me to avoid that 'gang' until their rage should subside. But soon I realized the absurdity of this hope, especially because they would accuse me as the perpetrator. I would not have been afraid at all of the comedy of trial, except for the fact that I was accused as perpetrator without a shred of proof (which they could not have, since I had nothing to do with the bomb), made me lose what little faith I had in the comedy of trial entirely; and as I later saw, with justice.

"The day after the Haymarket occurrence, I went to work without any evil expectations. During the forenoon, my employer informed me that the editors of the *Arbeiter-Zeitung* are arrested and that the place is closed. As a trustee I felt it my duty to find out what I could do, and so I went there. A thieving band of detectives were carrying on like vandals in the print-shop, throwing down set up type, destroying forms, etc. They also found material for the 'Manufacture of bombs,' namely: old type and stereotype!

"My brother-in-law, Mr. Schwab, was also arrested, although he was not present at the Haymarket gathering. I thought that they would let him out on bail, but I was altogether mistaken in that! I went to work again the following day, where I was requested sometime in the forenoon by two police loafers to come with them to their chief. There I underwent an examination and though it is true that I afterwards had to go again, I thought it wiser to get out of the way for a short time. I remained in the neighborhood of Chicago until I received the news that my unworthy person was much sought after. As it has been said, I was supposed to be the one who threw the bomb. That I was found worthy of such an honor is, I grant, very complimentary, but I don't deserve it and I decisively decline it. I thought it would be much 'cooler' than they wanted to make it for me, wherever I might be, and I betook myself to the cool North to await-from there the dropping of the temperature. . . .

> "With revolutionary regards,
> "R. Schnaubelt." [10]

This did not touch upon Schnaubelt's experiences after he decided to leave Chicago, and in the closing words of the letter he said that he might later describe his journey more fully. That Schwab should have questioned the first letter is not surprising. He was undoubtedly in indirect contact with Schnaubelt and he certainly knew that his brother-in-law was then in London. The letter was dated from Christiania. Schwab was evidently not informed that this obvious ruse was adopted to mislead the police. Schnaubelt, as far as it is known, never made public his full story. But Joseph Peukert, a comrade whom he had known some years earlier, has supplied fairly reliable information which supplements Schnaubelt's account.[11]

Peukert was in London sometime at the close of September or early in October, 1886, when he was informed that a "mysterious stranger" wished to see him. The stranger was Schnaubelt. He told Peukert that after he was questioned by the Chicago police, he stayed on a farm on the outskirts of the city. When the cry was raised that he was the bomb-thrower, he first intended to prove how groundless the accusation was. The advice of friends and the actions of the police led him to abandon this decision. He concluded that he would be safer elsewhere, and he struck out for the Canadian border. Avoiding frequented roads, he continued north to Quebec. In the environs of that city he found employment on a farm. Believing that he could trust his employer, Schnaubelt confided in him his desire to get to another part of the world. Schnaubelt was shortly provided with the necessaries—including dye for his hair and beard—for a journey to Europe, and landed safely in London, where he sought out Peukert.

He remained under cover in London until the spring of 1887. It was felt that he would run less risk of detection there than elsewhere if he took the necessary precautions. His presence in the city was kept as secret as possible, and Peukert, through a false address, cared for his correspondence. Before long, however, Schnaubelt gave signs of being psychologically disturbed. Granting his innocence in the Haymarket tragedy, it may be assumed that lack of employment, the strain of his flight, the fear that his Canadian confidant might not remain silent, the developments in Chicago, and the reports in the English press of a reward offered for his discovery,[12] served to upset him. According to Peukert, however, Schnaubelt's morbidity and melancholia quickly disappeared after he secured employment.

For some reason, Peukert suspected that Schnaubelt was being looked for in London. Schnaubelt himself felt that he could not remain permanently in that city. After consideration, he selected the Argentine as his next destination. Meanwhile the search for Schnaubelt apparently grew more pronounced. To draw attention away from London, Schnaubelt published his first letter in *Die Autonomie* under the Christiania dateline. Schwab's blunt assertion that the letter was not genuine, however, spoiled that game. He definitely knew that Schnaubelt was not in Norway.

Evidently early in the spring of 1887, Peukert secured

passage and introductions to comrades in Argentina, and Schnaubelt set sail for Buenos Aires, leaving the second letter for publication in *Die Autonomie* with Peukert. The latter never heard from Schnaubelt again. Malatesta, then living in the Argentine, informed Peukert years later that Schnaubelt arrived safe and sound. After the Chicago executions, however, he became extremely nervous and unwilling to meet people. He mistrusted Malatesta and his friends, and they shortly after broke off all relationship.[13]

What happened to Schnaubelt after this is not definitely known. It is sometimes said that he went to Mexico, where he remained until his death. According to another account, he returned to Europe. Lucy Parsons asserts that he came back to the United States, and that at the time Frank Harris had him penning his "death-bed confession"—whenever that might be—he was on the Pacific coast.[14]

Nothing in all of this proves Schnaubelt's culpability. Two considerations cast doubt upon his innocence: his flight from Chicago and his later attacks of nervousness and melancholia. These might be the work of a disturbed conscience, and they fit in with the portrait of the guilty fugitive. Yet, his departure from the scene of the bombing is at best negative evidence. Chicago, after May 4, was not a healthy environment for anyone related to those charged with the crime. Had he remained, the number of "anarchist martyrs" would have been increased by one. To flee might strengthen the presumption of guilt, but it would at least assure his life. His distressed state in London and in Buenos Aires may be explained without assuming that he participated in the bombing. He was in a new country among strangers, and was forced to lose his identity. He was, after all, whether guilty or not, a fugitive. On the basis of the known evidence, there is no solid reason to conclude that Schnaubelt threw the bomb.

With the same readiness with which the police pinned the bombing upon the "anarchists," radicals have charged municipal and private police with the crime. Parsons, for example, laid the bombing upon the shoulders of the police. Some present-day communists, self-constituted heirs of the militant tradition of the Chicago revolutionaries, are in thorough agreement with this. "Everyone . . . knows," writes Mr. Bimba, "the Haymarket explosion was the work of the Chicago police." [15] In terms of motivation and the known activities of *agents provocateurs*, radicals have not found it difficult to make out a case for this hypothesis. The history of the radical movement, they argue, shows many instances where police agents have perpetrated even worse deeds. That detectives and Pinkertons had been spying upon the Chicago revolutionaries and their movement is incontestable. That a bomb, were one to explode in Chicago, would be immediately taken to be a product of the propaganda of the revolutionaries is self-evident. Furthermore, they assert, many Chicagoans would regard the failure of the eight-hour movement and the destruction of the radical movement with undisguised pleasure. Both these ends could be attained through a display of extremist tactics which could be ascribed to the social-revolutionaries. Their activities in the labor movement supplied the link through which the eight-hour movement could be attacked. Thus, the logical setting is established for a police or Pinkerton bomb-thrower.

The *agent provocateur* hypothesis is not limited to radical circles. Henry Demarest Lloyd also inclined to it for "reasons" which were "cogent" with him. [16] There are stories in apparent confirmation of this hypothesis, but they are distressingly vague and unreliable. It was said, for example, that Louis F. Post was informed by a leading New Jersey attorney, "that a Chicago reporter, to the lawyer well known, and at one time on a New York paper, had, while in his cups . . . , boasted that he was paid by some Chicago journals to take a vacation from that city for the present and until the Anarchists' cases were settled as he knew who threw the bomb, and the organs of monopoly did not want him around." [17] Such tales, however, prove nothing.

Many of those who might be expected to snatch at the

agent provocateur hypothesis because it completely exculpates the eight men, repudiate this explanation of the bombing. Dyer D. Lum bluntly wrote that it was "puerile" to ascribe "the Haymarket bomb to a Pinkerton." [18] Max Nettlau, the leading historian of modern Anarchism, also rejects the *agent provocateur* hypothesis. Finally, it is somewhat unlikely that the Chicago police or Pinkertons were so wholly inhuman that they would sacrifice the lives of their own associates to wreck the radical movement. This end could have been accomplished with less disastrous consequences. The facts necessary to affirm the *agent provocateur* hypothesis have never appeared, but as long as the bomb-thrower is unknown, it cannot be completely excluded as the solution to the problem.

Another suggested answer to the puzzle involves the police indirectly. This assumes that the bomb was thrown by a workingman, free from all connection with the revolutionary movement, who had been harshly treated by the Chicago gendarmerie. Police tactics during labor disturbances for many years before 1886 were notoriously brutal. Pacification with club and revolver does not breed good-feeling, and there was a large number of aggrieved police victims. The bomb, therefore, could have been the work of a victimized workingman.

No one felt more strongly than Governor Altgeld that this was the proper solution to the problem. "To my mind," he wrote to Lloyd in 1893, "the police brutality is most important since it furnished an explanation and a motive." [19] With characteristic disdain of the hornet's nest he was stirring up, he made the same point so bluntly in his pardon message that it became an indictment of Capt. Bonfield.

"While some men may tamely submit to being clubbed and seeing their brothers shot down," he wrote, "there are some who will resent it and will nurture a spirit of hatred and seek revenge for themselves, and the occurrences that preceded the Haymarket tragedy indicate that the bomb was thrown by someone who, instead of acting on the advice of anybody, was simply seeking personal revenge for having been clubbed, and that Capt. Bonfield is the man who is really responsible for the deaths of the police officers." [20]

Though this hypothesis does offer "an explanation and a motive," it suffers from many vital weaknesses. Is it likely that a workingman, wholly unrelated to the revolutionary movement would employ a bomb for retaliation upon the police? And, if so, was the bomb of his own manufacture, or was it one of Lingg's? The very instrument of destruction chosen, throws suspicion upon someone other than an ill-used worker. It is only remotely possible that a workingman, having no connection with any of the social-revolutionary groups, might have picked up one of Lingg's bombs at the time they were so inexplicably deposited at Neff's Hall. Finally, the necessary positive evidence is lacking. The rejection of Gov. Altgeld's explanation of the bomb-throwing does not absolve Capt. Bonfield from blame. The latter's unwarranted presence at the meeting unquestionably led to the bomb-throwing.

As late as 1933, another suspect made his appearance for the first time. Early in that year a German anarchist, Carl Nold,[21] was corresponding with several old-timers who had been in Chicago in 1886-1887, concerning a reunion there during the existence of the World's Fair. In the answer from one of them he found the following sentence: "The old timers are mostly dead, including the bomb-thrower, who died in 1924 in the Poor-hospital in Blackwell's Island, without leaving anything behind." Carl Nold, well acquainted with the history of the radical movement in this country, was surprised by this. "This is the first time I heard that the bomb-thrower was known to anybody," he wrote. "I hope to be able to find out more about it." [22] He finally learned from one of the oldest living "comrades," [23] who knew this suspect, that he was George Schwab, a German shoemaker. His informant had "no proof that he was the bomb-thrower." [24] This most recent candidate for the honors—the indigent shoemaker—must be rejected.

What of the bomb-thrower so definitely referred to in the

telegram received by Black only the day before the execution? That message, it will be recalled, stated that August P. Wagener, who sent it, possessed proof that the condemned men were innocent and that the actual criminal was located in New York City.[25] It now appears quite certain that this telegram provides no clue to the actual criminal. It only leads one into an extremely ugly chapter in the history of the New York social-revolutionary movement.

Several wholly unscrupulous members of the I.W.P.A. or the Social Revolutionary Club of New York expressed their questionable revolutionary fervor in the form of an insurance "racket." They insured on a dwelling, set fire to it, and then collected from the insurance company. Before being exposed in the spring of 1886, they were responsible for some thirty-four fires in New York and Brooklyn. A good number of the members of this arson ring were arrested, and finally found guilty of defrauding an insurance company.[26] Mr. Wagener was associated in a legal capacity with Franz Mayhoff, one of the men implicated. In November of 1887, while Mayhoff was serving a four and a half year prison term in Sing Sing, he made an affidavit in which he asserted that in January, 1887, he was introduced to one Klemana Schuetz,[27] an anarchist. The latter informed Mayhoff that he had been forced to leave Chicago about the time of the Haymarket episode. Several weeks later, according to Mayhoff, Schuetz urged Mayhoff to assist him kill a man so as to rob him of $3,000. Schuetz also boasted that he had thrown the Haymarket bomb. Subsequently, Mayhoff declared, Schuetz showed him two bombs and swore that if the condemned men died on the gallows, Grinnell and the jury would be killed "like dogs." [28]

Little faith can be placed in these charges, since Schuetz was the principal witness against Mayhoff when the latter was convicted for attempting to defraud the Greenwich Insurance Company. Both the affidavit and the telegram based upon it, were probably produced by three different but related motives: Mayhoff's desire for revenge upon Schuetz; the hope that his story would reduce his stay in Sing Sing; and its employment by some New York comrades in a last minute effort to postpone the executions. Mr. Wagener's rôle was quite innocent and well-meaning. He accepted the affidavit at face value, and possessed no additional information implicating Schuetz. There is no choice but to abandon this solution to the mystery.[29]

When the motion for a new trial was argued, an affidavit was introduced which pointed to still another bomb-thrower. The affiant, John Philip Deluse of Indianapolis, swore that he believed he had seen and spoken to the bomb-thrower before May 4, 1886. Early in May, 1886, a man carrying a satchel entered his saloon in Indianapolis. While drinking, he asked several questions concerning the condition of the labor movement there. Informed that everything was "quiet," the stranger volunteered the information that he had come from New York and was going on to Chicago. Pointing to his satchel, he is reported to have said: "You will hear of some trouble there [Chicago] very soon. I have got something here that will work. You will hear of it." As he left, he raised his bag, and, pointing to it once more, announced, "You will hear of it soon." After May 4, Mr. Deluse concluded that his strange customer was the bomb-thrower.[30] Nothing more is known about this mysterious stranger, and the story probably merits no more consideration than the telling of it.

A week before November 11, a carpenter at Homestead, Penn.,[31] fell from a roof and broke his neck. It was reported that this unhappy person, Thomas Owen [32] by name, either confessed before dying that he threw the Haymarket bomb, or earlier informed a fellow-worker that he had stood next to the man who hurled it.[33] According to one account Owen declared before dying: "I was at the Haymarket riot and am an anarchist and say that I threw a bomb in that riot." [34] Investigation apparently showed that Thomas Owen had been in Chicago around May 4, and that he was regarded as an anarchist. Of the different versions of Mr. Owen's confession, the one that seems most plausible is that he was present at the Haymarket

gathering and that he saw someone near him hurl the bomb.
It also seems likely that Owen disclosed this long before his
fatal accident, and enjoined silence upon his confidant. How
much of the tale is to be ascribed to reportorial imagination
cannot be said. It is possible that Owen sought to save the
condemned men by manufacturing a "confession" when he
was about to die. In any case, both he and the reporters should
have known that only one bomb was thrown. Mr. Owen cannot seriously be suspected of the bomb-throwing.

The eight men found guilty of the murder of Degan
protested their profound ignorance of the identity of the
criminal agent. It was never charged during the trial that any
of them perpetrated the deed, but at least one story has gone
the rounds which makes Louis Lingg the bomb-thrower.[35] Of
all eight men, it is true that Lingg alone was temperamentally
fitted to commit the deed. He failed to express any regret that
the bomb had been thrown, and had he been guilty, it is likely
that he would have proudly admitted it. There is no basis for
regarding him as the criminal agent.

If any of the eight had any knowledge of the bomb-
thrower, they kept it a secret remarkably well. Fischer, pointedly
asked by William Salter who the bomb-thrower was, replied:
"I don't know, Mr. Salter, but I suppose it was some excited
workingman." [36] Neebe, asked the same question in 1890,
answered that he thought some "crank" did it.[37]

Unless the bomb-thrower was unusually discreet and never
revealed his act, there is some ground for assuming that the
identity of the bomb-thrower was at one time known. There
are hints that people in key positions have never disclosed all
they know. It is rumored that someone, now on the Pacific
Coast, definitely knows who threw the bomb. Another person
lays claims to this knowledge, and promises to make it public
on the fiftieth anniversary of the Haymarket tragedy. When
Robert Reitzel returned to Detroit after the burial of his four
comrades, he is said to have informed a Dr. U. Hartung that
"the Bomb-thrower is known, but let us forget about it; even if

he had confessed, the lives of our comrades could not have been saved." [38]

Perhaps the bomb-thrower died immediately after May 4, and his secret was buried with him. One version of the events of May 4 follows this scheme. According to it, the bomb was thrown by a Chicago comrade by the name of Reinold Krüger, familiarly known as "Big" Krüger to distinguish him from an August Krüger also in the movement. He is supposed to have been present at the Monday night conspiracy meeting, and to have been killed by the police on May 5, during one of the disturbances which followed the fatal fourth. [39]

It may be possible some day to say, without fear of contradiction, "so-and-so threw the bomb." At present, the personal identity of the man who committed the deed remains a mystery. Though he cannot be identified by name at this moment, there is reason for believing that he was associated with the Chicago movement. There is no certainty in this assertion, but the identification of the bomb-thrower with the social-revolutionary movement is more than an extreme possibility. There is more reason to assume that the man who hurled the bomb was a member of the Chicago movement rather than a disgruntled workingman, a tool of police or capitalists, or a "crank." Robert Reitzel's statement, the Krüger story, the rumors that the identity of the bomb-thrower was known to social-revolutionaries, as well as so much else that has been considered, point to this conclusion.

Before much news had been received from Chicago, Johann Most assumed that the bomb was thrown by someone associated with the movement. [40]

"Among the crowd," he wrote, "there was one of those few who took the advice of the anarchists to heart, in order to be in a position to defend himself eventually. This man had a bomb with him, and as he saw that hundreds of human lives, as well as his own, were in unavoidable danger from the raving police, he let fly his hand-grenade among the privileged murderers." [41] Most regarded the bomb as a product of the Chicago movement. In his long editorial, "The Chicago Bomb," this is patent. Considering the episode from the "juridical" and the "strategical" points of view, he concluded that the throwing of the bomb was fully justifiable, since it was thrown in defense. The social-revolutionaries had urged this type of action against police aggression. He found the bomb an enormous "success" with reference to the military tactics of the social revolution. In the "Civil War" of the future, Most saw such pocket bombs playing a vital rôle. Having decided that the Chicago bomb was "legally justified and militarily advantageous," he paid "All respects to the one who produced it and used it." There is not the slightest hint in this that the bomb was thrown by an *agent provocateur*.[42]

Most's editorial expressions were probably in large part the product of wish-fulfillment. He hoped rather than knew that the bomb bore some relationship to the revolutionary movement. But he was also—assuming that he had no direct information from Chicago—arguing from the logic of the situation. In this he was thoroughly justified. For years the revolutionaries had been recommending the use of force in answer to police aggression. For years they had urged the employment of dynamite and bombs. The Haymarket meeting was the ideal setting for a bomb to be thrown. It was a harmless gathering attacked by police. Both motive and explanation for the deed are there.

This does not mean, of course, that the bomb was the outcome of a conspiracy to inaugurate the social revolution. It cannot be denied that a scheme had been adopted by some of the social-revolutionaries providing for defense for themselves and workers against the police. Nor can it be denied that some individuals among the social-revolutionaries manufactured bombs. Most of the leaders and members of the movement were not temperamentally equipped for actually carrying out the deeds they urged in their written and spoken propaganda. In fact, they were not realists enough to understand fully the implications of what they advocated. There was, however, a handful of persons in the movement who would not stop short with verbal violence. In a movement which sanctified propaganda by deed, there undoubtedly were a few present who had the courage of their convictions, whose idealism completely justified recourse to bullets or dynamite. How many men of this type there were, one cannot say. Unquestionably their number was very small. But to assert that there was not a single one in the movement is patently ridiculous. There undoubtedly were one or two others cut out in Lingg's pattern. Engel's associates, it will be recalled, found Parsons, Spies and Schwab tame. Whatever logic can be read into the Haymarket episode leads one to conclude that it is highly probable that the bomb was a product of the Chicago movement. Of course, the possibility still remains that its relationship to the social-revolutionary movement was wholly casual and in no way causal.[43]

It is no longer necessary to whitewash the Chicago movement of all responsibility for the sake of those who were charged with the crime, and more than one physical-force revolutionary of the old school now credits the movement with the deed.[44] Even Lucy Parsons, in her strong insistence that the bomb-thrower is unknown, does not categorically deny that he might have been associated with the movement.[45] The leading living historian of Anarchism, Dr. Max Nettlau, prefers this interpretation of the Haymarket episode.[46] He has written that he sees no good reason for ascribing the bomb to anyone outside of the movement, and tells of a contemporary letter which places responsibility for the bomb upon a member of the movement. Dr. Nettlau, it should be observed, never set eyes on this letter. Nor has anyone who actually saw it recorded its existence. His knowledge of it came from Victor Dave who informed him that William Morris, to whom the letter was addressed, showed it to him. Dr. Nettlau received this information immediately after the letter is supposed to have been received. Dave was then intimate both with Morris and Nettlau, and the latter sees no reason for doubting either the existence of the epistle or Dave's version of its contents. A subsequent search for the letter among the correspondence of Morris and the *Commonweal,* which Morris was then editing, failed to disclose it. But the probability that the letter is genuine is supported by the assertion that it was written by William Holmes who was then in constant communication with William Morris. The existence of the letter may also be confirmed by an independent source.[47] Many people intimately acquainted with the Haymarket Affair have never even heard of the letter. Lucy Parsons bluntly denies its genuineness. She points out that she knew both Holmes and William Morris extremely well, and that neither of them had ever mentioned it.[48]

Genuine or not, and the first seems likely, the version of the bomb-throwing which the letter contains fits in with the available data. According to that version, a small group of social-revolutionaries decided to meet police violence with force and to use bombs. This decision, however, was recalled on May 4, and one member of the group who was out of the city during the day was not aware of the change in plan. Consequently, when the police appeared at the gathering which he attended, he hurled a bomb, expecting the others to follow suit. He is also supposed to have expected an uprising of the people as a result of this resistance to the police.[49]

Whether William Holmes, if he penned the letter, *was writing out of intimate knowledge, or whether he was simply offering a reasonable explanation of how the bomb came to be thrown in the light of the plan adopted by Engel's group, cannot be determined.* This question is, of course, a critical one. If the letter is genuine and Holmes was confiding to Morris positive information which he had secured from someone on the "inside," then the bomb-thrower was a member of the movement. On the other hand, it may be that Holmes was merely relating *how he thought* the bomb came to be thrown. In this event, Holmes' version is hypothetical and proves nothing.

Even if the letter be discounted, the setting of the bomb-throwing and the logic of the whole situation compel one to conclude that the bomb did not violate the propaganda of the movement, and was probably a product of it. This judgment, however, does not permit the conclusion *that the eight individuals convicted of the murder of Degan were guilty. On the basis of the reliable evidence, they must be considered innocent.*

NOTES CHAPTER XXIII

1. See above, pp. 264-271.
2. Definitive American edition, New York, 1920.
3. *Ibid.*, p. 9.
4. See the Foreword, *ibid.*, pp. 5-6.
5. Interview with Schilling.
6. Letter to author, April 7, 1930.
7. See below, pp. 523-524.
8. It was a communist-anarchist fortnightly paper published in London.
9. Author's translation.
10. Author's translation.
11. Joseph Peukert, *Erinnerungen eines Proletariers aus der revolutionären Arbeiterbewegung,* Berlin, 1913.
12. Peukert says it ranged from $10,000 to $30,000.
13. *Ibid.*, pp. 252-256, 268-269; *Die Autonomie,* August 3, 1889. This last contains a letter from Peukert defending himself against charges concerning something else, several paragraphs of which are given over to his relations with Schnaubelt. For an interesting and critical comment on Peukert and his volume of reminiscences, see Karl Kautsky, "Peukerts Erinnerungen," *Die neue Zeit,* March 20, 1914, pp. 924-932.
14. If Lucy Parsons means by this the time that Frank Harris wrote *The Bomb,* it would be as late as 1907. In a letter to Carl Nold, dated January 17, 1933, she writes with utter disregard for soft words and orthodox spelling:
    "Frank Harris 'Bomb' (which was a lie from cover to cover) had Schneb [Schnaubelt] making his 'Schbelt's death bed confession' in Monheim [Mannheim], Germany.
    "I write a most scathing denuncion [denunciation] on that lieing fraud, also of E. G. [Emma Goldman] endorcement of it, as being of 'more importance to the Anarchist movement than the monument in Waldheim Cemetary.'
    "At the time Harris had Schnabelt 'making his death bed confession,' I knew he was alive, because I personally had met him on the Pacific [Coast] at that time."
    In speaking to the author in 1933, Mrs. Parsons was less definite. She said that she was certain that Schnaubelt was living

in California *after The Bomb* was published, and that she and his sister, Michael Schwab's wife had a good laugh over the story in Harris' book. The rumor that someone in California, whose name cannot be divulged, actually knows who threw the bomb, may be linked with Schnaubelt's alleged presence there. There is no attempt to deal here with all the information and misinformation which the author has gathered about Schnaubelt through conversations with members of the radical movement.

15. *The Communist,* vol. 13, no. 11, November, 1934, p. 1182; see also, *The Daily Worker,* April 28, 1934, April 27, 1935.

16. Lloyd, *op. cit.,* vol. 1, p. 106.

17. *Social Science,* vol. 1, no. 15, October 12, 1887, p. 9. General Parsons, the brother of Albert Parsons, told this story in an interview first appearing in the New York *World.*

18. *Alarm,* December 29, 1888.

19. Quoted in Lloyd, *op. cit.,* vol. 1, p. 107.

20. *Pardon Message,* p. 23.

21. He died in Detroit, October 15, 1934.

22. Letter from Carl Nold to Lucy Parsons, January 12, 1933.

23. Claus Timmerman by name.

24. Letter of Carl Nold, March 1, 1933. Lucy Parsons, before she was informed by Nold of this, wrote to him in the letter already quoted:

    "Regarding that guy—that wise guy, who had the bomb-thrower die in a hospital on Blackwell's Island in 1924. Please tell him that this bomb-thrower stuff has been exploited by sensation mongers until it is noisating [nauseating]"

25. See above, pp. 459 *et seq.*

26. *Liberty,* vol. 3, no. 26, March 27, pp. 1, 8, vol. 4, no. 1, April 17, pp. 1, 4, no. 2, May 1, p. 5, no. 3, May 22, 1886, p. 8; New York *Sun,* May 3, 1886; W. C. Hart, *Confessions of an Anarchist,* London, 1906, pp. 10-12. The whole business seems to have been disclosed by M. Bachman. Tucker gave it publicity in *Liberty,* and criticized Most very sharply for not openly repudiating the men and their deeds.

27. Also given as Klimann Scheutz.

28. According to another account, Schuetz showed little concern for the prisoners.

29. Detroit *Evening Journal,* November 11, 1887; Chicago *Tribune,* November 11, 1887; conversations with individuals in the movement. Corroborative information was also supplied by Mr. Klaus of New York City who spoke to Wagener on this point.

30. *Brief and Argument,* p. 285; *Abstract of Record,* vol. 1, pp. 28-29.

31. Some accounts give Pittsburgh.

32. Or Owens.

33. New York *Tribune* and Chicago *Inter Ocean,* November 5, 1887, give the first and the New York *Times,* November 5, 1887, the second version.

34. New York *Tribune*, November 5, 1887.
35. According to this tale Lingg escaped an earlier arrest, when a meeting place of the "anarchists" was raided, by donning the garments of a charwoman and setting to work cleaning the floors.
36. Quoted in Lloyd, *op. cit.*, vol. 1, p. 88.
37. *The Open Court*, vol. 4, September 25, 1890, p. 2538. His questioner was Dr. Paul Carus. When further asked whether Lingg was the crank, Neebe said that he did not know since he did not meet Lingg until after the latter's arrest.
38. Letter of Carl Nold to Lucy Parsons, Feb. 6, 1933.
39. *Freiheit*, July 24, 1886.
40. *Freiheit*, May 8, 1886.
41. *Ibid.*, May 15, 1886.
42. *Idem.*
43. It can be noted in this connection that Charles Edward Russell relates that he undertook an investigation of the revolutionary groups in Chicago for the New York *World* after the bombing and found that the vast mass of the so-called revolutionaries would never actually practise propaganda by deed, but that there were some two dozen men equipped with both the desire and strength of purpose who would not hesitate to commit such a deed. Russell, *loc. cit.*, p. 411.
44. Dr. B. R. of Chicago, for example.
45. Interviews with Lucy Parsons.
46. Nettlau, *op. cit.*, p. 387.
47. Mr. Samuel Klaus of New York City claims to have heard of the letter from a source presumably unrelated to Dr. Nettlau.
48. Interviews with Lucy Parsons. Schilling, too, is extremely skeptical.
49. Nettlau, *op. cit.*, p. 387; a letter from Dr. Nettlau which the author examined gives a much fuller version of his source of information and also expresses more strongly his conviction that the bombing was a product of the movement.

XXIV. CONCLUSION

THE Haymarket bomb was responsible for the first major "red-scare" in American history, and produced a campaign of "red-baiting" which has rarely been equalled. So expertly was this campaign waged that it molded the popular mind for years to come, and played its part in conditioning the mass response to the imaginary threat of the "social revolution" frequently displayed in the United States since 1886. It led to the immediate popular condemnation of Socialism, Communism and Anarchism. Of these, for obvious reasons, the last was subjected to the most abuse. The common conception of the anarchist as a ragged, unwashed, long-haired, wild-eyed fiend, armed with smoking revolver and bomb—to say nothing of the dagger he sometimes carried between his teeth—dates from this period. The term "Anarchism" became a verbal bludgeon with which anything disreputable or mad was attacked, and "anarchist" became an epithet of defamation synonymous with "vermin," "rattlesnake," "cutthroat."

Four years after the executions, the Supreme Court of Illinois held that in accusing someone of being an anarchist, the Chicago *News* "laid itself open to damages for libel." The Court pointed out "That a man may be brought into hatred, contempt, or ridicule by professing vicious, degrading, or absurd principles . . . seems too plain for argument; and in a community where anarchy is clearly seen to be . . . the enemy of all government and the natural foe of each good citizen, the courts will protect a man from being charged with fellowship in this unpleasant school of philosophy." [1] Years later, at the

St. Louis Exposition of 1904, portraits of Parsons, Spies, Engel, Fischer, Lingg, Fielden, Neebe and Schwab were exhibited in a "gallery of notorious criminals—among highwaymen, murderers, robbers, bank embezzlers and car-barn bandits. . . ." [2]

The various proposals made in 1886 for ridding the country of anarchists and undesirable aliens did not vanish with the executions. Early in 1888, Congressman Adams of Chicago, introduced a bill "to provide for the removal of dangerous aliens from the territory of the United States." [3] In the following year a measure was proposed in the House to prevent "avowed" anarchists or nihilists from entering the United States, even though they had formerly been residents. Similar provisions failed to become part of the immigration laws of 1891. Three years later, Senator Hill presented a bill to prevent the entrance of and to deport anarchists. In the same year, Representative Stone proposed to define by law an anarchist as a person belonging to an organization "which provides . . . for the taking of human life unlawfully or for the unlawful destruction of buildings or other property where the taking of human life would be the probable result. . . ." The attempt of an anarchist, thus defined, upon the life of a government official was to be punished with death. These measures were in part inspired by the assassination of President Carnot of France, who was stabbed by the Italian anarchist Caserio. But they also stemmed from the hysteria created by the Haymarket catastrophe, which called forth the first efforts to secure national legislation against Anarchism.

The assassination of McKinley by Czolgosz, popularly regarded as a typical anarchist, produced a veritable flood of plans to free the nation from the anarchist menace. Senator Hoar seriously suggested that an uninhabited island be purchased to which all anarchists were to be banished, and Senator Hawley was reported to have offered "$1,000 for a good shot at an Anarchist." [4] The anti-anarchist war was also waged in the State legislatures, and in 1902 New York passed a law drastically punishing the advocacy of anarchistic principles and the publication and distribution of anarchistic literature.[5] In the following year, there came the first Federal legislation directed against anarchists. The immigration act of March 3, 1903, banned alien anarchists from entering the United States, and prohibited their naturalization.[6] In the subsequent acts of 1906 and 1907 these principles were reiterated, and naturalization was more rigidly forbidden to anarchists.[7] Thus passed the tradition that this country was a haven for the politically oppressed elsewhere.

The most active baiting of radicals took place naturally enough in Chicago, as has been seen. There were "sporadic outbursts" of the revolutionary movement in the city, but it was regarded as thoroughly under control until the radicals decided to celebrate, on August 5, 1900, the assassination of King Humbert I of Italy by the anarchist Bresci. In attempting to prevent the celebration, the police precipitated a riot in which thirty persons, ten of them children, were injured. This occurrence led to discussions of the Haymarket catastrophe, and the Chicago *Inter Ocean* observed that "The anarchists had been held in complete subjection in Chicago since 1886 until the outbreak yesterday." The police declared that they had learned an invaluable lesson in 1886: the revolutionary movement must be carefully observed and crushed if it showed signs of growth.[8] The events of May 4 did not pass quickly from Chicago's memory, and whenever the occasion offered they were employed to prevent the dissemination of radical doctrines. Thus, at the close of 1902, the mayor of the city was warned that if he permitted Emma Goldman to lecture publicly, he was inviting "another Haymarket tragedy." [9]

In New York City the radicals were also harassed. Here the silencing of Johann Most was early made the objective of the anti-anarchist campaign which the bomb inspired. He was regarded as the high-priest of the revolutionary movement, and his arrest shortly after May 4 was expected. The authorities hoped to have him prosecuted with the other defendants for the murder of Degan, but they failed. He was arrested once more in November, 1887, after delivering an alleged "incendiary" address on the twelfth dealing with the executions. He did not receive a fair trial and was sentenced to a year's imprisonment. His case was unsuccessfully appealed, and he served his term in 1891-92.[10]

Morris Hillquit writes that the Haymarket bomb "was practically the closing chapter in the history of Anarchism as an active element in the labor movement of this country."[11] This assertion has a triple implication: that the social-revolutionary movement with its two foci in Chicago and New York was distinctly and unquestionably anarchist in nature; that it played a vital rôle in the labor movement; and, finally, that the Haymarket bomb led to its rapid disintegration. The first has been shown to be false by a study of the "doctrines" of the social-revolutionary movement. The second is only true in so far as certain Chicago leaders were labor-minded and had labor affiliations, and it does not hold for the New York movement. The third is not borne out by the evidence, although even later day American anarchists have frequently asserted that since 1887 "no English oral agitation" of significant scope "has been carried on."[12] It is, of course, erroneous to assume that the social-revolutionary movement ever did have national scope, or that its English element was powerful.

Despite the buffeting it received at the hands of the police and the press, the revolutionary movement in Chicago was not destroyed.[13] Nor does it appear that it suffered irreparable injuries elsewhere. Contemporaries who were certain that the outcome of the "anarchist" case was resulting in the decline of radical movements of all shades throughout the country were mistaken.[14] On the contrary, radicalism in general probably received a stimulus, because the whole affair induced a widespread discussion of revolutionary theories. However mistaken these discussions frequently were, they were at times intelligent and constituted to some extent an educative process.[15] A Boston radical reported in 1888 that "the martyrs . . . did not die in vain!" The executions of November 11 "aroused so deep an indignation here [Boston] that it gave the anarchists an opportunity to engage in public agitation." Benjamin Tucker founded an anarchist club, which drew large crowds at its fortnightly gatherings, and was invited to read a paper before "The Round Table," a circle of intellectuals of social position.[16] The affair inspired debates on Anarchism in Knights of Labor Assemblies.[17] In Chicago the bomb-throwing led to a recognition of the need for adjusting industrial ills. Under the leadership of William Salter a series of economic conferences between business men and workingmen addressed by representatives of both groups were held in 1888.[18] Investigations of working-class conditions in Chicago which occurred about the same time were related to this development.[19]

The nature and outcome of the trial in some cases won the radicals a more sympathetic hearing than they would have normally received. William Holmes felt that the whole case resulted in a broadening of agitation which augmented the movement "ten-fold." [20] It has been asserted that in the East after the Haymarket episode "the Anarchist movement in New York and adjacent cities grew stronger than ever." [21] The size of the gatherings in Chicago commemorating the executions further makes it clear that the revolutionary movement was not shattered in that city.[22] It became, however, more definitely anarchistic, and in 1893 a number of Chicago "comrades" issued a call for a convention of anarchists which met in Chicago at the close of September. In number of delegates, groups represented and subjects discussed it does not compare very unfavorably with the Pittsburgh Congress, even though it was banned by the municipal authorities and the meetings were held secretly.[23]

The Haymarket Affair did have a positive effect upon the nature of the revolutionary movement in Chicago. It led to the abandonment of the advocacy of propaganda by deed and a reduction of the emphasis upon force. When the *Alarm* reappeared on November 5, 1887, under Dyer D. Lum's guidance, a leading editorial declared that force was not essential "to a revolution, nor is its use generally successful." A revolution is not made by "Barricades, revolts, riots . . . ; they are but incidents of one." The files of the *Alarm* during the remainder of its existence show that greater reliance was placed upon the efficacy of social "evolution," and that the use of force was urged primarily in answer to aggression. The *Arbeiter-Zeitung* during the same period seems to have been moving slowly toward authoritarian Socialism, and the *Vorbote,* as early as the summer of 1886, was bitterly attacked by the *Freiheit* for being receptive to political action.[24] Johann Most, however, did not repudiate his earlier position. By the 'nineties, it may be added, both the New York and Chicago movements became more distinctly anarcho-communist, due largely to the influence of Kropotkin.[25]

Few individuals were as profoundly affected by the Haymarket Affair as Henry Demarest Lloyd. In a sense, it constituted a turning point in his life.[26] In his note-book for 1887 he added to Parsons' cry, "Let the voice of the people be heard!" the words, *"The voice of the people shall be heard."* He felt that the four men "have died in vain, unless out of their death come a resurrection and a new life. . . . They have been killed because property, authority, and public believed that they came to bring not reform but revolution, not peace but a sword. . . ." After 1887, "he took his place on the side of the working men."

"In all issues," he said, "the principle of but one side can be right. The workingman is often wrong, but his is always the right side." The whole affair led him to ponder deeply the question of force.[27] William Salter, too, was deeply influenced by the "anarchist" case. It induced him to study Anarchism with some care,[28] and broadened his interest in working-class problems.

The affair probably did as much as any single factor to make Emma Goldman an ardent revolutionary. The bomb-throwing and the trial led her to become acquainted with the literature of Anarchism. The executions unnerved her completely and, she writes, "The next morning I woke as from a long illness. . . . I had a distinct sensation that something new and wonderful had been born in my soul. A great ideal, a burning faith, a determination to dedicate myself to the memory of my martyred comrades, to make their cause my own, to make known to the world their beautiful lives and heroic deaths." [29] Alexander Berkman, whose attempt upon Frick's life is a notable case of propaganda by deed, admired Lingg, and was convinced by "the hanging of the Chicago anarchists . . . that America was as despotic as Russia." [30] John Turner, English labor leader and radical, is reputed to have become an anarchist as a result of the Haymarket Affair.[31] Eugene Debs and Bill Haywood were both significantly impressed by it; the former spoke of the men involved as "the first martyrs in the cause of industrial freedom . . ." [32] Voltairine de Cleyre publicly testified that she was made an anarchist by "The Hanging in Chicago." [33] How many individuals were similarly affected, can never be determined, but it is safe to say that their number was not inconsequential.[34]

The Haymarket Affair created America's first revolutionary martyrs. Revolutionaries of almost every classification the world over have, since 1887, cherished the memory of and paid homage to the eight victims of the "anarchist" trial, and especially to the five who met with death. In 1888, Peter Kropotkin declared that the "commemoration of the Chicago martyrs has almost acquired the same importance as the commemoration of the Paris Commune." [35] Their speeches in court have been countless times reprinted in most modern languages. Their pictures have been hung in the homes and gathering-places of radicals. November 11, has become a consecrated day, and has been appropriately observed in Europe and America with a religious constancy and fidelity. Waldheim has become a place of pilgrimage. The State of Illinois made its contribution to the development of the "martyr cult" whose appearance distinguished the European revolutionary movement in the closing years of the nineteenth century.[36]

With the passage of time, Spies, Parsons, Engel, Neebe, Fischer, Schwab, Fielden, and Lingg also became, to a certain degree, labor heroes. This development came more or less naturally when the Haymarket episode was utilized to attack the labor movement at large, and a considerable portion of the working-class defended the men involved. It is not without significance that more copies of the speeches of the "Chicago martyrs" were purchased in the 'eighties and 'nineties by labor organizations than by radical groups.[37] Present-day communists who proudly claim the "tradition of the Haymarket" regard the eight men as "experienced working-class fighters. . . . solidly committed to a united and revolutionary struggle of the working class to overthrow capitalism." [38]

It is generally assumed that the Haymarket bomb adversely affected not only the eight-hour movement but the entire American labor movement. Powderly was convinced that it "did more injury to the good name of labor than all the strikes of that year, and turned public sentiment against labor organizations . . ." [39] Gompers felt that the trade-union movement "suffered for years" through the unwisdom of the Chicago "anarchists." [40] Prof. Ware strongly implies that the affair was a significant factor in the decline of the Knights of Labor because Parsons was identified with the Order and because the bomb "abruptly alienated" public "sympathy, which had grown steadily in favor of the Knights and the trade unions . . ." [41] As early as May 11, 1886, the Chicago *Herald* declared that the "bomb broke up" the eight-hour movement, arguing that the "necessity of putting down Anarchists has made public sentiment impatient with disputes as to hours and wages." The *Arbeiter-Zeitung* early ascribed the collapse of the movement to the bomb.[42] The journal of the Chicago Knights of Labor similarly felt that it "actually ended the [eight-hour] struggle among a great number of trades and occupations. . . ." [43] Gompers was certain that it "killed the eight-hour movement" of 1886, and "halted" the eight-hour program of the American Federation of Labor until 1890.[44] It has been asserted that the "failure of four-fifths of those who struck was in large measure due to the fatal bomb. . . ." [45]

Though these judgments have been so widely accepted that they are almost traditional, some of them may be questioned. It is doubtful whether the fact that Parsons was a Knight caused members to leave the Order. It is more likely that the official stand of the Order on the whole affair, dictated by Powderly, produced a wider revulsion of feeling in working-class circles and was responsible for some loss of membership. It undeniably provided another source for schism in the Order.[46] The loss of "public sympathy" for the Knights, if measured in terms of newspaper and periodical opinion, is perhaps to be more accurately ascribed to the tremendous expansion of the Order and to the recognition of the power which might be wielded by a national organization of great size motivated by the principle of labor solidarity. Prof. Ware himself dates the decline of the Order from May 1, 1886, although the great drop in membership was not apparent until after October. There were so many more potent forces operating to bring about the decline and subsequent disintegration of the Knights,[47] that the least that can be said is that the burden of proof still rests with those who assert that the Haymarket bomb was a vital factor in the process due to Parsons' membership and the loss of public sympathy.

It is in a sense somewhat misleading to declare that the "good name of labor" suffered and that "public sentiment was turned against labor organizations" because of the Haymarket bomb. It is more nearly correct to say that the tragedy was consciously used by capital interests through a willing press to effect these ends. The whole affair was thus pressed into service against labor. The degree of success achieved, however, cannot be definitely determined. The trade-union movement certainly was not checked as a result,[48] and it is doubtful whether labor's "good name" was lost in circles where it had been hitherto highly regarded.

Labor did unquestionably suffer directly and indirectly from the wave of reaction which followed the bomb-throwing. The most striking legislative manifestation of the reactionary spirit to which the affair gave full play was the Merritt Conspiracy Law.[49] Passed by the Illinois legislature before the State Supreme Court decision was handed down, it was frankly described as a measure to crystallize Judge Gary's theory of conspiracy into statutory law.[50] Organized labor fought the law bitterly, and the Chicago *Knights of Labor* charged that it was framed "to hold for murder every member of a labor organization, if in an attempt to secure remunerative wages a man is killed by anybody."[51] Labor finally managed to secure the repeal of the vicious statute in 1891. The victory, however, was a hollow one, for the law was so infamous that no official had had the courage to enforce it, and the decision of the Court upholding the theory of conspiracy was unaffected.[52] A more lasting and harmful product of the wave of reaction in Illinois was the Cole Anti-Boycott Law, approved June 16, 1887. This amended an earlier act to make boycotting a conspiracy punishable by five years' imprisonment, $2,000 fine, or both. Though the act also banned the black-list, it was widely assumed that it would be enforced primarily, if not solely, against labor. Extended efforts by organized labor failed to repeal or even amend the law.[53] Other measures placed upon the statute books of Illinois during 1887 are also to be related to the Haymarket Affair. Aliens were forbidden to hold or acquire property in the State except for a limited time under certain conditions. This reflected the anti-foreign feeling which it aroused. Another law provided that those suffering property injury from mobs and riots could sue for compensation. Other acts were designed to strengthen the police power in industrial disputes by extending the police jurisdiction of cities to adjoining towns and villages and by making it easier for sheriffs to secure aid in suppressing disturbances.[54] The passage of reactionary legislation in Georgia, Montana, Oregon, Texas, and Wisconsin, either broadening the definition of conspiracy or delimiting collective working-class action, may apparently be partly ascribed to the strikes of 1886 and the bomb-throwing.[55] Another characteristic product of the Haymarket tragedy was the purchase of a tract of land by capitalists who presented it to the Federal government on condition that it be occupied by the United States army forces. In 1889, wealthy Chicagoans started a fund to secure money to build an armory in the city.[56]

In precipitating the noteworthy political movement on the part of labor in 1886-1887 the Haymarket bomb had its most positive effect upon the American labor movement. "Labor felt that the tragedy of the bomb was laid at its door only to discredit it in its economic demands, and it turned to politics to save itself. By this act it brought into existence the most successful labor party that ever appeared in Chicago. It elected eight legislators, one alderman, and in one mayoralty election forced the two old parties to combine." [57] In August, 1886, the United Labor Party was established, and in its ranks there were found Republicans, Democrats, trade-unionists, Knights, single-taxers, reformists, and radicals of every shade. The new party was shortly split by internal difficulties, but it scored a notable success at the polls, electing seven State assemblymen, one State senator, five of the six judges it endorsed, and was only sixty-four votes shy of electing a Congressman. In the spring of 1887, the Republicans and Democrats were forced to fuse on the mayoralty candidate to defeat the labor forces. Inner dissensions caused the appearance of other political groups, however, and by 1889 the movement collapsed. The success in Chicago was matched by the Henry George campaign in New York City, the victories of the Union Labor Party in Milwaukee, and the peak vote achieved by labor parties wherever they appeared in New England, the mid- and northwest, New Jersey, Pennsylvania, and Colorado.[58]

It is difficult to determine what direct effects the bomb had upon the eight-hour movement. It must be remembered that preparation for the May 1 struggle was inadequate, that the demand quickly was modified into one for a shorter day, that the Knights of Labor were officially opposed, that the trade-unions were divided, and that there was a large supply of strike-breakers available.[59] In addition, labor spent much of its forces in extensive strikes before May 1 in which the demand for a shorter day was only one among other issues. As a plan for securing the eight-hour day, the movement was conceded to be a failure even before May 1.[60] Powderly firmly believed that the eight-hour strikes would have been doomed to defeat even if they had been supported by the Knights and the Federation and even if the bomb had not been thrown, because conditions were not ripe.[61]

The eight-hour movement, however, cannot be called a *complete* failure. It was estimated that by May 15, 42,000 workers through strikes and 150,000 without striking won a shorter day and other concessions. In Chicago alone, it was estimated, 47,500 won gains without stopping work. It must be noted, however, that in a very large number of cases employees were forced to give up their gains by the fall of 1886. This was strikingly true in Chicago, and throughout the country at large the lock-out was extensively employed to increase hours.[62] From government statistics, it can be computed that of some 665 strikes for a shorter day called in 1886, about 500 occurred in May and about 200 started on May 1. Of the total number, 169 were successful, 117 were partly successful, and the remainder (381) failed. For the entire year, the average weekly working time of those who struck was reduced, over the country at large, from just under sixty-two hours a week to slightly less than fifty-nine. Though the available statistics do not make possible precise judgments, it is clear that the eight-hour movement was not a complete failure, and that it resulted in some gains. From the dates of the duration of the May strikes no correlation can be made, when all other factors are taken into consideration, showing that the bomb-throwing directly caused the abandonment of strikes for a shorter day.[63]

Though it did have an adverse effect upon the spirit of the movement and it gave employers a powerful opposition weapon, it is doubtful whether the bomb was responsible for the "failure of four-fifths of those who struck . . ."

In the popular mind, the international May Day celebration is frequently connected with the Haymarket bomb. There is, however, no causal relationship between the two. May Day can in part be traced to the fixing of May 1 as the date for engaging in the eight-hour struggle by the Federation of Organized Trades and Labor Unions. After 1886, the date became traditional. The American Federation of Labor voted to revive the eight-hour movement on May 1, 1890. At an international congress of socialists—which body subsequently became the Second International—held in Paris, July, 1889, a resolution was adopted calling for a world-wide demonstration by workers for the eight-hour day on the date set by the A. F. of L. It is said that this was a result of the Federation's desire to secure as much support as possible for the movement. The resolution adopted by the congress appears to have been presented by an American Knight of Labor delegate. With the passage of years, the May 1 demonstration broadened to one for general working-class demands, labor solidarity, international peace and the like.[64]

In his monumental history of the United States James Ford Rhodes wrote:

"There can be no question that the punishment meted out to the anarchists was legally just."

"The historical judgment confirms the legal."[65]

In his extended "A History of the United States Since the Civil War," Ellis Paxson Oberholtzer declares:

"The Haymarket anarchists merited and would receive their punishment. . . . No fewer than seven of the wretches, who assumed an impudent front during . . . the trial . . . were found guilty of murder and were sentenced to be hanged."

He further observes that "On November 11, 1887, four met their not unmerited end on the scaffold." [66]

These judgments are historically false; they spring from a powerful property-sense and unsurmountable bias. Parsons, Spies, Fielden, Neebe, Engel, Fischer, Schwab, and Lingg were not guilty of the murder of Officer Degan in the light of the evidence produced in court. A biased jury, a prejudiced judge, perjured evidence, an extraordinary and indefensible theory of conspiracy, and the temper of Chicago led to the conviction. The evidence never proved their guilt. Nor can the conclusion that the bomb was probably thrown by a member of the social-revolutionary movement affect this statement. Even Lingg cannot be linked to the bomb unless it be assumed that the bomb was of Lingg's manufacture and that he was a party to a plan—if it existed—to throw bombs. No valid defense can be made for the verdict which sent four to their death by the noose, one by suicide, and three to prison for six years. If the eight men were guilty of Degan's death because they had urged the use of force, then William Randolph Hearst should have been tried as an accessory to the murder of McKinley because he wrote, in an editorial attacking the President, that "if bad institutions and bad men can be got rid of only by killing, then the killing must be done." [67]

One legal student who justified the verdict because it saved Chicago from destruction has nevertheless recognized the gross partiality of the trial and the force of public clamor, and has declared that the application of the same "legal doctrine . . . in a Boston court" six years before the Civil War, "would have convicted and hanged . . . Wendell Phillips and William Lloyd Garrison. . . ." [68] In a letter to Capt. Black, Ben Butler wrote of the "men who were unlawfully convicted and unwisely executed," and described their end as "palpable judicial murders. . . ." [69] No open-minded person can today disagree with his judgments.

Taken alone, the bomb of May 4 constitutes a highly dramatic episode in the broad stream of recent American history. In its relationship to the labor and social-revolutionary movements, in the black chapter it produced in the history of American justice, and in its multiple effects upon the American scene, it has taken on, as the Haymarket Affair, a broader and profounder significance.

NOTES CHAPTER XXIV

1. *Harvard Law Review,* vol. 5, no. 6, Jan. 15, 1892.
2. *Free Society,* July 10, 1904, p. 2.
3. *Alarm,* February 11, 1888.
4. *Free Society,* December 29, 1901, pp. 1, 2, January 5, 1902, pp. 1-2, 3, March 30, 1902, p. 4, June 8, 1902, p. 4.
5. *Ibid.,* April 20, 1902, p. 2, May 18, 1902, p. 1.
6. *United States Statutes at Large, 1901-1903,* vol. 32, Part I, Washington, 1903, pp. 1214, 1221, 1222.
7. *United States Statutes at Large, 1905-1907,* vol. 34, Part I, Washington, 1907, pp. 597, 598-599.
8. Chicago *Inter Ocean,* August 6, 1900.
9. Cited in *Free Society,* November 30, 1902.
10. Rocker, *op. cit.,* pp. 320-326, 337; *Alarm,* December 17, 1887; New York *World,* November 13, 1887; Chicago *Herald,* November 13, 1887; clippings, scrap-book Labadie Collection.
11. Hillquit, *op. cit.,* pp. 229-230.
12. *Mother Earth,* vol. 2, no. 9, November, 1907, pp. 378-388 *passim.*
13. See above, pp. 479 *et seq.*
14. Adams, *loc. cit.,* pp. 731, 733.
15. C. L. James, "Anarchism vs. Socialism," *Twentieth Century,* vol. 12, no. 1, January 4, 1894, p. 10.
16. *Alarm,* March 10, 1888.
17. *Advance and Labor Leaf,* September 24, 1887.
18. William Salter, *Address Before the American Federation of Labor Convention, at Philadelphia, Pa., December, 1892,* n.p., n.d., pp. 6-7.
19. See above, p. 21.
20. *Alarm,* August 4, 1888.
21. *Mother Earth,* vol. 2, no. 8, October, 1907, p. 326.
22. *Cf., Alarm,* November 17, 1888; *Free Society,* December 4, 1898.
23. *Free Society,* 44, November 13, 1904, pp. 5-6 (William Holmes, "The Anarchist Convention of 1893").
24. *Alarm,* March 10, 1888; *Freiheit,* August 14, 21, 1886.
25. See above, pp. 101-102.
26. Lloyd, *op. cit.,* vol. 1, chap. VI *passim.*
27. *Ibid.,* pp. 107, 108, 109.
28. See above, p. 398-399.
29. Emma Goldman, *Living My Life,* 2 vols., New York, 1931, vol. I, p. 10; *cf.,* p. 31.

30. *Ibid.*, p. 31.
31. *Ibid.*, p. 346.
32. *Free Society*, June 19, 1898, pp. 4-5; William D. Haywood, *Bill Haywood's Book; The Autobiography of William D. Haywood*, New York, 1929.
33. *Free Society*, December 16, 1900.
34. See the interesting communication "The Farcical Trial Made Her Think" in *ibid.*, December 4, 1898, p. 3.
35. *Freedom* (London), vol. 3, no. 27, December, 1888, p. 11.
36. *Ibid.*, pp. 9-10; *Social Science Review*, vol. 1, no. 21, November 30, 1887, p. 13; *Alarm*, February 25, December 1, 8, 15, 1888; *Mother Earth*, vol. 7, no. 9, November, 1912; *Le Procès des Anarchistes de Chicago*, Paris, 1892, p. 2; collection of circulars in Columbia University Library; Dubois, *op. cit.*, pp. 253-254; Gompers, *op. cit.*, vol. 2, p. 182.
37. Statement of Lucy Parsons.
38. *Daily Worker*, November 12, 1932.
39. Powderly, *op. cit.*, p. 543.
40. Gompers, *op. cit.*, vol. 2, p. 177.
41. Ware, *op. cit.*, pp. 69, 148, 149 (quoted section), 253, 293.
42. June 8, 1886.
43. Quoted in Staley, *op. cit.*, p. 70.
44. Quoted in Lloyd, *op. cit.*, vol. 1, p. 99; Gompers, *op. cit.*, vol. 1, p. 294, vol. 2, p. 178.
45. Commons, *op. cit.*, vol. 2, p. 386.
46. See above, pp. 413-418.
47. These appear somewhat inadequately considered in Ware's volume.
48. This is shown by the labor history of the following years and the growth of membership of the A. F. of L. for which the official figures read:

      1886—140,000
      1887—160,000
      1888—175,000
      1889—200,000
      1890—220,000
      1891—225,000
      1892—250,000

American Federation of Labor, History, Encyclopaedia, Reference Book, Washington, 1919, vol. 1, p. 63.
49. See above, pp. 370-371.
50. Chicago *Tribune*, May 5, 1887.
51. April 16, 1887, cited in Beckner, *op. cit.*, p. 15. State Senator Streeter asserted that the law was an invention of Chicago capitalists to oppress labor (*idem.*), while Arthur of the railroad brotherhood praised it as a safeguard of American institutions! (*Alarm*, July 21, 1888.)
52. Beckner, *op. cit.*, pp. 15-16.

53. The courts later distinguished between the primary and secondary boycotts, holding that the latter alone is illegal. Beckner, *op. cit.*, pp. 34-39; Staley, *op. cit.*, p. 71; *Third Annual Report of the Commissioner of Labor*, p. 1151; *Appleton's Annual Cyclopaedia, 1887*, p. 375.

54. *Appleton's Annual Cyclopaedia, 1887*, p. 375; *Annual Report of the Citizens' Association of Chicago, October, 1887*, Chicago, 1887, pp. 30-31.

55. *Third Annual Report of the Commissioner of Labor*, pp. 1149, 1156, 1159, 1162, 1163. A New York statute of June, 1886, was apparently a product of the bombing. It amended an older law to limit parades, giving police very wide powers over their control. It did not apply to parades of the national guard, police and fire departments and veterans. *Fifth Annual Report of the Bureau of Labor Statistics of the State of New York, for the Year 1887*, Troy, 1888, p. 731.

56. New York *Sun*, March 17, 1889.

57. Mittelman, *loc. cit.*, pp. 417-418.

58. *Ibid.*, pp. 419-423; Hillquit, *op. cit.*, pp. 247-248; Fine, *op. cit.*, pp. 53-55; Scudder, *op. cit.*, p. 86; *John Swinton's Paper*, files for September and October, 1886; *Social Science*, vol. 1, no. 5, August 3, 1887, p. 13, no. 11, September 14, 1887, p. 9, no. 16, October 19, 1887, p. 13; *Proceedings of G. A., K. of L., 1887*, p. 1505; *Alarm*, July 7, 1888.

59. See above, pp. 169 *et seq.*

60. *Fourth Biennial Report of the Bureau of Labor Statistics of Illinois*, pp. 479, 498.

61. Powderly, *op. cit.*, pp. 503-504.

62. *Fourth Biennial Report of the Bureau of Labor Statistics of Illinois*, pp. 479, 480, 491-492, Table II, 482-490; *Third Annual Report of the Commissioner of Labor*, Table XXII, pp. 1023-1024; *Twenty-First Annual Report of the Commissioner of Labor*, Washington, 1907, pp. 20, 70-71, 74-75, 80.

63. These conclusions are drawn from the *Third Annual Report of the Commissioner of Labor*, Table I, pp. 36-615.

64. Alexander Trachtenberg, *The History of May Day. International Pamphlets*, no. 14, New York, 1931, pp. 3, 14, 15, 16, 18; Boris Reinstein, *International May Day and American Labor. A Holiday Expressing Working Class Emancipation Versus a Holiday Exalting Labor's Chains*, New York, (1918?), p. 9; Ramus, *op. cit.*, p. 11; *Free Society*, May 14, 1899, p. 2; *Mother Earth*, vol. 5, no. 3, May 10, 1910, pp. 73-79 *passim*.

65. *Op. cit.*, vol. 8, p. 283.

66. In 5 vols., New York, 1931, vol. 4, p. 423.

67. New York *Journal*, April 10, 1901.

68. *Amer. St. Tr.*, vol. 12, pp. vi-vii (editor's comment).

69. Quoted in *Life of Albert R. Parsons*, pp. 261-263 (quoted sections, p. 261).

SELECTED BIBLIOGRAPHY

Abbot, Willis John, *Carter Henry Harrison. A Memoir*, New York, 1895.

Acht Opfer des Klassenhasses (Nach den Berichten der New Yorker Volkszeitung), New York, 1890.

Adams, Charles Kendall, "Contemporary Life and Thought in the United States," *Contemporary Review*, vol. 52, November, 1887.

Adams, Thomas Sewall, and Sumner, Helen L., *Labor Problems*, eighth edition, New York, 1911.

Addams, Jane, *Twenty Years at Hull House*, New York, 1911.

Advance and Labor Leaf.

Alarm.

Albany *Evening Journal.*

Albany Law Journal.

Altgeld, John P., *Live Questions: Including Our Penal Machinery and Its Victims*, Chicago, 1890.

—— *Reasons for Pardoning Fielden, Neebe, and Schwab*, Springfield, Ill., 1896.

The American.

American Federation of Labor, History, Encyclopaedia, Reference Book, Washington, 1919, vol. 1.

American Law Review.

Ames, Sarah E., *An Open Letter to Judge Joseph E. Gary, who in 1893 seeks to justify his participation (in 1887) in the lynching, under the hypocritical guise of the law, of men who entertained and expressed unpopular opinions*, Chicago, 1893.

Anarchism: Its Philosophy and Scientific Basis as Defined by Some of Its Apostles, Chicago, 1887.

The Anarchist (London).

Anarchist Case. Advance Sheets of the Illinois Reporter, Comprising Pages 1 to 267, Inclusive, of Volume 122, November 5, 1887, Springfield, Ill., 1887.

Anarchy at an End. Lives, Trial and Conviction of the Eight Chicago Anarchists. How They Killed and What They Killed With, Etc., Chicago, 1886.

Andrews, Stephen Pearl, *The Science of Society,* Boston, 1888.

Annual Reports of the Citizens' Association of Chicago. 1879-1887, Chicago, 1879-1887.

Appleton's Annual Cyclopaedia, 1886, 1887.

Arbeiter-Zeitung.

Atkinson, Edward, "The Hours of Labor," *North American Review,* vol. 142, May, 1886.

Die Autonomie.

Aveling, Edward, *An American Journey,* New York, n.d.

Aveling, Edward, and Eleanor Marx, "The Chicago Anarchists," *To-Day,* vol. 8, no. 48, November, 1887.

Bailie, William, *Josiah Warren, The First American Anarchist. A Sociological Study,* Boston, 1906.

Banker's Magazine and Statistical Register.

Barnes, William E., editor, *The Labor Problem. Plain Questions and Practical Answers,* New York, 1886.

Beckner, Earl H., *A History of Labor Legislation in Illinois (Social Science Studies directed by the Local Community research committee of the University of Chicago,* no. 13), Chicago, 1929.

Bergstresser, Genevieve Le Cron, *The History of the Haymarket Riot,* University of Chicago Master of Arts Thesis, MS. copy in New York Public Library.

Bernstein, Samuel, *The Beginnings of Marxian Socialism in France,* New York, 1933.

Das Blut-Urtheil. Die am 14 September 1887. Abgegebene Entscheidung des Ober-Staatsgerichts von Illinois in dem Monster-Prozess gegen die Chicagoer Anarchisten, n.p., n.d.

Bogart, Ernest Ludlow, and Thompson, Charles Manfred, *The Industrial State, 1870-1893 (The Centennial History of Illinois,* vol. 4), Chicago, 1922.

Bradford, Gamaliel, *Damaged Souls,* Boston, 1923.

Bradstreet's.

Brigham, Clifford, "Strikes and Boycotts as Indictable Conspiracies at Common Law," *American Law Review,* vol. 21, January-February, 1887.

Brissenden, Paul Frederick, *The I.W.W. A Study of American Syndicalism (Columbia Studies in History, Economics and Public Law,* vol. 83), New York, 1919.

Brooklyn *Eagle.*

Brooks, John Graham, *American Syndicalism. The I.W.W.,* New York, 1913.

Brooks, Van Wyck, *The Ordeal of Mark Twain,* new and revised edition, New York, 1933.

Browne, Francis F., "The Presidential Contest. I—Altgeld of Illinois," *The National Review* (London), vol. 38, no. 166, December, 1896.

Browne, Waldo E., *Altgeld of Illinois. A Record of His Life and Work,* New York, 1924.

—— *Man or the State?* New York, 1919.

Bryan, William Jennings, and Mary Baird, *The Memoirs of William Jennings Bryan,* Chicago, 1925.

Bryce, James, *The American Commonwealth,* 2 vols., New York, 1927.

Buchanan, Joseph R., *The Story of a Labor Agitator,* New York, 1903.

Cahill, Marion Cotter, *Shorter Hours. A Study of the Movement since the Civil War (Studies in History, Economics and Public Law,* edited by the Faculty of Political Science of Columbia University), New York, 1932.

Central Law Journal.

Cherouny, Henry W., *The Burial of the Apprentice. A True Story from Life in a Union Workshop . . . and Other Essays on Present Political and Social Problems,* New York, 1900.

The Chicago Anarchists and the Haymarket Massacre. Complete History of the Growth of Anarchism in Chicago—The Great Dynamite Conspiracy—The Haymarket Bomb-Throwing— Official Police Report of Casualties—The Trial, Evidence, Conviction and Sentence of the Accused, Speeches of Counsel and Defendants, Etc., Chicago, 1887.

Chicago *Daily News.*

Chicago *Evening Journal.*

Chicago *Globe*.

Chicago *Herald*.

Chicago *Inter Ocean*.

Chicago *Knights of Labor*.

Chicago *Labor Enquirer*.

Chicago *Mail*.

Chicago *Times*.

Chicago *Tribune*.

The Chicago Martyrs; Their Speeches in Court. With a Preface and Abstract of Record Prepared for the Supreme Court of Illinois to which Is Added the Reasons for Pardoning Fielden, Neebe and Schwab, by John Altgeld, Governor of Illinois, Glasgow (1893?).

The Chicago Martyrs. The Famous Speeches of the Eight Anarchists in Judge Gary's Court, October 7, 1886, and Reasons for Pardoning Fielden, Neebe and Schwab, by John P. Altgeld, San Francisco, 1899.

Clay, Sir Arthur, *Syndicalism and Labour, Notes upon Some Aspects of Social and Industrial Questions of the Day*, New York, 1911.

Clews, Henry, "Shall Labor or Capital Rule?" Part I, "The Labor Crisis," *North American Review*, vol. 142, June, 1886.

Columbia University Library Collection of Circulars.

Columbia University Library Scrap-Books of Clippings on Radicalism and Radical Movements.

Commons, John R., and Associates, *History of Labour in the United States*, 2 vols., New York, 1926.

Commonweal (London).

The Communist.

Cross, Ira B., *A History of the Labor Movement in California*, Berkeley, Calif., 1935.

Dabney, Virginius, *Liberalism in the South*, Chapel Hill, 1932.

Daily Worker.

Danryid, Lemuel, *History and Philosophy of the Eight-Hour Movement*, fourth edition, Washington, 1899.

Darrow, Clarence, *The Story of My Life*, New York, 1932.

Dawson, William H., *The German Empire, 1867-1914, and the Unity Movement*, 2 vols., London, 1919.

Dennett, Tyler, *John Hay. From Poetry to Politics,* New York, 1933.

Detroit *Evening News.*

Detroit *Journal.*

Donald, Robert, "The Eight Hours Movement in the United States," *The Economic Journal,* vol. 2, March, 1892.

Douglas, Paul H., "An Analysis of Strike Statistics, 1881-1921," *Journal of the American Statistical Association,* n.s. no. 143, September, 1923.

Dubois, Félix, *Le Péril anarchiste,* Paris, 1894.

Dunbar, William H., "The Anarchists' Case," *Harvard Law Review,* vol. 1, no. 7, February 15, 1888.

Ebert, Justus, *American Industrial Revolution. From the Frontier to the Factory; Its Social and Political Effects,* New York, 1902.

Ehlert, John, "Anarchists in Chicago," *America. A Journal of Today* (Chicago), vol. 1, no. 34, November 22, 1888.

Eight Hours for a Day's Labor. Address No. 2 by the National Eight-Hour Association of Chicago. Liberty Library, vol. 1, no. 2, Chicago, March 13, 1886.

Elkins, S. B., *The Industrial Question in the United States. Address Delivered before the Alumni Association of the University of the State of Missouri. June 3, 1885,* New York, n.d.

Eltzbacher, Paul, *Anarchism,* translated by Steven T. Byington, New York, 1908.

Ely, Richard T., *The Labor Movement in America,* new revised edition, New York, 1905.

—— *Recent American Socialism* (*Johns Hopkins University Studies in Historical and Political Science,* Third Series, vol. 4), Baltimore, 1885.

Endicott, Charles E. *Capital and Labor. Address before the Central Trades Union . . . at Boston, March 28, 1886,* n.p., n.d.

Engels, Friedrich, *Herr Eugen Dühring's Revolution in Science* [*Anti-Dühring*] (*Marxist Library, Works of Marxism, Leninism,* vol. 18), translated by Emile Burns, New York, n.d.

The Epoch.

Fackel.

Fifth Annual Report of the Bureau of Labor Statistics of the State of New York, for the Year 1887, Troy, 1888.

Fine, Nathan, *Labor and Farmer Parties in the United States, 1828-1928,* New York, 1928.

The First Annual Report of the Commissioner of Labor, March, 1886. Industrial Depressions, Washington, 1886.

Flinn, John J., *History of the Chicago Police, from the Settlement of the Community to the Present Time, under Authority of the Mayor and Superintendent of the Force,* Chicago, 1887.

Foran, M. A., *The Other Side. A Social Study Based on Fact,* Washington, 1886.

Fourth Biennial Report of the Bureau of Labor Statistics of Illinois. 1886, Springfield, 1886.

Frankfurter, Felix, and Greene, Nathan, *The Labor Injunction,* New York, 1930.

Free Society.

Freedom (London).

Freiheit.

[Frost, T. Gold], "The Anarchists' Cases," *Columbia Law Times,* vol. I, no. I, October, 1887.

Garraud, R., *L'anarchisme et la répression,* Paris, 1895.

Gary, Joseph E., "The Chicago Anarchists of 1886: the Crime, the Trial and the Punishment," *Century Magazine,* vol. 45, no. 6, April, 1893.

George, Jr., Henry, *The Life of Henry George,* 2 vols., Garden City, 1911.

Ghio, Paul, *L'anarchisme aux États-Unis,* Paris, 1903.

Gide, Charles, and Rist, Charles, *A History of Economic Doctrines from the Time of the Physiocrats to the Present Day,* translated from the second revised edition by William Smart, Boston, n.d.

Godwin, William, *An Enquiry Concerning Political Justice and Its Influence on General Virtue and Happiness,* edited and abridged by Raymond A. Preston, 2 vols., New York, 1926.

Goldman, Emma, "Johann Most," *American Mercury,* vol. 8, no. 30, June, 1926.

—— *Living My Life,* 2 vols., New York, 1931.

Gompers, Samuel, *The Eight-Hour Day. Its Inauguration, Enforcement and Influences,* Washington, n.d.

—— *Seventy Years of Life and Labor,* 2 vols., New York, 1925.

Greene, William B., *Mutual Banking,* New York, 1870.

Gretton, R. H., *A Modern History of the English People,* New York, 1930.

Groat, George Gorham, *Attitude of American Courts in Labor Cases* (Columbia University *Studies in History, Economics and Public Law,* vol. 42, whole no. 108), New York, 1911.

Hacker, Louis M., and Kendrick, Benjamin B., *The United States since 1865,* revised edition, New York, 1934.

Hamon, A., *Psychologie de l'anarchiste-socialiste,* Paris, 1895.

Handbook of Labor Statistics, 1929 Edition. Bulletin of the United States Bureau of Labor Statistics, Miscellaneous Series, no. 491, Washington, 1929.

Harper's Weekly.

Harris, Frank, *The Bomb,* definitive American edition, New York, 1920.

Hart, W. C., *Confessions of an Anarchist,* London, 1906.

Harvard Law Review.

Hatch, Rufus, "Strikes, Boycotts, Knights of Labor," Part II, "The Labor Crisis," *North American Review,* vol. 142, June, 1886.

The Haymarket Monument. What Is It Erected For? Chicago, 1889.

Haynes, Fred E., *Social Politics in the United States,* Boston, 1924.

Haywood, William D., *Bill Haywood's Book; the Autobiography of William D. Haywood,* New York, 1929.

Head, Franklin H., *Studies in Medieval and Modern History,* Chicago, n.d. (photostatic copy in New York Public Library).

Helm, Lyn, "Legal Aspects of the Boycott," *Chicago Law Times,* vol. 1, no. 1, November, 1886.

Herrick, Robert, *The Memoirs of an American Citizen,* New York, 1905.

Hicks, John D., *The Populist Revolt,* Minneapolis, 1931.

Hicks, Granville, *The Great Tradition. An Interpretation of American Literature since the Civil War,* New York, 1933.

Hill, Frederick Trevor, *Decisive Battles of the Law,* New York, 1907.

Hill, Walter B., *Anarchy, Socialism, and the Labor Movement. An Address Delivered before the Literary Societies of the University of Georgia, July 19, 1886,* Columbus, Ga., 1886.

Hillquit, Morris, *History of Socialism in the United States,* fifth edition, New York, 1910.

Hook, Sidney, *Toward the Understanding of Karl Marx,* New York, 1933.

House of Representatives, 51st Congress, 1st Session, Report No. 489, Adjustment of Accounts, Eight Hour Law, in *The Reports of Committees of the House of Representatives for the First Session of the Fifty-First Congress, 1889-'90,* vol. 2, Washington, 1891.

Hsiao, Kung Chuan, *Political Pluralism. A Study in Contemporary Political Theory,* New York, 1927.

Hull House Maps and Papers. A Presentation of Nationalities and Wages in a Congested District of Chicago, together with Comments and Essays on Problems Growing out of the Social Conditions, by Residents of Hull House, New York, 1895.

Hyndman, Henry Mayers, *The Chicago Riots and the Class War in the United States,* London, 1886.

The Independent.

Ingersoll, Robert G., *Works,* 13 vols., New York, 1912, vol. 8.

Iswolsky, Hélène, *La vie de Bakounine,* Paris, 1930.

James, C. L., "Anarchism vs. Socialism," *Twentieth Century,* vol. 12, no. 1, January 4, 1894.

—— "Judge Gary on the Anarchists," *Twentieth Century,* vol. 10, no. 16, April 30, 1893.

James, Edmund J., "Socialists and Anarchists in the United States," *Our Day,* vol. 1, no. 2, February, 1888.

John Swinton's Paper.

Johnson, Claudius O., *Carter Henry Harrison I, Political Leader* (*Social Science Studies directed by the Local Community research committee of the University of Chicago*), Chicago, 1928.

Journal of United Labor.

Kamman, William Frederick, *Socialism in German American Literature* (*Americana Germanica,* no. 24), Philadelphia, 1917.

Kautsky, Karl, "Peukerts Erinnerungen," *Die Neue Zeit,* March 20, 1914.

King, Willford Isbell, *The Wealth and Income of the People of the United States,* New York, 1923.

Kohlsaat, H. H., *From McKinley to Harding. Personal Recollections of Our Presidents*, New York, 1923.

Kropotkin, Peter, *Memoirs of a Revolutionist*, Boston, 1899.

Labadie Collection, University of Michigan Library, Scrap-Book of Clippings on the Haymarket Affair. Compiled by Agnes Inglis.

Labadie Collection, University of Michigan Library, Scrap-Book of Clippings on the Minneapolis Assembly of the Knights of Labor. Compiled by Agnes Inglis.

Labor: Its Rights and Wrongs. Statements and Comments by the Leading Men of Our Nation on the Labor Question of To-Day. With Platforms of the Various Labor Organizations, Knights of Labor, Federation of Trades, Agricultural Wheels of the South, Farmers' Alliance, and Full Proceedings of the General Assembly of the K. of L., at Cleveland, May 25 to June 3, 1886, Washington, 1886.

Labor Library, no. 12, New York, June, 1894.

Labor Leaf.

Lagardelle, Hubert, "Michel Bakounine," *Revue Politique et Parlementaire*, vol. 61, no. 182, August, 1909.

Lawson, John D., editor, *American State Trials. A Collection of the Important and Interesting Criminal Trials Which Have Taken Place in the United States from the Beginning of Our Government to the Present Day*, 13 vols., St. Louis, 1919, vol. 12.

Leroy-Beaulieu, Paul, *Collectivism, A Study of Some of the Leading Social Questions of the Day*, translated and abridged by Sir Arthur Clay, London, 1908.

Levine, Louis, *Syndicalism in France* (Columbia University Studies in History, Economics and Public Law, vol. 46, no. 3), second edition, New York, 1914.

Lewis, Leon, *The Ides of November. An Appeal for the Seven Condemned Leaders and a Protest Against Their Judicial Assassination*, Greenpoint, N. Y., 1887.

Lewis, Lloyd, and Smith, Henry Justin, *Chicago, the History of Its Reputation*, New York, 1929.

Liberty.

Life of Albert R. Parsons with Brief History of the Labor Movement in America. Also Sketches of the Lives of A. Spies,

Geo. Engel, A. Fischer and Louis Lingg, second edition, Chicago, 1903.

Lloyd, Caro, *Henry Demarest Lloyd (1847-1903), A Biography,* 2 vols., New York, 1912.

Lombroso, Cesare, *Études de sociologie. Les anarchistes,* translated by A. Hamel and A. Marie, Paris, n.d.

Lum, Dyer D., *A Concise History of the Great Trial of the Chicago Anarchists in 1886. Condensed from the Official Record,* Chicago (1886?).

McConnell, Samuel P., "The Chicago Bomb Case. Personal Recollections of an American Tragedy," *Harper's Magazine,* vol. 168, no. 1008, May, 1934.

McLaughlin, Andrew C., *A Constitutional History of the United States,* New York, 1935.

McNeill, George E., editor, *The Labor Movement, the Problem of To-Day, Comprising a History of Capital and Labor, and Its Present Status,* New York, 1887.

Mackay, John Henry, *"The Anarchists," A Picture of Civilization at the Close of the Nineteenth Century,* translated by George Schumm, Boston, 1891.

Man!

[*Manifesto of the*] *Pittsburgh Congress of the International Working People's Association, October 16, 1883,* New York, n.d.

Means, D. McGregor, "Labor Unions under Democratic Government," *Journal of Social Science* (containing the *Transactions of the American Association*), no. 21, September, 1886.

Michel, Louise, *Mémoires,* Paris, 1886.

Minneapolis *Evening Journal.*

Mittelman, Edward B., "Chicago Labor in Politics 1877-96," *The Journal of Political Economy,* vol. 28, no. 5, May, 1920.

Mordell, Albert, *Quaker Militant. John Greenleaf Whittier,* New York, 1933.

Most, Johann, *The Social Monster,* New York, 1890.

Mother Earth.

Mott, Rodney L., "The Political Theory of Syndicalism," *Political Science Quarterly,* vol. 37, no. 1, March, 1922.

Nation.

The National Cyclopaedia of American Biography, vols. 7, 9.

Nelles, Walter, "Commonwealth v. Hunt," *Columbia Law Review,* vol. 32, no. 7, November, 1932.

Nettlau, Max, *Anarchisten und Sozial-Revolutionäre. Die historische Entwicklung des Anarchismus in den Jahren 1880-1886 (Beiträge zur Geschichte des Sozialismus, Syndikalismus, Anarchismus,* Band V), Berlin, 1931.

—— *Bibliographie de l'anarchie,* Paris, 1897.

Nevins, Allan, *Grover Cleveland. A Study in Courage,* New York, 1933.

Newton, R. Heber, *The Present Aspect of the Labor Problem. Four Lectures Given in All Souls Church, New York, May, 1886,* New York, 1886.

New York *Commercial Advertiser.*

New York *Enquirer.*

New York *Evening Post.*

New York *Herald.*

New York *Journal.*

New York *Leader.*

New York *Sun.*

New York *Times.*

New York *Tribune.*

New York *World.*

New York Public Library Scrap-Books on Labor.

Nomad, Max, "Nechayev, 'The Possessed,' A Study," *Hound and Horn,* vol. 7, no. 1, October, December, 1933.

N. W. Ayer and Sons' American Newspaper Annual, 1883-1886, Philadelphia, 1883-1886.

Oberholtzer, Ellis Paxson, *A History of the United States since the Civil War,* 5 vols., New York, 1931, vol. 4.

Open Court.

Osgood, Herbert L., "Scientific Anarchism," *Political Science Quarterly,* vol. 4, no. 1, March, 1889.

The Pardon of the Anarchists [Chicago, 1893].

Parrington, Vernon Louis, *The Beginnings of Critical Realism in America, 1860-1920,* New York, 1930.

Peck, Charles F., *A Summary of the Third Annual Report of the Bureau of Statistics of Labor of the State of New York,* Albany, 1886.

Peixotto, Jessica, *The French Revolution and Modern French*

Socialism. A Comparative Study of the French Revolution and the Doctrines of Modern French Socialism, New York, 1901.

[Pentecost, Hugh], *El crimen de Chicago (11 de Novembre de 1887)*, New York, 1889.

The People (San Francisco).

Perlman, Selig, *A History of Trade Unionism in the United States*, New York, 1929.

—— *A Theory of the Labor Movement*, New York, 1928.

Peukert, Joseph, *Erinnerungen eines Proletariers aus der revolutionären Arbeiterbewegung*, Berlin, 1913.

Philadelphia *Press*.

Plan of Organization, Method of Propaganda and Resolutions, Adopted by the Pittsburgh Congress of the International Working Peoples' Association . . . , n.p., n.d.

Plechanoff, George, *Anarchism and Socialism*, translated by Eleanor Marx Aveling, Chicago (1907?).

Powderly, Terence Vincent, "The Army of the Discontented," *North American Review*, vol. 140, April, 1885.

—— "The Organization of Labor," *North American Review*, vol. 135, July, 1882.

—— *Thirty Years of Labor, 1859 to 1889*, Columbus, Ohio, 1889.

Pringle, Henry F., *Theodore Roosevelt. A Biography*, New York, 1931.

Proceedings of the General Assembly of the Knights of Labor of America. Eleventh Regular Session, Held at Minneapolis, Minnesota, October 4 to 19, 1887, n.p., 1887.

Le Procès des anarchistes de Chicago, Paris, 1892.

Public Opinion.

Raléa, Michel, *L'Idée de révolution dans les doctrines socialistes. Étude sur l'évolution de la tactique révolutionnaire*, Paris, 1923.

Ramus, Pierre, *Der Justizmord von Chicago. In Memoriam. 11 November, 1887. Nach urkundlichen Dokumenten und historischen Quellen dargesteelt . . . bearbeitet . . . von Pierre Ramus*, Zürich, 1912.

Record of the Proceedings of the Seventh Regular Session of the General Assembly [of the Knights of Labor], Held at Cincinnati, Ohio, Sept. 4-11, 1883, n.p., 1883.

Record of tne Proceedings of the Ninth Regular Session of the General Assembly [of the Knights of Labor], Held at Hamilton, Ont., October 5-13, 1885, n.p., 1885.

Record of Proceedings of the General Assembly of the Knights of Labor of America, vol. IV. Commencing with Session at Richmond, Virginia, October 4 to 20, 1886, n.p., 1886.

Reinstein, Boris, *International May Day and American Labor. A Holiday Expressing Working Class Emancipation Versus Holiday Exalting Labor's Chains*, New York (1918?).

Report of the Committee on Tenement Houses of the Citizen Association of Chicago. September, 1884, Chicago, 1884.

Report of the [Education and Labor] Committee of the Sena upon the Relations between Labor and Capital, and Tes mony Taken by the Committee, 4 vols., Washington, 1885.

Report of the Fourth Annual Congress of the International Wo ing Men's Association, Held at Basle, in Switzerland. Fr the 6th to the 11th September, 1869, London, (1869?).

Le Révolté.

Reynolds, Marcus T., *The Housing of the Poor in Amer Cities. The Prize Essay of the American Economic Asso tion for 1892 (Publications of the American Economic sociation*, vol. 8, nos. 2 and 3), London, 1893.

Rhodes, James Ford, *History of the United States from the C promise of 1850 to the End of the Roosevelt Administra 9 vols.*, New York, 1929, vol. 9.

The Road to Freedom.

Rocker, Rudolph, *Johann Most, das Leben eines Rebellen, E 1924.

Roosevelt, Theodore, *The Works of Theodore Roosevelt, 2c New York, 1926, vol. 14.

Russell, Charles Edward, "The Haymarket and Afterwards Personal Recollections," *Appleton's Magazine*, vol. 10 October, 1907.

Salter, William M., *Address [on Economic Conferences] the American Federation of Labor Convention, at P phia, Pa., December, 1892*, n.p., n.d.

—— *Anarchy or Government? An Inquiry in Fundamen tics*, New York, 1895.

Salter, William M., "Second Thoughts on the Treatment Anarchy," *Atlantic Monthly*, vol. 89, no. 535, May, 1902.

—— "What Shall Be Done with the Anarchists?" *Open Cou* vol. 1, no. 19, October 27, 1887.

Sartorius Freehern von Waltershausen, A., *Der Moderne Sozia. ismus in den Vereinigten Staaten von Amerika*, Berlin, 1890.

Sayre, Francis B., "Criminal Conspiracy," *Harvard Law Review*, vol. 35, no. 4, February, 1922.

Scudder, Jr., M. L., *The Labor-Value Fallacy*, third edition, Chicago, 1887.

Schaack, Michael J., *Anarchy and Anarchists*, Chicago, 1889.

Schuster, Eunice Minette, *Native American Anarchism. A Study of Left-Wing American Individualism* (*Smith College Studies in History*, vol. 17, nos. 1-4, October, 1931-July, 1932), Northampton, Mass., n.d.

Shannon, Fred Albert, *Economic History of the People of the United States*, New York, 1934.

Shepard, Elliot F., *Labor and Capital Are One*, New York, 1886.

Siringo, Charles A., *Two Evil Isms. Pinkertonism and Anarchism*, Chicago, 1915.

Smith, Richmond Mayo, "American Labor Statistics," *Political Science Quarterly*, vol. 1, no. 1, March, 1886.

Social Science.

Social Science Review.

Socialism and Anarchism. Antagonistic Opposites (*Socialistic Library*, no. 6), New York, 1886.

Sombart, Werner, *Socialism and the Social Movement*, translated by M. Epstein, London, 1909.

Sorel, George, *Reflections on Violence*, translated by T. E. Hulme, third edition, New York, 1912.

Spahr, Charles B., *An Essay on the Present Distribution of Wealth in the United States*, New York, 1896.

Spies, August, *Autobiography. His Speech in Court, Notes, Letters, Etc.*, Chicago, 1887.

Staley, Eugene, *History of the Illinois State Federation of Labor* (*Social Science Studies* directed by the Local Community research committee of the University of Chicago, no. 15, [i.e., 16]), Chicago, 1930.

Statist (London).

Steklov, Yu, *The History of the First International,* translated by Eden and Cedar Paul, New York, 1928.

Stepniak, "Terrorism in Russia and Terrorism in Europe," *Contemporary Review,* vol. 45, March, 1884.

Stone, Melville E., *Fifty Years a Journalist,* Garden City, N. Y., 1921.

Strong, Josiah, *Our Country. Its Possible Future and Its Present Crisis,* revised edition, New York, 1891.

A Summary of the Third Annual Report of the Bureau of Labor Statistics of New York, January 21, 1886, Albany, 1886.

Sumner, W. G., "Industrial War," *Forum,* vol. 2, September, 1886.

In the Supreme Court of Illinois, Northern Grand Division. March Term, A.D. 1887. August Spies et al., vs. The People of the State of Illinois. Abstract of Record, 2 vols., Chicago, 1887.

In the Supreme Court of Illinois, Northern Grand Division. March Term, A.D. 1887, August Spies et al., vs. The People of the State of Illinois. Argument of W. P. Black for Plaintiffs in Error, Chicago, 1887.

In the Supreme Court of Illinois, Northern Grand Division. March Term, A.D. 1887. August Spies et al., vs. The People of the State of Illinois. Brief and Argument for Plaintiffs in Error, Chicago, 1887.

In the Supreme Court of Illinois, Northern Grand Division, March Term, A.D. 1887. August Spies et al., vs. The People of the State of Illinois. Brief on the Facts for Defendants in Error, Chicago, 1887.

In the Supreme Court of Illinois, Northern Grand Division, March Term, A.D. 1887. August Spies et al., vs. The People of the State of Illinois. Brief on the Law for Defendants in Error, Chicago, 1887.

Swett, Leonard, *In the Supreme Court of Illinois. The Anarchists' Cases. Brief for the Defendants,* Chicago, 1887.

Sylvis, James C., *The Life, Speeches, Labors and Essays of William H. Sylvis,* Philadelphia, 1872.

Thayer, James B., " 'Law and Fact' in Jury Trials," *Harvard Law Review,* vol. 4, no. 4, November 15, 1890.

Third Annual Report of the Commissioner of Labor. Strikes and Lockouts, 1887, Washington, 1888.

Trachtenberg, Alexander, *The History of May Day. International Pamphlets,* no. 14, New York, 1931.

Train, George Francis, *My Life in Many States and in Foreign Lands, Dictated in My Seventy-Fourth Year,* New York, 1902.

Trumbull, M. M., "Judge Gary and the Anarchists," *Arena,* vol. 8, no. 47, October, 1893.

—— *The Trial of the Judgment,* Chicago, 1888.

—— *Was It a Fair Trial? An Appeal to the Governor of Illinois.* Chicago, 1887.

Truth.

The Truth Seeker.

Tucker, Benjamin R., *Henry George, Traitor,* New York, 1896.

—— *Instead of a Book. By a Man Too Busy to Write One. A Fragmentary Exposition of Philosophical Anarchism,* New York, 1893.

Twentieth Century.

Twenty-First Annual Report of the Commissioner of Labor. Strikes and Lockouts, 1906, Washington, 1907.

United States Statutes at Large, 1901-1903, vol. 32, Part I, Washington, 1903.

United States Statutes at Large, 1905-1907, vol. 34, Part I, Washington, 1907.

The University (Chicago).

Vorbote.

Walker, Francis A., *The Labor Problem of Today. An Address Delivered before the Alumni Association of Lehigh University, June 22d, 1887,* New York, 1887.

Ware, Norman J., *The Labor Movement in the United States, 1860-1895. A Study in Democracy,* New York, 1929.

Warren, Josiah, *Practical Details in Equitable Commerce,* New York, 1852.

Webb, Sidney, and Cox, Harold, *The Eight Hours Day,* London, 1891.

Wheeler, A. S., *The Labor Question. A Paper Read before the Commercial Club of Boston. October 16, 1886. Reprinted from the Andover Review for November, 1886,* Boston, 1886.

Whitlock, Brand, *Forty Years of It,* New York, 1925.

The "Why I Ams." An Economic Symposium, second edition (No. 11 *Unsettled Questions.* Fortnightly, New York, August 30, 1891), New York, 1892.

Wigmore, John H., "The Boycott and Kindred Practises as Grounds for Damages," *American Law Review,* vol. 21, July-August, 1887.

—— "Interference with Social Relations," *American Law Review,* vol. 21, September-October, 1887.

Willoughby, William Franklin, *Inspection of Factories and Workshops* (No. VII in *Monographs on American Social Economics* edited by Herbert B. Adams and Richard Waterman, Jr.), Boston, 1900.

Wolff, George D., "The Wage Question," *The Catholic Quarterly Review,* vol. 11, no. 42, April, 1886.

Woodford, Stewart L., *The Labor Problem. Annual Oration before the New York Delta of Phi Beta Kappa* [New York, 1886].

Workmen's Advocate.

Young, Art, *On My Way,* New York, 1928.

Zeisler, Sigmund, *Reminiscences of the Anarchist Case,* Chicago, 1927.

Zenker, E. V., *Anarchism. A Criticism and History of the Anarchist Theory,* New York, 1897.

INDEX

Abbot, Willis J., quoted, 92
Abbott, Lyman, 175
Adams, Charles Kendall, quoted, 11
Adams, G. W., 247
Adams, J. Coleman, on socialists, 210
Addams, Jane, on social conditions in Chicago, 16
Advance, on clemency, 439
Advance and Labor Leaf, opposed to executions, 409
Alarm, established, 113; 114, 115, 116, 119, 120, 121, 124, 127, 129 n. 17, 137, 138, 141, 145, 148, 149, 167, 169, 211, suspension of, 225; 230, 290, 295, 331, 339, 342, on Lingg's suicide, 455; on executions, 470; revived, 480; 481, 532, 533
Albany Law Journal, on strikes, 41-42; on radicals, 217-218; on Illinois Supreme Court decision, 377; on U. S. Supreme Court opinion, 386; on commutation of sentences, 458
Altgeld, John P., elected governor, 288; and pardon movement, 489 ff.; decides to pardon men, 492; pardon message, 493-496; denounced, 496-499; supported, 499-501; as politician, 501-502; on bomb-thrower, 516-517
Alena *Labor Journal,* on executions, 473
Amalgamated Association of Iron and Steel Workers, 174

American Federation of Labor, urges clemency, 418; 443, 536, 540
American Group, 110, 112, 117, 149, 277, 279
American Labor Budget, on Socialism, 406-407
Ames, Sarah E., 226
Amnesty Association, 411, 427, 430, disheartened, 439; clemency hearings, 440 ff.; petition of, 441-442; 458, 485, second, 487 ff., 500
Anarchism, in U. S. in 1881, 75-76; American philosophic, 76; Most and, 84-85, 103, 109; 101, 103, 112, conception of by Chicago social-revolutionaries, chaps. V-VI *passim;* 142, 143, 208, 223, 231, attitude of jurors toward, 247-248; 302, 320, 332, Spies on, 333; Schwab on, 335; 337; conception of by Engel, 339-340; 343, 366, 406, 412, 414, K. of L. and, 415 ff.; 419, 420, 469, 516, Haymarket Affair and, 528 ff.
Anarchist, 142, 290, 336
Anarchy and Anarchists, 223
Andrews, Stephen Pearl, 75
Anti-Monopolist, on verdict, 325
Anti-Monopoly Party, 82, 83
Appleton's Annual Cyclopaedia, 498
Arbeiter-Zeitung, 59, 111, 113, 114, 119, 120, 127, 129 n. 17, 184, 190, 191, 192, 193, 194, 211, 222, suspension of, 225; 230, 253, 258, 259, 261, 270, 276, 280, 290, 292, 293, 301, on verdict, 323; 330, 334, 336,